PRAISE FOR
THE LAND OF PAINTED CAVES

"This novel, the last in the series, is sweeping, grand, infinitesimally detailed, and ties up several loose ends. Ayla fulfills her destiny here, which is exactly what fans have been waiting for, for three decades." —RealAspen

"[Auel] does paint a convincing picture of ancient life. And readers who fell in love with little Ayla will no doubt revel in her prehistoric womanhood." —*People*

"After building her characters up to legendary proportions throughout *The Land of Painted Caves,* Auel wisely lets them have their flaws—and her most devoted fans will be left longing for at least one more book before Ayla's journey ends." —*Los Angeles Times*

"The millions of readers who have been with Ayla from the start will want to once again lose themselves in the rich prehistoric world Auel conjures and see how this internationally beloved series concludes." —*Booklist*

"The book is compelling and will be in high demand by Auel's fans." —*Library Journal*

"As with her other books, Auel spins her tale with credible dialogue, believable situations and considerable drama. More than that, she deftly creates a whole world, giving a sense of the origins of class, ethnic and cultural differences that alternately divide and fascinate us today. Among modern epic spinners, Auel has few peers." —*Kirkus Reviews*

"Like all of Auel's books, the research is extensive, with brilliantly re-imagined scenes of daily life and early forms of religion. The realism feels just as important as the mysticism, and the painstaking detail grounds the story with a sense of familiarity. Readers will find the people charming for their early discoveries, such as learning to count and creating glue." —*BookPage*

PRAISE FOR THE EARTH'S CHILDREN SERIES

"Shiningly intense . . . sheer story-telling skill holds the reader in a powerful spell." —*Publishers Weekly*

"Jean Auel has established herself as one of our premier storytellers. . . . Her narrative skill is supreme."
—*Chicago Tribune*

"She has gone beyond the cliché of leopard-skin-covered, club wielding grunters and presented a panorama of human culture in its infancy." —*The New York Times*

"Lively and interesting." —*The Washington Post*

PRAISE FOR
THE PLAINS OF PASSAGE

"Pure entertainment at its sublime, wholly exhilarating best." —*Los Angeles Times*

"Thrilling . . . This magical book is rich in details of all kinds . . . but it is the depth of the characters' emotional lives . . . that gives the novel such a stranglehold."
—*Cosmopolitan*

"Auel brings alive a world that has been irretrievably lost to us." —*Chicago Sun-Times*

"A gripping story . . . a major book that truly has something for everyone and can only enhance her high reputation as a writer, storyteller, and historian." —*Boston Sunday Herald*

"An admirable job . . . exhilarating, exciting and believable." —*Miami Herald*

"As welcome as letters from a long-lost friend . . . impeccably researched . . . as warm and inviting as its campfire milieu." —*Publishers Weekly*

"Has an ending so good I will be standing in line when book five gets here." —*Houston Chronicle*

By Jean M. Auel

The Land of Painted Caves

The Shelters of Stone

The Plains of Passage

The Mammoth Hunters

The Valley of Horses

The Clan of the Cave Bear

THE LAND OF PAINTED CAVES

EARTH'S CHILDREN®

JEAN M. AUEL

BANTAM BOOKS
NEW YORK

2011 Bantam Mass Market Edition

Copyright © 2011 by Jean M. Auel

EARTH'S CHILDREN is a trademark of Jean M. Auel.

All rights reserved.

Published in the United States by Bantam Books, an imprint of The Random House Publishing Group, a division of Random House, Inc., New York.

BANTAM BOOKS and the rooster colophon are registered trademarks of Random House, Inc.

Originally published in hardcover in the United States by Crown Publishers, a division of Random House, Inc., in 2011.

ISBN 978-0-553-28943-5
eBook ISBN 978-0-307-88665-1

Cover illustration: Ron Wood/Wood Ronsaville Harlin, Inc.
Cover typography: Anthony Bloch
Map illustration: Rodica Prato after Jean Auel
Insert map: copyright © Palacios after Jean Auel

Printed in the United States of America

www.bantamdell.com

9 8 7

Bantam Books mass market edition: November 2011

For RAEANN
> First born, last cited, always loved,

and for FRANK,
> who stands by her side,

and for AMELIA and BRET, ALECIA, and EMORY,
> fine young adults,
>> with Love.

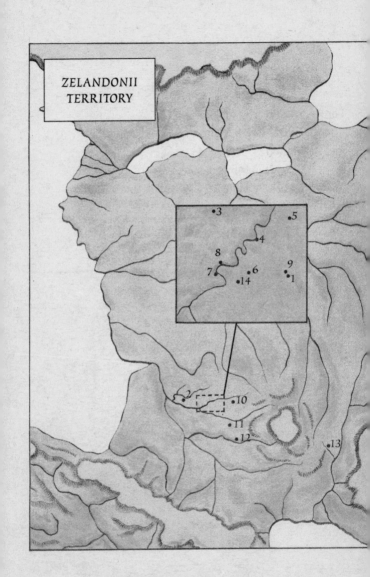

ZELANDONII
TERRITORY

SACRED SITES

1. Horsehead Rock—The Seventh Cave of the Zelandonii
2. New small cave at Sunview—The Twenty-sixth Cave of the Zelandonii
3. Mammoth Cave
4. Forest Cave—West Holding of the Twenty-ninth Cave
5. The Fifth Cave of the Zelandonii
6. The Women's Place
7. Little Valley—Fourteenth Cave of the Zelandonii
8. Ninth Cave of the Zelandonii
9. Horse Heart
10. White Hollow
11. Sacred Site of the Fourth Cave of the South Land Zelandonii
12. Sacred Site of the Seventh Cave of the South Land Zelandonii
13. The Great Earth Mother's Most Ancient Sacred Site
14. The Deep of Fountain Rocks

EARTH'S CHILDREN®

PREHISTORIC EUROPE DURING THE ICE AGE

Extent of ice and change in coastlines during 10,000-year interstadial, a warming trend during the Wurm glaciation of the late Pleistocene Epoch extending from 35,000 to 25,000 years before present.

CAVES OF THE SACRED SITES

1. Comarque
2. Gabillou
3. Rouffignac
4. La Foret
5. Castelmerle
6. Combarelles
7. Gorge d'Enfer
8. Laugerie Haute
9. Cap Blanc
10. Lascaux
11. Cougnac
12. Pech Merle
13. Chauvet
14. Font-de-Gaume

ACKNOWLEDGMENTS

I am grateful for the assistance of many people who have helped me to write the Earth's Children® series. I want to thank again two French archeologists who have been particularly helpful over the years, Dr. Jean-Philippe Rigaud and Dr. Jean Clottes. They have both enabled me to understand the background and to visualize the prehistoric setting of these books.

Dr. Rigaud's help has been invaluable beginning with my first research visit to France, and his assistance has continued over the years. I particularly enjoyed the visit, which he arranged, to a stone shelter in Gorge d'Enfer, which is still much the way it was in the Ice Age: a deep protected space, open in the front, with a level floor, a rock ceiling, and a natural spring at the back. It was easy to see how it could be made into a comfortable place to live. And I appreciated his willingness to explain to reporters and other media people from many countries the interesting and important information about some of the prehistoric sites in and around Les Eyzles de Tayac when Book 5, *The Shelters of Stone,* was launched internationally from that location in France.

I am most grateful to Jean Clottes, who arranged for Ray and me to visit many remarkable painted caves in the south of France. Particularly memorable was the visit to the caves on the property of Count Robert Begouen in the Volp Valley—l'Enlene, Trois-Freres, and Tuc-d'Audoubert—whose art is often pictured in texts and art books. To actually see some of that remarkable art in its environment, escorted by both Dr. Clottes and Count Begouen, was a treasured experience, and for that thanks in great measure are also due to Robert Begouen. It was his grandfather and two brothers who first explored the caves and began the practice of maintaining them, which continues to this day. No one visits the caves without the permission of Count Begouen, and usually his accompaniment.

We visited many more caves with Dr. Clottes, including Gargas, which is one of my favorites. It has many handprints, including those of a child, and a niche large enough for an adult to enter, whose inner rock walls are completely covered with a rich red paint using the ochers from the region. I am convinced Gargas is a woman's cave. It feels like the womb of the earth. Above all, I am grateful to Jean Clottes for the visit to the extraordinary Grotte Chauvet. Even though he became too ill with the flu to accompany us, Dr. Clottes arranged for Jean-Marie Chauvet, the man who discovered it and for whom it was named, and Dominique Baffier, curator of Grotte Chauvet, to show us that remarkable site. A young man who was working at the site was also with us and helped me through some of the more difficult parts.

It was a deeply moving experience that I will never forget and I am grateful to both Mr. Chauvet and Dr. Baffier for their clear and astute explanations. We went in through the ceiling, much enlarged since Mr. Chauvet and his colleagues first found their way in, and down a ladder that was attached to the rock wall—the original entrance was closed by a landslide many thousands of years ago. They explained some of the changes that have occurred during the past thirty-five thousand years since the first artists made their magnificent paintings.

In addition, I would like to thank Nicholas Conard, an American who lives in Germany and is in charge of the Archeology Department at the University in Tubingen, for the opportunity to visit several of the Caves along the Danube in that region of Germany. He also showed us several of the ancient carved ivory artifacts that are more than thirty thousand years old, including mammoths, a graceful flying bird that he found in two parts several years apart, and a most amazing lion-human figure. His latest find is a female figure that was created in the same style as others from France, Spain, Austria, Germany, and the Czech Republic from the same era, but that is unique in its execution.

I also want to thank Dr. Lawrence Guy Strauss, who has

been so willing and helpful in arranging for visits to sites and caves and often accompanying us on several trips to Europe. There were many highlights during those trips, but one of the most interesting was the visit to Abrigo do Lagar Velho, Portugal, the site of the "lapedo valley child," whose skeleton showed evidence that contact between Neanderthals and anatomically modern humans resulted in interbreeding. The discussions with Dr. Strauss about those Ice Age humans were not only informative, but always fascinating.

I have had discussions and asked questions of many other archeologists, paleoanthropologists and specialists whom I have met about that particular time in our prehistory, when for many thousands of years both kinds of humans occupied Europe at the same time. I have appreciated their willingness to answer questions and discuss the several possibilities of how they lived.

I want to give special thanks to the French Ministry of Culture for the publication of a book which I found invaluable: *L'Art des Cavernes: Atlas des Grottes Ornées Paléolithiques Francaises,* Paris, 1984, Ministère de la Culture. It contains very complete descriptions, including the floor plans, photographs, and drawings, as well as an explanatory narrative of most of the known painted and engraved caves in France, as of 1984. It does not include Cosquer, whose entrance is below the surface of the Mediterranean, or Chauvet, neither of which were discovered until after 1990.

I have visited many caves, some many times, and I can remember the ambiance, the mood, the feeling of seeing exceptional art painted on the walls inside caves, but I couldn't recall precisely what the first figure was, or on which wall it appeared, how far into the cave it was, or what direction it was facing. This book gave me the answers. The only problem was that it was published in French, of course, and while I have learned some French over the years, my command of the language is far from adequate.

So I am deeply indebted to my friend Claudine Fisher, Honorary French Consul for Oregon, French professor and director of Canadian Studies at Portland State University. She is a native speaker who was born in France, and she translated all the information I needed of every cave I wanted. It was a lot of work, but without her help, I could not have written this book, and I am more grateful than I can begin to express. She has been helpful in many other ways, too, besides just being a good friend.

There are several other friends I'd like to thank for their willingness to read a long and not-quite-polished manuscript, and make comments as readers: Karen Auel-Feuer, Kendall Auel, Cathy Humble, Deanna Sterett, Gin DeCamp, Claudine Fisher, and Ray Auel.

I want to offer gratitude in memoriam to Dr. Jan Jellnek, who was an archeologist from Czechoslovakia, now known as the Czech Republic, who helped me in many ways, from the beginning when we first exchanged letters, and then visits that Ray and I made to see the Paleolithic sites near Brno, and then he and his wife's (Kveta) trip to Oregon. His help was invaluable. He was always kind, and generous with his time and knowledge, and I miss him.

I am lucky to have Betty Prashker as my editor. Her comments are always insightful, and she takes my best efforts and makes them better. Thank you.

Gratitude always to the one who has been there from the beginning, my wonderful literary agent, Jean Naggar. With every book, I appreciate her more. I also want to thank Jennifer Weltz, Jean's partner at the Jean V. Naggar Literary Agency. They continue to perform miracles with this series, which is translated into many foreign languages and available all over the world.

For the past nineteen years Delores Rooney Pander has been my secretary and personal assistant. Unfortunately, she has become ill and has retired, but I want to thank her for her many years of service. You don't really know how much you count on someone like that until she is gone. I miss more than the work she did for me, I miss our conversations and discussions. Over the years she became a good friend. (Delores died of cancer in 2010.)

And most of all, for Ray, my husband, who is always there for me. Love and gratitude beyond measure.

Part One

The band of travelers walked along the path between the clear sparkling water of Grass River and the black-streaked white limestone cliff, following the trail that paralleled the right bank. They went single file around the bend where the stone wall jutted out closer to the water's edge. Ahead a smaller path split off at an angle toward the crossing place, where the flowing water spread out and became shallower, bubbling around exposed rocks.

Before they reached the fork in the trail a young woman near the front suddenly stopped, her eyes opening wide as she stood perfectly still, staring ahead. She pointed with her chin, not wanting to move. "Look! Over there!" she said in a hissing whisper of fear. "Lions!"

Joharran, the leader, lifted his arm, signaling the band to a halt. Just beyond the place where the trail diverged, they now saw pale-tawny cave lions moving around in the grass. The grass was such effective camouflage, however, that they might not have noticed them until they were much closer, if it hadn't been for the sharp eyes of Thefona. The young woman from the Third Cave had exceptionally good vision, and though she was quite young, she was noted for her ability to see far and well. Her innate talent had been recognized early and they had begun training her when she was a small girl; she was their best lookout.

Near the back of the group, walking in front of three horses, Ayla and Jondalar looked up to see what was causing the delay. "I wonder why we've stopped," Jondalar said, a familiar frown of worry wrinkling his forehead.

Ayla observed the leader and the people around him closely, and instinctively moved her hand to shield the warm bundle that she carried in the soft leather blanket tied to her chest. Jonayla had recently nursed and was sleeping, but moved slightly at her mother's touch. Ayla had an uncanny ability to interpret meaning from body language, learned young when she lived with the Clan. She knew Joharran was alarmed and Thefona was frightened.

Ayla, too, had extraordinarily sharp vision. She could also pick up sounds above the range of normal hearing and feel the deep tones of those that were below. Her sense of smell and taste were also keen, but she had never compared herself with anyone, and didn't realize how extraordinary her perceptions were. She was born with heightened acuity in all her senses, which no doubt contributed to her survival after losing her parents and everything she knew at five years. Her only training had come from herself. She had developed her natural abilities during the years she studied animals, chiefly carnivores, when she was teaching herself to hunt.

In the stillness, she discerned the faint but familiar rumblings of lions, detected their distinctive scent on a slight breeze, and noticed that several people in front of the group were gazing ahead. When she looked, she saw something move. Suddenly the cats hidden by the grass seemed to jump into clear focus. She could make out two young and three or four adult cave lions. As she started moving forward, she reached with one hand for her spear-thrower, fastened to a carrying loop on her belt, and with the other for a spear from the holder hanging on her back.

"Where are you going?" Jondalar asked.

She stopped. "There are lions up ahead just beyond the split in the trail," she said under her breath.

Jondalar turned to look, and noticed movement that he interpreted as lions now that he knew what to look for. He reached for his weapons as well. "You should stay here with Jonayla. I'll go."

Ayla glanced down at her sleeping baby, then looked up at him. "You're good with the spear-thrower, Jondalar, but there are at least two cubs and three grown lions, probably more.

If the lions think the cubs are in danger and decide to attack, you'll need help, someone to back you up, and you know I'm better than anyone, except you."

His brow furrowed again as he paused to think, looking at her. Then he nodded. "All right . . . but stay behind me." He detected movement out of the corner of his eye and glanced back. "What about the horses?"

"They know lions are near. Look at them," Ayla said.

Jondalar looked. All three horses, including the new young filly, were staring ahead, obviously aware of the huge felines. Jondalar frowned again. "Will they be all right? Especially little Gray?"

"They know to stay out of the way of those lions, but I don't see Wolf," Ayla said. "I'd better whistle for him."

"You don't have to," Jondalar said, pointing in a different direction. "He must sense something, too. Look at him coming."

Ayla turned and saw a wolf racing toward her. The canine was a magnificent animal, larger than most, but an injury from a fight with other wolves that left him with a bent ear gave him a rakish look. She made the special signal that she used when they hunted together. He knew it meant to stay near and pay close attention to her. They ducked around people as they hurried toward the front, trying not to cause any undo commotion, and to remain as inconspicuous as possible.

"I'm glad you're here," Joharran said softly when he saw his brother and Ayla with the wolf quietly appear with their spear-throwers in hand.

"Do you know how many there are?" Ayla asked.

"More than I thought," Thefona said, trying to seem calm and not let her fear show. "When I first saw them, I thought there were maybe three or four, but they are moving around in the grass, and now I think there may be ten or more. It's a big pride."

"And they are feeling confident," Joharran said.

"How do you know that?" Thefona asked.

"They're ignoring us."

Jondalar knew his mate was very familiar with the huge felines. "Ayla knows cave lions," he said. "Perhaps we should ask her what she thinks." Joharran nodded in her direction, asking the question silently.

"Joharran is right. They know we're here. And they know how many they are and how many we are," Ayla said, then added, "They may see us as something like a herd of horses or aurochs and think they may be able to single out a weak one. I think they are new to this region."

"What makes you think so?" Joharran said. He was always surprised at Ayla's wealth of knowledge of four-legged hunters, but for some reason it was also at times like this that he noticed her unusual accent more.

"They don't know us, that's why they're so confident," Ayla continued. "If they were a resident pride that lived around people and had been chased or hunted a few times, I don't think they would be so unconcerned."

"Well, maybe we should give them something to be concerned about," Jondalar said.

Joharran's brow wrinkled in a way that was so much like his taller though younger brother's, it made Ayla want to smile, but it usually showed at a time when smiling would be inappropriate. "Perhaps it would be wiser just to avoid them," the dark-haired leader said.

"I don't think so," Ayla said, bowing her head and looking down. It was still difficult for her to disagree with a man in public, especially a leader. Though she knew it was perfectly acceptable among the Zelandonii—after all, some leaders were women, including, at one time, Joharran and Jondalar's mother—such behavior from a woman would not have been tolerated in the Clan, the ones who raised her.

"Why not?" Joharran asked, his frown turning into a scowl.

"Those lions are resting too close to the home of the Third Cave," Ayla said quietly. "There will always be lions around, but if they are comfortable here, they might think of it as a place to return when they want to rest, and would see any people who come near as prey, especially children or elders. They could be a danger to the people who live at Two Rivers Rock, and the other nearby Caves, including the Ninth."

Joharran took a deep breath, then looked at his fair-haired brother. "Your mate is right, and you as well, Jondalar. Perhaps now is the time to let those lions know they are not welcome to settle down so close to our homes."

"This would be a good time to use spear-throwers so we can hunt from a safer distance. Several hunters here have been practicing," Jondalar said. It was for just this sort of thing that he had wanted to come home and show everyone the weapon he had developed. "We may not even have to kill one, just injure a couple to teach them to stay away."

"Jondalar," Ayla said, softly. Now she was getting ready to differ with him, or at least to make a point that he should consider. She looked down again, then raised her eyes and looked directly at him. She wasn't afraid to speak her mind to him, but she wanted to be respectful. "It's true that a spear-thrower is a very good weapon. With it, a spear can be thrown from a much greater distance than one thrown by hand, and that makes it safer. But safer is not safe. A wounded animal is unpredictable. And one with the strength and speed of a cave lion, hurt and wild with pain, could do anything. If you decide to use these weapons against those lions, they should not be used to injure, but to kill."

"She's right, Jondalar," Joharran said.

Jondalar frowned at his brother, then grinned sheepishly. "Yes she is, but, as dangerous as they are, I always hate to kill a cave lion if I don't have to. They are so beautiful, so lithe and graceful in the way they move. Cave lions don't have much to be afraid of. Their strength gives them confidence." He glanced at Ayla with a glint of pride and love. "I always thought Ayla's Cave Lion totem was right for her." Discomfited by showing his strong inner feelings for her, a hint of a flush colored his cheeks. "But I do think this is a time when spear-throwers could be very useful."

Joharran noticed that most of the travelers had crowded closer. "How many are with us that can use one?" he asked his brother.

"Well, there's you, and me, and Ayla, of course," Jondalar said, looking at the group. "Rushemar has been practicing a lot and is getting pretty good. Solaban's been busy making some ivory handles for tools for some of us and hasn't been working at it as much, but he's got the basics."

"I've tried a spear-thrower a few times, Joharran. I don't have one of my own, and I'm not very good at it," Thefona said, "but I can throw a spear without one."

"Thank you, Thefona, for reminding me," Joharran said. "Nearly everyone can handle a spear without a spear-thrower, including women. We shouldn't forget that." Then he directed his comments to the group at large. "We need to let those lions know that this is not a good place for them. Whoever wants to go after them, using a spear by hand or with the thrower, come over here."

Ayla started to loosen her baby's carrying blanket. "Folara, would you watch Jonayla for me?" she said, approaching Jondalar's younger sister, "unless you'd rather stay and hunt cave lions."

"I've gone out on drives, but I never was very good with a spear, and I don't seem to be much better with the thrower," Folara said. "I'll take Jonayla." The infant was now thoroughly awake, and when the young woman held out her arms for the baby, she willingly went to her aunt.

"I'll help her," Proleva said to Ayla. Joharran's mate also had a baby girl in a carrying blanket, just a few days older than Jonayla, and an active boy who could count six years to watch out for as well. "I think we should take all the children away from here, perhaps back behind the jutting rock, or up to the Third Cave."

"That's a very good idea," Joharran said. "Hunters stay here. The rest of you go back, but go slowly. No sudden moves. We want those cave lions to think we are just milling around, like a herd of aurochs. And when we pair off, each group keep together. They will probably go after anyone alone."

Ayla turned back toward the four-legged hunters and saw many lion faces looking in their direction, very alert. She watched the animals move around, and began to see some distinguishing characteristics, helping her to count them. She watched a big female casually turn around—no, a male, she realized when she saw his male parts from the backside. She'd forgotten for a moment that the males here didn't have manes. The male cave lions near her valley to the east, including one that she knew quite well, did have some hair around the head and neck, but it was sparse. This is a big pride, she thought, more than two hands-ful of counting words, possibly as many as three, including the young ones.

While she watched, the big lion took a few more steps into the field, then disappeared into the grass. It was surprising how well the tall thin stalks could hide animals that were so huge.

Though the bones and teeth of cave lions—felines that liked to den in caves, which preserved the bones they left behind—were the same shape as their descendants that would some-day roam the distant lands of the continent far to the south, they were more than half again, some nearly twice as large. In winter they grew a thick winter fur that was so pale, it was al-most white, practical concealment in snow for predators who hunted all year long. Their summer coat, though still pale, was more tawny, and some of the cats were still shedding, giving them a rather tattered, mottled look.

Ayla watched the group of mostly women and children break off from the hunters and head back to the cliff they had passed, along with a few young men and women with spears held in readiness whom Joharran had assigned to guard them. Then she noticed that the horses seemed particularly nervous, and thought she should try to calm them. She signaled Wolf to come with her as she walked toward the horses.

Whinney seemed glad to see both her and Wolf when they approached. The horse had no fear of the big canine preda-tor. She had watched Wolf grow up from a tiny little ball of fuzzy fur, had helped to raise him. Ayla had a concern, though. She wanted the horses to go back behind the stone wall with the women and children. She could give Whinney many com-mands with words and signals, but she wasn't sure how to tell the mare to go with the others and not follow her.

Racer whinnied when she neared; he seemed especially agi-tated. She greeted the brown stallion affectionately and patted and scratched the young gray filly; then she hugged the sturdy neck of the dun-yellow mare that had been her only friend dur-ing the first lonely years after she left the Clan.

Whinney leaned against the young woman with her head over Ayla's shoulder in a familiar position of mutual support. She talked to the mare with a combination of Clan hand signs

and words, and animal sounds that she imitated—the special
language she had developed with Whinney when she was a
foal, before Jondalar taught her to speak his language. Ayla
told the mare to go with Folara and Proleva. Whether the horse
understood, or just knew that it would be safer for her and her
foal, Ayla was glad to see her retreat to the cliff with the other
mothers when she pointed her in that direction.

But Racer was nervous and edgy, more so after the mare
started walking away. Even grown, the young stallion was accustomed to following his dam, especially when Ayla and
Jondalar were riding together, but this time he did not immediately go with her. He pranced and tossed his head and neighed.
Jondalar heard him, looked over at the stallion and the woman,
then joined them. The young horse nickered at the man as he
approached. With two females in his small "herd," Jondalar
wondered if Racer's protective stallion instincts were beginning
to make themselves felt. The man talked to him, stroked and
scratched his favorite places to settle him, then told him to go
with Whinney and slapped him on the rump. It was enough to
get him started in the right direction.

Ayla and Jondalar walked back to the hunters. Joharran and
his two closest friends and advisers, Solaban and Rushemar,
were standing together in the middle of the group that was left.
It seemed much smaller now.

"We've been discussing the best way to hunt them," Joharran
said when the couple returned. "I'm not sure what strategy to
use. Should we try to surround them? Or drive them in a certain direction? I will tell you, I know how to hunt for meat:
deer, or bison or aurochs, even mammoth. I've killed a lion or
two that were too close to a camp, with the help of other hunters, but lions are not animals I usually hunt, especially not a
whole pride."

"Since Ayla knows lions," Thefona said, "let's ask her."

Everyone turned to look at Ayla. Most of them had heard
about the injured lion cub she had taken in and raised until he
was full grown. When Jondalar told them the lion did what she
told him the way the wolf did, they believed it.

"What do you think, Ayla?" Joharran asked.

"Do you see how the lions are watching us? It's the same

way we're looking at them. They think of themselves as the hunters. It might surprise them to be prey for a change," Ayla said, then paused. "I think we should stay together in a group and walk toward them, shouting and talking loudly, perhaps, and see if they back off. But keep our spears ready, in case one or more come after us before we decide to go after them."

"Just approach them head-on?" Rushemar asked, with a frown.

"It might work," Solaban said. "And if we stay together, we can watch out for each other."

"It seems like a good plan, Joharran," Jondalar said.

"I suppose it's as good as any, and I like the idea of staying together and watching out for each other," the leader said.

"I'll go first," Jondalar said. He held up his spear, already on his spear-thrower ready to launch. "I can get a spear off fast with this."

"I'm sure you can, but let's wait until we get closer so we can all feel comfortable with our aim," Joharran said.

"Of course," Jondalar said, "and Ayla is going to be a backup for me in case something unexpected happens."

"That's good," Joharran said. "We all need a partner, someone to be a backup for the ones who throw first, in case they miss and those lions come at us instead of running away. The partners can decide who will cast first, but it will cause less confusion if everyone waits for a signal before anyone throws."

"What kind of signal?" Rushemar asked.

Joharran paused, then said, "Watch Jondalar. Wait until he throws. That can be our signal."

"I'll be your partner, Joharran," Rushemar volunteered.

The leader nodded.

"I need a backup," Morizan said. He was the son of Manvelar's mate, Ayla recalled. "I'm not sure how good I am, but I have been working at it."

"I can be your partner. I've been practicing with the spear-thrower."

Ayla turned at the sound of the feminine voice and saw that it was Folara's red-haired friend, Galeya, who had spoken.

Jondalar turned to look, too. That's one way to get close to the son of a leader's mate, he thought, and glanced at Ayla, wondering if she had caught the implication.

"I can partner with Thefona, if she would like," Solaban said, "since I'll be using a spear like her, not a spear-thrower."

The young woman smiled at him, glad to have a more mature and experienced hunter close by.

"I've been practicing with a spear-thrower," Palidar said. He was a friend of Tivonan, the apprentice of Willamar, the Trade Master.

"We can be partners, Palidar," Tivonan said, "but I can only use a spear."

"I haven't really practiced much with that thrower either," Palidar said.

Ayla smiled at the young men. As Willamar's apprentice trader, Tivonan would no doubt become the Ninth Cave's next Trade Master. His friend, Palidar, had come back with Tivonan when he went to visit his Cave on a short trading mission, and Palidar was the one who had found the place where Wolf had gotten into the terrible fight with the other wolves, and took her to it. She thought of him as a good friend.

"I haven't done much with that thrower, but I can handle a spear."

It's Mejera, the acolyte of Zelandoni of the Third, Ayla said to herself, remembering that the young woman was with them the first time Ayla went into the Deep of Fountain Rocks to look for the life force of Jondalar's younger brother when they tried to help his elan find its way to the spirit world.

"Everyone has already picked a partner, so I guess we're left. Not only have I not practiced with the spear-thrower, I have hardly ever seen it used," said Jalodan, Morizan's cousin, the son of Manvelar's sister, who was visiting the Third Cave. He was planning to travel with them to the Summer Meeting to meet up with his Cave.

That was it. The twelve men and women who were going to hunt a similar number of lions—animals with greater speed, strength, and ferocity that lived by hunting weaker prey. Ayla began having feelings of doubt and a shiver of fear gave her a chill. She rubbed her arms and felt an eruption of bumps. How could twelve frail humans even think of attacking a pride of lions? She caught sight of the other carnivore, the one she knew, and signaled the animal to stay with her, thinking, twelve people—and Wolf.

"All right, let's go," Joharran said, "but keep together."

The twelve hunters from the Third Cave and the Ninth Cave of the Zelandonii started out together walking directly toward the pride of massive felines. They were armed with spears, tipped with sharpened flint, or bone or ivory sanded to a smooth, round sharp point. Some had spear-throwers that could propel a spear much farther and with more power and speed than one thrown by hand, but lions had been killed with just spears before. This might be a test of Jondalar's weapon, but it would test the courage of the ones who were hunting even more.

"Go away!" Ayla shouted as they started out. "We don't want you here!"

Several others picked up the refrain, with variations, shouting and yelling at the animals as they approached, telling them to go away.

At first the cats, young and old, just watched them come. Then some began to move around, back into the grass that hid them so well, and out again, as though they weren't sure what to do. The ones who retreated with cubs returned without them.

"They don't seem to know what to make of us," Thefona said from the middle of the advancing hunters, feeling a little more secure than when they started, but when the big male suddenly snarled at them, everyone jumped with a start, and stopped in their tracks.

"This is not the time to stop," Joharran said, forging ahead.

They started out again, their formation a little more ragged at first, but they pulled together again as they continued on. All the lions started moving around, some turning their backs and disappearing into the tall grass, but the big male snarled again, then rumbled the beginning of a roar as he stood his ground. Several of the other big cats were arrayed behind him. Ayla was picking up the scent of fear from the human hunters; she was sure the lions were, too. She was afraid herself, but fear was something that people could overcome.

"I think we'd better get ready," Jondalar said. "That male doesn't look happy, and he has reinforcements."

"Can't you get him from here?" Ayla asked. She heard the series of grunts that was usually a precursor to a lion's roar.

"Probably," Jondalar said, "but I'd rather be closer, so I can be more sure of my aim."

"And I'm not sure how good my aim would be from this distance. We do need to be closer," Joharran said, continuing to march forward.

The people bunched together and kept going, still shouting, though Ayla thought their sound was more tentative as they drew closer. The cave lions became still and seemed tense as they watched the approach of the strange herd that didn't behave like prey animals.

Then, suddenly, everything happened at once.

The big male lion roared, a staggering, deafening sound, especially from such close range. He started toward them at a run. As he closed in, poised to spring, Jondalar hurled his spear at him.

Ayla had been watching the female on his right. About the time that Jondalar made his cast, the lioness bounded forward running, then vaulted to pounce.

Ayla pulled back and took aim. She felt the back of the spear-thrower with the spear mounted on it rise up almost without her knowing it as she hurled her spear. It was so natural for her, it didn't feel like a deliberate move. She and Jondalar had used the weapon during their entire yearlong Journey back to the Zelandonii and she was so skilled, it was second nature.

The lioness soared into her leap, but Ayla's spear met her more than halfway. It found its mark from beneath the big cat, and lodged firmly in her throat in a sudden fatal slash. Blood spurted out as the lioness collapsed to the ground.

The woman quickly grabbed another spear from her holder, and slapped it down on her spear-thrower, looking around to see what else was happening. She saw Joharran's spear fly, and a heartbeat later another spear followed. She noticed that Rushemar was in the stance of one who had just thrown a spear. She saw another large female lion fall. A second spear found the beast before she landed. Another lioness was still coming. Ayla cast a spear, and saw that someone else had, too, just a moment before her.

She reached for another spear, making sure it was seated right—that the point, which was affixed to a short length of tapering shaft made to detach from the main spear shaft, was firmly in place and the hole in the butt of the long spear shaft was engaging the hook at the back of the spear-thrower. Then she looked around again. The huge male was down, but moving, bleeding but not dead. Her female was also bleeding, but not moving.

The lions were disappearing into the grass as fast as they could, at least one leaving a trail of blood. The human hunters were gathering themselves together, looking around and beginning to smile at each other.

"I think we did it," Palidar said, a huge grin starting.

He had barely gotten the words out when Wolf's menacing growl caught Ayla's attention. The wolf bounded away from the human hunters with Ayla on his heels. The heavily bleeding male lion was up and coming at them again. With a roar, he sprang toward them. Ayla could almost feel his anger, and she didn't really blame him.

Just as Wolf reached the lion and leaped up to attack, keeping himself between Ayla and the big cat, she flung her spear as hard as she could. Her eye caught another one hurled at the same time. They landed almost simultaneously with an audible *thunk,* and *thunk.* Both the lion and the wolf crumpled in a heap. Ayla gasped when she saw them fall, swathed in blood, afraid that Wolf was hurt.

2

Ayla saw the heavy paw of the lion moving, and caught her breath, wondering if the big male could still be alive with all the spears in him. Then she recognized Wolf's bloody head working its way out from under the huge limb, and rushed toward him, still not sure if he was injured. The wolf squirmed free of the forearm of the lion, then grabbed the paw with his teeth and shook it with such vigor, she knew it had to be the blood of the lion on him, not his own. Jondalar was at her side the next moment and they walked toward the lion together, smiling with relief at the wolf's antics.

"I'm going to have to take Wolf to the river to get him cleaned up," Ayla said. "That's all lion's blood."

"I'm sorry we had to kill him," Jondalar said quietly. "He was such a magnificent beast, and only defending his own."

"I feel sorry, too. He reminded me of Baby, but we had to defend our own. Think how much worse we would feel if one of those lions had killed a child," Ayla said, looking down at the huge predator.

After a pause, Jondalar said, "We can both lay claim to him; only our spears reached him, and only yours killed this female who stood by his side."

"I think I may have hit another lioness, too, but I don't need to claim any part of that one," Ayla said. "You should take what you want of the male. I'll take this female's pelt and tail, and her claws and teeth as tokens of this hunt."

They both stood silently for a while, then Jondalar said, "I am grateful that the hunt was a success and no one was hurt."

"I would like to honor them in some way, Jondalar, to

acknowledge my respect for the Cave Lion Spirit, and show gratitude to my totem."

"Yes, I think we should. It is customary to thank the spirit when we make a kill, and to ask the spirit to thank the Great Earth Mother for the food she has allowed us to take. We can thank the Cave Lion Spirit and ask the spirit to thank the Mother for allowing us to take these lions to protect our families and our Caves." Jondalar paused. "We can give this lion a drink of water so the spirit won't arrive in the next world thirsty. Some people also bury the heart, give it back to the Mother. I think we should do both for this great lion who gave his life defending his pride."

"I will do the same for the female who stood with him, fighting at his side," Ayla said. "I think my Cave Lion Totem protected me, and maybe all the rest of us. The Mother could have chosen to let the Cave Lion Spirit take someone to compensate for the pride's great loss. I am grateful She didn't."

"Ayla! You were right!"

She spun around at the sound of the voice and smiled at the Ninth Cave's leader coming up behind them. "You said, 'A wounded animal is unpredictable. And one with the strength and speed of a cave lion, hurt and wild with pain, could do anything.' We shouldn't have assumed that because that lion was down and bleeding, he wouldn't try to attack again." Joharran addressed the rest of the hunters who had come to see the lions they had killed. "We should have made sure he was dead."

"What surprised me was that wolf," Palidar said, looking at the animal, still covered with blood, nonchalantly sitting at Ayla's feet, with his tongue lolling out of the side of his mouth. "He's the one who warned us, but I never imagined a wolf would attack a cave lion, wounded or not."

Jondalar smiled. "Wolf protects Ayla," he said. "It doesn't matter who or what it is, if it threatens her, he'll attack it."

"Even you, Jondalar?" he asked.

"Even me."

There was an uncomfortable silence; then Joharran said, "How many lions did we get?" Several of the big cats were down, some with a number of spears in them.

"I count five," Ayla said.

"The lions with spears from more than one person should be shared," Joharran said. "Those hunters can decide what to do with them."

"The only spears in the male and this female belong to Ayla and me, so we can claim them," Jondalar said. "We did what was necessary, but they were defending their family and we want to honor their spirits. We don't have a Zelandoni here, but we can give each a drink of water before we send them on their way to the spirit world, and we can bury their hearts, give them back to the Mother."

The other hunters nodded in agreement.

Ayla walked to the lioness that she had killed and took out her waterbag. It was made of the carefully washed stomach of a deer, with the lower opening tied off. The upper opening was pulled up around a deer vertebra, with the projections cut away, and sinew wrapped tightly around it. The natural hole in the center of the section of spine made a more than serviceable pour spout. The stopper was a thin leather thong that had been knotted several times in the same place, and stuffed into the hole. She pulled out the knotted leather cord stopper, and took a mouthful. Then she kneeled over the head of the lioness, pulled it around and opened the jaws, and squirted the water from her mouth into the mouth of the big cat.

"We are thankful, Doni, Great Mother of All, and we are grateful to the Spirit of Cave Lion," she said aloud. Then she began speaking with the silent hand signs of the formal language of the Clan, the one they used when addressing the spirit world, but in a quiet voice, she translated the meaning of the signs she was making. "This woman is grateful to the Spirit of the Great Cave Lion, the totem of this woman, for allowing a few of the Spirit's living ones to fall to the spears of the people. This woman would express sorrow to the Great Spirit of the Cave Lion for the loss of the living ones. The Great Mother and the Cave Lion Spirit know it was necessary for the safety of the people, but this woman wants to express gratitude."

She turned around to the group of hunters who were watching her. It wasn't done in quite the manner they were used to, but it was fascinating to watch her, and felt utterly right to those hunters who had faced their fears to make their territory safer for themselves and for others. It also made them understand why their Zelandoni Who Was First had made this foreign woman her acolyte.

"I will not make a claim to any other lions that may have been pierced by one of my spears, but I would like the spear back," Ayla said. "This lion has only my spear in it, so I will claim it. I will keep the skin and tail, the claws and the teeth."

"What about the meat?" Palidar said. "Are you going to eat some?"

"No. The hyenas can have it as far as I'm concerned," Ayla said. "I don't like the taste of the meat of meat-eaters, especially cave lions."

"I've never tasted lion," he said.

"Neither have I," said Morizan of the Third Cave, who had paired up with Galeya.

"Did none of your spears reach a lion?" Ayla asked. She saw them shake their heads in a sadly negative response. "You're welcome to this one's meat, if you want it, after I bury the heart, but I wouldn't eat the liver if I were you."

"Why not?" Tivonan asked.

"The people I grew up with believed the liver of meat-eaters could kill you, like a poison," she said. "They told stories about it, especially of a selfish woman who ate the liver of a cat, a lynx, I think, and died. Perhaps we should bury the liver, too, with the heart."

"Is the liver of animals who eat any meat bad for you?" Galeya asked.

"I think bears are all right. They eat meat, but they eat everything else, as well. Cave bears don't eat much meat at all, and they taste good. I knew some people who ate their liver and didn't get sick," Ayla said.

"I haven't seen a cave bear in years," Solaban said. He'd been standing close by, listening. "There aren't many around here anymore. Have you really eaten cave bear?"

"Yes," Ayla said. She considered mentioning that cave bear meat was sacred to the Clan, eaten only for certain ritual feasts, but decided it would just encourage more questions that would take too long to answer.

She looked at the lioness, and took a deep breath. It was big and would be a lot of work to skin. She could use some help, and observed the four young people who had been asking her questions. None of them had used spear-throwers, but she guessed that might change now, and though they hadn't landed a spear, they had been a willing part of the hunt and exposed themselves to danger. She smiled at them. "I'll give each of you a claw if you'll help me skin this lioness," she said, and watched them smile back.

"I'll be glad to," Palidar and Tivonan said almost simultaneously.

"Me too," said Morizan.

"Good. I can use the help." Then she said to Morizan, "I don't think we have been formally introduced."

She faced the young man and held out both her hands, palm up, in the formal gesture of openness and friendship. "I am Ayla of the Ninth Cave of the Zelandonii, acolyte of Zelandoni, First Among Those Who Serve The Great Earth Mother, mated to Jondalar, Master Flint-Knapper and brother of Joharran, leader of the Ninth Cave of the Zelandonii. Formerly I was Daughter of the Mammoth Hearth of the Lion Camp of the Mamutoi, Chosen by the spirit of the Cave Lion, Protected by the Cave Bear, and friend of the horses, Whinney, Racer, and Gray, and the four-legged hunter, Wolf."

It was enough of a formal introduction, she thought, watching his expression. She knew the first part of the formal recitation of her names and ties was probably somewhat overwhelming—her associations were among the highest ranked of all the Zelandonii, and the last part would be completely unfamiliar to him.

He reached for her hands and began his names and ties. "I am Morizan of the Third Cave of the Zelandonii," he started nervously, then seemed to be trying to think what to say next. "I am the son of Manvelar, leader of the Third Cave, cousin of . . ."

Ayla realized he was young and not accustomed to meeting new people and making formal recitations. She decided to make it easy for him, and ended the formal meeting ritual. "In

the name of Doni, the Great Earth Mother, I greet you, Morizan of the Third Cave of the Zelandonii," she said, then added,
"and I welcome your help."

"I want to help, too," Galeya said. "I'd like to have a claw as
a memory of this hunt. Even if I didn't get a spear into any of
them, it was exciting. A little frightening, but exciting."

Ayla nodded in understanding. "Let's get started, but I should
warn you to be careful when you cut out the claws, or the
teeth; don't let them scratch you. You have to cook them before they can be safely handled. If you get a scratch, it can turn
into a foul wound, one that swells up and suppurates with a
bad-smelling discharge."

She looked up and noticed in the distance that some people
were coming around the jutting wall. She recognized several
from the Third Cave who had not been with the first group that
joined them before. Manvelar, the strong and vigorous older
man who was their leader, was among them.

"Here come Manvelar and some others," Thefona said. She
had obviously seen and recognized them too.

When they reached the hunters, Manvelar walked up to Joharran. "I greet you, Joharran, leader of the Ninth Cave of the
Zelandonii, in the name of Doni, the Great Earth Mother," he
said, holding both hands out.

Taking both hands in his, Joharran returned the short formal greeting to acknowledge the other leader. "In the name of
Great Earth Mother, Doni, I greet you, Manvelar, leader of the
Third Cave of the Zelandonii." It was a customary courtesy
between leaders.

"The people you sent back came up and told us what was
going on," Manvelar said. "We've seen the lions around here
the past few days, so we came to help. They were returning
regularly and we were wondering what we should do about
them. It looks like you have taken care of the problem. I see
four, no, five lions down, including the male. The females will
have to find a new male now; maybe they'll separate and find
more than one. It will change the entire structure of the pride.
I don't think they will be back bothering us soon. We need to
thank you."

"We didn't think we could pass them safely, and didn't want them threatening Caves in the vicinity, so we decided to chase them away, especially since we had several people with us who could use spear-throwers. It's a good thing we had them. Even though he was badly wounded, that big male attacked again, after we thought he was down," Joharran said.

"Hunting cave lions is dangerous. What are you going to do with them?"

"I think the hides, teeth, and claws have all been claimed, and some say they want to taste the meat," Joharran said.

"It's strong," Manvelar said, wrinkling his nose. "We'll help you with the skinning, but it will take some time. I think you should plan on spending the night with us. We can send a runner ahead and tell the Seventh that you've been delayed, and why."

"Good. We will stay. Thank you, Manvelar," Joharran said.

The Third Cave served a meal to the visitors from the Ninth before they set out the next morning. Joharran, Proleva, Proleva's son, Jaradal, and new baby daughter, Sethona, were seated together with Jondalar, Ayla, and her daughter, Jonayla, out on the sunny stone front porch, enjoying the view along with their food.

"It would seem that Morizan is taking quite an interest in Folara's friend Galeya," Proleva said. They were watching the group of not-yet-mated young people with the indulgent eye of older siblings with families.

"Yes," Jondalar said, with a grin. "She was his backup yesterday during the lion hunt. Hunting together and depending on each other like that can create a special bond quickly, even if they didn't land a spear so they could lay claim to a lion. But they helped Ayla skin out her lioness, and she gave each of them a claw. They were done so fast, they came over and helped me, and I gave each of them a small claw, too, so they all have mementos of the hunt."

"That's what they were showing off last night over that cooking basket," Proleva said.

"Can I have a claw for a memento, Ayla?" Jaradal asked. The youngster had obviously been listening closely.

"Jaradal, those are mementos of a hunt," his mother said. "When you get old enough to go on hunts, you'll get your own mementos."

"That's all right, Proleva. I'll give him one," Joharran said, smiling gently at the son of his mate. "I got a lion, too."

"You did!" the six-year boy said excitedly, "and I can have a claw? Wait until I show Robenan!"

"Make sure you cook it before you give it to him," Ayla said.

"That's what Galeya and the rest were cooking last night," Jondalar said. "Ayla insisted that everyone cook the claws and fangs before they handled them. She says a scratch from a lion claw can be dangerous unless it's cooked."

"Why should cooking make a difference?" Proleva asked.

"When I was little, before I was found by the Clan, I was scratched by a cave lion. That's how I got the scars on my leg. I don't recall much about getting scratched, but I do remember how much my leg hurt until it healed. The Clan liked to keep the teeth and claws of animals, too," Ayla said. "When she was teaching me to be a medicine woman, one of the first things Iza told me was to cook them before they were handled. She said they were full of evil spirits, and the heat of cooking them drove the foulness out."

"When you think of what those animals do with their claws, they must be full of evil spirits," Proleva said. "I'll make sure Jaradal's claw gets cooked."

"That lion hunt did prove out your weapon, Jondalar," Joharran said. "Those who just had spears probably would have been good protection, if the lions had gotten closer, but the only kills were made with spear-throwers. I think it's going to encourage more people to practice."

They saw Manvelar approach, and greeted him cordially.

"You can leave your lion skins here and pick them up on your way back," he said. "We can store them in the back of the lower abri. It's cool enough down there that they should keep for a few days; then you can process them when you get home."

The tall limestone cliff they had passed just before the hunt, called Two Rivers Rock because Grass River joined The River there, had three deeply indented ledges, one above the other, that created protective overhangs for the spaces below them. The Third Cave used all of the stone shelters, but they lived mainly in the large middle one, which enjoyed an expansive panorama of both rivers and the area around the cliff. The others were mainly for storage.

"That would be a help," Joharran said. "We're carrying enough, especially with babies and children, and we've already been delayed. If this trip to Horsehead Rock hadn't been planned for some time, we probably wouldn't be making it. After all, we'll be seeing everyone at the Summer Meeting, and we still have a lot to do before we leave. But the Seventh Cave really wanted Ayla to visit, and Zelandoni wants to show her the Horsehead. And since it's so close, they want to go to Elder Hearth and visit the Second Cave, and see the ancestors carved in the wall of their lower cave."

"Where is the First Among Those Who Serve The Great Earth Mother?" Manvelar asked.

"She's already there, has been for a few days," Joharran said. "Conferring with several of the zelandonia. Something to do with the Summer Meeting."

"Speaking of that, when are you planning to leave?" Manvelar asked. "Perhaps we can travel together."

"I always like to leave a little early. With such a large Cave, we need extra time to find a comfortable place. And now we have animals to consider. I've been to the Twenty-sixth Cave before, but I'm not really familiar with the area."

"It's a large, flat field right beside West River," Manvelar said. "It's good for a lot of summer shelters, but I don't think it's a good place for horses."

"I like the site we found last year, even if it was rather far from all the activities, but I don't know what we'll find this year. I was thinking of scouting it out earlier, but then we got those heavy spring rains and I just didn't want to slog through the mud," Joharran said.

"If you don't mind being a bit out of the way, there may be a more secluded place nearer Sun View, the shelter of the Twenty-sixth Cave. It's in a cliff near the bank of the old riverbed, somewhat back from the river now."

"We may try that," Joharran said. "I'll send a runner after

we decide when to leave. If the Third Cave wants to go then, we can travel together. You have kin there, don't you? Do you have a route in mind? I know that West River runs in the same general direction as The River, so it isn't hard to find. All we have to do is go south to Big River, then west until we reach West River, and then follow it north, but if you know a more direct way, it might be a little faster."

"In fact, I do," Manvelar said. "You know my mate came from the Twenty-sixth Cave, and we visited her family often when the children were younger. I haven't been back since she died and I'm looking forward to this Summer Meeting and seeing some people I haven't seen for a while. Morizan and his brother and sister have cousins there."

"We can talk more when we return for the lion skins. Thank you for the hospitality of the Third Cave, Manvelar," Joharran said, as he turned to leave. "We need to be going. The Second Cave is expecting us, and Zelandoni Who Is First has a cave with a surprise to show Ayla."

Spring's first shoots had made a watercolor smear of emerald on the cold, brown defrosting earth. As the short season advanced and jointed stems and slender sheathing leaves reached their full growth, lush meadows replaced the cold colors along the floodplains of the rivers. Billowing in the warmer winds of early summer, the green of rapid growth fading to the gold of ripening maturity, the fields of grass ahead named the river beside them.

The group of travelers, some from the Ninth Cave and some from the Third, walked beside Grass River, retracing their steps from the previous day. They walked around the jutting stone in single file along the trail between the clear running water of Grass River and the cliff. As they continued, some people moved forward to walk two or three abreast.

They took the path that angled toward the crossing place—it was already being called the Place of the Lion Hunt. The way the rocks had been placed naturally was not an easy crossing. It was one thing for agile young men to leap from stone to slippery stone; it was quite another for a woman who was pregnant or carrying a baby, and perhaps other packs of food, clothing, or implements, or for older women or men. Therefore, more rocks had been carefully positioned between those the lower water level had uncovered to make the spaces between the stepping-stones closer. After they all had reached the other side of the tributary, where the trail was wide enough, they tended to walk two or three abreast again.

Morizan waited for Jondalar and Ayla, who were bringing up the rear in front of the horses, and stepped in beside them. After a casual exchange of greetings, Morizan commented, "I didn't realize how good your spear-throwing weapon could be, Jondalar. I've been practicing with it, but watching you and Ayla use it has given me a new appreciation for it."

"I think it's wise of you to make yourself familiar with the spear-thrower, Morizan. It is a very effective weapon. Is it something Manvelar suggested, or did you decide to do it on your own?" Jondalar asked.

"I decided, but once I started, he encouraged me. He said I was setting a good example," Morizan said. "To be honest, I didn't care about that. It just looked like a weapon I wanted to learn."

Jondalar grinned at the young man. He had thought it might be the younger ones who would be willing to try out his new weapon first, and Morizan's response was exactly what he had hoped would happen.

"Good. The more you practice, the better you will get. Ayla and I have been using the spear-thrower for a long time, all during the yearlong Journey back home, and for more than a year before that. As you can see, women can handle a spear-thrower very effectively."

They followed Grass River upstream for some distance, then came to a smaller tributary that was called Little Grass River. As they continued upstream along the smaller waterway, Ayla began to notice a change in the air, a cool, moist freshness filled with richer smells. Even the grass was a darker shade of green, and in places the ground was softer. The path skirted marshy areas of tall reeds and cattails as they proceeded through the lush valley and approached a limestone cliff.

Several people were waiting outside, among them two young women. Ayla grinned when she saw them. They had all mated at the same Matrimonial during last year's Summer Meeting, and she felt especially close to them.

"Levela! Janida! I was looking forward to seeing you so much," she said, walking toward them. "I heard you had both decided to move to the Second Cave."

"Ayla!" Levela said. "Welcome to Horsehead Rock. We decided to come here with Kimeran to see you, so we wouldn't have to wait until you came to visit the Second. It's so good to see you."

"Yes," Janida concurred. She was considerably younger than the other two women, and rather shy, but her smile was welcoming. "I am glad to see you, too, Ayla."

The three women embraced, though they were all rather careful about it. Both Ayla and Janida were carrying infants, and Levela was pregnant.

"I heard you had a boy, Janida," Ayla said.

"Yes, I named him Jeridan," Janida said, showing her baby.

"I had a girl. Her name is Jonayla," Ayla said. The infant was already awake from the commotion and Ayla lifted her out of the carrying blanket as she spoke, then turned to look at the baby boy. "Oh, he's perfect. May I hold him?"

"Yes, of course, and I want to hold your daughter," Janida said.

"Why don't I take your baby, Ayla," Levela said. "Then you can take Jeridan, and I'll give . . . Jonayla?" she saw Ayla nod, "to Janida."

The women shifted infants and cooed at them, while they looked them over and compared them with their own.

"You know Levela is pregnant, don't you?" Janida said.

"I can see that," Ayla said. "Do you know how soon you will have yours, Levela? I'd like to come and be here with you, and I'm sure Proleva would, too."

"I don't know for sure, some moons yet. I would love to have you with me, and definitely my sister," Levela said. "But you won't need to come here. We'll probably all be at the Summer Meeting."

"You're right," Ayla said. "It will be nice for you to have everyone around you. Even Zelandoni the First will be there, and she is wonderful at helping a mother to deliver."

"There may be too many," Janida said. "Everyone likes Levela, and they won't let everyone stay with you. It would be too crowded. You may not want me; I'm not very experienced, but I would like to be there with you, the way you were with me, Levela. I'll understand, though, if you would rather have someone that you've known longer."

"Of course I want you with me, Janida, and Ayla, too. After all, we shared the same Matrimonial, and that's a special bond," Levela said.

Ayla understood the feelings that Janida had expressed. She, too, wondered if Levela would rather have friends she had known longer. Ayla felt a flush of warmth for the young woman, and was surprised at the sting of tears she fought to hold back at Levela's willing acceptance of her. Growing up, Ayla hadn't had many friends. Girls of the Clan mated at a young age, and Oga, the one who might have been close, had become Broud's mate, and he wouldn't allow her to be too friendly with the girl of the Others that he had come to hate. She loved Iza's daughter, Uba, her Clan sister, but she was so much younger, she was more like a daughter than a friend. And while the other women had grown to accept her, and even care about her, they never really understood her. It wasn't until she went to live with the Mamutoi and met Deegie that she understood the fun of having a woman friend her own age.

"Speaking of Matrimonials and mates, where are Jondecam and Peridal? I think Jondalar feels a special bond for them, too. I know he was looking forward to seeing them," Ayla said.

"They want to see him, too," Levela said. "Jondalar and his spear-throwing weapon is all Jondecam and Peridal have talked about since we knew you were coming."

"Did you know that Tishona and Marsheval are living at the Ninth Cave now?" Ayla said, referring to another couple who had mated at the same time as they did. "They tried living at the Fourteenth, but Marsheval was at the Ninth Cave so often—or I should say at Down River learning how to shape mammoth ivory, and staying overnight at the Ninth—that they decided to move."

The three Zelandonia were standing back, watching, as the young women continued to chat. The First noticed how easily

Ayla fell into conversation with them, comparing babies and talking excitedly about the things that were of interest to young mated women with children, or expecting them. She had begun teaching Ayla some of the rudiments of the knowledge she would need to become a full-fledged Zelandoni, and the young woman was without doubt interested and quick to learn, but the First was now realizing how easily Ayla could get distracted. She'd been holding back, letting Ayla enjoy her new life as a mother and mated woman. Maybe it was time to push her a little harder, get her so involved that she would voluntarily choose to devote more time to learning what she needed to know.

"We should go, Ayla," the First said. "I would like you to see the cave before we get too involved with meals and visiting and meeting people."

"Yes, we should," Ayla said. "I left all three horses and Wolf with Jondalar, and we need to get them settled. I'm sure he has people he wants to see, too."

They walked toward the steep wall of limestone. The setting sun was shining directly on it and the small fire that had been built nearby was almost invisible in the bright sunlight. A dark hole was visible but not obvious. There were several torches propped against the wall and each of the Zelandonia lit one. Ayla followed the others into the dark hole, shivering as the darkness enveloped her. Inside the cavity in the rock cliff, the air suddenly felt cool and damp, but it wasn't only the abrupt drop in temperature that chilled her. She hadn't been there before and Ayla felt a touch of apprehension and trepidation when she entered an unfamiliar cave.

The opening was not big, but high enough so that no one had to bend over or stoop to enter. She had lit a torch outside and held the light in her left hand high in front of her, reaching for the rough stone wall with her right to steady herself. The warm bundle that she carried close to her chest with the soft carrying blanket was still awake, and she moved her hand from the wall to pat the baby to quiet her. Jonayla probably notices the change in temperature too, Ayla thought, looking around as she moved inside. It was not a large cave but it was naturally divided into separate smaller areas.

"It's here in the next room," said Zelandoni of the Second Cave. She was also a tall blond woman, though somewhat older than Ayla.

The Zelandoni Who Was First Among Those Who Served The Great Earth Mother stepped aside to let Ayla move in behind the woman who was leading them. "You go ahead. I've seen it before," she said, shifting her considerable size out of the way.

An older man stepped back with her. "I, too, have seen it before," he said, "many times." Ayla had noticed how much the old Zelandoni of the Seventh Cave resembled the woman who was leading the way. He was also tall, though a little stooped, and his hair was more white than blond.

Zelandoni of the Second Cave held her torch up high to cast its light ahead; Ayla did the same. She thought she saw some indistinct images on some of the cave walls as they passed by, but since no one had stopped to point them out, she wasn't sure. She heard someone begin to hum—a rich, lovely sound—and recognized the voice of her mentor, the Zelandoni Who Was First. Her voice echoed in the small stone chamber, but especially as they entered another room and turned a corner. As the Zelandonia held their torches up to highlight a wall, Ayla gasped.

She wasn't prepared for the sight in front of her. The profile of the head of a horse was carved so deeply into the limestone wall of the cave, it appeared to be growing out of it, and so realistically, it almost seemed alive. It was larger than life-size, or else it was a carving of a much larger animal than she had ever seen, but she knew horses and the proportions were perfect. The shape of the muzzle, the eye, the ear, the nose with its flaring nostril, the curve of the mouth and jaw, everything was exactly as it would be in real life. And in the flickering torchlight, it looked as if it were moving, breathing.

She let out a sobbing burst of air; she had been holding her breath and didn't realize it. "It's a perfect horse, except it's just the head!" Ayla said.

"That's why the Seventh Cave is called Horsehead Rock," the old man said. He was just behind her.

Ayla stared at the image, feeling a sense of awe and wonder, and reached out to touch the stone, not even questioning whether she should have. She was drawn to it. She held her hand on the side of the jaw, just where she would have touched a living horse, and after a time the cold stone seemed to warm as though it wanted to be alive and come out of the stone wall. She took her hand away, and then put it back. The rock surface still held some warmth, but then it cooled again, and she realized that the First had continued to hum while she touched the stone, but had stopped when she let go.

"Who made it?" Ayla asked.

"No one knows," said the First. She had come in after Zelandoni of the Seventh Cave. "It was made so long ago, no one remembers. One of the Ancients, of course, but we have no legend or history to tell us who."

"Perhaps the same carver who made The Mother of Elder Hearth," said the Zelandoni of the Second Cave.

"What makes you think so?" asked the old man. "They are entirely different images. One is a woman holding a bison horn in her hand; the other is the head of a horse."

"I have studied both carvings. There seems to be a similarity of technique," she said. "Notice how carefully the nose and the mouth, and the shape of the jaw of this horse are made? When you go there, look at the hips on the Mother, the shape of the belly. I've seen women who look just like that, especially those who have had children. Like this horse, the carving of the woman that represents Doni in the cave at Elder Hearth is very true to life."

"That's very perceptive," said the One Who Was First. "When we go to Elder Hearth, we'll do as you suggest, and look closely." They stood quietly, staring at the horse for a while; then the First said, "We should go. There are some other things in here, but we can look at them later. I wanted Ayla to see the Horsehead before we got involved with visiting and such."

"I'm glad you did," Ayla said. "I didn't know carvings in stone could look so real."

3

"There you are!" Kimeran said, getting up from a stone seat on the ledge in front of the shelter of the Seventh Cave to greet Ayla and Jondalar, who had just climbed up the path. Wolf followed behind them and Jonayla was awake and propped up on Ayla's hip. "We knew you had come, and then no one knew where you were."

Jondalar's old friend Kimeran, the leader of Elder Hearth, the Second Cave of the Zelandonii, had been waiting for him. The very tall light-haired man bore a superficial resemblance to six-foot-six-inch Jondalar with his pale yellow hair. Though many men were tall—over six feet—both Jondalar and Kimeran had towered over their other age-mates at their puberty rites. They were drawn to each other and quickly became friends. Kimeran was also the brother of the Zelandoni of the Second Cave, and the uncle of Jondecam but more like a brother. His sister was quite a bit older, and she had raised him after their mother died, along with her own son and daughter. Her mate had also passed on to the next world, and not long afterward she began training for the zelandonia.

"The First wanted Ayla to see your Horsehead, and then we needed to get our horses settled," Jondalar said.

"They are going to love your field. The grass is so green and rich," Ayla added.

"We call it Sweet Valley. The Little Grass River runs through the middle of it, and the floodplain has widened into a large field. It can get marshy in spring from snowmelt, and when the rains come in fall, but in summer when everything else is dried out, that field stays fresh and green," Kimeran said, as they continued walking toward the living space beneath the overhanging upper shelf. "It attracts a nice procession of grazers through here all summer long and makes hunting easy. Either the Second or the Seventh Cave always has someone watching."

They approached more people. "You remember Sergenor, the leader of the Seventh Cave, don't you?" Kimeran said to the visiting couple, indicating a middle-aged dark-haired man who had been standing back eyeing the wolf warily, and letting the younger leader greet his friends.

"Yes, of course," Jondalar said, noting his apprehension, and thinking that this visit might be a good time to help people get more comfortable around Wolf. "I remember when Sergenor used to come to talk to Marthona when he was first chosen as leader of the Seventh. You have met Ayla, I believe."

"I was one of the many to whom she was introduced last year when you first arrived, but I haven't had a chance to greet her personally," Sergenor said. He held out both hands, palms up. "In the name of Doni, I welcome you to the Seventh Cave of the Zelandonii, Ayla of the Ninth Cave. I know you have many other names and ties, some quite unusual, but I will admit, I don't remember them."

Ayla grasped both of his hands in hers. "I am Ayla of the Ninth Cave of the Zelandonii," she began, "acolyte to Zelandoni of the Ninth Cave, First Among Those Who Serve"; then she hesitated, wondering how many of Jondalar's ties to mention. At the Matrimonial Ceremony last summer, all of Jondalar's names and ties were added to hers, and it made for a very long recitation, but it was only during the most formal of ceremonies that the whole list was required. Since this was her official meeting of the leader of the Seventh Cave, she wanted to make the introduction formal, but not go on and on.

She decided to cite the closest of his ties and continue with her own, including her previous ties. She finished with the appellations that had been added in a more lighthearted vein, but that she liked to use. "Friend of the horses, Whinney, Racer, and Gray, and the four-legged hunter, Wolf. In the name of the Great Mother of all, I greet you, Sergenor, leader of the

Seventh Cave of the Zelandonii, and I would like to thank you for inviting us to Horsehead Rock."

She is definitely not a Zelandonii, Sergenor thought, as he heard her speak. She may have Jondalar's names and ties, but she's a foreigner with foreign customs, especially about animals. As he dropped her hands, he eyed the wolf, who had come closer.

Ayla saw his uneasiness around the big carnivore. She had noticed that Kimeran was not particularly comfortable near the animal either, though he had been introduced to Wolf last year shortly after they arrived, and he had seen him several times. Neither of the leaders was accustomed to seeing a hunting meat-eater moving so easily among people. Her thoughts were similar to Jondalar's: this might be a good time to get them more accustomed to Wolf.

The people of the Seventh Cave were noticing that the couple everyone talked about from the Ninth Cave had arrived, and more people were coming to see the woman with the wolf. All the nearby Caves had known within a day when Jondalar returned from his five-year-long Journey the summer before. Arriving on horseback with a foreign woman guaranteed it. They had met people from most of the nearby Caves at the Ninth Cave when they came to visit, or at the last Summer Meeting, but this was the first time they had paid a visit to the Seventh or the Second Cave.

Ayla and Jondalar had planned to go the previous fall, but never quite made it. It wasn't that their Caves were so far away from each other, but something always seemed to interfere, and then winter was upon them, and Ayla was getting along in her pregnancy. All the delayed expectation had made their visit an occasion, especially since the First had decided to have a meeting here with the local zelandonia at the same time.

"Whoever carved the Horsehead in the cave below must have known horses. It is very well made," Ayla said.

"I always thought so, but it is nice to hear it from someone who knows horses as well as you do," Sergenor said.

Wolf was sitting back on his haunches with his tongue hanging out of the side of his mouth, eyeing the man, his bent ear giving him a cocky, self-satisfied look. Ayla knew he was expecting to be introduced. He had watched her greet the leader of the Seventh Cave and he had come to expect to be presented to any stranger that she greeted in that way.

"I also want to thank you for allowing me to bring Wolf. He's always unhappy if he can't be near me, and now he feels that way about Jonayla, since he loves children so much," Ayla said.

"That wolf loves children?" Sergenor said.

"Wolf didn't grow up with other wolves, he was raised with the Mamutoi children of the Lion Camp and thinks of people as his pack, and all wolves love the young of their packs," Ayla said. "He saw me greet you and now he expects to meet you. He has learned to accept anyone that I introduce him to."

Sergenor frowned. "How do you introduce a wolf?" he said. He glanced at Kimeran and saw him grinning.

The younger man was remembering his introduction to Wolf, and though he might still be somewhat nervous around the carnivore, he was rather enjoying the older man's discomfiture.

Ayla signaled Wolf to come forward and knelt down to put her arm around him, then reached for Sergenor's hand. He jerked it back.

"He only needs to smell it," Ayla said, "so he becomes familiar with you. It's the way wolves meet each other."

"Did you do this, Kimeran?" Sergenor said, noticing that most of his Cave and their visitors were watching.

"Yes, in fact I did. Last summer, when they went to the Third Cave to hunt before the Summer Meeting. Afterward, whenever I saw the wolf at the Meeting, I had the feeling that he recognized me, though he ignored me," Kimeran said.

He didn't really want to, but with all the people watching, Sergenor was feeling pressed to comply. He didn't want anyone to think that he was afraid to do what the younger leader had already done. Slowly, tentatively, he stretched out his hand toward the animal. Ayla took it and brought it to the animal's nose. Wolf wrinkled his nose and, with his mouth closed, bared his teeth so that his large carnassial shearing teeth showed, in what Jondalar always thought of as his feeling-full-of-himself grin. But that wasn't how Sergenor saw it. Ayla could feel him shaking, and noticed the sour smell of his fear. She knew Wolf did, too.

"Wolf won't hurt you, I promise," Ayla said softly, under her breath. Sergenor gritted his teeth, forcing himself to hold steady while the wolf brought his tooth-filled mouth close to his hand. Wolf sniffed, then licked.

"What's he doing?" Sergenor said. "Trying to see what I taste like?"

"No, I think he's trying to calm you, like he would a puppy. Here, touch his head." She moved his hand away from the sharp teeth, and was speaking in a soothing voice. "Have you ever felt the fur of a living wolf? Do you notice that behind his ears and around his neck, the fur is a little thicker and rougher? He likes being rubbed behind his ears." When she finally let go, the man moved his hand away and held it in his other hand.

"Now he will recognize you," she said. She had never seen anyone so afraid of Wolf, or more brave in overcoming his fear. "Have you ever had any experience with wolves before?" she asked.

"Once, when I was very young, I was bitten by a wolf. I don't really remember, my mother told me about it, but I still have the scars," Sergenor said.

"That means the Wolf spirit chose you. The Wolf is your totem. That's what the people who raised me would say." She knew totems were not viewed the same way by the Zelandonii as they were by the Clan. Not everyone had one, but they were considered lucky by those who did. "I was clawed by a cave lion when I was young, when I could count perhaps five years. I still have the scars to show for it, and I still dream about it sometimes. It is not easy to live with a powerful totem like a Lion or a Wolf, but my totem has helped me, taught me many things," Ayla said.

Sergenor was intrigued, almost in spite of himself. "What did you learn from a cave lion?"

"How to face my fears, for one thing," she said. "I think you have learned to do the same. Your Wolf totem may have helped you without your knowing it."

"Perhaps, but how would you know if you have been helped

by a totem? Has a Cave Lion Spirit really helped you?"
Sergenor asked.

"More than once. The four marks that the lion's claw left on
my leg, that is a Clan totem mark for a Cave Lion. Usually it
is only a man who is given such a strong totem, but they were
so clearly Clan marks, the leader accepted me even though I
was born to the Others—that's their name for people like us.
I was very young when I lost my people. If the Clan hadn't taken
me in and raised me, I would not be alive now," Ayla explained.

"Interesting, but you said 'more than once,'" Sergenor reminded her.

"Another time, after I became a woman and the new young
leader forced me to leave, I walked for a long time looking for
the Others as my Clan mother, Iza, had told me to do before
she died. But when I couldn't find them, and I had to find a
place to stay before winter came, my totem sent a pride of
lions to make me change my direction, which led me to find a
valley where I could survive. It was even my cave lion who led
me to Jondalar," Ayla said.

The people who were standing around listening were fascinated with her story. Even Jondalar had never heard her explain her totem in quite that way. One of them spoke out.

"And these people who took you in, the ones you call the
Clan, are they really Flatheads?"

"That's your name for them. They call themselves the Clan,
the Clan of the Cave Bear, because they all venerate the Spirit
of the Cave Bear. He is the totem of all of them, the Clan
totem," Ayla said.

"I think it's time to let these travelers know where they can
put down their sleeping rolls and get settled so they can share
a meal with us," said a woman who had just arrived. She was
a pleasantly round, attractive woman with the glint of intelligence and spirit in her eyes.

Sergenor smiled with warm affection. "This is my mate,
Jayvena of the Seventh Cave of the Zelandonii," he said to
Ayla. "Jayvena, this is Ayla of the Ninth Cave of the Zelandonii. She has many more names and ties, but I'll let her tell
you."

"But not now," Jayvena said. "In the name of the Mother,

welcome, Ayla of the Ninth Cave. I'm sure you would rather get settled now than recite names and ties."

As they were starting to leave, Sergenor touched Ayla's arm and looked at her, then said, quietly, "I sometimes dream of wolves." She smiled.

As they were leaving, a voluptuous young woman with dark brown hair approached, holding two children in her arms, a dark-haired boy and a blond girl. She smiled at Kimeran, who lightly brushed her cheek with his, then turned to the visitors. "You met my mate, Beladora, last summer, didn't you?" he said, adding in a voice filled with pride, "and her son and daughter, the children of my hearth?"

Ayla recalled meeting the woman briefly the summer before, though she hadn't had a chance to get to know her. She knew that Beladora had given birth to her two-born-together at the Summer Meeting around the time of the First Matrimonial, when she and Jondalar were mated. Everyone had been talking about it. That meant the two would soon be able to count one year, she thought.

"Yes, of course," Jondalar said, bestowing a smile on the woman and her twins, then without really being aware of it, paying closer attention to the attractive young mother, his vivid blue eyes full of appreciation. She smiled back. Kimeran moved closer and put an arm around her waist.

Ayla was adept at reading body language, but she thought anyone could have understood what had just transpired. Jondalar found Beladora attractive, and couldn't help showing it, just as she couldn't help responding to him. Jondalar was unaware of his own charisma, didn't even realize he projected it, but Beladora's mate was very aware of it. Without saying a word, Kimeran had stepped in and made his claim known.

Ayla observed the byplay and was so intrigued that even though Jondalar was her mate, she didn't feel any jealousy. She did, however, begin to appreciate the comments she had been hearing about him ever since they had arrived. At a deeper level she knew that Jondalar was only appreciating; he had no desire to do more than look. There was another side to him, one that he rarely showed even to her, and then only when they were alone.

Jondalar's emotions had always been too strong, his passions too great. All his life he had struggled to control them and had finally managed only by learning to keep his feelings to himself. It was not easy for him to show the full intensity of his feelings. That was why he never displayed publicly the depth of his love for her, but sometimes when they were alone he couldn't control it. It was so powerful, it sometimes overwhelmed him.

When Ayla turned her head, she noticed Zelandoni Who Was First observing her, and understood that she, too, had been aware of the unspoken interactions and was trying to judge her response. Ayla gave her a knowing smile, then turned her attention to her baby, who was squirming in her carrying blanket, trying to find a way to nurse. She approached the handsome young mother who was standing beside Jayvena.

"Greetings, Beladora. I am glad to see you, especially with your children," she said. "Jonayla has soaked her padding. I brought some extra to replace it; would you show me where I can change it?"

The woman with a baby on each hip smiled. "Come with me," she said, and the three women started toward the shelter.

Beladora had heard people talk about Ayla's unusual accent, but she hadn't really heard her speak before. She was in labor during the Matrimonial when Jondalar mated his foreign woman, and she'd had little occasion to talk to Ayla later. She was busy with her own concerns, but now she knew what they meant. Though Ayla spoke Zelandonii very well, she just couldn't make some of the sounds exactly right, but Beladora was rather pleased to hear her. She had come from a region far to the south, and though her speech wasn't as unusual as Ayla's, she spoke Zelandonii with her own distinctive accent.

Ayla smiled when she heard her talk. "I think you were not born a Zelandonii," she said. "Just as I was not."

"My people are known as the Giornadonii. We are neighbors of a Cave of Zelandonii far south of here, where it's much warmer." Beladora smiled. "I met Kimeran when he traveled with his sister on her Donier Tour."

Ayla wondered what a "Donier Tour" was. Obviously, it had something to do with being a Zelandoni, since "donier" was another word for One Who Served The Great Mother, but Ayla decided she would ask the First later.

The fire's lambent flames cast a comforting ruddy glow beyond the confines of the oblong hearth that contained it, and painted a warm dancing light on the limestone walls of the abri. The rock ceiling of the overhanging ledge above the fire reflected the glowing hue down on the scene, giving the people a radiant look of well-being. A delicious communal meal that had taken many people a great deal of time and effort to prepare had been consumed, including a huge haunch of megaceros roasted on a sturdy spit stretched across large forked branches over that same extended rectangular firepit. Now the Seventh Cave of the Zelandonii along with many relatives from the Second Cave and their visitors from the Ninth and Third Caves were ready to relax.

Beverages had been offered: several varieties of tea, a fermented fruity wine, and the alcoholic brew called barma made from birch sap, with additions of wild grains, honey, or various fruits. They had each taken a cup of their favorite drink, and were milling about, looking for a place to sit near the welcoming hearth. A heightened feeling of anticipation and delight permeated the group. Visitors always brought a bit of excitement, but the foreign woman with her animals and exotic stories promised to be more stimulating than usual.

Ayla and Jondalar were in the midst of a group that included Joharran and Proleva, Sergenor and Jayvena, and Kimeran and Beladora, the leaders of the Ninth, Seventh and Second Caves, and several others, including Levela and Janida and their mates, Jondecam and Peridal. The leaders were discussing with the people of the Seventh Cave when the visitors should leave Horsehead Rock and go to Elder Hearth, with jocular asides, in a friendly rivalry with the Second Cave about where the visitors should stay the longest.

"Elder Hearth is senior and should be higher ranking and accorded more prestige," Kimeran said with a teasing grin. "So we should have them longer."

"Does that mean because I'm older than you, I should be

accorded more prestige?" Sergenor countered with a telling smile. "I'll remember that."

Ayla had been listening and smiling with the rest, but she had been wanting to ask a question. At a break in the conversation, she finally said, "Now that you have brought up the ages of the Caves, there is something I would like to know." They all turned to look at her.

"You have only to ask," Kimeran said with exaggerated courtesy and friendliness that intimated the suggestion of more. He had drunk a few cups of barma and was noticing how attractive his tall friend's mate was.

"Last summer Manvelar was telling me a little about the counting-word names of each Cave, but I'm still confused," Ayla said. "When we went to the Summer Meeting last year, we stopped overnight at the Twenty-ninth Cave. They live at three separate shelters around a big valley, each with a leader and a zelandoni, but they are all called by the same counting word, the Twenty-ninth. The Second Cave is closely related to the Seventh Cave, and you live just across a valley, so why do you have a Cave with a different counting word? Why aren't you part of the Second Cave?"

"That's one I can't answer. I don't know," Kimeran said, then gestured toward the older man. "You'll have to ask the more senior leader. Sergenor?"

Sergenor smiled, but pondered the question for a moment. "To be honest, I don't know, either. It never occurred to me before. And I don't know of any Histories or Elder Legends that tell about it. There are some that tell stories of the original inhabitants of the region, the First Cave of the Zelandonii, but they have long since disappeared. No one even knows for sure where their shelter was."

"You do know that the Second Cave of the Zelandonii is the oldest settlement of Zelandonii still in existence?" Kimeran said, his voice slightly slurred. "That's why it's called Elder Hearth."

"Yes, I knew that," she said, wondering if he would need the "morning after" drink she had concocted for Talut, the Mamutoi leader of the Lion Camp.

"I'll tell you what I think," Sergenor said. "As the families of the First and Second Caves grew too large for their shelters, some of them, offshoots of both Caves as well as new people who had come into the region, moved farther away, taking the next counting words when they established a new Cave. By the time the group of people from the Second Cave who founded our Cave decided to move, the next unused counting word was 'seven.' They were mostly young families—some newly mated couples, the children of the Second Cave—and they wanted to stay close to their relatives, so they moved here, just across Sweet Valley, to make their new home. Even though the two Caves were so closely related, they were the same as one Cave, I think they chose a new number because that's the way it was done. So we became two separate Caves: Elder Hearth, the Second Cave of the Zelandonii, and Horsehead Rock, the Seventh Cave. We are still just different branches of the same family."

"The Twenty-ninth is a newer Cave," Sergenor continued. "When they moved to their new shelters, I suspect they all wanted to keep the same counting-word name, because the smaller the counting word, the older the settlement. There is a certain prestige in having a lower counting word and Twenty-nine was rather large already. I suspect none of the people founding the new Caves wanted a larger one. They decided to call themselves Three Rocks, the Twenty-ninth Cave of the Zelandonii, and then use the names they had already given to the locations to explain the difference.

"The original settlement is called Reflection Rock, because from certain places you can see yourself in the water below. It is one of the few shelters that face north and is not quite as easy to keep warm, but it is a remarkable place and has many other advantages. It is the South Holding of the Twenty-ninth Cave, or sometimes the South Holding of Three Rocks. South Face became the North Holding, and Summer Camp became the West Holding of the Twenty-ninth Cave. I think their way is more complicated and confusing, but it's their choice."

"If the Second Cave is the oldest, then the next-oldest group still in existence must be Two Rivers Rock, the Third Cave of the Zelandonii. We stayed there last night," Ayla said, nodding as she understood more.

"That's right," Proleva said, joining in.

"But there is no Fourth Cave, is there?"

"There was a Fourth Cave," Proleva replied, "but no one seems to know what happened to it. There are Legends that hint at some catastrophe that struck more than one Cave, and the Fourth may have disappeared around that time, but no one knows. It's a dark time in the Histories, too. Some fighting with the Flatheads is inferred."

"The Fifth Cave, called Old Valley, upstream along The River, is next after the Third," Jondalar said. "We were going to visit them on our way to the Summer Meeting last year, but they had already left, remember?" Ayla nodded. "They have several shelters on both sides of Short River Valley, some for living, some for storage, but they don't give them separate counting words. All of Old Valley is the Fifth Cave."

"The Sixth Cave has disappeared, too," Sergenor continued. "There are different stories about what happened to it. Most people think illness reduced their numbers. Others believe there was a difference of opinion between factions. In any case, the Histories indicate that the people who had once been the Sixth Cave joined up with other Caves, so we, the Seventh Cave, are next. There is no Eighth Cave, either, so your Cave, the Ninth, comes after ours."

There was a moment of silence while the information was absorbed. Then, changing the subject, Jondecam asked Jondalar if he would look at the spear-thrower he had made, and Levela told her older sister, Proleva, that she was thinking about going to the Ninth Cave to have her baby, which elicited a smile. People started having private conversations and soon split up into other groups.

Jondecam was not the only one who wanted to ask questions about the spear-thrower, especially after learning about the lion hunt the day before. Jondalar had developed the hunting weapon while he lived with Ayla in her eastern valley and had demonstrated it shortly after he had returned to his home the previous summer. He had held further exhibitions at the Summer Meeting.

Earlier in the afternoon, when Jondalar was waiting for Ayla to visit Horsehead cave, several had practiced casting spears with throwers they had made, patterned after the ones they had seen him use, while Jondalar gave them instructions and advice. Now a group of people, primarily men but including some women, were gathered around him, asking questions about the techniques of making spear-throwers, and the light-weight spears that had proved to be so effective with it.

Across the hearth, near the wall that helped contain the heat, several women who had babies, Ayla among them, were gathered together feeding, rocking, or keeping an eye on sleeping ones while they chatted.

In a separate, more isolated area of the shelter, Zelandoni Who Was First had been talking with the other Zelandonia and their acolytes, feeling just a little annoyed that Ayla, who was her acolyte, had not joined them. She knew she had pushed her into it, but Ayla was already an accomplished healer when she had arrived, and had other remarkable skills besides, including knowing how to control animals. She belonged in the zelandonia!

The Zelandoni of the Seventh had asked the First a question and was waiting for an answer with a patient expression. He had noticed that the Zelandoni of the Ninth Cave seemed distracted and a bit annoyed. He had been observing her since the visitors had arrived and had seen her irritation grow, and guessed why. When Zelandonia visited each other with their acolytes, it was a good time to teach the novices some of the knowledge and lore they had to learn and memorize, and her acolyte was not here. But, he thought, if the First was going to choose an acolyte who had a mate and a new baby, she had to know her full attention would not be devoted to the zelandonia.

"Excuse me for a moment," the First said, pulling herself up from a mat on a low stone ledge and walking toward the group of chattering young mothers. "Ayla," she said, smiling. She was adept at hiding her true feelings. "I'm sorry to interrupt, but the Zelandoni of the Seventh Cave just asked me a question about setting broken bones, and I thought you might have some thoughts to contribute."

"Of course, Zelandoni," she said. "Let me get Jonayla; she's right over there."

Ayla got up, but hesitated when she looked down at her sleeping baby. Wolf looked up at her and whined, beating his tail against the ground. He was lying beside the infant that he considered to be his special charge. Wolf had been the last of the litter of a lone wolf that Ayla had killed for stealing from her traps, before she knew it was a nursing mother. She had tracked back to the den, found one living cub, and had brought him back with her. He had grown up in the close confines of the Mamutoi winter dwelling. He was so young when she found him—he would have counted perhaps four weeks—that he had imprinted on humans, and he adored the youngsters, especially the young one born to Ayla.

"I hate to disturb her. She just fell asleep. She's not used to visiting and has been overexcited this evening," Ayla said.

"We can watch her," Levela said, then grinned. "At least help Wolf. He won't let her out of his sight. If she wakes, we'll bring her over. But now that she has finally settled down, I don't think she'll stir for some time."

"Thank you, Levela," Ayla said, then smiled at her and the woman beside her. "You really are Proleva's sister. Do you know how much you are like her?"

"I know I've missed her since she mated Joharran," Levela said, looking at her sister. "We were always close. Proleva was almost a second mother to me."

Ayla followed the One Who Was First back to the group of Those Who Served The Mother. She noticed that most of the local zelandonia were there. In addition to the First, who was the Zelandoni of the Ninth Cave, and of course the Zelandonia of the Second and Seventh Caves, there were also the Zelandonia of the Third and Eleventh Caves. The Zelandoni of the Fourteenth had not come, but she had sent her first acolyte. There were several other acolytes. Ayla recognized the two younger women and a young man, from the Second and Seventh Caves. She smiled at Mejera from the Third Cave and greeted the elderly man who was the Zelandoni of the Seventh, and then the woman who was the daughter of his hearth, the Zelandoni of the Second, who was also the mother of Jondecam. Ayla had been wanting to get to know the Second better. Not many of the Zelandoni had children, but she was a woman who had been mated and had raised two children—and her brother Kimeran after their mother died—and now was a Zelandoni.

"Ayla has had more experience than most in setting bones, Zelandoni of the Seventh. You should ask her your question," the First said, settling back down and indicating a mat next to her for Ayla.

"I know if a fresh break is set straight, it will heal straight— I've done it many times—but someone was asking me if anything could be done if a break was not set straight and it healed crooked," the older man asked immediately. He was not only interested in her response, he had heard so much about her skill from the One Who Was First, he wanted to see if she would be flustered by a direct question from someone of his age and experience.

Ayla had just dropped down to the mat and turned to face him. She had a way of lowering herself that was particularly fluid and graceful, he noticed, and a way of looking at him that was direct yet not quite, that somehow conveyed a sense of respect. Though she had expected to be formally introduced to the other acolytes, and was surprised to be questioned so quickly, she responded without hesitation.

"It depends on the break and how long it has been healing," Ayla said. "If it's an old break, it's hard to do much. Healed bone, even if it healed wrong, is often stronger than bone that was not injured. If you try to rebreak it to set it right, the uninjured bone is likely to break instead. But if the break has just started to mend, sometimes it can be broken again and set straight."

"Have you ever done it?" the Seventh asked, a bit put off by the way she spoke; it was odd, not like the way Kimeran's pretty mate spoke, with a rather pleasant shift in certain sounds. When Jondalar's foreign woman spoke, it was almost as though she swallowed certain sounds.

"Yes," Ayla said. She had the feeling she was being tested, something like the way Iza used to ask her questions about healing practices and plant uses. "On our Journey here, we stopped to visit some people that Jondalar had met earlier, the Sharamudoi. Nearly a moon before we arrived, a woman he knew had taken a bad fall and had broken her arm. It was healing wrong, bent in such a way that she couldn't use it, and it was very painful. Their healer had died earlier that winter, and they did not have a new one yet, and no one else knew how to set an arm. I managed to rebreak her arm and reset it. It was not perfect, but it was better. She would not have full use, but she would be able to use it, and by the time we left, it was healing well and not causing her pain anymore," Ayla explained.

"Didn't breaking her arm cause her pain?" a young man asked.

"I don't think she felt the pain. I gave her something to make her sleep and relax her muscles. I know it as datura . . ."

"Datura?" the old man interrupted. Her accent was particularly heavy when she said the word.

"In Mamutoi it's called a word that might mean 'thorn apple' in Zelandoni, because at one stage it bears a fruit that could be described that way. It's a strong-smelling large plant with big white flowers that flare out from the stem," Ayla said.

"Yes, I believe I know the one," the old Zelandoni of the Seventh Cave said.

"How did you know what to do?" asked the young woman who was sitting beside the old man, in a tone that sounded full of wonder that someone who was just an acolyte could have known so much.

"Yes, that is a good question," the Seventh said. "How did you know what to do? Where did you get your experience? You seem quite knowledgeable for one so young."

Ayla glanced at the First, who seemed rather pleased. She wasn't sure why, but she had the impression that the woman was satisfied by her recitation.

"The woman who took me in and raised me when I was a little girl was a medicine woman of her people, a healer. She was training me to be a medicine woman, too. Men of the Clan use a different kind of spear than Zelandonii men when they hunt. It's longer and thicker and they don't usually throw it; they jab with it, so they have to get close. It's more dangerous and they were often hurt. Sometimes the hunters of the Clan traveled quite a long distance. If someone broke a bone, they weren't always able to return right away and the bone would start to heal before it could be set. I assisted Iza a few times when she had to rebreak and reset bones, and I also helped the medicine women at the Clan Gathering do the same."

"These people you call the Clan, are they really the same as Flatheads?" the young man asked.

She had been asked that question before, and she thought by the same young man. "That is your word for them," Ayla said again.

"It's hard to believe they could do so much," he said.

"Not for me. I lived with them."

There was an uncomfortable silence for a few moments, then the First changed the subject. "I think this would be a good time for the acolytes to learn or, for some of you, to review counting words, some of their uses and meanings. You all know the counting words, but what can you do if there are large amounts to count? Zelandoni of the Second Cave, would you explain?"

Ayla's interest was quickened. Suddenly fascinated, she leaned forward. She knew counting could be more complex and powerful than just the simple counting words, if one understood how to do it. The First noted her attention with satisfaction. She was sure that Ayla had a particular curiosity about the concept of counting.

"You can use your hands," the Second said, and held up both hands. "With the right hand, you count on your fingers as each word is said up to five." She made a fist, and lifted each finger in turn as she counted, beginning with the thumb. "You can count another five on your left hand until you get to ten, but that is as far as you can go with just counting. But instead of using the left hand to count the second five, you can bend down one finger, the thumb, to hold the first five," she held up her left hand with the back facing out, "then count again on the right hand, and bend down the second counting finger of the left hand to hold it." She bent her index finger on top of her thumb, so that she was holding open both hands, except for the index finger and thumb of her left hand. "That means ten," she said. "If I hold down the next finger, that means fifteen. The next finger is twenty, and next one twenty-five."

Ayla was amazed. She comprehended the idea immediately, though it was more complex than the simple counting words

Jondalar had taught her. She remembered the first time she learned the concept of calculating the number of things. It was Creb, the Mog-ur of the Clan, who had shown her, but essentially he could only count to ten. The first time he showed her his way of counting, when she was still a girl, he placed each finger of one hand on five different stones and then, since one arm had been amputated below the elbow, he did it a second time imagining that it was his other hand. With great difficulty, he could stretch his imagination to count to twenty, which was why it had shocked and upset him when she had counted to twenty-five with ease.

She didn't use words, the way Jondalar did. She did it with pebbles, showing Creb twenty-five by placing her five fingers on different stones five times. Creb had struggled to learn to count, but she understood the concept with ease. He told her never to tell anyone what she had done. He knew she was different from the Clan, but he hadn't understood how different until then, and he knew it would distress them, especially Brun and the men, perhaps enough to drive her out.

Most of the Clan could count only one, two, three, and many, though they could indicate some gradations of many, and they had other ways of understanding quantities. For example, they didn't have counting words for the years of a child's life, but they knew that a child in his birthing year was younger than a child who was in his walking year or his weaning year. It was also true that Brun didn't have to count the people of his clan. He knew the name of everyone and with just a quick glance, he knew if someone was not there, and who it was. Most people shared that ability to some degree. Once they were with a limited number of people for a period of time, they intuitively sensed if someone was missing.

Ayla knew that if her understanding of counting upset Creb, who loved her, it would disturb the rest of the Clan even more, so she never mentioned it, but she hadn't forgotten. She used her limited knowledge of counting for herself, especially when she lived alone in the valley. She had marked the passing of time by cutting marks on a stick every day. She knew how many seasons and years she had lived in the valley even without having counting words, but when Jondalar came, he was able to tally the marks on her sticks and tell her how long she had been there. To her, it was like magic. Now that she had an idea how he had done it, she was hungry to learn more.

"There are ways to count even higher, but it is more complicated," the Second continued, then smiled, "as with most things associated with the zelandonia." Those watching smiled back. "Most signs have more than one meaning. Both hands can mean ten or twenty-five, and it's not hard to understand what is meant when you are talking about it, because when you mean ten, you face the palms out; when you mean twenty-five, you turn the palms inward. When you hold them facing in, you can count again, but this time use the left hand, and hold the number with the right." She demonstrated and the acolytes mimicked her. "In that position, bending down the thumb means thirty, but when you count and hold to thirty-five, you don't hold the thumb down; you just bend the next finger down. For forty, you bend down the middle finger, for forty-five the next; for fifty the small finger of the right hand is bent, and all the other fingers on both hands are out. The right hand with bent fingers is sometimes used alone to show those larger counting words. Even larger counting words can be made by bending more than one finger."

Ayla had trouble bending just her little finger and holding that position. It was obvious that the rest of them had more practice, but she had no trouble understanding. The First saw Ayla grinning with amazement and delight, and nodded to herself. This is the way to keep her involved, she thought.

"A handprint can be made on a surface like a piece of wood or the wall of a cave, even on the bank of a stream," the First added. "That hand sign can mean several different things. It may mean counting words, but it may mean something else entirely. If you want to leave a handprint sign, you can dip your palm in color and leave the mark, or you can place your hand on the surface and blow color on and around the back of it, which leaves a different kind of handprint. If you want to make a sign that means a counting word, dip the palm in color for the smaller ones, and blow color on the back of your hand to show the larger ones. One Cave to the south and east of here makes the sign of a large dot using color on only the palm, without showing the fingers."

Ayla's mind was racing, overwhelmed with the idea of counting. Creb, the greatest Mog-ur of the Clan, could, with great effort, count to twenty. She could count to twenty-five and represent it with just two hands in a way that others could understand it, and then increase that number. You could tell someone how many red deer had congregated at their spring calving grounds, how many young were born; a small number like five, a small group, twenty-five, or many more than that. It would be harder to count a large herd, but it could all be communicated. How much meat should be stored to last how many people through the winter? How many strings of dried roots? How many baskets of nuts. How many days will it take to reach the Summer Meeting place? How many people will be there? The possibilities were incredible. Counting words had tremendous significance, both real and symbolic.

The One Who Was First was talking again, and Ayla had to wrench her mind away from her contemplations. She was holding up one hand. "The number of fingers on one hand, five, is an important counting word in its own right. It represents the number of fingers on each hand, and the toes on each foot, of course, but that is only its superficial meaning. Five is also the Mother's sacred counting word. Our hands and feet only remind us of that. Another thing that reminds us of that is the apple." She produced a small, unripe hard apple and held it up. "If you hold an apple on its side and cut it in half, as if you were cutting through the stem within the fruit," she demonstrated as she spoke, "you will see that the pattern of the seeds divides the apple into five sections. That is why the apple is the Mother's sacred fruit."

She passed out both sections to be examined by the acolytes, giving the top half to Ayla. "There are other important aspects of the counting-word five. As you will learn, you can see five stars in the sky that move in a random pattern each year, and there are five seasons of the year: spring, summer, autumn, and the two cold periods, early winter and late winter. Most people think the year starts with spring when new green starts growing, but the zelandonia know that the beginning of the year is marked by the Winter Shortday, which is what divides early winter from late winter. The true year begins with late winter, then spring, summer, autumn, and early winter."

"The Mamutoi count five seasons, too," Ayla volunteered. "Actually three major seasons: spring, summer and winter, and two minor seasons: fall and midwinter. Perhaps it should be called late winter." Some of the others were rather surprised that she would interject a comment when the First was explaining a basic concept, but the First smiled inwardly, pleased to see her getting involved. "They consider three to be a primary counting word because it represents woman, like the three-sided triangle with the point facing down represents woman, and the Great Mother. When they add the two others, fall and midwinter, seasons that mean changes are coming, it makes five. Mamut said five was Her counting word of hidden authority."

"That's very interesting, Ayla. We say five is Her sacred counting word. We also consider three to be an important concept, for similar reasons. I'd like to hear more about the people you call the Mamutoi, and their customs. Perhaps the next time the zelandonia meet," the First said.

Ayla was listening with fascination. The First had a voice that captured attention, demanded it, when she chose to focus it, but it wasn't only the voice. The knowledge and information she was imparting were stimulating and absorbing. Ayla wanted to know more.

"There are also five sacred colors and five sacred elements but it's getting late and we'll get into that next time," said the One Who Was First Among Those Who Served The Great Earth Mother.

Ayla felt disappointed. She could have listened all night, but then she looked up and saw Folara coming with Jonayla. Her baby was awake.

4

Anticipation for the Summer Meeting intensified after the Ninth Cave returned from visiting the Seventh and Second Caves. Everyone's time and attention was occupied with the hectic rush of getting ready to leave, and the excitement was palpable. Each family was busy with its own preparations, but the various leaders had the additional duty of planning and organizing for their entire Cave. That they were willing to assume the responsibility and able to carry it out was why they were leaders.

The leaders of all the Zelandonii Caves were anxious before a Summer Meeting, but Joharran was especially so. While most Caves tended to have some twenty-five to fifty people, some as much as seventy or eighty, usually related, his Cave was an exception. Nearly two hundred individuals belonged to the Ninth Cave of the Zelandonii.

It was a challenge to lead so many people, but Joharran was up to the task. Not only had Joharran's mother, Marthona, been a leader of the Ninth Cave, but Joconan, the first man to whom she was mated and to whose hearth Joharran had been born, was the leader before her. Joharran's brother, Jondalar, who was born to the hearth of Dalanar, the man Marthona mated after Joconan died, had specialized in a craft in which he showed both skill and inclination. Like Dalanar, he was recognized as an expert flint-knapper because it was what he did best. But Joharran grew up immersed in the ways of leadership and had a natural propensity to take on those responsibilities. It was what he did best.

The Zelandonii had no formal process for selecting leaders, but as people lived together, they learned who the best person

was to help them to resolve a conflict or sort out a problem.
And they tended to follow the ones who took on the organiza-
tion of an activity and did it well.

If several people decided to go hunting, for example, it
wasn't necessarily the best hunter they chose to follow, but the
one who could direct the group in a way that made the hunt
most successful for everyone. Often, though not always, the
best problem solver was also the best organizer. Sometimes
two or three people, who were known for their specific areas
of expertise, worked together. After a while, the one who dealt
with conflicts and managed activities most effectively was acknowledged as the leader, not in any kind of structured way,
but by unspoken consent.

Those who obtained leadership positions gained status, but
such leaders governed by persuasion and influence; they had
no coercive power. There were no specific rules or laws requiring compliance, or means of enforcing them, which made
leadership more difficult, but peer pressure to acknowledge
and accept suggestions by the head of the Cave was strong.
The spiritual leaders, the zelandonia, had even less authority to
compel, but perhaps more power to persuade; they were greatly
respected and a little feared. Their knowledge of the unknown
and their familiarity with the terrifying world of the spirits,
which was an important element in the lives of the community,
commanded respect.

Ayla's excitement about the upcoming Summer Meeting increased as the time to leave approached. She hadn't noticed it as
much the previous year, but they had arrived at Jondalar's home
not long before the annual gathering of the Zelandonii after
traveling for a year, and she had felt excitement and tension
enough just meeting his people and getting accustomed to their
ways. This year she had been aware of her mounting enthusiasm
since the beginning of spring, and as the days passed, she was as
rushed and eager as everyone. It was a lot of work to get ready
for the summer, especially knowing that they would be traveling around, not staying at any single place for the whole season.

The Summer Meeting was where people gathered together
after the long cold season to reaffirm their ties, to find mates,

and to exchange goods and news. The location became a sort of base camp from which individuals and smaller groups would be going on hunting expeditions and gathering excursions, exploring their land to see what had changed, and visiting additional Caves to see other friends and kin, and some more distant neighbors. Summer was the itinerant season; the Zelandonii were essentially sedentary only in winter.

Ayla had finished changing and nursing Jonayla and had put her down to sleep. Wolf had gone out earlier, probably to hunt or explore. She had just spread out their traveling sleeping roll to see what repairs it might need when she heard a tapping on the post beside the drape that closed the entrance to their dwelling. Her home was located near the back of the protected space, but closer to the southwestern, downriver end of the living area, since it was one of the newer constructions. She got up and pulled aside the drape and was pleased to see the One Who Was First standing there.

"How nice to see you, Zelandoni," she said, smiling. "Come in."

After the woman entered, Ayla caught a sense of movement outside and glanced up at another construction that she and Jondalar had made somewhat farther on across the vacant space as a place for the horses to shelter when the weather was especially disagreeable. She noticed that Whinney and Gray had just come up from the grassy edge of The River.

"I was going to make some tea for myself—can I make some for you?"

"Thank you, yes," the large woman said as she headed for a block of limestone with a large cushion on top that had been brought inside especially for her to use as a seat. It was sturdy and comfortable.

Ayla busied herself placing some cooking stones on the hot coals she had stirred up in the fireplace, and adding more wood. Then she poured water from the waterbag—the cleaned stomach of an aurochs bulging with fullness—into a tightly woven basket, and added some broken pieces of bone to protect the cooking basket from the sizzling-hot cooking stones.

"Is there a particular tea you'd like?" she asked.

"It doesn't matter. You choose—something calming would be nice," Zelandoni replied.

The padded rock had appeared in their dwelling shortly after they returned from the Summer Meeting the year before. The First had not asked for it, and she wasn't sure whether it was Ayla's idea or Jondalar's, but she knew it was meant for her and she appreciated it. Zelandoni had two stone seats of her own, one in her dwelling and one near the back of the exterior common work area. In addition, Joharran and Proleva provided her a solid place to sit comfortably in their dwelling. Though she could still get down on the floor if it was necessary, as time went on and she continued to grow fatter, she was finding it harder to get up. She assumed that since she was chosen to be First by the Great Earth Mother, She had a reason for making her look more like Her every year. Not every Zelandoni who had become First was fat, but she knew most people liked seeing her that way. Her size seemed to lend presence and authority. A little less mobility was a small price to pay.

With wooden tongs Ayla picked up a hot stone. The tongs were made from a thin piece of wood from just under the bark of a living tree, peeled in a long strip, the top and bottom cut, then bent around with steam. Fresh wood kept its springiness longer, but to keep the tree from dying, it was best if taken from only one side. She tapped the cooking stone against one of the rocks that circled the firepit to shake off the ashes, then dropped it into the water amid a cloud of steam. A second hot stone brought the water to the boil, though it settled down quickly. The pieces of bone kept the hot rocks from scorching the bottom of the basket, giving the fiber cooking pot a longer life.

Ayla looked through her supply of dried and drying herbs. Chamomile was always calming, but it was so commonplace, she wanted something more. She noticed a plant she had picked recently and smiled to herself. The lemon balm wasn't entirely dry yet, but she decided it didn't matter. It was entirely usable for tea. A little added to the chamomile along with some linden for a bit of sweetening would make a nice calming infusion. She put the chamomile leaves, the lemon balm, and linden into the water and let it steep a while, then poured two cups and brought one to the Donier.

The woman blew on it a bit then, sipped it carefully, and cocked her head, trying to identify the taste. "Chamomile, of course, but . . . let me think. Is it lemon balm, with perhaps some linden flowers?" she asked.

Ayla smiled. It was exactly what she did when she was given something unknown; she tried to identify it. And of course Zelandoni had known the ingredients. "Yes," Ayla said. "I had dried chamomile and linden flowers, but I just found the lemon balm a few days ago. I'm glad it grows nearby."

"Perhaps you could collect some lemon balm for me the next time you get some for yourself. It could be useful to take to the Summer Meeting."

"I'd be happy to. I could even get it today. I know exactly where it grows. On the plateau above, near the Falling Stone," she said. Ayla was referring to the unique formation of an ancient columnar section of basalt that had once found its way to the bottom of the primordial sea and was now eroding out of the limestone in a way that made it appear to be falling, though it was still firmly embedded into the upper face of the cliff.

"What do you know about the uses of this?" Zelandoni asked, holding up the cup of tea.

"Chamomile is relaxing and if you take it at night, it can help you to fall asleep. Lemon balm is calming, especially if you feel nervous and stressful. It will even relieve the stomach upset that sometimes comes with stress and it will help you sleep. It has a pleasant taste that is good with chamomile. Linden helps with headaches, especially when you feel tight and tense, and adds a little sweetening." Ayla thought of Iza, and the way she would test her with similar questions to see how much she remembered of the knowledge Iza was teaching her. She wondered if Zelandoni was also trying to find out how much she knew.

"Yes, this tea could be used as a mild sedative, in sufficient strength."

"If someone is really excitable, anxious and can't sleep, and something a little stronger is needed, the liquid from boiled valerian roots is settling," Ayla said.

"Particularly at night, to bring on sleep, but if the stomach is also upset, then vervain, a tea of the flower stems and leaves, may be better," the First said.

"I've also used vervain for someone recovering from a long illness, but it should not be given to a pregnant woman. It can stimulate labor, and even milk flow." The two women stopped, looked at each other, and chuckled, then Ayla said, "I can't tell you how happy it makes me to have someone to talk to about medicines and healing. Someone who knows so much."

"I think you may know as much as I do—in certain ways, more, Ayla, and it is a pleasure to discuss and compare ideas with you. I look forward to many years of such rewarding discussions," Zelandoni said; then she looked around and motioned toward the sleeping roll spread out on the floor. "It appears you're getting ready for the trip."

"I was just checking the sleeping roll to see if it needed mending. It's been a while since we've used it," Ayla said. "It's a good one for traveling in all kinds of weather."

The sleeping roll consisted of several hides sewn together to make a long top and bottom to accommodate Jondalar's height. They were attached at the foot, and removable thongs were threaded through holes down the sides that could be lashed tightly together or left loose, or even removed if it was especially warm. Thick furs were on the outside of the bottom piece, to create an insulating cushion against the hard and often cold ground. Any of several furs could be used, but it was usually made from an animal killed in cold weather. On this one, Ayla had used the supremely dense, naturally insulating winter fur of reindeer. The top of the sleeping roll was lighter weight; she had used the summer hides of megaceros, which were large and didn't require as much piecing together. An extra hide or fur could be thrown on top if it cooled down, or if it got really cold, additional furs could be put inside and the sides laced up.

"I think you'll get some use out of that," Zelandoni said, recognizing the versatility of the sleeping roll. "I came to talk to you about the Summer Meeting, or rather, about after the early ceremonial part of it. I was going to suggest that you make sure you have adequate traveling equipment and supplies with you. There are some sacred sites in this area you should see. Later, in a few years, I want to show you some of the sacred sites and take you to meet some of the zelandonia that live farther away."

Ayla smiled. She liked the idea of seeing new places, so long as it wasn't too far. She'd done enough long-distance traveling. She remembered just seeing Whinney and Gray, and an idea occurred to her that could make traveling with the First easier. "If we use the horses, we could travel much faster."

The woman shook her head and took a sip of tea. "There is no way I could get up on the back of a horse, Ayla."

"You wouldn't have to. You can ride on the pole-drag behind Whinney. We can make a comfortable seat on it." She had been thinking of how to convert the travois so that it could be used to carry passengers, especially Zelandoni.

"What makes you think that horse could pull someone my size on that dragging thing?"

"Whinney has pulled much heavier loads than you. She's a very strong animal. She could take you and your traveling things, and medicines. In fact, I was going to ask if you would like her to carry your medicines along with mine to the Summer Meeting," Ayla said. "We won't be taking passengers on the way there. We won't even be riding ourselves. We've promised several people that Whinney and Racer would carry certain things to the Meeting. Joharran wanted us to haul some poles and other building parts for some of the Ninth Cave's summer dwellings. And Proleva wanted to know if we could take some of her special large cooking baskets, and bowls and serving equipment for feasts and shared community meals. And Jondalar wants to lighten Marthona's load."

"It appears that your horses are going to be put to good use," the First said, taking another sip of her tea, her mind already formulating plans.

The First had various journeys planned for Ayla. She wanted to take her to meet some of the Zelandonii Caves that were farther away and visit their sacred places, and perhaps meet some of the people who were neighbors of the Zelandonii who lived near the boundaries of their territory. But Zelandoni had a feeling that the young woman, after coming so far to get here, might not be especially interested in making the extended trip she had in mind for her. She hadn't really mentioned anything about the Donier Tour that acolytes were expected to make.

She began to think that, perhaps, she ought to agree to allowing the horses to pull her on that thing; it might encourage Ayla to make the excursions. The large woman wasn't really interested in being dragged around by horses, and if she were honest with herself, she'd have to admit that the idea actually frightened her, but she had faced worse fears in her life. She knew the effect Ayla's control of the animals would have on people; they likely would be a little frightened, and very impressed. Maybe one day she ought to see what it would be like to sit on this pole-drag thing.

"Perhaps sometime we'll try to see if your Whinney can pull me," Zelandoni said, and watched a large grin expand across the young woman's face.

"This is as good a time as any," Ayla said, thinking it might be best to take advantage of the woman's agreeable mood before she changed her mind, and watched the startled look appear on the face of the One Who Was First.

Just then, the drape covering the entrance was pulled back and Jondalar strode in. He could see Zelandoni's startled expression and wondered what had brought it on. Ayla stood up and they greeted each other with a light embrace and a touching of cheeks, but their strong feelings for each other were obvious and did not escape their visitor's attention. Jondalar glanced toward the baby's place and noticed that she was sleeping, and then he walked to the older woman and greeted her in a similar fashion, still wondering what had disconcerted her.

"And Jondalar can help us," Ayla added.

"Help you with what?" he said.

"Zelandoni was talking about making some trips this summer to visit other Caves, and I thought it would be easier and faster using horses."

"It probably would, but do you think Zelandoni could learn to ride?" Jondalar asked.

"She wouldn't have to. We could make a comfortable seat on the pole-drag for her and Whinney could pull her," Ayla said.

Jondalar's forehead wrinkled as he thought about it, then he nodded his head. "I don't see why not," he said.

"Zelandoni said sometime she'd be willing to try to see if Whinney could pull her, and I said, 'This is as good a time as any.'"

Zelandoni glanced at Jondalar and detected a glint of enjoyment in his eyes, then looked at Ayla and tried to think of a way to put it off. "You said you would have to make a seat. You don't have one made yet," she said.

"That's true, but you didn't think Whinney could pull you. You don't need a seat to try it and see if she can. I don't have any doubt, but it might reassure you, and give us a chance to think about how to make a seat," Ayla said.

Zelandoni felt that somehow she had been snared. She didn't really want to do this, especially not right away, but she didn't think she could get out of it now. Then, recognizing that in her eagerness to have Ayla begin her Donier Tour, she had done it to herself, she heaved a big sigh and stood up. "Well, let's get it over with, then," she said.

When she lived in her valley, Ayla had thought of a way to use her horse to transport things of considerable size and weight, such as an animal she had hunted—and once, Jondalar, wounded and unconscious. It consisted of two poles attached together at the shoulders of the horse with a kind of strap made of thongs that went across Whinney's chest. The opposite ends of the poles spread out and rested on the ground behind the horse. Because only the very small surface area of the ends of the poles were dragged on the ground, it was relatively easy to pull them, even over rough terrain, especially for the sturdy horses. A platform made of planks or leather hides or basketry fibers was stretched across the poles to carry the loads, but Ayla wasn't sure if the flexible platform would hold the large woman without bending down to the ground.

"Finish your tea," Ayla said as the woman started to get up. "I need to find Folara or someone to watch Jonayla. I don't want to wake her up."

She returned quickly, but not with Folara. Instead Lanoga, Tremeda's daughter, followed Ayla in, carrying her youngest sister, Lorala. Ayla had tried to assist Lanoga and the rest of the children almost since she arrived. She couldn't ever remember being so angry with anyone as she was with Tremeda and Laramar because of the way they neglected their children, but there was nothing she could do about it—nothing anyone could do—except help the young ones.

"We won't be gone long, Lanoga. I should be back before Jonayla wakes up. We're just going to the horse shelter," Ayla said, then added, "There's some soup behind the fireplace with several good pieces of meat left and a few vegetables, if you or Lorala are hungry."

"Lorala might be. She hasn't eaten since I brought her to Stelona to nurse this morning," Lanoga said.

"You have something, too, Lanoga," Ayla said as they were leaving. She thought Stelona had probably given her something to eat, but was sure the girl hadn't eaten since the morning meal either.

When they were some distance from the dwelling, and Ayla was sure she wouldn't be overheard, she finally voiced her anger. "I'm going to have to go over there and check to see if there's any food for the children."

"You brought food over there two days ago," Jondalar said. "It shouldn't be all gone yet."

"You must know that Tremeda and Laramar are eating it, too," Zelandoni said. "You can't prevent them. And if you bring grain or fruit, or anything that will ferment, Laramar will take it and add it to the birch sap for his barma. I'll stop by on the way back for the children and take them with me. I can find someone to give them an evening meal. You shouldn't be the only one feeding them, Ayla. There are enough people in the Ninth Cave to make sure those children get enough to eat."

When they reached the horse shelter, Ayla and Jondalar gave Whinney and Gray some individual attention. Then from the end of a post, Ayla got the special harness she used for the pole-drag and led the mare outside. Jondalar wondered where Racer was, and looked over the edge of the stone porch at The River to see if he could catch sight of him, but he didn't seem to be nearby. He started to whistle for him, then changed his mind. He didn't need the stallion now. He would look for him later, after they got Zelandoni on the travois.

Ayla looked around the horse shelter and noticed some planks that had been pried out of a log with wedges and a maul. She had planned to make additional feeding boxes for the horses with them, but then Jonayla was born, and they kept using ones she had made before, and she never got around to making more.

Since they were kept under the overhanging ledge, protected from the worst of the weather, they seemed to be usable.

"Jondalar, I think we need to make a platform that won't bend so easily, for Zelandoni. Do you think we could fasten these planks across the poles to use as a base for a seat?" Ayla asked.

He looked at the poles and the planks, and then at the abundantly endowed woman. His forehead wrinkled in a familiar knot. "It's a good idea, Ayla, but the poles are flexible, too. We can try it, but we may have to use sturdier ones."

There were always thongs or cords around the horse shelter. Jondalar and Ayla used some to fasten the planks across the poles. When they were done, the three of them stood back and looked at their handiwork.

"What do you think, Zelandoni? The planks are slanting, but we can fix that later," Jondalar said. "Do you think you could sit on them?"

"I'll try, but it may be a little high for me."

While they were working, the Donier had become interested in the apparatus they were making, and was curious herself to see how it would work. Jondalar had devised a halter for Whinney similar to the one he used for Racer, though Ayla seldom used it herself. She usually rode bareback with only a leather riding blanket, directing the animal with her position and the pressure of her legs, but for special circumstances, especially when other people were involved, it gave her an added measure of control.

While Ayla put the halter on the mare, making sure Whinney was calm, Jondalar and Zelandoni went to the reinforced travois behind the horse. The planks were a bit high, but Jondalar lent his strong arm and gave her a boost. The poles did bend under her weight, enough that her feet could touch the ground, but it gave her the feeling that she could get down easily enough. The slanting seat did feel somewhat precarious, but it wasn't as bad as she thought it would be.

"Are you ready?" Ayla asked.

"I'm as ready as I'll ever be," Zelandoni said.

Ayla started Whinney at a slow walk in the direction of Down River. Jondalar walked behind, smiling encouragingly at Zelandoni. Then Ayla led the horse under the overhanging shelf and made a wide complete turn until they were facing in the opposite direction, and headed toward the east end of the front ledge, toward the dwellings.

"I think you should stop now, Ayla," the woman said.

Ayla stopped immediately. "Are you uncomfortable?" she said.

"No, but didn't you say you wanted to make a real seat for me?"

"Yes."

"Then the first time you take me for everyone to see on this, I think it would be better to have the seat fixed up the way you want it, because you know people will be looking and appraising," the large woman said.

Ayla and Jondalar were taken aback for a moment, then Jondalar said, "Yes, you are probably right."

In the next breath, Ayla said, "That means you would be willing to ride on the pole-drag!"

"Yes, I think I could become used to it. It's not like I couldn't get off anytime I wanted to," the great Donier said.

Ayla wasn't the only one working on traveling gear. The entire Cave had various items spread out in their dwellings or outside workplaces. They needed to make or repair sleeping rolls, traveling tents, and certain structural elements of the summer shelters, although most of the materials to make them would be gathered at the campsite. Those who had made objects as gifts or for trade, especially those who were proficient in certain crafts, had to make decisions regarding what and how much to bring. Those walking could carry only a limited amount with them, especially since they also had to carry food, both for immediate use and for gifts and special feasts, clothing, and sleeping rolls and other necessities.

Ayla and Jondalar had already decided to make new pole-drags for Whinney and Racer—the ends of the poles that dragged on the ground were the part that wore down first, especially when dragging heavy loads. After several people had made requests, they had offered the additional carrying power of the horses to family and close friends, but even the sturdy horses could take only so much.

From the beginning of spring, the Cave had hunted meat and collected plants—berries, fruits, nuts, mushrooms, edible stems, leaves and roots of vegetables, wild grains, even lichen and the inner bark of certain trees. Though they would bring a small amount of fresh food recently hunted or foraged, most of their food was dried. Drying preserved food for a long time and it weighed less, allowing them to carry more to eat while traveling and after they arrived until hunting and gathering patterns could be established at the location of the current year's Summer Meeting.

The site of the annual gathering changed every year in a regular cycle of suitable places. There were only certain areas that could accommodate a Summer Meeting and any area could only be used for one season and then had to rest for several years before it could be used again. With so many people congregated in one place—somewhere between one and two thousand people—by the end of the summer they would have used up all the resources for some distance around, and the earth needed to recover. The year before they had followed The River north about twenty-five miles. This year they would be traveling west until they reached another waterway, West River, which ran generally parallel to The River.

Joharran and Proleva were inside their dwelling finishing a midday meal along with Solaban and Rushemar. Ramara, Solaban's mate, and her son Robenan, had just left with Jaradal, Proleva's son, both of whom could count six years. Sethona, her baby daughter, had fallen asleep in Proleva's arms and she had just stood up to put her down. When they heard a tapping on the hard rawhide panel beside the entrance, Proleva thought that Ramara had probably forgotten something and returned, and was surprised when a much younger woman entered at her call to come into the dwelling.

"Galeya!" Proleva said, rather surprised. Though Galeya had been friends with Joharran's sister, Folara, almost from birth, and often came to their dwelling with her friend, she seldom came alone.

Joharran looked up. "Are you back already?" he said, then

turned to the others. "Since she's such a fast runner, I sent Galeya to the Third Cave earlier this morning to find out when Manvelar plans to leave."

"When I got there, he was just going to send a runner to you," Galeya said. She was a little out of breath, and her hair was wet from the sweat of her effort. "Manvelar said the Third Cave is ready to leave. He wants to start tomorrow morning. If the Ninth Cave is ready to go, he would like to travel with us."

"That's a little sooner than I had planned, I was thinking of leaving in the next day or so," Joharran said, his frown lines showing. He looked at the others. "Do you think we can be ready to go by tomorrow morning?"

"I can," Proleva said, without hesitation.

"We probably can," Rushemar said. "Salova has finished the last of the baskets she wanted to take with her. We haven't packed, but I have everything ready."

"I'm still sorting through my handles," Solaban said. "Marsheval came by yesterday to talk about what he should bring. He seems to have a talent for working with ivory, too, and is gaining skill," he added with a smile. Solaban's craft was making handles, mostly for knives, chisels, and other tools. Though he could make handles out of antler and wood, he particularly liked working with mammoth tusk ivory and had begun making other objects from it, like beads and carvings, especially since Marsheval had become his apprentice.

"Can you be ready to leave by tomorrow morning?" Joharran asked. He knew Solaban often agonized to the last moment over the decision of which handles to bring with him to the Summer Meeting, for gifts and for trading.

"I suppose I can," Solaban said, then coming to a decision, "Yes, I'll be ready, and I'm sure Ramara can be, too."

"Good, but we need to find out about the rest of the Cave so I can send a runner back to Manvelar. Rushemar, Solaban, we need to tell everyone that I'd like to have a short meeting, as soon as possible. You can say what it's about if anyone asks and tell them that whoever comes to represent each hearth should be able to decide for the rest," he said. He dumped the last remnants left in his personal eating bowl into the fire, then wiped it and his eating knife with a damp piece of buckskin before putting them into a carrying pouch attached to his belt. He'd run them under water when he had a chance. As he got up he said to Galeya, "I don't think you need to run back there again. I'll send another runner."

She looked rather relieved, then smiled. "Palidar runs fast. We were racing with each other yesterday, and he almost beat me."

Joharran had to stop and think a moment; the name wasn't immediately familiar to him. Then he remembered the lion hunt. Galeya had hunted with a young man from the Third Cave, but Palidar had also been with them on the hunt. "Isn't he a friend of Tivonan, the young man Willamar has been taking with him on trading missions?"

"Yes. He came back with Willamar and Tivonan last time, and decided he might as well go with us to the Summer Meeting and meet his Cave there." Galeya said.

Joharran nodded. It was acknowledgment enough. He didn't know if he would send the visitor, or someone else who was a member of the Ninth Cave, but he was aware that Palidar seemed to be of interest to Folara's friend Galeya, and obviously the young man had found a reason for staying. If there was a possibility that he might someday become a member of the Ninth Cave, Joharran wanted to know more about him, and tucked the thought away in his memory. He had more pressing issues to think about at the moment.

Joharran knew that at least one person from each dwelling would be present at his meeting, but as people started coming out, he saw that nearly everyone wanted to find out why the leader was calling a sudden meeting. When they had gathered in the work area, Joharran stepped up on the large flat stone that had been placed there so that he, or anyone who had something to say, could be seen more easily.

"I spoke with Manvelar not long ago," Joharran began without preamble. "As you know, the site of the Summer Meeting this year is the big field near West River and a tributary near the Twenty-sixth Cave. Manvelar's mate was from the Twenty-sixth Cave, and when her children were young they used to visit often to see her mother and family. I know how to get there by going south to Big River, then west to another river that joins with West River, and then following it north to the Summer Meeting place, but Manvelar knows a more direct way, starting out at Wood River and going west from here. We'd get there more quickly, and I had hoped we could travel with the Third Cave, but they are leaving tomorrow morning."

There was a murmuring from the gathered assembly, but before anyone could speak out, Joharran continued. "I know you like to have a few days' warning before we leave, and I usually try to do that, but I'm sure most of you are nearly ready to go. If you can pack and be ready by morning, we can travel with the Third Cave and get there much faster. The sooner we get there, the better our chances will be of finding a good place to set up our camp."

The crowd broke out in conversation and Joharran heard various comments and questions. "I don't know if we can be ready by then." "I need to talk to my mate." "We aren't packed yet." "Won't he wait another day or so?" The leader let it go on for a few moments; then he spoke again.

"I don't think it's fair to ask the Third Cave to wait for us. They want to find a good place, too. I need an answer now so I can send a runner back to him," he said. "One person from each hearth must make the decision. If most of you think you can be ready, we'll leave in the morning. Those who want to go then, come and stand to my right."

There was an initial hesitation, then Solaban and Rushamar walked up and stood on Joharran's right. Jondalar looked at Ayla, who smiled and nodded; then he moved to stand beside them on his brother's right. Marthona did the same. Then a few more came up and joined them. No one moved to his left side, which would have indicated an unwillingness to leave so soon, but several were hanging back.

Ayla was using the counting words as each person joined the group, saying the word under her breath and tapping a finger on her thigh at the same time. "Nineteen, twenty, twenty-one— how many hearths are there?" she wondered. When she reached thirty, it was obvious that most of the people had decided they could be ready by the following morning. The idea of getting there faster and finding a more desirable location was a powerful incentive. After five more people joined them, she tried to count the hearths left. There were quite a few still undecided people milling around, but she thought they represented only seven or eight hearths.

"What about those who are not ready by then?" a voice from the undecideds spoke out.

"They can come along later, on their own," Joharran said.

"But we always go as a Cave. I don't want to go alone," a person said.

Joharran smiled. "Then make sure you are ready by morning. As you can see, most people have decided they can leave then. I'm sending a runner to Manvelar to tell him we'll be ready to join the Third Cave tomorrow morning."

With a Cave the size of the Ninth, there were always a few who couldn't make the trip, at least not then—people who were sick or injured, for example. Joharran assigned a few people to stay with them to hunt and help take care of those left behind. The helpers would be replaced after about a half a Moon, so they wouldn't miss out on the entire Summer Meeting.

The people of the Ninth Cave were up much later than usual, and in the morning when everyone started gathering, a few were obviously tired, and grumpy. Manvelar and the Third Cave had arrived fairly early and were waiting in the open area that was just beyond the dwellings, toward Down River, not far from the place where Ayla and Jondalar lived. Marthona, Willamar, and Folara were ready early and had come to their dwelling, so some of their things could be packed on the horses or the travoises.

They also brought some food for a morning meal to share with Manvelar and a few others. The evening before, Marthona had suggested to her sons that it might be appropriate for her and Jondalar to entertain Manvelar and his family at Ayla's dwelling—so called since Jondalar had made it for her—and therefore allow Joharran and Proleva to get the rest of the Cave organized for the trek across country to Sun View, the home of the Twenty-sixth Cave of the Zelandonii, the place of the Summer Meeting.

5

It was a large group—nearly two hundred fifty people—
that started out later that morning, most of the Ninth and Third
Caves. Manvelar and the Third Cave took the lead, heading
down the slope from the eastern end of the stone shelter. Unlike the vegetation of Grass River Valley near the Third Cave,
where they found the lions, the path from the northeastern
edge of the stone porch of the Ninth Cave led down to a small
tributary of The River, called Wood River, because its protected valley was unusually rich with trees.

Wooded areas were rare during the Ice Age. The edge of
the glaciers that covered a quarter of the earth's surface were
not very far to the north, and created conditions of permafrost
in the nearby periglacial regions. In the summer the top layer
melted to various depths, depending on conditions. In cool,
shaded areas with heavy moss or other insulative vegetation,
the ground melted only a few inches, but where the land was
exposed to direct sunlight, it softened more, enough to allow
an abundant grass cover.

For the most part, conditions did not favor the growth of trees
with their deeper root systems, except in certain locations. In
places that were protected from the coldest winds and the hardest frosts, several feet of topsoil might be thawed, enough for
trees to take root. Gallery forests often sprung up alongside the
water-saturated edges of rivers.

Wood River Valley was one of those exceptions. It had a
relative abundance of both coniferous and deciduous trees
and brush, including varieties of fruit and nut trees. It was an
amazingly rich resource that provided a wealth of materials,

especially firewood, for those who lived near enough to benefit, but it wasn't a dense forest. It was more like a narrow valley parkland with open clearings of meadows and lovely glades between heavier wooded patches.

The large band traveled northwest through Wood River Valley for about six miles of gentle upgrade, a very pleasant beginning of the trek. At a tributary that cascaded down a hillside on the left, Manvelar stopped. It was time for a rest and to let some of the stragglers catch up. Most people built small fires to make tea; parents fed children and snacked on traveling food, dried strips of meat or pieces of fruit or nuts saved from the previous year's harvest. A few ate some of the special traveling cakes that nearly everyone had, a mixture of dried meat ground fine, dried berries or small chunks of other fruit, and fat, shaped into patties or cakes and wrapped in edible leaves. They were filling, high-energy food but they took some effort to prepare and most people saved them for later when they wanted to cover long distances quickly or were stalking game and didn't want to start a fire.

"This is where we turn," Manvelar said. "From now on, if we just continue due west, when we reach West River, we should be close to the Twenty-sixth Cave and the floodplain, which is where the Summer Meeting will be held." He was sitting with Joharran and several others. They looked at the hills rising up on the west bank and the tumultuous tributary tumbling down the slope.

"Should we camp here tonight?" Joharran asked, then looked up at the sun to check its path across the sky. "It's a little early, but we got off to a late start this morning, and that looks like a hard climb. We might be able to handle it better after a good night's rest." He feared it might be hard for some.

"Only for the next few miles, then it levels out on higher ground, more or less," Manvelar said. "I usually try to make the climb first, then stop and set up camp for the night."

"You're probably right," Joharran said. "It's better to have this behind us and start out fresh in the morning, but some people may find this climb more difficult than others." He looked hard at his brother, then flicked his eyes toward their mother, who had just arrived, and seemed grateful to sit and

rest. He had noticed that she seemed to be having a harder
time than usual.

Jondalar caught the silent signal, and turned toward Ayla.
"Why don't we stay back and bring up the rear, and direct any
stragglers who may have fallen behind." He motioned toward
a few others who were still coming.

"Yes, that's a good idea. The horses would rather be behind
everyone, anyway," she said, lifting Jonayla up and patting her
back. She had finished nursing, but seemed to want to play
around at her mother's breast. She was awake and lively, and
giggled at Wolf, who happened to be behind them. He reached
out and licked her face and the milk dribbling down her chin,
which made her giggle more. Ayla, too, had seen the signal
pass between Joharran and Jondalar, and like Joharran, she
had noticed that Marthona seemed to be slowing as the day
progressed. She had noticed that Zelandoni, who had just arrived, had been falling back also, but she wasn't sure if it was
because she was tiring, or if she was slowing down to keep
pace with Marthona.

"Is there some hot water to make tea?" Zelandoni said when
she reached them, pulling out the pouch in which she kept
her medicines, and bustling around preparing to make her
tea. "Have you had any tea yet, Marthona?" Even before the
woman shook her head from side to side to indicate that she
hadn't, the Donier continued, "I'll make some for you along
with mine."

Ayla watched them both closely and quickly realized that
Zelandoni had also noticed that Marthona seemed to be having some difficulty with the hike, and was preparing some
medicinal tea for her. Marthona knew it, too. Many people
seemed to be concerned for the woman, but they were keeping it at a subtle undercurrent. Ayla could tell, however, that
no matter how they tried to minimize it, they were genuinely
worried. She decided to see what Zelandoni was doing.

"Jondalar, will you take Jonayla? She's fed and wide awake
and wants to play," Ayla said, giving the baby to him.

Jonayla waved her arms and smiled at him and Jondalar
smiled back as he took her. It was obvious that he adored this
baby girl, this child of his hearth. He never seemed to mind

taking care of her. To Ayla he seemed more patient with her than she was. Jondalar himself was a little surprised at the strength of his feeling for her, and wondered if it was because for a time, he had doubted that there would ever be a child of his hearth. He feared he had offended the Great Earth Mother when he was young by wanting to mate with his donii-woman, and wasn't sure She would ever choose a piece of his spirit to mix with the spirit of a woman to create a new life.

That was what he had been taught. The creation of life was caused by the spirits of women mingling with the spirits of men with the help of the Mother, and most people he knew, including those he had met on his Journey, believed essentially the same thing . . . except for Ayla. She had a different view of the way new life came to be. She was convinced that there was more to it than just the mixing of spirits. She had told him that it wasn't only his spirit that had combined with hers to create this new person, but his essence when they shared Pleasures. She said Jonayla was as much his child as hers, and he wanted to believe her. He wanted this child to be as much his as hers, but he didn't know.

He knew Ayla had come to that belief when she lived with the Clan, though it wasn't what they believed either. She had told him that they thought it was totem spirits that caused a new life to start growing inside a woman, something about the male totem overpowering the female totem spirit. Ayla was the only one he knew who thought that a new life was begun by something more than spirits. But Ayla was an acolyte, training to become a Zelandoni, and it was the zelandonia that explained Doni, the Great Earth Mother, to Her Children. It made him wonder what would happen when the time came for her to explain how new life began to the people. Would she say that the Mother chose the spirit of a particular man to combine with her spirit the way the other Zelandonia did, or would she insist that it was a man's essence, and what would the zelandonia have to say about it?

When Ayla approached the two women, she noticed Zelandoni looking through her bag of medicinal herbs, and Marthona sitting on a log in the shade of a tree near Wood River. Jondalar's mother did look tired, though it seemed to Ayla that she was trying not to make an issue of it. She was smiling and chatting with some people nearby, but she looked as if she would rather just close her eyes and rest.

After she greeted Marthona and the others, Ayla joined the One Who Was First. "Do you have everything you need?" she asked quietly.

"Yes, though I wish I had time to prepare a fresh foxglove mixture properly, but I'll have to use the dried preparation I have," the woman said.

Ayla noticed that Marthona's legs seemed a little swollen. "She needs to rest, doesn't she? Not visit with those people who just want to be sociable," Ayla said. "I'm not as good as you at letting people know they should let her be for a while, without embarrassing her. I don't think she wants people to know how tired she feels. Why don't you tell me how to make the tea for her."

Zelandoni smiled and said almost inaudibly, "That was perceptive of you, Ayla. They are friends from the Third Cave whom she hasn't seen recently." Then she quickly explained how to make the infusion she wanted, and approached the chatting friends.

Ayla was concentrating on the instructions she had been given, and when she looked up, she saw that Zelandoni was walking away with Marthona's friends, and Marthona had closed her eyes. Ayla nodded to herself; that will discourage others from stopping to talk, she thought. She waited awhile to let the hot drink cool, and just as she was bringing it to Marthona, Zelandoni returned. They both hovered around the former leader of the Ninth Cave, making a point of showing their backs while she sipped her tea, blocking the view of passersby. Whatever was in Zelandoni's mixture, after a while it seemed to help, and Ayla thought that she would ask the Donier about it later.

When Manvelar started out again, leading the way up the incline, Zelandoni followed, but Ayla stayed seated beside Marthona. Willamar had joined them, and was seated on the other side of his mate. "Why don't you wait with us and let Folara go ahead," she said. "Jondalar has volunteered to stay until the last, to make sure everyone gets started in the right direction.

Proleva has promised to save something for us to eat whenever we get to the camp."

"I will," Willamar said, without hesitation. "Manvelar said from here, it's straight west for the next few days. How many days depends on how fast someone wants to go. No one has to be in a hurry. But it's good if someone follows along at the end just to make sure no one is delayed because they got hurt or ran into some other problem."

"Or has to wait for a slow old woman," Marthona said. "There may come a time when I won't be going to Summer Meetings."

"That's true for all of us," Willamar said, "but not yet, Marthona."

"He's right," Jondalar said, holding a sleeping baby in one arm. He had just arrived after talking to a family group with several young children, making sure they got started in the right direction. The wolf was following behind, keeping watch on Jonalya. "It doesn't matter if we take a little longer to get there. We won't be the only ones." He motioned toward the family starting the climb. "And once we get there, people will still be wanting your counsel and advice, mother."

"Do you want me to take Jonayla in my carrying blanket, Jondalar?" Ayla said. "We seem to be the last ones."

"I'm fine with her, and she seems comfortable. She's sound asleep, but we have to find an easy way for the horses to get to the top of that waterfall," he said.

"I'm looking for the same thing. An easy way. Perhaps I should follow your horses," Marthona said, not entirely in jest.

"It's not so much the horses—they are good climbers—it's getting up there with the heavy pole-drags and the loads on their backs," Ayla said. "I think we need to traverse our way up, making wide turns to allow for the poles they are dragging behind them."

"So you want an easy way with a gentle slope," Willamar said. "As Marthona said, that's what we want. If I'm not mistaken, I think we passed a gentler slope on our way here. Ayla, why don't we walk back a ways and see if we can find it?"

"Since Jondalar is so comfortable holding the baby, he can stay and keep me company," Marthona added.

And watch out for her, Ayla thought as she and Willamar started out. I don't like the idea of her waiting alone. There are many animals that might wander by and think of her as fair game: lions, bears, hyenas, who knows what? Wolf, who had been resting on the ground with his head between his paws, got up and seemed uneasy when he saw that Jonayla was staying, but Ayla was getting ready to leave.

"Wolf, stay!" she said, signaling the same thing to him. "Stay with Jondalar and Jonayla, and Marthona." The wolf lowered himself back down, but his head was up and his ears cocked forward, alert to any other words or signals from her as she walked away with Willamar.

"If we hadn't loaded the horses so heavily, Marthona could ride up that hill on a pole-drag," Ayla commented, after a while.

"Only if she were willing," Willamar said. "I've noticed something interesting since you came with your animals. She has absolutely no fear of that wolf, who is a powerful hunter that could easily kill her if he chose, but the horses are another matter. She doesn't like to get too close to them. She hunted horses when she was younger, but she fears them much more than the wolf, and they only eat grass."

"Perhaps it's because she doesn't know them as well. They are bigger, and can be skittish when they are nervous, or if something startles them," Ayla said. "Horses don't come into the dwelling; maybe if she spent more time with them, she wouldn't be so anxious about them."

"Maybe, but first you'd have to persuade her, and if she gets it in her mind that she doesn't want to, she's very good at evading what you want and doing what she wants, without seeming to. She's a very strong-minded woman."

"Of that, I have no doubt," Ayla said.

Though they weren't gone very long, by the time Ayla and Willamar returned, Jonayla had awakened and was now being held by her grandam. Jondalar was with the horses, checking their loads, making sure everything was securely fastened.

"We found a better place to climb that ridge. In some places it's a little steep, but it is climbable," Willamar said.

"I'd better get Jonayla," the young woman said, heading

toward Marthona. "She's probably made a mess and doesn't smell too good. She usually does when she wakes in the afternoon."

"She did," Marthona said, holding the baby so that she was sitting on her lap, facing her. "I haven't forgotten how to take care of a baby. Have I, Jonayla?" She bounced the infant lightly and smiled at her, and saw her smile returned along with some soft cooing sounds. "She is such a sweet little thing," she added, giving up the child to her mother.

Ayla couldn't help smiling at her daughter when she picked her up, and saw the smile returned as she arranged her baby in her carrying blanket, tying it securely. Marthona seemed rested and more lively when she stood up, which pleased her. They headed back along Wood River and around a bend, then started up the easier slope. When they reached the top, they went north again until they reached the small stream that had been spilling down to the river below, then proceeded west. The sun was shining almost directly in their eyes as it neared the horizon before they reached the camp that had been set up by the Third and the Ninth Caves. Proleva had been watching out for them and was relieved to see them when they finally arrived.

"I kept some food warm by the fire. What took you so long?" she said, leading them to the traveling tent they were sharing. She seemed particularly solicitous of Joharran's mother.

"We walked back along Wood River and found a slope that was easier for the horses to climb, so it was easier for me, too," Marthona said.

"I didn't think that the horses would have difficulties. Ayla said they were strong and could carry the loads," Proleva said.

"It wasn't the size of the loads, it was those pole things trailing behind them," Marthona said.

"That's right," Jondalar said. "The horses need a wider, easier path up a steep hill. They can't turn as sharply when they are pulling the pole-drags. We found a way up that allowed them to traverse their way up the hill, but we had to backtrack a ways down Wood River."

"Well, it's nearly level and open for the rest of the way,"

Manvelar said. He and Joharran had just joined them, and had heard Jondalar's comments.

"That will make it easier for everybody. Keep the food warm for us, Proleva. We have to unload the horses and find a good place for them to graze," Jondalar said.

"If you have a nice bone with some meat left on for Wolf, I'm sure he'd appreciate it," Ayla added.

It was dark when they returned from settling the horses and were finally able to have their meal. Everyone using their family traveling shelter was gathered around the fire: Marthona and Willamar, and Folara; Joharran and Proleva, and her two children, Jaradal and Sethona; Jondalar, Ayla, and Jonayla, and Wolf; and Zelandoni. Although she wasn't technically part of the family, she didn't have any other family in the Ninth Cave and usually stayed with the leader's family when they traveled.

"How long until we reach the Summer Meeting, Joharran?" Ayla asked.

"It depends how fast we go, but Manvelar said probably no more than three or four days."

It rained off and on most of the way and everyone was glad when, by the afternoon of the third day, they saw some tents ahead. Joharran and Manvelar, and Joharran's two close aides, Rushemar and Solaban, hurried ahead to find a place to set up their camps. Manvelar chose a place along a tributary, near its confluence with West River, and claimed it with his backpack. Then he found the leader of Sun View, and they all went through a short form of the formalized greeting.

". . . In the name of Doni, I greet you, Stevadal, leader of Sun View, the Twenty-sixth Cave of the Zelandonii," Joharran finished.

"You are welcome to the Gather Field of the Twenty-sixth Cave, Joharran, leader of the Ninth Cave of the Zelandonii," Stevadal said, letting go of his hands.

"We are glad to be here, but I'd like to ask your advice about where to set up our camp. You know how big we are, and now that my brother has returned from his Journey with some rather unusual . . . companions, we need to find a place where they won't disturb neighbors, and won't feel too crowded by people they don't know yet."

"I saw the wolf and two horses last year. They are rather unusual 'companions,'" Stevadal said, grinning. "They even have names, don't they?"

"The mare is Whinney—that's the horse Ayla usually rides. Jondalar calls the stallion he rides Racer; the mare is his dam, but it's three horses now. The Great Mother saw fit to Bless the mare with another young one, a little female. They call her Gray, for the color of her coat."

"You may end up with a whole herd of horses at your Cave!" Stevadal said.

I hope not, Joharran thought, but he didn't say anything, just smiled.

"What kind of place are you looking for, Joharran?"

"You remember last year we found a place somewhat out of the way. At first I thought it might be too far away from all the activities, but it turned out to be just right. There was a place for the horses to graze and for the wolf to be away from the people of the other Caves. Ayla controls him perfectly, and he even pays attention to what I say sometimes, but I wouldn't want him frightening anyone. And most of us liked that we were able to spread out a bit."

"As I recall, you also had plenty of firewood right to the end of the season," Stevadal said. "We even came and got some the last few days."

"Yes, we were fortunate. We weren't even looking for that. Manvelar told me he thought there might be a place for us a little closer to your Sun View. A little valley with some grass?"

"Yes, we sometimes have small gathers there with nearby Caves. Hazelnut grows there and blueberries," Stevadal said. "It's actually not far from a Sacred Cave. It's a little distance from here, but it might work for you. Why don't you come and take a look at it?" Joharran beckoned to Solaban and Rushemar and they followed after him and Stevadal.

"Dalanar and his Lanzadonii stayed with you last year, didn't they? Are they coming this year?" Stevadal asked as they walked.

"We haven't heard. He didn't send us a runner, so I rather doubt it," Joharran said.

Some members of the Ninth Cave, who had planned to stay with other kin or friends, left the group to find them. Zelandoni went to find the large special dwelling that was always set up for the zelandonia, right in the middle of everything. The rest waited just beyond the field where most of the Caves had gathered for the Summer Meeting, greeting many friends who came to see them. While they waited, the rain began to let up.

When Joharran returned, he went to the waiting group. "With Stevadal's help, I think I've found a place for us," he said. "Like last year, it's a little distance away from the main meeting place, but it should work."

"How far is it?" Willamar asked. He was thinking of Marthona. The trek to the Meeting had not been easy on her.

"You can see it from here, if you know where to look."

"Well, let's go look at it," Marthona said.

A group of more than one hundred and fifty trailed along after Joharran. By the time they reached the place, the rain had stopped and the sun broke through, highlighting a pleasant little blind valley, with room enough for all of those who were staying together with the Ninth Cave, at least for the beginning of the Summer Meeting. After the first ceremonies that marked the initial coming together, the peripatetic summer life of foraging, exploring, and visiting would begin.

Zelandonii territory was much larger than the immediate region. The number of people who identified themselves as Zelandonii had grown so large, their territory had had to expand to accommodate them. There were other Zelandonii Summer Meetings and some individuals or families or Caves did not go to Summer Meetings with the same people every year. Sometimes they went to Meetings that were farther away, especially if they had goods to trade or distant kin. It was a way of maintaining contact. And some Summer Meetings were held jointly between Zelandonii and neighboring people who lived near the ill-defined boundary of their territory.

Because they were such a large and prosperous people, in comparison to the other groups, the name Zelandonii carried a certain prestige, a cachet that others wanted to be associated with. Even those who did not think of themselves as Zelandonii liked to claim a relationship with them in their names and ties. But although their population was large in relation to other people, in reality it was insignificant in terms of their actual numbers and the territory they occupied.

People were in the minority among the inhabitants of that cold ancient land. Animals were far more numerous and diversified; the list of different kinds of living creatures was long. While some of them, such as roe deer or moose, lived singly or in small family groups in the few scattered woodlands or forests, most of them were dwellers of open grasslands—steppes, plains, meadows, parklands—and their numbers were huge. At certain times of year in regions not all that distant from each other, herds of mammoths, megaceros, and horses gathered together in the hundreds; bison, aurochs, and reindeer in the thousands. Migrating birds could darken the sky for days.

There were few disputes between the Zelandonii and their neighbors, partly because there was so much land and so few people, but also because their survival depended on it. If a living site became too crowded, a small group might splinter off, but they only went as far as the nearest available, desirable location. Few wanted to move very far from family or friends, not only because of ties of affection, but in times of adversity they wanted and needed to be close to those they could rely on for help. Where the land was rich and able to support them, people tended to cluster together in rather large numbers, but there were sizable tracts of land that were totally unoccupied by people, except for an occasional hunting foray or gathering expedition.

The world during the Ice Age with its glittering glaciers, transparently clear rivers, thundering waterfalls, and hordes of animals in vast grasslands was dramatically beautiful, but brutally harsh, and the few people who lived then recognized at a fundamental level the necessity of keeping strong affiliations. You helped someone today because you would likely need help tomorrow. It was why customs, conventions, mores, and traditions had developed that sought to diminish interpersonal hostility, ease resentments, and keep emotions in check. Jealousy was discouraged and vengeance dealt with by the society, with retribution meted out by the community that would give the injured parties satisfaction and ease their pain or anger, but that still would be fair to all concerned. Selfishness, cheating, and failing to assist someone in need were considered crimes, and the society found ways to punish such criminals, but penalties were often subtle and inventive.

The people of the Ninth Cave quickly decided on the individual locations for their summer lodges and began to construct semipermanent dwellings. They had been rained on enough and wanted a place where they could be dry. Most of the poles and stakes that were the major structural elements had been brought with them, carefully selected from their nearby wooded valley, cut and trimmed before they left. Many had been used for the traveling tents. They also had smaller, lighter-weight portable shelters that were easier to carry for overnight hunts or other treks.

The summer lodges were all made in generally the same way. They were round with room around the center pole so that several people could stand, with a thatched roof that slanted down toward the vertical outer walls, where the sleeping rolls were laid out. The top of the tall central pole of the traveling tent had been shaped into a long, tapering diagonal. It was made longer by attaching another pole with a similar tapering diagonal on the bottom facing the other way. They were held together with a sturdy rope wrapped round and round and pulled tight.

Another length of rope was used to mark off the distance from the central pole to the circular outer wall, and using that as a guide, they erected an enclosure of upright supports using the same posts that had been used for the tent, plus some additional ones.

Panels made of woven cattail leaves or reeds, or rawhide or other materials, some brought with them and some made on the spot, were fastened to both the outside and the inside of the posts, creating a double wall with air in between for insulation. The ground cloth only went a short distance up the inside wall, but it was enough to keep out drafts. Any moisture that condensed in the cool of the evenings would form on the inside of the outer wall, leaving the inside of the inner wall dry.

The roof of the shelter was made of thin poles of young fir or small-leaved deciduous trees, like willow or birch, which were placed from the central pole to the outer wall. Branches and sticks were fastened between them, and a rough thatch of grasses and reeds was added on top, making a waterproof ceiling. Since it only had to last for a season, most people didn't make the thatch particularly thick and it was usually made only well enough to keep out rain and wind. Before the end of summer, however, most roofs had to be patched more than once.

By the time most of the structures were finished and everything brought in and arranged, it was late afternoon and would be dark soon, but it didn't deter people from heading for the Main Camp to see who was there and greet friends and relatives. Ayla and Jondalar still had to make provisions for the horses. Remembering the year before, they fenced in an area somewhat away from the camp with support posts, some brought with them, some found. They used anything that would work, sometimes whole young trees that they dug up and replanted. Crosspieces might be wood or branches or even rope, mostly collected nearby. It wasn't that the horses couldn't have jumped over or broken out of the enclosure, it was more to define their space, both for them and for curious visitors.

Ayla and Jondalar were among the last to leave the camp of the Ninth Cave. When they finally started toward the main Summer Camp they passed by eleven-year Lanoga and her thirteen-year brother, Bologan, struggling to make a small summer lodge at the edge of the camp. Since no one wanted to share a dwelling with Laramar, Tremeda, and their children, it only needed to house their family, but Ayla noticed that neither parent was there helping the children.

"Lanoga, where is your mother? Or Laramar?" Ayla asked.

"I don't know. At the Summer Meeting, I suppose."

"Do you mean they've left you to make your summer lodge by yourselves?"

6

Ayla was appalled. The four younger children were standing around staring with eyes wide open. She thought they looked frightened.

"How long has this been going on?" Jondalar asked. "Who built your lodge last year?"

"Mostly Laramar and me," Bologan said, "with a couple of his friends, after he promised them some barma."

"Why isn't he building it now?" Jondalar asked.

Bologan shrugged. Ayla looked at Lanoga.

"Laramar got into a fight with mother and said he was going to stay in one of the fa'lodges with the men. He took his things and left. Mother chased after him, but she hasn't come back," Lanoga said.

Ayla and Jondalar looked at each other and without saying a word, they nodded. Ayla put Jonayla down on her carrying blanket, then they both started working with the children. Jondalar soon realized that they were using the poles from their traveling tent, which would not be enough to build a lodge. But they couldn't put up the tent because the wet leather hide was disintegrating, and the damp floor mats were falling apart. They had to make everything—wall panels, floor mats, and thatch for the roof—with materials found locally.

Jondalar started by looking for poles. He found a couple near their lodge, then cut down some trees. Lanoga had never seen anyone weave mats and panels quite the way Ayla did, or as fast, but the girl learned quickly when Ayla showed her. The nine-year girl, Trelara, and seven-year boy, Lavogan, tried to help as well, after they were given some instruction, but they were more occupied with helping Lanoga with one-and-a-half-year Lorala, and her three-year brother, Ganamar. Though he didn't say anything, Bologan noticed as they worked that Jondalar's techniques created a dwelling of a much sturdier construction than he had made before.

Ayla stopped to nurse Jonayla, and nursed Lorala, too, then got some food for the children from their lodge since apparently the parents hadn't brought any. They had to build a couple of fires to see what they were doing to finish the work. By the time they were nearly through, people were coming back from the Main Camp. Ayla had gone back to their dwelling for a covering for Jonayla since it was getting chilly. She had just put her baby down in their new summer lodge when she saw people approaching. Proleva, with Sethona on her hip, was walking with Marthona and Willamar, who was carrying a torch in one hand and guiding Jaradal with the other.

"Where did you go, Ayla? I didn't see you at the Main Camp," Proleva said.

"We never got there," Ayla said. "We've been helping Bologan and Lanoga build their lodge."

"Bologan and Lanoga?" Marthona said. "What happened to Laramar and Tremeda?"

"Lanoga said they got into a fight. Laramar decided to go to a fa'lodge, took his things and left, and Tremeda chased after him and didn't come back," Ayla said. It was obvious that she was having some trouble controlling her anger. "Those children were trying to build a lodge by themselves with nothing but tent posts and wet floor mats. They didn't have any food either. I nursed Lorala a little, but if you have any milk, Proleva, she could probably use some more."

"Where is their lodge?" Willamar said.

"At the edge of the camp, near the horses," Ayla said.

"I'll watch the children, Proleva," Marthona said. "Why don't you and Willamar see what you can do." She turned to Ayla. "I'll watch Jonayla, too, if you like."

"She's almost asleep," Ayla said, indicating where she was to Marthona. "Tremeda's children could use a few more floor mats, especially since they don't have enough sleeping rolls. When I left, Jondalar and Bologan were finishing up the roof."

The three of them hurried toward the nearly completed small dwelling. They could hear Lorala crying as they approached. To Proleva, it sounded like the fussiness of a baby who was overtired, and maybe hungry. Lanoga was holding her, trying to settle her down.

"Why don't you let me see if she'll nurse a little," Proleva said to the girl.

"I just changed her padding, stuffed it with her nighttime sheep's wool," Lanoga said, handing the toddler to Proleva.

When she offered her breast, the baby went for it eagerly. Since her own mother's milk had dried up more than a year before, many other women had taken turns feeding her and she was used to taking milk from any woman who offered. She also ate different kinds of solid food that Ayla had taught Lanoga to make for her. Considering her difficult beginning, Lorala was a remarkably healthy, happy, gregarious, though somewhat undersized child. The women who fed her took a certain pride in her good health and good nature, knowing that they had contributed to it. Ayla knew that they had kept the baby alive, but Proleva knew it was Ayla's idea originally, after she discovered that Tremeda's milk had dried up.

Ayla, Proleva, and Marthona found some additional skins and furs that they didn't mind giving up for the children to use as sleep coverings, and more food. Willamar, Jondalar, and Bologan collected some wood.

The structure was nearly finished when Jondalar noticed Laramar coming. He stopped some ways back, and stared at the small summer lodge, frowning.

"Where did this thing come from?" he asked Bologan.

"We built it," the boy said.

"You didn't build it by yourselves," Laramar said.

"No, we helped him," Jondalar interjected, "since you weren't here to do it, Laramar."

"No one asked you to butt in," Laramar sneered.

"Those children had no place to sleep!" Ayla said.

"Where's Tremeda? They're her children; she's supposed to see to them," Laramar said.

"She left after you did, chasing after you," Jondalar said.

"Then she's the one who left them, not me," Laramar said.

"They are the children of your hearth; they are your responsibility," Jondalar said with disgust, struggling to contain his anger, "and you left them without shelter."

"They had the traveling tent," Laramar said.

"The leather of your traveling tent was rotten. After it got soaked, it fell apart," Ayla said. "They had no food either, and several of them are hardly more than babies!"

"I assumed Tremeda would get some food for them," Laramar said.

"And you wonder why you are the lowest ranked," Jondalar said with scorn and a look of disgust.

Wolf was aware that something seriously distressing was going on between the people of his pack and the man he didn't like. He wrinkled his nose and started growling at Laramar, who jumped back to stay out of his way.

"Who are you to tell me what to do?" Laramar said. He was now getting defensive. "I shouldn't be the lowest ranked. It's your fault, Jondalar. You're the one who suddenly came back from a Journey with a foreign woman and you and your mother connive to put her ahead of me. I was born here; she wasn't. She should be the lowest ranked. Some people may think she's special, but anybody who lived with Flatheads is not special. She's an abomination, and I'm not the only one who thinks so. I don't have to put up with you, Jondalar, or your insults," Laramar said, then turned and stomped off.

Ayla and Jondalar looked at each other after Laramar left. "Is there truth in what he says?" Ayla asked. "Should I be ranked lowest because I am a foreigner?"

"No," Willamar said. "You brought your own bride price with you. Your Matrimonial outfit alone would put you among those with the highest status in any Cave you might choose, but you have also shown yourself to be a worthwhile and valuable person in your own right. Even if you had started out as a low-ranked foreigner, you wouldn't have stayed there for long. Don't let Laramar concern you about your place with us; everyone knows what his status is. Leaving these children alone to fend for themselves with no food or shelter bears it out."

As the builders of the small summer dwelling prepared to

return to their own lodge, Bologan touched Jondalar's arm.
When he turned back, Bologan looked down, and his face became a deep shade of red, noticeable even in the firelight.

"I . . . ah . . . just want to say, this place is nice, the best summer lodge we ever had," Bologan said, then quickly went in.

As they were walking back, Willamar said, under his breath, "I think Bologan was trying to thank you, Jondalar. I'm not sure if he has ever thanked anyone before. I'm not sure he knows how."

"I think you are right, Willamar. But he did just fine."

The morning dawned clear and bright and after the morning meal, and checking to see that the horses were comfortable, Ayla and Jondalar were eager to go to the Main Camp to see who was there. Ayla wrapped Jonayla in her carrying cloak and settled her on a hip, then signaled Wolf to come with her, and set out. It was a bit of a walk, but not bad, Ayla decided. And she did like having a place that was somewhat out of the way, when she wanted it.

People started hailing them as soon as they appeared, and it pleased Ayla that she recognized so many, unlike the summer before when she hardly knew anyone, and even those she had met, she didn't know well. Though most Caves looked forward to seeing certain friends and relatives every year, because they regularly changed locations for the Summer Meetings, and other groups of Zelandonii did the same, there usually was some difference in the mix of Caves from year to year that gathered at any particular place.

Ayla saw some people whom she was sure she had not seen before; they tended to be the ones who stared at Wolf, but the animal was welcomed with a smile or a greeting by many, especially children. He stayed close to Ayla, however, who was carrying the baby for whom he had a special affection. Large groups that included strangers were difficult for him. His instinct to protect his pack had grown more compelling as he matured, and various incidents in his life had reinforced it. In a sense, the Ninth Cave became his pack, and the territory they inhabited became the area he watched, but he couldn't protect the entire large group, much less the many additional people whom Ayla had "introduced" to him. He had learned not to treat them with hostility, but they were too many to fit into his instinctive conception of a pack. Instead, he decided that the people he knew were close to Ayla were his pack, the ones he was required to protect, especially the new young one he adored.

Though she had visited with them shortly before they left, Ayla was especially glad to see Janida with her baby and Levela. They were talking with Tishona. Marthona had told her that people often formed especially close friendships with the couples with whom they shared their Matrimonial, and it was true. She was glad to see all three women, and they all greeted Ayla and Jondalar, embracing each other and touching cheeks. Tishona had become so used to seeing the wolf, she hardly noticed him, but the other two, who still felt a little fear around him, took special pains to greet him, even if they didn't try to touch him.

Janida and Ayla fussed over each other's babies, talking about how much they had grown, and how wonderful they looked. Ayla noticed that Levela had also grown.

"Levela, you look like your baby will come anytime," Ayla said.

"I hope so. I'm ready," Levela said.

"Since we're all here, I can come and be with you when you have your baby, if you would like. And your sister Proleva can be with you, too," Ayla said.

"And our mother is here. I was so glad to see her. You've met Velima, haven't you?" Levela said.

"Yes," Ayla said. "But I don't know her well."

"Where are Jondecam, Peridal, and Marsheval?" Jondalar asked.

"Marsheval went with Solaban to look for an old woman who knows a lot about carving ivory," Tishona said.

"Jondecam and Peridal were looking for you," Levela said. "They couldn't find you last night."

"That's not surprising, since we weren't here last night," Jondalar said.

"You weren't? But I saw many people from the Ninth Cave," Levela said.

"We stayed at our camp," Jondalar said.

"Yes," Ayla said. "We were helping Bologan and Lanoga build a summer lodge."

Jondalar felt a twinge of indiscretion on her part when Ayla so openly revealed what he thought of as the confidential problems of their Cave. Not that there was anything expressly wrong with talking about them. It was just that he had been raised by a leader and knew how personally most leaders took unresolved situations within their Cave that they hadn't been able to settle. Laramar and Tremeda had been an embarrassment to the Ninth Cave for some time. Neither Marthona nor Joharran had been able to do much about them. They had lived there many years, and had the right to stay. As he suspected, Ayla's statement brought curious queries.

"Bologan and Lanoga? Aren't they Tremeda's children?" Levela said. "Why were you building their summer lodge?"

"Where were Laramar and Tremeda?" Tishona asked.

"They got in a fight, Laramar decided to move to a fa'lodge, Tremeda went after him, and didn't return," Ayla explained.

"I think I saw her," Janida said.

"Where?" Ayla asked.

"I think she was with some men who were drinking barma and gaming at the edge of the camp, near some of the men's far lodges," Janida said. She spoke softly, and seemed shy about speaking out. She shifted her baby and looked at him for a moment before she continued. "There were a couple of other women there, too. I remember being surprised to see Tremeda because I knew she had some little ones. I don't think those other women had young children."

"Tremeda has six children, the youngest little more than a one-year. The oldest sister, Lanoga, takes care of them, and she's barely an eleven-year, herself," Ayla said, trying to contain herself, but her irritation was obvious. "I think her brother Bologan tries to help, but he's only a thirteen-year. They were trying to put up a tent for themselves last night when we walked past on our way here. But it was wet and falling apart, and they didn't have any materials for a summer lodge. So we stayed and built one for them."

"You built a summer lodge by yourselves? With nothing but local materials?" Tishona said, looking at them with awe.

"It was a small one," Jondalar said, with a smile. "Just enough for their family. No one is sharing with them."

"I'm not surprised," Levela said, "but it is a shame. Those youngsters could use someone to help."

"The Cave helps," Tishona said, in defense of the Ninth Cave, of which she was now a member. "The other mothers even take turns nursing the baby."

"I was wondering about that when you said Tremeda didn't return and the youngest was little more than a one-year," Levela said.

"Tremeda ran dry a year ago," Ayla said.

It happens when you don't nurse enough, she thought, but didn't say it aloud. There were reasons, sometimes good ones, for a mother's milk to dry up. She recalled when she had grieved so much after the death of her Clan mother, Iza, that she was oblivious to the needs of her own son. The other nursing mothers of Brun's clan had been willing to feed Durc, but in her heart she would never quite get over it.

The other women of the Clan understood more than she that it was as much Creb's fault as anyone's. When Durc cried to be fed, instead of putting him in his grieving mother's arms and letting him rouse her, he brought the baby to one of the other women to be fed. They knew he meant well, he hadn't wanted to disturb Ayla in her sorrow, and they couldn't refuse him. But the lack of nursing had made her sick with milk fever, and by the time she recovered, she was dry. Ayla held the baby girl in her arms a little closer.

"There you are, Ayla!" Proleva said as she approached. She had four other women with her.

Ayla recognized Beladora and Jayvena, the mates of the leaders of the Second and Seventh Caves, and nodded at them. They acknowledged her as well. She wondered if the other two women were also the mates of leaders. She thought she recognized one of them. The other was drawing back from Wolf.

"Zelandoni has been looking for you," Proleva continued. "And several young men have been asking about you, Jondalar. I told them if I saw you, I'd tell you to meet them at Manvelar's lodge in the camp of the Third Cave."

"Proleva, where is the zelandonia lodge?" Ayla asked.

"Not far from the Third Cave's camp, right next to the camp of the Twenty-sixth Cave," Proleva said, pointing in the general direction.

"I didn't know the Twenty-sixth had set up a camp," Jondalar said.

"Stevadal likes to be in the middle of things," Proleva said. "His whole Cave isn't staying at the Meeting Camp, but there are a couple of lodges for those who happen to stay late and want a place to sleep. I'm sure there will be a lot of coming and going, at least until after the First Matrimonial."

"When will that be?" Jondalar asked.

"I don't know. I don't think they've decided yet. Maybe Ayla can ask Zelandoni," Proleva said, as she and the women with her continued on to wherever they were heading when she stopped to pass on the messages.

Ayla and Jondalar said their farewells and headed toward the camps to which they had been directed. When they neared the camp of the Third Cave, Ayla recognized the large zelandonia lodge with its ancillary lodges close by. Right now, she thought, recalling the Summer Meeting of the year before, the young women who were being prepared for their Rites of First Pleasures were cloistered in one of the special dwellings, while appropriate men were being selected for them. In the other lodge were the women who had decided to wear the red fringe, to be donii-women this season. They had chosen to make themselves available to the young men who were wearing puberty belts, to teach them how to understand a woman's needs.

Pleasures were a Gift from the Mother, and the zelandonia considered it a sacred duty to make sure the first experience of young adults was appropriate and educational. It was felt that both young women and young men needed to learn how to appreciate the Mother's Great Gift properly, and that older, more experienced people needed to demonstrate and explain, to share the Gift with them the first time under the discreet but watchful eyes of the zelandonia. It was a Rite of Passage too important to be left to chance encounters.

Both ancillary lodges were very well guarded since most men found them almost irresistible. Some men couldn't even look in the direction of either lodge without feeling aroused. Men, especially young men who had already had their manhood rites but were not yet mated, tried to peek in, and sometimes sneak into the lodge of the young women, and some older men liked to hover around it in hopes of catching a glimpse. Nearly every available man wanted to be selected for a young woman's First Rites, though there was also a certain anxiety involved if they were. They knew they would be observed and they feared they might not perform well, but there was also a special sense of satisfaction when they did. Most men also had exciting memories of their own donii-women when they first became men.

But there were restrictions imposed on those who had the important task of sharing and teaching the Mother's Gift of Pleasure. Neither the selected men nor the donii-women were to have any close ties with the younger ones for a year after the ceremony. They were considered too impressionable, too vulnerable, and not without reason. It wasn't unusual for a young woman who had had a pleasurable first experience with an older man to want to share it again, even though it was forbidden. After First Rites, she could have any other man she wanted—who also wanted her—but that made her first partner all the more appealing. Jondalar had been chosen often before he went on his Journey, and he had learned to gently evade sometimes persistent young women with whom he'd shared a loving and tender ceremonial experience, who tried to get him alone. But it was, in a sense, easier for the men. Theirs was a single event; one night of special Pleasure.

The donii-women were expected to be available for the entire summer, or more, especially if they were acolytes. Young men had frequent urges, and it took a while for them to learn that the needs of women were different, their satisfactions more varied. But the donii-women were required to make sure that the young men didn't form a lasting attachment, which was sometimes difficult.

Jondalar's donii-woman was The First, when she was known as Zolena, and she had taught him well. Later, after he returned to the Ninth Cave after spending several years with Dalanar, he was often chosen. But at the time of his puberty,

he became so enamored of Zolena, he would choose none of
the other donii-women. More, he wanted her to be his mate,
even though there was an age difference. The difficulty was
that she also developed strong feelings for the tall, handsome,
extremely charismatic young man with the pale blond hair and
unusually vivid blue eyes, and that had created problems for
both of them.

When they reached Manvelar's lodge, they knocked on a
wood panel near the entrance, and speaking in a louder voice,
said who they were. He called to them to come in.

"Wolf is with us," Ayla said.

"Bring him in," Morizan said as he pushed open the door
drape.

Ayla hadn't seen much of Manvelar's son since the lion
hunt, and she smiled cordially at him. After everyone had been
greeted, Ayla said, "I need to go to the zelandonia lodge. Could
you keep Wolf, Jondalar? Sometimes he creates such a distraction, he disrupts things. I like to ask Zelandoni first, before I
bring him there."

"If no one minds," Jondalar said, giving Morizan and
Manvelar and the others in the lodge a questioning look.

"It's fine. He can stay," Manvelar said.

Ayla stooped down and looked at the animal. "Stay with
Jondalar," she said, making the hand signal at the same time.
He nosed the baby and made her giggle, then sat down. Whining with concern, he anxiously watched her as she and the
baby left, but he didn't follow her.

When she reached the imposing lodge of the zelandonia,
she tapped on the panel, and said, "It's Ayla."

"Come in," she heard the familiar voice of the First Among
Those Who Served The Great Earth Mother say. The drape
covering the opening was pushed aside by a male acolyte and
Ayla stepped in. Though oil lamps were burning, it was dark
inside and she stood without moving for a while, waiting for
her eyes to adjust. When she could finally see where she was
going, she saw a group of people sitting near the large figure
of the First. "Come join us, Ayla," she said. She had waited

before speaking, knowing how the darkness inside left people momentarily blinded.

As Ayla headed toward them, Jonayla started fussing. The change in lighting had disconcerted the baby. A couple of acolytes made a space for her, and she sat down between them, but before she could focus her attention on the proceedings inside, she had to settle her child. Thinking that she might be hungry, she exposed her breast and brought the baby to it. Everyone waited. She was the only one there with a child and she wondered if she had interrrupted something important, but she had been given a message that Zelandoni wanted to see her.

When Jonayla settled down, the First said, "I'm glad to see you here, Ayla. We didn't see you last night."

"No, we didn't make it to the Meeting Camp," she said.

Some of the people who hadn't met her before were surprised at the way she said certain words. It made them curious. It wasn't like anything they had heard before. They had no trouble understanding her; she knew the language well, and had a pleasing low-pitched voice, but it was unusual.

"Were you or the baby not feeling well?" the First asked.

"No, we were fine. Jondalar and I went to check on the horses, and on our way back we saw Lanoga and Bologan trying to build a shelter. They didn't have any materials for a lodge, and were trying to put up the tent poles. We stayed and built a lodge for them."

The First frowned. "Where were Tremeda and Laramar?"

"Lanoga said they argued, Laramar left saying he was going to stay in a fa'lodge, Tremeda went after him, and neither one returned. Janida just told me that she saw Tremeda last night with some men who were drinking barma and gaming. I guess she got distracted," Ayla said.

"So it would seem," the Zelandoni of the Ninth Cave said. Though she was First, she was still responsible for the well-being of her Cave. "The children have a place now?"

"You built them an entire lodge?" said a man who was a stranger to Ayla.

"Not as big as this one," Ayla said with a smile, waving her hand to indicate the especially large shelter of the zelandonia. Jonayla seemed to have had enough. She let go and Ayla picked her up, put her over her shoulder and started patting her back. "They aren't sharing with anyone so it just had to be big enough for the family, the children and Tremeda and Laramar, if he decides to come back."

"How nice of you," someone said. The tone sounded rather derisive. Ayla looked and saw that it was Zelandoni of the Fourteenth who had spoken, an older, rather skinny woman whose thin hair always seemed to be falling out of her bun.

Ayla noticed that Madroman, who was sitting near the Fourteenth, along with the Zelandoni of the Fifth Cave, turned to look at her with a condescending expression. He was the one whose front teeth Jondalar had knocked out in a fight when they were younger. She knew that Jondalar didn't like him, and she suspected the feeling was mutual. She didn't much care for him either. With her ability to interpret nuances of attitude and expression, she always felt a certain deceit in his manner, a falseness in his smiling greetings, a lack of sincerity in his offers of welcome and friendliness, but she had always tried to treat him politely.

"Ayla has taken a special interest in the children of that family," the First said, careful to keep the exasperation out of her voice. The Zelandoni of the Fourteenth had been an annoyance ever since the Zelandoni of the Ninth Cave had become First, always trying to provoke someone, particularly her. The woman had felt she was next in line and had expected to be made First. She never quite got over the fact that the younger Zelandoni of the Ninth had been chosen instead.

"It seems they need it," said the same man who had commented earlier.

Jonayla had fallen asleep on her shoulder. Ayla took her carrying blanket and spread it out on the ground, the young acolyte on her right moved over to make room, then she put her infant down on it.

"Yes, they do," the First was saying, shaking her head; then she realized that Ayla didn't know the man, and though he had no doubt heard of her, he had not met her. "I don't think everyone here has met my new acolyte. Perhaps some introductions would be in order."

"What happened to Jonokol?" Zelandoni of the Fifth Cave asked.

"He moved to the Nineteenth Cave," the First said. "The White Hollow that was found last year enticed him. He always was more artist than acolyte, but he's serious about the zelandonia now. He wants to be sure that whatever is done with the new cave is appropriate . . . no, more than that. He wants it to be right. That white cave has called him now, more than any training could have done."

"Where are the Nineteenth Cave? Are they coming this year?"

"I believe they are, but they haven't arrived yet," the One Who Was First said. "I will be glad to see Jonokol; I miss his skills, but fortunately Ayla arrived with many skills of her own. She is already a fine healer, and brings some very interesting knowledge and techniques. I am pleased she has begun training. Ayla, will you stand so I can introduce you formally?"

Ayla got up and took a few steps to stand beside the First, who waited until everyone was looking at them, then said, "May I present to you Ayla of the Zelandonii, mother of Jonayla, Blessed of Doni, acolyte of the Zelandoni of the Ninth Cave, the One Who Is First Among Those Who Serve The Great Earth Mother. She is mated to Jondalar, son of Marthona, former leader of the Ninth Cave and brother to Joharran, present leader. Formerly she was a Mamutoi of the Lion Camp, the Mammoth Hunters who live far to the east, and an acolyte of Mamut, who adopted her as Daughter of the Mammoth Hearth, which is their zelandonia. She was also chosen and physically marked by the spirit of the Cave Lion, her totem, and is protected by the spirit of the Cave Bear. She is a friend of the horses, Whinney and Racer, and the new filly, Gray, and the four-legged hunter she calls Wolf."

Ayla thought it was a very comprehensive reciting of her names and ties, complete with explanations. She didn't know if she was actually an acolyte of Mamut, but he had adopted her to the Mammoth Hearth and he was training her. The Donier hadn't mentioned that she had also been adopted by the Clan, whom they called Flatheads. The only reference was that she was protected by the spirit of the Cave Bear. Ayla doubted if Zelandoni fully understood that it meant she was one of them, she was Clan—at least she was until Broud disowned her, cursed her, and made her leave.

The man who had spoken earlier approached Ayla and the First. "I am Zelandoni of the Twenty-sixth Cave, and in the name of Doni, I welcome you to this Summer Meeting Camp that we are hosting." He held out both hands.

Ayla took his hands. "In the name of the Great Mother of All, I greet you, Zelandoni of the Twenty-sixth Cave," she said.

"We have found a new deep hollow. It has wonderful resonance when we sing, but it is very small," the man said. He was obviously quite excited about it. "One must crawl in like a snake, and it is best for only one or perhaps two people, though three or four could go in. I think it is too small for the First, I am sorry to say, though I would certainly let her make that decision. I promised Jonokol I would show it to him when he came. Since you are now the First's acolyte, Ayla, perhaps you would like to see it, too."

The invitation caught her by surprise, but she smiled, then said, "Yes, I would like to see it."

7

T he Zelandoni Who Was First had mixed feelings upon hearing about the new cave. New discoveries of hollows that were likely to be entries to the Mother's Sacred Underworld were always exciting, but the thought that she might be excluded for purely physical reasons was disappointing, though the idea of crawling on her belly into a small space was not exactly appealing anymore. It did, however, please her that Ayla was accepted enough to be offered the opportunity in her place. She hoped it meant that her choice of a newcomer as an acolyte was already taken for granted. Of course, having a woman with such obviously unusual powers safely under the authority of the zelandonia was probably a relief to many. That she was also an inherently normal and attractive young mother made her acceptance easier.

"That is an excellent idea, Zelandoni of the Twenty-sixth Cave. I had planned to begin her Donier Tour later this summer, after the First Matrimonial and Rites of First Pleasures ceremonies. A visit to a new sacred hollow could be an early introduction, and give her a chance to understand from the beginning how sacred sites are known to the zelandonia," the First Donier said. "And while we are talking about introductions and training, I notice several of the newer acolytes here. This seems a good time to reveal some knowledge they will need to know. Who can tell me how many seasons there are?"

"I can," said a young man. "There are three."

"No," said a young woman. "There are five."

The First smiled. "One of you says three, another says five. Can anyone tell me which is correct?"

No one spoke for a while; then the acolyte next to Ayla on the left said, "I think both are."

The First smiled again. "You are correct. There are both three and five seasons, depending upon how you count them. Can anyone tell me why?"

No one spoke up. Ayla remembered some of Mamut's teachings, but she felt somewhat shy and hesitant to speak. Finally, when the silence grew awkward, she said, "The Mamutoi also have both three and five seasons. I don't know about the Zelandonii, but I can tell you what Mamut told me."

"I think that would be quite interesting," the First said, looking around and seeing nods of agreement from others of the zelandonia.

"The downward-pointing triangle is a very important symbol to the Mamutoi," Ayla began. "It is the symbol of woman, and it is made with three lines, so three is the number of the power of . . . I don't quite know the word . . . motherhood, giving birth, creating new life, and is very sacred to Mut, to the Mother. Mamut also said the three sides of a triangle represent the three major seasons, spring, summer, and winter. But the Mamutoi recognize two additional seasons, the ones that signal change, fall and midwinter, making five seasons. Mamut said five is the Mother's hidden power number."

Not only were the young acolytes surprised and interested, the older Zelandoni were fascinated by what she said. Even those who had met her the year before and had heard her talk noticed the way she spoke, her accent. To those who were seeing her for the first time, especially if they were young and had not traveled much, her voice seemed absolutely exotic. For most of the zelandonia she had spoken of information unknown to them but that essentially agreed with their way of thinking, which tended to confirm their own beliefs. That gave her added credence and an element of prestige. She was traveled, knowledgeable, but not really threatening.

"I didn't realize the ways of the Mother were so similar even from such a great distance," said Zelandoni of the Third. "We also speak of three main seasons—spring, summer, and winter—but most people recognize five: spring, summer, autumn, early winter, and late winter. We also understand that the inverted triangle represents woman and that three is the number of generative power, but five is a more powerful symbol."

"That is true. The ways of the Great Earth Mother are remarkable," the First said, then continued with the instruction. "We talked about the counting-word five before, the five parts of an apple, five fingers on each hand, five toes on each foot, and how to use the hands and counting words in a more powerful way. There are also five Primary, or Sacred, colors. All other colors are aspects of the main colors. The first color is Red. It is the color of blood, the color of life, but just as life does not last, the color Red seldom stays true for long. As blood dries it darkens, becomes brown, sometimes very dark.

"Brown is an aspect of red, sometimes called old Red. It is the color of the trunks and branches of many trees. The red ochers of the earth are the dried blood of the Mother, and though some can be very bright, almost new looking, they are all considered old Red. Some flowers and fruits show the true color of Red, but flowers are ephemeral, as is the red color of fruits. When red fruits, such as strawberries, are dried, they turn to old Red. Can you think of anything else that is Red, or an aspect of it?"

"Some people have brown hair," said an acolyte sitting behind Ayla.

"And some people have brown eyes," Ayla said.

"I've never seen anyone with brown eyes. The eyes of everyone I know are blue or gray, sometimes with a little green," said the young male acolyte who had spoken earlier.

"The people of the Clan who raised me all had brown eyes," Ayla said. "They thought my eyes were strange, perhaps even weak, because they were so light."

"You are talking about Flatheads, aren't you? They're not really people. Other animals have brown eyes, and a lot of them have brown fur," he said.

Ayla felt her anger flare. "How can you say that? The Clan are not animals. They are people!" she said through gritted teeth. "Have you ever even seen one?"

The First jumped in to quell the incipient disruption. "Acolyte of the Zelandoni of the Twenty-ninth Cave, it is true that some people have brown eyes. You are young and obviously inexperienced. That is one reason that before you become a full

Zelandoni, you need to make a Donier Tour. When you travel south, you will meet some people with brown eyes. But perhaps you should answer her question. Have you ever seen the 'animal' you call a Flathead?" she said.

"Well . . . no, but everyone says they look like bears," the young man said.

"When she was a child, Ayla lived among the ones that the Zelandonii know as Flatheads, but that she calls the Clan. They saved her life after she lost her parents; they took care of her, raised her. I think she has more experience with them than you. You also might ask Willamar, the Trade Master, who has had more contact with them than most. He says they may look a little different, but they behave like people and he believes they are. Until you have had some direct contact yourself, I think you should defer to those who have had personal experience with them," the First said, in a stern, lecturing tone.

The young man felt a flare of anger. He didn't like being lectured, and he didn't like that the ideas of a foreigner should be given more credence than those he had heard all his life. But after his Zelandoni signaled with a shake of his head, he decided not to dispute the One Who Was First Among Those Who Served The Great Earth Mother.

"Now, we were speaking of the Five Sacred Colors. Zelandoni of the Fourteenth Cave, why don't you tell us about the next one," the First said.

"The second primary color is Green," the Zelandoni of the Fourteenth began. "Green is the color of leaves and grass. It is also a color of life, of course, plant life. In winter you will see that many trees and plants are brown, showing that their true color is old Red, the color of life. In winter the plants are only resting, gathering strength for their new green growth in spring. With their flowers and fruits, plants also show most of the other colors,"

Ayla thought her delivery was flat, and if the information itself had not been so interesting, she could make it seem dull. No wonder the rest of the zelandonia didn't select her to be First. Then Ayla wondered if she just thought that because she knew how much the woman annoyed her Zelandoni.

"Perhaps the Zelandoni whose Cave is hosting this Summer

Meeting would tell us about the next Sacred Color?" the First interjected just as the Fourteenth was taking a breath to continue. The Fourteenth couldn't really object, under the circumstances.

"Yes, of course," he said. "The third primary color is Yellow, the color of the sun, Bali, and the color of fire, although there is also much Red in both, which shows that they have a life of their own. You can see the red in the sun mostly in the morning and in the evening. The sun gives us light and warmth, but it can be dangerous. Too much sun can make skin burn, and dry out plants and watering holes. We have no control over the sun. Not even Doni, the Mother, could control her son, Bali. We can only try to protect ourselves from him, get out of his way. Fire can be even more dangerous than the sun. We do have some control of it, and it is very useful, but we should never get careless with fire, nor take it for granted.

"Not all things that are Yellow are hot. Some soil is Yellow, there is yellow ocher as well as red ocher. Some people have yellow hair," he said, looking directly at Ayla, "and of course, many flowers show its true color. They always age to brown, which is an aspect of Red. It is for that reason that some argue that Yellow should be considered an aspect of Red and not a Sacred Color in its own right, but most agree that it is a primary color that attracts Red, the color of life."

Ayla found herself fascinated by the Zelandoni of the Twenty-sixth Cave, and observed him more closely. He was tall, muscular, with dark blond, almost brown hair with streaks of lighter color, and dark eyebrows that blended into his Zelandoni tattoo on his left forehead. The tattoo was not quite as ornate as some, but very precise. His beard was brown with a reddish tone, but small and with a distinct shape. She thought he must use a sharp flint blade to trim it, to keep it that way. He was probably approaching middle age, his face had some character, but he seemed young and vibrant and quietly in control.

She thought most people would think that he was handsome. She did, though she didn't fully trust her sense of who was attractive to her own kind of people, the "Others" to the Clan. Her perception of who looked good was strongly influenced by the standards of the people who raised her. She thought people of the Clan were handsome, but most of the Others did not, though many had never seen any, and most of those who had, had only seen them from a distance. She watched some of the young women acolytes and decided that they were attracted to the man who was speaking. Some of the older women seemed to be, too. In any case, he was very good at communicating the lore. The First seemed to agree. She asked him to continue.

"The fourth primary color is Clear," he said. "Clear is the color of the wind, the color of water. Clear can show all colors, as when you look in a still pond and see a reflection, or when drops of rain sparkle in all colors when the sun comes out. Both Blue and White are aspects of Clear. When you look at wind, it is clear, but when you look into the sky, you see blue. Water in a lake, or in the Great Waters of the West, is often blue, and the water seen on glaciers is a deep, vivid blue."

Like Jondalar's eyes, Ayla thought. She remembered when they were crossing the glacier that it was the only time she saw a blue color that matched his eyes. She wondered if the Zelandoni of the Twenty-sixth Cave had ever been on a glacier.

"Some fruit is blue," he was saying. "especially berries, and some flowers, although blue flowers are more rare. Many people have blue eyes, or blue mixed with gray, which is also an aspect of Clear. Snow is white, as are clouds in the sky, or gray when they are mixed with dark to make rain, but their true color is Clear. Ice is clear though it may appear white, but you know the true color of snow and ice as soon as they melt, and clouds when they rain. There are many white flowers, and one can find white earth in certain places. There is a location not far from the Ninth Cave where white earth, kaolin, can be found," he said, looking directly at Ayla, "but it is still an aspect of Clear."

The Zelandoni Who Was First picked up the lecture. "The Fifth Sacred Color is Dark, sometimes called black. It is the color of night, the color of charcoal after fire has burned the life out of the wood. It is the color that overcomes the color of life, Red, especially as it ages. Some have said that black is the darkest shade of old Red, but it is not. Dark is the absence of light, and the absence of life. It is the color of death. It does not even have an ephemeral life; there are no black flowers. Deep caves show the primary color of Dark in its truest form."

When she finished, she stopped and looked at the assembled

acolytes. "Are there any questions?" she said. There was a diffident silence, some shifting and shuffling, but no one spoke out. She knew there probably were questions, but no one wanted to be first, or appear not to understand if everyone else did, or seemed to. It was all right—questions could come later, and would. Since so many of the acolytes were there, and she had their attention, the First wondered if she should continue with the instruction. Too much at one time was hard to retain, and people's minds could wander. "Would you like to hear more?"

Ayla glanced at her baby and noticed that she was still asleep. "I would," she said softly. There were other murmurs and sounds from the group, most of them positive.

"Would someone like to talk about another way that we know five is a powerful symbol?" the One Who Was First asked.

"One can see five wandering stars in the sky," said the old Zelandoni of the Seventh Cave.

"That is true," the First said, smiling at the tall, elderly man, then announced to the rest, "and Zelandoni of the Seventh Cave is the one who discovered them and showed them to us. It takes time to see them, and most of you won't until your Year of Nights."

"What is the Year of Nights?" Ayla asked. There were several others who were glad she did.

"It is the year when you will have to stay awake at night and sleep during the day," the First replied. "It is one of the trials you will face in your training, but it is more than that. There are certain things you need to see that can only be seen at night, like where the sun rises and sets, especially during midsummer and midwinter, when the sun stops and changes direction, and the risings and settings of the moon. The Zelandoni of the Fifth Cave is the one who knows most about that. He made notations for half a year to keep track."

Ayla wanted to ask what other trials she would have to face in her training, but didn't speak up. She guessed she would find out soon enough.

"What else shows us the power of five?" the First asked.

"The Five Sacred Elements," the Zelandoni of the Twenty-sixth said.

"Good!" the large woman Who Was First said. She shifted to a more comfortable position on her seat. "Why don't you begin."

"It's always best to talk about the Sacred Colors before the Sacred Elements because color is one of their properties. The First Element, sometimes called a Principle or Essential, is Earth. Earth is solid, it has substance, it is soil and rock. You can pick up a piece of Earth with your hand. The color most associated with Earth is old Red. As well as being an element in its own right, Earth is the material aspect of all the other Essentials; it can hold them or be affected by them in some way," he said, then looked toward the First to see if she wanted him to continue. She was already looking at someone else.

"Zelandoni of the Second Cave, why don't you continue."

"The Second Element is Water," she said, standing up. "Water sometimes falls from the sky, sometimes rests on the surface of the earth or flows across it, or through it in caves. Sometimes it is absorbed and becomes part of the earth. Water is movable; the color of Water is usually Clear or blue, even when it looks muddy. When Water is brown, it is because you are seeing the color of Earth, which has mixed with Water. Water can be seen and felt, and swallowed, but you cannot pick it up with your fingers, though your hand can make a cup for it," she said, holding her two hands together to form a cup.

Ayla enjoyed watching her because she used her hands a lot when she was describing things, although it wasn't intentional the way it was with the Clan.

"Water must be held in something, a cup, a waterbag, your own body. Your body needs to hold water, as you will find out when you go through your trial of giving it up. All living things need water—plants and animals," the Second finished and sat down.

"Would anyone else like to say something about water?" the leader of the zelandonia asked.

"Water can be dangerous. People can drown in it," said the young acolyte sitting on the other side of Jonayla. She spoke softly and looked sad and Ayla wondered if she had personal knowledge of what she spoke.

"That's true," Ayla said. "On our Journey, Jondalar and I had to cross many rivers. Water can be very dangerous."

"Yes, I knew someone who broke through the ice on a river and drowned," said the Zelandoni of South Face, of the Twenty-ninth Cave. He started to embellish the story about drowning, but the main Zelandoni of the Twenty-ninth interrupted and cut him short.

"We understand water can be very dangerous, but so can Wind, and that is the Third Element." She was very pleasant with a nice smile, but an underlying strength, and she knew this was not a time for a digression into anecdotes. The First was discussing a serious matter with important information that needed to be understood.

The First smiled at her, knowing exactly what she had done. "Why don't you continue to tell us about the Third Element," she said.

"Like Water, Wind cannot be picked up, nor can it be held or seen, though its effects can be seen," she said. "When Wind is still, it cannot even be felt, but Wind can be so powerful it can pick up trees and knock them over. It can blow so hard, you can't move against it. Wind is everywhere. There is no place that you won't find it, not even in the deepest cave, though it is usually still there. You know it is present because you can make it move by flapping something. Wind also moves inside a living body. It can be felt when you suck in your breath and when you blow it out. Wind is essential for life. People and animals need Wind to live. When their Wind stops, you know they are dead," the Zelandoni of the Twenty-ninth Cave ended.

Ayla noticed that Jonàyla was beginning to squirm; she would be waking up soon. The First was aware of the baby, too, and an air of restlessness in the assembly. It was necessary to finish this session soon.

"The Fourth Element is Cold," the First continued. "Like Wind, Cold cannot be picked up or held, but it can be felt. Cold causes changes, makes things harder and slower. Cold can harden the Earth, and Cold can harden Water, turn it into ice and make it stop moving, and turn rain into snow or ice. The color of Cold is Clear or White. Some say that dark causes Cold. It does get cooler when the dark of night comes. Cold can be dangerous. Cold can help dark to drain life, but dark is unaffected by Cold, so things that are partly dark are less affected by Cold. Cold can be helpful, too. If food is put into a cold pit in the earth, or in water covered with ice, Cold can stop it from going bad. When Cold stops, things that are Clear can usually go back to the way they were, like ice back to Water. Old Red things or Elements can usually recover from Cold—the Earth, the bark of trees for example—but Green, Yellow, or true Red seldom do."

The First thought about asking for questions, but decided to hurry through. "The Fifth Element is Heat. Heat cannot be picked up or held, but it, too, can be felt. You know when you touch something hot. Heat also changes things, but where Cold makes slow changes, Heat is quick. As Cold drains life, Heat and warmth can restore it, bring it back. Fire and Sun can make Heat. The Heat from the sun softens the cold, hard Earth, and turns snow to rain, which helps green life sprout; it turns ice to Water, and helps it move again. The Heat of fire can cook food, both meat and vegetables, and warm the inside of a dwelling, but Heat can be dangerous. It can also help dark. The Primary Color of Heat is Yellow, often mixed with Red, but sometimes it is mixed with Dark. Heat can help the true Red of life, but too much Heat can encourage the Dark that destroys life."

The First's timing was just about right. Just as she finished, Jonayla woke up with a loud wail. Ayla quickly picked her up, rocked and bounced her to settle her, but knew she needed to be tended to.

"I want all of you to think about what you have learned today and remember any questions you may have so we can talk about them the next time we meet like this. Any of you who wish to leave can go now," the One Who Was First concluded.

"I hope we'll be able to meet again soon," Ayla said as she stood up. "This was very interesting. I'm looking forward to learning more."

"I'm glad, Acolyte of the Zelandoni of the Ninth Cave," the First said. Though Zelandoni called her Ayla when they were in a more casual situation, she always referred to everyone by formal titles when they were in the zelandonia lodge at Summer Meetings.

"Proleva, I need to ask you something," Ayla said, feeling uncomfortable.

"Go ahead, Ayla." All of the people who shared the dwelling were eating their morning meal, and turned toward her, their expressions full of curiosity.

"There is a Sacred Cave not far from the home of the Twenty-sixth Cave, and their Zelandoni has asked me to go with him to see it, since I am the First's acolyte. It is very small and the First would like me to go, to represent her."

Jondalar was not the only one whose attention was piqued. He glanced around and noticed that everyone was watching Ayla, and saw Willamar shudder. The Trade Master loved to travel great distances, but didn't much care for small, cramped spaces. He could make himself go into a cave if it was necessary, especially if it wasn't too small, but he preferred the open outdoors.

"I need someone to watch Jonayla, and feed her, if she needs it," Ayla explained. "I'll make sure she nurses before I leave, but I'm not sure how long it will take. I would take her with me, but I'm told one must crawl in like a snake, and I don't think I could do that with Jonayla. I think Zelandoni is pleased that I was asked."

Proleva thought for a moment. She was always busy at Summer Meetings, the Ninth was a large and important Cave, and she had many things planned for that day. She didn't know if she had time to take care of another baby besides her own, but she hated to refuse. "I'd be glad to feed her, Ayla, but I have promised to meet with some people today and I don't think I will be able to take care of her."

"I have an idea," Marthona said. Everyone turned to look at the former leader. "Perhaps we can find someone to go with Proleva to watch both Jonayla and Sethona while she is busy, and bring the babies to her when they need feeding."

Marthona looked hard at Folara, then surreptitiously poked her, wanting her to volunteer. The girl understood the message, and had thought about it even before, but wasn't sure if she wanted to spend a whole day taking care of the babies. On the other hand, she did love them both dearly, and it might be interesting to see what Proleva was going to be talking about at her meetings.

"I'll watch them," she said, then in a moment of inspiration added, "if Wolf will help me." That would bring her a lot of attention.

Ayla paused to think. She wasn't entirely sure if Wolf would obey the young woman in the middle of the Meeting area in the midst of so many strangers, though he would probably love to be around the little girls.

Adult wolves, aunts and uncles, were devoted to their young, and happily took turns watching them while the rest of the pack hunted, but a pack could not raise more than one litter. They had to hunt not only for themselves, but for several growing and hungry young wolves. To supplement nursing and to help wean the litter, the hunters brought back meat they had chewed and swallowed, regurgitating the partially digested food, making it easier for the pups to eat. It was the job of the alpha female to make sure no other females of the pack mated when they came into season, often interrupting her own mating to drive males away from them, so that her litter would be the one that was born and raised.

Wolf bestowed his normal wolfish adoration on the human babies of his pack. Ayla had observed and studied wolves when she was young, which was why she understood Wolf so well. As long as no one threatened the little ones, it was unlikely he would cause any trouble, and who would threaten them in the middle of a Summer Meeting?

"All right, Folara," Ayla said. "Wolf can help you watch the babies, but Jondalar, will you check on Wolf and Folara once in a while? I think he will mind her, but he may get too protective of the little ones, and not want to let anyone near them. He always does what you say when I'm not around."

"I was going to stay close to our camp and knap some tools this morning," he said. "I still owe special ones to some people for helping me build our dwelling at the Ninth Cave. There is a knapping area at the edge of the Meeting Camp, and it is paved with stones so it won't be muddy. I can work there and go to see how Folara and Wolf are doing occasionally. I did promise to meet with some people in the afternoon. After the lion hunt, many more are interested in the spear-thrower." His forehead wrinkled in a familiar frown as he thought about it. "But maybe we can meet where I can keep an eye on them."

"I hope we'll be back by afternoon, but I don't know how long the cave visit will take," Ayla said.

They all headed for the main encampment not long after, separating to go to their individual destinations when they reached the site. Ayla and Proleva, with their two babies, Folara, Jondalar, and the wolf, all went to the large zelandonia dwelling first. The donier of the Twenty-sixth Cave was already there waiting outside, and an acolyte Ayla had not seen for some time.

"Jonokol!" she said, rushing toward the man who had been the First's acolyte before her, and was considered one of the finest artists of the Zelandonii. "When did you arrive? Have you seen Zelandoni, yet?" she asked after they had embraced and touched cheeks.

"We got here just before dark last night," he said. "The Nineteenth Cave got off to a late start, and then the rain slowed us down. And yes, I have seen the First Among Those Who Serve The Mother. She's looking wonderful."

The other members of the Ninth Cave warmly greeted the man who had been, until recently, a valued member of their Cave and a good friend. Even Wolf sniffed him in recognition and was given a scratch behind the ears in return.

"Are you Zelandoni, yet?" Proleva asked.

"If I pass the testing, I may be at this Summer Meeting. Zelandoni of the Nineteenth is not well. She didn't come this year; she just couldn't walk so far."

"I'm sorry to hear that," Ayla said. "I was looking forward to seeing her."

"She has been a good teacher and I've been performing many of her tasks. Tormaden and the Cave would like me to take on the rest of the functions as soon as possible, and I think our Zelandoni wouldn't mind either," Jonokol said, then looking at the bundles Ayla and Proleva had in their carrying blankets, he added, "I see you have your little ones. I heard you both had girls, the Blessed of Doni. I am happy for you. May I see them?"

"Of course," Proleva said, taking her infant out of her carrying blanket and holding her up. "Her name is Sethona."

"And here is Jonayla," Ayla said, holding up her child as well.

"They were born within a few days of each other, and they are going to be great friends," Folara said. "I'm taking care of them today, and Wolf is going to help me."

"You are?" Jonokol said; then he looked at Ayla. "I understand we're going to visit a new sacred cave this morning."

"Are you coming with us, too? How wonderful," Ayla said; then she looked at the Zelandoni of the Twenty-sixth Cave. "Do you have any idea how long it will take? I would like to be back by afternoon."

"We should be back sometime in the afternoon," he said. He had been observing the reunion of the artist acolyte and his former Cave and their interactions. He had wondered how Ayla was going to handle visiting a difficult cave with a young baby and quickly understood that she had made arrangements for the care of her infant, which was wise. He wasn't the only one who wondered how a young mother was going to take on the full duties of a Zelandoni. Apparently with the help of family and friends in the Ninth Cave. There was a reason that few in the zelandonia chose to mate and have a family. In a couple of years, when the child was weaned, it would be easier for her . . . unless she were Blessed again. It would be interesting to watch the development of this young, and attractive, acolyte, he thought.

Saying she would be back soon, Ayla left with the others from the Ninth Cave to go with Proleva to her meeting. The Zelandoni of the Twenty-sixth Cave sauntered after them. She tried to nurse Jonayla, but the child was satisfied, and smiled at her mother while the milk dribbled out of the corner of her mouth; then she struggled to sit up. Ayla handed the baby over to Folara, and then stood in front of the wolf and tapped herself just under her shoulders. The animal jumped up, putting his large paws where she had tapped, as she braced herself to support his weight.

The demonstration that followed made people who hadn't seen it before stare in shocked disbelief. Ayla lifted her chin and exposed herself to the huge wolf. With great gentleness he licked her neck, then took her tender throat in his teeth in a wolfish gesture of acknowledgment of the alpha member of his pack. She returned the gesture near his mouth, getting a mouthful of fur; then holding him by his ruff, she looked into his eyes. He dropped down when she let go, and she stooped down to his level.

"I'm going away for a while," she said softly to the animal, repeating the meaning in the sign language of the Clan, though it was inconspicuous to most of those watching. Sometimes Wolf seemed to comprehend hand signals even better than words, but she generally used both when she was trying to communicate something important to him. "Folara is going to watch Jonayla and Sethona. You can stay here with the babies and watch them, too, but you must do what Folara tells you. Jondalar will be nearby."

She stood up and hugged her baby, and said good-bye to the others. Jondalar embraced her briefly as they pressed cheeks, and then she left. She wouldn't say even to herself that Wolf really understood everything she said, but when she talked to him like that, he paid close attention to her, and did seem to follow her instructions. She had noticed that the Zelandoni of the Twenty-sixth Cave had followed them and she knew he saw her with Wolf. His face still showed his surprise, though it wasn't obvious to everyone. Ayla was accustomed to reading meaning from subtle nuances; it was necessary in the language of the Clan, and she had learned to apply the skill to interpreting unconscious meaning in her own kind.

The man didn't say anything as they fell into step and walked back to the zelandonia dwelling together, but he had been astounded when she bared her throat to the wolf's fangs. The Twenty-sixth Cave had gone to a different Summer Meeting the year before and he hadn't seen her with the animal when she first arrived. First, he was surprised to see a hunting meat-eater calmly approaching with the people of the Ninth Cave, then he was amazed at the size of the animal. When he saw Wolf jump up on his hind legs, he was sure it was the biggest one of his kind he had ever seen. Of course, he'd never been quite so close to a living wolf before, but the animal was nearly as tall as the woman!

He had heard that the First's new acolyte had a way with animals and that a wolf followed her around, but he knew how people exaggerated and while he didn't deny what anyone said, he wasn't sure he fully believed it either. Perhaps a wolf had been seen near the Meeting and people were led to believe it was watching her. But this wasn't a creature skulking around the outskirts of the group, who may have been watching her from a distance, as he'd imagined. There was direct communication, understanding, and trust between them. The Zelandoni of the Twenty-sixth Cave had never seen anything like it and it piqued his interest in Ayla even more. Young mother or not, perhaps she did belong in the zelandonia.

It was well into the morning by the time the small group approached the unremarkable cave in the face of a low limestone cliff. There were four of them: the Zelandoni of the Twenty-sixth Cave; his acolyte, a quiet young man named Falithan, although he often referred to himself as the First Acolyte of the Zelandoni of the Twenty-sixth; Jonokol, the talented artist who had been the First's acolyte the year before; and Ayla.

She had enjoyed talking to Jonokol along the way, though it made her realize how much he had changed in the last year. When she first met him he was more artist than acolyte, and had joined the zelandonia because it allowed him to freely exercise his talent. He'd had no great desire to become a Zelandoni, he was content to remain an acolyte, but that had changed. He had become more serious, she thought. He wanted to paint the white cave that she, or rather Wolf, had found the previous summer, but not just for the joy of the art. He knew it was a remarkably hallowed place, a sacred refuge created by the Mother, whose white calcite walls offered a extraordinary invitation to be made into a distinctive place to commune with the world of the spirits. He wanted to know that world as a Zelandoni so he could do justice to its sanctity when he created the images from the next world that he was sure would speak to him. Jonokol would soon be Zelandoni of the Nineteenth Cave and give up his personal name, Ayla realized.

The entrance to the small cave seemed barely large enough for a person to enter and it seemed to get smaller as she looked farther inside. It made Ayla wonder why anyone would want to go inside it. Then she heard a sound that made the hair on the back of her neck stand on end, and gooseflesh appear on her arms. It was like a yodel, but faster and more high pitched, an ululating wail that seemed to fill the cave hole in front of them. She turned and saw that it was Falithan who was making the sound. Then a strange muted echo reverberated faintly back to them that did not quite synchronize with the original sound, but seemed to originate from deep inside the cave. When he finished, she saw Zelandoni of the Twenty-sixth smiling at her.

"It's quite a remarkable sound he makes, isn't it?" the man said.

"Yes, it is," Ayla said. "But why did he make it?"

"It's one way we test the cave. When a person sings or plays a flute or makes a sound like Falithan in a hollow, if the cave responds, sings back with a sound that is true and distinctive, it means the Mother is telling us that She hears, and She is telling us that one can enter the spirit world from here. Then we know it is a sacred place," the Twenty-sixth said.

"Do all sacred caves sing back?" Ayla asked.

"Not all, but most do, and some only in certain places, but there is always something special about sacred sites," he said.

"I'm sure the First would be able to test a cave like this, she has such a beautiful and pure voice," Ayla said, and then she frowned. "What if you want to test a cave but you can't sing, or play a flute, or make a sound like Falithan? I can't do any of those things."

"Surely you can sing a little."

"No, she can't," Jonokol said. "She speaks the words of the Mother's Song, and hums in a monotone."

"You have to be able to test a sacred site with sound," the Zelandoni of the Twenty-sixth Cave said. "That's an important part of being Zelandoni. And it must be a true sound of some kind. You can't just yell or scream." He seemed gravely concerned, and Ayla was crestfallen.

"What if I can't make the right kind of sound? A true sound?" Ayla said, realizing at that moment that she did want to be a Zelandoni someday. But what if she couldn't just because she couldn't make a proper sound?

Jonokol looked as unhappy as Ayla. He liked the foreigner Jondalar had brought back with him from his Journey, and he felt he owed her a debt. She was not only the one who found the beautiful new cave; she had made sure he was among the first to see it, and had agreed to become the First's acolyte, which had allowed him to move to the Nineteenth Cave, which was near it.

"But you can make a true sound, Ayla," Jonokol said. "You can whistle. I have heard you whistle just like a bird, and you can

make many other animal sounds. You can whinny like a horse,
you can even roar like a lion."

"That I'd like to hear," the Donier said.

"Go ahead, Ayla. Show him," Jonokol said.

Ayla closed her eyes and gathered up her thoughts to concentrate. She put her mind back to the time when she was living in
her valley and raising a young lion alongside a horse, as though
they were both her children. She remembered the first time Baby
managed to make a full-throated roar. She had decided to practice making the sound, too, and a few days later answered him
with a roar of her own. It wasn't quite as thunderous as his, but
he recognized it as a respectable roar. Like Baby, she had always built up to it with a series of distinctive grunts, and began
with a series of *unhk, unhk, unhk* sounds that grew louder with
each repetition. Finally she opened her mouth and pushed out
the loudest roar she could. It filled the small cave. Then after a
period of silence the roar echoed back on itself with a distant,
muted sound that with a chill of gooseflesh made each of them
feel that a different lion had answered from a place far away,
deep in the cave and beyond.

"If I didn't know better, I'd vow there was a lion in here," the
young acolyte of the Twenty-sixth said with a smile when the
echoes died down. "Can you really whinny like a horse, too?"

That one was easy. It was the true name of Ayla's horse, Whinney, the one she named her when she was a foal, though now she
more often said it like a word rather than a whinny. She made the
sound the way she usually greeted her friend when she hadn't
seen her for a while, a happy, welcoming *whiiinnneeey.*

This time the Donier of the Twenty-sixth Cave laughed out
loud. "And I imagine you can whistle like a bird, too."

Ayla smiled, a big delighted grin, then whistled through a series of birdcalls that she had taught herself when she was still
alone in her valley, and had learned to coax birds to eat out of her
hand. The bird trills and chirps and whistles reverberated with
the strangely muted echoing of the cave.

"Well, if I had any doubts about this being a Sacred Cave, I
couldn't anymore. And you won't have any problem testing with
sound, Ayla, even if you can't sing or play a flute. Like Falithan,
you have your own way," the Zelandoni said. Then he signaled to

his acolyte, who removed his backframe and took out of it four small bowls with handles that had been carved out of limestone.

The acolyte next brought out an object that looked like a small white sausage; it was a piece of the intestine of some animal filled with fat. He untwisted one end and squeezed out some of the slightly congealed fat into the bowl of each lamp, then put a strip of a dried boletus mushroom into each. Then he sat down and prepared to make a small fire. Ayla watched him, and almost offered to make a fire with one of her firestones, but the First had made a point the previous year to make a ceremony of showing the firestone, and though many of the Zelandonii now knew how to use it, Ayla wasn't sure how she wanted to show those who hadn't seen it the first time.

Using materials he had brought with him, Falithan soon had a small fire going and from it, using another strip of dried mushroom to transfer the fire, he melted some of the fat to make it more easily absorbed, then lit the mushroom wicks.

When the fire was well established in each grease lamp, the Zelandoni of the Twenty-sixth said, "Well, shall we explore this tight little cave? But you will have to assume that you are another animal, Ayla, a snake. Do you think you can slither in here?"

Ayla nodded her assent, though she felt some doubt.

Holding on to the handle of the small bowl-shaped lamp, the Zelandoni of the Twenty-sixth Cave put his head into the small opening first, getting down on his knees and one hand, and finally down on his stomach. Pushing the small oil lamp in front of him, he squirmed into the unique little space. Ayla followed him, then Jonokol and finally Falithan, each of them holding a lamp. She now understood why the Zelandoni had discouraged the First from attempting to enter the place. Though Ayla had occasionally been surprised at what the large woman could do if she set her mind to it, this cave really was too small for her.

The short walls were more or less perpendicular to the floor, but curved together at the ceiling, and appeared to be rock covered with a damp soil. The floor was a wet clayey mud that stuck to them, but actually helped them to slide through some of the tighter places, but it didn't take long for the cold clammy muck to seep into their clothing. The chill made Ayla aware that her breasts were full of milk and she tried to get up on her elbows so she wouldn't have to put all her weight on them, though it was difficult while holding the lamp. Small spaces didn't particularly bother Ayla, but when she got stuck in one place that curved sideways, she began to feel a touch of panic.

"Just relax, Ayla. You can make it," she heard Jonokol say, then felt a push against her feet from behind. With his help she squeezed through.

The cave was not uniformly small. When they got beyond the constriction, the cave opened up a little. They could actually sit up, and holding their lamps up, see each other. They stopped and rested for a while, then Jonokol couldn't resist. He took a small, chisel-pointed piece of flint from a pouch tied to his waist thong and, with a few quick strokes, engraved a drawing of a horse on the wall on one side, and then in front of it, another.

It had always amazed Ayla how skilled he was. When he was still at the Ninth Cave, she had often watched him when he practiced on the outside wall of a limestone cliff, or a slab of stone that had broken off, or on a section of rawhide with a piece of charcoal, or even on a smoothed-out area of dirt on the ground. He did it so often and with such ease, he almost seemed profligate, wasteful of his talent. But just as she had had to practice to gain skill with her sling or Jondalar's spear-thrower, she knew Jonokol had needed to practice to gain his level of proficiency. It was just that to her the ability to think of a living, breathing animal and reproduce its likeness on a surface was so extraordinary, it couldn't be anything but a great and amazing Gift from the Mother. Ayla was not alone in those feelings.

After they rested awhile, the Zelandoni of the Twenty-sixth Cave continued leading the way into the cave. They encountered a few more tight places before they reached a place where slabs of rock blocked their way; it was the end of the cave. They could go no farther.

"I notice that you felt compelled to make drawings on the wall of this cave," the Zelandoni of the Twenty-sixth said, smiling at Jonokol.

Jonokol wasn't sure he would put it quite that way, but he had drawn two horses, so he nodded assent.

"I have been thinking that Sun View should have a ceremony for this space. I am now more sure than ever that it is sacred, and

I would like to acknowledge that. It could be a place for young people who want to test themselves to come, even those who are quite young."

"I think you are right," the artist acolyte said. "It's a difficult cave, but staightforward. It would be hard to get lost in here."

"Would you join us in the ceremony, Jonokol?"

Ayla guessed the Zelandoni wanted Jonokol to make more drawings in this Sacred Cave that was so close to them, and wondered if his drawings would add more status to the place.

"I believe a mark of closure is needed here, to show it is as far as one can go within the cave—in this world," Jonokol said, then smiled. "I think Ayla's lion spoke from the next world. Let me know when you plan to have the ceremony."

Both the Zelandoni and his acolyte, Falithan, smiled their pleasure. "You are welcome to come, too, Ayla," the Twenty-sixth said.

"I will have to see what the First has planned for me," she said.

"Of course."

They turned around and started back, and Ayla was glad. Her clothes were soggy and caked with mud, and she was getting cold. It didn't seem to take as long to return, and she was happy that she didn't get stuck again. When they reached the entrance, Ayla breathed a sigh of relief. Her oil lamp had gone out just before they saw light coming in from outside. This may be a truly Sacred Cave, she thought, but she didn't think it was a particularly pleasant cave, especially having to crawl on her stomach most of the way.

"Would you like to come to visit Sun View, Ayla? It's not very far," Falithan said.

"I am sorry. Some other time I would love to visit, but I told Proleva I would be back in the afternoon. She is watching Jonayla, and I really do need to go back to the camp," Ayla said. She didn't add that her breasts were aching; she was feeling the need to nurse and getting very uncomfortable.

8

When Ayla returned, Wolf was waiting at the edge of the Summer Meeting Camp to greet her. He had somehow known she was coming. "Where's Jonayla, Wolf? Find her for me." The animal dashed out in front of her, then turned to look back and make sure she was following him.

He led her directly to Proleva, who was at the camp of the Third Cave, nursing Jonayla. "Ayla! You're back! If I'd known you were coming, I would have held off. I'm afraid she's full now," the woman said.

Ayla took her child and tried to nurse her, but the infant just wasn't hungry, which seemed to make Ayla's breasts ache even more. "Has Sethona nursed? I'm full, too. Full of milk."

"Stelona was helping me today, and she always has plenty of milk, even though her baby is eating some regular food. She offered to feed Sethona not long ago when I was talking to Zelandoni about the Matrimonial. Since I knew I'd be feeding Jonayla soon, I thought that would be perfect. I just didn't know when you would be back, Ayla."

"I didn't either," Ayla said. "I'll see if I can find someone else who needs milk, and thank you for taking care of Jonayla today."

Walking toward the big zelandonia lodge, Ayla saw Lanoga carrying Lorala on her hip. Three-year Ganamar, the next to the youngest in the family, was holding on to her tunic with one hand, the thumb of his other hand firmly in his mouth. Ayla hoped that Lorala might want to nurse; she was usually ready anytime. When she mentioned it, Lanoga told her, much to her relief, that she was looking for someone to feed the child.

They sat on one of several logs with seating pads on them

that were arranged around a darkened fireplace outside the entrance of the big lodge and Ayla gratefully took the older baby in exchange for her own. Wolf sat down near Jonayla, and Ganamar plopped down beside him. All the children of Laramar's hearth were comfortable around the animal, though Laramar was not. He still tensed up and backed away when the big wolf came near him.

Ayla had to wipe her breast off before she could nurse the child; the wet mud had soaked through. While Ayla was feeding Lorala, Jondalar returned from an afternoon of spear-throwing practice and Lanidar was with him. He smiled shyly at her and more warmly at Lanoga. Ayla gave him a quick appraising look. He was a twelve-year now, close to a thirteen-year, and he'd grown quite a bit in the past year. Even more in self-confidence, she noticed. He was taller and he wore a unique spear-thrower holder, a kind of harness that she could see accommodated his deformed right arm. It also held a quiver of several of the specialized spears that were used with a spear-thrower, which were shorter and lighter than the usual spears meant to be cast by hand, more like long darts tipped with sharp flint. His well-developed left arm looked almost as strong as a grown man's, and she suspected he had been practicing with the weapon.

Lanidar was also wearing a manhood belt with a red fringe, a narrow finger-woven strip of various colors and fibers. Some were natural vegetal colors like ivory flax, beige dogbane, and taupe nettles. Others were the natural fibers of animal fur, usually the dense, long coat of winterkills like white mouflon, gray ibex, dark red mammoth, and black horsetail. Most of the fibers could also be dyed to change or intensify the natural colors. The belt not only announced that he had reached physical maturity and was ready for a donii-woman and manhood rites, but the designs indicated his affiliations. Ayla was able to identify the symbolism that proclaimed he was of the Nineteenth Cave of the Zelandonii, though she couldn't yet identify his primary names and ties by their distinctive patterns.

The first time Ayla had seen a manhood belt, she had thought it was beautiful. She'd had no way then of knowing its meaning, however, when Marona, the woman who had expected to mate

Jondalar, tried to embarrass her by tricking her into wearing it, along with the winter undergarments of a young man. She still thought the belt ties were beautiful, though they reminded her of the unpleasant incident. She had, however, kept the soft buckskin garments the woman had given her. Ayla wasn't born to the Zelandonii, and in spite of their intended use, she didn't have the ingrained culture-driven sense that they were inappropriate. They were comfortably soft suede leather, velvety to the touch, and she decided she would wear them sometimes, after she made some adjustments to the leggings and tunic so they fit her womanly shape better.

People of the Ninth Cave looked at her strangely the first time she wore the undergarments of a young man as casual outer clothing in warm weather to go hunting, but they got used to it. After a while she noticed that some of the younger women started wearing similar clothing. But it embarrassed and angered Marona when Ayla wore them, because she was reminded that her trick had not been appreciated by the Ninth Cave. Instead they felt that she had disgraced them by treating the foreigner, who was destined to become one of them, so maliciously. Distressing Marona had not been Ayla's original intention when she first wore teenage boy's undergarments publicly, but the woman's reaction was not lost on her.

As Ayla and Lanoga exchanged babies again, several laughing young men approached, most of them wearing manhood belts and several of them carrying spear-throwers. Jondalar attracted people wherever he went, but young men in particular looked up to him and liked to cluster around him. She was pleased to note that they greeted Lanidar in a friendly way. Since he had developed such skill with the new weapon, his deformed arm no longer caused the other young men to avoid him. She was also pleased to note that Bologan was among them, though he lacked both a manhood belt and a spear-thrower of his own. She knew Jondalar had made several of the hunting weapons for people to practice.

Ayla knew that both men and women went to the practice spear-throwing sessions that Jondalar had begun to hold, but although the two genders were very aware of each other, the young men liked to socialize with their age-mates who were going through the same stage of development and looking forward to the same rituals, and young women tended to avoid the "boys with belts." Most of the young men glanced at Lanoga but pretended to ignore her, except Bologan. He did look at his sister and she looked back, and though they didn't smile or nod a greeting, it was an acknowledgment.

The boys all smiled at Ayla in spite of her mud-caked clothing, most of them shyly, but a couple were more bold in their appraisal of the beautiful older woman whom Jondalar had brought home and mated. Donii-women were invariably older and knew how to handle cocky boys trying to be men, to keep them in check without discouraging them too much. The impudent smile of some whom she hadn't met before was exchanged for a fleeting expression of apprehension when Wolf got up at her signal.

"Have you spoken to Proleva yet about the plans for tonight?" Jondalar asked Ayla as she started toward the camp of the Ninth Cave. He smiled at the baby and tickled her, and received a delighted giggle in return.

"No. I just returned from the new Sacred Cave the First wanted me to see, and then went to find Jonayla. I'll ask her after I change," Ayla said, as they touched cheeks. A couple of the young men, primarily the ones who were nervous about Wolf, looked surprised when Ayla spoke; it proclaimed her distant origins.

"Your clothes really are coated with mud," Jondalar said, wiping his hand on his pants after touching her.

"The cave had a very wet clay floor, and we had to crawl like a snake most of the time. The mud is cold and heavy, too. That's why I have to change."

"I'll walk back with you," Jondalar said; he hadn't seen Ayla all day. He took Jonayla in his arms so she would not get full of mud.

When Ayla found Proleva again, she learned that the Ninth Cave, along with the Third Cave—at the Third's camp—were hosting a meeting of the leaders of the rest of the Caves, and their assistants, who were at this Summer Meeting. All their families would join them for the evening meal. Proleva had organized the preparation, which included some people to care for children so their mothers could help.

Ayla signaled Wolf to come along. She noticed one or two women who looked uneasily at the carnivore, but was glad to see several people who recognized and welcomed Wolf, knowing what a help he could be in watching over them. Lanoga stayed to help mind the children; Ayla returned to see what Proleva wanted her to do.

In the course of the evening, she did stop to nurse Jonayla, but there was so much work to do to prepare and cook the large feast, she hardly had the chance to hold her infant until after everyone ate, and then she was summoned to the zelandonia lodge. She took Jonayla with her, and signaled Wolf to follow.

It was late and dark outside as she walked toward the large summer lodge along a path that had been laid with a paving of flat stones. She carried a torch, though light from various fireplaces lit her way reasonably well. She left the torch outside, propped up in a pile of rocks constructed to hold hot torches. Inside, a small fire near the edge of a larger fire ring and a few flickering lamps scattered here and there were glowing softly but gave scant illumination. Little could be seen beyond the lambent flames in the fireplace. She thought she heard someone snoring softly on the other side of the shelter, but she only saw Jonokol and the First. They were just within the circle of light, sipping cups of steaming tea.

Without interrupting their conversation, the First nodded to Ayla and motioned for her to sit. Glad to finally have a chance to relax in quiet and comfort, she gratefully settled down on a well-stuffed seating cushion, one of several scattered around the fireplace, and began to nurse her child while she listened. Wolf sat down beside them. He was welcome inside the zelandonia lodge, most of the time. Ayla had been gone for some time during the day and he didn't want to leave her or Jonayla.

"What was your impression of the cave?" the large woman said, directing her comment to the young man.

"It is very small, hardly big enough to squeeze through in places, but quite long. An interesting cave," Jonokol said.

"Do you believe it is sacred?" she asked.

"Yes, I do believe it is."

The First nodded. She hadn't doubted the Zelandoni of the Twenty-sixth Cave, but it was nice to have a corroborating opinion.

"And Ayla found her Voice," Jonokol added, smiling at Ayla, who was listening to the conversation, unconsciously rocking in a desultory fashion as she nursed her child.

"She did?" the older woman said.

"Yes," Jonokol said with a smile. "The Twenty-sixth asked her to test the cave, and was surprised when she said she couldn't sing or play a flute or do anything to test it. His acolyte, Falithan, sings a strong, high-pitched ululating wail that's very unique. Then I suddenly remembered Ayla's birdcalls and reminded her that she could whistle like a bird, and whinny like a horse, even roar like a lion. So she did. All of them. Amazed the Twenty-sixth, too, especially that roar. Her test substantiated the cave. When the roar came back, it was diminished, but clear, more than audible, but seemed to be coming from a very distant place. The other place."

"What did you think, Ayla?" the First asked, as she poured a cup of tea and handed it to Jonokol to give to her. She had noted that the infant had stopped nursing and had fallen asleep in Ayla's arms with a dribble of milk running down the side of her mouth.

"It's a difficult cave to get into, and long, but not complicated. It could be frightening, especially where it narrows down to some very tight passages, but no one could get lost in it," Ayla said.

"From the way you describe this new cave, it makes me think that it might be especially good for young acolytes who want to test themselves, to find out if the life of a Zelandoni is actually for them. If they are afraid of a small dark place that offers no real danger, I doubt that they could handle some of the other ordeals that truly can be perilous," the Woman Who Was First said.

It made Ayla wonder what some of those ordeals might be. She had been in enough risky situations in her life already; she wasn't sure if she wanted to face more, but perhaps she should wait and see what would be asked of her.

The sun was still low in the eastern sky, but a brilliant band of red, fading to purple at the edges, announced the coming day. A tinge of pink highlighted the thin, nebulous bank of stratus clouds on the western horizon, reflecting the back side of the glowing sunrise. As early as it was, almost everyone was already at the Main Camp. It had rained, off and on, for several days but this day looked more promising. Camping out when it rained was only endurable, never enjoyable.

"As soon as the First Rites and Matrimonial Ceremonies are over, Zelandoni wants to do some traveling," Ayla said, looking up at Jondalar. "She wants to begin my Donier Tour with some of the closer Sacred Sites. We need to make that seat on a pole-drag for her." They were walking back from seeing to the horses before heading toward the Meeting Campground for a morning meal. Wolf had started out with them, but was distracted and dashed into the brush.

Jondalar's brow wrinkled. "A trip like that could be interesting, but some people are talking about a big hunt after the Ceremonies. Maybe going after a summer herd so we can begin drying meat for next winter. Joharran has been talking about how useful the horses can be in driving animals into surrounds. I think he's counting on us to help. How do we decide which one to do?"

"If she doesn't want to go too far, maybe we could do both," Ayla said. She wanted to go with the First to visit Sacred Sites, but she also loved to hunt.

"Perhaps," Jondalar said. "Maybe we should talk to both Joharran and Zelandoni and let them decide. But in any case, we could go ahead and make a pole-drag seat for Zelandoni. When we were making the summer shelter for Bologan and Lanoga and the rest of that family, I noticed some trees that I thought might work."

"When do you think would be a good time to make it?"

"This afternoon, perhaps. I'll ask around to see if I can get a few people to help," Jondalar said.

"Greetings, Ayla and Jondalar," a familiar young voice said. It was Lanoga's younger sister, nine-year Trelara.

They both turned around and saw all six of the children coming out of their summer shelter. Bologan tied the opening flap closed, then caught up with them. Neither Tremeda nor Laramar was with them. Ayla knew the adults used the shelter sometimes, but they either had left earlier or, more likely, had not returned the night before. Ayla thought the children were probably heading to the Meeting Camp, hoping to find something to eat. People often made too much food and someone was usually willing to give them the leftovers. They may not always have received the choicest selection, but they seldom went hungry.

"Greetings, children," Ayla said.

They all smiled at her except Bologan, who tried to be more serious. When she first became familiar with the family, Ayla knew that Bologan, the eldest, stayed away from home as often as he could, preferring to associate with other boys, especially those who were more rowdy. But lately, it seemed to her, he was becoming more responsible toward the younger children, especially his brother Lavogan, who was a seven-year. And she'd seen him several times with Lanidar lately, which she thought was a good sign. Bologan walked up to Jondalar, rather diffidently.

"Greetings, Jondalar," he said, looking down at his feet before raising his eyes to meet the man's.

"Greetings, Bologan," Jondalar said, wondering why he had been approached.

"Can I ask you something?" Bologan said.

"Of course."

The boy reached into a pocket-like fold of his tunic and pulled out a colorful manhood belt. "Zelandoni talked to me yesterday, then gave this to me. She showed me how to tie it, but I can't seem to make it look right," he said.

Well, he was a thirteen-year now, Ayla thought as she fought back a smile. He hadn't specifically asked Jondalar for help, but the tall man knew what he wanted. Typically it was the man of a boy's hearth who gave him his manhood belt, usually made by his mother. Bologan was asking Jondalar to stand in for the man who should have been there for him.

Jondalar showed the young man how to tie the belt, then Bologan called to his brother and started out toward the Main Camp, the others followed behind more slowly. Ayla watched them go, thirteen-year Bologan walking beside seven-year Lavogan, eleven-year Lanoga, with Lorala, one-year plus a half, on her hip, and nine-year Trelara holding the hand of three-year Ganamar. She remembered being told that one who would have been a five-year had died in infancy. Though she and Jondalar helped them, and several others from the Ninth Cave as well, the children were essentially raising themselves. Neither their mother nor the man of their hearth paid much attention to them, and did little to support them. She believed it was Lanoga who held them together, though now, she was glad to see, Trelara was helping her and Bologan was more involved.

She felt Jonayla moving in her carrying blanket, waking up. She pulled it around from her back to her front, and took the baby out of it. She was naked, with no absorbent padding. Ayla held her out in front of her while the child wet on the ground. Jondalar smiled. None of the other women did that, and when he asked her, Ayla told him that was how Clan mothers often took care of their children's wetting. Though she didn't do it all the time, it certainly saved time cleaning up messes and gathering materials that could soak up liquid. And Jonayla was getting so used to it, she tended to wait until she was out before she let go.

"Do you think Lanidar is still interested in Lanoga?" Jondalar asked, obviously thinking about Tremeda's children, too.

"He certainly gave her a warm smile when he first saw her this year," Ayla said. "How is he doing with the spear-thrower? He looks to me as though he's been practicing with his left arm."

"He's good!" Jondalar said. "Actually, it's amazing to watch him. He has some use of his right arm, and uses it to help place the spear on the thrower, but he throws with great force and accuracy with his left arm. He's become quite a hunter and has gained the respect of his Cave, and more status. Now everyone at this Summer Meeting is looking at him with new eyes. Even the man of his hearth, who left his mother after he was born, has been showing an interest in him. And his mother and grandmother are no longer insisting that he go berry-picking and food-collecting with them all the time for fear he won't be able to support himself any other way. They made that harness he wears, but he told them what he wanted. They give you credit for teaching him, you know."

"You taught him, too," she said; then after a while she added, "He may have become a good hunter, but I still doubt that most mothers would want him to mate their daughters. They would be afraid that the bad spirit that deformed his arm is still hovering and might give their daughter's children the same problem. When he said last year that he wanted to mate Lanoga when they grew up, and help her raise her sisters and brothers, Proleva said she thought that would be a perfect pairing. Since Laramar and Tremeda have the lowest status, no mother would want her son to mate with her, but I don't think anyone would put up much objection to Lanidar mating Lanoga, especially if he's a good hunter."

"No. But I'm afraid Tremeda and Laramar will find a way to take advantage of him," Jondalar said. "I notice Lanoga isn't ready for First Rites, yet."

"But she will be soon. She's beginning to show signs. Maybe before the summer is over, the last First Rites ceremony of the season. Have they asked you to assist with First Rites this summer?" she asked, trying to seem unconcerned.

"Yes, but I told them I wasn't ready to take on that responsibility yet," he said, grinning at her. "Why? Do you think I should?"

"Only if you want to. There are some young women who might be very happy if you did. Perhaps even Lanoga," Ayla said, turning to look at Jonayla so he wouldn't see her face.

"Not Lanoga!" he said. "That would be like sharing First Rites with the child of my own hearth!"

She turned and smiled at him. "You are probably closer to it than the man who is," Ayla said. "You've provided more for that family than Laramar has."

They were approaching the Main Camp and people had

started calling greetings to them. "Do you think it will take very long to make a pole-drag with a seat?" Ayla asked.

"If I can get some help and we start soon, maybe later this morning, we can probably have it done by afternoon," he said. "Why?"

"Then should I ask her if she would have time to try it this afternoon? She said that was what she wanted to do before she used it in front of other people."

"Go ahead and ask her. I'll ask Joharran and some others to help. I'm sure we'll get it done." Jondalar grinned. "It will be interesting to see how people react when they see her riding behind the horses."

Jondalar was working on cutting down a straight, sturdy sapling that was a good deal thicker than the size they usually selected for a travois. The stone axe-head he was using had been shaped so that the thicker top was tapered up to a kind of point, and the cutting end knapped into a narrow thinning cross-section with a sharp, rounded bottom edge. The wooden handle had a hole gouged all the way through in one end into which the tapered top of the axe-head could fit. It was affixed in such a way that each time a blow was struck, the axe-head would wedge more firmly into the hole of the handle. The two pieces were firmly lashed together with wet rawhide that shrank and pulled tighter as it dried.

A stone axe was not strong enough to cut straight across the trunk of a tree; the flint would shatter and break if used in that way. To fell a tree with such a tool, the cuts needed to be made at an angle, whittling down the tree until it broke apart. The stump often looked as though it had been chewed down by a beaver. Even then, stone chips usually spalled off the axe-blade, so that it needed constant resharpening. This could be done by using a carefully controlled hammerstone, or pointed bone punch hit by a hammerstone, to remove narrow slivers of stone to thin down the cutting edge again. Because he was a skilled flint-knapper, Jondalar was often called upon to cut down trees. He knew how to use an axe properly, and how to resharpen one efficiently.

Jondalar had just cut down a second tree of similar size when a group of men arrived: Joharran, along with Solaban and Rush-emar; Manvelar, the leader of the Third Cave, and the son of his mate, Morizan; Kimeran, leader of the Second Cave, and Jon-decam, his same-age nephew; Willamar, the Trade Master, and his apprentice, Tivonan, and his friend Palidar; and Stevadal, the leader of the Twenty-sixth Cave, within whose territory this year's Summer Meeting was being held. Eleven people had come to make one pole-drag, twelve counting Jondalar. If she counted herself, thirteen. Ayla had made her first one by herself.

They were curious, she thought; that's brought them. Most of the new arrivals were familiar with the contrivance she called a pole-drag, which Ayla used with her horses to trans-port goods. It began with two poles made from whole trees with tapering tops, and all the branches trimmed off. Depend-ing upon the variety, the bark was sometimes removed as well, especially if it slipped off easily. The narrow ends were fas-tened together and attached to a horse at the withers with a harness of sturdy cords or leather thongs. The two trees angled out slightly in front, and much more toward the back, with only the ends of the heavier base dragging on the ground, which created relatively little friction, making it fairly easy to pull even with a heavy load. Crosspieces of wood, leather, or cordage, anything that could support a load, were attached to both poles across the space between.

Jondalar explained to the ones who had come to help that he wanted to make a pole-drag with special crosspieces put together in a certain way. Before long, more trees had been cut down, and a few suggestions offered and tried before they worked out something that seemed suitable. Ayla concluded they didn't need her, and while they were working, decided to get Zelandoni.

Taking Jonayla with her, she slipped away heading toward the main Meeting Camp, thinking about the adaptations to a pole-drag and the one they had made on their long return Journey to Jondalar's home. When they came to a large river they had to cross, they constructed a bowl boat similar to the kind the Mamutoi used to cross rivers: a frame of wood bent into the shape of a bowl and covered on the outside with a heavy well-greased aurochs hide. It was simple to make but a little diffcult to control in the water. Jondalar told her about the boats the Sharamudoi made, dug out of a log, widened with steam, with a pointed prow on each end. They were much more difficult to make, but it was much easier to make them go where you wanted, he explained.

The first time they crossed a river, they used the bowl boat to hold their things, and themselves, and propelled it with small oars across the river, while the horses swam behind. They repacked their things in panniers and saddle-baskets, then decided to make a pole-drag for Whinney to take the boat with them. Later they realized that they could attach the bowl boat between the poles of the travois and let the horses swim across a river pulling the load while Ayla and Jondalar rode on their backs, or swam along beside them. The bowl boat was lightweight and since it floated, it kept their things dry. When they reached the other side of the next river, instead of emptying it, they decided to leave their things in the bowl boat. While the pole-drag with the boat made crossing rivers easy and usually presented no problems traveling across open plains, when they had to move through woods or areas of high relief that required sharp turns, the long poles and the bowl-shaped boat could be a hindrance. They almost left them behind a few times, but didn't abandon them until they were much closer and had a much better reason.

Ayla had told Zelandoni earlier what they were planning, so she was ready when Ayla came for her. When they got back to the camp of the Ninth Cave, the men had moved closer to the fenced enclosure that had been made for the horses and didn't see them. The First slipped into the sleeping lodge used by Jondalar's family with the sleeping baby while Ayla went to see what was happening with the pole-drag seat. Jondalar had been right. With all the help, it hadn't taken long to construct. It had a deep bench-like seat with a back between the two sturdy poles, with a step up to it. Jondalar had taken Whinney out of the enclosure and was strapping the conveyance on the mare with a harness arrangement of thongs across her chest and high on her shoulders.

"What are you going to do with that?" Morizan said. He was still young enough to ask directly.

It was not considered courteous for adults to be quite so blunt, but it was what all the the others were thinking. Such directness might not have been appropriate for a mature Zelandonii, but it wasn't wrong, just naive and unsophisticated. Experienced people knew how to be more subtle and implicit. Ayla, however, was used to candor. It was common and entirely appropriate for the Mamutoi to be frank and forthright. It was a cultural difference, although they had their own kinds of subtleties. And the Clan could read body language as well as their sign language and, though as a result they couldn't lie, they did understand nuances and could be extremely discreet.

"I do have a particular idea of how to use it, but I'm still not sure if it will work. I'd like to try it out first, and if it doesn't work, it is a sturdy and well-made pole-drag and I will probably find another use for it," Ayla said.

While her reply didn't really answer his question, it satisfied the men. They assumed that she just didn't want to announce an experiment that might not work. No one liked to advertise their failures. Ayla was actually fairly certain it would work; she just didn't know if the First would be willing to use it.

Jondalar started walking slowly back toward their camp, knowing that if he moved, the others would. Ayla went into the horse enclosure to settle the horses after all the excitement of so many people around, nodding to the men to acknowledge their leaving. She patted and stroked Gray, thinking what a beautiful young filly she was. Then she talked to Racer and scratched his favorite itchy parts. Horses were very social animals, and liked being around their kind and others for whom they had affection. He was of an age that if he were living with wild horses, he'd be leaving his dam to run with a bachelor herd. But since Gray and Whinney were his only equine companions, he had grown quite close to Gray and had become somewhat protective of his young sister.

Ayla went out of the enclosure and approached Whinney, who was standing patiently with the pole-drag behind her. As the woman hugged her neck, the mare put her head over Ayla's shoulder, a familiar position of closeness between the two. Jondalar had put a halter on the mare, since it was easier for him to direct her with it. Ayla thought it might be better to use

it while the First was trying out her new means of transportation. Taking the lead attached to the halter, she headed toward
their sleeping lodge. By the time she reached it, the men were
walking back to the Main Camp and Jondalar was inside the
lodge talking to Zelandoni and holding Jonayla, who was quite
content.

"Shall we try it out?" Jondalar said.

"Is everyone gone?" the large woman asked.

"Yes, the men are gone and no one else is in camp," Ayla
said.

"Then I suppose this is as good a time as any," the First said.

They walked out of the lodge, each of them glancing around
to make sure no one else was there, then approached Whinney.
They went around the back of the horse.

Suddenly Ayla said, "Wait a moment," and went into the
summer dwelling. She came back out holding a padded cushion
and placed it on the seat, which was made of several small logs
lashed firmly together with strong cordage. A narrow back, perpendicular to the seat and made the same way, kept the cushion
in place. Jondalar handed Ayla the infant, then turned to help
Zelandoni.

But when the Donier stepped onto the crosspiece of wooden
logs made into a step that was close to the ground, the springy
long poles gave a little, and Whinney took a step forward because of the shift in weight. The First quickly backed off.

"The horse moved!" she said.

"I'll go hold her steady," Ayla said.

She went around to the front of the mare to calm her, holding the lead rope with one hand and the infant with the other.
The horse sniffed at the baby's tummy, which made her giggle
and her mother smile. Whinney and Jonayla were familiar with
and completely comfortable around each other. The child had
frequently ridden on the horse, in her mother's arms or slung in
her carrying blanket on the woman's back. She had also ridden
on Racer with Jondalar, and had been placed lightly on Gray's
back, while the man kept a secure hold on her, just so the two
of them could get used to each other.

"Try it again," Ayla called out.

Jondalar held out his hand for support, smiling at the large woman encouragingly. Zelandoni wasn't used to being encouraged or urged to do anything. She was the one who usually took on that duty and she gave Jondalar a hard look to see if he was patronizing her. In truth, her heart was pounding though she did not want to admit to her fear. She wasn't sure why she had agreed to do this thing.

Again the fresh trees that were used as poles yielded as the First put her weight on the thinner logs that had been lashed together to form the step, but Ayla steadied the mare, and Jondalar's shoulder offered support to her. She reached for the seat, again logs tied close together with rawhide cordage, turned herself around, and sat on the cushion with a sigh of relief.

"Are you ready?" Ayla called back.

"Are you?" Jondalar asked the Donier quietly.

"As ready as I'll ever be, I suppose."

"Go ahead," Jondalar said, raising his voice a bit.

"Take it slow, Whinney," Ayla said, going forward while holding the lead.

The horse started walking, pulling the sturdy pole-drag and the First Among Those Who Served The Great Earth Mother behind her. The woman grabbed the front edge of the seat as she felt herself being moved, but once Whinney got started, it wasn't bad, though she didn't let go of the seat. Ayla looked back to see how things were going, and noticed Wolf, sitting on his haunches, watching them. Where have you been? You've been gone all day, she thought.

The ride wasn't smooth; there were a few bumps and dips along the way, and one place where one leg dropped into a ditch caused by a creek runoff, making the rider sway to the left, but the conveyance was soon righted when Ayla turned Whinney slightly. They headed toward the horse enclosure.

It was a strange sensation to move without using her own feet, Zelandoni thought. Of course, children who were carried by their parents were used to it, she realized, but she hadn't been small enough to be carried by anyone for many years, and riding on this pole-drag moving seat wasn't the same. For one thing, she was facing backward, looking at where she had been, not where she was going.

Before they reached the horse enclosure, Ayla started a wide turn that led them back to the Ninth Cave's camp. She saw a track that led in a direction different from the one they usually took to the Main Camp. She had noticed it before and wondered where it led, but never seemed to have time to follow it. This seemed like a good time. She started toward it, then looked back and caught Jondalar's eye. She indicated the unknown trail with a slight gesture and he nodded imperceptibly, hoping that their passenger wouldn't notice and object. Either she didn't notice or didn't object as Ayla continued. Wolf had been trotting beside Jondalar bringing up the rear, but loped to the front when Ayla changed direction.

She had draped the lead rope across Whinney's neck; the horse would follow the woman's signals more easily than a lead rope attached to a halter. Then she put Jonayla in her carrying blanket on her back where the child could look around but wasn't a constant weight on her mother's arm. The trail led to the waterway known to the Ninth Cave as West River, and followed it for a short distance. Just as Ayla was wondering if she should turn back, she saw several familiar people ahead. She stopped the horse and walked back to Jondalar and Zelandoni.

"I think we've reached Sun View, Zelandoni," she said. "Do you want to go ahead and visit, and if so, do you want to stay on the pole-drag?"

"Since we're here, we might as well visit. I might not get here again for some time. And I'm ready to get off. It's not bad sitting on the moving seat, but it can be a bit bumpy sometimes." The woman stood up, and using Jondalar for a bit of balance and support, stepped down.

"Do you think you would find it convenient to use when we go to visit the sacred sites you want Ayla to see?" Jondalar asked.

"I think it could be useful, at least for part of the Journey." Ayla smiled.

"Jondalar, Ayla, Zelandoni!" a familiar voice called out. Ayla noticed a smile on Jondalar's face as she was turning around. Willamar was walking toward them along with Stevadal, the leader of the Twenty-sixth Cave.

"How nice that you decided to come," Stevadal said. "I didn't know if the First would be able to visit Sun View."

"Summer Meetings are always full for the zelandonia, but I do try to make at least one courtesy visit to the Cave that hosts the Meeting, Stevadal. We do appreciate the effort," she said.

"It is an honor," the leader of the Twenty-sixth said.

"And our pleasure," said a woman who had just arrived and was standing beside Stevadal.

Ayla was sure the woman was Stevadal's mate, though she hadn't met her, and didn't remember seeing her at the Meeting Camp. It made her look closer. She was younger than Stevadal, but there was something else. Her tunic hung on her thin frame, and she seemed wan and frail. Ayla wondered if she had been ill, or had suffered some grievous loss.

"I'm glad you're here," Stevadal said. "Danella was hoping to see the First, and to meet Jondalar's mate. She hasn't been able to go to the Meeting Camp, yet."

"You didn't tell me she was ill, or I would have come sooner, Stevadal," the First said.

"Our Zelandoni has been here for her," Stevadal said. "I didn't want to bother you. I know how busy you are at Summer Meetings."

"Not too busy to see your mate."

"Perhaps later, after everyone else has seen you," Danella said to the First, then turned to the tall blond man, "but I would like to meet your mate, Jondalar. I've heard so much about her."

"Then you shall," he said, beckoning to Ayla. She approached the woman with both hands out, palms up, in the traditional greeting of openness, showing she had nothing to hide. Then Jondalar began.

"Danella, of the Twenty-sixth Cave of the Zelandonii, mate of the leader, Stevadal, may I present to you Ayla of the Ninth Cave of the Zelandonii . . ." He continued with her usual introduction until he got to "Protected by the spirit of the Cave Bear."

"You forgot 'Friend of horses and the four-legged hunter she calls Wolf,'" Willamar added, chuckling.

He had joined them along with the rest of the men who had come to help make the new pole-drag. Since they were in the area, Willamar suggested that they stop by to visit Sun View, the home of the Twenty-sixth Cave of the Zelandonii, who were hosting the Summer Meeting, and they had been invited to stay for a cup of tea.

Most of the people who lived there were at the Summer Meeting Camp, but a few were still at home, among them the leader's mate, who apparently was, or had been, ill, Ayla concluded, and wondered how long she had been sick, and what her problem was. She glanced at Zelandoni, who was looking at her. Their eyes met and while nothing was said, she felt that the First was thinking the same thing.

"My names and ties are not nearly so interesting, but in the name of Doni, the Great Earth Mother, you are welcome here, Ayla of the Ninth Cave of the Zelandonii," Danella said.

"And I greet you, Danella of the Twenty-sixth Cave of the Zelandonii," Ayla said as they took each other's hands.

"The sound of your speech is as interesting as your names and ties," Danella said. "It makes one think of faraway places. You must have some exciting stories to tell. I would like to hear some of them, Ayla."

Ayla couldn't help but smile. She was more than aware that her speech was different from that of other Zelandonii. Most people tried to hide it when they noticed her accent, but Danella had such a charming and forthright manner that Ayla was immediately drawn to her. She reminded Ayla of the Mamutoi.

Ayla wondered again what illness or difficulty had caused Danella's physical frailty, which contrasted so sharply with her warm and winning personality. She glanced at Zelandoni and understood that the First also wanted to know, and would find out before they left the camp. Jonayla was squirming, and Ayla thought she probably wanted to see what was going on, and whom her mother was talking to. She shifted the carrying blanket around so her baby could ride on her hip.

"This must be your 'Blessed of Doni' infant, Jonayla," Danella said.

"Yes."

"That's a beautiful name. After Jondalar and you?"

Ayla nodded.

"She is as beautiful as her name," Danella said.

Although it wasn't obvious, Ayla knew how to read the nuances of body language and detected a hint of sadness in the fleeting frown and slight wrinkling of her brow. And suddenly the reason for both Danella's weakness and sadness came to her. She has miscarried quite late, or had a stillborn baby, Ayla thought, and probably had a difficult pregnancy, and very hard birth, and now had nothing to show for it. She is recovering from the strain on her body and grieving for her lost child. She looked toward the First, who was surreptitiously studying the young woman. Ayla thought she had likely guessed the same thing.

She felt Wolf push against her leg and looked down. He was looking up at her, making a slight whine, which let her know that he wanted something. He looked at Danella, then back at her, and whined again. Did he sense something about the leader's mate?

Wolves were always sensitive to weakness in others. When living in a hunting pack, it was the weak ones they generally attacked. But Wolf had formed a particularly close bond with the weak half-Clan child whom Nezzie had adopted when the wolf was very young and imprinting on his Mamutoi pack. Wolves of a pack adore their puppies, but humans were Wolf's pack. She knew he was drawn to human babies and children, and those that his wolf-sense told him were weak, not to hunt them, but to bond with as wild wolves did with their puppies.

Ayla noticed that Danella seemed a little apprehensive. "I think Wolf wants to meet you, Danella. Have you ever touched a living wolf?" she asked.

"No, of course not. I have never been this close to one before. Why do you think he wants to meet me?"

"He is drawn to certain people sometimes. He loves babies—Jonayla crawls all over him and even if she pulls his hair or pokes at his eyes or ears, he never seems to mind. When we first arrived at the Ninth Cave, he acted like this when he saw Jondalar's mother. He just wanted to meet Marthona." Ayla suddenly wondered if Wolf had sensed that the woman, who had once been the leader of the largest Cave of the Zelandonii, had a weak heart. "Would you like to meet him?"

"What do I have to do?" Danella said.

The visitors to Sun View were standing around watching. The ones who were familiar with Wolf and his ways were smiling, others were interested, but Stevadal, Danella's mate, was concerned.

"I'm not sure about this," he said.

"He won't hurt her," Jondalar said.

Ayla handed Jonayla to Jondalar, then led Wolf to Danella. She took the woman's hand and went through the process of Wolf's introduction.

"The way Wolf recognizes someone is by scent, and he knows that when I introduce him to someone like this, they are friends." Wolf sniffed at Danella's fingers, then licked them.

She smiled. "His tongue is smooth, soft."

"Some of his fur is, too," Ayla said,

"He's so warm!" Danella said. "I've never touched fur on a warm body before. And right here, you can feel something throbbing."

"Yes, that's how a living animal feels." Ayla turned to the leader of the Twenty-sixth Cave of the Zelandonii. "Would you like to meet him, Stevadal?"

"You might as well," Danella said.

Ayla went through a similar process with him, but Wolf seemed eager to return to Danella, and walked near her when they continued on to Sun View. They found places to sit—logs, padded stones, sometimes on the ground. The visitors took out their cups from pouches attached to their waistbands. They were served tea by the few people who had not gone to the Meeting Camp, among them both Danella's and Stevadal's mothers, who had stayed to help the leader's mate. When Danella sat down, Wolf sat beside her, but he did look at Ayla, as though asking for permission. She nodded, and he put his head down on his paws that were stretched out in front of him. Danella found herself petting him now and then.

Zelandoni sat beside Ayla. After she drank her tea, Ayla nursed Jonayla. Several people had come to chat with the First and her acolyte, but when they were finally alone, they began to discuss Danella.

"Wolf seems to be offering her some comfort," Zelandoni said.

"I think she needs it," Ayla said. "She's still so weak. I think she may have had a late miscarriage or a stillborn, and probably a difficult time before."

The First gave her a look of interest. "What makes you say that?"

"Because she's so thin and frail, I'm sure she's been ill or has had some problem for some time, and I noticed a certain sadness when she looked at Jonayla. It made me think she had had a long, hard pregnancy, and then lost the baby," Ayla said.

"That's a very astute judgment. I think you are right. I was thinking something very similar. Perhaps we should ask her mother. I'd like to examine her, just to make sure she's recovering well," the Donier said. "There are some medicines that could help her." The First turned to Ayla. "What would you suggest?"

"Alfalfa is good for fatigue, and the stinging pain when you pass water," Ayla said, then paused to think. "I don't know the name, but there's a plant with a red berry that's very good for women. It grows along the ground as a small vine and the leaves are green all year. It can be used for the cramps that can come with the moontime bleeding, and can ease heavy bleeding. It can encourage birth, and make it easier."

"I'm familiar with that one. It grows so thick, it sometimes forms a mat on the ground, and birds like the berries. Some people call it birdberry," the First said. "Alfalfa tea might help restore strength, also a decoction of the roots and bark of spikenard . . ." She stopped when she saw the puzzled expression on Ayla's face. "It's a tall bush with big leaves and purple berries . . . the flowers are small, greenish white . . . I'll show you sometime. It can help if the sac that holds the baby inside a woman drops down, slips out of place. That's why I'd like to examine her, so I know what to give her. Zelandoni of the Twenty-sixth is a good general healer, but he may not be as knowledgeable about women's ailments. I'll have to talk to him before we leave today."

After a polite length of time, the men who came to help build the pole-drag and then went to visit the home shelter of the Twenty-sixth Cave finished their tea and got up to leave. The First stopped Joharran. Jondalar was with him.

"Will you go to the zelandonia camp and see if you can find Zelandoni of the Twenty-sixth?" the Donier said quietly. "Stevadal's mate has not been well and I'd like to see if there is anything we can do. He's a good healer, and he may have done everything that can be done, but I need to talk to him. I think it's a woman's problem, and we are women . . ." She left the rest unsaid. "Ask him to come here; we'll wait awhile."

"Should I wait here with you?" Jondalar asked the two women.

"Weren't you planning on going to the practice field?" Joharran said.

"Yes, but I don't have to."

"Why don't you go, Jondalar. We'll be along later," Ayla said, brushing his cheek with hers.

The two women joined Danella and the two mothers, and a few others. When he saw that the First and her acolyte were not leaving, Stevadal stayed behind as well. The head Zelandoni was adept at finding out what was wrong with people, and soon discovered that Danella had been pregnant, and the baby was stillborn as they suspected, but she sensed that the two older women were holding something back, especially around Danella and Stevadal. There was more to the story than they were willing to say. The Donier would have to wait for the Twenty-sixth. In the meantime, the women chatted. Jonayla was passed around to the women. Although at first Danella seemed reluctant to take her, once she did, she held her for quite a while. Wolf seemed happy to stay with both of them.

Ayla took the pole-drag off Whinney and let her graze, and when she returned, they asked some tentative questions about the horse and how Ayla came to have her. The First encouraged Ayla to tell them. She was developing into quite a good storyteller and enthralled her listeners, especially when she added the sound effects of horse-neighs and lion-roars. Just as she was finishing, the Zelandoni of the Twenty-sixth Cave appeared.

"I thought I heard a familiar lion-roar," he said, greeting them with a big smile.

"Ayla has been telling us how she adopted Whinney," Danella said. "Just as I guessed, she has some captivating stories to tell. And now that I've heard one, I want to hear more."

The First was getting anxious to leave, though she didn't want to show it. It was entirely appropriate for the First Among Those Who Served The Great Earth Mother to visit with the leader of the Cave that was hosting the Summer Meeting and his mate, but she had many things to do. The ceremony of the Rites of First Pleasures would be the day after next, and then the first Matrimonial of the season. Though there would be another mating ceremony near the end of the summer for those who wanted to finalize their decisions before they returned to their winter shelters, the first one was invariably the largest and most well attended. There were many plans yet to be made.

While people fussed around making more tea, since they had drunk all there was, the First and her acolyte managed to get the Twenty-sixth aside and speak privately with him.

"We learned that Danella delivered a stillborn," the First said, "but more happened, I'm sure. I'd like to examine her and see if there is anything I can do to help."

He breathed a long sigh and frowned.

9

"Yes, you are right, of course. It wasn't just a stillborn baby," the Twenty-sixth said. "They were two-born-together, or would have been, but they were more than born together, they were joined together."

Ayla remembered that the same thing had happened to one of the women of the Clan, two babies joined together with a monstrous result. She felt a great sadness for Danella.

"One was normal size, the other much smaller and not fully formed, and parts of the second were attached to the first one," the Twenty-sixth continued. "I'm glad there was no breath in them, or I would have had to take it. It would have been too hard for Danella. As it was, she bled so much, I'm surprised she survived. We, her mother, Stevadal's mother, and I decided not to tell either one of them. We were afraid it would make any later pregnancy even more distressing than a stillborn would. You can examine her if you want, but it happened some time ago, in late winter. She has healed well; she just needs to recover her strength, and get through her grief. Your coming to visit may have helped. I saw her holding Ayla's baby, and I think that's good. She seems to have made a friend of you, Ayla, and your wolf, too. Perhaps she'll feel more inclined to go to the Summer Meeting now."

"Jondalar!" Ayla said when she and the First arrived back at the camp of the Ninth Cave. "What are you doing here? I thought you were going to the Summer Meeting Camp."

"I am going there," he said. "I just decided to check on Racer and Gray while I was here. I haven't spent much time with Racer, and they both seemed to enjoy the company. Why are you here?"

"I wanted to let Whinney feed Gray, while I nurse Jonayla. I was going to leave Whinney here, but then we thought this would be a good time for Zelandoni to ride into Camp on the pole-drag," Ayla said.

Jondalar grinned. "Then I'll wait," he said. "In fact, why don't I ride in with you on Racer?"

"We'll have to take Gray with us, too," Ayla said, frowning slightly. Then she smiled. "We can use the small halter you made for her; she's getting used to wearing it. It might be good for her to get accustomed to being around people she doesn't know."

"That should make quite a show," Zelandoni said. "But I think I like it. I'd rather be part of a bigger production than the only one for people to stare at."

"We should bring Wolf, too. Most people have seen the animals, but not together. There are still a few who can't quite believe that Whinney allows Wolf near her baby. If they see that he is no danger to Gray, it could help them realize that he's no danger to them, either," Ayla said.

"Unless someone attempted to harm you," Jondalar said, "or Jonayla."

Jaradal and Robenan came running into the summer dwelling of the leader of the Seventh Cave. "Weemar! 'Thona! Come and see!" Jaradal shouted.

"Yes, come and see!" Robenan echoed. The two boys had been playing just outside.

"They brought all the horses, and Wolf; even Zelandoni is riding! Come and see!" Jaradal exclaimed.

"Calm down, boys," Marthona said, wondering what Jaradal meant. It did not seem possible that Zelandoni could be sitting on the back of a horse.

"Come and see! Come and see!" both boys were yelling, while Jaradal tried to pull his grandam up from the cushion upon which she was seated. Then he turned to Willamar. "Come and see, Weemar."

Marthona and Willamar were visiting Sergenor and Jayvena

to discuss their part in an upcoming ceremony that would involve all leaders and former leaders in a small way. They had taken Jaradal with them to keep him out from underfoot of his mother. Proleva, as usual, was involved in meal planning for the event. Solaban's pregnant mate, Ramara, and her son, Robenan, who was Jaradal's age-mate and friend, had come along so the boys could play.

"We're coming," Willamar said, helping his mate up.

Sergenor pushed aside the drape that covered the entrance and all of them crowded out. A most surprising sight met them. Parading toward the zelandonia lodge were Jondalar on Racer's back, leading Gray, and Ayla riding the mare with Jonayla in her carrying blanket sitting in front of her. Whinney was pulling a pole-drag upon which the First was seated, facing backward. The wolf was padding along beside them. It was still unexpected for most people to see horses with people on their backs, not to mention the wolf nonchalantly walking with them. But to see the First Among Those Who Served The Great Earth Mother riding on a seat that was being pulled by a horse was nothing less than astonishing.

The procession passed quite near the camp of the Seventh Cave and although Marthona and Willamar and the rest of the people of the Ninth Cave were quite familiar with the animals, they gawked at the demonstration as much as anyone. The First caught Marthona's eye and, though she smiled in a decorous way, Marthona detected a sparkle of impish delight in the woman's gaze. It was more than a parade, it was a spectacle, and if there was one thing members of the zelandonia enjoyed staging, it was a spectacle. When they reached the entrance to the big lodge, Jondalar stopped and let Ayla and Whinney pull ahead, then dismounted and offered a hand to the First. For all her size, she stepped down from the seat on the travois gracefully and, perfectly aware that everyone was watching her, entered the lodge with great dignity.

"So that's what he wanted us to help him make," Willamar commented. "He said he needed to build a very sturdy pole-drag, with shelves. It wasn't shelves he wanted, but it was clever of him to say that. None of us could imagine that they would turn out to be a seat for Zelandoni. I'll have to ask her what it's like to sit on a seat that is pulled by a horse."

"It is brave of her to do that," Jayvena said. "I'm not sure that I would want to try it."

"I would!" Jaradal said, his eyes full of excitement. " 'Thona, do you think Ayla would let me sit on a pole-drag seat while Whinney pulled it?"

"I'd like to do it, too," Robenan said.

"The young are always willing to try something new," Ramara said.

"I wonder how many similar conversations are going on around this Camp right now," Sergenor said. "But if she lets one boy do it, every other boy in camp will be clamoring to do the same."

"And quite a few girls, too," Marthona added.

"If I were her, I would wait until we get back to the Ninth Cave," Ramara said. "Then it wouldn't be much different from letting a child or two ride on the mare's back while Ayla leads her around, the way she does now."

"It does make quite a demonstration, though. I recall how I felt when I first saw those animals. It could be frightening. Didn't Jondalar tell us that people ran away from them when they were on their Journey here? Now that we're used to them, it just seems rather impressive," Willamar said.

Not everyone was so pleasantly impressed by the demonstration. Marona, who loved to be the center of attention, felt a surge of jealousy rise up. She turned to her cousin Wylopa, and remarked, "I don't know how anyone can stand to be around those dirty animals all the time. When you get close to her she smells for horse, and I've heard she sleeps with that wolf. It's disgusting."

"She sleeps with Jondalar, too," Wylopa said, "and I'm told he won't share Pleasures with anyone else."

"That won't last," Marona said, giving Ayla a venomous stare. "I know him. He'll be back in my bed again. I promise you."

Brukeval saw the two cousins talking, recognized the nasty look Marona gave Ayla, and felt two opposing emotions. He knew it was hopeless, but he loved Ayla and wanted to protect her from the spitefulness of the woman who was also his cousin—he had been the brunt of her malice himself and knew how hurtful she could be. But he was also afraid that Ayla would suggest that he was a Flathead again and he couldn't stand that, even though he knew in his heart that she didn't mean it in the unkind way that most people did. He never looked at a polished blackened-wood reflector, but sometimes he caught glimpses of himself in still water and hated what he saw. He knew why people called him by that hateful name, but he couldn't bear the idea that there might be some truth to it.

Madroman was also scowling at Ayla and Jondalar. He resented the way Ayla was getting so much attention from the First. Yes, she was her acolyte, but he didn't think it was right for the one who was supposed to be overseeing all the acolytes to favor her so much when they were together at a Summer Meeting. And of course Jondalar had to be in the middle of things. Why did he have to come home? Things were better while the big oaf was gone, especially after the Zelandoni of the Fifth Cave decided to take him as an acolyte, though he thought he should have been a Zelandoni by now. But what could he expect with the Fat One in control? I'll think of a way, he thought.

Laramar turned his back on the whole thing and walked away, thinking his own thoughts. He'd seen enough of those horses and that wolf, especially that wolf. As far as he was concerned, they lived too close to his dwelling in the Ninth Cave, and they had spread out so far, the horses were on the other side of him. Before they came he could cut across the space they occupied. Now every time he went home, he had to make a wide circle around their lodge to avoid the wolf. The few times he got too close, the animal got his hackles up, wrinkled his nose, and showed his teeth, as though the whole place belonged to him.

Besides, she interfered, coming over and bringing food or blankets as though she was being nice, but she was really checking up on him. Now he didn't even have a lodge to go to. Not one where he felt he belonged. The children acted as though it was theirs. But it was still his hearth, and what he did at his own hearth wasn't any of her business.

Well, there were still the fa'lodges. He actually liked staying there. He wasn't bothered by children crying in the night, or his drunken mate coming in and starting an argument. At the fa'lodge where he was staying, the other men were mostly older and didn't bother each other. It wasn't boisterous and loud like the fa'lodges of the younger men, though if he offered one of his lodge-mates a drink of his barma, they were more than happy to drink with him. Too bad there were no fa'lodges at the Ninth Cave.

Ayla rode Whinney slowly around the outside of the large zelandonia lodge pulling the pole-drag, then started out of the Summer Meeting Camp back the way she had come. Jondalar followed leading Racer and Gray. The area where the Summer Meeting had been set up, called Sun View after the name of the nearby Cave, was often used as a campground for large gatherings. When it rained, stones were brought from the river and the nearby cliffs to pave the ground, especially when it was unusually muddy. Each year more were added until the campsite was now defined by the large area paved by the stones.

When they were somewhat outside the boundary of the Camp, beyond the paving stones and in the middle of a grassy field on the floodplain of the river, Ayla stopped. "Let's take off Whinney's pole-drag and leave the horses here for a while," she said, "where they can graze. I don't think they will wander far, and we can whistle them back, if we have to."

"Good idea," Jondalar said. "Most people know not to bother them if one of us isn't around and we can check on them. I'll take their halters off, too."

As they were tending to the horses, they saw Lanidar approaching, still wearing his specially made spear-thrower holder. He waved, then whistled a greeting, and received a welcoming neigh from Whinney and Racer in return.

"I wanted to see the horses," he said. "I liked watching out for them last year and getting to know them, but I haven't spent any time with them this summer, and I don't know Whinney's baby at all. Do you think they will remember me?"

"Yes. They answered your whistle, didn't they?" Ayla said.

He had brought some dried wild apple slices with him in a

fold of his tunic and fed the young stallion and then his dam
from his hand; then the young man squatted down and held
out a hand with a piece of the fruit to the little filly. She stayed
near Whinney's back legs at first. Though Gray was still nursing, she had started mouthing grass in imitation of her dam,
and it was obvious that she was curious. Lanidar was patient,
and after a while, the filly started edging toward him.

The mare watched, but neither encouraged nor restricted her
foal. Eventually, Gray's curiosity won out and she nosed Lanidar's open hand to see what it held. She got a piece of apple
in her mouth, then dropped it. Lanidar picked it up and tried
again. Though she wasn't as experienced as her dam, she managed to use her incisors and flexible lips and tongue to get it in
her mouth and bite. It was a new experience for her, and a new
taste, but she was more interested in Lanidar. When he began
to stroke her and scratch her favorite places, she was won over.
When he stood up, he had a big smile.

"We were going to leave the horses here in this field for a
while, and check on them every so often," Jondalar said.

"I'd be happy to watch them, like I did last year," Lanidar
said. "If there are any problems, I'll look for you, or whistle."

Ayla and Jondalar looked at each other, then smiled. "I
would be grateful for that," Ayla said. "I wanted to leave them
here so people would get more used to seeing them, and they'd
get more comfortable around people, especially Gray. If you
get tired or have to go, whistle loud or come and find one of
us and let us know."

"I will," he said.

They left the field feeling much more relaxed about the
horses. When they returned in the evening to invite Lanidar
to share a meal with their Cave, they found that several young
men, and a few young women, including Lanoga carrying her
youngest sister, Lorala, were visiting with him. When Lanidar
had watched the animals the year before, it was at the enclosure and nearby field that was close to the camp of the Ninth
Cave, which was some distance from the Main Camp. Not
many people went there and he had few friends then, anyway,
but since he had developed his skill with the spear-thrower and

was hunting regularly, he had gained more status. He had also gained several friends and, it seemed, a few admirers.

The young people were involved with each other and didn't notice Ayla and Jondalar coming. Jondalar was pleased to see that Lanidar was acting very responsibly, not allowing the group of youngsters to crowd in around the horses, especially Gray. He had obviously allowed the visitors to stroke and scratch them, but only let one or two at a time get close. He seemed to sense when the horses were tired of all the attention and just wanted to graze, and quite firmly told one of the youngsters to leave them alone. The couple didn't know that he had banished some young men earlier who had become too rambunctious by threatening to tell Ayla, who, he reminded them, was the acolyte of the First Among Those Who Served The Great Earth Mother.

The zelandonia were the ones whom people went to for help and assistance, and though they were respected, often revered, and many of them were loved, the feeling for them was always tempered with a little fear. The zelandonia were intimate with the next world, the world of spirits, the fearsome place where one went when the elan—the life force—left their body. They had other powers that went beyond the ordinary, too. Youngsters often spread rumors, and boys in particular liked to scare each other by telling stories about what a zelandoni might do, especially to their male parts, if one of them made one angry.

They all knew that Ayla seemed to be a normal woman with a mate and a baby, but she was still an acolyte, a member of the zelandonia, and a foreigner. Just listening to her speak emphasized her strangeness and made them aware that she was from some other place, a distant place, farther away than anyone had ever traveled, except for Jondalar. But Ayla also exhibited extraordinary abilities, like having control over horses and a wolf. Who knew of what she might be capable? Some people even looked askance at Jondalar, though he was born to the Zelandonii, because of the strange ways he had learned while he was gone.

"Greetings, Ayla and Jondalar, and Wolf," Lanidar said, which caused some of his young visitors who had not noticed their arrival to turn around sharply. They seemed to appear so suddenly. But Lanidar knew they were coming. He had noticed a change in the behavior of the horses. Even in the darkening twilight, the animals were aware of their approach and were edging toward them.

"Greetings, Lanidar," Ayla said. "Your mother and grandmother are at the camp of the Seventh Cave, along with most of the Ninth Cave. You have been invited to share a meal with them."

"Who will watch the horses?" he said, leaning down to pet Wolf, who had come to him.

"We have already eaten. We'll take them back to our camp," Jondalar said.

"Thank you for looking out for them, Lanidar," Ayla said. "I appreciate your help."

"I liked doing it. I'll watch them anytime," Lanidar said. He meant it. Not only did he enjoy the animals, he liked the attention it brought him. Being responsible for them had brought several curious young men, and young women, to visit.

With the arrival of the First Among Those Who Served, the Summer Meeting Camp was soon caught up in the usual hectic activity of the season. The Rites of First Pleasures had the usual complications, but none that had been as difficult as the one Janida had posed the year before when she turned up pregnant before she'd had her First Rites. Especially when Peridal's mother had objected to the mating of her son with the young woman. The mother's opposition was not entirely unreasonable, since her son could count only thirteen years and a half, and Janida could count only thirteen.

It wasn't only their youth. Although Peridal's mother didn't want to admit it, the First was sure she also objected because a young woman who shared Pleasures before her First Rites lost status. But, because Janida was pregnant, she also gained status. Several older men had been more than willing to offer her their hearths and welcome her child, but Peridal was the only one with whom she had shared Pleasures, and she wanted him. She had done it not only because he had pressed her so persistently, but because she loved him.

After the ceremony of First Rites, it was time to organize the first Matrimonial of the summer. Then a large herd of bison was spotted nearby, and the leaders decided that a major hunt was in order before the Matrimonial Rites. Joharran discussed it with the First, and she was agreeable to postponing the ceremony.

He was anxious to have Jondalar and Ayla use the horses to help drive the bison into the surround that was constructed to corral the animals. The value of the spear-throwers could be shown in hunting down the ones that evaded the surround trap. The leader of the Ninth Cave continued to encourage people to see how a spear could be cast from a much greater, and safer, distance with the spear-thrower. The implements were already becoming the weapon of choice for most of the people who'd had a chance to see them in action. The lion hunt was already common knowledge at the Meeting; the lion hunters had been enthusiastically telling the story of the dangerous confrontation.

Younger hunters were especially excited about the new weapon, and quite a few of the older ones were as well. Many of those who were less keen were the ones who were skilled in using a hand-flung spear. They were comfortable hunting the way they always had and not eager to learn a new method at such a late stage in their lives. By the time the hunt was over and the meat and skins preserved or put aside for further processing, the First Matrimonial had already been delayed too long to suit many.

The day of the communal Mating Ceremony had dawned bright and clear, and an air of anticipation filled the whole Camp, not just those who would be participating. It was a celebration that everyone looked forward to, one that they all took part in. The ceremony included the voiced approval of the newly mated couples by all the people at the Summer Meeting. The matings created changes in the names and ties of more than the new couples and their families; the status of nearly everyone shifted to some degree, some more than others, depending on the closeness of their relationships.

The Matrimonial the year before had been a stressful time for Ayla. Not only because it was her Mating Ceremony, but because she had so recently arrived and was the center of so much attention. She wanted Jondalar's people to like and accept her and was trying to fit in. Most of them did, but not all of them.

This year the leaders and former leaders, as well as the zelandonia, were seated strategically so they could answer when the First asked for responses from those present, which to her meant approvals. The First had not been pleased with the hesitation from some of the crowd the year before when she asked for the endorsement responses for Ayla and Jondalar, and she did not want that to become a practice. She liked her ceremonies to run smoothly.

The accompanying festivities were anticipated with great relish. People prepared their best dishes and wore their best clothes, but the Mating Festival was not only a joyous occasion for the ones who were mating, it was also the most appropriate occasion for a Mother Festival. Then everyone was encouraged to honor the Great Earth Mother by sharing Her Gift of Pleasure, with joinings and couplings as often as one was able, and with whomever one chose so long as the feeling was reciprocated.

People were encouraged to honor the Mother, but it was not required. Certain areas were set aside for those who did not wish to participate. Children were never required, though if some of them bounced around with each other in imitation of the adults, it usually drew indulgent smiles. Some adults just didn't feel like it, especially those who were sick or hurt or recovering from accidents or just tired, or women who had recently given birth, or were having their moontime and bleeding. A few of the zelandonia, who were undergoing certain trials that required abstaining from Pleasures for a period of time, volunteered to tend to the young children and help the others.

The One Who Was First was inside the zelandonia dwelling, sitting on a stool. She swallowed the last of her cup of hawthorn flowers and catmint tea and pronounced, "It's time." She gave the empty cup to Ayla, got up, and walked toward the back of the lodge to a small, secondary, somewhat concealed access that was camouflaged on the outside by a construction used to hold additional wood.

Ayla sniffed the cup; it was an automatic, habitual action, and almost as subconsciously, she noted the ingredients and reflected that it was probably the woman's moontime. Catmint, the waist-high, downy-leafed perennial with the whorls of white, pink, and purple flowers, was a mild sedative that could relieve tension and cramps. She wondered about the hawthorn, however. It had a distinctive taste and maybe she liked the flavor, but it was also one of the ingredients the First used in the medicinal preparation that she made for Marthona. Ayla was now aware that the medicines the Zelandoni gave Jondalar's mother were for the heart, the muscle in her chest that pumped blood. She had seen similar heart muscles in the animals she hunted and subsequently butchered. Hawthorn helped it to pump more vigorously and more rhythmically. She put the cup down and exited out the main entrance.

Wolf was waiting outside and looked expectantly at Ayla. She smiled, shifted Jonayla who was asleep in her carrying blanket, and hunkered down in front of the animal. Taking his head in both hands, she looked in his eyes.

"Wolf, I am so glad that I found you. Every day you are here for me, and you give me so much," she said, ruffling his shaggy hair. Then she bent her forehead to touch his. "Are you coming with me to the Matrimonial?" Wolf continued to look at her. "You can come if you want, but I think you'll get tired of it. Why don't you go hunt?" She stood. "You can go, Wolf. Go ahead, hunt for yourself," she said, moving her hand toward the boundary of the Camp. He looked up at her a little longer, then jogged off.

Ayla was wearing the clothing that she had worn when she mated Jondalar, her Matrimonial outfit, which she had carried with her for the entire yearlong Journey from the home of the Mamutoi far to the east to the home of Jondalar's people, the Zelandonii, whose territory extended to the Great Waters of the West. The Matrimonial did remind many people of the previous year's event. Several people talked about Ayla's unusual outfit when she appeared wearing it again. But it also reminded Zelandoni of the objections to her that some people had put forth. Although they weren't usually direct about it, the First knew it was primarily because Ayla was a stranger, and a stranger with uncanny abilities.

Ayla was going as a spectator rather than a participant this time and was looking forward to just watching the ritual. Recalling her Mating Ceremony, she knew the ones who were Promised were gathering in the smaller lodge nearby, dressed in their finery and feeling nervous and excited. Their witnesses and guests were also congregating in the front section of the viewing area, with the rest of the Camp filing in behind them.

She walked toward the large area where people gathered for various functions that involved the whole Camp. When she arrived, she stopped to scan the crowd, then headed toward the recognizable faces of the Ninth Cave. Several people smiled when she approached, including Jondalar and Joharran.

"You are looking particularly nice this evening," Jondalar said. "I haven't seen those clothes since this time last year." He was wearing the simple pure white tunic, decorated only with ermine tails, that she had made for him for their mating. On him, it looked stunning.

"That Mamutoi outfit does become you," his brother said. He did think so, but the leader of the Ninth Cave also understood how much wealth it displayed.

Nezzie, the mate of the headman of the Lion Camp, and the woman who had persuaded the Mamutoi to adopt her, had given the garments to Ayla, but their creation had been requested by Mamut, the holy man who had actually adopted her as a daughter of the Mammoth Hearth. They originally had been made for her when it was thought that she would mate Ranec, who was the son of the mate of Nezzie's brother, Wymez. Wymez had traveled far to the south in his youth, mated an exotic dark-skinned woman, and returned after ten years, unfortunately losing his woman on the way.

He brought with him fantastic stories, new flint-knapping techniques, and an amazing child with brown skin and tight black curls, whom Nezzie raised as her own. Among his light-skinned, fair-haired northern kin, Ranec was a unique boy who always caused an exciting stir. He grew into a man with a delicious wit,

laughing black eyes that women found irresistible, and a remarkable talent for carving.

Like the rest, Ayla had been fascinated by Ranec's unusual
coloring, and charm, but she also found the beautiful stranger
enthralling, and showed it, which brought out a jealousy in
Jondalar that he didn't know he had. The tall blond man with
the compelling blue eyes had always been the one that women
couldn't resist, and he didn't know how to handle the emotion
he had never experienced before. Ayla didn't understand his
erratic behavior, and finally promised to mate Ranec because
she thought Jondalar no longer loved her, and she did like the
dark carver and his laughing eyes. The Lion Camp grew fond
of Ayla and Jondalar that winter they lived with the Mamutoi,
and they all had been more than aware of the emotional difficulties of the three young people.

Nezzie in particular developed a strong bond with Ayla because of her care and understanding of another unusual child
the woman had adopted, who was weak, unable to speak, and
half Clan. Ayla treated his weak heart and made his life more
comfortable. She also taught Rydag the Clan sign language,
and the ease and speed with which he learned it made her
understand that he did have the Clan memories. She taught
the whole Lion Camp a simpler form of the unspoken language so he could communicate with them, which made him
extremely happy, and Nezzie overjoyed. Ayla quickly grew to
love him—in part because Rydag reminded her of her own
son, whom she'd had to leave behind, but more for himself,
though ultimately she hadn't been able to save him.

When Ayla decided to return home with Jondalar instead
of staying to mate Ranec, though Nezzie knew how much
Ayla's leaving hurt the nephew she had raised, she gave the
young woman the beautiful garments that had been made for
her, and told her to wear them when she mated Jondalar. Ayla
didn't quite realize how much wealth and status the Matrimonial clothing conveyed, but Nezzie did and so did Mamut,
the perceptive old spiritual leader. They had guessed from his
bearing and manner that Jondalar came from people of high
status, and that Ayla would need something to give her a good
standing among them.

Though Ayla didn't quite understand how much status her Matrimonial outfit displayed, she did understand the quality of the workmanship. The hides for the tunic and leggings had come from both deer and saiga antelope and were an earthy, golden yellow, almost the color of her hair. Part of the color was the result of the types of wood that were used to smoke the hides to keep them supple, and part the result of the mixtures of yellow and red ochers that were added. It had required a great deal of effort to scrape the skins to make them soft and pliable, but rather than being left with the velvety suede-like finish of buckskin, the leather had been burnished, rubbed with the ochers mixed with fat using an ivory smoothing tool that compacted the hide to a lustrous, shiny finish that made the soft leather almost waterproof.

The long tunic, sewn together with fine stitches, fell to a downward-pointing triangle at the back. It opened down the front with the sections below the hips tapering so that when it was brought together, another downward-pointing triangle was created. The full leggings were close fitting except around the ankle, where they could bunch softly or be brought down below the heel, depending on the footwear that was chosen. But the quality of the basic construction only laid the groundwork for the extraordinary outfit. The effort that went into the decoration made it an exquisite creation of rare beauty and value.

The tunic and lower part of the leggings were covered with elaborate geometric designs made primarily of ivory beads, some sections solidly filled in. Colored embroideries added definition to the geometric beaded pattern. They began with downward-pointing triangles, which horizontally became zigzags and vertically took on the shapes of diamonds and chevrons, then evolved into complex figures such as rectangular spirals and concentric rhomboids. The ivory beads were highlighted and accentuated by amber beads, some lighter and some darker than the color of the leather, but of the same tone. More than five thousand ivory beads made from mammoth tusks were sewn onto the garments, each bead carved, pierced, and polished by hand.

A finger-woven sash in similar geometric patterns was used

to tie the tunic closed at the waist. Both the embroidery and the belt were made of yarns whose natural color needed no additional dyeing: deep red woolly mammoth hair, ivory mouflon wool, brown musk-ox underdown, and deep reddish-black woolly rhinoceros long hair. The fibers were prized for more than their colors; they all came from animals that were difficult and dangerous to hunt.

The workmanship of the entire outfit was superb in every detail; it was evident to knowledgeable Zelandonii that someone had acquired the finest materials and assembled the most skillful and accomplished people to make the garments.

When Jondalar's mother had first seen it the year before, she knew that whoever had directed the outfit to be made commanded great respect and held a very high position within his community. It was clear that the time and effort it took to make it were considerable, yet the outfit had been given to Ayla when she left. None of the benefits of the resources and work that went into making it would stay within the community that made it. Ayla said she had been adopted by an old spiritual man she called Mamut, a man who obviously possessed such tremendous power and prestige—in effect, wealth—that he could afford to give away the mating outfit and the value it represented. No one understood that better than Marthona.

Ayla had, in effect, brought her own bride price, which gave her the status that she needed to contribute to the relationship so that mating her would not lower the position of Jondalar or his kin. Marthona made a point of mentioning that to Proleva, who she knew would tell her husband, Joharran, Marthona's eldest son, leader of the Ninth Cave. Joharran was glad to have an opportunity to see the prized possession again, now that he fully understood its value. He realized that if properly cared for—and he was sure it would be—the clothing would last a long time. The ochers used to burnish the leather did more than add color and make it water resistant; they helped to preserve the material, and make it resistant to insects and their eggs. It would likely be used by Ayla's children, and perhaps their children, and when the leather finally disintegrated, the amber and ivory beads could be reused for many more generations.

Joharran knew the value of ivory beads. Recently, he'd had occasion to trade for some, for himself but especially for his mate, and recalling the transaction, he looked at Ayla's rich and luxurious clothing with new appreciation. As he looked around he noticed that many people were surreptitiously watching her.

Last year, when Ayla wore it for her Matrimonial, everything about her was strange and unusual, including the woman herself. Now people had become more accustomed to her, to the way she spoke, and to the animals she controlled. She was looked upon as a member of the zelandonia and therefore her strangeness seemed more normal, if one could consider any Zelandoni normal. But the outfit made her stand out again, made people recall her foreign origins, but also the wealth and status she brought with her.

Among those watching her were Marona and Wylopa. "Look at her flaunting that outfit," Marona said to her cousin, her eyes full of envy. She would have been more than happy to flaunt it. "You know, Wylopa, that wedding outfit should have been mine. Jondalar Promised me. He should have come back and mated me, and given that outfit to me." She paused. "Her hips are too broad for it anyway," Marona said with scorn.

As Ayla and the others were making their way to a place that the Ninth Cave had claimed for watching the festivities, both Jondalar and his brother saw Marona. She was staring at Ayla with such malevolence, it made Joharran apprehensive, for Ayla's sake. He glanced at Jondalar, who had also seen Marona's glare of hatred, and a look of shared understanding passed between the two brothers.

Joharran moved closer to Jondalar. "You know that if she can, she will cause trouble for Ayla someday," the leader said under his breath.

"I think you're right, and it's my fault, I'm afraid," Jondalar said. "Marona thought I Promised to mate her. I didn't, but I understand why she may have thought so."

"It's not your fault, Jondalar. People have a right to make their own choices," Joharran said. "You were gone a long time. She had no claim on you, and shouldn't have had any expectations. After all, she mated and separated in the time you were gone. You made a better choice, and she knows it. She just can't stand it that you brought back someone who has more to offer than she does. That's why she'll try to cause trouble someday."

"Perhaps you are right," Jondalar said, though he didn't quite want to believe it. He wanted to give Marona the benefit of the doubt.

As the ceremony got under way, the two brothers got caught up in it, and thoughts of the jealous woman were forgotten. They hadn't noticed another pair of eyes that were also watching Ayla: their cousin, Brukeval. He had admired the way Ayla stood up to the derisive laughter of the Cave when Marona tricked her into wearing inappropriate clothing that first day. When they met that evening, Ayla recognized his look of the Clan and felt comfortable with him. She treated him with an easy familiarity that he wasn't used to, especially from beautiful women.

Then, when Charezal, that stranger from a distant Zelandonii Cave, began to make fun of him, derisively referring to him as a Flathead, Brukeval flew into a rage. He had been teased with that name by the other children of the Cave for as long as he could remember, and Charezal had obviously got wind of it. He had also heard that the way to get a reaction from the strange-looking cousin of the leader was to make innuendos about his mother. Brukeval never knew his mother; she died soon after he was born, but that only gave him reason to idealize her. She was not one of those animals! Could not be, and neither was he!

Though he knew Ayla was Jondalar's woman, and there was no way he could ever win her from his tall, handsome cousin, in his mind, seeing her stand up to everyone's laughter and not giving in to the ridicule made him admire her. For him it was love at first sight. Though Jondalar had always treated him well and never joined in when the others teased him, at that moment, he hated him, and hated Ayla as well because he couldn't have her.

All the hurt that Brukeval had felt in his life, together with the nasty remarks from the young man who was trying to take Ayla's attention away from him, erupted into uncontrollable anger. Afterward he noticed that Ayla seemed more distant, and no longer spoke to him with that familiar ease.

Jondalar didn't say anything to Brukeval about her change in feeling toward him after his outburst, but Ayla had told him that Brukeval's anger reminded her too much of Broud, the son of the leader of her clan. Broud had hated her from the beginning, and had caused her more pain and heartache than she ever could have imagined. She had learned to hate Broud as much as he hated her and, with good reason, to fear him. It was because of him that she was finally forced to leave the Clan, and to leave her son as well.

Brukeval remembered the warm glow he'd felt when they first met and watched Ayla from a distance whenever he could. The more he watched, the more enamored he became. When he saw the way she and Jondalar interacted, Brukeval would imagine himself in his cousin's place. He even followed them when they went to some secluded place to share Pleasures, and when Jondalar tasted her milk, he hungered to do the same.

But he was wary of her, too, afraid she would call him a Flathead again, or her word for them, the Clan. Just their name, Flatheads, had caused him so much pain as he was growing up that he couldn't bear the sound of it. He knew she didn't think of them the way most people did, but that made it worse. She sometimes spoke of them fondly, with affection and even love, and he hated them. Brukeval's feelings for Ayla were at cross-purposes. He loved Ayla, and he hated her.

The ceremonial part of the Matrimonial was long and drawn out. It was one of the few times when the complete names and ties of each of the Promised mates were recited. The matings were accepted by the members of their Caves agreeing aloud, and then by all the Zelandonii in attendance doing the same. Finally they were physically joined by a thong or cord that was wrapped, usually, around the right wrist of the woman and the left wrist of the man, although it could be the reverse, or even both left or both right wrists. After the cord was knotted, it would stay that way for the rest of the evening's festivities.

People always smiled at the inevitable stumblings and bumpings of the newly mated ones, and while it might be funny to watch, many observed carefully to see how they reacted, how quickly they learned to accommodate each other. It was the first test of the bond to which they had just committed, and the elders made whispered opinions to each other about the quality and longevity of the various matings based on how well they became accustomed to the restriction of being physically bound to each other. Mostly, they would smile or laugh at each other and themselves and make efforts to work things out until later, when they were alone and could untie—never cut—the knot.

As difficult as it might be for couples, it was even more so for those who had decided on a triple, or more rarely a foursome, but that was considered only proper, since such a relationship would require more adaptation to succeed. Each person had to have at least one free hand, so it was usually the left hands of multiples that were bound together. Walking from place to place, getting food and eating, even passing water or more solid elimination all had to be synchronized whether it was two or more that had joined. Occasionally, a person just couldn't stand the restraint and would become frustrated and angry, which never boded well for the mating, and rarely, the knot would be severed to break the relationship before it ever began. The severed knot was always the sign of the end of a mating, just as the tying of the knot symbolized the beginning of one.

10

The Matrimonial usually began in the afternoon or early evening to leave plenty of time for the festivities as it grew dark. The singing or reciting of the Mother's Song always ended the formal Mating Ceremony and signaled the beginning of the feasting and other celebratory activities.

Ayla and Jondalar stayed through the entire formal ceremony, and though she was feeling bored before it was over, she would never admit it. She had watched people coming and going throughout the afternoon, and realized that she was not the only one who grew tired of the long recitation of names and ties, and the repetition of ritual words, but she knew how important the ceremony was to each couple or multiple and to their immediate kin, and part of that was the acceptance by all the Zelandonii in attendance. Besides, all of the zelandonia were expected to remain until the end, and she was included among them now.

Ayla had counted eighteen individual ceremonies, when she saw the First gather them all together. She had been told there might be twenty or more, but some of them were not certain. There were any number of reasons why participation in the formal Mating Ceremonial might be postponed, especially the first one of the season, ranging from uncertainty if the couple was ready to make the commitment to an important relative being delayed. There was always the Matrimonial at the end of the season for final decisions, late-arriving kin, arrangements not yet completed, or new summer liaisons.

Ayla smiled to herself when she heard the rich full tones of the First singing the opening verse of the Mother's Song:

Out of the darkness, the chaos of time,
The whirlwind gave birth to the Mother sublime.
She woke to Herself knowing life had great worth,
The dark empty void grieved the Great Mother Earth.
The Mother was lonely. She was the only.

Ayla had loved the Legend of the Mother the first time she heard it, but she particularly loved the way it was sung by the One Who Was First Among Those Who Served The Great Earth Mother. The rest of the Zelandonii joined in, some singing, some reciting. Those who played flutes added their harmonies, and the zelandonia chanted a fugue in counterpoint.

She could hear Jondalar, who was standing beside her, singing. He had a good true voice, though he didn't sing often, and when he did it was usually with the group. Ayla, on the other hand, couldn't carry a tune; she never learned how, and didn't seem to have a natural inclination for singing. The best she could do was a singsong monotone, but she had memorized the words and spoke them with deep feeling. She particularly identified with the part where the Great Earth Mother had a son, "The Mother's great joy, a bright shining boy," and lost him. Tears came to her eyes whenever she heard:

The Great Mother lived with the pain in Her heart,
That She and Her son were forever apart.
She ached for the child that had been denied,
So She quickened once more from the life force inside.
She was not reconciled. To the loss of Her child.

Then came the part where the Mother delivered all the animals, also Her children, and especially when She gave birth to First Woman and then First Man.

To Woman and Man the Mother gave birth,
And then for their home, She gave them the Earth,
The water, the land, and all Her creation.
To use them with care was their obligation.
It was their home to use, But not to abuse.

For the Children of Earth the Mother provided,
The Gifts to survive, and then She decided,
To give them the Gift of Pleasure and sharing,
That honors the Mother with the joy of their pairing.
> *The Gifts are well earned, when honor's returned.*

The Mother was pleased with the pair she created,
She taught them to love and to care when they mated.
She made them desire to join with each other,
The Gift of their Pleasures came from the Mother.
> *Before She was through, Her children loved too.*
> *Earth's Children were blessed. The Mother could rest.*

That was the part everyone was waiting for. It meant the
formalities were over, it was time for feasting and other festivities.

People started milling around waiting for the feast to be set
out. Jonayla, who had been sleeping contentedly while Ayla
was sitting quietly, started to squirm around when they all
joined in on the Mother's Song. She woke up when her mother
got up and started moving. Ayla took her out of her carrying
blanket and held her out over the ground, where she let go of
her water. She had learned quickly that the sooner she went,
the sooner she'd be out of the cold and held close to a warm
body again.

"Let me take her," Jondalar said, reaching for the child.
Jonayla smiled at the man, which elicited a smile in return.

"Wrap her in this blanket," Ayla said, handing him the soft
hide of a red deer that she was using to carry her. "It's getting
chilly, and she's still warm from sleep."

Ayla and Jondalar walked toward the camp of the Third Cave.
They had enlarged their space to include room for their neighboring Cave in the main Summer Meeting area. The Ninth put
up a couple of shelters for their own use especially during the
day, but they still referred to it as the camp of the Third Cave.
They also tended to share meals and join together for feasts,
but Matrimonial Feasts were always prepared and shared by
the entire group.

They joined the rest of Jondalar's family and friends who were bringing food to the large meeting area of the Summer Camp near the zelandonia lodge. Proleva, as usual, organized the entire affair, assigning tasks and delegating individuals to be responsible for various jobs. People were coming from all directions bringing the components of the great feast. Each camp had developed their own variations on the standard ways of cooking the substantial quantity and diversity of foods that were available in the region.

The abundant grasslands and gallery forests along rivers provided rich feed for the many varieties of large grazing or browsing animals, including aurochs, bison, horse, mammoth, woolly rhinoceros, megaceros, reindeer, red deer, and several other types of deer. Some animals that in later times retreated to mountains spent certain seasons on the cold plains, like the wild goat known as ibex, the wild sheep called mouflon, and a goat-antelope referred to as chamois. A sheep-antelope named saiga lived on the steppes all year. In the coldest part of winter musk-oxen also appeared. There were also small animals, usually caught in traps, and fowl, often brought down with stones or throwing sticks, including Ayla's favorite, ptarmigan.

A wide selection of vegetables was available, including roots such as wild carrots, cattail rhizomes, flavorful onions, spicy little pignuts, and several different kinds of starchy biscuit roots and ground nuts that were collected with digging sticks, then eaten raw, cooked, or dried. Thistle stems, held up by the flower head so the sharp thorns could be scraped off before cutting, were delicious when lightly cooked; burdock stems required no special handling but needed to be picked young. The green leaves of lamb's quarter made a wonderful wild spinach; stinging nettles were even better, but had to be picked with a large leaf from another plant to protect the hand from the stinging, which disappeared when they were cooked.

Nuts and fruits, especially berries, were also in abundance, and an assortment of teas was provided. The steeping of leaves, stems, and flowers in hot water, or just letting them sit out in the sun for a while, was usually enough to make an infusion with the desired flavors and characteristics. But steeping was not a sufficiently rigorous process to extract the flavors and natural constituents from hard organic substances; barks, seeds, and roots usually required boiling to make the proper decoctions.

Other beverages were available, like fruit juices, including fermented varieties. Tree saps, particularly birch, could be boiled down to bring out the sugar and then fermented. Grains and, of course, honey could also be made into an alcoholic drink. Marthona provided a limited quantity of her fruit wine, Laramar some of his barma, and several others had brought their own varieties of drinks with variable alcoholic content. Most people brought their own eating utensils and bowls, although a supply of wood or bone platters, and carved or tightly woven bowls and cups, were offered for those who wanted to use them.

Ayla and Jondalar walked around greeting friends and sampling the foods and drinks offered by different Caves. Jonayla was often the center of attention. Some people were curious to see if the foreigner who had grown up with Flatheads, whom some still considered animals, had given birth to a normal child. Friends and relatives were just pleased to see that she was a happy, healthy, and very pretty little girl, with fine, almost white, soft curly hair. Everyone also knew immediately that it was Jondalar's spirit that the Great Mother had selected to mix with Ayla's to create her daughter; Jonayla had the same extraordinarily vivid blue eyes.

They passed by a group of people who had set up camp on the edge of the large communal area, and Ayla thought she recognized some of them. "Jondalar, aren't those people Traveling Storytellers?" she asked. "I didn't know they were coming to our Summer Meeting."

"I didn't know either. Let's go and greet them." They hurried to the camp. "Galliadal, how nice to see you," Jondalar called out as they neared.

A man turned around and smiled. "Jondalar! Ayla!" he said, approaching them with both hands stretched out to them.

He clasped Jondalar's hands. "In the name of the Great Earth Mother, I greet you," Galliadal said.

The man was nearly as tall as Jondalar, somewhat older, and nearly as dark as the Zelandoni man was light. Jondalar's hair was light yellow, Galliadal's was dark brown but with lighter streaks, and thinning on top. His blue eyes were not as striking as Jondalar's, but the contrast to his darker skin coloring made them intriguingly noticeable. His skin is not brown like Ranec's, Ayla thought. It's more like he has been out in the sun a lot, but I don't think it fades much in winter.

"In the name of Doni, you are welcome to our Summer Meeting, Galliadal, and welcome to the rest of your Traveling Cave," Jondalar replied. "I didn't know you had come. How long have you been here?"

"We arrived before noon, but we shared a meal with the Second Cave before we set up camp. The leader's mate is a far-cousin of mine. I didn't even know she had two-born-together."

"You're related to Beladora? Kimeran and I are age-mates; we went through our manhood rites together," Jondalar explained. "I was the tallest one there and felt out of place, until Kimeran came. I was so glad to see him."

"I understand how you felt, and you are even taller than me." Galliadal turned his attention to Ayla. "Greetings to you," he said, grasping her outstretched hands.

"In the name of the Great Mother of All, welcome," Ayla replied.

"And who is this pretty little thing?" the visitor said, smiling at the baby.

"This is Jonayla," Ayla said.

"Jon-Ayla! Your daughter, with his eyes, that's a good name," Galliadal said. "I hope you are coming tonight. I have a special story for you."

"For me?" Ayla said with surprise.

"Yes. It's about a woman who has a special way with animals. It's been very well liked everywhere we've been," Galliadal said with a big grin.

"Do you know someone who understands animals? I'd like to meet her," Ayla said.

"You already know her."

"But, the only person I know like that is me," Ayla said, then blushed when she understood.

"Of course! I couldn't pass up such a good story, but I don't give her your name, and I changed some other things. Many people ask if the story is about you, but I never tell them. It makes it more interesting. I'll be telling it when we get a good crowd. Come and listen."

"Oh, we will," Jondalar said. He had been watching Ayla and from her expression, he didn't think she was particularly happy about the idea of a storyteller making up stories about her and telling them to all the Caves. He knew many people who would love the attention, but he didn't think that she would. She already got more attention than she wanted, but he couldn't blame Galliadal. He was a storyteller and Ayla's story was a good one.

"It's about you, too, Jondalar. I couldn't leave you out," the storyteller said, with a wink. "You're the one who was gone on a Journey for five years and brought her back with you."

Jondalar winced to himself to hear that; it wasn't the first time that stories had been told about him, and they weren't always ones he wanted to have spread around. But it was best not to complain or make anything out of it; that would just add to the story. Storytellers loved to tell stories about individuals who were known, and people loved to hear them. Sometimes they used real names and other times, especially if they wanted to embellish the story, they would make up a name so people would have to guess who the story was about. Jondalar grew up hearing such stories, and he loved them, too, but he loved the Elder Legends and Histories of the Zelandonii better. He'd heard many stories about his mother when she was leader of the Ninth Cave, and the story about the great love of Marthona and Dalanar had been told so many times, it was almost legend.

Ayla and Jondalar chatted with him awhile, then wandered toward the camp of the Third Cave, stopping along the way to talk with various people they knew. As the evening deepened, it grew quite dark. Ayla stopped for a moment to look up. The moon was new, and without its glowing light to moderate their brilliance, the stars filled the night sky with an awe-inspiring profusion.

"The sky is so . . . full . . . I don't know the right word," Ayla said, feeling a touch of impatience with herself. "It is beautiful, but more than that. It makes me feel small, but in a way that makes me feel good. It is greater than us, greater than everything."

"When the stars are bright like that, it is a wondrous sight," Jondalar said.

While the bright stars did not bestow as much radiance as the moon would have, it did provide almost enough illumination to see their way. But the multitude of stars was not the only light. Every camp had great bonfires, and torches and lamps had been placed along paths between camps.

When they reached the camp of the Third Cave, Proleva was there with her sister, Levela, and their mother, Velima. They all greeted each other.

"I can't believe how much Jonayla has grown in just a few moons," Levela said. "And she's so beautiful. She has Jondalar's eyes. But she looks like you."

Ayla smiled at the compliment to her baby, but deflected the one directed at her. "I think she looks like Marthona, not me. I'm not beautiful."

"You don't know what you look like, Ayla," Jondalar said. "You never look at a polished reflector, or even a pool of still water. You are beautiful."

Ayla changed the subject. "You are really showing now, Levela," Ayla said. "How are you feeling?"

"Once I got over feeling sick in the morning, I've been feeling good," Levela said. "Vigorous and strong. Although, lately, I get tired easily. I want to sleep late and take naps in the day, and sometimes if I stand for a long time, my back hurts."

"Sounds about right, wouldn't you say," Velima said, smiling at her daughter. "Just the way you are supposed to feel."

"We're setting up an area to take care of children so their mothers and mates can go to the Mother Festival and relax," Proleva said. "You can leave Jonayla, if you want. There will be singing and dancing, and some people had already drunk too much before I left."

"Did you know the Traveling Storytellers are here?" Jondalar asked.

"I heard they were supposed to come, but I didn't know they had arrived," Proleva said.

"We talked to Galliadal. He said he wanted us to come and

listen. He said he has a story for Ayla," Jondalar said. "I think it's a thinly disguised story about her. We should probably go and listen so we'll know what people will be talking about tomorrow."

"Are you going, Proleva?" Ayla asked as the woman was putting down her sleeping baby.

"It was a big feast, and I've been working on it for many days," Proleva said. "I think I'd rather stay here and watch the little ones with just a few women. It would be more restful. I've been to my share of Mother Festivals."

"Maybe I should stay and watch the children, too," Ayla said.

"No. You should go. Mother Festivals are still new to you, and you need to become familiar with them, especially if you are learning to be a Zelandoni. Here, give me that little one of yours. I haven't cuddled her for days," Proleva said.

"Let me nurse her first," Ayla said. "I'm feeling rather full anyway."

"Levela, you should go, too, especially since the storytellers are here. You too, mother," Proleva said.

"The storytellers will be here for many days. I can see them later, and I've been to my share of Mother Festivals, too. You've been so busy, we haven't had much time to visit. I'd rather stay here with you," Velima said. "But you should go, Levela."

"I'm not sure. Jondecam is already there, and I told him I'd meet him, but I am tired already. Maybe I'll just go for a while, to hear the storytellers," she said.

"Joharran is there, too. He almost has to be, just to keep an eye on some of the young men. I hope he takes some time to enjoy himself. Tell him about the storytellers, Jondalar. He always enjoys them."

"I will if I can find him," Jondalar said.

He wondered if Proleva was staying away to give her mate the freedom to enjoy the Mother Festival. Although everyone knew they could take partners other than their mates, he knew that some people didn't necessarily want to watch their own mate couple with someone else. He knew he didn't. It would be very hard for him to see Ayla go off with some other man.

Several men had already shown an interest in her, the Zelandoni of the Twenty-sixth, for example, and even the storyteller Galliadal. He knew that such jealousy was frowned on, but he couldn't help how he felt. He just hoped he would be able to hide it.

When they returned to the large gathering area, Levela quickly spied Jondecam and hurried ahead, but Ayla stopped at the edge just to watch for a while. Almost all the people who were attending the Summer Meeting at this location had already arrived and she was still not entirely comfortable with so many people in one place, especially in the beginning. Jondalar understood and waited with her.

At first glance the large space seemed filled with a vast amorphous throng surging in an eddying mass, like a great roiling river. But as she watched, Ayla began to see that the crowd had formed itself into several groups, generally around or near a large fire. In one area near the edge, close to the Storytellers' camp, many people were gathered around three or four people talking with exaggerated gestures, who were standing on a platform-like construction made of wood and hard rawhide that raised them somewhat above the crowd so they could be seen more easily. Those nearest to the platform were sitting on the ground or on logs or rocks that had been dragged closer. Almost directly opposite, across the gathering area, other people were dancing and singing to the sound of flutes, drums, and other percussion musical instruments. Ayla felt drawn to both and was trying to decide where to go first.

In another area people were gambling, using various tokens and gaming pieces, and in a nearby area, people were getting refills of their favorite beverages. She noticed Laramar doling out portions of his barma, with a false smile.

"Garnering favors," Jondalar said, almost as though he knew what she was thinking. She wasn't aware of the look of distaste that had appeared on her face when she saw the man.

Ayla saw that Tremeda was among those who were standing around waiting for more of his barma, but Laramar wasn't offering any to her. She turned toward the nearby group who were picking at what was left of the food, which had been gathered together and offered for whoever wanted more.

Throughout the entire space, people stood together talking and laughing, or drifting from one place to another for no apparent reason. Ayla didn't immediately notice the undercurrent of activity around the darker edges of the crowd. Then she happened to catch sight of a young woman with bright red hair whom she recognized as Folara's friend Galeya. She was walking away from the eating area with the young man from the Third Cave who had joined the lion hunt, Ayla recalled. They had chosen to partner together to watch out for each other.

Ayla watched the young couple as they headed for the darkened periphery of the gathering and saw when they paused to embrace. She felt a moment of embarrassment; she hadn't meant to observe them when they were being intimate. Then she saw that there were others in certain areas away from the main activities who also appeared to be closely involved with each other. Ayla felt herself flush.

Jondalar smiled to himself. He had seen where she was looking. The Zelandonii tended not to stare at such activity either. It wasn't so much a matter of embarrassment; intimacy was commonplace and they just ignored it. He had traveled far and was aware that people's customs could be different, but she had too; he knew that she had seen people together before—they lived in such close quarters it couldn't be avoided. She must have seen similar activity at the Summer Meeting the year before. He wasn't quite sure what was causing her discomfort. He was going to ask, but then he saw Levela and Jondecam returning and decided to wait until later.

Her discomfiture stemmed from her early years when she had lived with the Clan. It had been strongly stressed to her that some things, even though they could be observed, were not supposed to be seen. The stones that outlined each hearth in the cave of Brun's clan were like invisible walls. One did not see past the boundary stones, did not look into the private areas of another man's hearth. People averted their eyes, or assumed the far-off look of gazing into space, anything to avoid seeming to stare into the area enclosed by the stones. And as a rule they were careful not to stare inadvertently. Staring was part of the body sign language of the Clan, and had specific meanings. An intense look from a leader, for example, could be a reprimand.

When she realized what she had seen, Ayla had quickly looked in another direction, and saw Levela and Jondecam approaching. She felt an odd sense of relief. She touched cheeks and greeted them affectionately, as though she hadn't seen them for a while.

"We're going to watch the storytellers," Levela said.

"I was just trying to decide if I wanted to listen to stories or music," Ayla said. "If you are going to watch the storytellers, maybe I'll go with you."

"So will I," Jondalar said.

When they arrived at the place, there seemed to be a break in the performance. A narrative had apparently just been concluded and a new one hadn't yet begun. People were milling around; some were leaving, some were arriving, some changing positions. Ayla looked over the area to get a sense of the place. The low platform, though empty now, was big enough to hold three or four people with room to move about. There were two somewhat rectangular fire trenches not directly in front of the platform, but on either side, for light rather than heat. In between and on either side of the fires were several logs arranged somewhat haphazardly in rows and a few good-size stones, all of them covered with stuffed pads for easier sitting. There was an open space in front of the logs where people were sittting on the ground, many on some kind of ground covering, like woven grass floor mats or hides.

Several people, who had been sitting on a log near the front, stood up and walked away. Levela headed purposefully in that direction and sat down on the soft pad that covered the tree trunk. Jondecam quickly sat beside her; then they claimed space beside them for their friends who had been delayed by someone who greeted them along the way. While they were exchanging pleasantries, Galliadal approached.

"You did decide to come," he said, bending down to greet Ayla, touching his cheek to hers and, Jondalar thought, holding it there too long. Ayla felt Galliadal's warm breath on her neck and noticed his pleasant manly smell, different from the one she was most familiar with. She also noticed the tension in Jondalar's jaw, in spite of his smile.

Several people were crowding around them and Ayla thought they probably wanted the storyteller's attention. She had noticed that many people liked to flock around Galliadal, especially young women, and some were looking at her with a kind of expectancy, as though they were waiting for something. She didn't think she liked it.

"Levela and Jondecam are holding places in front for us," Jondalar said. "We should go and claim them."

She smiled at Jondalar, and they went to join their friends, but when they arrived, some other people were also sitting on the log, taking some of the space Levela and Jondecam had been holding. They all crowded together, then waited.

"I wonder what's taking so long," Jondecam said, getting a bit impatient.

Jondalar noticed that more people were arriving. "I think they are waiting to see how many are coming. You know how it is: once they start, storytellers don't like to have a lot of people moving around; it disrupts the telling. They don't mind a few slipping in quietly, but most people don't like to come in the middle of a story either. They'd rather hear it from the beginning. I think a lot of people were waiting until they were done with the story they were on. When they saw people moving away, they decided that was the time to come."

Galliadal and several other people had stepped up to the low platform. They waited until people noticed them. When everyone stopped talking and it became quiet, the tall dark-haired man began.

"Far away in the land of the dawning sun . . ."

"That's the way all stories start," Jondalar whispered to Ayla, as though he was pleased that it had begun right.

". . . there lived a woman and her mate and her three children. The eldest was a boy named Kimacal." When the storyteller mentioned the first of the woman's offspring, a young man who was also on the platform stepped forward and made a slight bow, implying that he was the one referred to. "The next one was a girl named Karella." A young woman did a pirouette that ended in a bow when he mentioned the second child. "The youngest one was a boy named Wolafon." Another young man pointed to himself and grinned proudly when the third child was announced.

There was a slight murmur in the audience, and a few chuckles when the name of the youngest child was mentioned as people perceived a connection with Ayla's name for her four-legged hunter.

Although he wasn't shouting, Ayla noticed that the story-teller's voice could be heard very well by the entire audience. He had a special way of speaking that was powerful, clear, and expressive. It made her think of her visit to the cave with the Zelandoni of the Twenty-sixth and his acolyte and the sounds the three of them had made in front of the cave before crawl-ing in. It occurred to her that Galliadal could have become one of the zelandonia, if he wished.

"Though they were old enough, none of the young people were mated yet. Their Cave was small and they were closely related to most of the people near their age. The mother was beginning to worry that they would have to go far away to find mates, and she might not see them again. She had heard of an old Zelandoni who lived alone in a cave some distance up the river to the north. Some people talked in whispers about her, saying she could make things happen, but she might exact a payment that would be hard to make. The mother decided to go and find her," the storyteller said.

"One day after she returned, the woman sent her children out to the edge of a stream to collect cattail roots. When they arrived they met three other young people, a girl about the age of Kimacal, a boy about the age of Karella, and a girl about the age of Wolafon."

This time the first young man on the platform smiled coquett-ishly when the older girl was mentioned, the young woman took a bravado stance, and the other young man assumed the posture of a shy young girl. There was laughter from the audi-ence. When Ayla and Jondalar looked at each other, both were smiling.

"The three newcomers were strangers who had recently ar-rived from the land to the south. As all of them had been taught was appropriate, they greeted each other and introduced themselves, reciting their important names and ties.

"'We have come looking for food,' the eldest visitor explained." Galliadal changed the timbre of his voice when he spoke as the young woman.

"'There are many cattails here; we can share them,' Karella said." The young woman mouthed the words Galliadal spoke, again changing his tone. "They all started pulling cattail roots out of the soft mud by the edge of the stream, Kimacal helping the older foreign girl, Karella showing the middle boy where to dig, and Wolafon pulling out some roots for the shy younger girl, but the fair young woman wouldn't accept them. Wolafon could see that his brother and sister were enjoying the company of their pleasurable new friends, becoming very friendly."

The laughter was now quite loud. Not only were the innuendos obvious, the young man portraying the older brother and the young woman on the platform were in an exaggerated embrace, while the younger brother looked on with envy. When Galliadal narrated, he changed his voice for each character as he spoke for them, while the others on the raised platform demonstrated, often very dramatically.

"'These are good cattails. Why won't you eat them?' Wolafon asked the appealing stranger, 'I cannot eat cattails,' the young woman said. 'I can only eat meat.'" When he spoke as the woman, he pitched his voice quite high.

"Wolafon didn't know what to do. 'Maybe I can hunt for some meat for you,' he said, but he knew he wasn't a very good hunter. He usually went along on game drives. He meant well, but he was a little lazy and never tried very hard to hunt himself. He went back to the home of his mother's Cave.

"'Kimacal and Karella shared cattails with a woman and man from the south,' he told his mother. 'They have found mates, but the woman I want can't eat cattails. She can only eat meat, and I'm not a very good hunter. How can I find food for her?'" Galliadal related.

Ayla wondered if "sharing cattails" had some second meaning that she wasn't familiar with, like a joke she didn't understand, since the storyteller went from eating cattails together to being mated in the next breath.

"'There is an old Zelandoni who lives alone in a cave north of here near the river,' his mother said. 'She may be able to help you. But be careful what you ask for. You may get exactly what you want.'" Galliadal again changed the timbre of his voice when he spoke as the mother.

"Wolafon set out to find the old Zelandoni. He traveled upriver for many days, looking into all the caves he happened to see along the way. He was almost ready to give up, but he saw a small cave high up in a cliff and decided that would be the last cave he would investigate. He found an old woman sitting in front of it, who seemed to be sleeping. He approached quietly, not wanting to disturb her, but he was curious and looked at her carefully," Galliadal continued.

"Her clothes were nondescript, the same kind of thing most people wore, though rather shapeless and shabby. But she wore many necklaces made of a variety of materials: beads and shells; several pierced animal teeth and claws; animals carved out of ivory, bone, antler, and wood; some of stone and amber; and disk-shaped medallions with animals carved on them. There were so many objects on the necklaces, Wolafon couldn't even see them all, but even more impressive were her facial tattoos. They were so intricate and embellished, he could hardly see her skin under all the squares, swirls, curlicues, and flourishes. She was without doubt a Zelandoni of great stature and Wolafon was a little fearful of her. He didn't know if he should bother her with his little request."

The woman on the platform had seated herself and although she hadn't changed clothes, the way she wrapped them around herself gave the impression of an old woman in the shapeless clothing Galliadal had described.

"Wolafon decided to leave, but as he turned to go, he heard a voice. 'What do you want from me, boy?' she said." Galliadal's voice took on the sound of an older woman, not thin and quavery, but powerful and mature.

"Wolafon gulped, then turned around. He introduced himself properly, then said, 'My mother told me you might be able to help me.'

" 'What is your problem?'

" 'I met a woman, who came from the south. I wanted to share cattails with her, but she said she couldn't eat cattails, she could only eat meat. I love her and I would hunt for her but I am not a very good hunter. Can you help me to become a good hunter?'

" 'Are you sure she wants you to hunt for her?' the old Zelandoni asked. 'If she doesn't want your cattails, it may be that she won't want your meat, either. Did you ask her?'

" 'When I offered her the cattails, she said she couldn't eat them, not that she didn't want to, and when I told her I would hunt for her, she didn't say no,' Wolafon said." The voice Galliadal used for the young man sounded hopeful, and the expression of the young man on the platform mimicked the tone.

" 'You know that all it takes to become a good hunter is practice, lots of practice,' the old Zelandoni told him.

" 'Yes, I know. I should have practiced more.'" The young man on the platform looked down, as though contrite.

" 'But you didn't practice, did you? Now, because a young woman interests you, you want to suddenly become a hunter, is that right?'" Galliadal's tone as the old Zelandoni became a reprimand.

" 'I suppose so.'" The young man looked even more ashamed. " 'But I adore her.'"

" 'You must always earn whatever you get. If you don't want to make the effort to practice, you must pay for the skill some other way. You give your effort to practice, or you give something else. What are you willing to give?' the old woman asked.

" 'I'll give anything!'" The audience gasped, knowing it was the wrong thing to say.

" 'You could still take the time to practice and learn how to hunt,' the old Zelandoni said.

" 'But she won't want to wait until I learn how to hunt well. I adore her. I just want to bring her meat so she will love me. I wish I was born knowing how to hunt.'"

Suddenly the audience and the ones on the raised platform detected a commotion in their midst.

11

Wolf was slipping through the crowd, occasionally brushing against someone's leg but gone before they could catch more than a glimpse of what had touched them. Though most people were familiar with him, he was still a surprise that could bring a gasp or a squeal of apprehension when he was noticed. He even surprised Ayla when he appeared so unexpectedly and sat in front of her, looking up at her face. Danella was startled, because he had appeared so quickly, but she wasn't afraid.

"Wolf! You've been gone all day. I was beginning to wonder where you were. Exploring the whole area, I think," Ayla said as she rubbed the ruff of fur around his neck and scratched behind his ears. He reached up to lick her neck and chin, then put his head in her lap, seeming to enjoy her welcoming strokes and caresses. When she stopped, he curled up in front of her and laid his head on his paws, relaxed, but watchful.

Galliadal along with the others on the platform watched him, and then the man smiled. "Our unusual visitor has come at an appropriate time in the story," he said. Then back in character, he continued.

"'Is that what you want? To be a natural-born hunter?' the old Zelandoni asked.

"'Yes! That's it. I want to be a natural-born hunter,' Wolafon said.

"'Then come into my cave,' said the old woman." The tone of the story was no longer at all humorous; it was ominous.

"As soon as Wolafon walked into the cave, he became very sleepy. He sat down on a pile of wolf furs, and was instantly asleep. When he finally woke up, he felt that he had slept for a long time, but he didn't know how long. The cave was empty, with no sign that it had ever been inhabited. He quickly ran outside." The young man on the platform ran out of the imaginary cave, using both hands and feet.

"The sun was shining and he was thirsty. As he headed for the river, he began to notice that something was strange. For one thing, he was seeing things from a different angle, as though he were lower to the ground. When he reached the edge of the stream, he felt the cold water on his feet as though he didn't have any foot-coverings on. When he looked down, he didn't see feet at all; he saw paws, the paws of a wolf.

"At first he was confused. Then he realized what had happened. The old Zelandoni had given him exactly what he asked for. He wanted to become a natural-born hunter, and now he was. He had become a wolf. That wasn't what he meant when he asked to be a good hunter, but it was too late now.

"Wolafon was so sorry he wanted to cry, but he had no tears. He waited at the water's edge, and in the stillness, began to be aware of the woods in a new way. He could hear things he had never heard before, and smell things he hadn't even known existed. He picked up the scent of many things, especially animals, and when he focused on a large rabbit, a white hare, realized that he was hungry. But now he knew exactly what to do. Quietly, slowly, he stalked the creature. Though the hare was very fast, and could turn in an instant, the wolf anticipated his moves and caught him."

Ayla smiled to herself at this part of the story. Most people did believe that wolves and other meat-eaters were born knowing how to hunt and kill their prey, but she knew better. After she had mastered the use of the sling, practicing in secret, she wanted to take the next step, to actually hunt with it, but hunting was forbidden to the women of the Clan. Many carnivores often stole meat from Brun's clan, particularly smaller meat-eaters like martens, stoats, and other weasels, small wild cats, foxes, and middle-size hunters like vicious wolverines, tufted lynxes, wolves, and hyenas. Ayla justified her decision to defy the Clan taboo by resolving that she would hunt only meat-eaters, animals that were destructive to her clan, leaving the hunting of food animals to the men. As a result, she not only excelled as a hunter, but she learned a great deal about her chosen prey. She spent the first few years observing them before she managed to make her first kill. She knew that while the tendency to hunt was strong in meat-eaters, they all had to be taught by their elders in one way or another. Wolves weren't born knowing how to hunt; young ones learned from their pack.

She was drawn back into Galliadal's storytelling. "The taste of warm blood running down his throat was delicious and Wolafon quickly devoured the hare. He went back to the river for another drink and cleaned the blood off his fur. Then he nosed around looking for a secure place. When he found one, he curled up and using his tail to cover his face, he went to sleep. When he woke up again, it was dark, but he could see better at night than he ever had before. He stretched languorously, lifted his leg and sprayed a bush, then went out hunting again." The young man on the platform did a good job of mimicking a wolf's actions, and when he lifted his leg, the audience laughed.

"Wolafon lived in the cave that had been abandoned by the old woman for some time, hunting for himself and enjoying it, but after a while he began to get lonely. The boy had become a wolf, but he was still a boy, too, and he began to think about returning home to see his mother, and the attractive young woman from the south. He headed back toward the Cave of his mother, running with the ease of a wolf. When he saw a young deer who had strayed away from its mother, he remembered that the girl from the south liked to eat meat, and decided he would hunt it and bring it to her.

"When Wolafon got close, some people saw him coming and were afraid. They wondered why a wolf was dragging a deer toward their home. He saw the attractive young woman, but he didn't notice the tall, handsome, fair-haired man standing beside her holding a new kind of weapon that enabled him to throw spears very far and fast, but as the man was preparing to cast a spear, Wolafon dragged the meat to the woman and dropped it at her feet. Then he sat down in front of her and looked up. He was trying to tell her that he loved her, but

Wolafon couldn't speak anymore. He could only show his love by his actions and the look in his eyes, and it was obvious that he was a wolf who loved a woman."

All of the people in the audience turned to stare at Ayla and the wolf at her feet, most of them smiling. Some began to laugh, then others started to slap their knees in applause. Although it wasn't quite where Galliadal had intended to end the story, the response from the listeners made him realize that it was a good place to stop.

Ayla felt embarrassed to be the center of so much attention, and looked at Jondalar. He was smiling, too, and slapping his knees.

"That was a good story," he said.

"But none of it is true," she said.

"Some of it is," Jondalar said, looking down at the wolf who was now standing in an alert and protective posture in front of Ayla. "There is a wolf who loves a woman."

She reached down to stroke the animal. "Yes, I think you are right."

"Most of the stories that storytellers tell are not true, but they often have some truth in them, or satisfy a desire for an answer. You have to admit, it was a good story. And if someone didn't know that you found Wolf as a very young cub alone in his den, with no siblings, or pack, or mother left alive, Galliadal's story could indulge their wish to know, even if they understood that it probably wasn't true."

Ayla looked at Jondalar and nodded; then they both turned and smiled at Galliadal and the others on the platform. The storyteller acknowledged them with an elaborate bow.

The audience was getting up and moving around again, and the storytellers stepped down from the platform to make room for a different set of people to tell a story. They joined the group around Ayla and Wolf.

"It was incredible when the wolf appeared. He came at just the right time," said the young man who had portrayed the boy-wolf. "It couldn't have been better if we'd planned it. I don't suppose you'd like to come and bring him every night?"

"I don't think that would be a good idea, Zanacan," Galliadal said. "Everyone will be talking about the story we told this evening. If it happened all the time, it would take away the special quality of tonight. And I'm sure Ayla has other things to do. She is a mother, and the First's acolyte."

The young man flushed a little red and looked embarrassed. "You're right, of course. I'm sorry."

"Don't be sorry," Ayla said. "Galliadal is right, I have many things to do, and Wolf wouldn't always be here just when you might want him, but I think it would be fun to learn something about storytelling the way you do it. If no one would mind, I'd like to visit sometime when you are practicing."

Zanacan, and the others, became very aware of Ayla's unusual accent as she spoke, especially because they all knew the effect of different tonal qualities and voices, and had traveled around the region much more than most.

"I love your voice!" Zanacan said.

"I've never heard an accent like yours," the young woman said.

"You must come from very far away," the other young man added.

Ayla was usually a little embarrassed when people mentioned her accent, but the three young people seemed so excited and genuinely pleased, she could only smile.

"Yes. She does come from very far away. Much farther than you can imagine," Jondalar said.

"We would love it if you came to visit us anytime you want while we're here, and would you mind if we tried to learn your way of speaking?" the young woman said. She looked up at Galliadal for approval.

The storyteller looked at Ayla. "Gallara knows that sometimes our camp is not open to casual visitors, but, yes, you would be welcome to visit our camp anytime."

"I think we could make a wonderful new story of someone who comes from very far away, maybe even farther than the land of the dawning sun," said Zanacan, still full of excitement.

"I think we could, but somehow I doubt if it would be as good as the real story, Zanacan," Galliadal said, then to Ayla and Jondalar he added, "The children of my hearth sometimes get very excited over new ideas, and you have given them many."

"I didn't know Zanacan and Gallara were the children of your hearth, Galliadal," Jondalar said.

"And Kaleshal, too," the man said. "He's the eldest. Perhaps we should make proper introductions."

The young people who had portrayed the characters of the story seemed quite pleased to meet the living counterparts of their tale, especially when they got to Ayla's names and ties. as Jondalar recited them.

"May I present to you Ayla of the Zelandonii," Jondalar began. When he got to where she came from, he changed the introduction somewhat. "Formerly she was Ayla of the Lion Camp of the Mamutoi, the Mammoth Hunters who live far to the east, in 'the land of the dawning sun,' and adopted as Daughter of the Mammoth Hearth, which is their zelandonia. Chosen by the spirit of the Cave Lion, her totem, who physically marked her, and protected by the spirit of the Cave Bear, Ayla is friend to the horses, Whinney and Racer, and the new filly, Gray, and loved by the four-legged hunter she calls Wolf."

They understood the names and ties that Jondalar brought to the list when they mated, but when he spoke of Mammoth Hearth, and Cave Lion and Cave Bear, not to mention the living animals she brought with her, Zanacan opened his eyes very wide. It was a mannerism of his when he was surprised.

"We can use that in the new story!" Zanacan said. "The animals. Not exactly the same, of course, but the idea of hearths named for animals, and maybe Caves, too, and the animals she travels with."

"I told you her real story is probably better than any story we could make up," Galliadal said.

Ayla smiled at Zanacan. "Would you like to meet Wolf? All of you," she said.

All three young people looked surprised, and Zanacan's eyes opened again. "How do you meet a wolf? They don't have names and ties, do they?"

"Not exactly," Ayla said. "But the reason that we give our names and ties is to learn more about each other, isn't it? Wolves learn more about people and many things in their world by scent. If you let him smell your hand, he will remember you."

"I'm not sure . . . would that be good or bad?" Kaleshal said.

"If I introduce you, he will count you as a friend," Ayla said.

"Then I think we should," Gallara said. "I wouldn't want to be counted as anything but a friend of that wolf."

When Ayla reached for Zanacan's hand and brought it to Wolf's nose, she could feel the slight resistance, a tendency to pull back at first. But once he realized that nothing bad would happen, his innate curiosity and interest were aroused. "His nose is cold, and wet," he said.

"That means he's healthy. How did you think a wolf's nose should feel?" Ayla said. "Or his fur? What do you think that feels like?" She moved his hand to stroke his head, and feel the fur along his neck and back. She went through a similar process with the other two young people, while many others stood back and watched.

"His fur is smooth and rough, and he's warm," Zanacan said.

"He's alive. Living animals are warm, most of them. Birds are very warm, fish are cool, and snakes can be either," Ayla said.

"How do you know so much about animals?" Gallara said.

"She's a hunter, and she's caught almost every kind of animal there is," Jondalar said. "She can kill a hyena with a stone, catch a fish with her bare hand, and birds come to her whistle, but she usually lets them go. Just this spring, she led a lion hunt, and killed at least two with her spear-thrower."

"I didn't lead the hunt," Ayla said, frowning. "Joharran did."

"Ask him," Jondalar said. "He says you led the hunt. You were the one who knew about lions, and how to go after them."

"I thought she was a Zelandoni, not a hunter," Kaleshal said.

"She's not a Zelandoni yet," Galliadal said. "She's an acolyte, in training, but I understand a very good healer already."

"How can she know so many things?" Kaleshal asked, doubt in his tone.

"She had no choice," Jondalar said. "She lost her people when she was a five-year, was adopted by strangers and had to learn their ways, then lived alone for a few years before I found her, or I should say, she found me. I had been attacked by a lion. She rescued me, and treated my wounds. When you lose everything at such a young age, you have to adapt and learn quickly or you won't survive. She's alive because she was able to learn so many things."

Ayla was paying attention to Wolf, stroking him and rubbing behind his ears, keeping her head down, trying not to listen. It always embarrassed her when people talked about her as though the things she had done were accomplishments. It made her feel as though she thought she was important, and that made her uncomfortable. She didn't think she was important, and she didn't like being singled out as different. She was just a woman, and a mother, who had found a man to love and people like herself, most of whom had come to accept her as one of them. Once she had wanted to be a good Clan woman; now she just wanted to be a good Zelandonii woman.

Levela walked up to Ayla and Wolf. "I think they are getting ready to tell the next story," she said. "Are you staying to hear it?"

"I don't think so," Ayla said. "Jondalar may want to stay. I'll ask him, but I think I'll come back another time to listen to stories. Are you staying?"

"I thought I might see if there is anything good left to eat. I'm getting a little hungry, but I'm tired, too. I may go back to our camp soon," Levela said.

"I'll go with you to get something to eat. Then I have to pick up Jonayla from your sister." Ayla took a few steps to where Jondalar and the others were talking, and waited until there was a break in the conversation. "Are you going to stay to hear the next story?" she asked.

"What do you want to do?"

"I'm getting tired and so is Levela. We thought we'd go and see if there is anything good left to eat," Ayla said.

"That sounds fine to me. We can come back another time to listen to more stories. Is Jondecam coming?" Jondalar said.

"Yes, I am." They heard his voice coming toward them. "Wherever you are going."

The four of them left the storytellers' camp and headed for the area where the food had been gathered together. Everything was cold, but cold slices of bison and venison were still tasty. Globular root vegetables of some variety were soaking in a rich broth that had a thin layer of congealed fat on top, which added flavor. Fat was a desirable quality, relatively rare on free-ranging wild animals, and necessary for survival. Hidden behind some empty bone platters they found a woven bowl with some round blue-colored berries left in it, several varieties mixed together like huckleberries, bearberries, and currants, which they gladly shared. Ayla even found a couple of bones for Wolf.

She gave one to the canine, which he carried in his mouth until he found a comfortable place to settle down and gnaw on it, near the place where his people ate. Ayla wrapped the other one that had more meat on it in some large leaves that had lined a platter to make a nice presentation, to carry back to the camp for later. She tucked the bone into the small one-sided haversack that she used to carry things, especially things for Jonayla like a hard rawhide scrap that the baby liked to chew on, a hat and a small extra blanket, and some soft absorbent material like mouflon wool that she stuffed around the baby. She also carried her tinder kit for starting fires in a pouch tied to her waist, and her personal dishes and eating knife. They found some logs with pads on them nearby, obviously dragged there for seating.

"I wonder if any of mother's wine is left," Jondalar remarked.

"Let's go see," Jondecam said.

There was not even a drop, but Laramar had noticed them, and hurried over with a freshly opened waterbag of barma. He filled the personal cups of both the men, but both Ayla and Levela said they didn't want much, and would just take a sip from the men's drinks. Ayla didn't want to make pleasant talk with the man for too long. After a few minutes, they went back to the logs with pads on them that were near the food. When they finished, they strolled back to Proleva's shelter at the camp of the Third Cave.

"There you are. You're back early," Proleva said, after they brushed each other's cheeks in greeting. "Did you see Joharran?"

"No," Levela said. "We only listened to one story, then got some food. It was a story about Ayla, sort of."

"Actually, it was about Wolf. It was a story about a boy who turned into a wolf that loved a woman," Jondalar said. "Wolf came and found Ayla right in the middle of it, which pleased Galliadal and the three young people of his hearth, who were helping him tell the story."

"Jonayla is still sleeping. Would you like a nice cup of hot tea?" Proleva said.

"I don't think so. We're going back to our camp," Ayla said.

"You're not going back, too?" Velima said to Levela. "We've hardly had any time to visit. I want to know about your pregnancy and how you are feeling."

"Why don't you stay here tonight," Proleva said. "There's room for all four of you. And Jaradal would love to see Wolf when he wakes up."

Levela and Jondecam quickly agreed. The camp of the Second Cave was nearby, and the idea of spending some time with her mother and her sister was appealing to Levela, and Jondecam didn't mind.

Ayla and Jondalar looked at each other. "I really should check on the horses," Ayla said. "We left early and I don't know of anyone who stayed at camp today. I just want to know they are all right, especially Gray. She can be a tempting treat for some four-legged hunter, though I know Whinney and Racer will protect her. I would just feel better going back."

"I understand. She's a little like your baby, too," Proleva said.

Ayla nodded and smiled in agreement, "And where is my baby?"

"She's over there, sleeping with Sethona. It's a shame to disturb her—are you sure you won't stay?"

"We'd like to, but one of the problems with having horses as friends is that you feel responsible for them, especially if you keep them in an enclosure that is not closed to four-legged hunters," Jondalar said. "Ayla is right. We need to check on them."

Ayla had wrapped her child in her carrying blanket and was hoisting the baby onto her hip. She woke briefly, but then settled down next to her mother's warmth and went back to sleep. "I really appreciate your watching her, Proleva. The storytelling was interesting, and it made it much easier to watch and listen without interruption," Ayla said.

"It was my pleasure. Those two girls are getting to know each other and they are starting to entertain each other. I think they are going to be real friends," Proleva said.

"It was fun watching them together," Velima said. "It's good if close cousins spend time with each other."

Ayla signaled Wolf, who picked up his bone, and they all left the summer dwelling. Jondalar selected a torch that was stuck in the ground, one of many lighting a path outside the shelter, and checked it to see how much burning material was left to make sure it would last until they reached their camp.

They left the warm glow of fires in the Main Camp and moved into the deep soft obscurity of night. The enveloping darkness wrapped itself around them with an intensity that absorbed the light and seemed to smother the flame of the torch.

"It's so dark; there's no moon tonight," Ayla said.

"But there are clouds," Jondalar said. "They are blocking out the stars. You can't see many."

"When did it cloud up? I didn't notice them when we were in Camp."

"That's because all the fires are distracting, and the light from them fills your eyes." They walked quietly side by side for a while, then Jondalar added, "Sometimes you fill my eyes, and I wish there weren't so many people around."

She smiled and turned to look at him. "On our way here when it was just the two of us and Whinney, Racer, and Wolf, I was often lonely for people. Now we have people and I'm glad, but sometimes I remember when it was just the two of us and we could do whatever we wanted whenever we felt like it. Maybe not always, but most of the time."

"I think about that, too," Jondalar said. "I remember when, if I looked at you and felt you fill my manhood, we could just stop and share Pleasures. I didn't have to go with Joharran to meet some people to make arrangements for something, or do something for mother, or just see so many people around that there is no place to stop and relax and do what I want with you."

"I feel the same way," Ayla said. "I remember when I could

look at you and feel inside how only you could make me feel, and know that if I gave you the right signal, you would make me feel that way again because you know me better than I know myself. And I wouldn't have to think about taking care of a baby, and maybe several others at the same time, or plan a feast with Proleva, or help Zelandoni take care of someone who is sick or hurt, or learn about some new treatments, or remember the Five Sacred Colors, or how to use counting words. Although I love all of it, sometimes I miss you, Jondalar, I miss being with just you."

"I don't mind having Jonayla around. I like to watch you with her; sometimes that fills me even more, but I can wait until she's content. The trouble is that usually someone comes and interrupts, and I have to go someplace, or you do." He stopped to kiss her tenderly; then they continued, walking in silence.

The walk was not long but as they neared the camp of the Ninth Cave, they almost stumbled over a cold fireplace before they noticed it. There were no fires anyplace, not a single dying ember or tent glowing from the light within or line of light from a crack between planks. They could smell the vestiges of old fires, but it appeared that no one was there and hadn't been for some time. Every single person from the most populous Cave in the region had left their camp.

"No one is here," Ayla said, very surprised. "Everyone is gone. Except for the ones who may have gone hunting or visiting, they must all be at the Main Camp."

"Here's our dwelling, at least I think it is," Jondalar said. "Let's build a fire inside to warm it up, then go check on the horses."

They brought in some wood and dried aurochs dung patties that had been stacked outside and started a fire in the small fireplace they had created near their sleeping places. Wolf came in with them and parked his bone in a small hole near an area of the wall that was seldom used by anyone but him. Ayla checked the large waterbag near the main hearth.

"We should bring in some water, too," she said. "There's not much left in this. Let's go find the horses. Then I'm going to have to feed Jonayla; she's starting to fuss around."

"I'd better get a new torch. This one will go out soon," Jondalar said. "I should spend some time tomorrow making new ones."

He lit a new torch off the old one, then put the remains of the first in the fireplace. When they left the shelter, Wolf followed them out. Ayla heard him make a low throaty growl as they approached the fence of the horse surround.

"Something's wrong," she said, hurrying.

Jondalar held the torch high to spread the light it gave off. There was a strange lump of something near the center of the enclosed space. As they neared it, Wolf's growl grew louder. When they got closer they could see pale gray, spotted, rather fluffy fur with a long tail, and a lot of blood.

"It's a leopard, a young snow leopard, I think. It's been trampled to death. What's a snow leopard doing here? They like the highlands," Ayla said. She ran toward a roofed shelter they had constructed for the horses to get out of the rain, but it was empty.

"Whiiinnney," she called, "Whiiiinnney!" making it a loud neigh that sounded to Jondalar exactly like a horse.

It was the name she had originally given the mare. The name she was called by most people, Whinney, was an accommodation Ayla had made to the language of people. She whinnied again, then blew her special call whistle very loudly. Finally, from a distance, they heard an answering neigh.

"Wolf, go find Whinney," she said to the canine. The animal raced off in the direction of the neigh with Ayla and Jondalar following behind. They went through the fence where the horses had stomped it down to break through, and she understood how they got out.

They found all three horses near a creek at the back of the area the Ninth Cave was using for their camp. Wolf was sitting on his haunches guarding them, but, Ayla realized, he wasn't too close. They had obviously had a bad scare, and somehow the wolf sensed that even the friendly carnivore felt threatening at the moment. Ayla rushed to Whinney, but slowed down when she noticed that Whinney was watching her intently, her mouth tight, her ears, nose, and eyes pointed toward her, focused on her, sometimes swinging her head slightly.

"You're still afraid, aren't you?" Ayla began talking to the mare softly in their special language. "I don't blame you, Whinney." Again she said her name the way a horse would, but more softly. "I'm sorry I left you alone to fight off that leopard by yourselves, and I'm sorry no one was here to hear you when you were screaming for help."

She had been slowly walking toward the horse as she spoke until finally she reached her and put her arms around the sturdy neck. The horse relaxed, put her head over the woman's shoulder and leaned into her as Ayla leaned back in the familiar comforting stance that had been their custom since the early days in the valley.

Jondalar followed her lead, whistling his call to Racer, who was also still feeling frightened. He stuck the torch in the ground, then approached the young stallion, and stroked and scratched him in his favorite places. The handling by their familiar friends comforted the animals, and soon Gray also joined in, nursing from her dam for a while, then going to Ayla for some affectionate touching and scratching. Jondalar also joined in stroking the little filly. But it was only after the five of them were all together—six including Jonayla, who was awake and squirming in her carrying blanket—that Wolf joined them.

Even though Whinney and Racer had known him from the time he was a four-week-old pup and had helped to raise him, his underlying scent was still of a carnivore, a meat-eater whose wild cousins often preyed on horses. Wolf had sensed their discomfort when they saw him, probably from their scent of fear, and knew to wait until they were comfortable again before approaching them. He was welcomed to the pack of people and horses that he had imprinted on, the only pack he had known.

About then Jonayla decided it was her turn. She let out a hungry wail. Ayla took her out of her carrying blanket and held her out in front to pass her water on the ground. When she was through, Ayla propped her up on Gray's back for a moment, holding her with one hand while she straightened out the carrying blanket and exposed a breast with the other hand. Soon the infant was wrapped up again, held close to her mother, happily nursing.

On the way back, they made a detour around the enclosure, knowing that the horses would never go into it again. Ayla thought that she would get rid of the leopard carcass later and she wasn't sure about the enclosure. At the moment she never wanted to put the horses in one again and would be happy to give the wooden poles and planks to whoever wanted them, for firewood if nothing else. When they reached their lodge, they led the horses around to an area on the back side of the summer dwelling that was used infrequently, where some grass still grew.

"Should we put a halter on them and tie them to a ground stake?" Jondalar said. "It would keep them close by."

"I think it would upset Whinney, and Racer, after their scare, if they couldn't run freely. For now I think they will want to stay close, unless something scares them again, and we'd hear them. I think I'm going to leave Wolf out here to guard them, at least for tonight." She went to the animal and bent down close. "Stay here, Wolf. Stay here and watch Whinney, and Racer and Gray. Stay and guard the horses." She wasn't entirely sure if he understood, but when he lowered his hindquarters and looked toward the horses, she thought he might. She pulled out the bone she had tucked away for him and gave it to him.

The small fire they had started inside the shelter had long since gone out, so they started a new one, bringing in more fuel to keep it going. About then, Ayla noticed that the nursing was encouraging Jonayla to generate more than water. She quickly spread out a small pile of soft absorbent cattail fibers, and laid the child's bare bottom on it.

"Jondalar, would you get the large waterbag and bring me whatever is left in it, so I can clean her up, then go and fill it with fresh water, and our small one, too," Ayla said.

"She is a smelly little thing," he said with an adoring smile at the little girl he thought was utterly beautiful.

He found the bowl made of tightly woven osier willow withes with an ocher-stained red cord worked in near the top, which was often used to clean especially dirty messes of various kinds. It was marked with the color so it wouldn't inadvertently

be used for drinking water or cooking. He brought it and the
nearly empty waterbag to their hearth, filled the bowl, then
took their waterbag, made of the stomach of an ibex, the same
one that provided the hide for Jonayla's carrying blanket, along
with the large general one to the entrance. He picked up one
of the unlit torches that was nearby, took it to their fireplace
to light it, and picking up the waterbags on the way, went out.

Animal stomachs, when thoroughly cleaned and with extra
holes at the bottom sewed or tied off, were nearly waterproof
and made excellent waterbags. When Jondalar came back with
the water, the soiled water bowl was beside the night basket
near the door, and Ayla was nursing Jonayla again in hopes of
putting her to sleep.

"I suppose I should empty the bowl and the night basket,
while I'm at it," he said, planting the end of the lighted torch
in the ground.

"If you want, but hurry," Ayla said, looking at him with a
languorous yet mischievous smile. "I think Jonayla is almost
asleep."

He felt an immediate tightening in his loins and smiled
back. He brought the large, heavy waterbag to the main hearth
and hung it in its accustomed place, a peg on one of the strong
posts that supported the structure, then brought the second one
to their sleeping place.

"Are you thirsty?" he asked, as he watched her nurse the
baby.

"I wouldn't mind a little water. I was thinking of making
some tea, but I think I'll wait until later," she said.

He poured some water in a cup and gave it to her, then went
back to the door. He poured the contents of the bowl into the
night basket, then picked up the torch and went back outside
taking the night basket and soiled bowl with him. Propping
the torch in the ground, he dumped the large, malodorous
night basket in one of the trenches the people used for passing
their wastes. Dumping such wastes was a job no one liked to
do. Picking up the torch, he then took them both to the lower
end of the stream, far away from the place upstream that they
had designated as their source of water. He rinsed them both
out, letting the water flow through them; then with a shovel

made of the scapula of some animal, with one edge thinned and sharpened, that was left there for the purpose, he filled the night basket something less than half full of dirt. Then, using clean sand from the bank of the waterway, he carefully washed and scoured his hands. Finally, with the torch to guide his way, he picked up the basket and bowl and headed back to the dwelling.

He put the night basket in its usual place, the bowl beside it, and the flaming torch in a holder made for it near the entrance. "That's done," he said, smiling at Ayla as he walked toward her. She was still holding the baby. He kicked off his sandals made of woven grass—the usual foot-coverings worn in the summer—and lay down beside her, propping himself up on one elbow.

"It will be someone else's turn next," she said.

"That water is cold," he said.

"And so are your hands," she said, reaching for them. "I should warm them up," she added, the hint of suggestion in her voice.

He looked at her with glowing eyes, his pupils enlarged with desire, and the dim light inside the dwelling.

12

Jondalar enjoyed watching Jonayla, whatever she was doing, whether it was nursing or playing with her feet or putting things in her mouth. He even liked to look at her when she was sleeping. Now he gazed at her trying to resist falling to sleep. She would start to let go of her mother's nipple, then suckle a few more times and hold on for a moment, then begin to let go, and repeat the process. Finally she lay quietly in her mother's arms. He was fascinated as a drop of milk formed at the end of the nipple and fell.

"I think she's asleep," he said, softly.

"Yes, I think so," Ayla said. She had packed the baby in clean mouflon wool, which she had washed a few days before, and wrapped her up in her usual swaddling nightclothes. The woman stood up and gently carried her infant to a nearby small sleeping roll. Ayla didn't always move Jonayla out of her bed when she went to sleep, but on this night she definitely wanted their sleeping roll for just Jondalar and her.

When she went back, the man who was waiting watched her as she slipped back into her place beside him; she looked directly at him, which still took some conscious thought for her. Jondalar had taught her that among his people, and most of his kind—and hers—it was considered impolite, if not devious, if you didn't look directly at the person to whom you were speaking.

While Ayla was looking at him, she started thinking about how other people saw this man she loved, how he appeared, his physical look. What was it about him that drew people to him before he even said a word? He was tall, with yellow hair lighter than hers, and he was strong and well made, with good proportions for his height. Though she couldn't see the color in the dim light of the shelter, she knew that his eyes, which always caught people's attention, matched the extraordinary blue of glacier water and the ice of its depths. She had seen both. He was intelligent and skilled in making things, like the flint tools he crafted, but more than that, she knew he had a quality, a charm, a charisma that attracted most people, but especially women. Zelandoni had been known to say that not even the Mother could refuse him if he asked.

He didn't quite know he had it—it was an unconscious appeal—but he did tend to take for granted that he would always be welcomed. Though it wasn't something he used on purpose, exactly, he knew he had an effect on people and benefited from it. Even his long Journey had not disabused him of the notion, or changed his perception that wherever he went, people would accept him, approve of him, like him. He had never really had to explain himself or find out how to fit in, and he never learned how to ask for pardon for doing something inappropriate or unacceptable.

If he seemed contrite or acted sorry—feelings that were usually genuine—people tended to accept that. Even when he was a young man and had beat Ladroman so badly that he knocked out his permanent front teeth, Jondalar didn't have to find the words to say he was sorry, then face him, and say them. His mother paid a heavy compensation for him, and he was sent away to live with Dalanar, the man of his hearth, for a few years, but he didn't have to do anything himself to make amends. He didn't have to beg forgiveness, or even say he was sorry for doing something wrong and injuring the other boy.

Though to most people he was considered an amazingly handsome, masculine man, Ayla thought of him in a somewhat different way. Men of the people who raised her, men of the Clan, had features that were more rugged, with large round eye sockets, generous noses, and pronounced brow ridges. From the first moment she saw him, unconscious, almost dead, after being attacked by her lion, the man had aroused an unconscious memory of people she hadn't seen in many years, a memory of people like herself. To Ayla, Jondalar's features were not as strong as those of the men with whom she had grown up, but they were so perfectly shaped and arranged, she thought that he was incredibly beautiful, like a fine-looking animal, a healthy young horse or lion. Jondalar had explained to her that it was not a word usually used to describe men, but though she didn't say it often, she did think he was beautiful.

He looked at her as he lay beside her, then bent his head to kiss her. He felt the softness of her lips and slowly moved his tongue between them, which she obligingly opened. He felt a tightening of his loins again.

"Ayla, you are so beautiful, and I am so lucky," he said.

"I am so lucky," she said. "And you are beautiful."

He smiled. She knew it wasn't quite the word to use, though she used "beautiful" correctly in all other instances. Now, when she said it to him in private, he just smiled. She hadn't closed the ties at the top of the opening of her tunic, though her breast had slipped back inside. He reached in and pulled it out again, the same one she had just used to nurse, and ran his tongue around the nipple, then suckled on it, tasting her milk.

"It feels different inside me when you do it," she said softly. "I like it when Jonayla nurses, but it doesn't feel the same. You make me want you to touch me in other places."

"You make me want to touch you in those places."

He undid all the ties and opened her tunic wide, exposing both breasts. When he suckled her again, her other nipple dribbled milk, and he reached over to lick that one.

"I'm coming to like the taste of your milk, but I don't want to take what belongs to Jonayla."

"By the time she's hungry again, more milk will be there."

He let go of the nipple and ran his tongue up to her neck and then kissed her again, this time more fiercely, and felt a need so strong he wasn't sure he could control it. He stopped and buried his face in her neck, trying to regain his composure. She began tugging on his tunic to pull it over his head.

"It's been a while," he said, sitting up on his knees. "I can't believe how ready I am."

"Are you?" she said, with a teasing grin.

"I'll show you," he said.

He stripped off his tunic with a two-handed pull over his head, then, standing, untied the drawstring around his waist and pulled off his short-legged trousers. Under those he wore a protective pouch that covered his man parts, tied on around his hips with thin strips of leather. Usually made of chamois or rabbit or some other soft skin, the thong pouches tended to be worn only in summer. If the weather became very warm or a man was working especially hard, he could strip down to just that and still feel protected. Jondalar's pouch was bulging with the member it contained. He slipped the thongs down, releasing his straining manhood.

Ayla looked up at him, a slow smile showing her response. There was a time when the size of his member had frightened women, before they knew with what care and gentleness he used it. His first time with Ayla he was afraid she might be nervous, before they both understood how suited they were to each other. Sometimes Jondalar really couldn't believe how lucky he was. Whenever he wanted her, she was ready for him. She never acted coy or disinterested. It was as if she always wanted him as much as he wanted her. He responded with a grin of such happiness and delight that in response her smile grew into the glorious manifestation that transformed her in his eyes, and those of most men, into a woman of unsurpassed beauty.

The fire in their small hearth was burning down, not yet out, but not giving much light or heat. It didn't matter. He dropped down beside her and began to remove her clothing, first the long tunic, stopping to suck on her nipples again, before untying the thongs around her waist holding up her half-leggings. He loosened the waist ties, and pulled the leggings down, running his tongue down her stomach, dipping into her navel, then pulling them down more, uncovering her pubic hair. When the top of her slit showed, he dipped his tongue there, savoring her familiar taste and searching for the small knob. She made a small squeal of pleasure when he found it.

He pulled off her leggings, and bent down to kiss her again, then tasted milk and worked his way down and tasted her essence again. He spread her legs, opened her lovely petals, then found her swelling nodule. He knew just how to stimulate her; he suckled it and worked it with his tongue while he put his fingers inside her and found other places that stirred her senses.

She cried out, feeling jolts of fire rising through her. Almost too soon he felt a spurt of fluid, tasted her, and his urge to let himself go was so strong, he very nearly couldn't hold back. He raised up, found her opening with his swollen manhood, and pushed in, grateful that he didn't have to fear that he would hurt her, that she could take him all, that he fit so well.

She cried out again, and again each time he pulled out and moved in. And then he was there. With a groaning shout that he seldom expressed when others were around, he reached an intensely powerful peak and surged into her. As she heard his cries, she felt herself matching his movements, not even hearing her own sounds as the waves of sensation, matching his, flooded over her. She arched her back, pushing into him as he pushed against her. They held for a moment, shaking with the convulsions, pushing against each other as though trying to get inside each other and become one, and then they dropped down, panting to catch their breaths. He lay on top of her, the way she liked it, until he thought he must be too heavy on her and rolled over.

"I'm sorry it was so fast," he said.

"I'm not. I was just as ready as you were, maybe more."

They lay together for a while, then she said, "I'd like to take a quick dip in the stream."

"You and your cold-water baths. Do you have any idea how cold that water is? Remember when we stayed with the Losadunai on our Journey here? The hot water that came out of the ground, and the wonderful hot baths they built?" Jondalar said.

"They were wonderful, but cold water makes you feel fresh and tingly. I don't mind cold-water baths," she said.

"And I've become accustomed to them. All right. Let's build up the fire so it's warm when we come back, and go take a cold wash, a quick cold wash."

When glaciers covered the land not far to the north, even at the height of summer the evenings could be cool at latitudes midway between the pole and the equator. They took with them the soft chamois drying skins that had been given to them by their Sharamudoi friends on their Journey, and wrapping themselves in them, ran out to the stream, downriver of their usual water source, but not as far down as the waste basket washing place.

"This water is cold!" Jondalar protested when they ran in.

"Yes, it is," Ayla said, crouching down so that the water reached her neck and covered her shoulders. She splashed cold water on her face, then used her hands to rub herself all over under the water. She ran out, picked up the chamois towel and wrapped it around herself, and dashed toward their shelter. Jondalar was close on her heels. They hovered over the fire and dried off quickly, then hung the wet skins on a peg. They crawled into their sleeping roll and cuddled close to get warm.

Once they felt comfortable again, he whispered in her ear, "If we go slowly, do you think you can be ready again?"

"I think so, if you can."

Jondalar kissed her, searching with his tongue to open her mouth, and she responded in kind. This time, he didn't want to rush it. He wanted to linger over her, explore her body, find all the special places that gave her pleasure, and let her find his. He ran his hand down her arm and felt her cool skin that was beginning to warm, then caressed her breast, feeling the contracted, hardened nipple in his palm. He manipulated it between his thumb and finger, then ducked his head under the cover to take it in his mouth.

There was a noise outside. They both lifted their heads above the covers to listen. There were voices, coming closer, and then the flap over the entry was pushed aside as people walked in. They both lay still, listening. If everyone went right to bed, they could continue their new explorations. Neither one of them felt entirely comfortable sharing Pleasures while other people were sitting nearby fully awake and talking, although some people didn't seem to mind. It wasn't all that unusual, Jondalar realized, and tried to remember what he did when he was younger.

He knew they had grown used to seclusion when they spent a year traveling alone together to his home, but he thought that he was always a man who liked his privacy, even when Zolena was teaching him. Especially when the teaching became more than a donii-woman and her young charge, when they actually became lovers, and he wanted her to be his mate. Then he recognized her voice along with that of his mother and Willamar. The First had come with them to the camp of the Ninth Cave.

"Let me get some water heating for tea," Marthona said. "We can get a light from Jondalar's hearth."

"She knows we're awake," Jondalar whispered to Ayla. "I think we're going to have to get up."

"I think you're right," Ayla said.

"I'll bring you some fire, mother," Jondalar said, pushing the covers back and reaching for his pouch thong.

"Oh, did we wake you?" Marthona said.

"No, mother," he said. "You didn't wake us." He got up and found a long, thin piece of kindling and held it to the fire until it caught, then brought the fire to the main hearth in the shelter.

"Why don't you have some tea with us," his mother said.

"I guess we might as well," he said. He knew that they were all fully aware that they had interrupted the young couple.

"I've been wanting to talk to both of you anyway," Zelandoni said.

"Let me go back and put some warmer clothes on," he said.

Ayla had already dressed herself when Jondalar got back to their small sleeping area. He quickly put on his clothing and both of them went to the main hearth, carrying their personal drinking cups.

"Someone filled up the waterbag," Willamar said. "I think you saved me the trouble, Jondalar."

"Ayla noticed it was empty."

"I saw Wolf and your horses out back of the dwelling, Ayla," Willamar said.

"No one was in camp all day, and a snow leopard tried to get Gray. Whinney and Racer fought him off and killed him, but they broke out of the surround," Jondalar said.

"Wolf found them way in the back of this meadow, near the cliffs and a small stream. It must have been terrible for them. They were even afraid of him and us at first," Ayla said.

"And they wouldn't go anywhere near that surround, so we brought them here," Jondalar said.

"Wolf is watching them now, but we'll have to find some other place to keep the horses," Ayla said. "I was going to find someplace to get rid of that snow leopard carcass tomorrow, and give away the wood from that surround. It would make good firewood."

"There are some good planks on that surround. It's good for more than firewood," Willamar said.

"You can have it all, Willamar. I don't even want to see it again," Ayla said, with a shudder.

"Yes, why don't you decide what to do with that wood, Willamar. There are some good pieces," Jondalar said, thinking to himself that the snow leopard had scared Ayla even more than it did the horses. It made her angry, too. She'd probably burn the surround herself just to get rid of it.

"How do you know it was a snow leopard? They are not usually found around here," Willamar said, "and never in summer, that I can remember."

"When we got to the enclosure, we found the remains of the leopard, but no sign of the horses," Jondalar said. "Ayla found a long fluffy tail of grayish white fur with dark spots and recognized it as belonging to a snow leopard."

"Sounds right to me," Willamar said, "but snow leopards like the highlands and mountains, and go after ibex, chamois, and mouflon, not usually horses."

"Ayla said she thought it was a young one, possibly male," Jondalar said.

"Maybe the mountain feeders are coming down early this year," Marthona said. "If that is true, it could mean a short summer."

"We'd better tell Joharran. It might be wise to plan some major hunts soon, and lay in a good store of meat early. A short summer can mean a long, cold winter," Willamar said.

"And we'd better pick all we can of whatever ripens before any cold weather comes," Marthona said. "Even before it ripens, if necessary. I remember one year many years ago when we collected very little fruit, and had to dig roots out of almost frozen ground."

"I remember that year," Willamar said. "I think it was before Joconan was leader."

"That's right. We weren't even mated yet, but we were interested," Marthona said. "If I remember correctly, there were several bad years around that time."

The First had no recollection of the event. She was probably a very young child at the time. "What did people do?" she asked.

"At first, I don't think anyone believed the summer could be over so fast," Willamar said. "And then everybody started hurrying to lay in food for the winter. It was good that they did. It turned out to be a long cold season."

"People should be warned," the First Among Those Who Served The Great Earth Mother said.

"How can you be sure it means a short summer? It's just one snow leopard," Jondalar said.

Ayla was thinking the same thing, but didn't say anything.

"No one has to be sure," Marthona said. "If people dry extra meat or berries, or store more roots or nuts early, and it doesn't turn cold, it won't hurt anything. It will get used up later. But if we don't have enough, people could go hungry, or worse."

"I told you I wanted to talk to you, Ayla. I've been thinking about when we should start your Donier Tour. I wasn't sure if we should go early, or wait until the end of summer, maybe even after the Second Matrimonial. Now I think we should start as soon as we can. We can warn people of the possibility of a short season at the same time," the First said. "I'm sure the Fourteenth would be more than happy to conduct the Late Matrimonial. I don't think there will be many couples anyway. Just the few who may meet and decide this summer. I know of two couples who aren't sure if they want to mate yet, and one whose Caves are slow in coming to agreements. Do you think you can be ready to go in a few days?"

"I'm sure we can," Ayla said. "And if we leave, I won't have to find another place for the horses."

"Look at the crowd," Danella said, watching the people who had congregated in groups and pockets around the large zelandonia dwelling. She was walking with her mate, Stevadal, the leader of Sun View, and with Joharran and Proleva.

They were watching the crowd who were gathered around the large shelter, watching to see who would come out, not that there wasn't enough to see anyway. The special pole-drag with the seat that had been made for the First had been hitched to the dun-yellow mare of Jondalar's foreign woman, and Lanidar, the young hunter from the Nineteenth Cave with the deformed arm, was holding a rope attached to a halter, a device made of rope that went around the horse's head. He was also holding a lead attached to the young brown stallion, who had a similar pole-drag hitched to him, loaded with bundles. The gray foal was standing near him, as though looking to him for protection from the crowd. The wolf was beside them, sitting on his haunches, watching the entry, too.

"You were still weak and weren't here when they arrived," Stevadal said to his mate. "Do they always get so much attention, Joharran?"

"It's always like that when they load up," Joharran said.

"It's one thing to have the horses around the edges of the Main Camp, and the wolf at Ayla's side; you get used to seeing the animals being friendly to a few people. But when they attach those things they pull, and load them up, when they ask the horses to work and the horses are willing, I think that's what comes as a real surprise," Proleva said.

There was a stir of excitement as people started leaving the summer dwelling. The four of them hurried so they could make their farewells. When Jondalar and Ayla came out, Wolf stood up, but stayed where he was. They were followed by Marthona, Willamar, and Folara, several Zelandonia, and then the First. Joharran was already planning a large hunt, and though Stevadal was a little reluctant to accept their warning of a short summer entirely, he was more than willing to go along on the hunt.

"Will you be coming back here, Ayla?" Danella asked, after she had brushed cheeks. "I've hardly had time to get to know you."

"I don't know. I think that depends on the First," Ayla said.

Danella also brushed Jonayla's cheek with hers. The child was wide awake, held to her mother's hip with her carrying blanket, and seemed to be sensing the excitement in the air. "I wish I'd had the chance to know this little one better, too. She is such a delight, and so pretty."

They walked to where the horses were waiting, and took the lead ropes. "Thank you, Lanidar," Ayla said. "I am grateful for your help with the horses, especially these past few days. They trust you, and feel comfortable around you."

"I've enjoyed it. I like the horses and both of you have done so much for me. If you hadn't asked me to watch them last year, and taught me how to use the spear-thrower, and given me my first one, I never would have learned how to hunt. I'd still be following my mother around picking berries. Now I have some friends, and some status to offer Lanoga, when she's older."

"So you still plan to mate with her," Ayla said.

"Yes, we are making plans," Lanidar said. He stood for a moment, as though he wanted to say more. Finally he did. "I want to thank you and Jondalar for the summer dwelling you built for them. It made such a difference. I have stayed there a few times—well, most nights—to help her with the little ones. Her mother came back two, no three times. Tremeda always asks me for something, but not until the next morning. At night, she can hardly walk. Laramar even spent the night once. I don't think he noticed that I was there. He left in the morning right after he got up."

"How about Bologan? Does he stay there at night and help with the younger children?" Ayla asked.

"Sometimes. He's learning to make barma, and he stays with Laramar whenever he makes it. He's also been practicing with the spear-thrower. I've been showing him. Last summer, he didn't seem interested in hunting, but this year, I think after he saw what I've learned, he wants to show that he can do it."

"Good. I'm glad to hear that. Thank you for telling me about them and yourself," Ayla said. "If we don't come back here after our travels, I will look forward to seeing you next year." She brushed her cheek with his and gave him a hug.

Ayla noticed the crowd's attention was drawn to Whinney's pole-drag. The large woman who was the Zelandoni of the Ninth Cave, and the First Among Those Who Served was walking toward it. Ayla had some idea how nervous she was, but she didn't show it. She walked with an air of confidence, as though it were nothing at all. Jondalar was standing there with a smile, and held out his hand to assist her. Ayla stayed at Whinney's head, to steady her when she became aware of the added load. The woman stepped up on the lower step, and felt it give as the poles bent with her weight, but no more than the normal spring of the wood. Still holding Jondalar's hand for balance, and reassurance, she continued up, then turned around and sat down. Someone had made a very comfortable pad for the seat and backrest, and once she had seated herself, she felt better. She noticed arm supports that she could hold on to once they started moving, which also eased her concerns.

Once Zelandoni was settled, Jondalar went to Ayla, and locked both hands together to make a place for her foot. He stood beside Whinney and helped Ayla, carrying Jonayla, get up on her horse. When she was carrying her baby, it was difficult to jump up in her usual way. The man tied the long lead that was attached to Gray's small halter to the frame of the pole-drag, then went to Racer, who was beside them, and easily climbed on.

Ayla started out, leading the way out of the Main Camp of the Summer Meeting. In spite of all her encumbrances, supporting a rider and hauling a heavy load on the pole-drag, Whinney was not about to let her offspring get in front of her. She was lead mare, and in a herd, the lead mare always led the way. Ayla smiled down at him as Wolf fell in beside her.

Racer and Jondalar fell in behind them. He was glad to be bringing up the rear. It gave him the opportunity to keep an eye on Ayla and her baby, not to mention Zelandoni, to make sure nothing went wrong. Since the First was facing backward, he could smile at her, and if he got close enough, even have a conversation, or at least say a few words.

The Donier waved sedately at the receding Camp of people, and continued to watch them until they were too far to see clearly. She, too, was glad Jondalar was behind her. She was still a little nervous about riding behind the horse, and just watching the place she had been and the landscape passing by was not terribly interesting after the first few miles. It was a bumpy ride, especially when the going was a little rough, but all in all, it was not a bad way to travel, she decided.

Ayla headed back the way they had come until they came to a stream coming down from the north, near a landmark they had discussed the night before; then she stopped. Jondalar, with his long legs, had to do little more than step off the young

stallion and went ahead to help Ayla, but she had already
swung her leg over and slid down.

The horses were compact animals, not ponies, but wild horses
in their natural state were not tall. They were, however, sturdy,
robust, and exceedingly strong, with a rather thick neck capped
by a short mane that stood upright. They had tough hooves that
could run over any land—sharp stones, hard ground, or soft
sand—without needing protection. They both walked back to
Zelandoni and held out hands, which she took to help her balance as she got down.

"It's not difficult to travel like that," the First said. "A little
bumpy, sometimes, but the seat pad eases that and the arm
rests give you something to hang on to. It feels good to stand
up and walk, though." She looked around, then nodded. "From
here we travel north for a while. It's not too far, but it will be
uphill and the climb is steep."

Wolf had raced ahead, following his nose to explore the area,
but returned when they stopped. He loped back into sight as
they were helping Zelandoni back on the pole-drag; then they
got up on their horses. They crossed the stream and followed
it north, upstream on the left bank. Ayla noticed cut marks on
trees and knew the trail had been blazed by someone who had
gone that way before. When she looked closely at one of the
marks used to indicate the path, she could see it was just a
fresh renewal of an older blaze that had darkened and was not
as readily seen; there was an older mark that was partly grown
over and, she thought, another even older one.

Ayla kept the horses at a slow walk so as not to tire them.
Zelandoni talked to Jondalar, who felt like walking and had gotten off Racer and was leading the brown horse along the marked
trail. It was a rigorous uphill climb and as they ascended, the
landscape changed with deciduous trees that became brush that
was interspersed with taller conifers. Wolf kept disappearing
into the woods, then would materialize from another direction.

After about five miles, the trail led them to the entrance of
a large cave high up in the hills of the watershed between The
River and West River. It was well into the afternoon by the
time they reached the place.

"That was much easier than walking up," Zelandoni said

as she stepped down from her seat on the pole-drag, not even waiting for help from Jondalar this time.

"When do you want to go in?" Jondalar asked, going to the entrance and looking in.

"Not until tomorrow," Zelandoni said. "It's a long way in. It will take all day to go in and come back."

"Do you plan to go all the way in?"

"Oh, yes. All the way to the back."

"Then we should probably set up camp here since we'll be staying at least two nights," Jondalar said.

"It's still early. After we set up camp, I think I'll look and see what is growing around here," Ayla said. "I may find something nice for our evening meal."

"I'm sure you will," Jondalar said.

"Do you want to come? We can all go," Ayla said.

"No. I've already seen some outcroppings of flint coming out of the rock walls, and I know there's some inside the cave, too," Jondalar said. "I'm going to take a torch and go in and look."

"What about you, Zelandoni?" Ayla said.

"I don't think so. I want to meditate a bit about this cave, and I want to check the torches and lamps and think about how many we will need. And what else we should bring in with us," the One Who Was First said.

"It looks like a huge cave," Ayla said, stepping inside, peering into the darkness, then looking up at the roof.

Jondalar followed her in. "Look, here's another piece of flint coming out of the wall, right near the entrance. I'm sure there's more deeper inside," he said, his excitement evident from the sound of his voice. "It would be heavy to carry very much of it out, though."

"Is it this high all the way in?" Ayla asked the woman.

"Yes, more or less, except at the very end. This is more than a cave. It is a huge cavern—actually there are many large rooms and tunnels. There are even lower levels, but we won't need to explore them this time. Cave bears have come in here in winter; you can see their wallows and scratchings on the walls," the First said.

"Is it big enough for the horses to walk in?" Ayla asked.

"Maybe with a pole-drag, so we could take some of Jondalar's flint out?"

"I think so," Zelandoni said.

"We'll have to make blaze marks on our way in to make sure we can find our way out," Jondalar said.

"I'm sure Wolf could help us get out if we get turned around," Ayla said.

"Will he come in with us?" Zelandoni asked.

"If I ask him to," Ayla said.

The area had obviously been used before; outside the entrance, the ground in places had been leveled, and several fireplaces set up, evident by the ashes and charcoal, and fire-burned rocks around them. They selected one to reuse, but added stones from another one around the edge, and made a spit for roasting using some forked branches wedged in with stones and greenwood sticks that would be used to impale the food. Jondalar and Ayla unhitched the horses, removed their halters, and led them to an open patch of grass nearby. They could take care of themselves, and would come at the sound of their whistles.

Then they all set up a traveling tent that was bigger than usual. They had put two together and tried it out before they left to make sure it would be comfortable for all of them. They had dried traveling food with them, plus some cooked leftovers from their early meal, but they had also brought some fresh meat from a red deer kill that had been made by Solaban and Rushemar. Leaning the poles from the pole-drags together, Jondalar and Ayla made a high tripod construction fastened at the top from which they suspended rawhide-wrapped packages of food to keep animals from getting it. To leave it in the tent would have been to invite a carnivore in to search for it.

They collected fuel for the fire, mostly deadwood from downed trees, and brush, but also the dried twigs and branches of the coniferous trees, low down on the trunks below the last living ones, dried grasses, and the dried droppings of the animals that ate grass. Ayla started a fire and banked it to make coals for later. They all had a lunch of leftovers, and even Jonayla mouthed the end of a bone after she nursed. Then they went to their separate tasks. Zelandoni began checking the bundles that had been on Racer's pole-drag, looking for torches and lamps, bags of fat for lamp fuel, and lichen, dried mushroom, and various other wick materials. Jondalar picked up his bag of flint-knapping tools, lit a torch from the fire, and went into the large cavern.

Ayla put on her haversack, the Mamutoi carrrying bag that was worn over one shoulder, somewhat softer than Zelandoni backframes, though still roomy. She wore it on her right side along with her quiver with its spear-thrower and spears. She tied her baby high up on her back with the carrying blanket on the other side, but Jonayla could be easily shifted around to sit on her left hip. In front on her left side, she shoved her digging stick under the sturdy leather thong she wore around her waist, while the sheath with her knife hung down the right. Several pouches hung from her waistband, too. She wore her sling around her head, but she carried the stones for her weapon in another pouch fastened to her waist thong. Another pouch was for general things like eating dishes, a fire-starting kit, a small hammerstone, a sewing kit that included thread of various sizes, from fine twists of sinew to sturdy cord that fit through the holes of the larger ivory needles. She also had some coils of larger cordage, and a few other odds and ends. The last object was her medicine bag.

She carried her medicine bag attached to her waist thong. The otter-skin pouch was something she seldom went anywhere without. It was very unusual; even Zelandoni had never seen one like it, although she immediately grasped that it was an object of spiritual power. It was made like the first one Iza, Ayla's Clan mother, had made for her out of a whole otter skin. Instead of cutting through the stomach in the usual way of field-dressing an animal, the throat had been cut not quite all the way around, so that the head, with the brains removed, was attached at the back by a flap of skin. The innards, including the backbone, had been carefully drawn out of the neck opening, while the feet and tail were left in place. Two red-dyed cords were threaded around the neck in opposite directions making the closure secure, and the head, dried and somewhat compressed, was used as a cover flap.

Ayla checked the quiver, which held four spear-darts and her spear-thrower; then she picked up her collecting basket, signaled Wolf to come with her, and started down the trail back the way they had come. When they were approaching the cave, she had seen and evaluated most of the vegetation that was growing along the way and had assessed its uses. It was something she had learned as a girl, and was, by now, second nature. It was an essential practice for people who lived off the land, whose survival depended on what could be hunted or gathered or found as they foraged each day. Ayla always categorized the medicinal as well as the nutritional properties of what she saw. Iza was a medicine woman, and had been determined to teach her knowledge to her adopted daughter along with her own daughter. But Uba was born with memories inherited from her mother, and she only needed to be reminded once or twice to know and understand what her mother showed or explained.

Since Ayla didn't have the Clan memories, Iza discovered it was much more difficult to train her. She had to teach her by rote; only by constant repetition could the girl of the Others be made to remember. But then Ayla surprised Iza because once she did learn, she could think about the medicine she had been taught in a new way. For example, if one medicinal plant wasn't available, she was quick to think of a substitute, or a combination of medicines that would bring together similar properties or actions. She was also very good at diagnosis, at being able to determine what was wrong when someone came with a vague complaint. Although she couldn't explain it, it gave Iza a sense of the differences in the way the Clan and the Others thought.

Many in Brun's clan believed that the girl of the Others who lived in their midst wasn't very smart because she couldn't remember as quickly or as well as any of them. Iza had realized that she wasn't less intelligent, but that she thought differently, in another way. Ayla had come to understand it as well. When people of the Others would make comments about the people of the Clan being none too bright, she would try to explain that they were not less intelligent, but differently intelligent.

Ayla walked back along the trail to a place she distinctly remembered, where the trail through the woods they had been following went over a slight rise and opened out to a field of low-growing grass and brush. She had noticed it when they passed by before, and as she approached it again, she detected the delicious fragrance of ripe strawberries. She untied the carrying blanket and spread it out on the ground, then put Jonayla in the middle of it.

She picked a tiny berry, squashed it a little to bring out the sweet juice and put it in her baby's mouth. Jonayla's expression of surprise and curiosity made Ayla smile. She put a few in her own mouth, gave another to her baby, then looked around to see what she could use to bring some back to camp.

She spied a stand of birch trees nearby and signaled Wolf to watch Jonayla while she went to examine them. When she reached the trees, she was glad to see that some of the thin bark had started to peel. She pulled several wide strips off and brought them back with her. From the sheath that was attached to her waistband she withdrew a new knife, which Jondalar had recently given to her. It was made of a flint blade he had knapped and inserted into a beautiful handle of yellowing old ivory shaped by Solaban with some carvings of horses done by Marsheval. She cut the birch bark into symmetrical pieces, then scored them to make it easier to fold into two small containers with lids. The berries were so tiny, it took a long time to pick enough to give three people a reasonable taste, but the flavor of the wild strawberries was so luscious, it was worth it. From the pouch in which she carried her personal drinking cup and bowl, she always carried a few other items, including coils of twine. Cordage of various sizes was always useful. She used some to tie the birch-bark containers together, then put them in her gathering basket.

Jonayla had fallen asleep, and Ayla covered her with a corner of the soft buckskin carrying blanket, which was getting a little tattered at that end. Wolf was lying beside her, his eyes half closed. When Ayla looked over at him, he thumped his tail on the ground, but stayed close to the newest member of his pack. Ayla got up, picked up the gathering basket, and walked across the grassy field toward the woods on the fringe.

The first thing she saw in a hedge bank were the starlike whorls of the narrow leaves of cleavers, growing abundantly up and through other plants, aided by the tiny hooked bristles that covered them. She pulled out several of the long, trailing stems by the roots, bunching them up together easily because the bristles made them stick together. In that state they could be used as a strainer and for that quality alone they were useful, but they had many other properties, both nutritional and medicinal. The young leaves made a pleasant spring green, the roasted seeds an interesting dark beverage. The pounded herb mixed with fat into an ointment was helpful for women whose breasts were swollen with caked milk.

She was drawn to a sunny dry, grassy place, detected a delightful aromatic fragrance, and looked for the plant that liked to grow there. She quickly found hyssop. It was one of the first plants Iza had taught her about and she remembered the occasion well. It was a woody little shrub that grew something more than a foot high, with narrow evergreen leaves, small and dark green, crowding together along the branching stems. The intense blue flowers, circling the stem among the upper leaves on long spikes, had just started to appear and several bees were buzzing around them. She wondered where the hive was, since honey flavored with hyssop was especially tasty.

She picked several of the stalks, planning to use the flowers for tea, which was not only delicious, but especially good for coughs, hoarseness, and deep chest conditions. The leaves when bruised were also good for relieving cuts and burns, and for reducing bruises. Drinking the tea of the leaves and soaking the limbs in a bath of it were a good treatment for rheumatism. Thinking of that brought a sudden thought of Creb, which made her smile even as it brought a memory of sadness. One of the other medicine women at the Clan Gathering had explained that she also used hyssop for the swelling of the legs caused by retaining too much fluid. Ayla glanced up and saw Wolf still lying beside her sleeping baby, then turned and went more deeply into the woods.

On a shady bank near some spruce trees Ayla spied a patch of woodruff, a little plant about ten inches high with leaves growing in circles, similar to cleavers, but with a weak stem. She bent down on her knees to carefully pick the plant with its leaves and tiny white four-petaled flowers. It had its own delicious scent and made a tasty tea, and Ayla knew the fragrance would grow stronger when it was dried. The leaves could be used for wounds, and when boiled they were good for stomachaches and other internal disorders. It was useful to disguise the sometimes unpleasant smell of other medicines, but she also liked to spread it around her dwelling, and to stuff pillows with it because of its natural perfume.

Not far away she saw another familiar plant that liked shady banks in woods, this one close to two feet high, wood avens. The toothed leaves, shaped somewhat like wide feathers and covered with small hairs, were sparsely scattered along its wiry stems, which branched slightly. The leaves were not uniform in size or shape, depending upon their position on the stem. On the lower branches, the leaves grew on long stalks and had irregular spaces between the leaflets, with the terminal one large and rounder. The intermediate pairs were smaller and somewhat different in shape and size. The higher-up leaves were three-fingered and narrow, the lower ones rounder. The flowers, which rather resembled buttercups, had five bright yellow petals with green sepals between, and seemed too small for such a tall plant. The fruits, which appeared together with the flowers, were more conspicuous and ripened into the small, bristly heads of dark-red burrs.

But Ayla dug down for the rhizome from which the plant grew. She wanted the small, wiry rootlets that had the scent and flavor of cloves. She knew they were good for many things, for stomach problems, including diarrhea, for sore throat, fever, and the stuffiness and mucus of a cold, even for bad breath, but she especially liked to use them as a pleasant, mildly spicy, clove-like seasoning for food.

She saw plants some distance away that she thought at first were a patch of violets, but which on closer inspection turned out to be ground ivy. The flowers were different in shape and grew from the base of leaves that grew in whorls of three or four around the stem. The kidney-shaped leaves with rounded teeth and a network of veins grew opposite each other on long stalks on alternate sides of square stems and stayed green all year, but the color varied from bright to dark green. She knew ground ivy was strongly aromatic and sniffed it to confirm the identity. She had made a thick infusion along with licorice root for coughs, and Iza had used it to soothe inflamed eyes. One Mamut at the Mamutoi Summer Meeting had recommended ground ivy for humming noises in the ears, and for wounds.

The damp ground led to a marshy area and a small stream, and Ayla was delighted to see an extensive stand of cattails, a tall reedlike plant six feet or more in height and among the most useful of all plants. In spring, the young shoots of new roots could be pulled loose from the rootstalk, exposing a tender young core; the new shoots and the core could be eaten raw or cooked lightly. Summer was the season for the green flower stalks growing at the top of the tall stems, which when boiled and gnawed off the stem were deliciously edible. Later they would turn into brown cattails, and the long pollen spike above each cattail would ripen, making the protein-rich yellow pollen available for harvesting. Then the cattail would burst into tufts of white down, which could be used as stuffing for pillows, pads, or diapers, or as tinder for starting fires. Summer was also the season when the tender white sprouts that represented next year's plant growth were growing out of the thick underground rhizome, and with such a large concentration, gathering a few would not harm next year's crop.

The fibrous rootstalk was available all year, even in winter if the ground wasn't frozen or covered with snow. A white, starchy flour could be extracted by pounding it in a shallow, wide bark container of water so that the heavier flour would settle to the bottom while the fibers floated, or the rhizome could be dried and later pounded to remove the fibers, leaving the dry flour. The long, narrow leaves could be woven into mats for sitting upon or could be turned into envelope-like pouches, or waterproof panels, several of which could be made into a temporary shelter, or into baskets or cooking bags that could be filled with roots, stalks, leaves, or fruits, lowered into boiling water, and easily retrieved, and if they cooked long enough, the leaves could also be eaten. The dried stalk from the previous year's growth could be used as a fire drill when spun between the palms against a suitable platform to make fire.

Ayla put her gathering basket down on dry ground, pulled her digging stick, which was made from an antler of a red deer, out of her waistband, and waded into the marsh. With the stick and her hands she dug down through the mud about four inches and pulled out the long rootstalks of several plants. The rest of the plant came with, including the large sprouts attached to the rhizome, and the six-inch-long, nearly inch-thick, cattail-shaped green flower-seed heads, both of which she was planning to cook for their evening meal. She wrapped some cordage around the long cattail stalks, making a bundle that was more easily managed, and headed back to the open field.

She passed an ash tree along the way, and she recalled how prevalent they had been near the home of the Sharamudoi, although there were a few in Wood Valley. She thought about preparing the ash keys the way the Sharamudoi did, but the winged fruit had to be picked when very young, crisp but not stringy, and these were already past their prime. The tree had many medicinal uses, though.

When she returned to the meadow, she was immediately alarmed. Wolf was standing near her baby, staring at some high grass, making a low, menacing growl. Was something wrong?

13

She hurried to find out. When she reached them, she saw that Jonayla was awake and oblivious to the danger the canine seemed to sense, but she had somehow turned herself over from her back to her stomach and was holding herself up on her arms looking around.

Ayla couldn't see what Wolf was looking at, but she heard movement and snuffling sounds. She put down her collecting basket and the bundle of cattails, picked up her baby, and put her on her back with the carrrying blanket. Then she loosened the ties and reached into the special pouch for a couple of stones as she pulled her sling off her head. She couldn't see what was there; no point in using a spear if there was nothing to aim at, but a stone flung hard in the general direction might scare it off.

She cast one stone, followed quickly by another. The second hit something with a *thump* and a yelp. She heard something moving in the grass. Wolf was straining forward, whining softly, eager to go.

"Go ahead, Wolf," she said, making the signal at the same time.

Wolf dashed ahead while Ayla quickly wrapped her sling back around her head, then took her spear-thrower out of its holder, and reached for a spear as she followed behind.

When Ayla reached Wolf, he was facing off with an animal the size of a bear cub, but much more fierce. The dark brown fur with a lighter band that ran along its flanks to the upperside of its bushy tail was the distinctive marking of a wolverine. She had dealt with this largest of the weasel family before, and had seen them drive bigger four-legged hunters away from their own kills. They were nasty, vicious, and fearless predators that often hunted and killed animals much larger than themselves. They could eat more than looked possible for a creature their size, which probably accounted for their other name, "glutton," yet sometimes, it seemed, they slaughtered for pleasure, not hunger, leaving behind what they killed. Wolf was more than ready to defend her and Jonayla, but in any fight a wolverine could inflict serious injury, or worse, if not on a pack, certainly on a solitary wolf. But he wasn't a lone wolf; Ayla was part of Wolf's pack.

With cool deliberation, she fitted a spear onto her thrower, and without hesitation hurled it at the animal, but Jonayla made a crying sound that alerted the wolverine. The creature had seen the woman's swift movement at the last moment, and started to scurry away. It might well have dashed out of her line of fire entirely if it hadn't been distracted by having to watch the wolf. As it was, it moved enough that her spear missed its mark slightly. Though the animal was hurt and bleeding, the sharp tip had only penetrated the hindquarters, which was not immediately fatal. The flint point of her spear was attached to a short, tapering length of wood that fit into the front of a longer shaft, and had separated from the long end of the spear as it was supposed to.

The wolverine ran for cover in the wooded underbrush with the point still embedded in him. Ayla could not leave the injured animal. Though she thought it was mortally wounded, she needed to finish it. It was probably hurting and she didn't want anything to hurt unnecessarily. Besides, wolverines were bad enough under normal circumstances—who knew what kind of damage it might inflict if it was frantic with pain, perhaps to their own camp, which wasn't so far away. In addition, she wanted to retrieve her shaped flint point, to see if it was still usable. And she wanted the fur. She took out another spear, noting where the shaft of the first lay so she could come back for it.

"Find him, Wolf!" she signaled without saying the words, and followed behind.

Wolf, running in front, quickly sniffed out the animal. Not far ahead, Ayla found the canine snarling threateningly at a mass of dark brown fur snarling back from within a coppice of bushes.

Ayla quickly studied the position of the animal, then flung her second spear, hard. It pierced deeply, going all the way through the neck. A spurt of blood declared that an artery was severed. The wolverine stopped snarling and dropped to the ground.

Ayla disengaged the second spear shaft and considered dragging the wolverine back by its tail, but the nap of the fur lay in the other direction and pulling with the grain rather than against it would make it easier to tow the animal across the grass. Then she noticed more wood avens with their strong, wiry stems growing nearby, and yanked them out by the roots. She wrapped the stems around the head and jaws, and hauled the wolverine back to the clearing, stopping to pick up her first spear shaft on the way.

When she reached the place where she had left her gathering basket, Ayla was shaking. She dropped the animal a few feet away, loosened the carrying blanket, and shifted Jonayla around to the front. She hugged her daughter as tears rolled down her cheeks, finally letting her fear and anger out. She was sure the wolverine had been after her baby.

Even with Wolf on guard—and she knew he would have fought to his death for her—the large, vicious weasel could have hurt the healthy young canine, and attacked her child. There were very few animals that would go up against a wolf, especially one as big as Wolf. Most large cats would have backed off, or just passed them by, and those were the predators that were most on her mind. That was the only reason she had left Jonayla, not wanting to disturb her sleeping infant while she went to gather a few greens. After all, Wolf was watching her. Jonayla wasn't out of her sight more than a few moments, just when she was in the marsh getting the cattails. But she hadn't considered a wolverine. She shook her head. There was always more than one kind of predator around.

She nursed the baby for a while, as much to comfort herself as the child, and praised Wolf, petting him with her other hand and talking to him.

"Right now I have to skin out that wolverine. I would rather have killed something we could eat, though I suppose you could eat him, Wolf, but I do want that fur. It's the one thing wolverines are good for. They are mean and vicious and steal food from traps and when meat is drying, even if people are around. If they get inside a shelter, they destroy everything they can and make a big stink, but their fur makes the best trim around a winter hood. Ice doesn't cling to it when you breathe. I think I'll make a hood for Jonayla, and a new one for me, and maybe Jondalar, too. But you don't need one, Wolf. Ice doesn't cling much to your fur, either. Besides, you'd look funny with wolverine fur around your head."

Ayla recalled the wolverine that had been bothering the women of Brun's clan when they were cutting up an animal from a hunt. It kept dashing into their midst and stealing the freshly cut strips of meat they had set out to dry on cords stretched close to the ground. Even when they threw stones, it wasn't deterred for long. Finally some of the men had to go after it. That incident had given her one of the reasons she had used to rationalize her decision when she resolved she would teach herself to hunt with the sling she had secretly learned to use.

Ayla put her baby down on the soft buckskin carrying blanket again, this time on her stomach, since she seemed to like pushing up and looking around. Then she dragged the wolverine carcass a few more paces away and turned it on its back. First she cut out the two flint points that were still embedded in the animal. The one stuck in the hindquarters was still good—she would only need to wash off the blood—but the one she had thrown with such force that it went clear through the neck had a broken tip. She could resharpen it and use it for a knife if not a spear point, but Jondalar could do it better, she thought.

With the new knife he had recently given her, she turned to the wolverine. Starting at the anus, she cut away his genital organs and made a deft cut up toward the stomach but stopped short of the ventral scent gland. One of the ways wolverines marked their territory was to straddle low logs or bushes and rub the strong-smelling material that issued from the gland on them. They also marked territory with urine and feces, but it was the gland that could ruin the fur. It was almost impossible to get the smell out and unbearable to wear the fur around the face if it was contaminated by the gland, whose smell was almost as strong as a skunk's.

Carefully pulling the skin away to avoid cutting through the stomach lining and breaking into the intestines, she cut all the way around the gland, then gingerly feeling with her hand, reached under it with the knife and cut it free. She was going to just toss it toward the woods, then realized that Wolf would likely pick up the odor and go after it, and she didn't want him smelling terrible either. She cautiously picked it up by the edge of the skin and walked back toward the woods where she had killed the creature. There was a fork in a tree above her head and she laid the gland on top of a branch. When she came back, she finished cutting through the skin, making a slit up the stomach to the throat.

Next she went back to where she started, at the anus, and began to slice through both skin and flesh. When she got to the pelvic bone, she felt for the ridge that was between the left and right sides, and cut through the muscle down to the bone. Then forcing the legs apart and again feeling for just the right spot, she exerted more pressure, and split the bone, cutting the stomach membrane just a bit to relieve tension. Now the bowel could be removed with the rest of the innards after she finished cutting the opening. Once this delicate task was accomplished cleanly, she cut the meat up to the breastbone, being careful not to penetrate the intestines.

Cutting through the breastbone would be somewhat more difficult, and would require more than just her stone knife. She needed a hammer. She knew she had a small hammerstone in the same pouch in which she kept her bowl and cup, but she looked around first to see if she could find something else to use. She should have taken the rounded stone out before she started the task of field-dressing the wolverine, but she had been a little disconcerted and forgot. She had some blood on her hands and didn't want to reach into her pouch and leave wolverine blood inside. She saw a stone sticking out of the ground and, using her digging stick, tried to pry it out, but it turned out to be bigger than it seemed. Finally, she wiped her hand on the grass and removed the hammerstone from her pouch.

But she needed more than a stone. If she just hit the back of her new flint knife with a hammerstone, it would chip. She needed something to soften the blow. Then she remembered that a corner of the baby's carrying blanket was getting tattered. She got up and walked back to where the baby was kicking her feet and trying to reach for Wolf. Ayla smiled at her then cut off a piece of soft leather from the ragged corner. When she got back to her chore, she placed the blade of her knife lengthwise along the sternum, put the folded-up soft leather over the back of the blade, then picked up the hammerstone and hit the blade. The knife made a cut, but did not split the bone. She hit it again, and then a third time before she felt the bone give way. Once the breastbone was split open, she continued to cut up to the throat to free the windpipe.

She stretched the rib cage apart, then with her knife she cut the diaphragm, which separated the chest from the stomach, free from the walls. She got a good hold on the slippery windpipe and began to pull out the viscera, using her knife to free them from the backbone. The whole connected package of internal organs fell out on the ground. She turned the wolverine over to let it drain. It was now field dressed.

The process was essentially the same for any animal, small or large. If it was an animal that was intended for food, the next step would be to cool it as quickly as possible, by skinning it, rinsing it with cool water, and if it had been winter, laying it on snow. Many of the internal organs of herbivorous animals like bison or aurochs or any of the various deer, or mammoth or rhinoceros, were edible and quite tasty—the liver, the heart, the kidneys—and some parts were usable. The brains were almost always used for tanning the hides. The intestines could be cleaned out and stuffed with rendered fat, or cut-up pieces of meat, sometimes mixed with blood. Well-washed stomachs and bladders made excellent waterbags, and were good containers for other liquids. They also made effective cooking utensils. Cooking could also be done in a fresh skin spread out and stuffed loosely into a hole dug in the ground, adding water, then boiling it with heated rocks. When used for cooking, stomachs, hides, and all organic materials shrank some because they also cooked, so it was never a good idea to fill them too full of liquid.

Though she knew some people did, she never ate the meat of carnivores. The Clan that raised her didn't like to eat animals that ate meat, and Ayla found it distasteful the few times she had tried it. She thought that if she was really hungry, she might be able to stomach it, but she was sure she'd have to be starving. These days, she didn't even like horsemeat, though it was the favorite of many people. She knew it was because she felt so close to her horses.

It was time to gather up everything and head back to camp. She stashed the spear shafts in the special quiver, along with her spear-thrower, and put the points she had retrieved into the cavity of the wolverine. She put Jonayla on her back with the carrying blanket, then picked up her gathering basket, and tucked the bundled long stems of cattails under one arm. Then grabbing the avens stems still tied to the head of the wolverine, she started out dragging it behind her. She left its innards where they had fallen; one or more of the Mother's creatures would come along and eat them.

When she walked into their camp, both Jondalar and Zelandoni gawked for a moment. "It's looks like you've been busy," Zelandoni said.

"I didn't think you were going hunting," Jondalar said, walking toward her to relieve her of some of her burdens, "especially for a wolverine."

"I didn't plan to," Ayla said, then told him what had happened.

"I wondered why you were taking your weapons with you just to gather some growing things," Zelandoni said. "Now I know."

"Usually women go out in a group. They talk and laugh and sing, and make a lot of noise," Ayla said. "It can be fun, but it also warns animals away."

"I hadn't thought of it that way," Jondalar said, "but you're right. Several women together probably would keep most animals away."

"We always tell young women whenever they leave their homes, to visit, or to pick berries, or gather wood, or whatever, to go with someone," Zelandoni said. "We wouldn't have to tell them to talk and laugh, and make noise. That happens whenever they get together, and it is a measure of safety."

"In the Clan, people don't talk as much, and they don't laugh, but they make rhythms as they walk by banging digging sticks or rocks together," Ayla said, "and sometimes shouting and making other loud noises along with the rhythms. It's not singing, but it feels something like music when you do it."

Jondalar and Zelandoni looked at each other, at a loss for words. Every so often Ayla would make a comment that gave them an insight into her life when she was young and living with the Clan, and how dissimilar her childhood had been from theirs, or anyone they knew. It also gave them an insight into how much the people of the Clan were like themselves— and how much different.

"I want that wolverine fur, Jondalar. I could make a new lining around the face of a hood for you with it, and for me and Jonayla, too, but I need to skin it right away. Would you watch her?" Ayla asked.

"I'll do better than that. I'll help you with it, and we can both keep an eye on her," Jondalar said.

"Why don't you both work on that animal, and I'll watch the baby," Zelandoni said. "It's not like I haven't cared for babies before. And Wolf will help me," she added, looking at the large, usually dangerous animal, "won't you, Wolf?"

Ayla dragged the wolverine to a clearing some distance beyond the boundaries of their camp; she didn't want to invite any passing scavengers into their living area. Then she took her salvaged flint points out of its belly cavity.

"Only one has to be reworked," she said, giving them to Jondalar. "The first spear went into his hindquarters. He saw me make the throw and moved fast. Then Wolf chased him and cornered him in some bushes. I threw the second spear hard, harder than I needed to. That's why the tip broke, but I knew he was going after Jonayla, and I was angry."

"I'm sure you were. I would have been, too. I think my day was much less exciting than yours," Jondalar said as they began skinning the wolverine. He made a cut through the pelt down the left hind leg to the belly cut Ayla had made earlier.

"Did you find flint in the cave today?" Ayla asked, making a similar cut down the left foreleg.

"There's a lot there. It's not the finest quality, but it's serviceable, especially for practice," Jondalar said. "Do you remember

Matagan? The boy who was gored in the leg by the rhino last year? The one whose leg you fixed?"

"Yes. I didn't get a chance to talk to him, but I saw him. He walks with a limp, but he seems to get around fine," she said, making a cut in the right front leg, while Jondalar worked on the right hind leg.

"I talked to him and to his mother and her mate, and some others from their Cave. If it's agreeable to Joharran and the Cave—and I can't imagine why anyone would object—he's going to come and live at the Ninth Cave at the end of summer. I'm going to show him how to knap flint, and see if he has any talent or inclination for it," Jondalar said. Then, looking up, "Do you want to save the feet?"

"Those are sharp claws, but I don't know what I'd use them for," Ayla said.

"You can always trade them. I'm sure they'd make good decorations, for a necklace, or sewn on a tunic. The teeth, too, for that matter. And what do you want to do with this gorgeous tail?" Jondalar said.

"I think I'll keep the tail along with the pelt," Ayla said, "but I may trade the claws and the teeth . . . or maybe I could use a claw as a hole-maker."

They cut off the feet, breaking through the joints and cutting the tendons, then pulled the furry skin off the right side to the backbone, using their hands to tear it off more than their knives. They balled up fists to break through the membrane between the body and the hide as they got to the meatier part of the legs. Then they turned it over and started on the left side.

Talking as they worked, they continued separating the hide from the carcass by pulling and tearing, wanting to make as few cuts in the skin as possible. "Where will Matagan stay? Does he have any family at the Ninth Cave?" Ayla asked.

"No, he doesn't. We haven't decided yet where he should stay."

"He'll miss his home, especially at first. We have a lot of room, Jondalar; he could stay with us," Ayla said.

"I was thinking of that, and was going to ask if you'd mind. We'd have to rearrange some things, give him his own sleeping space, but that might be the best place for him. I could work with him, watch what he does, see how much interest he shows.

No point in making him work at it if he doesn't like it, but I wouldn't mind having an apprentice," Jondalar said. "And with his bad leg, it would be a good skill for him to learn."

They had to use their knives more to release the skin from the backbone and around the shoulders, where it was tight and the membrane between the meat and the skin was not as defined. Then they had to remove the head. With Jondalar holding the animal taut, Ayla found where the head met the neck and swiveled easily, then cut through the meat to the bone. With a twist, a quick break, and a cut through membranes and tendons, the head was off, and the pelt was free.

Jondalar held up the luxuriant hide, and they admired the thick, beautiful fur. With his help, skinning the wolverine had been short work. Ayla recalled the first time that he had helped her cut up a kill, when they were living in the valley where she found her horse, and he was still recovering from being mauled by the lion. It had come as a surprise to her not only that he was willing, but that he was able. Men of the Clan didn't do that kind of work, they didn't have the memories for it, and Ayla still forgot sometimes that Jondalar could help her with tasks that in the Clan had been women's work. She was accustomed to doing it herself and seldom asked for assistance, but she was as grateful now as she had been then for his help.

"I'll give this meat to Wolf," Ayla said, looking down at what was left of the wolverine.

"I was wondering what you were going to do with it," Jondalar said.

"I'll wrap the hide up now, with the head inside, and make us an evening meal. Maybe tonight I can start scraping the skin," Ayla said.

"Do you have to start on it tonight?" Jondalar said.

"I'll need the brains for softening it, and they'll go bad fast if I don't start using them soon. This is such beautiful fur, I don't want to spoil it, especially if it is going to be as cold next winter as Marthona thinks it will."

They started to leave, but Ayla spied a patch of plants with coarsely toothed heart-shaped leaves growing about three feet tall in the rich, moist soil along the stream they were using for water. "Before we go back to camp, I want to collect some of those stinging nettles," Ayla said. "They'll be good to eat tonight."

"They sting," Jondalar said.

"Once they are cooked, they don't sting, and they taste good," Ayla said.

"I know, but I wonder how people first thought of cooking nettles for food. Why would they even think of eating them?" Jondalar said.

"I don't know if we'll ever find out, but I have to find something to pick them with. Some big leaves to cover the hands so the nettles won't sting me." She looked around, then noticed a tall, stiff plant with showy thistle-like purple flower heads, and big heart-shaped soft, downy leaves growing from the ground around the stems. "There's some burdock. Those leaves feel like fine buckskin, they'll work."

"These strawberries are delicious," Zelandoni said. "A perfect ending to a wonderful meal. Thank you, Ayla."

"I didn't do much. The roast came from the hindquarters of a red deer that Solaban and Rushemar gave me before we left. I just made a stone oven and roasted it, and cooked up some cattails and greens."

Zelandoni had watched Ayla dig a hole in the ground with a small shoulder bone that had been shaped and sharpened at one end and used like a trowel. To remove the loose dirt, she transferred it by small shovelfuls onto an old hide; then gathering the ends together, she hauled the hide away. She lined the hole with stones, leaving a space not much bigger than the meat, then built a fire in it until the rocks were hot. From her medicine bag, she took out a pouch and sprinkled some of the contents on the meat; some plants could be both medicinal and flavorful herbs. Then she added some of the tiny rootlets growing out of the wood avens rhizome, which tasted like cloves, along with hyssop and woodruff.

She wrapped the red deer roast in the burdock leaves. Then she covered the hot coals in the bottom of the hole with a layer of dirt so they wouldn't burn the meat, and dropped the leaf-wrapped roast in the little oven. She piled wet grasses on top and more leaves, and covered it all with more dirt to make it airtight. She topped it with a large, flat stone that she had also heated over a fire, and let the roast cook slowly in the residual heat and its own steam.

"It wasn't just cooked meat," Zelandoni insisted. "It was very tender and had a flavor that I wasn't familiar with, but it tasted very good. Where did you learn to cook like that?"

"From Iza. She was the medicine woman of Brun's clan, but she knew more than the healing uses of plants; she knew how they tasted," Ayla said.

"That's exactly how I felt when I first tasted Ayla's cooking," Jondalar said. "The flavors were unfamiliar, but the food was delicious. I've gotten accustomed to it now."

"It was also a smart idea to make those little cooking bags out of the cattail leaves, then putting the nettle greens and the green cattail tops and shoots in them before putting them in the boiling water. It was so easy to pull them out. You didn't have to fish around in the bottom of the pot," the First said. "I'm going to use that idea for making decoctions and tisanes." She saw a frown of puzzlement on Jondalar's face and added a clarification. "Cooking medicines and steeping teas."

"I learned that at the Summer Meeting of the Mamutoi. A woman there was cooking that way, and many of the other women started doing it too," Ayla said.

"I also liked the way you put a little fat on top of the hot flat stone and cooked those cattail flour cakes on it. You put something in them as well, I noticed. What is in that pouch that you use?" the Woman Who Was First asked.

"The ashes of coltsfoot leaves," Ayla said. "They have a salty flavor, especially if you dry them first and then burn them. I like to use sea salt, when I can get it. The Mamutoi traded for it. The Losadunai live near a mountain made of salt, and they mine it. They gave me some before we left, and I still had some when we arrived here, but it's gone now, so I use the ashes of coltsfoot leaves made the way Nezzie did. I used coltsfoot before, but not the ashes."

"You have learned a lot from all your travels, and you have many talents, Ayla. I didn't realize cooking was one of them, but you are very good at it." Ayla didn't quite know what to say. She didn't consider cooking a talent. It was just something you did. She still didn't feel comfortable with direct praise and didn't know if she would ever be, so she didn't respond to it. "Big, flat rocks like that are hard to find. I think I'll keep that one. Since Racer is pulling a pole-drag, I can pack it and won't have to carry it," Ayla said. "Would anyone like some tea?"

"What kind are you making?" Jondalar said.

"I thought I'd start with the cooking water that was used for the nettles and cattails, and add some hyssop," Ayla said, "and maybe woodruff."

"That ought to be interesting," Zelandoni said.

"The water is still warm. It won't take much to heat it up again," she said, putting cooking stones in the fire again.

Then she started putting things away. She carried aurochs fat in a cleaned intestine, and had used some to cook with. To close it, she twisted the end of the intestine, then put it in the stiff rawhide container that held meats and fats. The fat had been rendered in simmering water to a smooth white tallow and was used both for cooking and for light when it got dark, and on this trip when going into a cave. The food left over from their evening meal was wrapped in large leaves, tied with cord, and hung from the tripod of tall poles along with the meat container.

Tallow was the fuel that was put in the shallow stone lamps. Wicks could be any of a number of absorbent materials such as lichen or dried boletus mushrooms. When lit in the absolute dark of a cave, the light shed by the lamps was much brighter than seemed possible. They would be using them in the morning when they went into the nearby cave.

"I'm going to the river to clean our bowls. Would you like me to clean yours, too, Zelandoni?" Ayla asked as she added hot stones to the liquid, watched it boil up in a hiss of steam, then added whole fresh hyssop plants.

"Yes, that would be nice."

When she returned she found her cup filled with hot tea, and Jondalar holding Jonayla, making her laugh with funny sounds and faces. "I think she's hungry," he said.

"She usually is," Ayla said, smiling as she took the child and settled down near the campfire, with her cup of hot tea nearby. Jondalar and Zelandoni had been talking before the baby started fussing, apparently about his mother, and picked up the conversation once Jonayla was content and quiet again.

"I didn't know Marthona all that well when I first became a Zelandoni, though there were always stories about her, stories of her great love for Dalanar," the First said. "Once I became the acolyte of the Zelandoni before me, she told me about the relationships of the woman who was known for her competent leadership of the Ninth Cave so I would understand the situation.

"Her first man, Joconan, had been a powerful leader and she learned a great deal from him, but in the beginning, I was told, she didn't so much love him as admire and respect him. I had the feeling that she almost worshipped him, but that isn't the way Zelandoni put it. She said Marthona worked very hard to please him. He was older, and she was his beautiful young woman, though he had been ready to take on two women at the time, perhaps even more. He hadn't chosen to mate before, and didn't want to wait long to have a family once he decided to have one. More than one mate would give him more assurance that there would be children born to his hearth.

"But Marthona was soon pregnant with Joharran, and when she gave birth to a son, Joconan wasn't in such a hurry anymore. Besides, not long after her son was born, Joconan started to get sick. It wasn't obvious at first and he kept it to himself. Soon he discovered that your mother was more than beautiful, Jondalar; she was also intelligent. She found her own strength in helping him. As he grew weaker, she took on more and more of his responsibilities as leader, and did it so well that when he died, the people of her Cave wanted her to stay on as leader."

"What kind of man was Joconan? You said he was powerful. I think Joharran is a powerful leader. He usually manages to persuade most people to agree with him and do what he wants," Jondalar said. Ayla was fascinated. She had always wanted to know more about Marthona, but she was not a woman to speak much about herself.

"Joharran is a good leader, but not powerful in the same way that Joconan was. He's more like Marthona than her mate. Joconan could be daunting sometimes. He had a very commanding presence. People found it very easy to go along with him, and difficult to oppose him. I think some people were afraid to disagree with him, though he never threatened anyone, that I was aware of. Some people used to say he was the Mother's chosen. People, young men in particular, liked to be around him, and young women threw themselves at him. They say almost all young women wore fringes then, trying to snare him. It's no wonder he waited until he was older before he mated," Zelandoni said.

"Do you think fringes really help a woman snare a man?" Ayla asked.

"I think it depends on the man," the Donier said. "Some people think that when a woman wears a fringe, it suggests her pubic hair, and that she is willing to expose it. If a man is easily excited, or interested in a particular woman, a fringe can arouse him and he'll follow her around until she decides to capture him. But a man like Joconan knew his own mind, and I don't think he was interested in a woman who felt she needed to wear a fringe to attract a man. It was too obvious. Marthona never wore fringes and she never lacked for attention. When Joconan decided he wanted her and was willing to take the young woman from the distant Cave to be trained as a Zelandoni, since they were like sisters, they all agreed. It was the Zelandoni who objected to the double mating. He had promised that the visitor would be returned to her people after she learned the necessary skills."

Ayla knew the Donier was a good storyteller, and she found herself totally enraptured, partly by the storytelling, but more by the story that was being told.

"Joconan was a strong leader. It was under his leadership that the Ninth Cave grew so large. The cave always had the size to accommodate more people than usual, but not many leaders were willing to be responsible for so many," Zelandoni said. "When he died, Marthona was overcome with grief. I think for a time she wanted to follow him to the next world, but she had a child, and Joconan left a big hole in the community. It needed to be filled.

"People started coming to her when they needed the kind of help that a leader provides. Things like resolving disputes, organizing visits to other Caves, travels to Summer Meetings, planning hunts and deciding how much each hunter needed to share with the Cave, both immediately and for the next winter. After Joconan got sick, they got used to coming to Marthona, and she to handling the problems. Their need and her son may be what kept her going. After a while, she became the acknowledged leader, and eventually her grief eased, but she told the Zelandoni before me that she didn't think she would ever mate again. Then Dalanar walked into the Ninth Cave."

"Everyone says that he was the great love of her life," Jondalar said.

"Dalanar was the great love of her life. For him, Marthona could almost have given up her leadership, but not quite. She felt they needed her. And though he loved her as much as she loved him, after a while, he needed something of his own. He wasn't content to sit in her shadow. Unlike you, Jondalar, his skill in working with the stone wasn't enough."

"But he is one of the most skilled I have ever met. His work is known by everyone, and they all acknowledge him as the best. The only flint-knapper I've ever known who can compare with him is Wymez, of the Lion Camp of the Mamutoi. I always wished the two of them could meet," Jondalar said.

"Perhaps, in a sense they have, through you," the large woman said. "Jondalar, you must know that if you aren't already, you will soon be the most renowned flint-knapper of the Zelandonii. Dalanar is a skilled toolmaker, there's no question of that, but he's Lanzadonii now. Anyway, his real skill was always people. He is happy now. He has founded his own Cave, his own people, and though in a way he will always be Zelandonii, his Lanzadonii will someday come into their own.

"And you are the son of his heart, as well as the son of his hearth, Jondalar. He's proud of you. He loves Jerika's daughter, Joplaya, too. He's proud of you both. Although in a hidden place in his heart, he might always love Marthona, he adores Jerika. I think he loves that she looks so exotic, and that she is so little, yet so fierce. That's part of what attracts him. He's so big that next to him she looks half his size, she looks delicate, but she is more than a match for him. She has no desire to be leader; she's happy to let him do it, although I have no doubt that she could. Her strength of will and character are formidable."

"You are certainly right about that, Zelandoni!" he said, with a laugh, one of his big, lusty warm laughs, its spontaneous enthusiasm all the more astonishing because it was unexpected. Jondalar was a serious man, and though he smiled easily, he seldom laughed out loud. When he did, the unreserved exuberance of it came as a surprise.

"Dalanar found someone after he and Marthona severed the knot, but many doubted that she would ever find a man to replace him, would ever love another man in the same way, and she didn't, but she found Willamar. Her love for him is not less than her love for Dalanar, but of a different character, just as her love for Dalanar was not the same as her love for Joconan. Willamar also has a skill with people—that's true of all the men in her life—but he satisfies it as the Trade Master, traveling, making contacts, seeing new and unusual places. He has seen more, learned more, and met more people than anyone, including you, Jondalar. He loves to travel, but even more, he loves coming home and sharing his adventures and knowledge about the people he met. He has established trading networks all across the Zelandonii land and beyond, and has brought back useful news, exciting stories, and unusual objects. He was a tremendous help to Marthona as leader, and now to Joharran. There is no man I respect more. And, of course, her only daughter was born to his hearth. Marthona always wanted a daughter, and your sister, Folara, is a lovely young woman," Zelandoni said.

Ayla understood the feeling. She too had wanted a daughter very much, and she glanced down at her sleeping infant with a strong feeling of love.

"Yes, Folara is beautiful, and also intelligent and fearless," Jondalar said. "When we first arrived, and everyone else was so uneasy about the horses and all, she didn't hesitate. She ran down the path to greet me. I'll never forget that."

"Yes, Folara makes your mother proud, but more, with a daughter one always knows that her children are your own grandchildren. I'm sure she loves the children born to her sons' hearths, but with a daughter there is no doubt. Then, of course, your brother Thonolan was also born to Willamar's hearth and though she played no favorites, he was the one who made her smile. But he made everyone smile. He had a way with people that was even more winning than Willamar's, warm, open friendliness—qualities no one could resist, and he had the same love of travel. I doubt that you would ever have gone on such a long Journey if not for him, Jondalar."

"You're right. I never thought of making a Journey until he decided to go. Visiting the Lanzadonii was far enough for me."

"Why did you decide to go with him?" Zelandoni asked.

"I don't know if I can explain it," Jondalar said. "He was always fun to be around, so I knew it would be easy traveling with him, and he did make the trip sound exciting, but I didn't think we'd go as far as we did. I think part of it was that sometimes he could be a little reckless and I felt a need to look out for him. He was my brother and I think I loved him more than anyone I knew. I knew I'd come home someday, if it was possible, and I felt that if I was with him, he'd come back home with me, eventually. I don't know . . . something was pulling me," Jondalar said. He glanced at Ayla, who had been listening even more intently than Zelandoni.

He didn't know it, but my totem and maybe the Mother pulled him, Ayla thought. He had to come and find me.

"What about Marona? Obviously you didn't feel enough for her to make you want to stay. Did she have anything to do with your decision to go?" the First asked. This was the first time since his return that the Donier had an opportunity to really talk to him about why he took his long Journey, and she was going to take advantage of it. "What would you have done if Thonolan had not decided to make a Journey?"

"I guess I would have gone to the Summer Meeting and probably mated Marona," Jondalar said. "Everyone expected it, and there wasn't anyone I cared for more, at that time." He looked up and smiled at Ayla. "But to be honest, I wasn't thinking about her when I decided to go, I was worried about mother. I think she guessed Thonolan might not return, and I was afraid she might worry that I wouldn't either. I did plan to come back, but you never know. Anything can happen on a Journey, and many things did, but I knew Willamar wouldn't be going away, and she had Folara and Joharran."

"What makes you think Marthona did not expect Thonolan to return?" the First asked.

"It was something that she said to us when we left to go visit Dalanar. Thonolan was the one who noticed it. Mother said 'Good Journey' to him, not 'Until you return,' as she did to me. And remember when we first told mother and Willamar about Thonolan? Willamar said that mother never expected him to return, and as I feared, she was afraid I wouldn't come back either when she found out I had gone with him. She said she was afraid she had lost two sons," Jondalar said.

That was why he couldn't stay with the Sharamudoi when Tholie and Markeno asked us to, Ayla thought. They were so welcoming and I had grown so fond of them during our visit, I wanted to stay, but Jondalar couldn't. Now I know why, and I'm glad we came all the way back. Marthona treats me like a daughter and a friend, and so does Zelandoni. I really like Folara, and Proleva and Joharran, and many others. Not everyone, but most people have been nice.

"Marthona was right," Zelandoni said. "Thonolan was favored with many Gifts, and he was greatly loved. Many people used to say he was a favorite of the Mother. I never like it when people say that, but in his case it was prophetic. The other side of being one of Her favorites is that She can't stand to be separated from them for too long and tends to take Her favorites back early, when they are still young. You were gone so long, I wondered if you were a little too favored, also."

"I didn't think I'd be gone five years," Jondalar said.

"Most people doubted that you or Thonolan would ever return after you were gone two years. Occasionally someone would mention that you and Thonolan had gone on a Journey, but they were already starting to forget you. I wonder if you know how stunned people were when you returned. It wasn't only that you appeared with a foreign woman, and those horses and a wolf," Zelandoni said, and smiled wryly. "It was that you came back at all."

14

"Do you think we should even try to take the horses inside that cave?" Ayla said the next morning.

"Most of the cave has high ceilings, but it is a cave. That means once we get away from the entrance, it's dark, except for the light we bring with us, and the floor is uneven. You have to be careful because it falls down to a lower level in several places. It should be empty now, but bears use it in winter. You can see their wallows and their scratch marks," Zelandoni said.

"Cave bears?" Ayla asked.

"From the size of the scratches, it's very likely that some cave bears have been inside. There are smaller marks, but I don't know if they are from smaller brown bears, or young cave bears," the Donier explained. "It's a very long walk to the primary area, and just as long back. It will take us, or at least it will take me, all day. I haven't done it for some years and, to be honest, I suspect this will be my last time."

"Why don't I take Whinney inside and see how she behaves," Ayla said. "I should take Gray, too. I think I will use halters for both of them."

"And I'll take Racer," Jondalar said. "We can walk them in by themselves, and see how they take to it, before we connect the pole-drags."

Zelandoni watched as they put halters on the horses and walked the animals toward the mouth of the large cave. Wolf followed them. The Donier didn't plan to take them through the entire cavern. She herself didn't know exactly how extensive this sacred site was, though she had a good idea.

It was a massive cavern more than ten miles long made up of a maze of galleries, some connected and some going off in every direction, with three underground levels, and about seven miles to the part she wanted to show them. It would be a long walk, but she had mixed feelings about using the pole-drag. Even if she was slower, she felt she could still make the trek and while it might be easier, she didn't really want to be going into the sacred cavern looking backward.

When Jondalar and Ayla came out, they were shaking their heads and comforting the horses. "I'm sorry," Ayla said. "I think it could be the scent of bears, but both Whinney and Racer were very nervous in that cave. They shied away from the bear wallows, and the darker it got, the more uneasy and agitated they became. I'm sure Wolf will come with us, but the horses don't like it in there."

"I'm sure I can walk it, but it will take more time," Zelandoni said with a feeling of relief. "We will need to bring food and water with us, and warm clothes. It will get cold in there. And plenty of lamps and torches. Also those thick mats you made out of the cattail leaves, in case we want to sit. There will be some rocks or cave growths on the ground, but they will likely be damp and muddy."

Jondalar packed most of their supplies in his sturdy back-frame, but Zelandoni also had one, like Jondalar's though not as big, made of stiff rawhide attached to a frame. The slender round poles of the frame came from the new stems of fast-growing trees, like the variety of willow known as poplar that shot up straight in one season. Jondalar and Zelandoni also had implements and pouches dangling from their waist thongs. Ayla had her haversack, and the rest of her equipment, and of course, Jonayla.

They made one last check of their campsite before they left, with Ayla and Jondalar also trying to make sure the horses would be fine for the day while they were deep in the cavern. They lit one torch to start with from the fire before they banked it down. Then Ayla signaled to Wolf to stay with them, and they started into Mammoth Cavern.

Though the entrance was rather large, it was nothing to the actual size of the cave, but it gave natural light for the first part of the trek and their single torch was sufficient. As they continued into the enormous space, the only thing to be seen was the inside of a huge cave that had obviously been used by bears. Ayla wasn't sure, but she thought that no matter how big a cave was, only one bear at a time would use it in any one season. Many large oval depressions cratered the ground, which implied that bears had used the cave for a very long time, and the bear claw scratches on the walls left no doubt about what had made the bear hollows. Wolf stayed close, walking beside her, occasionally brushing against her leg, which was reassuring.

After they had proceeded deeply enough into the cave that no outside light could be detected and the only way they could find their way was with the light sources they brought with them, Ayla began to feel the cold inside the cave. She had brought a warm tunic with long sleeves and a separate head covering for herself, and an elongated parka with a hood for her infant. She stopped and untied Jonayla's carrying blanket, but as soon as she was away from her mother's warmth, she too noticed the cold and began to fuss. Ayla quickly dressed both of them, and when the baby was close to her mother again and felt her warmth, she settled down. The others also put on warmer clothing.

When they started out again, the First began to sing. Both Ayla and Jondalar looked at her, rather surprised. She started with a soft hum, but after a while, though she didn't use words, her singing grew louder, with greater changes in scale and in pitch, more like tonal exercises. Her voice was so full and rich it seemed to fill the huge cave, and her companions thought it was beautiful.

They had gone about a half mile into the cavern, and were walking three abreast in the large space, with Zelandoni in the middle between Ayla and Jondalar, when the sound of the woman's voice seemed to change, to gain an echoing resonance. Suddenly Wolf surprised them all and joined in with the eerie howl of wolfsong. It sent a shiver down Jondalar's back, and Ayla felt Jonayla squirming and seeming to crawl up her back. Then suddenly without saying a word but still singing, the Donier reached out with both hands and stopped her companions. They looked at her and seeing that she was gazing at the left wall, they also turned to see what was there. That was when they saw the first sign that the cavern was more than a huge, rather frightening, empty grotto that seemed to go on forever.

At first Ayla didn't see anything except some reddish-colored rounded flint outcroppings, which had been a common sight on all the walls. Then, high on the wall, she noticed some black marks that did not look natural. Suddenly her mind made sense of what her eyes were seeing. Painted on the wall in black outline were the shapes of mammoths. As she observed more closely, she saw three mammoths facing left, as though marching out of the cave. Then behind the last one, the outline of the back of a bison, and slightly confused with that, the distinctive shape of the head and back of another mammoth facing right. A short distance and a little higher up was a face with a distinctive beard shape, an eye, two horns, and the hump of another bison. Six animals in all, or enough of an impression to identify that many, had been painted on the wall. Ayla felt a sudden chill and shuddered.

"I've camped in front of this cave many times, and I didn't know these were here. Who made these paintings?" Jondalar asked.

"I don't know," Zelandoni said. "No one knows for sure—the Ancients, the Ancestors. They are not mentioned in the Elder Legends. It is said that long ago there were many more mammoths around here, and woolly rhinoceroses, too. We find many old bones and tusks yellowed with age, but now we rarely see the animals. It has become quite an event when they are spotted, like the rhinoceros those boys tried to kill last year."

"There seemed to be quite a few where the Mamutoi live," Ayla said.

"Yes, we went on a big hunt with them," Jondalar said, and added thoughtfully, "but it is different there. It's much drier and colder. Not as much snow. When we hunted mammoth with the Mamutoi, the wind just blew the snow around the dry grass still standing on the open land. Here, when you see mammoths heading north in a hurry, you know a big snow storm is on the way. The farther north you go, the colder it is, and after a certain distance, it gets drier too. Mammoths flounder in heavy snow, and cave lions know it and follow them. You know the saying 'Never go forth, when mammoths go north,'" Jondalar said. "If the snow doesn't catch you, the lions will."

Since they had stopped, Zelandoni took out a new torch from her backframe and used the one Jondalar was holding to light it. Although his was not burned out yet, it was smoldering and had been giving off a lot of smoke. When she was through, he hit his torch against a stone to knock off the burnt charcoal from the end, which caused it to burn brighter. Ayla felt her baby still squirming a little in the blanket on her back. Jonayla had been sleeping, the darkness and the motion of her mother walking lulling her, but she might be waking, Ayla thought. Once they started walking again, the infant settled down.

"The men of the Clan hunted mammoth," Ayla said. "I went along with the hunters once, not to hunt—women of the Clan don't hunt—but to help dry the meat and carry it back." Then, as an afterthought, she added, "I don't think the people of the Clan would ever come into a cave like this."

"Why not?" Zelandoni asked as they walked deeper into the cave.

"They wouldn't be able to talk, or maybe I should say they couldn't understand each other very well. It's too dark, even with torches," Ayla said. "Besides, it's hard to talk with your hands when you are holding a torch."

The comment made Zelandoni again aware of her odd way of saying certain sounds, as was often the case when Ayla talked about the Clan, especially the differences between them and the Zelandonii. "But they can hear and they have words. You've told me some of their words," she said.

"Yes, they have some words," Ayla said, then continued to explain that to the Clan, the sounds of speech were secondary. They had names for things, but movement and gestures were primary. It wasn't only hand signs; body language was even more important. Where the hands were held when the signs were made; the posture, bearing, and stance of the person communicating; the ages and genders of those both making the signs and to whom they were given; and often barely perceptible indications and expressions, a slight movement of a foot or hand or eyebrow, were all part of their sign language. One couldn't even see it all if one focused only on looking at the face, or just listening to the words.

From an early age, children of the Clan had to learn how to perceive language, not just hear it. As a result, very complex and comprehensive ideas could be expressed with very little obvious movement and even less sound—but not over a great distance or in the dark. That was a major disadvantage. They had to see it. Ayla told them of one old man who had been going blind, who finally gave up and died because he couldn't communicate anymore; he couldn't see what people were saying. Of course, sometimes the Clan did need to speak in the dark, or shout over a distance. That was why they had developed some words, used some sounds, but their use of speaking words was much more limited. "Just as our use of gestures is limited," she said. "People like us, the ones they call 'the Others,' also use posture, expression, and gesture to speak, to communicate, but not as much."

"What do you mean?" Zelandoni said.

"We don't use sign language as consciously, or as expressively, as the Clan. If I make a beckoning gesture," she said, showing the movement as she explained, "most people know it means to 'come.' If I make it quickly or with some agitation, it implies urgency, but from any distance there's usually no way to tell if the urgency is because someone is hurt or if the evening meal is getting cold. When we look at each other and see the shape of the words or the expressions on a face, it tells us more, but even in the dark, or in a fog, or from a distance we can still communicate with almost as much understanding. Even shouting from a great distance, we can explain very complete and difficult ideas. Such ability to speak and understand under almost any circumstance is a real advantage."

"I never thought of it that way," Jondalar said. "When you taught the Mamutoi Lion Camp to 'speak' the Clan way with signs, so Rydag could communicate, everyone, particularly the youngsters, made a game of it, had fun giving each other signals. But when we got to the Summer Meeting, it became more serious when we were around everybody else but wanted to let someone from the Lion Camp know something privately. I remember one time in particular when Talut was telling the Lion

Camp not to say something until later, because there were some people nearby whom he didn't want to know. I don't recall what it was now."

"So, if I understand you correctly, you could say something in words, and at the same time say something else, or clarify some meaning privately, with these hand signs," the One Who Was First said. She had stopped walking, and the frown of concentration indicated that she was thinking of something she felt was important.

"Yes, you could," Ayla said.

"Would it be very difficult to learn this sign language?"

"It would be if you tried to learn it completely, with all of its shades of meaning," Ayla said, "but I taught the Lion Camp a simplified version, the way children are taught at first."

"But it was enough to communicate," Jondalar said. "You could have a conversation . . . well, maybe not about the finer points of some intricate idea."

"Perhaps you should teach the zelandonia this simplified sign language," the First said. "I can see where it could be quite useful, to pass on information, or to clarify a point."

"Or if you ever met one of the Clan and wanted to say something," Jondalar said. "It helped me when we met Guban and Yorga just before we crossed the small glacier."

"Yes, that too," Zelandoni said. "Maybe we could make arrangements for a few teaching sessions next year, at the Summer Meeting. Of course, you could teach the Ninth Cave during the next cold season." She paused again. "You're right, though, it wouldn't work in the dark. So they don't go into caves at all?"

"They go into them; they just don't go in very far. And when they do, they light the way very well. I don't think they would go this far into a cave," Ayla said, "except alone, or for special reasons. The mog-urs sometimes went into deeper caves." Ayla vividly recalled a cave at the Clan Gathering, where she followed some lights and saw the mog-urs, the holy men.

They started walking again, each caught up in private thoughts. After a while Zelandoni started singing again. When they had gone another distance that was not quite as far as it had been to the first paintings on the walls, the sound of Zelandoni's voice developed more resonance, seemed to echo from the walls of the cave, and Wolf began to howl again. The First stopped and this time faced the right wall of the cave. Ayla and Jondalar again saw mammoths, two of them, not painted but engraved, plus a bison, and what appeared to be some strange marks made with fingers in softened clay or something similar.

"I always knew he was a zelandoni," the First said.

"Who?" Jondalar asked, although he thought he knew.

"Wolf, of course. Why do you think he 'sings' when we come to the places where the spirit world is near?"

"The spirit world is near, here in this place?" Jondalar said, looking around and feeling a touch of apprehension.

"Yes, we are very close to the Mother's Sacred Underworld here," said the Spiritual Leader of the Zelandonii.

"Is that why you are sometimes called the Voice of Doni? Because when you sing you can find these places?" Jondalar said.

"It's one reason. It also means that sometimes I speak for the Mother, as when I am the Surrogate of the Original Ancestress, the Original Mother, or when I am the Instrument of She Who Blesses. A Zelandoni, especially One Who Is First, has many names. That's why she usually gives up her personal name when she serves the Mother."

Ayla was listening carefully. She really didn't want to give up her name. It was all she had left of her own people, the name her mother had given her, although she suspected "Ayla" wasn't exactly her original name. It was only as close as the Clan could say it, but it was all she had.

"Can all Zelandonia sing to find these special places?" Jondalar asked.

"They don't all sing, but they all have a 'Voice,' a way to find them."

"Is that why I was asked to make a special sound when we were examining that small cave?" Ayla asked. "I didn't know that would be expected."

"What sound did you make?" Jondalar asked, then smiled. "I'm sure you didn't sing." Then turning to Zelandoni he explained, "She can't sing."

"I roared like Baby. It brought back a nice echo. Jonokol

thought it sounded like there was a lion in the back of that little cave."

"What do you think it would sound like here?" Jondalar asked.

"I don't know. Loud, I suppose," Ayla said. "It doesn't feel like it would be the right sound to make here."

"What would be the right sound, Ayla?" Zelandoni asked. "You will have to be able to make some sound when you are Zelandoni."

She paused to think about it. "I can make the sound of many different birds; maybe I could whistle," Ayla said.

"Yes, she can whistle like a bird, like many birds," Jondalar said. "She is such a good whistler, they will actually come and eat out of her hand."

"Why don't you try it now?" the Donier said.

Ayla thought for a while, then decided on a meadowlark, and brought forth a perfect imitation of a soaring lark. She thought she heard more resonance, but she would have to do it again in another part of the cave, or outside, to be sure. Somewhat after that, the sound of Zelandoni's singing changed again, but in a slightly different way than it had before. The woman motioned to the right and they saw that a new passageway opened out.

"There is a single mammoth down that tunnel, but it's quite a long ways, and I don't think we should take the time to visit it now," the Donier said, and added in an offhand way, "There's nothing in there," indicating another opening almost directly across on the left. She continued singing past another passage opening off to the right. "There's a ceiling in there that brings us close to Her, but it's a long walk in and I think we should wait until we're coming out to decide if we want to visit it." Somewhat farther on she warned them, "Be careful ahead. The passageway changes direction. It makes a sharp turn to the right, and at the turn there is a deep hole that leads to an underground section of the cave, and it's very wet. Perhaps you should follow me now."

"I think I should light another torch, too," Jondalar said. He stopped and took another one out of his backframe, and lit it from the one he was holding. The floor was already wet with small puddles and damp clay. He snuffed out the torch that was nearly burned out and put the stub in a pocket of the pack he was carrying. It had been drilled into him from a young age that one didn't litter the floor of a sacred place unnecessarily.

To rid it of the burned ash, Zelandoni tapped the torch she was holding on a stalagmite that seemed to be growing up from the ground. It burned more brightly immediately. Ayla smiled when she caught sight of Wolf. He brushed against her leg and she scratched behind his ears, a reassuring touch for both of them. Jonayla was moving around again as well. Whenever Ayla stopped walking, the baby noticed it. She would have to feed her soon, but it seemed that they were heading into a more dangerous part of the cave, and she wanted to wait until they were past it. Zelandoni started out again. Ayla followed and Jondalar brought up the rear.

"Watch your footing," the First said, holding the torch high so that the light spread out more. It lit a stone wall on the right, then suddenly the torchlight disappeared, but a glowing light outlined the edge. The floor was very uneven, rocky, and covered with slippery clay. The moisture had seeped through Ayla's footwear, but the soft leather soles gripped well. When she reached the lighted edge of the stone wall and looked around, Ayla saw the large woman standing behind it, and a passageway continuing on to the right.

North, I think we're heading north now, she said to herself. She had been trying to pay attention to the direction they had been moving since they entered the cave. There had been a few slight turns in the passageway, but they had traveled essentially west. This was the first major change in direction. Ayla looked ahead and saw nothing beyond the light of the torch held by Zelandoni, except the dark, yawning intensity found only in subterranean depths. She wondered what else there was farther on in this cavernous hollow.

Jondalar's torchlight preceded him around the edge of the wall that changed their direction. Zelandoni waited until they were all together, including Wolf, before she spoke. "A little ways ahead, where the ground levels out, there are some good stones to sit on. I think we should stop there and have something to eat and fill our small waterbags," she said.

"Yes," Ayla said. "Jonayla has been moving around waking

up, and I need to feed her. I think she would have been awake some time ago, but the darkness and movement while I walked have kept her quiet."

Zelandoni started humming again until they reached a place where the cave resonated with a different sound. She sang with more tonal clarity as they neared a small side tunnel on the left. She stopped where it opened out.

"This is the place," she said.

Ayla was glad to unload her haversack and spear-thrower. They each found a comfortable stone and Ayla took out three mats woven of the cattail leaves to sit upon. As soon as she moved her infant to her breast, Jonayla was more than ready to nurse. Zelandoni took three stone lamps out of her pack, a decorated one made of sandstone, which Ayla had seen her use before, and two of limestone. The stone of all of them had been shaped and abraded into small bowls with straight handles formed on a level with the rim. The First also found the carefully wrapped package of wicking materials and extracted six strips of dried boletus mushroom.

"Ayla, where is that tube of tallow you had?" the woman asked.

"It's in the meat parfleche in Jondalar's backframe." Ayla said.

Jondalar took out the food packages and the large waterbag that he had been carrying on his back as well and brought them to Ayla. He opened the rawhide meat container and she pointed out the intestine stuffed with clean white grease that had been rendered from the hard fat near the kidneys, which gave it a little more body. He brought it to the Donier.

While Jondalar refilled the small waterbags they had with them from the large one he carried, Zelandoni put some globs of the tallow into the bowls of each of the three stone lamps, and used her torch to start them melting. She then laid two dried mushroom wicks into the pools of melted fat in each of the lamps so that more than half the length of each absorbent strip was in the liquid fat, leaving two small ends sticking out over each rim. When she lit them they sputtered a bit, but the heat drew the fat into the wicks and soon they had three

additional sources of light, which made it seem quite bright
inside the absolute darkness of the cave.

Jondalar passed out the food that had been cooked during their morning meal for their trek inside the cave. They
put pieces of roasted red deer meat into their personal eating
bowls, and used their cups for cold broth with cooked vegetables from another waterbag. The long pieces of wild carrots,
small round starchy roots, trimmed thistle stems, shoots from
hops, and wild onions were quite soft and required little chewing; they drank them into their mouths with the soup.

Ayla had also cut up some meat for Wolf. She gave it to him,
then settled down to eat her own food while she finished nursing her daughter. She had noticed that though he explored a
little during their walk, Wolf didn't stray too far. Wolves could
see amazingly well in the dark and sometimes she could see
his eyes from the dark recesses of the cave reflecting even
their small light. Having him nearby gave her a feeling of security. She felt sure that if something unforeseen happened to
make them lose their fire, he would be able to lead them out of
any cave using only his nose. She knew his sense of smell was
so keen, he could easily retrace their steps.

While everyone was quietly eating, Ayla found herself paying attention to her surroundings, using all her senses. The
light from their lamps illuminated only a limited area around
them. The rest of the cave was black, a rich, all-encompassing
darkness that was never found outside even in the deepest
gloom of night, but while she could not see beyond the glow
of the small double fires in each of their lamps, if she tried she
could hear the the soft mutterings of the cave.

She had seen that in some areas the ground and stones were
fairly dry. Others glistened with shimmering wetness as water
from rain and snow and melting runoff seeped slowly, with
inestimable patience, through earth and limestone, accumu-
lating calcareous residue on its way, and depositing it drop by
drop to create the stone icicles above them and the rounded
stumps of stone below. She could hear faint soft drips, both
nearby and farther away. After time beyond measure, they
joined into the pillars and walls and draperies that shaped the
inside of the cave.

There were tiny scrabblings and chitterings of minute creatures, and an almost undetectable movement of air, a muted soughing that she had to strain to perceive. It was almost drowned out by the noise of the breathing of the five living beings who had entered the silent space. She tried to smell the air and opened her mouth to sample it. It felt moist with a slight decaying taste of raw earth and ancient seashells compressed into limestone.

After their meal, Zelandoni said, "There is something I'd like you to see in this small tunnel. We can leave the packs here and pick them up on the way back, but each of us should carry a lamp."

They all found a private corner to pass water and relieve themselves first. Ayla held the baby out to let her pass her wastes as well and cleaned her with some soft fresh moss she had brought with her. Then she used the carrying blanket to hold Jonayla on her hip, picked up one of the limestone lamps, and followed Zelandoni into the passageway that split off toward the left. The woman started singing again. Both Ayla and Jondalar were becoming familiar with the echoing timbre of the tone that informed them they were near a sacred site, a place that was closer to the Other World.

When Zelandoni stopped, she was looking at the right wall. They followed her gaze and saw two mammoths facing each other. Ayla thought they were particularly remarkable, and wondered what all the different placements of mammoths in this cave meant. Since they were created so long ago that no one knew who made them, or even the Cave or the People to whom the artists belonged, it wasn't likely that anyone would know, but she couldn't resist asking.

"Do you know why the mammoths are facing each other, Zelandoni?"

"Some people think they are fighting," the woman said. "What do you think?"

"I don't think so," Ayla said.

"Why not?" the First said.

"They don't look fierce or angry. They seem to be having a meeting," Ayla said.

"What do you think, Jondalar?" Zelandoni asked.

"I don't think they are fighting, or planning to fight," he said. "Maybe they just happened to meet."

"Do you think whoever put them there would go to the trouble if they just happened to meet?" the First asked.

"No, probably not," he said.

"Maybe each mammoth represents the leader of a group of people who are coming together to make a decision about something important," Ayla said. "Or perhaps they have made the decision and this commemorates it."

"That's one of the more interesting ideas I've heard," Zelandoni said.

"But we'll never know for sure, will we?" Jondalar said.

"No, not likely," the One Who Was First said. "But the guesses people make often tell us something about the one doing the guessing."

They waited together in silence; then Ayla had an urge to touch the wall between the mammoths. She reached out with her right hand and placed it palm down on the stone, then closed her eyes and held it there. She felt the hardness of the rock, the cold, rather damp sensation of the limestone. And then she thought she felt something else, like an intensity, a concentration, heat—maybe it was her own body heat warming the stone. She took her hand down and looked at it, then shifted her baby into a slightly different position.

They went back to the main passageway and headed north, with lamps for light now instead of torches. Zelandoni continued using her voice, sometimes humming, sometimes expressing greater tonal qualities, stopping when she thought there was something she wanted them to see. Ayla was particularly fascinated by the mammoth that had lines indicating fur hanging below, but that also had marks, perhaps bear claw marks, scratching through it. She was intrigued by the rhinoceroses. When they got to a place where the song in the large cave grew more resonant, Zelandoni stopped again.

"We have a choice here of which way to go," she said. "I think we should go straight first, then turn around and come back to here and take the left passage for a while. Then turn around and go back the way we've come, and out of the cave. Or we can just take the left way, and then return."

"I think you should decide," Ayla said.

"I think Ayla's right. You have a better sense of the distance, and you know how tired you are," Jondalar said.

"I am a little tired, but I may never come here again," Zelandoni said, "and tomorrow I can rest, either in camp, or with a horse dragging me on that seat thing you made. We'll go straight ahead until we find the next place that could lead us closer to the Mother's Sacred Underworld."

"I think this whole cave is close to Her Underworld," Ayla said, feeling a tingling sensation in the hand that had touched stone.

"You are right, of course, which is why it's more difficult to find the special places," the First said.

"I think this cave could take us all the way to the Other World, even if it's in the middle of the earth," Jondalar said.

"It is true that this cave is much larger and there is much more to see than we will in this one day. We won't go into the caves below at all," Zelandoni said.

"Has anyone ever gotten lost in here?" Jondalar said. "I should think it would be easy enough."

"I don't know. Whenever we come here, we always make sure we have someone with us who is familiar with the cave and knows the way," she said. "Speaking of familiar, I think this is where we usually replenish the fuel in the lamps."

Jondalar got out the fat again and after the woman added some to the stone bowls, she checked the wicks and pulled them out of the oil and up a little higher, making them burn brighter. Before they started out again, she said, "It helps to find which way to go if you can make sounds that resonate, that make a sort of echo. Some people use flutes, so I think your bird whistling should work, Ayla. Why don't you try it."

Ayla felt a little shy about it and wasn't sure which bird to choose. Finally she decided on a skylark and thought about the bird with its dark wings and long tail framed in white, with bold streaks on its breast and a small crest on its head. Skylarks walked rather than hopped and roosted on the ground in well-hidden nests made of grass. When flushed out, a skylark warbled a rather liquid *chirrup,* but its early morning song was

sustained for a long time as it flew high up in the sky. That was
the sound she produced.

In the absolute dark of the deep cave, her perfect rendering
of the song of a skylark had an eerie incongruity, a strangely
inappropriate haunting quality that caused Jondalar to jerk
with a shudder. Zelandoni tried to hide it, but she also felt an
unexpected quiver. Wolf felt it, too, and didn't even try to hide
it. His astonishing howl of wolfsong reverberated throughout the massive enclosed space, and that set Jonayla off. She
began to cry, but Ayla soon understood it wasn't so much a
cry of fear or distress as a loud wail that sounded like an accompaniment to Wolf.

"I knew he belonged to the zelandonia," the First said, then
decided to join in with her rich operatic voice.

Jondalar just stood there, astonished. When the sounds
ended, he laughed rather tentatively, but then Zelandoni also
laughed, which brought out his hearty animated laughter that
Ayla loved and caused her to join in.

"I don't think this cave has heard so much noise in a long
time," said the One Who Was First. "It should please the Mother."

As they started out again, Ayla displayed a virtuosity of bird
calls, and before very long, she thought she detected a change
in the resonance. She stopped to look at the walls, first right,
then on the left, and saw a frieze of three rhinoceroses. The
animals were only outlined in black, but the figures contained
a sense of volume and an accuracy of contour that made them
remarkably realistic. It was the same with the animals that were
engraved. Some of the animals she had seen, especially the
mammoths, were drawn with just an outline of the head and the
distinctive shape of the back, some added two curved lines for
tusks, and others were remarkably complete, showing eyes and
a suggestion of their woolly coats. But even without the tusks
and other additions, the outlines were sufficient to display the
sense of the complete animal.

The drawings made her wonder if the quality of her whistles, and Zelandoni's songs, had really changed in certain regions of the cave, and if some Ancestor had heard or felt the
same qualities there, and marked them with mammoths and
rhinos and other things. It was fascinating to imagine that the

cave itself told people where it should be marked. Or was it the Mother who was telling Her children through the medium of the cave where to look and where to mark? It made her wonder if the sounds they made really led them to places that were closer to the Mother's Underworld. It seemed that they did, but in a small corner of her mind, she had reservations and only wondered.

As they set out again, Ayla continued her bird whistles. Somewhat farther along, she wasn't sure, but felt almost compelled to stop. She didn't see anything at first, but after taking a few more steps she looked on the left side of the broad cave. There she saw a rather remarkable engraved mammoth. It must have been in its full shaggy winter coat. It showed the hair on its forehead, around the eyes and on the face, and down the trunk.

"He looks like a wise old man," Ayla said.

"He's called the 'Old One,'" Zelandoni said, "or sometimes the 'Wise Old One.'"

"He does make me think of an old man who can claim many children to his hearth, and their children, and perhaps theirs," Jondalar said.

Zelandoni started singing again, returning to the opposite wall, and came to more mammoths, many of them, painted in black. "Can you use the counting words and tell me how many mammoths you see?" she said to both Jondalar and Ayla.

They both walked close to the cave wall, holding out their lamps to see better, and made a game of counting out the number word for each one they saw. "There are some facing left, and others facing right," Jondalar said, "and there are two in the middle facing each other again."

"It looks like those two leaders that we saw before have met again and brought some of their herd with them," Ayla said. "I count eleven of them."

"That's what I got, too," Jondalar said.

"That's what most people count," Zelandoni said. "There are a few more animals to see if we continue this way, but they are much farther on, and I don't think we need to visit them this time. Let's go back and take that other passage. I think you'll be quite surprised."

They returned to the place where the two tunnels diverged, and Zelandoni led them into the other one. She hummed or sang softly as they went. They passed by more animals, mostly mammoths, but also a bison, perhaps a lion, Ayla thought, and she noticed more finger markings, some in distinctive shapes; others seemed more random. Suddenly the First raised the tone and timbre of her voice, and slowed her steps. Then she began the familiar words of the Mother's Song.

> Out of the darkness, the chaos of time,
> The whirlwind gave birth to the Mother sublime.
> She woke to Herself knowing life had great worth,
> The dark empty void grieved the Great Mother Earth.
>   The Mother was lonely. She was the only.
>
> From the dust of Her birth She created the other,
> A pale shining friend, a companion, a brother.
> They grew up together, learned to love and to care,
> And when She was ready, they decided to pair.
>   Around Her he'd hover. Her pale shining lover.

Her full, rich voice seemed to fill the entire space and depth of the great cave. Ayla was so moved, she not only felt shivers, she felt her throat constricting and tears forming.

> The dark empty void and the vast barren Earth,
> With anticipation, awaited the birth.
> Life drank from Her blood, it breathed from Her bones.
> It split Her skin open and sundered Her stones.
>   The Mother was giving. Another was living.
>
> Her gushing birth waters filled rivers and seas,
> And flooded the land, giving rise to the trees.
> From each precious drop new grass and leaves grew,
> And lush verdant plants made all the Earth new.
>   Her waters were flowing. New green was growing.
>
> In violent labor spewing fire and strife,
> She struggled in pain to give birth to new life.

Her dried clotted blood turned to red-ochered soil,
But the radiant child made it all worth the toil.
  The Mother's great joy. A bright shining boy.

Mountains rose up spouting flames from their crests,
She nurtured Her son from Her mountainous breasts.
He suckled so hard, the sparks flew so high,
The Mother's hot milk laid a path through the sky.
  His life had begun. She nourished Her son.

He laughed and he played, and he grew big and bright.
He lit up the darkness, the Mother's delight.
She lavished Her love, he grew bright and strong,
But soon he matured, not a child for long.
  Her son was near grown. His mind was his own.

The deep cave seemed to be singing back to the One Who Was First, the rounded shapes and sharp angles of the stone causing slight delays and altering tones so that the sound coming back to their ears was a fugue of strangely beautiful harmony.

For all that her full-bodied voice filled the space with sound, there was something comforting about it to Ayla. She didn't hear every word, every sound—some verses just made her think more deeply about the meaning—but she had the feeling that if she were ever lost, she could hear that voice from almost anywhere. She watched Jonayla, who seemed to be listening hard too. Jondalar and Wolf both seemed to be as enraptured by the sound as she was. As the singing continued, Ayla was lulled into feeling the story but not really hearing every word, until Zelandoni came to the verse that Ayla loved best.

The Great Mother lived with the pain in Her heart,
That She and Her son were forever apart.
She ached for the child that had been denied,
So She quickened once more from the life force inside.
  She was not reconciled. To the loss of Her child.

Ayla always cried at this part. She knew what it was like to lose a son and felt as one with the Great Mother. Like Doni, she also had a son who still lived, but from whom she would be forever apart. She hugged Jonayla to her. She was grateful for her new child, but she would always miss her first one.

> With a thunderous roar Her stones split asunder,
> And from the great cave that opened deep under,
> She birthed once again from Her cavernous room,
> And brought forth the Children of Earth from Her womb.
>   From the Mother forlorn, more children were born.

> Each child was different, some were large and some small,
> Some could walk and some fly, some could swim and some
>   crawl.
> But each form was perfect, each spirit complete,
> Each one was a model whose shape could repeat.
>   The Mother was willing. The green earth was filling.

> All the birds and the fish and the animals born,
> Would not leave the Mother, this time, to mourn.
> Each kind would live near the place of its birth,
> And share the expanse of the Great Mother Earth.
>   Close to Her they would stay. They could not run away.

Both Ayla and Jondalar looked around the great cavern, and caught each other's eye. This was certainly a sacred place. They had never been in such a huge cave and suddenly they both understood the meaning of the sacred-origin story better. There might be others, but this had to be one of the places from which Doni gave birth. They felt they were in the womb of the Earth.

> They all were Her children, they filled Her with pride
> But they used up the life force She carried inside.
> She had enough left for a last innovation,
> A child who'd remember who made the creation.
>   A child who'd respect. And learn to protect.

> First Woman was born full-grown and alive,
> And given the Gifts she would need to survive.

Life was the First Gift, and like Mother Earth,
She woke to herself knowing life had great worth.
  First Woman defined. The first of her kind.

Next was the Gift of Perception, of learning,
The desire to know, the Gift of Discerning,
First Woman was given the knowledge within,
That would help her to live, and pass on to her kin.
  First Woman would know. How to learn, how to grow.

Her life force near gone, the Mother was spent,
To pass on Life's Spirit had been Her intent.
She caused all of Her children to create life anew,
And Woman was blessed to bring forth life, too.
  But Woman was lonely. She was the only.

The Mother remembered Her own loneliness,
The love of Her friend and his hovering caress.
With the last spark remaining, Her labor began,
To share life with Woman, She created First Man.
  Again She was giving. One more was living.

Both Zelandoni and Ayla looked at Jondalar and smiled, and their thoughts were similar. They both felt that he was a perfect example, he could have been First Man, and they were both grateful that Doni had created man to share life with woman. From their expressions, Jondalar could almost guess their thoughts, and felt a little embarrased, though he didn't know why he should.

To Woman and Man the Mother gave birth,
And then for their home, She gave them the Earth,
The water, the land, and all Her creation.
To use them with care was their obligation.
  It was their home to use, but not to abuse.

For the Children of Earth the Mother provided,
The Gifts to survive, and then She decided,

To give them the Gift of Pleasure and sharing,
That honors the Mother with the joy of their pairing.
    The Gifts are well earned, when honor's returned.

The Mother was pleased with the pair She created,
She taught them to love and to care when they mated.
She made them desire to join with each other,
The Gift of their Pleasures came from the Mother.
    Before She was through, Her children loved too.
    Earth's Children were blessed. The Mother could rest.

As she always did when she heard the Mother's Song, Ayla wondered why there were two lines at the end. It felt like something was missing, but maybe Zelandoni was right, it was just to give it finality. Just before the woman finished her song, Wolf felt the need to respond in the way wolves always communicated with each other. While the First continued her singing, he sang his wolfsong, yipping a few times then making a great, loud, eerie, full-throated howl, followed by a second, and a third. The resonances in the cave made it sound like wolves from a great distance were howling back, perhaps from another world. And then Jonayla started her wailing cry that Ayla had come to understand was her way of responding to wolfsong.

In her mind, Zelandoni thought, whether Ayla wants it or not, it seems that her daughter is destined to become part of the zelandonia.

15

As the First continued into the cave, she held her lamp high. For the first time they began to see a ceiling. As they neared the end of the passage, they entered an area where the ceiling was so low, Jondalar's head almost brushed it. The surface was almost, but not quite, level and very light colored, but more than that, it was covered with paintings of animals in black outline. There were mammoths, of course, some almost completely drawn, including their shaggy fur and tusks, and some showing just the distinctive shape of their backs. There were also several horses, one quite large that dominated its space; many bison, wild goats, and goat-antelopes; and a couple of rhinoceroses. There was no order to their placement or size. They faced all directions, and many were painted on top of others, as though they were falling out of the ceiling at random.

Ayla and Jondalar walked around, attempting to see it all and trying to make sense of it. Ayla reached up and brushed her fingertips across the painted ceiling. Her fingers tingled at the uniform roughness of the stone. She looked up and tried to take in the entire ceiling the way a woman of the Clan learned to see an entire scene with a quick glance. Then she closed her eyes. As she moved her hand across the rough ceiling, the stone seemed to disappear, and she felt nothing but empty space. In her mind a picture was forming of real animals in that space coming from a long distance, coming from the spirit world behind the stone ceiling and falling to the Earth. The ones that were larger or more finished had almost reached the world she walked in; the ones that were smaller or barely suggested were still on their way.

Finally she opened her eyes, but looking up made her dizzy. She lowered her lamp and looked down at the damp floor of the cave.

"It's overwhelming," Jondalar said.

"Yes, it is," Zelandoni said.

"I didn't know this was here," he said. "No one talks about it."

"The zelandonia are the only ones who come here, I think. There is a little concern that youngsters might try to look for this and lose their way," the First said. "You know how children love to explore caves. As you noticed, this cave would be very easy to get lost in, but some children have been here. In those passages we passed on the right near the entrance, there are some fingermarks made by children, and someone lifted at least one child up to mark the ceiling with fingers."

"Are we going any farther?" Jondalar asked.

"No, from here, we'll head back," Zelandoni said. "But we can rest here for a while first, and while we're here, I think we should fill the lamps again. We have a long way to go."

Ayla nursed her baby a little, while Jondalar and Zelandoni filled the lamps with more fuel. Then, after a last look, they turned around and began to retrace their steps. Ayla tried to look for the animals they had seen painted and engraved on the walls along the way, but Zelandoni was not constantly singing, and she wasn't making her bird calls, and she was sure she missed some. They reached the junction where the large passage they were in reached the main one, and continued south. It was quite a long walk, it seemed, before they reached the place where they had stopped to eat and then turned in to the place of the two mammoths facing each other.

"Do you want to stop here to rest and have a bite to eat, or go around the sharp bend first?" the First asked.

"I'd rather make the turn first," Jondalar said. "But if you are tired, we can stop here. How do you feel, Ayla?"

"I can stop or I can go on, whatever you want, Zelandoni," she said.

"I am getting tired, but I think I'd like to get past that sink-hole at the turn before we stop," she said. "It will be harder for me to get going once I stop, until I get my legs used to moving again. I'd like to have that hard part past me," the woman said.

Ayla had noticed that Wolf was staying closer to them on the way back, and he was panting a little. Even he was getting tired, and Jonayla was more restless. She had probably done her share of sleeping, but it was still dark and it confused her. Ayla shifted her from her back to her hip, then to the front to let her nurse awhile, then back to her hip. Her haversack was getting heavy on her shoulder, and she wanted to shift it to the other, but it would mean changing everything else around, too, and that would be difficult while they were moving.

They worked their way carefully around the turn, especially after Ayla slipped a little on the wet clay, and then Zelandoni slipped, too. After they made it around the difficult corner, with little effort they reached the turnoff that had been on their right and was now on their left and Zelandoni stopped.

"If you recall," she said, "I told you there is an interesting sacred space down that tunnel. You can go in and see it, if you want. I'll wait here and rest; Ayla can use her bird whistle to find it, I'm sure."

"I don't think I want to," Ayla said. "We've seen so much, I doubt that I could appreciate anything new. You said that you may not come back here again, but if you've been here several times before, I think it's likely I may come back again, especially since it's so close to the Ninth Cave. I'd rather see it with fresh eyes, when I'm not so tired."

"I think that's a wise decision, Ayla," the First said. "I will tell you it's another ceiling, but on this one, the mammoths are painted in red. It will be better to see it with fresh eyes. But I do think we should have a bite to eat and I need to pass water."

Jondalar breathed a sigh of relief, took off his backframe, and found a darkened corner for himself. He had been sipping on his small waterbag all day, and he felt a need to relieve himself, too. He would have gone in the new passage if the women had wanted to go, he thought as he stood hearing his stream on the stone, but he was tired of the marvelous sights of this cave for now, and tired of walking, and just wanted to get out. He didn't even care if they ate right now.

There was a small cup of cold soup waiting for him, and a bone with some meat on it. Wolf was working his way through a small pile of cut-up meat, too. "I think we can chew on the meat as we walk," Ayla said, "but save the bones for Wolf. I'm sure he'd like to gnaw on them while he's resting by a fire."

"We'd all like a fireplace about now," Zelandoni said. "I think we should also put the lamps away when they run out of fat, and use these torches for the rest of the way out." She had a fresh torch ready for each of them.

Jondalar was the first to light his as they walked by the other passage opening out on their left, across from the first painted mammoth they had seen.

"This is the place where you turn in to see the children's fingermarks, and there are other kinds of interesting things on the walls and ceilings, deep in that passageway and its several turnoffs," Zelandoni commented. "No one knows what they mean, though many have made guesses. Many are painted in red, but it's a bit of a walk from here."

Not long afterward, both Ayla and Zelandoni lit their torches. Ahead, where the tunnel split, they took the right-hand path, and Ayla thought she could see the hint of light ahead. When it angled farther to the right, she was sure, but it wasn't bright light, and when they finally walked out of the cave, the sun was setting. They had spent the entire day walking in the great cavern.

Jondalar stacked wood in the pit to light with his torch. Ayla dropped her haversack on the ground near the firepit, and whistled for the horses. She heard a distant whinny, and started in that direction.

"Leave the baby with me," Zelandoni said. "You've been carrying her all day. You both need a rest."

Ayla put the blanket down on the grass, and put Jonayla on it. She seemed glad to kick her feet in freedom, as her mother whistled again and ran toward the answering sounds of horses. She always worried when she was gone from them for some time.

They slept late the next morning, and didn't feel any particular rush to continue their travels, but by midmorning, they were getting restless and anxious to go. Jondalar and Zelandoni discussed what would be the best way to get to the Fifth Cave.

"It's east of here, maybe two days' travel, or three if we take our time. I think if we just headed in that direction, we'd get there," Jondalar said.

"That's true, but I think we are also a little north, and if we just go east, we'll have to cross both North River and The River," Zelandoni said. She picked up a stick and started drawing lines on the ground where it was bare. "If we start out going east but somewhat south, we can reach Summer Camp of the Twenty-ninth Cave before nightfall and stay with them tonight. North River joins The River near South Face of the Twenty-ninth Cave. We can cross The River at the ford between Summer Camp and South Face and have only one river to cross. The River is bigger there, but shallow, and then we can go on toward Reflection Rock and to the Fifth Cave the way we did last year."

Jondalar studied her scratchings on the ground, and while he was looking at them, Zelandoni added another comment. "The trail is fairly well blazed on the trees between here and Summer Camp, and there's a path on the ground the rest of the way."

Jondalar realized that he had been thinking about traveling the way he and Ayla did on their Journey. On horseback, with the bowl boat attached to the end of the travois to float their things across streams, they didn't need to concern themselves much about crossing any but the biggest of rivers. But with the First sitting on the pole-drag Whinney was pulling, it wasn't likely to float, and neither was the one Racer was dragging with all their supplies. Besides, it would be easier to find their way with blazed trails.

"You are right, Zelandoni," he said. "It might not be quite as direct, but your way would make it easier, and likely get us there just as fast or faster."

The trail blazes weren't quite as easy to follow as the First had remembered. It seemed that people hadn't been that way very often lately, but they renewed some of them as they went along so the trail would be easier for the next person to use. It was nearing sunset when they reached the home of Summer Camp, also known as the West Holding of the Twenty-ninth Cave, which was sometimes known as Three Rocks, meaning three separate locations.

The Twenty-ninth Cave had a particularly interesting and

complex social arrangement. They once had been three separate Caves that lived in three different shelters that looked out on the same rich expanse of grassland. Reflection Rock faced north, which would have been a major disadvantage except that what it had to offer more than compensated for its north face. It was a huge cliff, a half mile long, two hundred sixty feet high, with five levels of shelters and a vast potential for observing the surrounding landscape and the animals that migrated through it. And it was a spectacular sight that most people looked upon with awe.

The Cave called South Face was just that: a two-story shelter facing south, situated to get the best of the sunlight in summer and winter, high enough up to get a good view of the open plain. The final Cave was Summer Camp, which was on the west end of the plain and offered among other things a wealth of hazelnuts, which many of the people from the other Caves went to pick in late summer. It was also the one with the closest proximity to a small Sacred Cave, which was called by the people who lived in the vicinity simply Forest Hollow.

Since all three Caves utilized essentially the same hunting and gathering areas, hard feelings were developing, leading to fights. It wasn't that the area couldn't support all three groups— it was not only rich in itself, it was a major migration route— but often two or more gathering groups or hunting parties from different Caves went after the same things at the same time. Two uncoordinated hunts trying for the same migrating small herd interfered with the plans of both, and had been known to chase away the animals, with neither group getting a kill. If all three groups went after them independently, it was worse. All the Zelandonii Caves in the region were being pulled into the disagreements, one way or another, and finally, at the urging of all their neighbors, and after difficult negotiations, the three separate Caves decided to join together and become one Cave in three locations, and to work together to mutually harvest the plenty of their rich plain. Though there were still occasional differences, the unusual arrangement seemed to be working.

Because the Summer Meeting was still going on, not many people were at the West Holding of the Twenty-ninth Cave. Most of those who stayed back were old, or sick, and unable to make the trip, plus the ones who stayed to care for them. In rare cases, someone who was working on something that couldn't be interrupted or could only be done in summer also stayed. Those who were at West Holding welcomed the travelers enthusiastically. They seldom had visitors this early in the summer and since they were coming from the Summer Meeting, they could bring news. In addition, the visitors themselves made news wherever they went: Jondalar, the returned traveler, and his foreign woman and her baby, and the wolf and horses, and the First Among Those Who Served The Great Earth Mother. The travelers were especially welcomed by those who were ill or failing, because of who they were: healers, and at least one who was acknowledged as among the best of their people.

The Ninth Cave had always had a particularly good relationship with the people of Three Rocks who lived at the place called Summer Camp. Jondalar recalled going there when he was a boy to help harvest the nuts that grew so abundantly in their vicinity. Whoever was invited to help harvest always got a share of the nuts, and they didn't invite everyone, but they always invited the other two Caves of Three Rocks, and the Ninth Cave.

A young woman with light blond hair and pale skin stepped out of a dwelling that was under the abri and looked at them with surprise. "What are you doing here?" she said, then caught herself. "I'm sorry, I didn't mean to be so rude. It's just such a surprise to see you here. I wasn't expecting anyone."

Ayla thought she looked sad and drawn; a darkness circled her eyes.

Zelandoni knew it was the acolyte to the Zelandoni of the West Holding of the Twenty-ninth Cave. "Don't be sorry," said the First. "I know we caught you by surprise. I am taking Ayla on her first Donier Tour. Let me introduce you." The First went through an abbreviated version of a formal introduction, then said, "I'm wondering why an acolyte would stay behind. Is someone especially sick here?"

"Perhaps no more than others here who are close to the Next World, but she's my mother," the acolyte said. Zelandoni nodded with understanding.

"If you like, we can take a look at her," the One Who Was First said.

"I'd be grateful if you would, but I didn't want to ask. My Zelandoni seemed to help her when she was here, and she did give me some instructions, but mother seems to have gotten worse. She's much more uncomfortable, but I can't seem to help her," the young acolyte said.

Ayla remembered meeting the Zelandoni of Summer Camp the year before. Since each one of the Caves of Three Rocks had a Zelandoni who lived with them, it had been concluded that if all three had a deciding voice at the meetings of the zelando-nia, it would give the Twenty-ninth Cave too much influence. Therefore, a fourth Donier was chosen to represent the entire group, but she functioned more as a mediator, not only between the three other Zelandonii, but also between the three separate leaders, and it took much time and a great deal of skill with people. The other three Doniers were called colleagues. Ayla remembered the Zelandoni of Summer Camp as a middle-aged woman, nearly as fat as the One Who Was First, but rather than tall, she was quite short and seemed warm and motherly. Her title was Complementary Zelandoni of the West Holding of the Twenty-ninth Cave, although she was a full Zelandoni, and accorded the complete respect and status of her position.

The young acolyte seemed relieved to have someone else look at her mother, especially someone of such prominence and knowledge, but seeing that Jondalar was just beginning to unpack the things from the pole-drag, and Ayla's baby, who was riding her back, seemed to be getting fussy, she said, "You should get yourselves settled in first."

They greeted everyone who was there, put down their sleeping rolls, settled the horses to a good open space of fresh grass, and got Wolf acquainted with the people, or rather, the people familiar with him. Then Zelandoni and Ayla approached the young acolyte.

"What is it that is troubling your mother?" Zelandoni asked.

"I'm not entirely sure. She complains about stomachaches or cramps, and lately she has no appetite," the young woman said. "I can see that she's getting thin, and now she doesn't want to get out of bed. I am very worried."

"That's understandable," Zelandoni said. "Do you want to come with me to see her, Ayla?"

"Yes, but let me ask Jondalar to watch Jonayla first. I just nursed her, so she should be fine."

She took the baby to Jondalar, who was talking to an older man who didn't seem weak or ill. Ayla supposed he was there on behalf of someone else, like the young acolyte. Jondalar was delighted to look after Jonayla, smiling as he reached for her. Jonayla smiled back; she liked being with him.

Ayla returned to the place where the other two women waited and followed them into a dwelling, similar to the ones made by the Ninth Cave, but this one was much smaller than most of those she had seen. It seemed made to house only the woman who occupied the sleeping place within. It wasn't much bigger than the bed, just a small space around it and a small storage and cooking area. Zelandoni alone seemed to fill it, with very little extra room for the two younger women.

"Mother. Mother!" the acolyte said. "There are some people here to see you."

The woman moaned and opened her eyes, and then opened them wider when she saw the large figure of the First.

"Shevola?" she said with a raspy voice.

"I'm here, mother," the acolyte said.

"Why is the First here? Did you send for her?"

"No, mother. She just happened to stop by and said she'd look in on you. Ayla is here, too," Shevola said.

"Ayla? Isn't she Jondalar's foreign woman with the animals?"

"Yes, mother. She brought them with her. If you feel up to it later, you can go out and see them."

"What is your mother's name, Acolyte of the West Holding of the Twenty-ninth Cave?" Zelandoni asked.

"Vashona of Summer Camp, the West Holding of the Twenty-ninth Cave. She was born at Reflection Rock before Three Rocks joined together," the young woman explained, then felt slightly embarrassed, aware that she didn't need to go through so much explanation. This wasn't a formal introduction.

"Would you mind if Ayla examined you, Vashona?" the First asked. "She is a skilled healer. We may not be able to help you, but we'd like to try."

"No," the woman said softly, and it seemed with some hesitation. "I wouldn't mind."

Ayla was a little surprised that the First wanted her to look at the woman. Then it occurred to her that the space inside the dwelling was so cramped, the large woman might have some difficulty getting down to the bedside. She knelt down and looked at the woman. "Are you feeling pain now?" she asked.

Both Vashona and her daughter suddenly became aware of Ayla's unusual way of speaking, her exotic accent.

"Yes."

"Will you show me where it is?"

"It's hard to say. Inside."

"Higher up or lower down?"

"All over."

"May I touch you?"

The woman looked at her daughter, who looked at Zelandoni. "She does need to examine her," the First said.

Vashona nodded agreement and Ayla pulled down the cover and opened her clothing, exposing her stomach. She noted immediately that the woman was bloated. She pressed down on her stomach, starting at the top and working her way down over the rounded bulge. Vashona winced, but didn't cry out. Ayla felt her forehead and around the back of her ears, then bent closer and smelled her breath. Then she sat back on her heels and looked thoughtful.

"Do you get a burning pain in your chest, especially after you eat?" Ayla asked.

"Yes," the woman replied, with a questioning look.

"And does air come out of your mouth with a loud noise in the throat, like when you burp a baby?"

"Yes, but many people belch," Vashona said.

"That's true, but have you spit up blood, too?" Ayla asked.

Vashona frowned. "Sometimes," she said.

"Have you noticed blood or a dark sticky mass in your excrement?"

"Yes," the woman said, almost in a whisper. "More lately. How did you know?"

"She knows from her examination of you," Zelandoni interjected.

"What did you do for your pain?" Ayla asked.

"I did what everybody does for pain. I drank willow-bark tea," Vashona said.

"And do you also drink a lot of peppermint tea?" Ayla said.

Both Vashona and Shevola, her acolyte daughter, looked at the stranger with surprise. "It's her favorite tea," Shevola said.

"Licorice root or anise tea would be better," Ayla said, "and no more willow bark, either, for now. Some people think that since everybody uses it, it can't hurt you. But too much can. It is a medicine, but it's not good for everything, and should not be used too frequently."

"Can you help her?" the acolyte asked.

"I think so. I believe I know what is wrong. It's serious, but there are things that can help. I must tell you, though," Ayla added, "that it could be something even more serious that is much harder to treat, although we can at least relieve some of her pain."

Ayla caught the eye of Zelandoni, who was nodding slightly with a knowing expression on her face.

"What would you suggest for treatment, Ayla?" she asked.

Ayla looked thoughtful for a moment, then said, "Anise or licorice root to settle the stomach. I have some dried in my medicine bag. And I think I have dried sweet flag—although it is so sweet it's almost bitter—which can stop cramping spasms, and there are plenty of dandelions around to cleanse her blood and help her insides work better. I just picked some cleavers, which can purge her body of residues of wastes, and a decoction of the woodruff I just gathered is good for stomachs, can help her feel better all over, and tastes good. I may be able to find more of those wood avens rootlets I used for flavoring the other evening. They're especially good for stomach disorders. But what I'd really like to have is celandine; that would be most helpful. It's a good treatment for either one of her possible problems, especially the more serious one."

The young woman looked at Ayla with awe. The First knew she wasn't Summer Camp's Zelandoni's First Acolyte. She was still new to the zelandonia and had much to learn. And Ayla could still surprise even the First with the depth of her knowledge. She turned to the young acolyte.

"Perhaps you could assist Ayla with the preparation of your

mother's medicine. It will be a way for you to learn how to make it after we leave," Zelandoni said.

"Oh, yes. I'd like to help," the young woman said, then looked at her mother with tenderness in her eyes. "I think this medicine will make you feel much better, mother."

Ayla watched the fire sending flickering sparks up into the night as though trying to reach their twinkling brethren far up in the sky above. It was dark; the moon was young and had already set. No clouds obscured the dazzling display of stars that were so thick, they seemed to be strung together on skeins of light.

Jonayla was asleep in her arms. She had finished nursing some time before, but Ayla was comfortable relaxing by the fire holding her. Jondalar was sitting beside her and a little behind, and she leaned into his chest and the arm that had found its way around her. It had been a busy day and she was tired. There were only nine people of the Cave who had not gone to the Summer Meeting, six who were too sick or weak to make the long walk—she and Zelandoni had looked at all six—and three who had stayed behind to care for them. Some of those who couldn't make the journey were nonetheless well enough to help with certain chores like cooking and gathering food. The older man Jondalar had been talking with earlier, who was staying for a while to help, had gone hunting and brought down a deer, so they put together a venison feast for their guests.

In the morning, Zelandoni took Ayla aside and told her that she had arranged for the young acolyte to show their Sacred Cave to her. "It isn't very big, but it is very difficult. You may have to crawl through parts of it, so wear something to climb through caves and cover your knees. When I was young, I went into it once, but I don't think I could do it now. I think the two of you will manage just fine, but it will be slow going. You are both strong young women, so it shouldn't take too long, but because it is difficult, you might want to consider leaving your baby here." She paused, then added, "I will watch her if you like."

Ayla thought she detected a reluctance in Zelandoni's voice. Taking care of babies could be tiring, and the First might have other plans. "Why don't I ask Jondalar if he will. He likes to spend time with Jonayla."

The two young women started out together, with the young acolyte showing the way. "Should I call you by your full title, a short version of it, or by your name?" Ayla asked after they had walked a short distance. "Different acolytes seem to have different preferences."

"What do people call you?"

"I am Ayla. I know I'm the acolyte of the First, but I still have trouble thinking of myself that way, and 'Ayla' is what everyone calls me. I like it better. My name is the only thing I have left from my real mother, my original people. I don't even know who they were. I don't yet know what I'm going to do when I become a full Zelandoni. I know we're supposed to leave our personal names behind, and I hope when the time comes, I'll be ready to, but I'm not yet."

"Some acolytes are happy to change names, some would rather not, but it all seems to work out. I think I'd like you to call me Shevola. It seems more friendly than 'acolyte.'"

"So please call me Ayla."

They walked farther along a trail through a narrow canyon, dense with woods and brush, between two imposing cliffs, one of which held the stone shelter of the people. Wolf suddenly bounded up. He startled Shevola, who wasn't used to wolves appearing suddenly. Ayla grabbed his head between her hands, roughing up his mane, and laughed.

"So you didn't want to be left behind," she said, actually glad to see him. She turned toward the acolyte. "He always used to follow me everywhere I went, unless I told him not to, until Jonayla was born. Now he's drawn between us when I am in one place and she is in another. He wants to protect both of us, and can't always make up his mind. I thought I'd let him choose this time. I think he must have decided that Jondalar could protect Jonayla well enough and came to find me."

"Your control over animals is amazing, the way they go where you want and do what you want. One gets used to watching you after a while, but it is still hard to believe," Shevola said. "Did you always have these animals?"

"No. Whinney was the first, unless you count the rabbit I found when I was a little girl," Ayla said. "He must have gotten away from some predator, but he was hurt, and didn't, or couldn't, run away when I picked him up. Iza was the healer and I took him back to the cave so she could help him. She was more than surprised, and told me that healers were supposed to help people, not animals, but she helped him anyway. Maybe to see if she could. I suppose the idea that people could help animals must have stayed with me when I saw the little foal. I didn't realize at first that the animal that fell into my pit trap was a nursing mare, and I don't know why I killed the hyenas that were after her baby, except I hate hyenas. But once I did, I felt that the foal had become my responsibility, that I had to try to raise her. I'm glad I did. She has become my friend."

Shevola was fascinated by the story Ayla told with such casualness, as though it were an ordinary thing. "Still, you have control over those animals."

"I don't know if I would call it that. With Whinney, I was like her mother. I took care of her and fed her and we came to understand each other. If you find an animal when it is very young and raise it like a child, you can teach it how to behave, the same way a mother teaches a child how to behave," Ayla tried to explain. "Racer and Gray are her son and daughter, so I was there when they were born."

"What about the wolf?"

"I set some traps for ermines, and when Deegie—she was my friend—and I went to check them, I discovered that something was stealing them from my snares. When I caught sight of a wolf eating one, it made me angry. I killed her with my sling; then I saw that she was a nursing mother. I didn't expect it. It was out of season for a wolf to have cubs young enough to still be nursing, so I backtracked her trail to her den. She was a lone wolf, didn't have a pack to help her, and something must have happened to her mate, too. That's why she was stealing from my snares. There was only one puppy left alive, so I took him back with me. We were living with the Mamutoi then, and Wolf was raised with the children of the Lion Camp. He never knew what it was like to live with wolves; that's why he thinks people are his pack," Ayla said.

"All people?" Shevola asked.

"No, not all people, although he has gotten used to large crowds. Jondalar and I, and now Jonayla, of course—wolves love their young—are his primary pack, but he also counts Marthona and Willamar and Folara among his family, Joharran and Proleva and her children, too. He accepts people I bring to him to sniff, that I introduce to him, as friends, sort of temporary pack members. He ignores everyone else, so long as they offer no harm to those he feels close to, those he considers his pack," Ayla explained to the avidly interested young woman.

"What if someone did try to harm someone that he felt close to?"

"On the Journey Jondalar and I made to get here, we met a woman who was evil, who took pleasure in hurting people. She tried to kill me, but Wolf killed her first."

Shevola felt a chill, a rather delicious thrill, like she did when a good storyteller recounted a scary tale. Although she didn't doubt Ayla—she didn't think the acolyte of the First would make up something like that—nothing like that had ever happened in her life and it just didn't seem quite real. But there was the wolf, and she knew what wolves could do.

As they continued along the trail between the cliffs, they came to an offshoot toward the right that led up to a split in the stone face, an entrance into the cliff. It was a rather steep climb, and when they reached it they found that a large block of stone partially closed off the way in, but there was an opening on both sides of it. The left side was narrow but passable; the right side was much larger, and it was obvious that people had stayed there before. She saw an old pad on the ground with grass stuffing sticking out where the leather was split on one side. Scattered around it was the familiar debitage of chips and pieces left from someone knapping flint to make tools and implements. Bones that someone had chewed on had been thrown at the wall nearby and fallen to the ground at the foot of it. They went inside and walked a ways into the cave. Wolf followed them. Shevola led them to some stones, then slipped off her backframe and propped it up on one.

"It will soon be too dark to see," Shevola said. "It's time to

light our torches. We can leave our packs here, but drink some
water first."

She started looking into her pack for fire-making material,
but Ayla already had her fire-starting kit out, and a small un-
woven basketlike shape made of dried shreds of bark pushed
together. She stuffed it with some of the quick-burning fire-
weed fluff that she liked to use for tinder. Then she withdrew a
piece of iron pyrite, her firestone, with a groove already worn
into it from the many times it had been used, and a fragment of
flint that Jondalar had shaped to fit the groove. Ayla struck the
firestone with the flint and drew off a spark that landed in the
flammable fluff. It sent up a faint curl of smoke. Ayla picked
up the bark basket and began to blow on the tiny ember, which
caused it to flare up in small licks of flame. She blew again,
then set the little basket of fire down on the stone. Shevola had
two torches ready and lit them from the small fire. Once the
torches were burning, Ayla squeezed the bark shreds together
and tamped them down to put out the fire so the bark that was
left could be used again.

"We have a couple of firestones, but I haven't learned to use
them yet," the young acolyte said. "Would you show me how
you do that so fast?"

"Of course. It just takes some practice," Ayla said. "But now
I think you should show me this cave." As the young woman
headed deeper in, Ayla wondered what this Sacred Place would
be like.

Some light was coming from the opening that led outside,
but without the light from the torches, they would not have been
able to see their way, and the floor of the cave was very uneven.
Pieces of the ceiling had fallen down and sections of walls had
collapsed in. They had to walk very carefully, climbing up and
over the stones. Shevola headed for the left wall and then stayed
close to it. She stopped where the cave narrowed and seemed
to divide into two tunnels. The right side was wide and easy to
enter; the other passage on the left side was quite narrow and
got smaller. As one looked into it, it appeared to be a dead end.

"This cave is misleading," Shevola said. "The larger opening is on the right, and you might think that would be the way

to go, but it leads nowhere. A little farther along, it divides again and both ways get smaller and smaller, then just end. Here on the left, the cave gets very narrow and small, but once you get past that, it opens out again." Shevola held up her torch, pointing out a few faint tracings on the left wall. "Those were put there to let someone who isn't familiar with this cave know that this is the way to go, if they understand what the markings mean."

"That would be someone in the zelandonia, I suppose," Ayla said.

"Usually," Shevola said, "but youngsters sometimes like to explore caves, and they often work out what the markings mean." After a short distance, the young woman stopped. "This is a good place to sound your Sacred Voice," she said. "Do you have one yet?"

"I haven't decided," Ayla said. "I've whistled like birds, but I also roared like a lion. Zelandoni sings and it is always beautiful, but when she sang in the mammoth cave, it was unbelievable. What do you do?"

"I sing, too, but not like the First. I'll show you." Shevola made a very high-pitched sound, then dropped to a low pitch, then continuously increased her pitch until she reached the first sound. The cave sang back a muted echo.

"That is remarkable," Ayla said, then whistled her medley of birdsong.

"Now, that is remarkable," Shevola said. "It really sounded like birds. How did you learn to do that?"

"After I left the Clan and before I met Jondalar, I lived in a valley far to the east. I used to feed the birds to entice them to come back, and then started to mimic their calls. Sometimes they would come when I whistled, so I practiced more."

"Did you say you could roar like a lion, too?"

Ayla smiled. "Yes, and whinny like a horse and howl like a wolf, and even laugh like a hyena. I started trying to make the sounds of many animals, because it was fun, and challenging." And something to do when you are alone, and birds and animals are your only company, she thought, but didn't say out loud. Sometimes she avoided mentioning things just because it would have required too much explanation.

"I know some hunters that can make pretty good animal sounds, especially to entice them closer, like the call of a male red deer and the bawl of an aurochs calf, but I've never heard anyone make a lion roar," Shevola said, looking at her with a hopeful expression.

Ayla smiled, took a deep breath, then faced the cave opening and started with a few preliminary grunts, the way a lion did. Then she let out a roar, like one Baby used to make after he reached maturity. It may not have been as loud as the roar of a real lion, but it had all the nuances and intonations and sounded so much like a real lion roar that most people who heard it believed it was real, and therefore believed it was louder than it actually was. Shevola paled for a moment at the sound, and then when the cave echoed it back, she laughed.

"If I had just heard that, I don't think I'd go into that cave. It sounds like there is a cave lion inside."

Just then Wolf decided to respond to Ayla's lion roar with his own sound, and howled his wolfsong. The cave resounded that back as well.

"Is that wolf a Zelandoni?" the young acolyte asked with surprise. "It sounded like he was using a Sacred Voice, too."

"I don't know if he is. To me he's just a wolf, but the First has made similar comments when he does something like that," Ayla said.

They started into the narrowed space, Shevola first, followed by Ayla, and then Wolf. It wasn't long before Ayla was thinking how glad she was that Zelandoni had told her to dress for clambering around in a cave. Not only did the walls of the cave narrow, but the level of the floor rose and the ceiling lowered. It left such a small, cramped space to work their way through, they couldn't even stand upright in it, and in some places they had to get on their knees to go forward. Ayla dropped her torch going through the narrow section, but managed to pick it up before it went out.

Progress became easier after the cave passage opened out, especially when they could walk upright again. Wolf, too, seemed happy to be beyond the tight space, even though he could go through it much more easily, but they still had some narrow sections to squeeze through. In one area the wall on the right had crumbled into a scree slope of loose dirt and small stones, leaving barely a level path on which to put their feet. As they carefully picked their way through, more stones and pebbles rolled down the rather steep grade. They both crowded closer to the opposite wall.

Finally, after another narrowing of the passage, Shevola stopped, held up her torch, and faced the right. Wet, shiny clay partially covered a small section of the wall, but it became part of the medium of expression. A sign was engraved on it, five vertical lines and two horizontal lines, one of which crossed all five of the upright lines, while the second only went about halfway across. Next to the sign was an engraving on stone of a reindeer.

By now Ayla had seen enough paintings, drawings, and engravings to have developed her own sense of those she considered good and those she thought were less well done. In her opinion, this reindeer was not as well made as some others she had seen, but she would never say anything like that to Shevola or the rest of the Cave, or anyone else. It was a private thought. Not so long ago, just the idea of drawing anything resembling an animal on a cave wall was unbelievable. She'd never seen anything like it. Even a partial drawing of a shape that suggested an animal was astonishing and powerful. This one, particularly by the shape of its antlers, she knew was a reindeer.

"Do you know who made this?" Ayla asked.

"There's nothing in the Elder Legends or Histories, except general references that could be alluding to almost any cave markings, but there are a few hints in some of the stories that are told about our Cave that suggest it could have been an ancient one of West Holding, perhaps one of the Founders," Shevola said. "I like to think it was an Ancestor who made them."

As they continued farther into the cave, the difficulties lessened only slightly. The floor was still very rough and the walls had projections that they had to watch out for, but finally at about fifty feet into the long, narrow space, Shevola stopped again. On the left side of the passage they came to a narrow room, and on the right wall of it was a projection near the

ceiling where there was a panel of several engraved figures at
an inclination of about forty-five degrees from the horizontal. It was the principal composition of the cave, consisting
of nine engraved animals on a limited surface area, perhaps
thirty inches by forty-five inches. Again, clay on the wall became part of the medium.

The first image on the left was partly carved in the clay; the
rest were incised into the stone, probably with a flint burin.
Ayla noticed that there was a fine transparent covering of calcite on the frieze, an indication that it was already old. The
projection was colored in part with a natural pigment of black
manganese dioxide. The fragility of the surface was extreme;
a small section of the carbonate material had flaked off, and
another looked as though it would soon detach from the rest
of the rock.

The central subject that dominated the frieze was a magnificent reindeer, with the head raised and antlers extended
back, and carefully drawn details like the single eye, the line
of the mouth, and the nostril. The flank was marked with nine
cuplike holes parallel to the line of its back. Behind it, facing
in the opposite direction, was another partial animal, probably a deer, or perhaps a horse, with another line of engraved
holes running across the body. On the far right of the panel
was a lion, and between them a series of animals, including
horses and a mountain goat. Under the chin of the central figure, and utilizing the same line as the neck of the reindeer, was
the head of a horse. In the lower part of the panel, below the
main figures, was an engraving of another horse. In all, Ayla
used the counting words to tally nine fully or partially drawn
animals.

"This is as far as we need to go," Shevola said. "If we go
straight, it just ends. There is another very tight passage to the
left, but once you get through it there's nothing except another
little room that also just ends. We should go back."

"Do you ever do ceremonies or rituals when you come
here?" Ayla asked as she turned around and stroked the wolf,
who was patiently waiting.

"The ritual was the making of these images," the young acolyte said. "The person who came here, perhaps once, or maybe

more times, was making a ritual Journey. I don't know, it may have been a Zelandoni, or an acolyte becoming a Zelandoni, but I can imagine that it was someone who felt a need to reach for the Spirit World, for the Great Earth Mother. There are some sacred caves that are meant for people to visit and conduct rituals, but I think this was done as a personal Journey. In my mind I try to acknowledge that person when I come here, in my own private way."

"I think you are going to be a very good Zelandoni," Ayla said. "You are already so wise. I was feeling the need to recognize this place and the one who created this work. I think I will follow your advice and reflect on it and the one who made it, and offer a personal thought to Doni, but I would like to do more, perhaps reach for the Spirit World, too. Have you ever touched the walls?"

"No, but you can if you want."

"Will you hold my torch?" Ayla asked.

Shevola took the torch and held both of them high to shed more light in the tiny cramped cave. Ayla reached up with both hands outstretched and put them palm down on the wall, not on any of the engravings or paintings, but near them. One hand felt the wet clay, the other the rough surface of the limestone. Then she closed her eyes. It was the clay surface that first gave her a tingling feeling; then a sense of intensity seemed to flow out of the rock wall. She wasn't sure if it was real or if she was imagining it.

For an instant, her thoughts flashed back to when she was living with the Clan and her trip to the Clan Gathering. She had been the one who was required to make the special drink for the mog-urs. Iza had explained the process to her. She had to chew the hard, dry roots, and spit the mash into the water in the special bowl, then stir it with her finger. She wasn't supposed to swallow any, but she couldn't help it, and she felt the effects. After Creb tasted it, he must have thought it was too strong, and gave each mog-ur less to drink.

After she consumed the women's special drink and danced with them, she went back and found the bowl with some of the white milky liquid still in the bottom. Iza had told her it should never be wasted, and Ayla wasn't sure what to do, so she drank

it, then found herself following the lights of lamps and torches
into a sinuous cave to the special meeting of the mog-urs. The
rest didn't know she was there, but The Mog-ur, her Creb, did.
She never did understand the thoughts and visions that filled
her head that night, but afterward they came back to her sometimes. That's how she was feeling now, not as strongly, but the
same sensation. She lifted her hands from the cave wall, and
felt a shiver of apprehension.

Both young women were quiet as they retraced their steps,
stopping for a moment to look again at the first reindeer and
its accompanying signs. Ayla noticed some curved lines that
she hadn't seen the first time. They continued past the unstable scree slope, which made Ayla shudder, and the narrowed
places until they reached the very difficult passage. This time
Wolf went first. When they reached the place that required
them to proceed ahead on hands and knees, one hand since the
other was holding the light, she saw that her torch was burning
low, and hoped it would last until they were through.

When they reached the other side, Ayla could see light coming in from the opening, and her breasts felt full. She hadn't
thought they were gone that long, but she knew Jonayla needed
feeding or would soon. They hurried to the stones where they
had left their backframes, and both young women reached for
their waterbags. They were thirsty. Ayla dug down in the bottom of her pack for a small bowl she kept for Wolf. She poured
some into the bowl for the animal, then took a drink from the
bag herself. When they were through, and she had repacked
Wolf's bowl, they hoisted their packs to their backs and started
out of the cave to return to the place called Summer Camp of
Three Rocks, the West Holding of the Twenty-ninth Cave of
the Zelandonii.

16

"There's Reflection Rock," Jondalar said. "Did you plan to stop at the South Holding of the Twenty-ninth Cave, Zelandoni?"

The small procession of people, horses, and Wolf came to a halt beside The River and looked up at the impressive limestone cliff divided into five and in some places six levels. Like most of the cliff walls in the region, there were naturally occuring black vertical streaks of manganese that gave a distinctive look to the face of the cliff. They noticed some movement of people who were looking at them but apparently didn't necessarily want to be seen. Ayla recalled that several people of this Cave, including the leader, were quite apprehensive around the horses and Wolf, and she rather hoped they would not be stopping here.

"I'm sure there are a few people there who stayed back from the Summer Meeting," the woman said, "but we visited last year and we didn't get the chance to visit the Fifth Cave. I think we should keep going."

They continued upstream, following the same trail that they had the year before, heading for the place where the river spread out and the water became shallow, and more easily crossed. If they had planned to follow The River, and if they had made arrangements before they left, they could have traveled by raft, a journey that required poling the bulky craft upstream. Or they could walk on the trail beside The River, which would require going due north, then east as the waterway started into a broad bend that curved around in a large loop, and then south and east again, making another large loop that would end up bearing north again, a trek of ten miles. After the large looping S curves, the path along The River proceeded upstream with gentler meandering turns toward the northeast.

There were some small living sites near the northern end of the first loop, but Zelandoni was planning to visit a sizable settlement at the southernmost end of the second loop, the Fifth Cave of the Zelandonii, sometimes known as Old Valley. It was easier to reach Old Valley by going across country rather than following the river around the extensive S curves. Starting from Reflection Rock on the left bank of The River, it was only a little more than three miles east and just slightly north to the large Fifth Cave, though the trail, following the easiest way across the hilly terrain, was not quite so direct.

When they arrived at the shallow crossing of The River, they stopped again. Jondalar got down from Racer's back and scrutinized the river crossing. "It's up to you. Would you rather get down and wade across, or stay on the pole-drag, Zelandoni?"

"I'm not sure. I think both of you would know better," the Donier said.

"What do you think, Ayla?" Jondalar said.

She was in front of the group, using the carrying blanket to secure Jonayla in front of her on the mare's back. She twisted around to look at the others. "The water doesn't look deep, but it could be deeper farther on and you might find yourself sitting in water," Ayla said.

"If I get out and wade, I will certainly get wet. Maybe I'll take a chance and see if this seat keeps me drier," the First said.

Ayla looked around at the sky. "It's a good thing we got here now while the river is low. I think it might rain, or . . . I don't know," she muttered. "It feels like something is coming."

Jondalar remounted his horse and Zelandoni stayed on the pole-drag. As they crossed, the horses were in water up to their bellies and the two on horseback got their lower legs and bare feet wet. The Wolf, who had to swim a short distance, actually got fully soaked, but he shook it off when they reached the opposite bank. But the wooden pole-drag floated a bit, and the water level was low. Except for a few splashes, Zelandoni stayed quite dry.

Once across The River, they followed a well-marked path heading away from the river, traversed up the side of a ridge, over a rounded top where another trail joined it, then down the opposite side and along the customary shortcut. The walking distance to the Fifth Cave of the Zelandonii was about four miles. As they were traveling, the First offered them some information and history about the Fifth Cave. Although Jondalar knew most of it, he still listened attentively; Ayla had heard some of it before, but learned much that was new.

"From the counting word in their name, you know that the Fifth Cave is the third oldest existing group of the Zelandonii," the Donier began, speaking in her instructional voice, which carried quite a distance though it was not excessively loud. "Only the Second and Third Caves are older. While the Histories and Elder Legends speak of the First Cave, no one seems to know what happened to the Fourth. Most people assume that some illness reduced its numbers until they were less than viable, or a difference of opinion among a number of the people caused some to leave, with the remaining ones then joining another Cave. Such an occurrence is not uncommon, as the missing counting words in a naming and tallying of all the various Caves will attest. Most Caves have Histories of assimilating members or joining other groups, but none has any stories about the Fourth Cave. Some people imagine that a terrible tragedy befell the Fourth Cave, which caused the death of them all."

The First Among Those Who Serve The Great Earth Mother continued to lecture as they proceeded, thinking that Ayla in particular needed to know as much as possible about her adopted people, especially since she would someday have to teach the younger ones of the Ninth Cave. Ayla found herself listening with fascination, watching the trail they were following only peripherally, guiding Whinney unconsciously with the pressure of a knee or a shift in her position as the woman behind her spoke, and though facing backward, filled the surrounding air with her voice.

The home of the Fifth Cave was a comfortable little valley between limestone cliffs below a high promontory with a clear stream running down the middle, which began in a lively spring and ended where it debouched straight into The River several hundred feet away. The high cliffs rearing up on both sides of the small stream offered nine rock shelters of various sizes, some rather high up on the walls, but not all of them had people living in them. The valley had been in use for as long as anyone could remember, which is why it was called Old Valley. The Histories and Elder Legends of the Zelandonii affirmed that many Caves had ties to the Fifth Cave.

Each one of the Caves in the Zelandonii territory was essentially independent, and could take care of its own basic needs. Members could hunt and fish, gather foods, and collect materials to make whatever they needed, not just to survive, but to live well. They were the most advanced society not only in their region, but perhaps in all the world in their time. The Caves cooperated with each other because it was in their best interests to do so. They sometimes went on group hunting expeditions, especially for larger animals like mammoth and megaceros, the giant deer, or for dangerous animals like the cave lion, and shared the dangers and the results. They sometimes gathered produce in large parties and were able to collect an abundance in a short ripening season before the food was past its prime.

They negotiated for mates from the larger group because they needed a more extensive pool of people to draw from than their own small Cave, and they exchanged goods not because they needed to, but because they liked what other people made. Their products were similar enough to be understandable, but offered interest and diversity, and when things went wrong, it was good to have friends or relatives they could turn to for help. Living in a periglacial region, an area that skirted glaciers, with exceedingly cold winters, things could go wrong.

Each Cave tended to specialize in various ways, partly as a result of where each one lived, and partly because certain people developed ways to do certain things especially well and passed on the knowledge to their closest kith and kin.

For example, the Third Cave were considered to have the best hunters, primarily because they lived high up on a cliff at the confluence of two rivers with large grassy meadows on the floodplains below that attracted most varieties of game as they migrated through, and they were usually the first to see them. Because they were considered the best, they were continually perfecting their hunting and observing skills. If it was a large herd, they would signal nearby Caves for a group hunt. But if it was only a few animals, their hunters often went out themselves, though they often shared their bounty with neighboring Caves, especially during gatherings or festivals.

The people of the Fourteenth Cave were known as exceptional fishers. Every Cave fished, but they specialized in catching fish. They had a fairly healthy stream running through their small valley that began many miles upstream and was home to several different varieties of fish, in addition to being a spawning creek for salmon in season. They also fished The River and used many different techniques. They developed weirs to trap fish, and were very skilled in spear-fishing, net fishing, and the use of fish gouges, a kind of hook that was straight and pointed at both ends.

The shelter of the Eleventh Cave was close to The River. They had access to trees, and had developed the skills to make rafts, which had been passed down and improved through several generations. They poled the rafts up and down The River, hauling their own goods as well as goods for the other Caves, thereby acquiring benefits and obligations from their neighbors, which could be traded for other goods and services.

The Ninth Cave was located next to Down River, a site that was used as a gathering place by the local artisans and craftspeople. As a result, many of those people moved to the Ninth Cave, which partly accounted for the fact that so many people lived there. If someone wanted a special tool or knife made, or rawhide panels that were used for constructing dwellings, or new cordage, whether heavy rope or strong twine or fine thread, or clothing or tents or the materials to make them, or wooden or woven bowls or cups, or a painting or carving of a horse or bison or any other animal, or any number of other creative things, they went to the Ninth Cave.

The Fifth Cave, on the other hand, thought of themselves as being very self-sufficient in every way. They counted themselves as having extremely skilled hunters, fishers, and artisans of every kind. They even made their own rafts, and claimed to be the Cave that invented them in the first place, though that claim was disputed by the Eleventh. Their Doniers were well respected and had always been. Several of the stone shelters in the small valley were decorated with paintings and carvings of animals, some in high relief.

However, most of the Zelandonii thought of the Fifth Cave as specializing in the making of jewelry and beads as personal decorations and ornamentation. When someone wanted a new necklace, or various kinds of beads to sew on clothing, they often went to the Fifth Cave. They were especially skilled at making beads out of ivory, and each single bead was a long and painstaking process to make. They also carved holes through the roots of the teeth of various animals for pendants and distinctive beads—fox teeth and red deer canines were favorites—and they managed to acquire seashells of various kinds from both the Great Waters of the West and the large Southern Sea.

When the travelers from the Ninth Cave reached the Fifth Cave's little valley, they were quickly surrounded. People were coming out of several stone shelters in the cliffs on both sides of the small river. Several were standing in front of the large opening of a shelter that faced southwest. Others emerged from another shelter just to the north of it, and on the other side of the valley more people were coming out of shelters. The travelers were surprised to find so many people, more than they expected. Either a large proportion of the Cave had decided not to go to any Summer Meeting, or they had come back early.

The people approached with curiosity, but none came too close. They were held back a little by fear and awe. Jondalar was a familiar figure to all the Zelandonii, except for the younger people who had come of age while he was gone. And everyone knew about his return from a long Journey and had seen the woman and animals he had brought with him, but the unusual procession of Jondalar and the foreign woman with her baby, the wolf, three horses, including a foal, and the One Who Was First sitting on a seat dragged by one of the horses made quite an impression. To many there was something eerily supernatural about animals behaving so docilely when they should be running away.

One of the first who saw them had run to tell the Zelandoni of the Fifth Cave, who was waiting for them. The man, who was among those in front of the shelter on the right, approached, smiling cordially. He was middle-aged, but on the young side of the range. He had long brown hair pulled back and wrapped around his head in a complicated coiffure, and the tattoos on his face that announced his important position were more elaborate than they needed to be, but he wasn't the only Zelandoni who had embellished his tattoos. There was a soft roundness about him, and the fleshiness of his face tended to make his eyes look small and gave him an air of shrewd cleverness, which wasn't entirely incorrect.

In the beginning, Zelandoni had reserved judgment of him, not sure if she could trust him, not even sure if she liked him. He could argue his opinions very strongly, even when they were opposed to hers, but he had proven his reliability and loyalty, and in meetings and councils, the First came to rely on the shrewdness of his advice. Ayla was still withholding her complete trust of him, but when she learned that Zelandoni thought well of him, she was more inclined to give him credence.

Another man followed him out of the stone shelter, one whom Ayla had distrusted the first time she met him. Madroman had been born to the Ninth Cave, though later he moved to the Fifth Cave, and obviously became an acolyte from that group. The Zelandoni of the Fifth Cave had several acolytes, and though Madroman may have been among the oldest of his acolytes, he was not the one ranked as first. But Jondalar was surprised to discover that he had been accepted into the zelandonia at all.

In his youth, when Jondalar had become enamored of the First, then an acolyte named Zolena, another young man, called Ladroman, had wanted Zolena for his donii-woman. He was

jealous of Jondalar and had spied on them, and heard Jondalar trying to persuade Zolena to become his mate. It was the
donii-women who was supposed to keep such entanglements in
check. The young men they were instructing were considered
too vulnerable to the knowing older women. But Jondalar was
tall and mature for his age, incredibly handsome and charismatic with striking blue eyes, and so appealing that she didn't
reject him immediately.

Ladroman told the zelandonia and everyone else that they
were breaking taboos. Jondalar got into a fight with him about
it, and for spying on them, which became a big scandal, not
only because of the liaison but because Jondalar knocked out
Ladroman's two front teeth in the confrontation. They were
permanent teeth that could never grow in again. It not only
left him talking with a lisp, but made normal biting difficult
for him. Jondalar's mother, who was leader of the Ninth Cave
at the time, had had to pay heavy compensation for her son's
behavior.

As a result of the whole affair, she decided to send him to live
with Dalanar, the man to whom she was mated when Jondalar was born, the man of his hearth. Although Jondalar was
upset at first, eventually he was thankful. The punishment—
as he interpreted it, although his mother thought of it more as
a cooling-off period until things settled down and people had
time to forget about it—gave the young man the chance to get
to know Dalanar. Jondalar resembled the older man to a remarkable degree, not only physically, but in certain aptitudes,
particularly flint-knapping. Dalanar taught him the craft,
along with his close cousin, Joplaya, the beautiful daughter of
Dalanar's new mate, Jerika, who was the most exotic person
Jondalar had ever met. Jerika's mother, Ahnlay, gave birth to
her during the long Journey she had made with her mate, and
had died before she reached the flint mine Dalanar had discovered. But her mother's mate, Hochaman, had lived to fulfill
his dream.

Hochaman was a Great Traveler who had walked all the
way from the Endless Seas of the East to the Great Waters
of the West, although Dalanar had walked for him at the end,

carrying him on his shoulders. When they returned Jondalar home to the Ninth Cave a few years later, Dalanar's Cave made a special trip a little farther west just so the diminutive old man, Hochaman, could see the Great Waters once more, again riding on the shoulders of Dalanar. He walked the last few feet himself and at the edge of the ocean dropped to his knees to let the waves wash over him and to taste the salt. Jondalar grew to love all of the Lanzadonii, and became grateful that he'd been sent away from home, because he discovered he had a second home.

Jondalar knew that Zelandoni didn't care much for Ladroman either after all the trouble he'd caused her, but in a way it made her more serious about the zelandonia and her duties as an acolyte. She developed into a formidable Zelandoni, who had been called on to be the First just before Jondalar left on the Journey with his brother. In truth, that was one of the reasons he went. He still harbored strong feelings for her and he knew that she would never become his mate. He was surprised, when after five years he returned with Ayla and her animals, to learn that Ladroman had changed his name to Madroman—though he never understood why—and had been accepted into the zelandonia. That meant that no matter who had proposed him, the One Who Was First had had to accept him.

"Greetings!" said the Zelandoni of the Fifth Cave, holding out both his hands to the First as she was stepping off the special travois. "I didn't think I'd have a chance to see you this summer."

She took both his hands, and then leaned forward to touch his cheek with hers. "I looked for you at the Summer Meeting, but was told you went to a different one with some of your neighboring Caves."

"It's true, we did. It's a long story that I'll tell you later, if you want to hear it." She nodded that she did. "But first let's find a place for you, and your . . . ahhh . . . traveling companions to stay," he said, looking significantly at the horses and Wolf. He led them across the small creek, and as he started walking down a well-worn path beside the stream in the middle of the small valley, he continued the explanation. "Essentially it was a matter of reinforcing friendships with closer Caves. It was a smaller Summer Meeting, and we took care of the necessary ceremonies rather quickly. Our leader and some of our Cave went hunting with them, others went visiting and gathering, and the rest of us came back here. I have an acolyte finishing her year of watching the sunsets and Marking the Moons, and I wanted to be here for the end, when the sun stands still. But what are you doing here?"

"I am also training an acolyte. You've met Ayla." The large woman indicated the young woman who was with her. "You may have heard that Ayla has become my new acolyte and we have begun her Donier Tour. I wanted to make sure she saw your Sacred Places." The two elder members of the zelandonia nodded to each other in recognition of their mutual responsibilities. "After Jonokol moved to the Nineteenth Cave, I needed a new acolyte. I think he fell in love with that new sacred cave Ayla found. He always was an artist first, but he puts his heart into the zelandonia now. The Nineteenth is not as well as she might be. I hope she lives long enough to finish training him properly."

"But he was your acolyte. I'm sure he was well trained before he moved," the Zelandoni of the Fifth Cave said.

"Yes, he's had training, but he wasn't really interested when he was my acolyte," the First said. "He was so good at creating images, I had to bring him into the zelandonia, but that was his real love. He was bright and he learned quickly, but he was content to remain an acolyte; he had no real desire to become a Zelandoni, until Ayla showed him White Hollow. Then he changed. Partly because he wanted to make images in there, I'm sure, but that wasn't all. He wants to make sure his images are right for that Sacred Space, so now he embraces the zelandonia. I think Ayla must have sensed that. When she first discovered the cave, she wanted me to see it, but it was more important to her that Jonokol see it."

The Fifth turned to Ayla. "How did you find White Hollow?" he asked. "Did you use your voice on it?"

"I didn't find it. Wolf did," Ayla said. "It was on a hillside buried in brush and blackberry canes, but he suddenly disappeared into the ground beneath the brush. I cut some of it back and went after him. When I realized it was a cave, I came out and made a torch and went back in. That's when I saw what it was. Then I went to find Zelandoni and Jonokol."

It had been some time since the Zelandoni of the Fifth Cave had heard Ayla speak, and her manner of speaking was noticeable, not only to him, but to the other members of his Cave, including Madroman. It reminded Madroman of all the attention Jondalar got when he came back with the beautiful foreign woman and her animals, and how much he hated Jondalar. He always gets noticed, the acolyte thought, especially by women. I wonder what they would think of him if he was missing his two front teeth? Yes, his mother paid reparations for him, but that didn't bring my teeth back.

Why did he have to come back from his Journey? And bring that woman with him? All the fuss they make about her and those animals. I've been an acolyte for years, but she's the one who is getting all the special attention from the First. What if she becomes Zelandoni before I do? She didn't pay much attention to him when they met; she was little more than polite, and she still ignored him. People gave her credit for finding the new cave, but by her own admission, she wasn't the one who found it. It was that stupid animal who did.

He was smiling while he was mulling his thoughts, but to Ayla, who wasn't watching him directly, but observing him closely the way a woman of the Clan would, with indirect glances that took in all of his unconscious body language, his smile was deceitful and devious. She wondered why the Fifth had taken him as an acolyte. He was such a shrewd and canny Zelandoni, he couldn't have been fooled by him, could he? She glanced at Madroman again and caught him staring directly at her with such a malevolent glare it made her shudder.

"Sometimes I think that Wolf belongs in the zelandonia," the One Who Was First said. "You should have heard him in Mammoth Cave. His howl sounded like a Sacred Voice."

"I'm glad you have a new acolyte, but I have always been surprised that you have only one," the Fifth said. "I always have several; right now I'm considering another. Not all acolytes can become zelandoni, and if one decides to give it up,

I always have someone else. You should consider that . . . not that I should tell you."

"You are probably right. I should consider it. I always have my eyes on several people who might make good acolytes, but I tend to wait until I need one," the First said. "The trouble with being First Among Those Who Serve The Great Earth Mother is that I'm responsible for more than one Cave and I don't have as much time to devote to training acolytes, so I'd rather concentrate on one. Before I left the Summer Meeting, I had to make a choice between my responsibility to the Zelandonii, and my obligation to train the next Zelandoni for the Ninth Cave. The Late Matrimonial had not yet been performed, but since there were only a few who were planning to mate then, and I knew the Fourteenth could handle it, I decided it was more important to start Ayla's Donier Tour."

"I'm sure the Fourteenth was quite pleased to take over for you," the Fifth said, with conspiratorial disdain. He was well aware of the difficulties the First had with the Zelandoni of the Fourteenth Cave, who not only wanted her position, but felt she deserved it. "Any of the Zelandoni would. We see the prestige, but the rest of us don't always see the problems . . . including me."

The abris that hovered around them were shelters of stone scoured out of the limestone cliffs by wind, water, and weather through eras of erosion. At any one time, only some were lived in, but others were available to be used for other things. Some of them were utilized for storage, or as a quiet place to practice a craft, or as a meeting place for a couple who wanted to be alone, or for small groups of young or old to plan activities. And one was usually set aside as a place for visitors to stay.

"I hope you will be comfortable here," the Fifth said as he led them into one of the natural stone shelters near the base of the cliff. The space within was quite roomy with a level floor and a high ceiling, open in the front but protected from rain. Near one side wall, several tattered padded cushions were strewn about, and a few lens-shaped dark circles of ash, a couple with some stones around them, showed where previous tenants had made fires.

"I'll send over some wood, and water. If there is anything

else you need, let me know," the Zelandoni of the Fifth Cave said.

"This looks fine to me," the First said. "Is there anything you think we might need?" she asked her companions.

Jondalar shook his head and grunted in the negative as he went to untie Racer's pole-drag to relieve him of his load, and to start unpacking. He wanted to set up the tent inside the shelter so it could air out and not be rained on. Ayla had mentioned that she thought it might rain, and he respected her sense of changing weather.

"I just want to ask something," Ayla said. "Would anyone mind if we bring the horses under the shelter? I've been noticing clouds building up, and it seems like rain, or something . . . is coming. Horses like to stay dry, too."

Just as Jondalar was leading the young stallion away, the horse defecated, leaving plops of brown, grassy dung on the ground behind him, which gave off a strong horsey odor.

"If you want to give your horses shelter from rain, go right ahead," the Zelandoni of the Fifth Cave said, then grinned. "If you don't mind, I doubt that anyone else will."

Several others smiled or snickered as well. It was one thing to look at the animals and those who had the ability to control them with awe, but seeing an animal perform its natural functions took some of the glamour away, made them seem less magical. Ayla had noticed the reserved reactions of the people when they first arrived and was glad Racer had chosen that moment to show he was just a horse.

Zelandoni collected the padded cushions and looked them over. Some were made of leather, some of woven vegetal fibers like grass, reeds, and cattail leaves, and several showed their stuffing material out of cracked or torn edges, which was likely why they were left in the seldom-used shelter. She banged several against the stone wall to clean them of dust and dirt, then stacked them up near the fireplace near where Jondalar had taken the folded tent. Ayla started to shift Jonayla around to her back so she could help him put up the tent.

"I'll take her," the large woman said, reaching for Jonayla. She watched the baby while Jondalar and Ayla raised their tent inside the stone shelter in front of one of the circles of ashes surrounded by stones and laid out fire-making and burning materials for a quick start whenever they wanted a fire. Then they spread out their sleeping rolls and other equipment inside; Wolf always stayed with them in the tent. Finally they put both pole-drags toward the back of the abri and arranged places for the horses under the shelter in front of them, moving Racer's recent droppings out of the way.

Some children from the local Cave stood around watching them but didn't venture too close, except for one girl, whose curiosity finally got the better of her. She approached the Zelandoni and the baby; the First thought the girl could probably count nine or ten years.

"I'd like to hold the baby," she said. "Could I?"

"If she'll let you. She has a mind of her own," the woman said.

The girl held out her arms to her. Jonayla hesitated, but smiled shyly at her, when she moved closer and sat down. Finally Jonayla let go of Zelandoni and crawled to the stranger, who picked her up and put her on her lap.

"What's her name?"

"Jonayla," the woman said. "What's yours?"

"Hollida," the child replied.

"You seem to like babies," Zelandoni said.

"My sister has a baby girl, but she went to visit her mate's family. He comes from a different Cave. I haven't seen her all summer," Hollida said.

"And you miss her, don't you?"

"Yes. I didn't think I would, but I do."

Ayla saw the girl as soon as she approached, and noticed the interaction. She smiled to herself, remembering how much she had wanted a baby when she was younger. It made her think about Durc and she realized that he could probably count about the same number of years now as the girl, but in the Clan he would be considered much closer to adulthood than the girl obviously was. He's growing up, she thought. She knew she would never see her son again, but she couldn't help thinking about him sometimes.

Jondalar noticed the wistful expression on her face while she was watching the girl play with Jonayla and wondered what was going through her mind. Then Ayla shook her head, smiled, called Wolf to her, and walked toward them. If the girl is going to spend time with Jonayla, Ayla thought, I'd better introduce her to Wolf so she won't be afraid of him.

After all three adults had unpacked and were settled in, they walked back to the first stone shelter. Hollida was with them, walking with the First. The rest of the children, who had been watching, raced ahead. When the visitors neared the shelter of the Zelandoni of the Fifth Cave, several people were in front of the large opening in the stone wall, waiting. Their coming had been announced by the children before they arrived. It also appeared a celebration was planned; several people were cooking at hearths in this one location. Ayla wondered if she should have changed out of her traveling clothes, and worn something more suitable, but neither Jondalar nor the First had changed. Some people emerged from the shelter to the north, and from the ones on the other side of the valley when they passed by. Ayla smiled to herself. It seemed obvious that the children had let the others know they were coming.

The area of the Fifth Cave suddenly made her think of the Third Cave at Two Rivers Rock and Reflection Rock of the Twenty-ninth Cave. Their living areas were spread out on residential terraces, one over another, in commanding walls of cliffs, with protective overhangs to shelter the interior spaces from rain and snow. Here, instead, there were several shelters closer to ground level on both sides of the small stream. But it was the close proximity of the several locations where people lived that made them one Cave. Then it occurred to her that the entire Twenty-ninth Cave was attempting to do the same thing, except that their living places were more widely dispersed. It was their mutual hunting and foraging area that brought them together.

"Greetings!" the Zelandoni of the Fifth Cave said when they neared. "I hope you find your place comfortable. We are going to have a community feast in your honor."

"It isn't necessary to go to so much trouble," the One Who Was First said.

He looked at the First. "You know how it is; people love to have an excuse for a celebration. Your coming is a particularly good excuse. We don't often have the Zelandoni of the Ninth Cave who is also the One Who Is First as a visitor. Come inside. You said you wanted to show your acolyte our Sacred Places." He turned to address Ayla. "We live in ours," he said, as he led them in.

The inside of the stone shelter made Ayla stop short with surprise. It was so colorful. Several of the walls were decorated with paintings of animals, which was not so unusual, but the background of many of them was painted a bright red shade with red ocher. And the renderings of the animals were more than outlines, or drawings; most of them were infilled with color, shaded to bring out the contours and shapes. One wall in particular caught Ayla's attention. It was a painting of two exquisitely portrayed bison, one of them obviously pregnant.

"I know most people carve or paint the walls of their abris, and may consider the images sacred, but we think of this entire space as sacred," the Zelandoni of the Fifth Cave said.

Jondalar had visited the Fifth Cave several times and had admired the wall paintings of their stone shelters, but he had never thought of them any differently than he did the paintings and engravings inside the shelter of the Ninth Cave, or any other cave or abri. He wasn't sure if he understood why this shelter should be any more sacred than any other, though it was more highly colored and decorated than most. He just assumed that it was the style that the Fifth Cave preferred, like the ornate tattoos and hair arrangement of their Zelandoni.

The Zelandoni of the Fifth Cave looked at Ayla with the wolf standing alertly at her side, then at Jondalar and the baby, who was tucked contentedly into the crook of the man's arm, looking around with interest, then at the First. "Since the feast is not yet ready, let me show you around," he said.

"Yes, that would be nice," the First said.

They walked out of the shelter and into another one that was immediately to the north. It was essentially a continuation of the first one. And it was also decorated, but in a very different way, which created the sense that they were two different shelters. There were paintings on the walls, like the mammoth that was painted in red and black, but some walls of this cave were deeply engraved and some were both engraved and painted. Other engravings intrigued Ayla. She wasn't sure what they meant.

She approached a wall to look more closely. There were some cuplike holes, but other oval carvings with a second oval around them and a mark like a hole extended into a line in the middle. She saw a horn core on the ground nearby that had been carved into a shape that appeared to be a man's organ. She shook her head and looked again, then almost smiled. That was exactly what it was, and when she looked at the oval shapes, it came to her that they might represent female organs.

She turned around and looked at Jondalar and the First, and then the Zelandoni of the Fifth. "Those look like man and woman parts," she said. "Is that what they are?"

The Fifth smiled and nodded. "This is where our donii-women stay, and often where we have Mother Festivals, and sometimes where we have Rites of First Pleasures. It is also where I have meetings with my acolytes when I am training them, and where they sleep. This is a very Sacred Place," the Fifth said. "That's what I meant when I said we live in our Sacred Sites."

"Do you sleep here, too?" Ayla asked.

"No, I sleep in the first shelter, the other side of this one, near the bison," he said. "I don't think it is good for a Zelandoni to spend all his time with his acolytes. They need to be able to relax, away from the restraining eye of their mentor, and I have other things to do and people to see."

As they walked back to the first part of the shelter, Ayla asked, "Do you know who made your images?"

The question caught him a little off guard. It was not a question usually asked by Zelandonii. The people were accustomed to their art; it had always been there, or they knew the ones who were currently making it, and no one had to ask.

"Not the engravings," he said after pausing to think for a moment. "They were made by the Ancient Ones, but several of our paintings were made by the woman who first taught Jonokol, when she was younger. The one who was Zelandoni of the Second Cave before the one who is now. She was acknowledged as the finest artist of her time, and she was the one who saw the potential in Jonokol even when he was just a boy. She saw potential in one of our young artists too. She now walks the next world, I am sorry to say."

"What about the carved horn?" Jondalar queried, indicating the phallus-shaped object, which he had also seen. "Who made that?"

"That was given to the Zelandoni before me, or perhaps the one before him," the Fifth said. "Some like to have it around during Mother Festivals. I'm not sure, it may have been used as a way to explain the changes in a man's organ. Or it may have been a part of First Rites, especially for girls who didn't like men, or were afraid of them."

Ayla tried not to show it in her expression, it wasn't for her to say, but she thought it would be uncomfortable, perhaps even painful, to use a hard carved object rather than the warm manhood of a caring man, but then she was used to the tenderness of Jondalar. She glanced at him.

He caught her eye and the facial expression she tried to hide, and smiled reassuringly. He wondered if the Fifth was making up a story because he didn't really know what the image meant. Jondalar was sure it had been symbolic of something at one time, probably having to do with a Mother Festival since it was an erect male organ, but that its exact meaning probably had been forgotten.

"We can go across the stream and visit our other Sacred Places. Some of us also live in them. I think you may find them interesting, as well," the Zelandoni of the Fifth Cave said.

They walked toward the small stream that divided the valley, and then upstream to where they had crossed before. There were two solid stepping-stones in the middle of the waterway, which they used to get to the other side; then they went back downstream toward the shelter in which they were staying. There were several abris on this side of the stream nestled into the slope of the valley that continued up to a high promontory that dominated the whole region, and served as a good lookout point. They walked to one that was about six hundred feet from where the spring-fed stream flowed into The River.

When they walked under the overhanging stone of the

shelter, they were struck immediately by a frieze of five animals: two horses and three bison all facing right. The third
figure in particular was a bison about three feet long, deeply
incised into the stone wall. Its voluminous body was carved in
such strong relief, it was almost a sculpture. Black coloration
was used to accentuate the outline. Several other engravings
covered the walls: cupules, lines, and animals, most not as
deeply carved.

They were introduced to several of the people who were
standing around watching them, looking rather proud. They
were no doubt pleased to show off their stunning home, and
Ayla didn't blame them. It was very impressive. After she had
carefully looked over the engravings, Ayla began to take in the
rest of the shelter. It was obvious that quite a few people lived
there, though there weren't very many at the moment. Like all
the rest of the Zelandonii, in summer people traveled; visiting,
hunting, gathering, and collecting various other materials that
they used to make things.

Ayla noticed an area that had been left recently by someone
who was working with ivory, judging from the material scattered around. She looked more closely. There were pieces in
different stages of production. The tusks first had been scored
over and over again to detach rod-shaped sections, and several
small rods were stacked together. A couple of rods had been
divided into sections of pairs, which were then worked into
two round segments attached together. The flattened piece between was pierced just above each round, then scored and cut
through to create two beads, which then had to be smoothed
into the final form, a rounded basketshape.

A man and a woman, both middle-aged, came and stood beside her as she was hunkered down to look closely; she wouldn't
dream of touching the beads. "These are remarkable—did you
make them?" Ayla said.

They both smiled. "Yes, bead-making is my craft," they said
together, then laughed at their inadvertent timing.

Ayla asked how long it took to make the beads, and was told
one person would be lucky to complete five or six beads from
first light until the sun was high and they stopped for a midday
meal. Enough beads for one necklace, depending upon how

long it was, took anywhere from several days to a moon or two. They were extremely precious.

"It looks like a difficult craft. Just looking at the various steps it takes makes me appreciate my Matrimonial outfit even more. There are many ivory beads sewn on it," Ayla said.

"We saw it!" the woman said. "It was beautiful. We went to see it afterward, when Marthona had laid it out on display. The ivory beads were expertly made, by a somewhat different process, I think. The hole seemed to go all the way through the bead, perhaps working from both sides. That is very difficult to do. If you don't mind my asking, where did you get it?"

"I was a Mamutoi—they live far to the east—and the mate of the leader gave it to me; her name was Nezzie of the Lion Camp. Of course, that was when she thought I was going to mate the son of her brother's mate. When I changed my mind and decided to leave with Jondalar, she told me to keep it for my mating with him. She was very fond of him, too." Ayla explained.

"She must have been fond of him, and you," the man said. He thought, but didn't say, that the outfit was not only beautiful, it was extremely valuable. To give so much to someone who would take it away meant she must have cared a great deal for the young woman. It made him better understand the status the foreign woman had been accorded, though she was not born a Zelandonii, as her speech certainly attested. "It is without doubt one of the most stunning outfits I have ever seen."

The Zelandoni of the Fifth Cave added, "They also make beads and necklaces out of seashells from both the Great Western Waters and the Southern Sea, and they carve ivory pendants, and pierce teeth. People especially like to wear fox teeth and those special shiny eyeteeth of deer. Even people from other Caves want their work."

"I grew up near a sea, far to the east," Ayla said. "I'd like to see some of your shells."

The couple—Ayla couldn't decide if they were mates or sister and brother—brought out bags and containers from where they were stored, and poured them out for display, eager to show their riches. There were hundreds of shells, mostly small, globular mollusks like periwinkles or long shapes such as dentalia that could be sewn onto clothes or strung into necklaces. There were also some scallop shells, but for the most part, the shells were from creatures that were essentially inedible, which meant they had been collected for their decorative value alone, not as food, and from a great distance away. They had either traveled to both seashores themselves, or traded for them from someone who had. The amount of time invested in acquiring items solely for display meant that as a society, the Zelandonii were not living on the edge of survival; they had abundance. According to the customs and practices of their time, they were wealthy.

Both Jondalar and the First had come to see what had been brought out and displayed for Ayla. Though they had both been aware of the Fifth Cave's status, partly because of their jewelry-makers, seeing so much at once was almost overwhelming. They couldn't help but make comparisons in their minds to the Ninth Cave, but when they thought about it, they knew that their Cave was equally wealthy, in a slightly different way. In fact, most of the Zelandonii Caves were.

The Zelandoni of the Fifth Cave took them into another shelter nearby, and again it was well decorated, primarily with engravings of horses, bison, deer, even a partial mammoth, often accented with both red ocher and black manganese paint. The antlers of an engraved deer, for example, had been outlined in black, while a bison had been painted mostly red. Again they were introduced to the people who were there. Ayla noticed that the children who had been around their shelter, which was on the same side of the small stream, had gathered around again; she recognized several of them.

Suddenly Ayla felt dizzy and nauseous, and had a very strong need to get out of the shelter. She couldn't explain her intense urge to leave, but she had to get outside.

"I'm thirsty, I want to get some water," she said, walking out quickly, and heading toward the stream.

"You don't have to go out," a woman said, following behind her. "We have a spring inside."

"I think we all need to go anyway. The feast must be ready,

and I'm hungry," the Zelandoni of the Fifth Cave said. "I should think you must be, too."

They returned to the main shelter, or what Ayla had come to think of as the main shelter, and found everything for the feast set up and waiting for them. Although extra dishes were stacked up for the visitors, Ayla and Jondalar got their personal eating cups, bowls, and knives out of their pouches. The First carried her own dishes as well. Ayla took out Wolf's water bowl, which also served as an eating dish if one was needed, and thought that she should start making eating dishes for Jonayla soon. Though she planned to nurse her until she could count at least three years, she would be giving her tastes of other food long before that.

Someone had recently hunted an aurochs; a roast haunch, turned on a spit over coals, was the main dish. Lately, they only saw the wild cattle in summer, but it was one of Ayla's favorite foods. The taste was similar to bison, except richer, but then they were similar animals, with hard, round, curving horns that grew to a point and were permanent, not shed every year like deer antlers.

There were summer vegetables, too: sow-thistle stems, cooked pigweed, coltsfoot, and nettle leaves flavored with sorrel, and cowslips and wild rose petals in a salad of young dandelion leaves and clover. Fragrant meadowsweet flowers gave a honey-like sweetness to a sauce of crabapples and rhubarb served with the meat. A mixture of summer berries required no sweetening. They had raspberries, an early ripening variety of blackberries, cherries, blackcurrants, elderberries, and pitted blackthorn plums, though pitting the small sloes was a time-consuming job. Rose leaf tea finished off the delicious meal.

When she took out Wolf's bowl and gave him the bone she had chosen with a little meat left on, one of the women looked at the wolf with disapproval, and Ayla heard her say to another woman that she didn't think it was right to feed a wolf food that was meant for people. The other woman nodded her head in agreement, but Ayla had noticed that both of them had looked at the four-legged hunter with trepidation earlier in the day. She had hoped to introduce Wolf to the women to perhaps reduce their fearfulness, but they made a point of avoiding both Ayla and the meat-eater.

After the meal, more wood was put on the fire to provide stronger light against the encroaching darkness. Ayla was nursing Jonayla and sipping a cup of hot tea with Wolf at her feet in the company of Jondalar, the First, and the Zelandoni of the Fifth. A group of people approached, including Madroman, though he stayed in the background. Ayla recognized others, and gathered that they were the acolytes of the Fifth, probably wanting to spend some time with the One Who Was First.

"I have completed Marking the Suns and Moons," said one of them. The young woman opened up her hand and revealed a small plaque of ivory covered with strange markings.

The Fifth picked it out of her hand and examined it carefully, turning it over to see the back side and even checking around the edges. Then he smiled. "This is about a half year," he said, then gave it to the First. "She is my Third Acolyte, and started the Marking this time last year. Her plaque for the first half is put away."

The large woman looked at the piece with the same careful scrutiny as the Zelandoni of the Fifth, but not as long. "This is an interesting method of marking," she said. "You show the turns by position and the crescents with curved marks for two of the moons you've marked. The rest are around the edge and on the back. Very good."

The young woman beamed under the praise from the First.

"Perhaps you could explain what you've done to my acolyte. Marking the Suns and Moons is something she has yet to do," the First said.

"I would have thought it was something she had already done. I've heard she is known for her medicinal knowledge, and she is mated. There are not many acolytes I know who are mated and have children, not even many Zelandonia," the Third Acolyte of the Zelandoni of the Fifth Cave said.

"Ayla's training has been unconventional. As you know, she was not born to the Zelandonii, so the order in which she has gained her knowledge is not the same as ours. She is an exceptional healer. She started young, but she is just beginning her Donier Tour, and hasn't yet learned to Mark the Suns and Moons," the Zelandoni Who Was First carefully explained.

"I'll be happy to explain the way I Marked them to her," the Third Acolyte of the Fifth said, and sat down next to Ayla.

Ayla was more than interested. This was the first she had heard of Marking the Suns and Moons, and didn't know it was another task she'd have to complete as part of her training. She wondered what else there was that she didn't know she would have to do.

"You see, I made one mark each night," the young woman said, showing her the marks she had etched into the ivory with a pointed tool of sharp flint. "I'd already marked the first half year on another piece, so I was getting an idea of how to keep track of more than just the count of the days. I started this just before the moon was new and I was trying to show where the moon was in the sky, so I began here." She indicated a mark that was in the middle of what seemed to be just random haphazard pitting. "The next few nights it snowed. It was a big storm and blocked out the moon and the stars, but I wouldn't have been able to see the moon anyway. It was the time when Lumi was closing his great eye. The next time I saw him, he was a thin crescent, waking up again, so I made a curved mark here."

Ayla looked where the young woman indicated and was rather surprised to see that what had appeared at first to be a hole made by a sharp point was indeed a small curved line. She looked more closely at the group of markings and suddenly they didn't look so random. There did seem to be a pattern to it, and she was interested in how the young woman would proceed.

"Since the time of Lumi's sleeping is the beginning of a Moon, that's here on the right where I decided to turn back to mark the next set of nights," the Third Acolyte continued. "Right about here was the first eye-half-closed; some people call it the first half-face. Then it keeps getting bigger until it's full. It's hard to tell when it's exactly full—it looks full for a few days—so that's here on the left where I turned back again. I made four curved marks, two below and two above. I kept marking until it was the second half-face, when Lumi starts to close his eye again, and you notice it's just above the first half-face.

"I kept marking until his eye was closed again—see here on the right, where I curved down? All the way around the line with the first right-end turn. You take it and see if you can follow it. I always make the turns when he's full face, on the right, or when he's sleeping, on the left. You'll see that you can count two Moons, plus another half. I stopped at the first half-face after the second Moon. I was waiting for Bali to catch up. It was the time when the sun is as far south as it goes and stands still for a few days, then changes direction and goes north again. It's the ending of First Winter and the beginning of Second Winter, when it's colder but has the promise of Bali's return."

"Thank you," Ayla said. "That was fascinating! Did you work it all out yourself?"

"Not exactly. Other Zelandonia showed me their way of marking, but I saw a plaque at the Fourteenth Cave once that was quite old. It wasn't marked in quite the same way, but it gave me the idea when it was my time to Mark the Moons."

"It's a very good idea," the First said.

It was very dark when they started back to their sleeping place. Ayla was holding the baby, who was sound asleep wrapped up in her carrying blanket, so both Jondalar and the First each borrowed a torch to see their way.

As they approached the visitors' shelter, they passed by some of the other shelters they had seen earlier. When she came to the one where she had felt so uncomfortable, Ayla shuddered again and hurried past.

"What's wrong?" Jondalar asked.

"I don't know," Ayla said. "I've been feeling strange all day. It's probably nothing."

When they reached their shelter, the horses were milling around outside, rather than in the large roomy space she had made for them inside. "Why are they out here? The horses have been acting up all day; that may be what's bothering me," Ayla said. As they turned into the shelter toward their tent, Wolf hesitated, then sat down on his haunches and refused to enter. "Now, what's wrong with Wolf?"

17

"W hy don't we take the horses for a run this morning?" Ayla said softly to the man who was lying beside her. "Yesterday they seemed restless and edgy. I am too. They don't really get to go free and fast when they are pulling the pole-drags. It's hard work, but not the kind of exercise they like."

Jondalar smiled. "That's a good idea. I don't get to exercise the way I'd like to either. What about Jonayla?"

"Maybe Hollida would like to watch her, especially if Zelandoni will keep an eye on them," Ayla said.

Jondalar sat up. "Where is Zelandoni? She's not here."

"I heard her get up earlier. I think she went to talk to the Fifth," Ayla said. "If we leave Jonayla, perhaps we should leave Wolf, too, though I'm not sure how the people of this Cave feel about him. They seemed a little nervous around him while we were eating last night. This is not the Ninth Cave. . . . Let's take Jonayla with us. I can take her in her carrying blanket. She likes to ride."

Jondalar pulled the top of their sleeping roll back and got up. Ayla got up too, leaving the baby who had been sleeping at her side to wake up while she went to pass her water.

"It rained last night," Ayla said when she got back.

"Now aren't you glad you stayed inside, in the tent and under cover?" Jondalar said.

Ayla didn't answer. She hadn't slept well. She just couldn't get comfortable, but they did stay dry and the tent aired out.

Jonayla had rolled over on her stomach and was kicking her legs and holding her head up. She had also rolled out of her swaddling, and the soiled absorbent wadding it held in place.

Ayla collected the unpleasant material and dumped it in the night basket, rolled up the damp, softened-leather swaddling blanket, then picked up the baby and headed down to the small stream to clean the little one, herself, and the blanket. She rinsed herself and the baby in the running water, a procedure to which the baby was now so accustomed, she didn't even fuss about it, though it was cold. Ayla hung the swaddling across some brush near the water, then got dressed and found a comfortable place to sit outside of the stone shelter to nurse her infant.

In the meantime, Jondalar had found the horses not far up the valley, brought them back to the abri, and was tying riding blankets on the backs of both Whinney and Racer. At Ayla's suggestion, he tied equally balanced pack baskets across the mare's rump as well, but had some difficulty when Gray started nuzzling her dam, trying to nurse. About the time they were ready to go to what Ayla thought of as the main shelter in this place of many shelters, Wolf returned. She assumed he had gone off to hunt earlier, but he appeared so suddenly, he spooked Whinney, which surprised the woman. Whinney was normally a calm horse and the wolf didn't usually alarm her; it was Racer who was more excitable, but all the horses seemed skittish, even the little filly. And Wolf, too, Ayla thought as he pressed against her as though looking for attention. She felt odd herself. Something seemed off, just not quite right. She looked at the sky to see if any storm threatened; a film of high clouds made the sky white with telltale traces of blue. They probably all needed a good run.

Jondalar put the halters on Racer and Gray. He had also made one for Whinney but Ayla used it only on special occasions. Before she even knew she was training Whinney, she had taught the mare to follow her; she still didn't think of it as training. When she showed Whinney what to do, and repeated the instruction many times until she understood, then the mare did it because she wanted to. It was similar to the way Iza had trained Ayla to remember the many different plants and herbs, and their uses, by repetition and rote memorization.

When they were all packed, they walked to the shelter of the Zelandoni of the Fifth Cave, and again the procession of man, woman, baby, wolf, and horses caused the people to stop what they were doing and watch, hard pressed to avoid the discourtesy of outright staring. Both the Fifth and the One Who Was First walked out from the shelter.

"Come and join us for a morning meal," the man said.

"The horses are agitated and we've decided to take them out for some exercise to run off their restlessness and settle them down," Jondalar said.

"We just arrived yesterday. Don't they get enough exercise traveling?" the First said.

"When we're traveling and they are pulling loads, they don't run or gallop," Ayla explained. "Sometimes they need to stretch their legs."

"Well, at least come and have some tea, and we'll pack up some food for you to take with you," the Zelandoni of the Fifth said.

Ayla and Jondalar looked at each other, and understood that although they would have preferred to just leave, it might offend the Fifth Cave, and that would not be appropriate. They nodded to each other in acquiescence.

"Thank you, we will," Jondalar said, reaching into the carrying pouch attached to his waist thong and pulling out his personal drinking cup. Ayla also found her cup and passed it down to a woman near the fireplace who was ladling out the hot liquid. She filled the drinking containers, and handed them back. Rather than settling down to graze while they were waiting, the horses were markedly apprehensive, displaying their anxiety. Whinney was dancing in place, sniffing loudly as furrows appeared over her eyes. Gray was picking up her dam's nervous symptoms, and Racer was sidestepping with his neck arched high. Ayla tried to comfort the mare, running her hand along the side of her neck, and Jondalar was having to hang on to the rope halter to keep the stallion from breaking away.

Ayla glanced across the stream dividing the valley and watched some children running and screaming alongside the waterway in some kind of game that to her seemed more frenzied than usual, even for excited youngsters. She watched them dashing in and out of the shelters, and suddenly had a feeling that it was dangerous, though she didn't see how it could be.

Just as she was about to speak to Jondalar and tell him they had to go, some people brought them rawhide-wrapped packages of food. The couple thanked everyone as they stashed the parfleches in the pack baskets on Whinney; then with the help of some nearby rocks, they climbed up onto the horses' backs and started riding out of the valley.

As soon as they reached a clear, open field, they eased their control and let the horses run. It was exhilarating and lessened Ayla's nervousness, but didn't eliminate it. Finally the horses grew tired and slowed down. Jondalar noticed a stand of trees in the distance and guided Racer in that direction. Ayla saw where he was heading and followed. The young filly, who could already run as fast as her mother, trailed behind. Young horses quickly learned to run fast; they had to if they were going to survive. The wolf raced along with them; he also enjoyed a good run.

As they neared the trees, they could see a small pool, obviously spring fed, that overflowed its banks in a rill that ran off across the field. But as they neared the pool, Whinney suddenly stopped short, which nearly knocked Ayla to the ground. She wrapped her arm around her baby, who had been sitting in front of her, and quickly slid down from the mare's back. She noticed Jondalar having trouble with Racer, too. The stallion reared up, neighing loudly, and the tall man slid back, then quickly stepped off. He didn't fall, but had trouble regaining his footing.

Ayla became aware of a loud rumbling, feeling it as much as hearing it, and realized it had been going on for some time. She glanced ahead and saw the water in the pool shoot up in a fountain as though someone had squeezed the spring and sent a squirt of liquid up in the air. It was only then that she noticed the ground was moving.

Ayla knew what it was—she had felt the earth shift beneath her feet before—and felt a gorge of panic rise up in her throat. The earth was not supposed to move. She struggled to keep her balance. Petrified, she clung to her baby, afraid to take a step.

She watched the knee-high grass of the open field perform a strange, quivering dance as the groaning earth moved in unnatural ways to unheard music deep within. Ahead, the small stand of trees near the spring amplified the movement. The water bounced up and fell back, swirled over its bank, churned up dirt from its bed, and spit out muddy globs. She smelled the stench of raw earth; then with a crack, one fir tree suddenly gave way and slowly began to tip over, pulling up and exposing half its circle of roots.

The shaking seemed to go on forever. It brought back recollections of other times, and the losses that had come with the moving, groaning earth. She shut her eyes tight, trembling, and sobbed with grief and fear. Jonayla started to cry. Then Ayla felt a hand on her shoulder, and arms wrap around her and the baby that offered solace and comfort. She leaned against the warm chest of the man she loved, and the baby quieted. Slowly, she became aware that the quaking had stopped and the shuddering earth had stilled, and she felt the tightness inside her lessen.

"Oh, Jondalar," she cried. "That was an earthquake. I hate earthquakes!" She trembled in his arms. She thought, but didn't want to say it aloud—voicing thoughts could give them power— that earthquakes were evil; bad things always seemed to happen when the earth shook.

"I don't much like them either," he said, holding his fragile little family close. Ayla looked around, and noticed the tilted fir tree near the spring. She shivered with an unexpected memory of a scene long ago.

"What's wrong?" Jondalar asked.

"That tree," she said.

He looked where she was gazing and saw the tree near the spring, canted over and roots exposed.

"I remember seeing many trees tipped over and leaning like that, and some on the ground and fallen across a river. It must have been when I was very young . . . ," she said, hesitating, "before I lived with the Clan. I think it was when I lost my mother, and family, and everything. Iza said that I could walk well and talk; I suppose I could count five years when she found me."

After she told him of her memory, Jondalar held her until she relaxed again. Though it was just a brief recitation, it gave him a better understanding of the terror she must have felt as a little girl when an earthquake had brought her world crashing down around her, and life as she had known it came to an abrupt end.

"Do you think it will come back? The earthquake? Sometimes when the earth moves like that, it doesn't settle down right away. It comes back," Ayla said, when they finally let go of each other.

"I don't know," he said. "But maybe we should get back to Old Valley, and make sure everyone there is all right."

"Of course! I was so scared, I wasn't thinking about anyone else. I hope everyone is safe. And the horses! Where are the horses?" Ayla cried, looking around. "Are they all right?"

"Aside from being as frightened as we were, I think they're fine. Racer reared up and made me slide off, but I managed not to fall. Then he started running in big circles. As far as I could tell, Whinney didn't move, and Gray stayed by her side. I think she must have run away after it stopped."

Off in the distance on the level field, Ayla spied the animals, and breathed out, relieved. She whistled her special summons loudly and saw Whinney's head go up, then start in her direction. Racer and Gray followed, and Wolf behind them.

"They're coming now, and there's Wolf, too. I think he must have run off with them," Jondalar said.

By the time the horses and Wolf arrived, Ayla was more composed. Since there was no convenient rock or stump of wood nearby to help her climb on Whinney's back, she gave Jonayla to Jondalar for a moment, and holding on to the mare's stand-up mane, she jumped up, threw her leg over, and found her seat. She took the child from the man and watched while Jondalar climbed up on Racer's back in much the same way, though he was so tall, he could almost step up onto the back of the compact, sturdy stallion.

She looked toward the spring, where the tree still leaned at a precarious angle. It would fall soon, she was sure. Though she had wanted to go there before, she didn't want to go near it now.

As they started toward Old Valley, they heard a loud crack, and when they glanced back, there was a more muffled boom as they watched the tall fir hitting the ground. Riding back to the Fifth Cave, Ayla wondered about the horses, and the implication of their recent actions.

"Do you suppose that the horses knew the ground was going to shake like that, Jondalar? Was that why they were behaving so strangely?" she asked.

"They definitely were nervous," Jondalar said, "but I'm glad they were. That's why we left and were out in the open when it happened. I think it's safer to be out here; you don't have to worry about things falling on you."

"But the ground can open up under you," Ayla said. "I think that's what happened to my family. I remember that smell of deep earth, of wetness and decay. But I don't think all earthquakes are the same. Some are more powerful than others. And most of them can be felt a long distance away, but not as strongly."

"When you were young, you must have been very close to the place where the shaking started, if all the trees toppled over and the ground opened up. I don't think we were as close to this one. Only one tree fell."

Ayla smiled at him. "There aren't many trees out here to fall, Jondalar."

He smiled a little ruefully. "That's true, and all the more reason to be out here when the ground shakes," he said.

"But how would you know when the ground is going to shake?"

"By paying attention to the horses!" he said.

"If only I could be sure that would always work," she said.

As they neared Old Valley, they noticed unusual activity. Almost everyone seemed to be outside of the shelters, and many of them were clustered around in front of one of them. They dismounted and walked the horses toward the shelter they had been using, which was just beyond the one where the people were gathered.

"There you are!" the First called out. "I was a little worried about you when the ground started shaking."

"We're fine. Are you all right?" Ayla said.

"Yes, yes, but the Fifth Cave has had some injuries, one serious," the woman said. "Perhaps you might take a look."

Ayla detected the note of concern in her voice. "Jondalar, would you take the horses and see how everything is? I'm going to stay here and help Zelandoni," she said.

She followed the large woman until they came to the place in front of the shelter where a boy was lying on a fur bedroll that was spread out on the ground, with the fur side down to make a padding underneath. Extra pads and blankets had been placed under him to elevate his head and shoulders slightly. Soft, pliable skins, covered with blood, were directly under his head, and blood was still seeping out. She took Jonayla out of her carrying blanket, set it out on the ground, and put the baby down on it. Wolf lay down next to her. Then Hollida appeared.

"I'll watch her," she said.

"I would be grateful," Ayla said. She saw a cluster of people nearby who seemed to be consoling a woman, and realized that it was probably the boy's mother. She knew how she would feel if he were her son. She exchanged a look with the First, held it for a moment, and understood that the boy's injury was more than serious. It was grim.

Ayla knelt down to examine him. He was lying in the open in the light of the sun, though high clouds shielded the brightness somewhat. The first thing she noticed was that he was unconscious, but breathing, though it was slow and irregular. He had bled a great deal, but that was usually the case with head wounds. Much more serious was the pink-tinged fluid draining from his nose and ears. That meant the bone of the skull was cracked and the substance inside injured, which did not bode well for the child. Ayla understood the First's concern. She lifted his eyelids and looked at both of his eyes; one of the pupils contracted in the light, and the other was larger than the first and did not react, another bad sign. She turned his head slightly to allow the bloody mucus coming from his mouth to drain to the side and not clog his breathing passages.

She had to control a reaction to shake her head so the mother wouldn't see how hopeless she thought it was. She got up and looked intently at the First, communicating her bleak prognosis. They went off to the side where the Zelandoni of the Fifth Cave was watching. Some people from his shelter had come to get the Zelandoni when the boy was hurt, and he had already examined him. He had asked the First to look at the child to confirm his diagnosis.

"What do you think?" the man said under his breath, looking at the older woman, then at the younger one.

"I don't think there's any hope for him," Ayla said in a very soft voice.

"I'm afraid I agree," the One Who Was First said. "There is very little that can be done for an injury like that. He has not only lost blood, but he is also losing other fluids from inside his head. Soon the wound will swell and that will be the end."

"That's what I thought. I will have to tell his mother," the Zelandoni of the Fifth said.

The three Zelandonia walked to the small group of people who were obviously trying to comfort the woman who was sitting on the ground not far from the boy. When she looked at the expressions on the faces of the three Zelandonia, the woman broke out in sobs. The Zelandoni of the Fifth Cave knelt down beside her.

"I am sorry, Janella. The Great Mother is calling Jonlotan back to Her. He was so full of life, such a joy, that Doni can't bear to be without him. She loves him too much," the man said.

"But I love him, too. Doni can't love him more than I do. He's so young. Why does She have to take him now?" Janella sobbed.

"You will see him again, when you return to the Mother's breast, and walk the next world," the Fifth said.

"But I don't want to lose him now. I want to see him grow up. Isn't there anything you can do? You are the most powerful Zelandoni there is," the boy's mother pleaded, looking at the First.

"You can be sure that if there were, I would be doing it. You don't know how much it hurts me to say it, but there is nothing I can do for someone with such a severe injury," the One Who Was First said.

"The Mother has so many, why does She want him, too?" Janella sobbed.

"That is one question to which we are not given to know the answer. I am sorry, Janella. You should go to him while he still breathes, and comfort him. His elan must find his way to the next world now and I'm sure he is frightened. Though he may not show it, he will be grateful for your presence," the large, powerful woman said.

"Since he's still breathing, do you think he might wake up?" Janella asked.

"It is possible," the First said.

Several people helped the woman up and led her to her dying son. Ayla picked up her child, held her close for a moment, and thanked Hollida, then walked toward the shelter in which they were staying. The two Zelandonia joined her.

"I wish there were something I could do. I feel so helpless," the Zelandoni of the Fifth Cave said.

"We all do at a time like this," the First said.

"How long do you think he'll live?" he asked.

"You never know. He could linger for days," the Zelandoni of the Ninth Cave said. "If you want us to stay, we will, but I wonder how extensive this earthquake was, and if it was felt at the Ninth Cave. We have a few people who didn't go to the Summer Meeting . . ."

"You should go and see how they are," the Fifth said. "You are right. There's no telling how long the boy will linger. You may be the First, but you are still responsible for the Ninth Cave, and seeing to their well-being. I can do whatever is necessary here. I have before. Sending someone's elan to the next world is not my most favorite part of taking care of one's Cave, but it needs to be done, and it is important that it be done right."

Everyone slept outside of the stone shelters that night, mostly in tents. They were too apprehensive to go inside, where rocks might still fall, except to run in and retrieve something they needed. There were a few aftershocks, and a little more rock shook loose from the walls and ceilings of the shelters, but nothing as heavy as the piece that fell on the boy's head. It would be a while before anyone would feel like being in a stone shelter, though when the cold and snow of the periglacial winter arrived, people would forget the peril of falling rocks and be glad for some protection from the weather.

The procession of people, horses, and a wolf started out in the morning. Ayla and the First stopped in to see the boy, but

more to see how his mother was bearing up. They both had
mixed feelings about leaving. They wanted to stay and help
the mother of the injured boy cope with her loss, but they
were both concerned about those who had stayed behind at the
stone shelter of the Ninth Cave of the Zelandoni.

They traveled south, following The River as it wound along
its sinuous course downstream. The distance was not too great,
though they had to cross back over The River and climb up
the highland and back down again because the curving stream
forced the water against the rock walls in one section, but the
horses made the trek both easier and faster. By late afternoon,
they were in sight of the sheer limestone cliff with the column
near the top that appeared to be falling, which housed the large
abri of the Ninth Cave. They strained to see if there were any
differences that might warn them of damage to their home, or
injury to its inhabitants.

They reached Wood Valley and made their way across the
small river that fed into The River. People were standing on
the northern end of the stone front porch that faced southwest
waiting for them as they started up the path. Someone had
seen them coming and told the others. When they passed by
the jutting corner that held the hearth of the signal fire, Ayla
noticed it was still smoldering from recent use and wondered
why.

Because the Ninth Cave had so many people, the number
who had stayed back from the Summer Meeting, for one reason or another, was nearly as great as those who made up the
total of some of the smaller Caves, though it was comparable
in proportion to the other groups. The Ninth Cave had the
greatest number of people of any of the Caves of the Zelandonii, including the Twenty-ninth and the Fifth, which had
several stone shelters. Their abri was extraordinarily large and
had plenty of room to comfortably house their large number,
and more. In addition, the Ninth Cave had individuals who
were very skilled in many ways and had much to offer. As a result they had a very high status among the Zelandonii. People
wanted to join them, but they could only take in so many and
tended to be selective, choosing those who reinforced their

standing, though once someone was born to them or became a member, they were very seldom turned out.

All who had not gone to the Summer Meeting, who were able, came out to watch the travelers arrive, many of them gaping with surprise; they had never seen their Donier sitting on a seat that was pulled by Ayla's horse. Ayla stopped to let Zelandoni step off the pole-drag, which she did with unruffled dignity. The First saw a middle-aged woman, Stelona, whom she knew to be levelheaded and responsible, she had stayed at the Ninth Cave to care for her ailing mother.

"We were visiting the Fifth Cave and felt a strong earthquake. Did you feel it here, Stelona?" the First said.

"We felt it, and people were frightened, but it didn't seem too bad. Some rocks fell, but mostly in the gathering area, not here. No one was hurt," Stelona said, anticipating the Zelandoni's next question.

"I'm glad to hear that. The Fifth Cave was not so lucky. A boy was severely injured when a large rock fell on his head. I'm afraid there's little hope for him. He may already be walking the next world," the Donier said. "Have you heard anything from the other Caves in this area, Stelona? The Third? The Eleventh? The Fourteenth?" the First said.

"Only smoke from their signal fires to let us know they were there and didn't need any immediate help," Stelona said.

"That's good, but I think I'll go see what damage, if any, they sustained," the Donier said, then turned to look at Ayla and Jondalar. "Would you like to come along? And perhaps bring the horses? They could be useful if anyone does need help."

"Today?" Jondalar asked.

"No, I was thinking of making a tour of our neighbors tomorrow morning."

"I'd be glad to go with you," Ayla said.

"Of course, I will, too," Jondalar said.

Ayla and Jondalar unloaded Racer's travois, except for their own things, and left the bundles on the ledge in front of the living section, then led the horses pulling the nearly empty pole-drags past the part of the shelter where most of the people lived. They lived at the the other end of the inhabited area, although the overhanging stone protected a much larger section, which was only used occasionally, except for the places they had made for the horses. As they walked along the front of the huge abri, they couldn't help but notice some newly fallen pieces of stone, but nothing too large, nothing much bigger than pieces that sometimes split off by themselves for no reason that anyone could determine.

When they reached the large, flat stone near the edge of the front porch that Joharran and others sometimes used to stand on when they wanted to address a group, Ayla wondered when it fell and what had caused it. Was it an earthquake or had it just sheared off by itself? Suddenly the stone shelters that had seemed so protective didn't feel quite so safe anymore.

As they started to lead the horses under the overhanging ledge toward their space, Ayla wondered if they would balk the way they had the night before. But the place was familiar to them and they apparently sensed no danger. They went right in, which gave her an immense feeling of relief. There is really no protection when the earth decides to shake, inside or out, but if the horses were to give her a warning again, she did think she would rather be outside.

They unhitched the two pole-drags and left them in their usual place, then led the horses to the corrals that they had made for them. They were not penned in. The structures they had constructed under the overhanging ledge were there for the animals' comfort; they were free to come and go at any time. Ayla brought water from the spring-fed stream that separated the Ninth Cave from Down River, and poured it into their troughs, although the horses could just as easily have gotten water from the stream themselves. She wanted to make sure that water was available in the middle of the night, especially for the little one.

Only during the spring rutting season were there any constraints on the horses. Then not only did they fasten the gates closed, put halters on the animals, and tie them to posts to keep them from getting free, but Ayla and Jondalar usually slept nearby to drive away the stallions that were drawn to the mare. Ayla didn't want Whinney to be captured by some stallion and driven to his herd, and Jondalar didn't want Racer running off to be hurt fighting with other stallions in an effort to mount the tempting females. He even had to be kept away from his dam, whose mating scent was so overpoweringly close. It was a difficult time for all of them.

Some hunters took advantage of Whinney's luring aroma, which could be detected by males more than a mile away, and killed a few of the wild horses, but they stayed out of sight of Ayla and made sure not to mention it to her. She was aware of the practice and couldn't really blame them. She had lost her taste for horsemeat, and chose not to eat it, but she knew most people enjoyed it. Just so long as they didn't go after her horses, she didn't object to others hunting the animals. They were a valuable food source.

They walked back to their own dwelling and unloaded their belongings. Although they hadn't been gone very long, not even as long as usual for a Summer Meeting, Ayla was happy to be back. Visiting other Caves and Sacred Sites along the way seemed to have taken more time than normal, and the effort left her tired. The earthquake had been particularly draining. She shuddered at the thought of it.

Jonayla had been fussing and she brought the baby to the changing place just outside the dwelling; then she went inside and settled down to nurse, happy to be there. The structure had rawhide-panel walls but no ceiling, at least none that was constructed. When she looked up, she saw the underside of the overhanging rock of the natural stone shelter. She could smell food cooking and knew they would share a meal with some of their usual community, and then she'd be able to crawl into her bedroll and cuddle up between Jondalar and Jonayla, with Wolf just beyond. She was glad to be home.

"There's a Sacred Cave nearby that you haven't really explored, Ayla," Zelandoni said while they were sharing their morning meal the day after their return. "The one we call the Women's Place, on the other side of Grass River."

"But I've been to the Women's Place," Ayla said.

"Yes, you've been there, but how far in did you go? There is much more to it than you've seen. It's on the way to Horsehead Rock and Elder Hearth. I think we should make a stop on our way back."

Ayla found the visits to the Sacred Caves fascinating, but it was exhausting, and she had seen so many recently, she was tired of visiting decorated caves. It was too much to take in all at once. She wanted some time to think about what she had already seen, but she couldn't bring herself to refuse Zelandoni's suggestion, any more than she could refuse her request to accompany her when she went to visit the other Caves in the region to see how they had fared during the earthquake. She wanted to know, too, though she was also tired of traveling and wouldn't have minded resting for a day or so.

The earthquake had been experienced by the Third, the Eleventh, and the Fourteenth Caves, their closest neighbors, as well as by Elder Hearth, the Second Cave, and Horsehead Rock, the Seventh, with little damage, if the signal fires had been interpreted right, but the first wanted to check on the Caves that were a little farther away just to make sure. A few people from the nearby Caves had some bruises from falling stones, and a beautiful lamp that had been carved out of sandstone was smashed. The Donier wanted to make sure that any injuries that might have been sustained really weren't serious. Ayla had the sense that the quake hadn't been as strong in this region as it had been at Old Valley, and wondered if it had been more severe farther north.

On the way to Horsehead Rock, they stopped by a couple of homesites of smaller Caves near Little Grass River that were being formed by some young people who were beginning to feel crowded out. Several caves and abris in the region were inhabited, at least part of the year, and people had started to refer to the area as New Home. They were all empty, even the most settled one, called Bear Hill. Zelandoni explained that the young people who lived there still thought of themselves as belonging to the Cave of their families and traveled with them to the Summer Meeting. Those who couldn't or didn't go gathered with the ones who stayed behind from their primary Cave. Though they didn't see any people, going that way allowed Jondalar and Zelandoni to show Ayla the "back way" to Horsehead Rock and Elder Hearth, and Sweet Valley, the rich, moist lowland between them.

After checking out Bear Hill, they crossed Little Grass

River—the stream was low at this time of year and easy to traverse, especially where it widened out—and headed over the highland toward Sweet Valley and Horsehead Rock, the Seventh Cave of the Zelandonii. The ones who had stayed back from the Second Cave had joined the Seventh Cave, but there were still just a few people left behind, and they welcomed the visitors eagerly, partly because the ones who were ill or failing were glad to see the Doniers, but mostly because it broke up the tedium of seeing only the same few people. The Zelandonii were a sociable folk, used to living in close quarters with a number of others, and most, even if they were unable to go, missed the excitement of the Summer Meeting. Since the people were still at the Summer Meeting, or doing some other summer activity—hunting, fishing, gathering, exploring, or visiting—it felt a bit strange to visit the Caves when they were nearly empty.

They had all felt the earthquake, but no one had been injured, though some were still nervous about it and sought out reassurance from the First. Ayla observed how the woman managed to comfort them with her words, though she didn't really say anything specific, and couldn't have done anything about the natural upheaval anyway. It was her way of speaking, her assured manner, her posture, the younger woman thought. Zelandoni even made her feel better. They stayed overnight; people had started preparing a place for them to sleep and making food for a small feast as soon as they had arrived. It would have been impolite, not to mention unkind, for them to have left any sooner.

On the way back the next day, Zelandoni wanted to check a place they had bypassed on the way out. They rode back over the raised ground again, toward Little Grass River but more upstream, to a community on the edge of the highland called Lookout. It was well named. A settled area around rocky outcrops that offered some protection from weather was unoccupied by its inhabitants at the moment, but from a rise nearby, they could see for a long distance in many directions, particularly toward the west.

Ayla felt unsettled from the moment they drew near to the place. She didn't know why, but she had an uncanny feeling in the middle of her back and as far as she was concerned, they couldn't get away fast enough. The moment she dismounted from her horse, Wolf sought her out, rubbing against her leg and whining. He didn't like the place either, but the horses seemed unperturbed. It was a perfectly normal summer day, with a warm sun and green grass growing on the hillside, and the place had an excellent view of the countryside. There was nothing she could see or detect to account for her discomfort, and she hesitated to say anything.

"Do you want to stop and rest, and have a midday meal here, Zelandoni?" Jondalar asked.

"I don't think there is any reason for us to stay here," the woman replied, heading back to the pole-drag, "especially if we are going to stop and see the Women's Place. And if we don't take too long, it's close enough to the Ninth Cave that we can get home before dark."

Ayla wasn't at all sorry that Zelandoni decided to continue and was glad now that the First had wanted to show her the sacred deep of the Women's Place. They worked their way down the western side of the highland to Little Grass River, and near its confluence with Grass River they crossed over. Just a short distance beyond was a small U-shaped valley surrrounded by tall limestone cliffs that opened out onto Grass River, and across that, the green valley that gave the waterway its name, Grass Valley.

The little meadow's lush grass often enticed various grazers, but the high walls of the sides eased to a comfortably climbable slope, especially for hoofed animals, some three hundred feet back, which made it not quite suitable for a hunting trap without extensive construction of fences and corrals. Such work had been started once, but never finished. Only part of a rotting back fence remained of the effort.

The area was known as the Women's Place. Men were not restricted, but since it was used primarily by women, few men outside of the zelandonia visited the site. Ayla had stopped there before, but it was usually to bring a message to someone, or she was with someone who was on the way to some other place. She had never had occasion to stay long. Usually she had come from the direction of the Ninth Cave, and she knew that when entering the small meadow with Grass River at her back, on the outside of the wall on the right was a small cave, a temporary shelter and sometime storage place. Another small cave penetrated the same limestone wall just after rounding the corner into the enclosed valley.

Of much greater importance were two caves, narrow winding fissures that opened out of a small rock shelter that was at the back of the meadow somewhat raised from the level of the floodplain floor. Those caves at the rear of the valley had contributed to the reluctance to make the site into a hunting site, though it would not have mattered if it had been ideally suited to the purpose. The first passage, on the right, wove its way within the limestone wall back toward the way they had come until it came out at a small, narrow exit not far from the first small cave in the right wall. Though it had many engravings on its walls, it and the rock shelter where it started were used primarily as a place to stay while visiting the other cave.

No one was there when Ayla, Jondalar, and Zelandoni arrived. Most people had not yet returned from their summer activities, and the few who stayed at their living sites had no reason to visit. Jondalar unhitched the pole-drags from the horses to give them a rest. The women who used it kept the area generally neat and orderly, but it was visited often and was well used, and a Women's Place was inevitably a children's place as well. When Ayla had visited before, the usual activities of ordinary living were apparent. There had been wooden bowls and boxes, woven baskets, toys, clothing, and racks and posts for drying or making things. Implements of wood, bone, antler, or flint were sometimes lost or broken, or carried off by children and ended up kicked aside or left in the cave, unnoticed in the dark. Food was cooked, trash piled up, and, particularly when the weather was bad, was disposed of inside the cave, but, Ayla had learned, only in the right-hand cave.

Some things were still around. Ayla found a log with a trough dug out of it that had obviously been used to hold liquid, but she decided to use their own utensils to make tea and soup. She gathered some wood and, using an existing black depression filled with charcoal, started a fire and added

cooking stones to heat water. Some logs and chunks of limestone had been dragged close to the fireplace by previous oc-
cupants, and Zelandoni took the stuffed pads from her travois
and placed them around to make the seating more comfortable. Ayla nursed, then put Jonayla down on her blanket on the
grass while she ate, and watched the baby fall asleep.

"Do you want to come along, Jondalar?" Zelandoni asked
when they had finished. "You probably haven't seen it since
you were a boy and made your mark inside."

"Yes, I think I will," he said.

Nearly everyone made a mark on the walls of this cave at
some time, occasionally more than once, although the males
of the community were usually children or young adolescents
when they made theirs. He remembered the first time he went
inside by himself. It was a simple cave with no passages leading off to get lost in, and youngsters were allowed to find their
own way. Generally, they went in alone or at most in pairs to
make their own private marks, whistling or humming or chanting along the way until the walls seemed to answer back. The
marks and engravings did not symbolize or represent names;
they were a way that people told the Great Earth Mother about
themselves, how they defined themselves to Her. Often they
only made finger tracings. It was enough.

After they finished their meal, Ayla wrapped her infant securely to her back and they each lit a lamp and started into
the cave, Zelandoni in front and Wolf bringing up the rear.
Jondalar recalled that the left cave felt exceedingly long—it
was more than eight hundred feet deep, winding through the
limestone—and that the beginning of the fissure was fairly
easy to enter, and unremarkable. Only a few markings on the
walls near the entrance indicated that someone had been there
before.

"Why don't you use your bird whistles to speak to the
Mother, Ayla," the First said.

Ayla had heard the woman humming, not loudly but very
melodically, and hadn't expected to be asked. "If you would
like me to," she said, and began a series of bird calls, the ones
she thought of as softer evening sounds.

About four hundred feet from the entrance, halfway in, the

cave narrowed and the sounds resonated differently. That was where the drawings started. From this point on, the walls were covered with drawings of every kind. The two walls of the winding subterranean passage were marked with almost uncountable, often undecipherably superimposed and intermingled engravings. Some were isolated and many that could be interpreted were very well made. Adult women frequented the cave most often and, consequently, the more accomplished, refined engravings were usually made by them.

Horses predominated, shown at rest and with lively movement, even galloping. Bison were also very prevalent, but there were many other animals: reindeer, mammoths, ibex, bears, cats, wild asses, deer, woolly rhinoceroses, wolves, foxes, and at least one saiga antelope, hundreds of engravings in all. Some were very unusual, like the mammoth with its trunk curled back; the head of a lion that utilized a naturally embedded stone for the eye was strikingly rendered; and a reindeer bending down to drink was outstanding for its beauty and realism, as were the two reindeer facing each other. The walls were fragile and didn't lend themselves well to painting, but were easy to mark and engrave, even with fingers.

There were also many parts of human figures, including masks, hands, and various silhouettes, but always distorted, never as clearly and beautifully drawn as the animals, such as the disproportionately large limbs on the seated figure, shown in profile. Many engravings were incomplete and buried in a network of lines, various geometric symbols, tectiform signs, and undefined marks and scribbles that could be interpreted many ways, sometimes depending on how the light was held. The caves were originally formed by underground rivers, and at the end of the gallery there was still a karstic area of active cave formation.

Wolf ran on ahead into some of the more inaccessible parts of the cave. He came back carrying something in his mouth and dropped it at Ayla's feet. "What is this?" she said as she bent to pick it up. All three of them focused their lamps on the object. "Zelandoni, this looks like a piece of a skull!" Ayla said. "And here is another piece, a part of a jaw. It's small. I think this may have been a woman. Where did he find these, I wonder?"

Zelandoni took them and held them in the light from the lamp. "There may have been a burial in here, long ago. People have lived near here for as long as anyone can remember." She saw Jondalar make an involuntary shudder. He preferred to leave things of the spirit world to the zelandonia, and she knew it.

Jondalar had helped with burials when he was required to do so, but he hated the duty. Usually when men returned from digging burial holes, or other activities that brought them dangerously close to the spirit world, they went to the cave called the Men's Place, on a highland across Grass River from the Third Cave, to be scrubbed and purified. Again, women were not prohibited from the Men's Place, but like a fa'lodge, it was mostly male activities that took place, and few women, outside of the zelandonia, went there.

"The spirit is long gone from these," she said. "The elan found its way to the world of the spirits so long ago that only pieces of bone are left. There may be more."

"Do you know why someone was buried in here, Zelandoni?" Jondalar asked.

"It is not what we usually do, but I am sure this person was put in this Sacred Place for a reason. I don't know why the Mother decided to let the wolf show them to us, but I will put these back farther on. I think it is best to return them to Her."

The One Who Was First went ahead into the twisting darkness of the cave. They watched her light weaving ahead, then disappear. Not long after, it reappeared, and soon they saw the woman returning. "I think it's time to go back," she said.

Ayla was glad to be leaving the cave. Besides being dark, the caves were always damp and chilly once you moved past the opening, and this one felt close and confined, but maybe it was just that she'd had her fill of caves for a while. She just wanted to go home.

When they arrived at the Ninth Cave, they found that more people had come home from the Summer Meeting, though some were planning to leave again soon. They had brought with them a young man who was smiling shyly at a woman seated near him. His hair was light brown and his eyes were gray. Ayla recognized Matagan, the young man of the Fifth

Cave who had been gored in the leg by a woolly rhinoceros the year before.

Ayla and Jondalar had been returning from their period of isolation after their Matrimonial when they saw several young men—inexperienced boys, really—who were baiting a huge, full-grown rhino. The youngsters had been sharing one of the bachelor fa'lodges, some for the first time, and were full of themselves, sure they would live forever. When they saw the woolly rhinoceros, they decided to hunt it themselves without going to find an older, more experienced hunter. They were thinking only of the praise and glory they would get when the people at the Summer Meeting saw their kill.

They were really quite young; some had barely gained hunter status, and only one of them had even seen hunters baiting a rhino, though they had all heard of the technique. They didn't know how deceptively quick the huge creature could be, or how important it was to keep focused and not allow their attention to stray for a moment. That was all it had taken. The rhino had shown signs of tiring, and the boy hadn't kept his attention closely enough on the animal. When it came for him, Matagan was unable to move fast enough. He was badly gored in the right leg below the knee. The injury was severe, with the lower part of his leg bent sharply backward and the jagged broken bones sticking out of the profusely bleeding wound. He would likely have died if Ayla hadn't happened to be there and, from her training in the Clan, knew how to set a broken leg and staunch the bleeding.

When he did survive, the fear was that he might never walk on that leg again. He did walk, but there was permanent damage and some paralysis. He could get around fairly well, but his ability to crouch down or stalk an animal was severely curtailed; he would never be a really good hunter. That was when discussions began about him becoming an apprentice to Jondalar to learn flint-knapping. The boy's mother and her mate, plus Kemordan, the leader of the Fifth Cave, Joharran, Jondalar, and Ayla, since he would be staying with them, had finally settled everything at the Summer Meeting before they left. Ayla liked the youngster and approved of the arrangement. The boy needed to have a skill that would give him respect and status, and she remembered when they were traveling, how much Jondalar had enjoyed teaching his craft to anyone willing to learn, especially youngsters. But she had hoped for a day or so of rest and quiet alone in her home. She took a deep, silent breath and walked over to greet Matagan. He smiled when he saw her coming, and hurried to scamble to his feet.

"Greetings, Matagan," she said, reaching for both of his hands. "In the name of the Great Earth Mother, I welcome you." She looked him over closely in her inconspicuous way, and noted that he seemed rather tall for his age, though he was still young and had not reached his full height. She hoped his injured leg would continue to grow to match the length of his good leg. It was hard to tell how tall he would be, but his limp could get worse if his legs became unequal in size.

"In the name of Doni, I greet you, Ayla," he replied, the polite greeting he had been taught to use.

Jonayla, tied to her mother's back with the carrying blanket, squirmed to see to whom she was talking. "I think Jonayla wants to greet you, too," Ayla said, loosening her blanket and shifting her around to the front. The baby sat wide-eyed in her mother's arms looking at the young man; then suddenly she smiled and held out her arms to him. Ayla was surprised.

He smiled back. "Can I hold her? I know how. I have a sister a little older than her," Matagan said.

And he's probably homesick and lonesome for her already, Ayla thought, as she handed Jonayla to him. It was obvious that he was comfortable holding a baby. "Do you have many brothers and sisters?" she asked.

"I guess so. She's the youngest, I'm the oldest, and there are four in between, including two born together," he said.

"I think you must be quite a help to your mother. She is going to miss you. How many years do you count?" she said.

"I'm a thirteen-year," he said. He became aware of her un-usual accent again. When he had first heard the foreign woman speak, the year before, he had thought her accent was quite strange, but when he was recovering, especially when he woke up after the accident and was in so much pain, he grew to look forward to that accent because she invariably brought some re-lief. And although the other Zelandonia also checked on him, she came regularly, and stayed to talk to him and straighten his bedding to make him comfortable, as well as giving him medicine.

"And you have reached your manhood and had your rites last summer," a voice behind Ayla said. It was Jondalar, who had been hearing the conversation as he approached them. The style of Matagan's clothing, the patterns that had been sewn on them, and the beads and jewelry he wore told Jondalar that the youngster was considered a man of the Fifth Cave of the Zelandonii.

"Yes, last summer at the Meeting," Matagan said. "Before I was hurt."

"Now that you are a man, it's time for you to learn a skill. Have you done much flint knapping?"

"Some. I can make a spear point and a knife, or reshape one that is broken. They aren't the best, but they work," the boy said.

"Perhaps the question I should ask is, do you like working the flint?" Jondalar said.

"I like it when it goes right. Sometimes it doesn't."

Jondalar smiled. "Even for me, sometimes it doesn't," he said. "Have you eaten?"

"I just finished," Matagan said.

"Well, we haven't yet," Jondalar said. "We just got back from a short trip to see some of our neighbors and find out if they suffered any injuries or damage from the earthquake. You know that Ayla is acolyte to the First, don't you?"

"I think everyone knows that," he said, shifting Jonayla around to lean against his shoulder.

"Did you feel the earthquake?" Ayla asked. "Was anyone in your traveling party hurt?"

"We felt it. Some people were knocked down, but no one was really hurt," he said. "I think everyone was scared, though. I know I was."

"I can't think of anyone who wouldn't be afraid during an earthquake. We'll get something to eat; then we'll show you where you can stay. We haven't set anything up special, yet, but we'll work it out later," Jondalar said as they headed toward the other side of the shelter where people were gathered.

Ayla reached for Jonayla.

"I can hold her while you get some food," Matagan said. "If she'll let me."

"Let's see if she will," Ayla said, turning toward the firepit where the food had been set out. Suddenly Wolf appeared. He had stopped for water when they reached the Ninth Cave, and then found that someone had put some food in his bowl. Matagan's eyes opened wider with surprise, but he had seen the wolf before and he didn't seem overly frightened of the animal. Ayla had introduced the wolf to Matagan the year before when she was taking care of him, and the animal sniffed the young man who was holding the baby of his pack, and recognized his scent. When the boy sat down, the wolf sat down beside him. Jonayla seemed happy with the arrangement.

By the time they finished eating, it was getting dark. There were always some prepared torches ready for lighting near the main fire where the group often gathered and Jondalar took one and lit it. They all had traveling gear with them—backframes, sleeping rolls, traveling tents. Jondalar helped Ayla with some of hers, while she carried the baby, but Matagan seemed to be able to handle his own, including a sturdy staff that he sometimes used to walk with. He didn't seem to need it all the time. Ayla suspected he had used it on the long walk from the Sun View, the place of the Summer Meeting, to the Ninth Cave, but probably could get by just fine for shorter distances.

When they reached their dwelling, Jondalar went in first, lighting the way, and held open the drape across the entrance. Matagan went in next, followed by Ayla.

"Why don't you set up your sleeping roll here in the main room near the fire for now. We'll work out something better tomorrow," Jondalar said, suddenly wondering how long Matagan would be living with them.

Part Two

18

"Matagan, have you seen Jonayla and Jondalar?" Ayla called out when she saw the young man walking with a limp, coming out of the addition that had been built next to her dwelling. There were three youths living there now: Matagan; Jonfilar, who had come from the west, near the Great Waters; and Garthadal, whose mother was the leader of his Cave, and had traveled with him from far to the southeast because she had heard of Jondalar's skill.

After four years, Matagan was the most senior of Jondalar's apprentices and had gained so much proficiency that he was helping the man train the younger ones. He could have gone back to the Fifth Cave, or almost any other Cave, as an experienced flint-knapper in his own right, but by now he thought of the Ninth Cave as his home and preferred to stay and work with his mentor.

"I saw them earlier heading toward the horse surround. I think I heard him promise her yesterday that he would take her riding today if it didn't rain. She's getting good at riding Gray, as little as she is, even if she can't get on or off by herself yet."

Ayla smiled to herself with the memory of Jondalar riding Racer with Jonayla sitting in front of him before she was even walking, and they both trained Gray with the child on her back in front of them, her little arms hugging the mare's thick neck. The young girl and the young mare grew up with each other, and Ayla thought the tie between them was as close as the one between Whinney and herself. Jonayla was good with all the horses, including the stallion—in some ways even better than her mother because she learned to direct him using the halter and lead rope, the way Jondalar did. Ayla still directed Whinney using body language and wasn't as comfortable riding a horse using Jondalar's technique.

"When they come back, would you tell Jondalar I'll be late tonight? I may not be back until morning. Do you know about the man who fell off the cliff near The Crossing this morning?" Ayla said.

"Yes. A visitor?" Matagan said.

"A neighbor from New Home. He used to be with the Seventh Cave; now he lives at Bear Hill. I can't understand why anybody would try to climb High Rock when it's so wet from all the rain. Mud has been sliding down some of the steeper slopes; it was probably muddy up there, too," Ayla said. This has been a wet spring, she thought. Springs have been more wet ever since we had that cold winter that Marthona predicted a few years ago.

"How is he?" Matagan asked. He knew what it was like to suffer the consequences of poor judgment.

"He's seriously hurt. Broken bones and I don't know what else. I'm afraid Zelandoni will be up all night with him. I'll be staying to help her," Ayla said.

"With you and the First there, I'm sure he's getting the best care possible," Matagan said, then smiled. "And I speak from experience."

Ayla smiled back. "I hope so. A runner was sent to tell his family. They should be arriving soon. Proleva is making a meal for them and some others at the main hearth. I'm sure there will be enough for you and the boys, and Jondalar and Jonayla, too," she added as she turned to hurry back.

She found herself still thinking about Jonayla and the animals as she walked back. When she had to be away, Wolf sometimes stayed with Jonayla, sometimes with her. If she went with Zelandoni to help someone at another Cave, Wolf usually came with her, but when she had to make "sacrifices" and endure "tests" as part of her training—go without sleep, give up Pleasures, fast for periods of time—she usually went alone.

She often stayed at the small shelter called the Little Hollow of Fountain Rocks, which was comfortable enough. It was right next to the Deep of Fountain Rocks, sometimes called Doni's Deep, the long cave that was the first Sacred Site she saw when she came to live with the Zelandonii. Fountain Rocks was about a mile away from the Ninth Cave, plus a gentle-sloped but long climb up the cliff. The long painted cave had other names, especially to the zelandonia, such as Entrance to the Womb of the Mother or the Mother's Birth Canal. It was the most Sacred Site in their immediate region.

Jondalar wasn't always happy when she had to be away, but he never minded taking care of Jonayla, and Ayla was glad for both of them that they were developing such a close relationship. He had even started teaching her to knap flint alongside his apprentices.

Ayla's musings were cut short when she noticed two women walking toward her on her way back, Marona and her cousin. Wylopa nodded in greeting and smiled whenever she saw her, and though it always looked insincere, Ayla smiled back. Marona usually acknowledged her only with the briefest of nods and Ayla responded in kind. The woman didn't even do that much if no one else was around, but this time Marona did smile at her. It made Ayla look at her again. It was in no way a pleasant smile. It was more like a sneer, a gloating sneer.

Ever since her return, Ayla couldn't help but wonder why Marona had moved back to the Ninth Cave. She thought the Fifth Cave had accepted her well enough, and the woman had been known to remark when she moved there that she liked it better. I like it better when she's there, too, Ayla thought.

It wasn't just because Marona and Jondalar had once been a couple. Rather that no one had been more malicious and spiteful to her, beginning with the trick of the boys' winter underwear so people would laugh at her. But Ayla had faced the laughter down and gained the respect of the Ninth Cave. Now, particularly when she was riding Whinney, she often wore a similar outfit on purpose, and so did many other women, much to Marona's vexation. Light leggings and a sleeveless tunic in soft leather were quite comfortable to wear when the days were mild.

Ayla had heard talk from some of Matagan's visiting relatives that Marona had angered some high-status women of the

Fifth Cave, kin of Kemordan, the leader, or his mate, for persuading a man who was Promised to one of them to run away with her instead. With her nearly white blond hair and dark gray eyes, she was an attractive woman, though Ayla thought the lines of the frown she wore so often were beginning to etch themselves more deeply on her face. Just like most of her relationships, the liaison didn't last very long, and after claiming his regret and making satisfactory reparations, he was accepted back, but she was looked upon with less favor. As Ayla neared Zelandoni's dwelling, her musings slipped into the back of her mind as thoughts of the injured man filled it.

Later in the evening, when she stepped out of the Donier's abode, which was both her home and an infirmary, she saw Jondalar sitting next to Joharran, Proleva, and Marthona. They had finished their meal and were sipping tea, watching Jonayla and Proleva's daughter, Sethona. Jonayla was a happy, healthy child and very pretty, everyone said, with fine, very light soft curly hair and Jondalar's extraordinarily vivid blue eyes. To Ayla, Jonayla was the most beautiful thing she had ever seen, but growing up in the Clan had taught her to be reticent in expressing such thoughts about her own child. It could bring bad luck, and when she tried to look at it objectively, she believed she was bound to feel that way about her own offspring, but in her heart, she could hardly believe such an amazing child could be hers.

Sethona, Jonayla's close cousin, born only a few days before her and a constant playmate, was gray-eyed with dark blond hair. Ayla thought she resembled Marthona; she already showed elements of the former leader's dignity and grace, and her clear direct gaze. Ayla turned her attention to Joharran and Jondalar's mother. Marthona was showing her age, her hair was more gray, her face more lined, but it wasn't just her physical appearance. She wasn't well and that worried Ayla. She and Zelandoni had discussed her situation, and every possible remedy and treatment they could think of to help her, but they both knew there was no way to keep Marthona from walking in the next world someday; they could only hope to delay it.

Though she had lost her own mother, Ayla felt herself lucky to have had Iza, the Clan medicine woman, as the mother who raised her as a girl, with Creb, the Mog-ur, as the man of her hearth. Nezzie of the Mamutoi was the mother who wanted to adopt her into the Lion Camp, although the Mamut of the Mammoth Hearth had done it instead. Jondalar's mother had treated Ayla like a daughter from the first, and she thought of Marthona as her mother, her Zelandonii mother. She felt close to Zelandoni as well, but she was more a mentor and friend.

Wolf was watching the girls, his head down on his front paws. He had noticed Ayla when she approached, but when she didn't immediately join them, he raised his head and looked at her, which caused everyone else to look, too. That made Ayla aware that she had been so lost in thought she had stopped walking. She continued toward them.

"How is he?" Joharran asked when she neared.

"It is still hard to know. We've put splints on the broken bones in his legs and arm, but we don't know what may be broken inside. He still breathes, but he hasn't roused. His mate and mother are in with him now," Ayla said. "Zelandoni feels she should stay with them, but I think someone could bring her something to eat, which might encourage his family to come out and eat, too."

"I'll take her the food and try to persuade them to come out here," Proleva said, getting up and walking toward the stack of visitors' dishes. She took an ivory plate, which had been flaked off a large mammoth tusk and smoothed with sandstone rocks, and selected some slices of meat from the whole mountain goat kid that had been roasted on a spit. It was a rare treat. Several hunters from the Ninth and neighboring Caves had gone ibex hunting, and had had some luck. Proleva added some leafy greens and lightly cooked spring stalks of new thistle and roots of some kind, then carried it to the entrance of Zelandoni's dwelling and scratched at the exposed side of a piece of rawhide next to the heavy leather drape across the entrance. A moment later she went in. Not long after, she walked out with the mate and mother of the injured man, brought them to the main hearth, and gave them visitor plates.

"I should go back in," Ayla said, looking at Jondalar. "Did Matagan tell you I will probably be late tonight?"

"Yes. I'll put Jonayla to bed," he said, standing and picking up the child. He embraced the woman, touching cheeks, while Ayla held them both close.

"I rode Gray today," Jonayla said. "Jondy took me out. He rode Racer. Whinney came too, but she didn't have anyone to ride her. Why don't you come, mama?"

"I wish I could have, Baby," Ayla said, hugging them both again. Her pet name for her child was similar to the word for "baby" that she had called the injured lion cub she had once found, nursed back to health, and then raised. It was a modification of the Clan word for "infant" or "little one." "But a man fell down and got hurt today. Zelandoni has been trying to make him feel better, and I've been helping her."

"When he gets better, will you come?" Jonayla said.

"Yes, when he gets better, I will come riding with you," Ayla said, thinking, *if* he gets better. Then she turned to Jondalar. "Why don't you take Wolf with you, too." She had noticed the mate of the man eyeing the animal warily. Everyone knew about the wolf and most had seen him, at least from a distance, but not everyone had tried to find a place to sit and eat with him nearby. The woman had also been looking askance at Ayla, especially after hearing the word she had used to refer to her child. Even modified, the word had a distinctly strange and unfamiliar sound.

After Jondalar left with Jonayla and Wolf, Ayla went back into Zelandoni's dwelling. "Has there been any improvement in Jacharal?" she asked.

"Not that I've been able to see," the One Who Was First said. She was glad the two women relatives had gone out so she could speak frankly. "Sometimes people languish in this condition for quite a while. If someone can manage to get them to take in water and food, they last longer, but if not they are gone within days. It's as though the spirit is confused, the elan is not sure if it wants to leave this world while the body still breathes, even if the rest of the body is damaged beyond repair. Sometimes they wake up, but may not be able to move, or some part of them won't move or doesn't heal right. Occasionally, given enough time, some people will heal from a fall like that, but most often they don't."

"Has he lost fluid from his nose or ears?" Ayla asked.

"Not since he's been here. There is an injury to his head, but it doesn't seem very deep, just a few superficial scratches. He has so many broken bones, I'm guessing his real damage is internal. I'll watch him tonight."

"I'll stay with you. Jondalar took Jonayla, and Wolf, with him. This man's mate seemed uncomfortable around Wolf," Ayla said. "I thought most people were used to him by now."

"I suspect she hasn't had time to get used to your wolf. She's not from here; Amelana is her name. Jacharal's mother told me the story. He went on a Journey to the south, mated her there, and brought her back with him. I'm not even sure if she was born in Zelandonii territory or only near it. The borders of territories are not always clear. She seems to speak it well enough, though with that southern inflection, a little like Beladora, Kimeran's mate."

"What a shame, to come all the way here, and then possibly lose her man. I don't know what I would have done if something had happened to Jondalar right after I got here, or even now," Ayla said, shuddering at the thought.

"You would stay here and become a Zelandoni, just as you are now. You said yourself, you don't really have anyplace to go back to. You're not going to make the long Journey all the way back to the Mamutoi alone, and weren't you adopted by them? You're more than adopted here. You belong. You are Zelandonii," the woman said.

Ayla was a little surprised at the vehemence of the First's statement, but more than that, she was gratified. It let her know she was wanted.

It wasn't the next morning, but early the day after, that Ayla finally returned to her home. The sun was just coming up, and she paused a moment to watch the glowing color, brighter in one spot, begin to saturate the sky across The River. The rain had stopped, but clouds hanging low on the horizon strung out in wispy threads of brilliant reds and golds. When the searing light first lifted above the cliffs, Ayla tried to shade her eyes to take notice of the formations nearby so she could compare the rising of the intense radiance with where it rose the day before.

Soon she would be required to note the risings and settings
of the sun and moon for a whole year. The hardest part of that,
she was told by others of the zelandonia, was missing sleep,
especially watching the moon, which sometimes first appeared or disappeared in the middle of the day, and sometimes
in the middle of the night. The sun, of course, always rose in
the morning and set in the evening, but some days were longer
than others, and it moved across the horizon in a predictable
way. For half the year as the days grew longer, it traveled a
little farther north every day until it stood still for a few days
in the middle of summer, when the days were longest, the time
of the Summer Longday. Then it reversed its direction, setting
a little farther south every day while the days got shorter, passing the time when day and night were the same length, and the
sun set nearly directly west, until it stood still again for a few
days in the middle of winter, the time of the Winter Shortday.

Ayla had talked with Jacharal's mother and Amelana, and
had become better acquainted with the young woman. They
had at least one thing in common: they were both foreign
women who had mated Zelandonii men. She was quite young,
Ayla realized, and a little unpredictable and capricious. And
she was pregnant, and still suffering some morning sickness.
She really wished they could do more for Jacharal, for Amelana's sake as well as his own.

Both Ayla and Zelandoni watched him closely, for themselves as well as for him. They wanted to see his progress to
try to learn more about conditions such as his. So far they had
managed to get some water into him, but it was only reflex action that caused him to swallow, and sometimes choke, when
they put water in his mouth. He didn't wake up as a result of
their efforts. While they were together, Zelandoni also spent
some time instructing Ayla in the ways of the zelandonia. They
discussed medicines and healing practices, and conducted
several ceremonies in an effort to elicit the help of the Great
Earth Mother. Ayla was familiar with only some of it. They
hadn't yet gotten the whole community involved in the healing
ceremonies, which would be much more elaborate and formal.

They also discussed a forthcoming Journey the older woman
wanted to make with her acolyte, a long Journey that would

take the entire summer, and she wanted to leave soon. There were several Sacred Sites to the south and the east that the First thought they should visit. They would not be going alone. Not only would Jondalar come, but Willamar, the Trade Master, and his two young assistants. They were discussing who else should make the trip with them, and Jonokol's name came up. The idea of traveling so far to see new places was exciting, but Ayla knew it would also be arduous, and was grateful for the horses. It would make traveling easier for her and the First. Besides, Zelandoni liked arriving on the pole-drag being pulled by Whinney. It created a commotion and she liked doing things that brought attention to the zelandonia, and the importance of the position of the First.

When Ayla arrived at her dwelling, she thought about making a morning tea for Jondalar, but she was so tired. She hadn't slept much, staying up so Zelandoni could rest. In the morning, the Donier had sent her home to get some sleep. It was so early, everyone was still sleeping, except Wolf, who was outside waiting to greet her. She smiled when she saw him. It amazed her how he always seemed to know when she was coming, or where she was going.

When she went in, Ayla noticed that Jonayla was sleeping beside Jondalar. She had her own smaller sleeping roll beside theirs, but she liked to crawl in with them, and when Ayla wasn't there, which was happening more often, she climbed in with him. Ayla started to pick Jonayla up to move her back to her own sleeping place, then changed her mind and decided to let them finish sleeping without being disturbed. They'd be up soon enough. She went to Jonayla's bed, and though it was small, there was extra bedding in the storage area. Rearranging her child's bedroll somewhat, she used it instead. When Jondalar woke up and saw Ayla sleeping in Jonayla's place, he smiled, then frowned. He thought she must have been very tired, but he missed having her beside him.

Jacharal died a few days later, without ever waking up. Ayla used the travois to transport him back to the Seventh Cave. His mother wanted the funeral ceremony to be held there and him to be buried nearby so his elan would be in a familiar area while he was finding his way to the next world. Ayla, Jondalar,

Zelandoni, and several others from the Ninth and neighboring Caves and all the people from Bear Hill took part in the burying ritual. Afterward Amelana approached Zelandoni and Ayla and asked to talk with them.

"Someone told me that you are planning to make a Journey south soon. Is that true?" Amelana said.

"Yes," Zelandoni said, wondering what the young woman wanted. She thought she knew and was already considering how to handle it.

"Will you take me with you? I want to go home," the young woman said, her eyes welling up with tears.

"But this is your home, isn't it?" the First said.

"I don't want to stay here," Amelana cried. "I didn't know that Jacharal wanted to move to New Home and live at Bear Hill. I don't like it. There's nothing there. Everything has to be made or built, even our dwelling, and it's still not finished. They don't even have a Zelandoni. I'm pregnant and I would have to walk to another Cave to have my baby. Now I don't even have Jacharal. I told him not to climb up High Rock."

"Have you talked to Jacharal's mother? I'm sure you could stay at the Seventh Cave."

"I don't want to stay at the Seventh Cave. I don't know the people there either, and some of them haven't been very nice to me because I come from the south. I am Zelandonii after all."

"You could move to the Second Cave. Beladora is from the south," the First said.

"She's south, but more east and she's a leader's mate. I don't really know her. And I just want to go home. I want to have my baby there. I miss my mother," Amelana said, and burst out into sobs.

"How far along are you?" Zelandoni asked.

"My bleeding stopped more than three Moons ago," she said, sniffling.

"Well, if you are sure you want to leave, we'll take you with us," Zelandoni said.

The young woman smiled through her tears. "Thank you! Oh, thank you."

"Do you know where your Cave is?"

"It's on the central highland, a little toward the east, not far from the Southern Sea."

"We may not be going there directly. There are some places we need to stop along the way."

"I don't mind if we stop," Amelana said, then added a little tentatively, "but I would like to get home before the baby comes."

"I think we can manage that," said the One Who Was First.

After Amelana left, Zelandoni mumbled under her breath, "The handsome stranger visits your Cave and it seems so romantic to run off with him to make a home in a new place. I have no doubt she pleaded just as hard with her mother to let her get mated and go live with him at his home. But once you arrive, you find it's not so different from the old one, only you don't know anyone. Then your exciting new mate decides to join with a group that wants to make a new Cave. They expect you to be as excited about making a place of your own as they are, but they have only moved around the hill from their old Cave, and they are with people they know.

"Amelana is a total stranger, with a slightly different way of speaking, and probably used to a little coddling, who has moved to a new place where customs and expectations are a little different. She doesn't need the excitement of making a new home; she has just moved to a new home. She needs to be able to settle down and learn about her new people. But her mate, who has already shown that he likes to take risks just by going on a Journey, is ready for the adventure of creating a new Cave with his—but not her—friends and relatives.

"They were probably both beginning to regret their hasty mating, beginning to argue about differences, perceived and real, and then she finds herself pregnant with no one to make a fuss over her. Her mother and aunts, and all her sisters and cousins and friends, are back at the home she left. And then her danger-loving mate takes one risk too many and dies. It's probably better for everyone if she goes back to her home, a little wiser for her adventure. She really doesn't have anyone here with whom she has a close attachment."

"I didn't have anyone here when I came," Ayla said.

"But you did. You had Jondalar," Zelandoni said.

"You said that her mate already had shown that he liked to take risks by going on a Journey. I met Jondalar on his Journey. Didn't that make him a man who liked risks?"

"He was not the one who loved to take risks; his brother was. He went along to be with Thonolan, to protect him, knowing of his tendency to rush into precarious situations. And he had no one here to hold him. Marona really had nothing to offer him, except an occasional interlude of Pleasures. He loved his brother more than her, and perhaps he wanted to get out of the implied Promise that she was assuming much more than he was, but he wasn't able to just come out and tell her. He was always looking for someone special. For a while he thought he found it with me, and I admit I was tempted, but I knew that it would never work. I'm glad that he found what he wanted with you, Ayla," the large woman said. "Your situation, though superficially similar, is not at all the same as Amelana's."

Ayla thought about how wise Zelandoni was; then she suddenly wondered how many people were going to be making this Journey south that the First had proposed. The Donier, Jondalar, herself, and Jonayla, of course; she was saying the counting words under her breath, and touching her leg with her fingers, tallying the people as she named them. That's four. Willamar and his two assistants are going, seven. He said he wanted to give them the full measure of his experience. He also said it would likely be his last extended trading mission, that he was tired of traveling. No doubt he is, Ayla thought, but she wondered if part of it was because he knew Marthona was not well and he wanted to spend more time with her.

And now Amelana is going; that's eight. And if Jonokol comes, nine: eight adults and one child. Ayla had a feeling there would be more. Almost as though someone had known what she was thinking, Kimeran and Beladora, with their five-year twins, sought out Zelandoni. They wanted to go south, too, and bring the children to visit her people. Beladora was almost certain that the First wouldn't mind visiting her Cave. It was near one of the most beautiful Sacred Sites in the land, and one of the oldest. But they didn't want to make the entire trip that the Donier had planned. They wanted to meet them along the way.

"Where do you want to meet?" Zelandoni asked.

"Perhaps at Jondecam's sister's Cave," Beladora said. "Camora is also Kimeran's sister, at least they were raised together, along with Jondecam. Camora lives at her mate's Cave, which is on the way to the Cave of my people."

Ayla smiled at the beautiful woman with dark wavy hair and a full rounded figure, who also spoke with an accent, though it was not as unusual as hers. She felt a special bond with her, another foreign woman who had mated a Zelandonii man and returned with him. Ayla knew about the special circumstances of Kimeran and his much older sister, who took care of him along with her own children following the death of their mother. Her mate had also died young. She became a Zelandoni after her children and her brother were grown.

"There is highland between here and Beladora's people if you try to go directly," Kimeran was saying. "Good hunting for ibex and chamois, but difficult climbing in places even if you follow rivers. I thought we'd travel south and then east, and go around it. I think it might be easier for Gioneran and Ginadela, and for us when we have to carry them. Their legs are short still." Kimeran smiled. "Not like mine, or yours, Jondalar." There was warm feeling between Jondalar and the tall, blond man.

"Are you going to travel alone?" Zelandoni asked. "That may not be wise if you are taking the children."

"We had thought of asking Jondecam, and Levela and her son, if they would like to come with us, but we wanted to ask you first, Zelandoni," Beladora said.

"I think they would make good traveling companions," the First said. "Yes, we could meet up with you along the way."

Ayla was tapping her fingers on the side of her leg again. That's sixteen in all, if Jonokol comes, she thought. But Amelana will only be with us on the way there, not the return visit, and we won't meet up with Kimeran and the others until later.

"Will we be going to the Summer Meeting?" Jondalar asked.

"Only for a few days, I think," Zelandoni said. "I will ask the Fourteenth and the Fifth to take care of my duties. Between them, I'm sure everything will get done, and I'll be interested to know how they work together. I'll send a runner to Jonokol before we go to the Meeting, to see if he wants to come along with us, and if he can. He may have other plans—after all, he is Zelandoni of the Nineteenth Cave now. I can't just tell him what to do anymore . . . not that I ever could, even when he was my acolyte."

The morning dawned sunny and bright the day the Ninth Cave left for the Summer Meeting. It had been raining on and off for several days before, but on this day the clouds were gone, and the sky shimmered with a crystalline brilliance that gave distant highlands an intense clarity. They traveled south-west this year, and the place where the Summer Meeting was being held was farther away than customary, which took them longer than usual to get there.

When they arrived, Ayla noticed that some people from more western Caves were there who were unknown to her. They were the ones who gawked a little longer at her with the three horses and the wolf, not to mention the pole-drags the horses were pulling, one of which carried the First. There was some disappointment when it was learned that the First and her acolyte with the unusual animals would not be stay-ing long. Ayla thought she would have liked to stay and get to know some of the Zelandonii she hadn't met, but she was also looking forward to the summer Journey the First had planned.

Jonokol did decide to join them. He had never made a very extensive Donier Tour, partly because in the beginning he hadn't really planned to become a full-fledged Zelandoni; he just wanted to make images and paintings, and the First hadn't pushed him. After he saw the beautiful white walls of the new Sacred Cave and became serious about the zelandonia, he moved to the Nineteenth Cave, which was closest to the new hallowed site. His Zelandoni there had been too old and weak to make any long Journeys, although her mind was sharp until the end. He had since heard remarkable things about some of the painted caves to the south and didn't want to pass up this opportunity to see them for himself; he might never have another chance.

Ayla was pleased. He had been welcoming to her from the beginning, and he could be good company. They stayed only four days at the Meeting, but almost everyone was there to see them off. A traveling band that had become the size of a small Cave, they made quite a spectacle as they started out, primarily because of the animals and the accoutrements, but the group included more than the ones who planned to make the long trip together. Several people from some of the Caves to the west had joined them who were unfamiliar to Ayla; they planned to go on in another direction. There were also some people from the neighboring Caves, particularly the Eleventh, including Kareja, their leader.

The First wanted to travel south following The River until they reached its mouth at its confluence with Big River. Once there they would have to cross the larger river, which as its name implied was deeper and wider than The River, with a swifter current. They could cross their familiar river at the Crossing Place, a wider, shallower section, using stepping-stones, or wading, sometimes up to the waist, depending on the season, but it would take more than that to cross Big River. To solve that problem, the First and Willamar had approached Kareja and some members of the Eleventh Cave, who were known for the rafts they made, to take the travelers and their gear down The River to its mouth and then across the larger expanse of Big River.

They started out heading back toward the Ninth Cave. With only adults—except for Jonayla—and the horses, their pace was much faster than when an entire Cave moved. Most of the travelers were young and healthy, and though the First was a big woman—a size that gave her a commanding presence— she was strong and walked much of the time. When she got tired and felt she couldn't keep up, she was able to ride on the travois, which did not in any way detract from her authority or dignified bearing, especially since she was the only one who rode on a seat on the pole-drag that was pulled by Ayla's horse.

That evening, when they camped for the night, the First and the Trading Master began discussions with Kareja, the leader of the Eleventh Cave, and some of the others who were familiar with the use of their rafts and could estimate how many rafts and people it would require to take the travelers on the next part of their Journey. Then the details for the exchange of goods and services for the use of the rafts had to be worked out. It was not a private discussion and the Zelandonii who were unfamiliar to the Ninth and Eleventh Caves were very interested. A couple of them even wondered if the rafts could be used to travel west on Big River to the Great Waters of the West, which of course they could, at least during the right seasons; it was coming back that was difficult.

As part of their bartering, Kareja of the Eleventh Cave had been asking Jondalar for a future service from the Ninth Cave in exchange for their service in handling the rafts. Jondalar had been sitting in on the talks along with the First, but was wishing Joharran were there. Promises of undeclared future services could be problematic and might require more than some wanted to give.

"I don't think I have the right to make a commitment like that for the Ninth Cave," Jondalar said. "I'm not the leader. Maybe Willamar or Zelandoni can."

Kareja had been waiting until the time was right in the negotiations to ask for a particular service from Jondalar that she wanted for a person in her Cave. "But you can make a commitment for yourself, Jondalar," Kareja said. "There is a young woman I know who has shown great promise as a worker of the flint. If you would take her as an apprentice, I would call this matter complete."

Zelandoni watched him, wondering how he would respond. She knew he had been asked by many to train a youngster, but he was very selective. He already had three apprentices and couldn't possibly take on all who asked. But this was his mate's Donier Tour and it wouldn't be inappropriate for him to contribute something to make it easier.

"A girl? I doubt that a woman could become a fully trained flint-knapper," a man from one of the western Caves commented. He had traveled with them from the Summer Meeting. "I've had a little training in working with flint, and it takes both strength and precision to make good tools. We all know of Jondalar's reputation as a flint-knapper. Why should he waste his time trying to train a girl?"

Ayla had become quite interested in the conversation. She didn't at all agree with the man. In her experience, women could knap flint as well as men, but if Jondalar took on a woman apprentice, where would she stay? He couldn't put her in with the young men apprentices, especially when her monthly bleeding came. Although the Zelandonii were not as strict about it as the Clan, where a woman couldn't even look at a man at that time, a woman did need privacy. That meant she would have to live in their dwelling with them, or some other arrangement would have to be made.

Jondalar had obviously been thinking the same thing. "I'm not sure we can take in a young woman, Kareja," he said.

"Are you saying a woman cannot learn to knap flint?" Kareja said. "Women make tools all the time. A woman isn't going to run to a flint-knapper every time a tool breaks when she's scraping a hide or butchering a kill. She reworks it or makes a new one herself."

Kareja appeared calm, but the First knew she was struggling to control herself. She wanted to tell the man from the west outright how absurd he was, but it seemed to her that Jondalar was agreeing with him. Zelandoni was watching the exchange with interest.

"Oh, I know a woman can make tools for her own uses, a scraper or a knife, but can a woman make a hunting tool? Spear points and darts have to fly straight and true, or you miss the kill," the man said. "I don't blame the flint-knapper for not wanting to take a woman as an apprentice."

Kareja was incensed. "Jondalar! Is he right? Do you think women can't learn to knap flint as well as any man?"

"That has nothing to do with it," Jondalar said. "Of course women can knap flint. When I was living with Dalanar and he was teaching me, he taught my close cousin, Joplaya, right alongside me. We were rather competitive, and when I was younger I'd never tell her, but now I wouldn't hesitate to say that in some ways she's better than I am. It's just that I don't know where a young woman would stay. I can't put her in with the three apprentices I have. They're men and a woman needs some privacy. We could take her in with us, but an apprentice needs a place to keep her tools, and her samples, and flint chips are sharp. Ayla gets upset if any have stuck on my clothes when I come in. She doesn't want them around Jonayla, and I don't blame her. If I took on your young woman, we'd have to build an addition to the apprentice dwelling, or a separate one."

Kareja immediately calmed down. That the young woman from the Eleventh Cave should have privacy was a reasonable response. With a woman like Ayla for a mate, who was a credible hunter besides being a Zelandoni acolyte, she should have known Jondalar wouldn't share the ludicrous views of that man from the west. After all, Jondalar's mother had been a leader. But he did bring up a good point, the tall, thin woman thought.

"A separate one would be better, I think," Kareja said. "And the Eleventh Cave will help you build it, or if you tell me where you want it, we can build it while you are gone on this Journey."

"Wait a heartbeat!" Jondalar said, his eyes opening wide with surprise at the speed with which Kareja had taken over. Zelandoni was smiling to herself and glanced at Ayla, who was fighting to keep her smile from showing. "I didn't say I would take her. I always have to test my prospective apprentices. I don't even know who she is."

"You know her. It's Norava. I saw you working with her last summer," Kareja said.

Jondalar relaxed and grinned. "Yes, I do know her. I think she could be an excellent flint-knapper. When we were on that aurochs hunt last year, she had broken a couple of points. She was reworking them when I walked by. I stopped for a moment to watch and she asked for some help. I showed her a few things, and she immediately caught on. She learns quick and has good hands. Yes, if you make sure she has a place to stay, Kareja, I'll take Norava as an apprentice."

19

M ost of the people from neighboring Caves who had not gone to the Summer Meeting were at the Ninth Cave when the travelers arrived; word had been sent ahead by a runner and others had been watching out for them. A meal was ready and waiting. Hunters had gone out and brought down a megaceros, whose massive palmate antlers were still in velvet, bringing the blood supply that enabled them to grow to their magnificent and increasing size every year.

In mature males a set of antlers could span in excess of twelve feet, each one three feet in width, or more. The projecting tines were often cut off for other purposes, leaving a large, rather concave palm section of strong bone-like keratin material that was very serviceable. It could be used as a serving platter, or with a sharpened edge as a shovel, especially for moving soft material like ashes from a fireplace, or soft sand on the river's edge, or snow. Shaped in a suitable way, it could also be used as an effective oar or rudder to help propel and steer rafts. The huge deer also supplied meat for a gathering of hungry travelers, as well as members of the Ninth Cave and their neighbors, with plenty left over for all.

The next morning the ones who were traveling with the First gathered their belongings, and some extra megaceros meat for the Journey, and walked the short distance to The Crossing. They waded across The River to the wooden dock in front of the shelter known as River Place, the Eleventh Cave of the Zelandonii. Several rafts made of small whole trees that were stripped into pliable logs, then lashed together, were tied up to the dock, a simple wooden structure that jutted out over the river. Some

were being repaired; the rest were ready for use. One new one
was being made. A series of logs laid out in a row on the beach
showed the process of construction. They were aligned with the
thicker end of the small trees at the back end, and the thinner,
upper part of the trunks brought together into a kind of prow
and pointing forward.

The horses had pulled the pole-drags to the Eleventh Cave
with most of the gear of the travelers, but now everything had
to be stowed on the rafts and tied down. Fortunately, the Zelandonii knew how to travel light. They brought only what they
could carry themselves. The only extra weight was the poles
and connecting pieces of the travoises. Except for Ayla and
Jondalar, they hadn't grown to depend on having the assistance
of horses and pole-drags to help them carry their things.

The people of the Eleventh Cave, who would be guiding the
rafts downstream, were directing the loading of the rafts, which
had to be well balanced or they could be difficult to control.
Jondalar and Ayla helped to load the long pole-drags onto the
raft that would run first, the one that would carry the First, Willamar, and Jonokol. The heavier pole-drag, the one with the seat,
had to be dismantled and was loaded on the second raft, which
would float behind. It would take Amelana and Willamar's two
young apprentice traders, Tivonan and Palidar.

Ayla and Jondalar, with Jonayla of course, would ride the
horses on the riverbank, if there was one, or they would wade or
swim, or in some cases ride farther inland. There was one area
of rapids in particular, places with high rock sides and rough
water, that Kareja strongly suggested they ride around inland.
She also pointed out that anyone who might be frightened by a
difficult passage might want to walk the inland trail as well. A
few years back they had lost a raft there and some people were
injured, but none died.

While they were waiting, a woman came down from the rock
shelter that was higher up and back from the water's edge and
went to talk with the First. She wanted the healer to look at
her daughter, who was in great pain from her teeth. Ayla asked
Jondalar to look after Jonayla; then she and the First followed
the woman back up to the living shelter. It was smaller than the
Ninth Cave's shelter, but then most were. The people who lived

there had made it comfortable. The woman took them to a small dwelling under the overhanging shelf. Inside, a young woman who could count perhaps sixteen years was tossing and turning on a sleeping roll, sweating profusely. One cheek was red and severely swollen. She was obviously suffering from a terrible toothache.

"I've had some experience with toothaches," Ayla said to the young woman, recalling the time she helped Iza pull one of Creb's teeth. "Would you let me look at it?"

The young woman sat up and shook her head, "No," she said in a muffled voice. She stood up and went to the First, and touched the side of her face. "Just stop the pain."

"Our Zelandoni gave us something for her pain before he left, but it seems so much worse now; the medicine doesn't do much good," the mother said.

Ayla watched Zelandoni. The big woman scowled and shook her head.

"I'll give her some strong medicine that will put her to sleep," the First said to the young woman's mother. "And leave some with you to give her later."

"Thank you. Thank you so much," the mother said.

As Ayla and Zelandoni walked back down to the water's edge, Ayla turned to her mentor with a questioning look. "Do you know what's wrong with her tooth?"

"She's had a problem since her teeth first started to grow in. She has too many, a double row," the First said. Then seeing Ayla's quizzical look, she explained. "She has two sets of teeth trying to grow into the same spaces at the same time, and they have grown in wrong, all crowded together. She had terrible teething pains when she was a baby, and again when her second teeth came in. After that she was fine for a while; the teeth didn't hurt her for several years, but then the very back teeth started growing in and she started getting painful toothaches again."

"Can't some of the teeth be taken out?" Ayla said.

"Zelandoni of the Eleventh has tried, but they are packed so tightly together, he couldn't get any out. The young woman tried herself a few moons ago, and ended up breaking some. Her toothaches have been worse since then. I think there may be suppuration and inflammation now, but she won't let anyone look. I'm not sure her mouth will ever heal. She will probably die from those teeth. It might be kinder to give her too much of the pain medicine and let her go to the next world quietly," the First said. "But that will be for her and her mother to decide."

"But she's so young, and she looks like a strong, healthy woman," Ayla said.

"Yes, and it's a shame she has to suffer so, but I'm afraid it won't stop now until the Mother takes her," the Donier said, "especially if she won't let anyone help her."

By the time they got back down to The River, the rafts were almost loaded. Two rafts were being used to hold the six travelers who would be floating downriver and some of the gear from the pole-drags. Ayla and Jondalar on horseback would wear their backframes and carry their own personal things. Of course, Wolf would manage quite well on his own. Kareja told them that they considered taking three rafts, but there were only enough people to handle two at the moment. They would have had to send for more people and wait until they arrived, so they decided two would be enough. They never took such long and possibly dangerous trips with fewer than two rafts.

The floating craft were pushed upstream by using one or more long poles to thrust against the bottom of the river, and were carried downstream by the current. Since that was their direction, once the rope that held a raft to the dock was released, the river made the work easy. The pole was used mainly to help steer the craft and to avoid jutting rocks. They used another steering mechanism as well: an antler of a megaceros with the tines removed and the central palm shaped into a rudder and attached to a handle. It was mounted in the center of the stern of the craft in such a way that it could be pivoted left or right to change direction. In addition, long oars were also shaped out of the palmate antlers of moose or megaceros and attached to poles to help propel and maneuver the floating wooden platforms. But it took skill and experience to keep the unwieldy, clumsy craft on course, and usually three people working closely together.

Ayla put the riding blankets on the backs of Whinney, Racer, and Gray, then attached a lead rope to the young mare, but put Jonayla in front of her on Whinney for now. There would be time enough to let Jonayla ride by herself when they weren't riding in and out of a river. As soon as the first raft was pushed off from the dock, Ayla looked around for Wolf, then whistled for him. He came bounding up, shaking with excitement. He knew something was happening. Ayla and Jondalar directed the horses into the river and when they reached the deepest part near the middle, the animals swam, following the rafts for a while before striking out for the opposite shore.

The rafts made good speed heading south, and the horses following along managed not to fall too far behind the rafts as long as they were swimming or there was land on the edge of the river. When the walls of the cliffs closed in, they turned back into the river and let the horses swim in the deep, swift water. The second raft used the oars to slow down so the horses could catch up. When they did, Shenora, the woman who was steering the rudder of the first raft, called out, "Just beyond the next turn, there's a low bank. You should get out there and go around the next series of cliffs. We'll be running into some whitewater beyond that turnoff. It's very rough and I don't think it's safe for you or the horses to stay in the water."

"What about you and the people on the raft? Will you be safe?" Jondalar called back.

"We've done it before," the woman said. "With a poler, a paddler, and me steering, we should be all right."

Jondalar, guiding Gray by her lead, directed Racer toward the left with the rope attached to his halter, so that it would be easier to go ashore when they reached the place to get out. Ayla, with her arm around Jonayla, followed after. Wolf was swimming behind them.

Amelana and Willamar's two apprentices, Tivonan and Palidar, were in the last raft, the one closest to them. Amelana seemed concerned, but she showed no inclination to get out and walk. The two young men were hovering around her; an attractive young woman was always appealing to young men, especially if she was pregnant. Zelandoni, Jonokol, and Willamar in the front raft were beyond the range of Jondalar's voice now, and they were the ones he was most concerned about. But if the First decided not to get off the raft here, he supposed she must have thought it was safe enough.

As the horses walked out of the river, both animals and

humans dripping water, the people on the rafts watched them go. Zelandoni observed the horses with the humans on their backs scrambling out of the water and up onto the riverbank, and was having second thoughts about her decision to stay on the platform of logs tied together with leather thongs, sinew, and fiber cordage. Suddenly she was longing for the feel of the earth beneath her feet. Although she had been poled upriver before, and had floated down calmer waters, she had never chosen to take the whitewater route to Big River before, but Jonokol and in particular Willamar had seemed so unconcerned, she couldn't bring herself to admit her fears.

Before she knew it, a bend in the river and a cliff alongside it blocked her view of the last place to escape from the churning water. Zelandoni turned her head back around to the front and frantically searched for the rope handles extending from the ties that held the logs together, which she had been shown when she climbed aboard the floating structure. She was sitting on a heavy cushion made of leather somewhat waterproofed with grease that had been burnished into the hide, but a good soaking was expected when riding a raft.

Ahead, the river was a raging mass of foaming white water. It came up between the logs, and splashed over the sides and front. She noticed the roar of the roiling river growing louder as the powerful current carried them between cliffs rising high on both sides of the rushing waterway.

Then they were in the middle of the maelstrom, with water splashing over rocks and around boulders that had been eroded away from the cliffs and outcrops by the forces of extreme cold, fierce winds, and rough water. The First stifled a gasp when she felt a spray of cold water on her face as the front of the raft dove into the churning, racing whitewater.

Usually, if there were no storms or tributaries adding more to the volume, the quantity of water in The River stayed about the same, but a change in the riverbed and channel changed the condition of the flow. At a crossing place, where the river widened out and became more shallow, the water rippled and bubbled easily around the rocks in the middle of the stream, but as the cliff walls drew closer together, and the slope of the riverbed dropped more steeply, the same amount of water confined to the narrower space surged through with more force. That force was taking the raft made of wooden logs with it.

Zelandoni was frightened, but excited, too, and her estimation of the expertise of the rafters of the Eleventh Cave rose immensely after watching them control the craft that was being so rapidly propelled down the lower reaches of The River. The man with the pole was now using it to push them away from boulders that emerged in the middle of the river, and to keep them away from the cliff walls that rose up at the water's edge. The rower sometimes did the same, and at other times tried to help steer the way through channels that had no obstructions, along with the woman who controlled the rudder and guided the cumbersome craft. They had to work together as a team, yet think independently.

They turned around a bend and the raft suddenly slowed, though the river spilled just as rapidly down around them, as the bottom of the watercraft scraped along a section of the river that flowed downhill across the smooth stone of barely submerged solid rock. This was the most difficult part of the river to navigate on their return, having to pole up the shallow, steep riverbed. Sometimes they got out of the river and carried the raft around the place. Coming off the rock, they skidded down through a small waterfall at the side and ended up in a notch in the rock wall to the left, a backflowing eddy holding them in place. They were floating but they were trapped, unable to continue downstream.

"This happens sometimes, though it hasn't for a while," said the woman controlling the rudder. Shenora was holding it up out of the water now, and had been since they started round the bend. "We have to push away from the wall, but it can be difficult. It's hard to swim out of here, too. If you got off the raft now, the water could grab you and pull you down. We need to get out of this back eddy. The second raft will be here soon, and they could help us, but they might run into us and get caught, too."

The man with the pole put his bare feet into the cracks between the logs of the raft for traction, to keep them from slipping, then pushed at the cliff wall with his pole, straining to make the raft move. The one with the oar was also trying to help push against the wall, although the handles of the paddles were shorter and not as strong. They could bend or break at the connection between the antler paddle and the wood handle.

"I think you need another pole or two," Willamar said, moving toward the poler with a long, thin log from one of Ayla's pole-drags. Jonokol was behind him with another.

Even with three men pushing, it took some effort to get them away from the back-eddy trap, but eventually they were into the current again. Once they were floating freely, the poler guided them to a jutting rock, and with him using his pole and the others using the paddle and rudder, they held the raft in place. "I think we should wait here and see how the second raft comes through," he said. "This is more treacherous than usual."

"Good idea," Willamar said. "I've got a couple of young traders on that raft, whom I'd rather not lose."

As they spoke, the second raft appeared around the bend, and was slowed down by the submerged rock riverbed as the first raft had been, but the current had pushed them a little farther out from the wall and they managed to avoid getting caught in the back eddy. Once they saw that the second raft was clear, the first raft started out again. There was still some rough water ahead, and in one place the raft behind them bumped into a jutting rock and started into a spin, but they managed to get out of it.

Zelandoni held on to her rope handles again as she felt the raft lift on a surging wave and then dive down into rushing water. It happened a few more times before they came to another bend in the river. Beyond that, suddenly, The river was calm, and on the left bank was a nice sandy level beach and a small dock of sorts. The raft headed toward it, and when they got close, one of the paddlers threw a loop of rope that was attached to the raft around a pole anchored sturdily into the ground at the edge of the river. The second paddler threw another rope, and between them they pulled the raft up close to the small dock at the shore.

"We should get off here and wait for the others. Besides, I need a rest," the man with the pole said.

"Yes, you do, we all do," the First said.

The second raft appeared as the ones who arrived first got off. The people from the first raft helped to tie the second log platform to the small dock and its passengers gladly got off to take a rest. A little later, Ayla and Jondalar and their menagerie came around the back edge of the cliff they had just passed. Getting caught in the backwater eddy had slowed the rafts down, giving the horses time to catch up.

They all greeted each other enthusiastically, glad to see that everyone was safe. Then a man of the Eleventh Cave started a fire in a pit that had obviously been used before. Rocks that were smooth and rounded from being tumbled around by The River had been collected earlier and piled near the edge of the stream to dry out. Dry rocks heated faster when put in the fire, and were less dangerous. Moisture trapped within rocks could cause them to explode when exposed to the heat of a fire. Water was drawn from The River and put in two cooking bowls and a kerfed box. When the hot cobbles were added to the water they produced a cloud of steam amid a welling up of bubbles. Additional rocks brought the water to cooking temperature.

Traveling by water was much faster, but they weren't able to forage for food along the way when they were on The River, so they used the food they brought with them. Various leaves for tea went into the kerfed box; dried meat made a flavorful base for soup and it went into one large bowl, along with dried vegetables and some of the roasted megaceros from the night before. In the second bowl, dried fruits were added to the hot water to soften them. It was a quick lunch so they could get back on the rafts and finish their water journey before it got dark.

Toward the mouth of The River, many small tributaries were adding to the size of the stream, and to the turbulence, but the water was never again as rough as it had been going through the whitewater rapids. They followed the left bank south until they came in sight of Big River; then as The River delta widened at the mouth, the Eleventh Cave river rafters kept the craft toward the middle of the waterway until it carried them into Big River. The conflicting currents of the two rivers had built up a bar, a ridge of sand and silt, that added another precarious aspect to their ride when they crossed over it. Then, suddenly they were in a much larger body of water, with a strong current carrying them toward the Great Waters. The pole was of little value now.

The man using it picked up a second oar that had been tied down near the edge. The two men with oars of megaceros antlers and Shenora, the woman who controlled the rudder, had the job of getting them across the fast-flowing river. She pulled the rudder over as far as it would go to steer it toward the opposite shore, while the rowers worked to guide the lumbering craft. The second raft followed them.

The horses and Wolf swam across somewhat more directly. They continued along the shore, keeping the raft in sight as it angled toward land. As they rode downstream, Jondalar remembered with fondness the boats used by the Sharamudoi who lived beside the Great Mother River. They lived so far downstream of the long and significant watercourse that it had become quite wide and swift, but the boats they used skimmed across the water. Small ones could be controlled by a single person using a double-ended paddle. Jondalar had learned to use one, though he'd had a mishap or two in the process. Large ones could be used to carry goods and people, though they also needed more than one person using oars to propel them, but they had much greater control.

He thought about how the boats were made. They started with a large log, dug out the center, using hot coals and stone knives, shaped both ends into a point, and stretched the log with steam to make it wider in the middle. Then planks, known as strakes, were added to the sides to enlarge the watercraft, attached with wooden pegs and leather ties. He had helped them build such a boat when he and Thonolan were living with them.

"Ayla, remember the boats of the Sharamudoi?" Jondalar said. "I think we could make one—at least I'd like to try—a small one, to show the Eleventh Cave. I have tried to explain the boats to them, but it's hard to make it clear. I think if I made a small boat, they'd get the idea."

"If you want me to help you, I'll be happy to," Ayla said. "We could also make one of those round bowl boats that the Mamutoi used to make. We made one on our Journey here. It held a lot of things when we attached it to Whinney's pole-drag, especially when we had to cross rivers." Then she frowned. "But sometimes Zelandoni might need me."

"I know," he said. "If you can help me, I'd appreciate it, but don't worry about it. Maybe I can get my apprentices to help. The bowl boats can be useful, but I think I'll try to make one of those small Sharamudoi boats first. It will take longer, but it'll be easier to control, and it would give us an opportunity to develop effective knives to make those kinds of boats. If the Eleventh Cave likes it as well as I think they will, I'm sure I can trade the boat for a future use of their rafts, and if they decide to make more boats, they might want to use knives especially designed for carving out the inside of logs, and I could make future trades for many trips on the river."

Ayla thought about the way Jondalar's mind worked, the way he was always thinking ahead, especially to gain some benefit for the future. She knew he was very conscientious about taking care of her and Jonayla, and she knew the Zelandonii concept of status was also involved in some way. It was important to him and he was very aware of what needed to be done in any given situation to achieve it. His mother, Marthona, was like that too, and he had obviously learned from her. Ayla understood the notion of status; it had been perhaps of even greater consequence to the Clan, but to her it didn't seem so crucial. Though she had gained status among various people, it always seemed to be something that came to her; she had never had to strive for it, and she wasn't sure if she would know how to.

The current carried the rafts quite some distance downstream before they were able to reach the other side. By then the sun was getting low in the west, and everyone was relieved when both rafts reached the far shore. While camp was being set up, Willamar's two young apprentice traders, along with Jondalar and Wolf, left to see if they could find anything to hunt. They still had some venison from the megaceros, but it wouldn't last too much longer and they wanted to look for fresh meat.

Soon after they started out, they saw a lone bull bison, but it saw them first and ran off too quickly for them to follow. Wolf flushed out a couple of nesting ptarmigans, resplendent in summer plumage. Jondalar got one with his spear-thrower, Tivonan missed with his spear-thrower, and Palidar didn't get his set up fast enough. One ptarmigan wasn't going to feed many people, but Jondalar retrieved it. It was going to be dark soon; they didn't have much time to look for anything else, so they headed back toward camp.

Then Jondalar heard a yelp and quickly turned to see Wolf trying to hold a young bull bison at bay. It was smaller than the one they had first seen, and it was likely that it had only recently left the maternal herd to roam with the bachelors, which grouped in looser, smaller herds at this time of year. Jondalar's spear was in his thrower in an instant, and Palidar was more ready this time. As the men closed in for the kill, Tivonan managed to get his spear-thrower armed as well.

The inexperienced young bison had been concentrating on the wolf, whom he instinctively feared, and wasn't paying much attention to the bipedal predators, for whom he had no instinctive sense, and no familiarity, but with three of them closing in, he had little chance. Jondalar, who was the most proficient spear-thrower, cast his spear the instant after it was mounted on the thrower. The other two men took a little more time to aim. Palidar cast the lightweight spear with the thrower next, quickly followed by Tivonan. All three spears hit their mark and brought the animal down. The young men let out a whoop; then each of the young traders grabbed a front leg by the hoof, and began skidding the bison toward camp. He would supply enough meat for several meals for all fourteen adults, plus the wolf, who certainly deserved a share for his part in hunting the animal.

"That wolf can be a real help sometimes," Palidar said, smiling at the wolf with the ear that was cocked at an odd angle. It made Wolf recognizable, distinguished him from any wild canines that happened to be in his area, but Palidar knew why it was that way and it hadn't been an occasion to smile. He was the one who had come upon the site of the wolf fight, which included a lot of blood, a badly torn-up dead female, and the body of one animal that Wolf had managed to kill. Palidar skinned it, thinking he could use the fur to decorate a carrying pouch or spear quiver, but when he went to visit his friend Tivonan to show him his find, Wolf picked up the scent of the wolf and attacked the young man. Even Ayla had trouble getting the four-legged hunter away from Palidar; the fact that Wolf was still weak from his injuries helped.

The Ninth Cave had never seen Wolf attack a person, and it

came as a surprise to them, but Ayla noticed the piece of wolf fur sewn onto Palidar's spear-holder, and when he told her where he obtained it, she put the story together. She asked him for the piece of fur and gave it to Wolf, who bit and tore and shook the thing until it was shredded to bits. It was almost funny to watch him, but not to Palidar, who was glad he hadn't come upon Wolf when he was alone. He took Ayla to the place where he found the fur, which was much farther than she had imagined. She was surprised at the distance Wolf had dragged himself to reach her, but she was grateful that he had.

She told Palidar what she thought had happened. She knew Wolf had found a lone female wolf companion and guessed they were trying to cut out a piece of territory for themselves, but obviously the local pack was too big and too well entrenched, and Wolf and his she-wolf too young. Wolf had another disadvantage. He had never play-fought with littermates and, beyond instinct, he didn't know how to fight wolves.

Wolf's mother was a female who had come into heat at the wrong time of year and was driven out of her pack by the alpha female. She happened to meet an elderly male who had left his pack, not able to keep up anymore. He felt invigorated for a while, having a young female to himself, but he died before the winter was out, leaving her to raise her litter alone when most mother wolves would have had the help of a whole pack.

When Ayla had rescued him, Wolf was barely four weeks old and the last survivor of her litter, but that was the age when a mother wolf would normally have brought her cubs out of their birthing den to imprint on the wolf pack. Instead Wolf imprinted on the human pack of Mamutoi, with Ayla as his alpha mother. He didn't know his canine siblings—he wasn't raised with other wolf cubs. He was raised by Ayla along with the children of the Lion Camp. Since a wolf pack and a human family group have many characteristics in common, he adapted to living with people.

After the fight, Wolf managed to drag himself close enough to the Camp of the Ninth Cave for Ayla to find him. Almost everyone at the Summer Meeting rooted for his recovery. The First even helped Ayla treat his wounds. His ear had been nearly torn off, and though Ayla stitched it back together, it healed with a cocky turn that many thought gave him a raffish air, a look of free-spirited charm, which made people smile when they saw him.

The incident had made her understand that he not only had to heal from his physical wounds, he had to heal from the stressful ones that had caused him to attack the young man who carried the skin of the wolf he had killed, and reminded him of the fight. The young canine had never been in a fight with wolves before. It made him much more wary of the scent that he recognized at a deep level as his own kind.

The Sacred Site that the First wanted to visit was a painted cave that was several days' walk to the east and south. And the Eleventh Cave had to negotiate the same swift current getting back across the major waterway they had just crossed. They needed to put in to the large river some distance upstream if they wanted to reach the other side anywhere near the mouth of The River, which would take them back home. They were both heading for a particular Cave that was, Ayla was told, near the place where a small stream joined Big River. The smaller waterway began in a highland to the south that was near the Sacred Site the First wanted Ayla to see next. They started east, back upstream along Big River, the next morning.

The Eleventh was not the only Cave of Zelandonii that used rafts to navigate the rivers of their territory. Many generations before some descendants of the same ancestors of river runners who had settled the Eleventh Cave decided to start a new Cave on the other side of Big River close to the place where they usually started back. They had camped in the area many times, often searching for caves and sheltering abris when the weather turned bad, and they explored the area while they hunted and gathered food. They came to know the region quite well.

Later, for the usual reasons—their home became too crowded, or someone had a disagreement with her brother's mate or his uncle—a small group broke off and formed a new Cave. There was still far more uninhabited land than people to fill it. For the original Cave, it was a definite advantage to have a place to go that had friends, food, and a place to sleep. The two closely related Caves worked out ways to exchange services and goods, and the new Cave thrived. They became known as the First Cave of Zelandonii in the land south of Big River, which was shortened over time to the First Cave of the South Land Zelandonii.

The Donier wanted to make arrangements with them to cross the river on their way back, and to give them advance warning that another group that the travelers were planning to meet later would be coming across Big River. She also wanted to speak with their Zelandoni, a woman she had known since before she became an acolyte. Then the group would split. The Eleventh Cave raft runners would start back across Big River; from the same place, the Donier Tour travelers would follow the small river upstream to reach the painted cave.

Running rivers required that sometimes they had to carry the raft, to portage around obstacles or extremely rough water or waterfalls, or areas so shallow that the craft scraped the bottom. For that reason, the rafts were built with slender logs anchored to supports that ran across them, so that the people who controlled each raft could carry it. This time the travelers helped, which made the job easier. The oars, rudders, and poles were loaded on the pole-drags pulled by the horses, along with the traveling tents and some extra belongings of the hikers. As they trudged upriver, they all carried their own backframes with their personal gear, and traded off carrying the rafts.

As they continued east, upstream, along the left bank, the south side of the large, west-flowing river, they knew they were near the mouth of The River when they came to the first of two large meandering loops of Big River. When they reached the bottom end of the first loop, the travelers didn't walk beside the river. It would have meant a great deal of extra walking to follow the loop when they could just hike across the land a short distance, until they met up with the bottom end of the second loop of Big River again. They were following a path that had begun as an animal trail and had been enlarged by human traffic. Where it forked, with one path heading north alongside the river and the other going east cross-country, it was the eastern track that was more heavily traveled.

They reached the lower end of the second loop, then followed the river only until it headed north again. The forking paths at the bottom of this loop, one toward the east and the other heading north, were more equally worn; it was the north end of the second loop that was opposite the mouth of The River, the place where it flowed into Big River, and that northern path was used as often as the other. Going east across the land, they reached the river again, then followed the trail beside it in a southeast direction. The volume of water in Big River was considerably less before the place where the water of the river entered the larger stream. It was there that they decided to camp for the night.

Everyone had finished their evening meal and most were sitting around the fire relaxing before settling down in their tents and sleeping rolls. Ayla was giving Jonayla a second helping, listening to some young people from the Eleventh talk about starting a new Cave farther downstream, near the place where the rafts had landed when they first crossed Big River. They planned to provide places to sleep and to have food available for travelers who crossed Big River either to continue south or to travel west farther downstream. For a previously agreed-upon exchange, tired raft runners and their passengers would have a place to rest without having to set up camp first. Ayla began to understand how communities of people spread out and grew, and why people might want to start a new Cave. Suddenly it seemed entirely reasonable.

It took a another day to reach the settlement of the First Cave of the South Land Zelandonii. They arrived late in the afternoon, and Ayla thought it definitely was more convenient to have a place to spread out their sleeping rolls without having to set up their tents, and to have cooked food available. The people of this Cave also traveled and hunted in the warm season just as all the other Caves did, and therefore had fewer people in residence, but they were not as few in relation to their number as most of the other Caves. The ones who stayed behind were not just those who could not travel, but also those who made themselves available to provide their services to others.

The travelers were encouraged to spend an extra few days with the South Land Zelandonii, who had heard about a wolf and horses that did the bidding of a foreign woman and a Zelandonii man who had returned from a long Journey. They were surprised to learn that so much of what they thought was exaggeration was actually true. They also felt honored to have the First Among Those Who Served The Great Earth Mother in their midst. All the Zelandonii, even those who seldom saw her, acknowledged her as First, but someone from the South Land Cave did mention another woman who lived near a Cave much farther south who was also very respected and honored. The First smiled; the woman was a person she knew of, and she hoped to see her.

The ones whom the South Land Cave knew best were the raft runners from the Eleventh and the Trading Master of the Ninth Cave. Willamar had come their way many times on his journeys. The two Caves of Zelandonii who built, propelled, and controlled rafts had stories to tell, talents to share, and skills to show each other, as well to any of the others who were interested. They explained some of the techniques they used to construct their crafts. Jondalar listened with great attention.

He talked about the Sharamudoi boats, but didn't go into great detail since he had decided to build one to show them rather than try to tell anyone about them again. His reputation as a flint-knapper was very well known and when they asked him, he was happy to demonstrate some of his techniques. He also talked about how he developed the spear-thrower, whose usage had spread rapidly, and with Ayla showed some of the finer points of controlling the effective hunting weapon. Ayla also demonstrated her skill with the sling.

Willamar told stories of some of his adventures while traveling as the Master Trader, and he was a good storyteller who enthralled his audience. Zelandoni used the opportunity to instruct, and recited or sang with her impressive voice some of the Zelandonii Histories and Elder Legends. One evening she persuaded Ayla to display her virtuosity in imitating animal voices and whistling birdsong. After telling a story about the Clan, Ayla showed them some ways to communicate in the Clan sign language, in case they happened to meet a band of Clan hunters or travelers. Before long, the whole group was having simple conversations without making a sound. It was like a secret language, used with a sense of fun.

Jonayla was an adorable little girl whom most were delighted to entertain, and being the only child among the travelers, she received a great deal of attention. Wolf did, too, because he allowed people to touch and pet him, but even more because of the way he responded to the requests of those he knew. It was, however, obvious to everyone that it was Ayla, Jondalar, and Jonayla to whom he responded best. The people were also intrigued with the way all three could handle the horses. The older mare, Whinney, who seemed most gentle and willing, was without doubt closest to Ayla. Jondalar was the one who controlled with finesse the more high-spirited stallion, whom he called Racer, but most surprising was the way the little one, Jonayla, rode and took charge of the young mare, Gray, though she had to be lifted onto the horse's back to ride her.

They also allowed a few other people to ride one or another of the horses, usually the two mares. The stallion could sometimes be difficult for strangers, especially if they were nervous. The people of the Eleventh Cave in particular became more aware of how useful horses could be to transport goods, and the raft runners understood the process of transporting goods better than most, but they also saw how much work it was to care for the animals even when they weren't being used. Rafts didn't have to be fed or watered; they didn't need shelter or brushing or attention other than some repair and maintenance, and the need to carry them occasionally.

The days they'd spent together made the Donier Tour travelers and the Eleventh Cave raft runners feel sad when they went their separate ways. They had been together through some difficult times on the water, and had shared the work of traveling on land. They had each found their role in doing whatever was necessary to set up camp, hunt, and gather food, and contribute to the chores and necessities of daily living. They had shared stories and skills, and they knew that they had formed special friendships that they hoped would be renewed later. When they started south, Ayla felt a loss. The people from the Eleventh Cave had begun to feel like part of her family.

20

Continuing their travels with only half as many people had some benefits. The traveling felt lighter, easier. There were fewer things to deal with, and no rafts to carry; less food had to be found, and not as much wood and other fuel had to be gathered to cook it. Fewer waterbags needed to be filled, and less space was required to make camp, which gave them a greater choice of where to camp. Though they missed their newfound friends, they traveled more quickly and soon settled down into a new, more efficient routine for the next few days. The small river provided a constant source of water and had a trail that was easy to follow, though it had an uphill grade almost the entire way.

The people who lived near the next Sacred Place that the First wanted to show Ayla were an offshoot of the First Cave of South Land. The First pointed out an abri as they passed by.

"That's the entrance to the painted cave I want you to see," the First said.

"Since it's a Sacred Site, can't we just go into it?" Ayla asked.

"It is in the territory of the Fourth Cave of South Land Zelandonii, and they consider it theirs to use and show," the First said. "They are also the ones who would add any new paintings, usually. If Jonokol felt moved to paint on the walls, they would probably welcome it, but it would be best if he made his wishes known to them first. One of their own might have been feeling the need to paint something in the same place. It's unlikely, but if that were true, it might mean that the spirit world is reaching out to the zelandonia for some reason."

She went on to explain that it was always fitting to recognize the territory that any Cave thought of as theirs. They didn't have a concept of private property; the notion that land could be owned did not occur to anyone. The earth was the embodiment of the Great Mother, given to Her children for all to use, but the inhabitants of a region thought of their territory as their home. Other people were free to travel anywhere, through any region, even distant ones, as long as they used consideration and generally accepted courtesies.

Anyone could hunt or fish or collect food that was needed, but it was considered polite to make one's presence known to the local Cave. That was especially true of neighbors, but also of those passing by so they would not disrupt any plans the local group might have. If a resident spotter had been watching an approaching herd, for example, and the hunters were planning a large hunt to fill out their own larder for the coming cold season, it could make for some short tempers if travelers, in going after only one animal, scattered the herd. If, instead, they checked in with the local Cave, they would likely be invited to come along on their organized hunt and keep a share for themselves.

Most Caves had spotters who were always on the lookout, primarily for migrating herds, but also for any unusual activity in their region, and people traveling with a wolf and three horses was definitely unusual—even more so if one or more of the horses was dragging a conveyance, upon which a large woman was sitting. By the time the visitors came within sight of the home of the Fourth Cave of the South Land Zelandonii, there was a small cluster of people waiting for them. After the large woman dismounted, a man with tattoos on his face that declared he was a Zelandoni stepped forward to greet her and the rest of the people. He had recognized her facial tattoos.

"Greetings to The One Who Is First Among Those Who Serve The Great Earth Mother," he said, approaching her with both hands open and extended in the usual manner to show candor and friendliness. "In the name of Doni, Great and Beneficent First Mother Who Provides For Us All, you are welcome."

"In the name of Doni, Original And Most Generous Mother, I greet you, Zelandoni of the Fourth Cave of the South Land Zelandonii," The One Who Was First said.

"What brings you this far south?" he asked.

"A Donier Tour for my acolyte," the First said.

He watched a tall, attractive young woman approach with an especially pretty little girl. The Zelandoni smiled, and approached the young woman with his hands outstretched; then he noticed the wolf, and glanced around nervously.

"Ayla, of the Ninth Cave of the Zelandonii . . ." The First began the formal introduction with her important names and ties.

"Welcome, Ayla of the Ninth Cave of the Zelandonii," he said, though he wondered about all her unusual animal names and ties.

Ayla stepped forward with both of her hands out. "In the name of Doni, Mother of All, I greet you, Zelandoni of the Fourth Cave of the South Land Zelandonii," she said.

The man struggled not to show his surprise at the way she spoke. It was obvious that she came from someplace far away. It was rare that a foreigner was accepted into the zelandonia, yet this foreign woman was acolyte to the First!

With her ability to detect nuances of gesture and expression, Ayla could clearly see his surprise, and his attempt to hide it. The First also noted his surprise, and repressed a smile. This was going to be an interesting Journey, she thought. With horses, a wolf, and a foreign acolyte, people were going to talk about their visitors for some time. The First thought she would give the Zelandoni a bit more information to show Ayla's status and introduce him to the rest of their party. She motioned to Jondalar, who had also picked up on the reactions of this Cave's Zelandoni and the First's response.

"Jondalar, please greet the Zelandoni of the Fourth Cave of the South Land Zelandonii." She turned to the man. "This is Jondalar of the Ninth Cave of the Zelandonii, Master Flint-Knapper of the Ninth Cave of the Zelandonii, brother of Joharran, leader of the Ninth Cave, son of Marthona, former leader of the Ninth Cave, born to the Hearth of Dalanar, leader and founder of the Lanzadonii," she said, "and mated to Ayla of the Ninth Cave of the Zelandonii, acolyte to the First, and mother of Jonayla, Blessed of Doni."

The two men clasped both hands and greeted each other in the formal way. The few people who had gathered to meet them were rather overwhelmed by all the high-status names and ties. The Ninth Cave itself had a high position in the ranking of the Caves.

Though such formality was seldom used in normal encounters, the First had the impression that this particular Zelandoni would not hesitate to tell stories of this meeting. And the reason she had wanted to take Ayla on a Donier Tour was not just to show her some of the Sacred Sites in Zelandonii territory, but to introduce her to many of the Caves. She had plans for Ayla that no one else was aware of, not even Ayla. She signaled Jonokol next.

"Since we were making this trip, I thought I should include my former acolyte. I never took him on a tour when he was just Jonokol, my artistic acolyte. Now he is not only a talented painter, with an exceptional new Sacred Place in which to work, but an intelligent and important Zelandoni," the First said.

The tattoos on the left side of his face had already announced that he was not an acolyte any longer. Zelandonia tattoos were always on the left side of the face, usually on the side of the forehead or the cheek, and sometimes quite elaborate. Leaders had tattoos on the right side, and other important people, like the Trade Master, had symbols that were in the middle of the forehead and generally smaller.

Jonokol stepped up and made his own introduction. "I am the Zelandoni of the Nineteenth Cave of the Zelandonii, and I greet you, Zelandoni of the Fourth Cave of the Zelandonii who live in the land south of Big River," he said, and reached out with both hands.

"Greetings, and you are welcome here, Zelandoni of the Nineteenth Cave" was the response.

Willamar came forward next. "I am Willamar of the Zelandonii, mated to Marthona, former leader of the Ninth Cave, who is the mother of Jondalar. I am known as the Trade Master of the Ninth Cave, and I have brought my two apprentices, Tivonan and Palidar."

The Zelandoni welcomed the master trader. When he saw the tattoo symbol in the middle of his forehead, he knew the man held an important position, but it was only when he saw it more closely that he knew Willamar was a Trader. He then welcomed the two young men, who returned formal greetings to him.

"I have stopped here before and have seen your remarkable Sacred Site. But this is my last trading mission. It is these two men that you will likely see from now on. I knew the Zelandoni before you. Is he still Zelandoni?" The question was Willamar's tactful way to ask if he was still alive. The former Zelandoni had been Willamar's contemporary, perhaps a little older, and this new one was young.

"Yes, he went to the Summer Meeting, but it was not easy for him. He is not well. Like you, he is giving up his calling. He said this will likely be his last Summer Meeting. Next year he plans to stay here to help care for those who can't go. But you seem to be in good health. Why are you passing your profession on to these young men?" the young Zelandoni asked.

"It is one thing to continue if you generally stay close to one region, but a Trade Master travels, and to be honest, I'm getting tired of traveling. I want to spend more time with my mate and her family." He motioned toward Jondalar, then continued. "This young man was not born to my hearth, but I feel as though he was. He lived there from the time he was a toddler. For a while I thought he'd never stop growing." Willamar smiled at the tall blond man. "And his mate, Ayla, feels like mine, too. Marthona, his mother, is a grandam and has some remarkable young ones, this pretty little one among them. I am grandfa to her," Willamar said, indicating Jonayla. "Marthona also has a daughter, who is the child of my hearth. She is of mating age. Marthona would be grandma and I am looking forward to being grandda to her children. It's time for me to stop traveling."

Ayla listened with interest to Willamar's explanation. She had guessed that he wanted to spend more time with Marthona, but she hadn't realized how strongly he felt about the children of his mate, and their children, and Folara, the child of his hearth. She realized then how much he must still miss Thonolan, the son of his hearth, who had died on the Journey he made with Jondalar.

The First continued with the last introductions. "We also have a young woman who is traveling with us, returning to her Cave. Her mate was a man whose home was near ours. He met her on a Journey and brought her back with him, but he now walks the next world. He was climbing a high cliff and fell. This is Amelana of the Southern Zelandonii," the First said.

The Zelandoni of the Fourth Cave of the South Land Zelandonii looked at the young woman, and smiled. She is quite lovely, he thought, and guessed that she was probably pregnant, not that she showed much yet, but he felt he had a good sense about those things. What a shame that she had lost her mate so young. He reached for her outstretched hands. "In the name of Doni, you are welcome, Amelana of the Southern Zelandonii."

His warm welcoming smile was not lost on her. She responded politely and smiled sweetly. He wanted to find a place for her to sit, but he felt he had to complete the introductions, and presented, in a general way, the people of his Cave who had not gone to the Summer Meeting, because it seemed that introductions were necessary.

"Our leader is not here. She's with the others at the Summer Meeting," the Zelandoni said.

"I assumed as much," the First said. "Where is your Summer Meeting this year?"

"Three or four days to the south, at the confluence of three rivers," volunteered one of the hunters who was there to help out those who had stayed behind. "I can take you there, or go and get her. I know she would hate to miss your visit."

"I am sorry. We can't stay long now. I have planned a very extensive Donier Tour for my acolyte and the Zelandoni of the Nineteenth Cave, all the way to the end of the central highland and then quite a ways east," the Zelandoni Who Was First explained. "We want to visit your Sacred Cave—it is a very important one—but we have many others to see and our Journey will be extensive. Perhaps on our way back . . . Wait, did you say at the confluence of three rivers? Isn't there an important Sacred Site near there, a large and richly painted cave?"

"Yes, of course," the hunter said.

"Then I think we will see your leader. I had planned to go there next," the First said, thinking how opportune it was that some of the South Land Caves had decided to have their Summer Meeting there this year. It would give her a chance to introduce many more Caves to Ayla, and arriving at the Meeting with the wolf and horses, and so many important people from the north side of Big River, should make quite an impression.

"You can join us for a meal and will spend the night, I hope," the Zelandoni was saying.

"Yes, yes, and thank you for inviting us. It is welcome after a long day of traveling. Where would you like us to set up our camp?" the First said.

"We have a visitors' lodging place, but I should check it out first. With only a few of us here, we haven't had to use it. I don't know what condition it's in."

In winter when the Cave, the semi-sedentary group of people who lived together, typically an extended family, were in residence at the stone shelter they thought of as home, they tended to break up into smaller households, thus spreading out to some extent. But the few who stayed behind during the summer liked to gather closer together. The other constructions used as dwellings, or as the rudiments of what would be finished into living places, were left alone, which tended to invite small creatures like mice and voles, newts, toads, and snakes, and various spiders and insects.

"Why don't you just show it to us. I'm sure we can clear it out and make do," Willamar said. "We've been setting up tents every night. Just having a shelter will be a welcome change."

"I should at least check to make sure there is adequate fuel for a fire," the local Zelandoni said, starting toward the lodge.

The travelers followed behind. When they were settled in, they went to the area where those who had not gone to the Summer Meeting were staying. Having visitors was usually a welcome event, a diversion, except for those who were too ill or in pain and couldn't move from their beds. The First always tried to make a point of checking in on the ones who were not well whenever she visited a Cave. Usually there wasn't much she could do, but most people enjoyed the attention, and sometimes she could help. They were often elderly and would soon be walking the next world, or they were sick or hurt, or in the late stages of a difficult pregnancy. They were left behind but not abandoned. Loved ones, relatives or friends, made sure that there was somebody to look after them, and the leaders of the Caves usually assigned a rotation of hunters to help provide for them and to serve as runners if messages needed to be communicated.

A communal meal was being prepared. The visitors brought their own contribution to it, and helped them prepare it. It was close to the time of the longest days of the year and after everyone had eaten, the First suggested to Ayla and the Zelandoni of

the Nineteenth, whom Ayla still referred to as Jonokol most of
the time, that they visit with the ones who were not at the meal
because they were sick or had some other physical condition,
while it was still light. Ayla left Jonayla with Jondalar while she
accompanied them, but Wolf came along.

No one had any immediate problems that hadn't been taken
care of. A young man had a broken leg, which Ayla thought
hadn't been set too well, but it was too late to do anything about
it now. It was nearly healed, and he was able to walk, though with
a bad limp. A woman had been severely burned on her arms and
hands, with splashes on her face. She was also nearly healed, but
had been left with some serious scarring and had avoided the
Summer Meeting. She hadn't even come out to meet the visitors.
This was a situation that would require a different kind of care,
the Donier thought. The rest were mainly older people, some
who suffered from sore knees, hips, or ankles, or shortness of
breath, or dizziness, or failing eyesight or hearing to such an extent that they hadn't wanted to make the long hike, though they
were glad to see the visitors.

Ayla spent some time with one man who was almost stone
deaf, and the people who cared for him, and showed them some
simple Clan talking signs so he could make his needs known
and understand their replies. Though it took a while for him to
understand what she was trying to do, once he did, he was quick
to learn. Later, the Zelandoni told her it was the first time that he
had seen the man smile in a long time.

As they were coming out of the structure under the overhanging shelter, Wolf left Ayla's side and started sniffing around a
structure in one corner. She heard a cry of fear in a woman's
voice. She left the others and immediately went to see what was
wrong. She found a woman who had covered her head and shoulders with a soft buckskin blanket, cringing in a corner. It was the
burned woman who had been hiding from the visitors. Wolf had
dropped down on his belly, whining a little as he tried to edge
closer. Ayla dropped down beside him and waited awhile, then
began to speak to the frightened woman.

"This is Wolf," Ayla said. She had named him the Mamutoi
word for the animal, so the woman heard only a strange sound.
She tried to squeeze farther back into the corner and covered her

head completely. "He won't hurt you." Ayla put her arm around the wolf. "I found him when he was a tiny little puppy, but he grew up with the children of the Lion Camp of the Mamutoi."

The woman became very conscious of Ayla's accent, especially after hearing her word for Wolf, and strange words for the name of the people she had mentioned. Despite herself, she was curious. Ayla could hear that her breathing had calmed down.

"There was a boy who lived with them who had been adopted by the leader's mate," Ayla continued. "Some people would call him an abomination, a mixture of Clan, the people some call Flatheads, and those who look like us, but Nezzie was a caring woman. She was nursing her own child and after the Clan woman who gave birth to him died, she fed the newborn infant. She just couldn't let him go to the next world, too, but Rydag was weak, and he couldn't talk the way we do.

"The people of the Clan mostly talk with hand movements. They have words, but not as many as we do, and they can't say many of the words we speak. I lost my family in an earthquake, but I was lucky because a clan found me and a woman of the Clan raised me. I learned to speak the way they do. Their words don't sound like ours, but those are the ones I learned to say when I was growing up. That's why I sound different when I talk, especially some of my words. As hard as I try, I still can't quite make certain sounds."

Although the light in the corner was quite dim, Ayla noticed that the cover had fallen away from the woman's head and she was obviously listening intently to Ayla's story. Wolf was still whining softly and straining to inch forward to reach her.

"When I brought Wolf back to the lodge of the Lion Camp, he developed a special closeness to that boy who was weak. I don't know why, but Wolf also loves babies and small children. They can poke at him, and pull his hair, and he never complains. It's as if he knows they don't mean to, and he just feels very protective toward them. You may think it's a strange way for a wolf to act, but that's how they behave toward their own puppies. The whole pack is protective toward the young ones and Wolf felt especially protective of that weak boy."

Ayla bent closer to the woman as Wolf crept closer. "I think he feels that way about you. I think he knows that you were hurt, and he wants to protect you. See, he's trying to reach you, but he's being very careful about it. Have you ever touched a living wolf before? Their fur is soft in some places and coarse in others. If you give me your hand, I'll show you."

Without warning, Ayla reached for the woman's hand and, before she could pull it away, put it on the top of Wolf's head, as the animal laid his head down on her leg. "He's warm, isn't he? And he likes it when you rub behind his ears."

Ayla felt her start to rub Wolf's head, then took her hand away. She had felt the scarring, and the stiffness where the skin had pulled tight as it healed, but she seemed to have the use of her hand. "How did it happen? Your burns?" Ayla asked.

"I filled a cooking basket with hot stones, and added a few more until it was boiling, then I tried to move it over. It split open and the hot water splashed all over me," she said. "It was so stupid! I knew that basket was wearing out. I should have stopped using it, but I was just going to make some tea, and it was nearby."

Ayla nodded. "Sometimes we don't stop to think. Do you have a mate? Or children?"

"Yes, I have a mate, and children, a boy and girl. I told him to take them to the Summer Meeting. No reason for them to pay the price for my stupidity. It was my fault that I can't go anymore."

"Why can't you go anymore? You can walk, can't you? You didn't burn your legs or feet."

"I don't want people looking at me with pity for my scarred face and hands," the woman said angrily, as tears came to her eyes. She moved her hand away from Wolf's head and put the blanket back over her head.

"Yes, some people will look at you with pity, but we all have accidents, and some people are born with worse problems. I don't think you can let it stop you from living. Your face is not that bad, and with time the scars will fade and won't show as much. The scars on your hands and probably your arms are worse, but you can use your hands, can't you?"

"Some. Not the way I used to."

"They will get better, too."

"How do you know so much? Who are you?" the woman said.

"I am Ayla of the Ninth Cave of the Zelandoni," Ayla said,

holding out her hands in formal greeting as she began reciting her names and ties, "Acolyte of the One Who Is First Among Those Who Serve The Great Earth Mother . . ." She went through all her usual names and ties because it gave her something to say. She ended with "Friend of the horses, Whinney, Racer, and Gray, and the four-legged hunter, Wolf—his name just means 'wolf' in the Mamutoi language. I greet you in the name of Doni, Mother of All."

"You are the acolyte of the First? Her First Acolyte?" the woman said, forgetting her manners for the moment.

"Her only acolyte, although her former acolyte is with us, too. He is Zelandoni of the Nineteenth Cave now." Ayla said. "We have come to see your Sacred Site."

The woman suddenly realized that she was going to have to extend her hands and take hold of the hands of this young woman to formally introduce herself to the acolyte of the First, who had obviously traveled far and seemed so accomplished. This was one of the main reasons she hadn't wanted to go to the Summer Meeting. She would have had to show not only her face but her burned hands to everyone she met. She bowed her head and thought about hiding them under the cover and saying she was unable to greet her properly, but the acolyte had already touched her hand and knew that wasn't true. Finally, she took a deep breath, then pushed the blanket away and held out her badly burned hands.

"I am Dulana of the Fourth Cave of the South Land Zelandonii," she said, beginning to recite her names and ties.

Ayla, holding both of her hands, concentrated on them. They were stiff and the skin was stretched, bumpy and irregular, and probably still a little painful, she thought.

". . . in the name of Doni, I welcome you, Ayla of the Ninth Cave of the Zelandonii."

"Are your hands still giving you some pain, Dulana?" Ayla asked. "Some willow-bark tea would probably help if they are. I have some with me if you need it."

"I can get some from our Zelandoni, but I didn't know if I should keep on taking it," Dulana said.

"If you are still feeling pain, then do it. It keeps the heat and redness away, too. And I was just thinking that maybe you, or someone you know, could make some fine soft skins, maybe rabbit skins, and put together some mittens for you, except with fingers. Then when you meet people, they probably wouldn't notice that your hands are a little rough. And do you have some nice clean white tallow? I can make a hand softening cream for you. Maybe add some beeswax, and rose petals to make it smell nice. I have some of both with me. You could rub it on during the day, and wear it under your finger-mittens, too. You can put it on your face to soften those burn scars and help them fade away," Ayla said, thinking as she was talking of what could be done to help the woman.

Suddenly Dulana started crying.

"What's wrong, Dulana?" Ayla said. "Did I say something to upset you?"

"No. It's just the first time anyone has said anything to me that gave me hope," Dulana sobbed. "I was feeling that my life was ruined, that everything had changed so much, nothing would ever be the same, but you make the burns and the scars seem like nothing, like no one will even notice, and you tell me all these things that can help. Our Zelandoni tries, but he's so young, and healing isn't his best talent." The young woman paused and looked directly at Ayla. "I think I know why the First chose you for her acolyte, even if you weren't born to the Zelandonii. She is the First, and you are First Acolyte. Should I call you that?"

Ayla gave her a wry smile. "I know that someday I will probably have to give up my name and be called 'Zelandoni of the Ninth Cave,' but not too soon, I hope. I like being called Ayla. It's my name, the name my real mother gave me, or close to it anyway. It's the only thing I have left from her."

"Ayla, then, and how do you say the name of this wolf?" He had put his head back down on her leg again, and she found it comforting.

"Wolf," Ayla said.

Dulana made an attempt at the name, and Wolf lifted his head and looked at her, acknowledging her effort.

"Why don't you come out and meet everyone," Ayla said. "The Trade Master is with us and he tells wonderful stories about his travels, and the First might sing some of the Elder Legends, and she has a beautiful voice. You shouldn't miss out."

"I guess maybe I could," Dulana said, softly. She had been feeling lonely staying inside her dwelling by herself while everyone else was enjoying the visitors. When she got up and walked out, Wolf stayed close to her. Everyone from the Cave, especially the Zelandoni, was surprised to see her, and even more to see the way the four-legged hunter seemed to have developed a protective closeness to her. Instead of Ayla, or even Jonayla, he chose to sit beside Dulana. The First glanced at her acolyte and gave her an inconspicuous nod of approval.

In the morning the visitors and some of the local residents prepared to visit the nearby painted cave. There were several stone shelters in the region, many of them home to various Caves, usually named with their own counting words, though on occasion two or three that lived close to each other joined together to make a single Cave. Most were empty now, with the people doing their usual summer traveling. A few people from nearby Caves who did not make the trek to their Summer Meeting had come to stay where there was a Zelandoni in residence.

All eight adults who were traveling on the Donier Tour, plus five who were staying at the Fourth Cave of the South Land Zelandonii, were in the group who came to see the Sacred Site, which included the two hunters who normally lived at the nearby stone shelter. Dulana had offered to watch Jonayla, Ayla suspected she missed her children. Jonayla was willing to stay with the woman, and Wolf was willing to stay with both of them, so Ayla agreed. Although the child could walk, she was only a four-year, so Ayla often carried her. Jondalar also carried her occasionally, but Ayla was so used to carrying her daughter, she felt as if she had forgotten something when they started out.

They reached the small stone shelter that the First had pointed out to Ayla on their way there. The opening faced east and it was obvious that the site had been used as a living space at times. The dark charcoal circle of a former fireplace was still partially surrounded with stones, though some were missing. A couple of larger chunks of limestone that had broken loose from wall or ceiling had been dragged closer to it for seating. A torn and discarded leather covering lay in a pile near a wall next to a few large and awkward pieces of wood that would likely last through the night if the fire was big and hot enough to get them started.

The entrance to the cave was at the north end of the abri under a short section of overhanging ledge, which was weathering and shedding pieces of broken rock that were beginning to pile up in front of the opening that led inside the wall of stone.

The Zelandoni had put some wood, tinder, and a fire-making drill and platform along with some stone lamps into a backframe that he slipped off near the firepit. Then he began to organize the materials. When she saw what he was doing, Ayla reached into a leather pouch hanging from her waist thong and retrieved two stones. One was a strong piece of flint in a sturdy blade shape, the other a walnut-size chunk of stone with a silvery-brassy metallic luster. A groove had been worn into the shiny stone from being struck repeatedly by the flint blade.

"Will you allow me to start a fire?" Ayla asked.

"I'm pretty good at it. It won't take me long," the Zelandoni said as he started to cut a notch in the platform for the pointed end of the wooden drill he would twirl between his hands.

"She can do it faster," Willamar said with a grin.

"You seem very sure," the young Zelandoni said, beginning to feel a bit competitive. He was rather proud of his fire-making skill. There were few who could make a fire from scratch faster than he could.

"Why don't you let her show you," Jonokol said.

"Fine," the young man said, then stood up and backed away. "Go ahead."

Ayla knelt down by the dark, cold fireplace, then looked up. "May I use your tinder and kindling, since it's here?" she asked.

"Why not?" the local Zelandoni said.

Ayla piled the light, dry tinder together, then bent down close to it. She struck the iron pyrite with the flint, and the young Zelandoni thought for a moment that he saw a flash of light. Ayla struck again, this time drawing off a large spark that landed on the desiccated, easily flammable material and brought forth a bit of smoke that she started blowing on. In a moment there was a small flame, which she fed with more tinder, then slightly larger pieces, then kindling, then small wood. When it was established, she sat back on her heels. The young Zelandoni stood with his mouth agape.

"You'll catch flies that way," the Trade Master said, grinning.

"How did you do that?" the young local Zelandoni asked.

"It's not that difficult with a firestone," Ayla said. "I'll show you before we leave, if you'd like."

After a few more heartbeats to let the surprising fire-making display settle in, the First spoke up. "Let's get the lamps lit. I notice you brought some—are there also some stored here?"

"Usually. It depends on who was here last," the young man said as he retrieved three shallow bowls gouged out of the local limestone from his backframe, "but I don't count on it." He also took out a small rawhide packet of wick materials and a hollow aurochs horn from a young animal—much more manageable than the huge horns of a mature adult specimen—with the open end covered by several layers of nearly waterproof intestine tied on with sinew. Inside was softened grease. He also had some torches made of leaves, grasses, and other vegetation tied tightly around a stick while they were still green enough to be pliable, left to dry for a short while, then dipped in warm pine pitch.

"Is it a very big cave?" Amelana asked. She was slightly nervous in deep caves, especially if they were difficult.

"No," the local Zelandoni said. "There's only one main room with a passage leading to it, a smaller side room on the left, and an ancillary passage on the right. The most sacred areas are in the principal room."

He poured a little softened grease into each of the three stone lamps, added mushroom wicks, then catching fire with a twig, used it to light the wicks once they had drawn up some of the fuel. He also lit one of the torches, then quickly put everything into his backframe again and shouldered it. He led the way into the cave, holding the torch high. One of the hunters brought up the rear to make sure no one got into trouble or fell behind. It was a large group and if it hadn't been a reasonably accessible cave, the First would not have allowed so many people to go in at one time.

Ayla was near the front, with the First and Jondalar behind her. She glanced down and noticed a broken piece of flint on the ground, and not far beyond another blade of flint that appeared whole, but she left them both. Once they were beyond the narrow entrance passage, the cave opened out in both directions.

"On the left is just a constricted little tunnel," the young Zelandoni said. "The right leads down to the ancillary passage. We'll go straight ahead, more or less."

He held the torch high and Ayla looked back. She saw people filing into the enlarged space. Interspersed among them were three lights, three people holding the stone lamps. In the absolute black inside the cave, the torch and small fires appeared to shed much more light than seemed possible, especially now that her eyes were adjusting to the darkness. As they continued, the passage ahead veered slightly to the left and back again to the right, but the way was essentially straight. After a slight widening, the passage narrowed and the Zelandoni stopped. He held the torch high toward the left wall and Ayla saw claw marks.

"At some time bears have hibernated in this cave, but I have never seen them," the young man said.

Just beyond them, some large rocks had fallen from the wall or ceiling, requiring everyone to go single file. On the other side of the rocks, the Zelandoni again held the torch toward the left. On the wall were the first definitive signs that people had been there before: looping, swirling traces done with the fingers adorned the space. A little farther and the passageway opened out again.

"On the left is the secondary room, but there's not much in there except red and black dots in certain places," the Zelandoni said. "Though they don't seem to be much, they are very meaningful, but you have to belong to the zelandonia to understand. We'll go straight ahead."

He went on straight ahead and after a little jog to the right, he stopped in front of a panel that contained finger traces in red ocher and six black fingerprints. The next panel was more complex. The young man held up the torch while people crowded around. There were what appeared to be human figures, but they were vague, almost ghostlike, and there were deer all interspersed with dots. It was very enigmatic, spiritual, numinous, and it gave Ayla a chill. She was not alone. It suddenly became very still. She realized she hadn't noticed that people had been quietly talking until they stopped.

The left wall had a small projection, a protrusion. Behind it was a niche that spread out into a panel. The first thing she noticed were two magnificent megaceroses painted in black outline, one superimposed on the other. The one in front was a male carrying an imposing rack of palmate antlers. His neck was thick with the muscles needed to support such a heavy load. His head seemed small in comparison to the powerfully built neck. The hump on his withers, more like a black bump, which she knew from butchering the giant deer, was a tight bundle of tendons and sinew that was also necessary to support the weight of the antlers he carried on his head. The megaceros behind the first one also displayed the powerful neck and the hump on the withers, but there were no antlers. She thought it could have been a female, but she believed it was probably another male who had shed his antlers after the fall rut. After the mating season, there was no need for the grand display that showed his enormous strength and attracted the females, and he would need to conserve his energy reserves to survive the glacial winter that would soon be upon them.

She had looked at the two megaceroses for quite a while before she suddenly saw the mammoth. It was inside the body of the first giant deer, and it wasn't a complete mammoth, just the line of the back and head, but the distinctive shape was enough. It made her wonder which was painted first, the mammoth or the megaceros. Seeing it made her look more closely at the rest of the wall. Above the back of the first megaceros, in front of the head of the second, two additional animals were painted in black outline, and again they were not complete. There was a side view of the head and neck of a mountain goat with its two horns that arched back, and a front view of just the horns of a different mountain goat–like animal, which she thought might be an ibex or a chamois.

Advancing a little farther, they came to another section of animals painted in black outline, which contained another megaceros with his giant antlers. There was also part of a smaller deer, a wild mountain goat, and the suggestion of a horse with the stand-up mane and the beginning of the back, and another figure that was more surprising and frightening. It was a partial figure, just the lower body and legs that looked human, with three lines either going into or emanating from his backside. Were they meant to be spears? Was someone suggesting that a human had been hunted with spears? But why put something like that on the wall? She tried to recall if she had ever seen an animal represented with spears in it. Or was it meant to represent something else, something coming out of the body? The lower back was not the most logical place to aim in order to hunt something. A spear in the buttocks, or even the lower back, was not likely to be fatal. Maybe it was meant to show pain, a pain in the back that hurt as much as a spear.

She shook her head. She could make all the guesses she wanted to, but that wouldn't bring her any closer to the real reason. "What do those lines in that figure mean?" she asked the local Zelandoni, pointing to the painting that was suggestively human.

"Everyone asks," he said. "No one knows. It was done by the Ancients." Then he turned to the First. "Do you know anything about it?"

"There is nothing specifically mentioned in the Histories or Elder Legends, but I can say this," the First said. "The meaning of any of the images in a Sacred Site is seldom obvious. You know yourself that when you travel to the spirit world, things are seldom what they seem. The fierce can be tame, the gentlest, the most ferocious. It's not necessary for us to know what something in here means. We already know it was important to the one who put it there, or it would not be here."

"But people always ask. They want to know," the young man said. "They make guesses and want to know if they are true, if they guessed right."

"People should know, you don't always get what you want," the First said.

"But I'd like to tell them something."

"I'm telling you something. It's enough," the woman said.

Although she had been tempted, Ayla was glad now that she hadn't been the one to ask what the young man had asked. The First always said anyone could ask her any question, but Ayla had noticed before that the woman who was her mentor could make a person feel less than bright for asking certain questions. The thought occurred to her that while anyone could ask her any question, it didn't mean she could necessarily answer every question that she was asked. But as the First she couldn't exactly say she didn't know. It wasn't what people wanted to hear from her, and even if she didn't always answer the question, she never lied. Everything she said was true.

Ayla didn't lie either. Children of the Clan learned early that their way of communicating made lying nearly impossible. After she met her own kind of people, she noticed that people had trouble keeping track of lies, and it seemed to her that lying was more trouble than it was worth. Perhaps, instead, the First had developed a way to avoid answering a question by making the one who asked question his own intelligence for asking. Ayla found herself turning aside and smiling to herself, thinking she had deduced something significant about the powerful older woman.

She had. The First saw her turn away, and caught the glimpse of a smile she had tried to hide. She thought she guessed the reason, and was glad Ayla had turned aside. She didn't mind that her acolyte learned some things on her own, but it was best not to make an issue of them. The time might come when she would have to employ similar strategies.

Ayla turned her attention back to the wall. The young Zelandoni had moved on and was now holding his torch up to show the next section, which had a pair of goats and some dots. Beyond that were two more goats, some dots, and some curved lines. Some of the animals, and lines and dots, were in red, some in black. They were entering a little antechamber with five black and red dots and in the back some red dots and lines. They came back out of the opening of the niche, and turned a corner. On the wall on the other side there was another humanlike figure with lines going into or emanating from it, seven of them going in all directions. It was a very roughly drawn figure, hardly even recognizable as human, except it really couldn't be anything else. There were two legs indicated, two very short arms, and a misshapen head drawn in black outline. She wanted to ask the First what it meant, but she probably didn't know either, though she might have some ideas. Perhaps later they could talk about it. Four mammoths painted in red were also in this section, very simplified, sometimes only suggested, just enough to identify the animal. There were also the horns of a goat and more dots.

"If we go to the middle of this room, we can see the whole wall, especially if the ones with lamps stay near it," the local Zelandoni said.

They all shuffled around until they were in position to see the entire display; then they looked at the entire wall of painted panels. At first there was some shuffling and clearing of throats, a few murmurs and whispers, but soon everything was still as the people focused on the stone wall that they had studied closely. When they saw all the images together, they began to feel the sense of the mystical potential the bare rock had acquired. For a moment in the flickering flames and wispy smoke of the lamps, the figures seemed to move and Ayla had the impression that the walls were transparent, that she was seeing through the solid stone and catching a vague glimpse of some other place. She felt a chill, then blinked a few times and the wall became solid again.

The Zelandoni led them out again, pointing out a few places where there were dots and marks on the walls. As they moved out of the decorated area of the cave, and got closer to the entrance, the daylight that penetrated the space made the cave seem more clear. They could see the shape of the walls and the rocks that had fallen to the ground. When they stepped out of the cave, the light seemed exceptionally bright after all that time in the dark. They squinted and closed their eyes, waiting for them to adjust. It took a while before Ayla noticed Wolf, and a moment longer before she saw his agitation. He yipped at her and started in the direction of the living shelter, then turned around and headed back toward her and yipped before he trotted the other way again.

She looked at Jondalar. "Something must be wrong," she said.

21

Jondalar and Ayla both ran back to the Cave, following Wolf. As they drew near, they could see a number of people in front of the shelter in the field where the horses grazed. When they got closer, they saw a scene that might have been funny if it hadn't been so frightening. Jonayla was standing in front of Gray with her arms outstretched as though to protect the young mare, facing down six or seven men armed with spears. Whinney and Racer were ranged behind them, watching the men.

"What do you think you are doing?" Ayla shouted, reaching for her sling since she didn't have her spear-thrower with her.

"What do you think we're doing? We're hunting horses," one of the men replied. He heard her odd accent and added, "Who wants to know?"

"I am Ayla of the Ninth Cave of the Zelandonii," Ayla said. "And you are not hunting those horses. Can't you see those are special horses?"

"What makes them so special? They look like ordinary horses to me."

"Open your eyes and look," Jondalar said. "How often do you see horses stand still for a child? Why do you think those horses are not running away from you?"

"Maybe because they're too stupid to know any better."

"I think maybe you are too stupid to understand what you are seeing," Jondalar said, getting angry at the insolent mouth of the young man who seemed to be speaking for the group.

He whistled a piercing series of tones. The hunters watched the stallion turn toward the tall blond man, then trot up to him.

Jondalar stood in front of Racer and made a point of arming his spear-thrower, though he didn't quite aim it at the men.

Ayla walked between her daughter and the men and signaled Wolf to her, then added a signal that meant "Guard the horses." The wolf bared his teeth and snarled at the men, which made them crowd closer together and back up a few paces. Ayla picked up Jonayla and put her on Gray's back. Then she grabbed Whinney's stand-up mane, leaped up and threw her leg over, and landed on her back. Every action caused the hunters to react with increasing surprise.

"How did you do that?" the young speaker said.

"I told you these were special horses, and not to be hunted," Ayla said.

"Are you a Zelandoni?"

"She's an acolyte, a Zelandoni in training," Jondalar said. "She's First Acolyte of the Zelandoni Who Is First Among Those Who Serve The Mother, who will be here shortly."

"The One Who Is First is here?"

"Yes, she is here," Jondalar said, looking more closely at the men. They were all young, probably recently initiated into manhood and sharing a fa'lodge at a Summer Meeting—likely the one at the site of the next Sacred Cave they were planning to visit. "Aren't you rather far from your Summer Meeting fa'lodge?" he asked.

"How do you know that?" the young man said. "You don't know us."

"But it's not hard to guess. This is the time of Summer Meetings, you are all about the age when young men decide to leave their mother's camp and stay in a fa'lodge, and to show how independent you are, you decided to go hunting and maybe even bring some meat back. But your luck hasn't been too good, has it? And now you are hungry."

"How do you know? Are you a Zelandoni, too?" the young man said.

"Just a guess," Jondalar said; then he noticed the First arriving and all the others following behind. The One Who Was First could walk rather fast when she had a mind to, and she knew that if the wolf had come looking for them, there must have been some kind of trouble.

The First took in the scene quickly: young men with spears, too young to be very experienced; the wolf in a defensive stance in front of the horses with both the young girl and the woman on their bare backs without any of the usual accoutrements for riding, and a sling in Ayla's hand, Jondalar with an armed spear-thrower standing in front of the stallion. Had Jonayla sent the wolf for her mother while she was trying to protect the horses from more than a handful of would-be hunters?

"Is there a problem here?" the Donier said. The young men knew who she was though none of them had ever seen her before. They had all heard descriptions of the First, and understood the meaning of the tattoos on her face, and the necklaces and clothing she wore.

"Not anymore, but these men were thinking of hunting our horses, until Jonayla stopped them," Jondalar said, restraining the urge to smile.

She is a plucky child, the Donier thought, when her initial evaluation of the situation was confirmed. "Are you from the Seventh Cave of the South Land Zelandonii?" she asked the young men. The Seventh Cave, where they were heading next, was the most important Cave in this region.

She had a good idea of their Cave from the designs on the clothing they wore. She knew all the differentiating patterns and designs of clothing and jewelry in her immediate area, but the farther away they traveled, the less she would be able to identify people, although she might be able to make some educated guesses.

"Yes, Zelandoni Who Is First," the young man who had spoken before replied, in a much more deferential tone. It was always smart to be careful around Zelandonia, but especially the One Who Was First.

The young Zelandoni of the local Cave arrived, and most of the others who had visited the Sacred Site. They were standing around watching to see what the powerful woman would do to the young men who had threatened the special horses.

The First turned to the hunters of the local Cave. "It appears that there are now seven more hungry mouths to feed. That will cut down on supplies in a hurry. I think we'll have to stay a little longer, until a hunting expedition can be organized. You will have help, fortunately. We have several experienced hunters in our group, and with some proper direction, even those young men should be able to make a contribution. I'm sure they will be disposed to help in any way they can, under the circumstances," she said, then gave the young man who seemed to speak for the group a hard stare.

"Yes, of course," he said. "Hunting is what we were doing."

"But not very well," someone in the crowd who was watching said, under his breath, but loud enough so that everyone heard. Some of the young men blushed and looked away.

"Has anyone spotted any herds recently?" Jondalar asked, directing his question to the two hunters of the Cave. "I think we'll need to hunt more than one animal."

"No, but it's the right season for red deer to be migrating through, especially the does and young. Someone could go out and look, but it usually takes a few days," one of the Cave hunters said.

"What direction would they be coming from?" Jondalar asked. "I can go and look this afternoon, on Racer. He can travel faster than anyone on foot. If I find anything, Ayla and I can go back and perhaps chase them this way. Wolf can help, too."

"You can do that?" the young man blurted out.

"We told you they were special horses," Jondalar said.

The deer meat had been spread out on cordage that was stretched across a slow, smoky fire overnight. As Ayla was packing it into her parfleche meat container, she wished it had had more time to dry, but they'd already stayed two days longer than the First had planned. Ayla thought she could continue drying it over fires along the way, or even after they arrived at the Seventh Cave of the South Land Zelandonii, since they would be staying for a while.

The Donier Tour group had grown again; the seven young men would be with them. They had proved quite helpful on the hunt, if a little too eager. They did know how to throw spears; they just didn't know how to cooperate to drive animals toward one another or into some kind of a cul-de-sac so they could be effectively hunted. The young men were quite impressed with the spear-throwers used by the travelers from north of Big River, including the First's acolyte, as were the two local hunters, who had heard of the weapon but had not seen one in action. With Jondalar's help, most had already made spear-throwers of their own and were practicing with them.

Ayla had also persuaded Dulana to come with them and enjoy at least part of her Summer Meeting. She was lonely for her mate and children and wanted to see them, though she was still nervous about the scars on her hands and face. She shared a sleeping place with Amelana. They had become friendly, especially since Dulana was willing to chat about pregnancy and giving birth from the point of view of her own experience. Amelana never felt comfortable just chatting with the First or her acolyte, even though Ayla had a child with her. The young woman had heard them discussing medicines and healing practices, and other knowledge and lore of the zelandonia, most of which she didn't understand, and felt intimidated by the accomplished women.

She did, however, like the attention she was getting from all the young men, both the young hunters and Willamar's apprentices, though the traders did back off when she was surrounded by all of the rather bumptious youths. They didn't need to vie for her attention. They knew the youngsters would be with them only a few days, and they had the rest of the trip. While Jondalar with the help of Jonokol and Willamar was hitching the First's special riding travois to Whinney, Ayla and the Donier were watching the byplay of Amelana and the young men.

"They remind me of a litter of wolf cubs," Ayla said.

"When did you see wolf cubs?" Zelandoni said.

"When I was young and still living with the Clan," Ayla said. "Before I started hunting meat-eaters, I used to watch them, sometimes for a long time, all morning, or all day, if I could stay away that long. I watched all kinds of four-legged hunters, not just wolves. That was how I learned to track very silently. Watching the young of any animal was always fascinating, but I particularly liked wolf cubs. They liked to play, just like those boys—I suppose I should call them young men, but they still act like boys. Look how they wrestle and punch and bump each other out of the way, all trying to get Amelana's attention."

"I notice Tivonan and Palidar are not with them," the Donier said. "I think they know they'll have plenty of time to pay attention to her after we reach the next Sacred Site and the youngsters go away, and when we start traveling again."

"You think those young men will go off someplace when we get to the next Cave? She's a very attractive young woman," Ayla said.

"She's also their only audience right now. They will be the center of attention of admiring friends and relatives when they arrive at their Camp with us, and bringing deer meat to share. Everyone will be asking them questions and be eager to hear the stories they have to tell. They won't have time for Amelana."

"Won't that make her sad or upset?" Ayla said.

"She'll have new admirers by then, and they won't all be boys. An attractive young, pregnant widow will not lack for attention, and neither will those young traders. I'm glad neither one of them seems overly infatuated with Amelana," the older woman said. "She's not the kind of woman who would make a good mate for either one of them. A woman mated to a traveler has to have strong interests of her own and not depend on her man to keep her occupied."

Ayla thought that she was glad Jondalar was not a trader, or involved in some other craft that would require him to travel long distances. It wasn't that she didn't have interests of her own or that she needed him to keep her occupied; it was that she would worry if he were gone for a long time. He occasionally took his apprentices to search out new sources of flint, and often examined likely sources when he was out with hunting parties, but traveling alone could be dangerous, and if he got hurt, or worse, how would she know? She would have to wait and wait, wondering if he would ever return. Traveling with a group or even two is better. Then one at least can come back and tell you.

It occurred to her that perhaps Willamar wouldn't choose just one of his apprentices to be the next Trade Master. He might choose both, and suggest that they travel together for company and to help each other. Of course, a trader's mate could travel with him, too, but once children came along she might not want to travel away from other women much anymore. It would have been much more difficult, when we were on our Journey, if I'd had a baby along the way. Most women would want the help and companionship of their mothers and other relatives and friends . . . just like Amelana does. I don't blame her for wanting to go home.

Once they were under way, the travelers settled into a routine quickly, and since they'd had such a good hunt before they left, they didn't have to allow time for hunting along the way, and traveled a little faster than usual. They did spend extra time collecting food that grew, however. Since the season had progressed, they had a greater selection and abundance of vegetables—roots, stems, leafy greens—and fruits to gather.

About midmorning on the day they left, as the temperature began to warm, Ayla began to notice a delicious aroma. Strawberries! We must be walking through a field of wild strawberries, she thought. She wasn't the only one who became aware of the favorite fruit, and everyone was glad to stop to make tea and to pick several small baskets of the tiny bright red berries. Jonayla didn't bother with a basket—she picked them right into her mouth. Ayla smiled at her, then looked at Jondalar, who was picking strawberries alongside her.

"She reminds me of Latie. Nezzie would never send her daughter out to pick strawberries for a meal. Latie ate everything she picked and never brought anything back, no matter how often her mother chided her. She loved strawberries too much," Ayla said.

"Is that right?" Jondalar said. "I didn't know that. I guess I was too busy with Wymez or Talut when you were talking to Latie or Nezzie."

"I even made excuses for Latie sometimes," Ayla said. "I'd tell Nezzie there weren't enough berries for everyone. It was true enough; by the time Latie got through, there weren't, and she could pick them fast." Ayla picked for a while in silence, but mentioning Latie brought up other memories. "Remember how much she loved the horses? I wonder if Latie ever managed to find a young one to bring home. Sometimes I miss the Mamutoi. I wonder if we'll ever see any of them again."

"I miss them, too," Jondalar said. "Danug was becoming a fine flint-knapper, especially with Wymez to train him."

When she finished picking her second basket of strawberries, Ayla noticed other things growing that could add to their evening meal, and asked Amelana and Dulana if they wanted to help her collect some. Ayla took Jonayla and headed first for the edge of the river they were following to collect cattails. Their rhizomes with their new roots and the corms and the lower stems were particularly succulent at this time of year. The top spike had also filled out with tightly packed green buds, which could be boiled or steamed and then chewed off. There were also several kinds of leafy greens. She saw the distinctive shape of sorrel and smiled when she thought of their spicy, tangy taste, and she was especially pleased to find nettles, delectable when cooked down to a delicious green mass.

Everyone enjoyed the meal that night. Spring foods were usually sparse—a few greens, some new shoots—and the larger variety and quantity of plant foods that summer brought were welcomed. The people sometimes craved vegetables and fruits because they provided essential nutrients that their bodies needed, especially after a long winter of primarily dried meat, fat, and roots. The morning meal was leftovers and hot tea, and a quick start. They planned to cover a lot of ground that day so they would arrive at the local Summer Meeting Camp early on the day after.

On the second day, shortly after they started out, the travelers ran into some difficulty. The river they were following had been spreading out and the banks near the stream were becoming boggy and overgrown with vegetation, making it difficult to walk close to the water. It was midmorning and they had been climbing up the sloping sides of a rise for some time. They finally came to the crest of a knoll, and looked out over a valley below. High hills ranged around a long, low area of land, dominated by a steep-sloped prominence that overlooked the confluence of three rivers: a major one that came from the east and meandered off toward the west, a large tributary originating in the northeast, and the small one they were following. Directly ahead of them in a field between two of the rivers was a profusion of summer shelters, lodges, and tents. They had reached the Summer Meeting Camp of the Zelandonii who lived in the land south of Big River, in the territory of the Seventh Cave.

One of the spotters came running into the zelandonia lodge. "Wait until you see what is coming this way!" he blurted out.

"What?" said the Zelandoni of the Seventh Cave of South Land Zelandonii.

"People, but that's not all."

"All the Caves are here," another Zelandoni said.

"Then they must be visitors," the Seventh said.

"Were we expecting any visitors this year?" the elder Zelandoni of the Fourth Cave of the South Land Zelandonii said as they all got up and headed toward the entryway.

"No, but that's the way it is with visitors," the Seventh said.

When the Zelandonia went out, the first thing they noticed heading their way was not the band of people, but the three horses, all of which were dragging some kind of contrivances; two also had people on their backs, one of them a man, another a child. A woman was walking in front of a horse dragging a different apparatus, and as they drew closer, movement beside the woman resolved itself into a wolf! Suddenly the Seventh started to recall stories from people who had stopped on the way back from a Journey north. They talked about a foreign woman and horses, and a wolf. Then it all came together.

"If I'm not mistaken," the tall, bearded, brown-haired man said, loud enough for the rest of the Zelandonia to hear, "we are being paid a visit by the First Among Those Who Serve The Great Earth Mother, and her acolyte." He added to an acolyte who was standing nearby, "Go and find as many of the leaders as you can and bring them here." The young man set out in a run.

"Isn't she supposed to be a large woman? Very impressive, I understand, but this would be a long way for a large woman to come," said a rather plump Zelandoni.

"We shall see," said the Seventh. Since the most Sacred Site in this region was near the Seventh Cave, the Zelandoni of the

Seventh Cave usually, though not always, became the acknowledged leader of the local zelandonia.

More people started gathering around, and the leaders of various Caves began appearing. The leader of the Seventh Cave came and stood beside the Zelandoni of the Seventh. "Someone said the First is coming to visit?" she said.

"I believe so," the Zelandoni said. "Do you remember those visitors we had a few years ago? The ones from far to the south?"

"Yes, I do. Now that you mention it, I think I remember that they said one of the northern Caves had a foreign woman living there who had great control over animals, horses in particular," the woman said. The tattoos on the side of her forehead were on the opposite side of the ones on the forehead of the Zelandoni, but similar.

"They told me she was an acolyte of the First. They didn't see much of her, at least not before they had to leave. Her mate was a Zelandonii man who went on a long Journey, five years or more, and brought her back home with him. He also had control of horses and even her child did, and they had a wolf, too. It looks to me like that's who's coming," the Zelandoni explained. "I'm guessing the First may be with them."

They have efficient spotters, the First said to herself as they pulled up to a rather large lodge, which she assumed was for the zelandonia. They seem to have gathered together quite a welcoming party. Ayla signaled Whinney to stop, and when the First was sure there would be no last-moment jerks, she stood up, and with great agility and grace the large woman stepped off the special travois. That's why she can travel so far, the plump Zelandoni thought.

All the Zelandonia, leaders, and visitors exchanged formal greetings and identified themselves. The leaders of the Caves from which the young hunters originally came were also glad to see them. Their fa'lodge was empty and no one had seen them for several days, and their families were beginning to worry and wanted a search party sent out to look for them. Since they arrived with the visitors, there was obviously a story here, which could be told later.

"Dulana!" a voice called out.

"Mother! You came!" two happy young voices shouted at the same time.

The elderly Zelandoni from the Fourth South Land Cave looked up, surprised to see the young woman. She had been so despondent after she burned herself, she couldn't even bring herself to come outside of her shelter, and here she was at the Summer Meeting. She would have to make some inquiries and find out what had changed her mind.

A major celebration, feast, and Mother Festival were immediately planned to welcome the visitors and the First, and when it was learned that they wanted to visit their Sacred Site, the Zelandoni of the Seventh began to make the arrangements. Most of the usual Summer Meeting ceremonies were over, except for the Last Matrimonial, and people had begun making plans to leave, but with the coming of the visitors, most people decided to stay a little longer.

"We may need to arrange a hunt and perhaps a foraging excursion," the leader of the Seventh said.

"The hunters, including your young men, did manage to intercept a herd of migrating red deer before we left," the First said. "They made several kills and we brought most of the animals with us."

"We only field-dressed them," Willamar said. "They'll need to be skinned, butchered, and either cooked or dried soon."

"How many deer did you bring?" the leader of the Seventh Cave asked.

"One for each of your young hunters, seven," Willamar said.

"Seven! How could you bring so many? Where are they?" a man said.

"Would you like to show them, Ayla?" Willamar said.

"I would be glad to," Ayla said.

The people nearby noticed her accent and knew she had to be the foreign woman they had heard about. Many of them followed her and Jondalar back to where the horses were patiently waiting. Behind both Racer and Gray were newly made pole-drags that appeared to be piled high with cattail leaves. As Ayla started to remove them, it was quickly revealed that beneath the vegetation were several whole carcasses of red deer of various sizes and ages, female and young. They were covered with cattails mainly to protect them from insects.

"Your young men were very enthusiastic hunters," Jondalar said. He refrained from adding, "But not very selective." "These are all their kills. They should make a hearty feast."

"We can use the cattails, too," a voice from the watching group said.

"And you are welcome to them," Ayla said. "There were more growing where we turned away from the river, and other good things to eat as well."

"I imagine plants growing near your Camp have been picked clean by now," the One Who Was First said. There were nods and comments of agreement.

"If some of you would be willing to ride on the pole-drags, we can take you to the river where they are, and bring you and your pickings back," Ayla said.

Several of the younger people looked at each other, then quickly volunteered. They went to get digging sticks and knives, and wide-mesh carrying bags and baskets. On a regular travois, two or three people could semi-recline, but on the one made especially for the First, two normal-size people could sit upright, side by side, three if they were very thin.

When they started out, Jondalar, Ayla, and Jonayla rode on the backs of Racer, Whinney, and Gray, while the horses pulled six more people on the pole-drags. Wolf followed after them. When they reached the place where the travelers had turned away from the river, they halted the horses and the young people got off, feeling rather pleased with themselves for taking the unusual ride; then everyone spread out in several directions to forage. Ayla unhitched the pole-drags to give the horses a rest, and the animals grazed while the gatherers worked. Wolf nosed around, then ran into the woods after a scent he wanted to follow.

They were back at the Camp by midafternoon. While they were gone, many hands had made short work of processing the red deer, and much of it was already cooking. Work had begun on turning some of the pelts into leather that could be worn or made into other useful products.

The feast and celebration went on into the night, but Ayla was tired and as soon as plans were made to visit the Sacred Site, and she could graciously leave, she went to her traveling tent with Jonayla and Wolf to settle in for the night. Jondalar met another flint-knapper and got involved in a discussion about the qualities of flint from various places; the area they were in was the source of some of the best stone in the region.

He told Ayla he would be along soon, but by the time he retired to the tent, both Ayla and Jonayla were sound asleep, along with some of their other tent-mates. The First stayed in the zelandonia lodge that night. Ayla had been invited to stay, and though she knew her Zelandoni would have liked her to get more involved with the local doniers, Ayla wanted to stay with her family and the First didn't press her. Amelana was the last to return. Though Ayla had told her that while she was pregnant, it probably wasn't a good idea to drink beverages that would make her intoxicated, she was more than a little tipsy. She went right to bed and hoped Ayla wouldn't notice.

Early in the morning Amelana was awakened and asked if she wanted to visit the Sacred Site, but she declined, saying she had overdone it the day before and felt she should rest. Both Ayla and the First knew she was suffering from the morning-after malady. Ayla was tempted to let her just suffer it out, but for the sake of her unborn child, she made her some of the special medicine she had developed for Talut, leader of the Lion Camp of the Mamutoi, to overcome the headache and upset stomach that came with too much indulgence. The young woman still wanted nothing more than to stay in her sleeping roll.

Jonayla didn't want to go either. After her experience with the men who wanted to hunt her horses, she was worried that someone else might make a try for them, and wanted to stay and guard them. Ayla tried to explain that everyone at the Camp knew they were special horses by now, but Jonayla said she was afraid someone new might come who didn't know about them. Ayla couldn't deny that her daughter had done the right thing before, and Dulana was more than happy to watch the child for Ayla, especially since her daughter was close to the same age. So Ayla let her stay.

The rest of those who wanted to see the painted cave started out. The group consisted of the One Who Was First; Jonokol,

her First Acolyte, who was now Zelandoni of the Nineteenth
Cave; Ayla, her current acolyte; and Jondalar. Willamar came,
but not his two apprentices; they had found other objects of interest to distract them. In addition, several of the Zelandonia
who were at the Summer Meeting wanted to see the site again,
especially if they were going to be led through it by the Seventh,
who knew it better than anyone alive.

There were ten satellite Caves in the region, each of which had
its own painted cave as a Sacred Site that was complementary to
the important one near the Seventh Cave, but many of them had
only rudimentary paintings and engravings in comparison. The
Fourth Cave of the South Land Zelandonii, which they had just
visited, was one of the better ones. The group started up a path
that traversed its way up the steep hill they had seen when they
first saw the valley.

"This is called Blackbird Hill," the Seventh explained.
"Sometimes the Hill of the Fishing Blackbird. Somebody invariably asks why, but I don't know. I have occasionally seen a
raven or a crow up here, but I don't know if that's relevant. The
one who was Seventh before me didn't know, either."

"The reason for names often gets lost in the depths of memory," the First said. The big woman was out of breath and huffing a bit as she climbed the hill, but continued doggedly on. The
zigzagging trail made the ascent a little easier, if longer.

Finally they reached an opening into the limestone hill at a
point that was quite high above the valley floor. The entrance
was not very exceptional, and if the path had not led to it, it
would hardly have been noticed. The opening was high enough
to enter without ducking or stooping and wide enough to accommodate two or three people, but a large bush growing in
front of it would have made it difficult to find unless one knew
exactly where to look. One of the acolytes brushed away a small
spill of rubble spalling off the rocky slope above that had accumulated in front of the entrance. Ayla showed her skill with
making fire quickly, which included a promise to show the Seventh how it was done; then lamps and torches were lit.

The Zelandoni of the South Land Seventh Cave led the way
into the cave, followed by the First, then Jonokol, Ayla, Jondalar, and Willamar. They were followed by the local zelandonia

who chose to come, including a couple of acolytes.The group numbered twelve in all. The entrance opened into the side of a passageway that required them to turn either right or left. They turned right and after a short distance, the passage widened and split into two tunnels. They had entered a room that had a stone blockage in the middle with a narrow passageway around it on one side and a wider one on the other.

"We could go either way; we'd end up in the same place, at a pile of rocks in the back with no way out except the way we came in, but there are some interesting things to see," the Seventh said.

They took the narrow right fork and immediately came upon some small red dots on the right wall, which the Seventh pointed out. There were more on the left wall; then a little farther on they stopped to look at a horse painted on the right wall and more dots, and near it a lion with a fantastic tail held up but curled toward the back. Ayla wondered if the person who made the image had perhaps seen a lion with a broken tail that had healed with an odd twist. She knew how strangely broken bones sometimes healed.

Then on the right wall, after a few more paces along the narrow passage, they came to a panel that the Seventh called "the Deer." The drawing made Ayla think of female megaceroses, and she remembered that they had seen the giant deer painted in the Sacred Cave near the South Land Fourth Cave. Across from it on the left were two large red dots. More red dots were painted on the wall beyond the deer, and then on the vaulted ceiling ahead were several rows of large dots.

Ayla was curious about the dots, but she was reluctant to ask questions. Finally she ventured a query. "Do you know what the dots represent?"

The tall man with the full brown beard smiled at the attractive acolyte, whose lovely features had a bit of a foreign aspect, which appealed to him. "They don't necessarily mean the same thing to everyone, but to me, when I am in the right state of mind, they seem to be pathways leading to the next world and, more important, they show the way back." She nodded at his answer, then smiled. He liked her look even better when she smiled.

They continued around the middle-section blockage through the narrow passage, which then opened wider. They kept veering toward the left until they were headed in the direction that led back to the place from which they started, through a much larger room that had obviously been used by bears, probably hibernating bears. The walls bore the traces of their claws as they raked them down the limestone. When they approached the opening through which they had entered the cave, the Seventh kept going straight ahead, the direction they would have been going if they had turned left when they first entered the cave.

They walked some distance, staying close to the right wall, through a long tunnel. It wasn't until they reached an opening to the right that they saw more markings; on the low vaulted ceiling of the passage were four red negative handprints, somewhat smeared, three red dots, and some black marks. Across the opening were a series of eleven large black dots and two negative handprints that had been made by placing a hand on the wall and spattering red color on and around it. When the hand was taken away, a negative impression of the hand remained surrounded by the red ocher. The Seventh then turned right into the opening of the vaulted passage.

Beyond the smeared negative handprints, the stone on the wall became soft, as though covered with clay. The cave was high above the river valley floor, and reasonably dry inside, but it was calcareous rock, which was naturally porous, and water saturated with calcium carbonate constantly seeped through it. Sometimes, drip by infinitesimal drip, over millennia, huge stalagmite pillars formed, which seemed to grow from the floor of a limestone cave below stalactite icicles of equal size but different shape suspended from the ceiling. But sometimes the water accumulated in the limestone and left the surface of the cave walls softened enough that marks could be made with only the fingers. Significant areas of the softened stone had formed in the small room to the right, which seemed to invite visitors to mark. Portions of the walls were covered with a scrawl of finger marks, which for the most part were unorganized scribbles, although one area included the partial drawing of a megaceros defined by a huge distinctive palmate antler and a small head.

There were other signs and dots painted in red or black color where the surface was hard enough, but except for the megaceros, Ayla felt the room was filled with disorganized marks that were meaningless to her. But she was beginning to learn that no one knew what everything in the painted caves meant. It was likely that no one actually knew what anything meant, except the person who put it there, and perhaps not even then. If something painted on the walls of a cave made you feel something, then whatever you felt was what it meant. It might depend on your state of mind, which could be altered, or how receptive you were. Ayla thought about what the Seventh said when she asked him about the rows of large dots. He put it in very personal terms and told her what the dots meant to him. The caves were Sacred Sites, but she was beginning to think it was a personal, individual sacredness. Maybe that's what she was supposed to be learning on this trip.

When they left the small room, the Seventh crossed to the left side of the main passageway that led to it. The tunnel at that point turned toward the left and they walked along the left wall for a short distance. Then the Seventh held up his lamp. It illuminated a long panel filled with animals painted in black, many superimposed on others. At first she saw the mammoths—there were many of them—then she saw the horses, the bison, and the aurochs. One of the mammoths was covered with black marks. The Seventh said nothing about the panel; he just stayed there long enough for everyone to see what they wanted to see. When he saw most people starting to lose interest, except Jonokol, who could probably have stayed much longer just to study the painting, the Seventh moved on. He next showed them a cornice on which were painted bison and mammoths.

There were several more markings and a few animals that the Seventh pointed out as they moved slowly through the cave, but the next place he stopped was truly remarkable. On a large panel were two horses painted in black, back-to-back, and the inside of the outlines of their bodies was filled with large black dots. In addition there were more dots and handprints around the outside of the horse outlines, but the most unusual aspect was the head of the right-facing horse. The painted head was quite small, but it was painted inside a natural contour of the rock that resembled the head of a horse and framed the painted

head. The shape of the rock itself had told the artist that a horse
needed to be painted there. All the visitors were very impressed.
The First, who had seen the horse panel before, smiled at the
Seventh. They had both known what was coming and they were
pleased that they got the response they had expected.

"Do you know who painted this?" Jonokol asked.

"An Ancestor, but not an ancient one. Let me show you some
things you may not notice immediately," the Seventh said, stepping up closer to the stone panel. He held his left hand up over
the back of the left-facing horse and bent the joint of his thumb.
When he held his hand beside a red outline, it was obvious
that the negative space was not a handprint, but a bent thumb.
Now that it had been pointed out, they could see that there were
several outlines of bent thumbs along the back of the left-hand
horse.

"Why was that done?" a young acolyte asked.

"You would have to ask the Zelandoni who painted it," the
Seventh replied.

"But you said it was done by an Ancestor."

"Yes," the Zelandoni said.

"But the Ancestor walks in the next world now."

"Yes."

"Then, how can I ask?"

The Seventh only smiled at the young man, who frowned and
fidgeted. There were some titters of laughter from those watching, which suddenly made the young acolyte blush.

"I can't ask, can I?"

"Perhaps when you learn to walk in the next world," the First
said. "There are some Zelandonia who can, you know. But it is
very dangerous, and not all choose to."

"I don't believe everything on that panel was made by the
same person," Jonokol said. "The horses probably were, and
the hands, and most of the dots, but I think some of them were
added later, and the thumbs, and I think I see a red fish on top of
that horse, but it's not clear."

"You may be right," said the Seventh. "That's very perceptive."

"He is an artist," Willamar said.

Ayla noticed that Willamar often tended to keep his opinions to himself, and wondered if that was something he had learned to do on his travels. When you traveled a lot and met many new people, it probably wasn't wise to advance your own opinions on strangers too readily.

The Seventh showed them many other marks and paintings, including a humanlike figure with lines either coming out of or going into his body, similar to those they had seen at the Fourth South Land Cave's Sacred Site, but after the unusual horses, nothing else seemed to stand out, except for some formations far older than any of the paintings. Large disks of calcite naturally formed by the same actions that had created the cave itself decorated one room in the cave and were left alone in their own space without any embellishments added, as though they were decorations in their own right made by the Mother.

After they returned from visiting the Sacred Site, the First was anxious for them to be on their way again, but she felt she had to stay for a while to fulfill her role as the First Among Those Who Served The Great Mother, especially for the zelandonia. It wasn't often that they had an opportunity to spend time with her. For some of the groups who lived within Zelandonii territory, the First was almost a mythical figure, a figurehead whom they acknowledged but seldom saw, and in reality, did not need to see. They were more than capable of performing their functions without her, but for the most part they were very pleased and excited to see her. It wasn't as though they thought of her as the Mother Herself, or even the Mother incarnate, but she was definitely Her representative, and with her huge size, she was impressive. Having an acolyte who could control animals added to her stature. She had to stay a little longer.

During the evening meal, the Seventh sought out the visitors. He sat beside the First with his plate of food and smiled, then spoke softly to her. It wasn't exactly a conspiratorial whisper, but Ayla was sure she would not have heard him if she hadn't been sitting on the other side of the First.

"We have been talking about having a special ceremony at the Sacred Cave later tonight, and would like you and your acolyte to join us if you feel up to it," he said.

The First smiled at him encouragingly. This might make her decision to stay a little longer a bit more interesting, she thought.

"Ayla, would you be interested in going to this special ceremony?"

"If you would like me to, I would be happy to join you," Ayla said.

"What about Jonayla? Can Jondalar watch her?" the First asked.

"I'm sure he could," Ayla said, not as excited about going since Jondalar wasn't invited, but then he wasn't a part of the zelandonia.

· "I'll come for you later," the Seventh said. "Dress warmly. It gets cool at night."

After things had quieted down and most people had gone either to their beds or to some other activity—talking, drinking, dancing, gambling, or whatever else they chose—the Zelandoni of the South Land Seventh Cave returned to their camp. Jondalar was waiting with Ayla and Zelandoni beside the fire. He wasn't particularly pleased about Ayla going off at night to participate in some secret ceremony, but he didn't say anything. A Zelandoni was, after all, what she was training to be. Part of that was secret ceremonies with other zelandonia.

The Seventh had brought some torches and lit them from the small fire that was still burning in the fireplace. He took the lead when they started out, followed by the First and then Ayla, each holding a torch. Jondalar watched them as they headed up the trail that led to the Sacred Cave. He was even tempted to follow them, but he had promised to watch Jonayla.

Wolf had apparently had the same inclination, but not long after they left, the wolf came back to the camp. He went into the tent and sniffed the child, then walked out, looked in the direction Ayla had taken, then went to Jondalar and sat down close beside him. Soon he laid his head on his front paws, still watching the direction she had gone. Jondalar put his hand on the animal's head and ran it down across his shoulders and back a few times, petting the great canine.

"She chased you away, too, didn't she?" the man said. Wolf whined softly.

22

T he Seventh led the two women along the path up toward the Sacred Cave. Some torches had been stuck in the ground beside the path to help guide them, and Ayla suddenly recalled the time she had followed the lamps and torches into the winding cave at the Clan Gathering until she came upon the mog-urs. She knew she wasn't supposed to be there then and had stopped just in time, hiding behind a huge stalagmite so they wouldn't see her, but Creb knew she was there. This time she was part of the group that had been invited to join the gathering.

It was a good walk up to the Sacred Cave and by the time they reached it they were all breathing hard. The First was thinking to herself that she was glad she had decided to make this trip now; in a few years she wouldn't be able to. Ayla had been aware of her difficulty and had purposely slowed down to make it easier for the woman. They knew they were close when they saw a fire burning ahead, and soon after noticed several people standing or sitting around it.

They were greeted with enthusiasm by the gathering, then stood and talked while they waited for a few more to arrive. Soon another group of three appeared, Jonokol among them. He had been visiting the camp of another Cave whose Zelandoni was also inclined to make images. They were also greeted by all; then the Seventh addressed them.

"We are very fortunate to have the First Among Those Who Serve The Great Mother with us. I don't think she has ever joined one of our Summer Meetings before and she makes this an especially memorable occasion. Her acolyte, and the

Zelandoni who was her acolyte, are both with her, and we are pleased to welcome them as well."

There were words and gestures of greeting and then the Seventh continued. "We should all make ourselves comfortable around the fire; we brought pads to sit on. I have a special tea to try, for any who would like to. It was given to me by a Zelandoni far to the south of here, in the foothills of the tall mountains that define the boundary of Zelandonii territory. She has watched over a very sacred cave there for many years and renews it frequently. All Sacred Caves are wombs of the Great Mother, but in some Her presence is so profound, we know they must be exceptionally close to Her; hers is one of those. I think the Zelandoni who maintains it for the Mother has pleased Her so well, it has made the Mother want to stay close to it."

Ayla noticed that Jonokol was paying very close attention to the words of the Seventh, and thought it might be because he wanted to learn how to please the Mother so she would stay close to the white cave. He never said it in so many words, but she knew he considered it his special Sacred Cave. She did, too.

Someone had put cooking rocks in the fire previously and were now taking them out with bentwood tongs, and dropping them into a tightly woven container of water. Then the Seventh added the contents of a leather pouch to the steaming water. The scent pervaded the area and Ayla tried to identify the ingredients. She thought it was a mixture, some of which seemed familiar, but some not at all. Overlying everything else was a strong odor of mint, which she thought might have been added to disguise the smell of some other ingredient or to mask an unpleasant odor or taste. After the tea had steeped for a while, the Seventh dipped some out into two cups, one larger than the other.

"This is a powerful drink," the Seventh said. "I have tried it once, and I will be very careful before using very much of it again. It can take you very close to the world of the spirits, but I think everyone can have a taste, if you are careful not to take too much. One of my acolytes has offered to drink a larger dosage so that she can be a way in, a conduit for us."

The larger cup was passed around and each one there took a small drink. When it reached the First, she smelled it first, then took a small sip and rolled it around in her mouth, trying to distinguish the elements. Then she took a slightly larger taste, and passed it on to Ayla. She had observed the First closely, and did the same thing. It was very potent. The scent alone was strong and made her feel a bit dizzy. The sip filled her mouth with a powerful taste that wasn't entirely unpleasant, but wasn't something she would want to drink every day like a normal cup of tea, and the small taste that she swallowed almost made her feel faint. She wished she knew what the ingredients were.

After tasting, everyone watched as the Seventh's acolyte drank the small cupful. It wasn't long before she was on her feet, weaving unsteadily toward the entrance to the Sacred Cave. The Seventh quickly got up to offer a hand to help her keep her balance. The rest of the zelandonia present followed them into the Sacred Cave, several of them carrying lit torches. They allowed the First, along with Ayla and Jonokol, to go ahead. Although it was quite a long way in, the acolyte went almost directly to the area of the cave where the painted horses that enclosed the large dots were. Several of those with torches went close to the wall to shine light on them.

Ayla was still feeling the effects of her small taste of the drink and wondered what sensations the acolyte who had drunk much more was experiencing. The young woman went to the panel and put both hands on it, then got in close and laid her cheek against the rough stone as though she was trying to get inside it. Then she began to cry. Her Zelandoni put his arm around her shoulders to calm her. The First took a few steps toward her and then began to sing the Mother's Song.

Out of the darkness, the chaos of time,
The whirlwind gave birth to the Mother sublime.
She woke to Herself knowing life had great worth,
The dark empty void grieved the Great Mother Earth.
The Mother was lonely. She was the only.

Everyone listened, and Ayla could feel a tension in her shoulders that she didn't know was there begin to ease. The young acolyte stopped crying, and after a while when they picked up the tune of the music, others joined in, especially when they got to the part where she sang about Her bringing forth the children of earth from her womb.

Each child was different, some were large and some small,
Some could walk and some fly, some could swim and some
*   crawl.*
But each form was perfect, each spirit complete,
Each one was a model whose shape could repeat.
*   The Mother was willing. The green earth was filling.*

All the birds and the fish and the animals born,
Would not leave the Mother, this time, to mourn.
Each kind would live near the place of its birth,
And share the expanse of the Great Mother Earth.
*   Close to Her they would stay. They could not run away.*

When the First was through, the acolyte was sitting on the ground in front of the painted panel. Several others were also sitting on the ground looking rather dazed.

When the First walked back to where Ayla was standing, the Seventh soon joined them. He said very softly, "It was remarkable the way your singing settled everyone down." Then he added, indicating the ones who were seated, "I think they took more than a sip. Some may be here awhile. I think I should stay until everyone is ready to go back, but you don't have to."

"We'll stay awhile longer," the One Who Was First said, noticing that several more people were sitting.

"I'll get some of those pads," the Seventh said.

When he returned, Ayla was ready to sit. "I think that tea keeps getting stronger," she said.

"I think you are right," the First said. "Do you have any more?" she asked the Seventh. "I would like to test it further when we get back home."

"I can give you some to take with you," he said.

As Ayla sat down on the pad, she looked at the painted wall again. It seemed almost transparent, as though she could see through it to the other side. She had the feeling there were more animals wanting to come out, getting ready to live in this world. As she continued to watch, she felt more and more drawn into the world behind the wall, and then it seemed she was in it, or rather high above it.

It seemed not much different from her world, at first. There were rivers flowing across grassy steppes and prairies, and cutting between high cliffs, trees in protected areas and gallery forests along riverbanks. Many animals of all kinds roamed the land. Mammoths, rhinoceroses, megaceros, bison, aurochs, horses, and saiga antelope preferred the open grasslands; red deer and other varieties of smaller deer liked the cover of a few trees; reindeer and musk-oxen were well adapted to cold. There were all the varieties of other animals and birds, and predators from the huge cave lion to the smallest weasel. It wasn't so much that she saw them as that she knew they were there, but there were differences. Things seemed strangely reversed. Bison and horses and deer were not avoiding the lions, but ignoring them. The landscape was clear, but when she looked in the sky she saw the moon and the sun, and then the moon moved in front of the sun and turned it black. Suddenly she felt herself being shaken by the shoulder.

"I think you may have fallen asleep," the First said.

"Perhaps, but it feels as though I was in another place," Ayla said. "I saw the sun turn black."

"You may have been, but it's time for us to leave. It's getting light out."

When they walked out of the cave, several people were standing around the fire, warming themselves. A Zelandoni handed each of them a cup of hot liquid.

"This is just a morning drink," he said, smiling. "It was a new experience for me," he added, "very powerful."

"For me, as well," Ayla said. "How is the acolyte who drank a whole cup?"

"She's still feeling the effects. They are very long lasting, but she is being carefully watched."

The two women walked back to the camp. Although it was very early in the morning, Jondalar was awake. Ayla wondered if he had gone to bed at all. He smiled and looked relieved when he saw Ayla and the First returning.

"I didn't think you'd be there all night," Jondalar said.

"I didn't think we would, either," Ayla said.

"I'm going to the zelandonia lodge. You may want to rest today, Ayla," the First said.

"Yes, I may, but right now, I want something to eat. I'm hungry."

It was another three days before the travelers with Ayla's Donier Tour left the Summer Meeting of the South Land Zelandonii, during which time Amelana had a small crisis. A very charming, somewhat older and apparently high-status man had been pressing her to stay and become his mate, and she was tempted. She told the First that she needed to talk to her, and maybe Ayla, too. When they met, she began by presenting reasons why she should stay and mate the man who obviously wanted her so much, cajoling and smiling as though she felt she needed permission and was trying to get their agreement. The First had been more than aware of what was going on, and had made a few inquiries.

"Amelana, you are a grown woman who has been mated and unfortunately widowed, and will soon be a mother who will have the responsibility of taking care of the new life that is growing inside you. The choice is entirely yours. You don't need my permission or anyone else's," the First began. "But since you asked to speak with me, I presume it is because you want some advice."

"Well, yes, I guess so," Amelana said. She seemed surprised that it had been so easy. She thought she would have to wheedle and coax the Zelandoni to agree to the proposed new mating.

"First of all, have you met the people of his Cave, or any of his relatives?" the woman asked.

"Sort of. I've shared a few meals with some cousins, but mostly there have been so many feasts and celebrations, we haven't needed to eat with his Cave," Amelana said.

"Do you remember what you said when you asked to come along on this Journey? You said that you wanted to go home so you could be with your mother and family to have your baby. More than that, you weren't happy when Jacharal moved with friends and relatives to start a new Cave—at least in part, I'm sure, because you didn't know them very well. They were all excited about starting in someplace new, but you had already left the familiar behind and were in a new place. You wanted to be settled and wanted people to be excited about your new baby. Isn't that right?" the First said.

"Yes, but he's older. He's settled. He's not going to start a new Cave. I asked him," Amelana said.

The First smiled. "At least you asked that. He is a charming, attractive man, but he is older. Did you wonder why he wants a new mate now? Did you ask if he already has a mate? Or if he ever had one?"

"Not exactly. He said he had been waiting for just the right woman," Amelana said, frowning.

"Just the right woman to help his first woman take care of her five children?"

"His first woman? Five children?" Amelana's frown deepened. "He didn't say anything about five children."

"Did you ask him?"

"No, but why didn't he tell me?"

"Because he didn't have to, Amelana. You didn't ask him. His mate told him to find another woman to help her, but everyone here knows he already has one woman and her children at his hearth. Since she's his first, she would have the status and the say. She's the one who brings the status to that arrangement, in any case. He doesn't have much besides good looks and a charming way. We're leaving tomorrow. If you decide to mate him, no one here will bring you back home to your mother's Cave."

"I am not staying here," Amelana said, angrily. "But why would he trick me like that? Why didn't he tell me?"

"You're an attractive woman, Amelana, but very young, and you like attention. He will no doubt find a second woman, but she won't be young and pretty, with no one to stand up for her once we're gone. That is what he'd rather have. That's why you are so right for him. The woman he'll find will likely be older, maybe not very attractive. She may have a couple of children of her own, or if he's lucky she'll be a woman who couldn't have children, and will be happy to find a charming man with

a family, willing to take her in and make her part of his family.
I'm sure that's what his first woman is hoping for, not a pretty
young woman who will leave with the first man who makes
her a better offer. I'm sure that's what you would do, even if it
means you would lose status."

Amelana looked shocked at the First's straightforward remarks; then she started to cry. "Am I really that bad?"

"I didn't say you were bad, Amelana. I said you were young,
and like most attractive young women, especially those with
high status, you are used to gettting your own way. But you
have a child on the way. You are going to have to learn to put
your child's needs ahead of your own wants."

"I don't want to be a bad mother," Amelana wailed. "But
what if I don't know how to be a good mother?"

"You will be," Ayla said, speaking for the first time, "especially once you are home with your mother. She will help
you. And even if you didn't have a mother, you would fall in
love with your baby just like most mothers do. It's the way the
Great Mother made women, at least most women, and many
men, too. You are a loving person, Amelana. You will be a fine
mother."

The First smiled. "Why don't you go and get your things
ready, Amelana," she said, more kindly. "We'll be leaving
early tomorrow."

The company of travelers set out the next day, following one
of the three rivers that came together near the Seventh Cave of
South Land Zelandonii. They used the shallow Crossing Place
at the Campsite to reach the other side, and kept to the river's
meandering course in the beginning. Then, rather than following the twists and turns of the waterway, they decided to strike
out across country heading more east than south.

This was all new country to Ayla and to Jonayla, of course,
but she was so young, it was unlikely that she would remember when she got older that she had been this way before. It
was unfamiliar to Jondalar as well, though he knew he had
been here with Willamar and his mother, and Marthona's other
children. Jonokol hadn't traveled much, so it was new to him
as well, and Amelana didn't recall anything about the region,

though she had come through it from her Southern Cave. It just wasn't anything she paid attention to at the time. Her mind had been filled with her exciting new mate, who couldn't seem to stay away from her, and daydreams about her new home. The First had been in the general vicinity several times, but not for quite a while, and she didn't recall it except in a general way. It was the Trade Master who knew it well. He had brought his two assistants before, but they would need to know it equally well. Willamar was looking for certain landmarks to help him guide the way.

As they traveled, the landscape was changing in subtle ways every day. They were gaining elevation and the country was becoming more rugged. There were more limestone outcrops, often accompanied by brush and even small woods growing around them, and less open grassland. Though they were increasing altitude, it was also gradually warming as the summer wore on, and the vegetation was changing as they journeyed south. They saw fewer coniferous trees, like spruces, firs, and junipers, and more deciduous types like larches, and the small-leaf variety such as willows and birches, also fruit and nut trees and occasionally big-leaf maples and oaks. Even the grasses changed, less rye grass and more of the wheat types such as emmer and spelt, although mixed fields were common that included triticale and many herbaceous plants.

While traveling, they hunted a variety of large and small game as they came upon it and gathered the vegetable produce that grew so abundantly at this time of year, but they weren't thinking about storing for future use, so their needs were not great. Except for Jonayla, they were healthy adults who were capable of foraging for food and taking care of themselves. The large woman did not hunt or gather, but as the First, she contributed in her own way. She walked some of the time, and the more she did, the more she was able to, but when she got tired, she rode the travois and did not slow them down. It was primarily Whinney who pulled her on her special pole-drag, but Ayla and Jondalar were training the other horses to pull the large travois as well. Though they moved slowly enough that the horses could graze along the way, especially in the

morning and evening, they made good time, and with the
weather remaining pleasant, their trek felt like an agreeable
excursion.

They had been traveling for several days, heading generally
southeast; then one morning Willamar started out due east, at
times even a little north, almost as though he were following
a trail. They climbed up around a jutting ridge and behind it
there was a trail, but barely wide enough for the extended legs
of the First's pole-drag.

"Perhaps you should walk, Zelandoni," Willamar said. "It's
not much farther."

"Yes, I think I will," she said. "If I recall right, the trail narrows more up ahead."

"There is a wide spot around the next bend. You might want
to leave the pole-drag there, Ayla," Willamar suggested. "I
don't think the trail will accommodate it."

"Pole-drags don't do well on steep trails. We found that out
before," she said, including Jondalar with a glance.

When they reached the wide place, they helped the Donier
down, and proceeded to unhitch the conveyance. Then they
continued walking up the trail, with Willamar in the lead and
the rest of the travelers behind him. Ayla, Jondalar, and Jonayla with the animals brought up the rear.

They traversed a few more legs of the zigzag path and one
steep climb up the trail and suddenly found themselves on a
relatively broad, grassy shelf at the back of which, amid the
smoke of a few fires, was a collection of rather substantial
shelters made of wood and hides, with grass thatch roofs. A
crowd of people was standing in front of the dwellings facing the approaching visitors, but Ayla could not tell if they
were especially glad to see them. They seemed defensive; no
one was smiling and some held spears, though they were not
aimed at anyone.

Ayla had seen that kind of reception before and subtly signaled the wolf to stay close. She could hear the slight rumble in his throat as he moved in front of her in a protective
stance. She looked at Jondalar, who had put himself in front of
Jonayla and held her there, though she struggled to see around
him. The horses were prancing lightly with nervousness, and

their ears were pricked forward. Jondalar took a better grip on the lead ropes of Racer and Gray and looked toward Ayla as she put a hand on Whinney's neck.

"Willamar!" a voice called out. "Is that you?"

"Farnadal! Of course it's me, and a few others, mostly from the Ninth Cave. I thought you'd be expecting us. Aren't Kimeran and Jondecam here yet?" Willamar said.

"No, they aren't," Farnadal said. "Should they be?"

"Are they coming?" a female voice said, with a happy touch of excitement.

"We expected them to be here already. No wonder you look so surprised to see us," Willamar said.

"You are not the one who surprises me," Farnadal said, with a sardonic look.

"I think some introductions are in order," Willamar said. "I'll begin with the First Among Those Who Serve The Great Earth Mother."

Farnadal gasped, then caught himself and stepped forward. Once he looked more closely he recognized her both from her general description and from her tattoos. He had met her before but it had been some time and they had both changed since then.

"In the name of Doni you are welcome, Zelandoni the First," he said, then held out both hands and continued with the formal greeting. The rest of the travelers were introduced, with Jondalar and Ayla last.

"This is Jondalar of the Ninth Cave of the Zelandonii, Master Flint-Knapper . . . ," the Master Trader began, then continued with Ayla's introduction.

"This is Ayla of the Ninth Cave of the Zelandonii, formerly of the Lion Camp of the Mamutoi . . . ," Willamar said. He noticed Farnadal's expression change as he gave her names and ties, and especially when she greeted him and he heard her speak.

The introductions, by inference, had told him quite a lot about the woman. First that she was a foreigner, which was obvious when she spoke, who had been adopted as a full Zelandonii, in her own right, not just mated to someone who was a Zelandonii, which was unusual in itself. Then that she belonged to the zelandonia, and had become an acolyte of the First. And although the man was holding ropes that had been tied around two horses and was controlling them, she was given the credit for all the animals. It was obvious that she had power over the other horse, and the wolf even without ropes. It seemed to him that she must already be a Zelandoni, not just an acolyte, even of the First.

Then he remembered a troupe of traveling Storytellers a year or so back that had some new and wildly imaginative stories about horses carrying people and a wolf who loved a woman, but he never dreamed there could be any truth in them. Yet, here they were. He hadn't seen the horses carrying people, but he was beginning to wonder how much truth was in those stories.

A tall woman, whom Ayla thought looked somehow familiar, came forward and asked Willamar, "Did you say you were expecting to see Jondecam and Kimeran here?"

"It has been a long time since you have seen them, hasn't it, Camora?" Willamar said.

"Yes, it has," she said.

"You resemble your kin, especially your brother, Jondecam, but Kimeran, too," Willamar said.

"We are all related," Camora said, explaining to Farnadal, "Kimeran is my uncle, but he was much younger than his sister, who was my mother. When my mother's mother joined the spirits of the next world, my mother raised him like a son, along with Jondecam and me. Then when the man to whom she was mated passed on to the next world, she became a Zelandoni. It runs in her family; her grandfa was also a Zelandoni. I wonder if he still walks this world?"

"Yes, he does, in fact, and while age has slowed his step, he is still Zelandoni of the Seventh Cave. Your mother is now the spiritual leader of the Second," Willamar said.

"The one who was Zelandoni of the Second Cave before her, the one who taught me to make images, walks the next world now," Jonokol added. "That was a sad day for me, but your mother is a good Donier."

"Why did you think Kimeran and Jondecam would be here?" Farnadal asked.

"They were supposed to leave shortly after we did and come straight here. We made stops along the way," the Zelandoni Who Was First said. "I am taking Ayla on her Donier Tour, and Jonokol, too—I should say Zelandoni of the Nineteenth. We never made much of a Tour when he was my acolyte, and he needs to visit some of the Sacred Sites. From here we were all going to travel together to see one of the most important painted caves. It is in the southeast of Zelandonii territory, and then we'll visit relatives of Kimeran's mate, Beladora. She is from the Giornadonii, the people who live on the long peninsula that juts into the Southern Sea, south of the eastern Zelandonii territory.

"As a young man, Kimeran traveled with his sister-mother on her Donier Tour to the northern end of the Giornadonii territory. He met Beladora, mated her, and brought her back with him. The story is similar to Amelana's," the First said, indicating the pretty, young woman in their group, "but this young woman's story is much less fortunate. Her mate now walks in the next world, and she wanted to return to her own people. She misses her mother. She is carrying new life, and would like to be near her mother when her child is born."

"That's understandable," Camora said, smiling sympathetically at Amelana. "No matter how kind people may be, a woman always wants her own mother with her when she gives birth, especially the first time."

Ayla and the First exchanged quick glances. Camora probably missed her people. Even though a woman might find a visitor from another place so attractive that she just had to go away with him, it apparently wasn't so easy to live with the strangers who were the kin of her mate. Though they might be people from the same territory, with beliefs and customs generally similar, each Cave had its own ways, and a new person was always at a disadvantage in terms of status.

Ayla recognized that her situation was not the same as the two young women. Although she was called Ayla of the Mamutoi, she had been more of a stranger to them than she had been to the Zelandonii, and they to her. When she left the Clan, she had hoped to find people like herself, but she didn't know where to look. She had lived alone in a pleasant valley for several years until she found Jondalar, who had been wounded by a lion. Except for him, the Mamutoi were the first of her kind she had met since she lost her family when she was a child of five. She had been raised by the Clan, who were not just people of a different Cave or territory, or with dissimilar hair or eyes or skin, or who spoke an unknown language. The people of the Clan were genuinely different. Their language capabilities were distinctive, the way they thought, the way their brains functioned was unusual, even the shape of their heads and to some extent their bodies were not quite the same.

There was no doubt that they were people, and there were many similarities between them and the ones they called "the Others." They hunted the animals in their vicinity, and gathered the food that grew. They shaped tools out of stone and with them made other objects like clothing and containers and shelters. They cared about each other and took care of each other, and even recognized that Ayla was a child when they found her, and though she was one of the Others, they took care of her. But they were different in some ways that, even though she grew up with them, she never fully understood.

Though she sympathized with the young women who lived far away from their families and missed them, she didn't fully empathize with them. At least they were living with people like themselves. She was grateful to have found her own kind, and especially to have found a man who cared about her among them. She couldn't even put into words how much she cared for Jondalar. He was more than she could ever have hoped for. He not only said he loved her, he treated her with love. He was kind, he was generous, he adored her daughter. If it weren't for him, she would not have been able to be an acolyte, to be a part of the zelandonia. He supported her, took care of Jonayla when she wasn't home, even though she knew he would rather she was there with him, and he could bring her to unbelievable joy when they shared Pleasures. She trusted him implicitly and completely, and could not believe how fortunate she was.

Camora looked at the Zelandoni Who Was First. "Do you think something might have happened to Kimeran and Jondecam?" she asked, with a worried frown. "Accidents can happen."

"Yes, they can, Camora, but it could also be that they were delayed and didn't start as soon as they planned. Or something may have occurred at their Cave that made them change their mind and decide not to go. They would have no way of letting us know. We will wait here a few days, if Farnadal doesn't mind," she glanced at him and he smiled and nodded, "before we continue on our Journey, to give them a chance to catch up."

"Perhaps we can do even more," Jondalar said. "Horses can travel much faster than people can. We can ride back along the trail they were on and see if we can find them. If they are not too far away, we might. At least we can try."

"That's a good plan, Jondalar," Ayla said.

"So they do carry you on their backs, like the Storytellers said," Farnadal said.

"Have the Storytellers been here recently?" Ayla asked.

"No, about a year ago. But I thought someone had just made up some remarkable new stories. I didn't know they were true," he said.

"We'll start in the morning," Jondalar said. "It's too late now."

Everyone from the Cave who could was gathered at the bottom of the slope that led up to the ledge where they lived. Ayla and Jondalar had tied riding blankets and carry-baskets that held their camping gear and supplies on all three horses, and put halters on the stallion and young mare. Then Jondalar lifted Jonayla up to Gray's back.

Does that little girl control a horse, too? Farnadal wondered. All by herself? She's so small and a horse is a big powerful animal. And those horses should be afraid of that wolf. Anytime I've seen a wolf get close to a horse before, they would shy and run away, or if they thought one was ready to attack, they would try to trample it.

What kind of powerful magic does that woman have? For a moment he felt a tingle of fear, then he shook himself. She seemed like just an ordinary woman; she talked to the other women, helped with the work, tended to the children. She is an attractive woman, especially when she smiles, and except for her accent, you wouldn't think there was anything remarkable about her, or even unusual. Yet, there she is leaping up onto the back of that dun-yellow mare.

He watched them start off, the man in the lead, the child in the middle, and the woman bringing up the rear. The man was big for the compact horse, which he called Racer, his feet nearly dragged the ground when he sat on the dark brown horse—an unusual color that he had not seen before. But as the animals began a fast trot, the man sat farther back on the horse, pulled up his knees, and hugged the body of the stallion with his legs. The girl sat forward, almost riding the neck of the taupe-colored young mare, her little legs sticking out. Again the grayish-tan horse's coat was an unusual color, though he had seen it before when he'd made a trip north. Some called the taupe color gruya; Ayla just called it gray, and it had became the mare's name.

Not long after they started out, the fast trot speeded up to a gallop. Without encumbrances, like the pole-drags, the horses liked to stretch their legs, especially on a morning ride. Ayla leaned forward low on Whinney's neck, which was her signal to the horse to go as fast as she wished. Wolf yipped and joined in the sprint. Jondalar leaned forward as well, keeping his knees bent and close to the animal. Jonayla grabbed Gray's mane with one hand, and with her cheek resting high on the horse's neck while she squinted to see ahead, she wrapped her other arm around as best she could. With the wind in their faces, the fast ride was exhilarating, and the riders let the horses have their run and delighted in it.

After they had worked out all the kinks, Ayla sat up somewhat, Jonayla sat lower near the base of Gray's neck, and Jondalar sat a little straighter and let his legs hang down. They all felt more relaxed and cantered on at a somewhat slower pace. Ayla gave Wolf a signal and said "Search," which he knew meant search for people.

There were very few people on earth at that time. They were far outnumbered by millions of other creatures from the very large to the very small, and those humans who were there tended to cluster close together. When Wolf sampled all the smells that were in the wind, he could identify many different animals in various stages of life, and death. He seldom detected the scent of human on the wind, but when he did, he knew it.

The rest of them also searched, scanning the landscape to see if they could find any sign that people had passed by recently. They didn't think they would discover anyone so close, sure that the other party of travelers would have sent a runner ahead if they were in any kind of trouble and that close to their destination.

Around midday, they took a break for a meal and to let the horses graze. When they continued, they scanned the countryside more intently. There was a trail of sorts that they followed: occasional blazes on trees, limbs on brush bent in certain ways, sometimes a small pile of stones tapering from front to back, and rarely a mark on a rock made with red-ocher paint. They searched until sundown, then made camp and set up their traveling tents near an active stream that had begun as a spring on higher ground.

Ayla took out some traveling cakes made with dried bilberries, rendered fat, and dried meat that had been ground with a pestle into small pieces, and broke them into boiling water, then added some extra dried meat to the soup. Jondalar and Jonayla took a walk in the rather flat meadow nearby, and the child returned with her hands full of onions they had found, mostly by smell. The level ground had been a wetland earlier in the season, the result of the stream flooding, and as it dried it became a suitable place for certain plants to grow. Ayla thought she might take a look at it the next morning to gather more onions and whatever else she might find.

They started out the next day after their meal, finishing the soup made the night before, which included some additional roots and greens that Ayla had found in her quick exploratory hike around the area. Their second day was as disappointing as the first; they found no sign that any people had passed that way recently. Ayla did see tracks of many animals and began pointing them out to Jonayla, showing her the subtle aspects that indicated the movements of various creatures. By the time they stopped for a midday meal on the third day, both Jondalar and Ayla were feeling some concern. They knew how much

Kimeran and Jondecam wanted to see Camora and they knew that Beladora was anxious to visit her family.

Had the ones they were expecting just not made the trip? Had something come up that caused them to cancel or postpone their planned journey, or had something happened to them along the way?

"We could go back to Big River and the First Cave of South Land Zelandonii and see if they made the crossing," Ayla said.

"You and Jonayla wouldn't have to make that long trip. I could go and you could return to let everyone know. If we don't return in a few days, they'll be worrying about us," Jondalar said.

"You are probably right," Ayla said, "but let's keep looking, at least until tomorrow. Then we can decide."

They made camp late, and avoided talking about the decision they knew they would have to make. In the morning, the air felt damp and they noticed clouds had formed in the north. In the early morning the wind was erratic, coming from every direction. Then it shifted and started blowing from the north, with some strong gusts, which made the horses nervous as well as the people. Ayla always packed extra clothing for warmth in case of shifts in the weather, or if they needed to be up late in the evening.

The glaciers, beginning in the farthest north and lying like a huge pancake on the curved top of the earth, presented walls of solid ice more than two miles thick only a few hundred miles away. On the hottest days of summer, the nights were usually cool and even the daytime weather could change abruptly. The north wind brought a chill and a reminder that even in summer, winter ruled the land.

But the north wind brought something else as well. In the bustle of striking camp and preparing a meal, no one noticed the shift in Wolf's posture. But a loud yip that was almost a bark got Ayla's attention. He was standing, almost leaning into the wind, with his nose high and forward. He had picked up a scent. Each time they started out from camp, she had given him the signal to search for people. The wolf's highly developed sense of smell had found something, some small whiff brought in by the wind.

"Look, mother! Look at Wolf!" Jonayla said. She had seen his bearing, too.

"He's located something," Jondalar said. "Let's hurry and finish packing."

They threw things into the pack baskets much less neatly than usual, and tied them on the horses along with the riding blankets, put the halters on Racer and Gray, doused the fire, and mounted.

"Find them, Wolf," Ayla said. "Show us which way to go." She made the Clan hand signals when she gave the command.

The wolf headed north, but took a more easterly direction than they had been traveling. If what he had scented was the group they were supposed to meet, they seemed to have veered off the infrequently marked trail, or perhaps they had traveled into the eastern highland for some other reason. Wolf moved with single-minded purpose using the ground-covering lope that was common to his species; the horses with Whinney in the lead followed behind. They traveled all morning and past the time when they would normally have stopped for a midday meal.

Ayla thought she caught a whiff of something burning, then Jondalar called out to her, "Ayla, do you see smoke ahead?"

She did see a faint trace of smoke rising in the distance and urged Whinney to a faster pace. She was holding Gray's lead rope, and glanced back at her beloved daughter on the young mare's back to make sure Jonayla was prepared for the increased speed. The girl smiled at her mother in excitement, which indicated that she was prepared. Jonayla loved riding her horse by herself. Even when her mother or Jondalar wanted her to ride in front on one of their mounts for safety because the trail was rough, or so she could rest and not have to hold on as firmly, the child resisted, though it seldom did any good.

When they saw a camp with people around it, they slowed down as they approached. They weren't sure who the people were. Someone else could also be traveling, and rushing into a camp of strangers on the backs of horses could cause distress for everyone.

23

T hen Ayla saw a man as tall as Jondalar with blond hair. He also saw her. "Kimeran! We've been looking for you! I'm so glad we found you," Ayla said, with relief in her voice.

"Ayla!" Kimeran said. "Is it really you?"

"And how did you find us?" Jondecam said. "How did you know where to look?"

"Wolf found you. He has a good nose," Ayla said.

"We went to Camora's Cave, expecting to meet you there, but they were surprised to see us," Jondalar said. "Everyone was getting worried, especially your sister, Jondecam. So I suggested we go back on the horses along the trail that I thought you would take, because they can go much faster than people."

"But we went off the trail to find a place to make a good camp when the children got sick," Levela said.

"You say the children are sick?" Ayla asked.

"Yes, and Beladora, too," Kimeran said. "Maybe you shouldn't come too close. Ginadela got it first. She was hot, feverish, then Levela's son, Jonlevan, and then Beladora. I thought Gioneran might avoid it, but about the time that Ginadela started to get red spots all over her, he started getting feverish."

"We didn't know what to do for them, except let them rest, make sure they drank plenty of water, and try to cool the fever with wet compresses," Levela said.

"You did the right thing," Ayla said. "I've seen something like this before. At the Mamutoi Summer Meeting, when I was spending a lot of time with the mamuti. They are like the zelandonia, the ones who know the spirit world, and are healers. One of the Camps arrived with several people who were sick, mostly children. The Mamuti made them stay at the far edge of the Meeting Camp, and posted several Mamuti to make everyone else stay away. They were afraid most of the people at the Summer Meeting would get the sickness."

"Then you should make sure that Jonayla doesn't play with the children," Levela said, "and you should stay away."

"Are they still hot and feverish?" Ayla asked.

"Not much anymore, but they are full of red spots."

"I'll take a look at them, but if they are not feverish, it may be all right. The Mamutoi think it is an ailment of childhood, and they say it's better if you get it as a child. Children tend to recover more easily," Ayla said. "It's harder on adults."

"That's true for Beladora. I think she was sicker than the children," Kimeran said. "She's still weak."

"The mamuti told me the fever is more intense and lingers, and the spots take longer to go away if you get it after you are grown," Ayla said. "Why don't you take me to see Beladora and the children."

Their tent had two tops. A primary pole held up the higher one, and a thin wisp of smoke was coming out of a hole near the top of that one. A smaller pole supported an extension of the tent, making more room. The entrance was a little low and Ayla ducked to go inside. Beladora was lying on a sleeping roll in the enlarged area. The three children were sitting up on their bedrolls but did not seem to feel very energetic. Three other sleeping places were in the other side, two together and one separate. Kimeran came in after Ayla. He could stand erect near the pole in that section, but had to bend over or stoop to move around in the rest of the tent.

Ayla first went to check on the children. The youngest, Levela's son Jonlevan, seemed to be over his fever, though he was still listless and covered with red spots that seemed to be itchy.

He smiled when he saw Ayla. "Where's Jonayla?" he asked. The woman recalled that she liked to play with him. He could count three years to her four, but he was approaching her in height. She liked to play his mother or sometimes his mate, and boss him around. They were cousins since his mother, Levela, was the sister of Proleva, who was mated to Jondalar's brother Joharran, close cousins who would not be allowed to mate.

"She's outside," Ayla said as she put the back of her hand on his forehead; it wasn't abnormally hot, and his eyes didn't have the glazed look of fever. "I think you are feeling better, aren't you? Not so hot anymore?"

"I wan' play wif' Jonayla."

"Not yet, maybe in a little while," Ayla said.

She checked out Ginadela next. She also seemed well on the way to recovery, though her red spots were certainly colorful. "I want to play with Jonayla, too," she said. The twins could count five years, and just as Kimeran and Jondalar resembled each other—both were tall and blond—though they were not related, Jonayla and Ginadela were also blond and fair with blue eyes, though Jonayla had the same vivid, startling blue color of Jondalar's eyes.

Gioneran, Ginadela's twin, had rather dark brown hair, and brownish-green hazel eyes, like his mother, but he seemed to have some of Kimeran's height. When Ayla put the back of her hand to his head, there was still some heat, and his eyes had the shiny look of fever. His spots were coming on strong, but they seemed a little raw, not as distinctly developed.

"I'll give you something to make you feel better in a little while," she said to the boy. "Would you like a drink of water now? Then I think you should lie down."

"All right," he said, with a weak smile.

She reached for the waterbag, and poured some into a cup that was beside his sleeping roll, then helped him hold it while he drank. He did lie down afterward.

Finally she went to Beladora. "How are you feeling?" Ayla asked.

"I've felt better," she said. Her eyes were still glazed, and she was sniffling. "I'm really glad you're here, but how did you find us?"

"When you weren't at Camora's Cave, we thought something must have delayed you. It was Jondalar's idea to take the horses and look for you. They can go faster than people, but it was Wolf who picked up your scent and brought us here," Ayla said.

"I didn't realize how useful your animals could be," Beladora said. "But I hope you don't get this sickness. It's terrible, and now I'm feeling itchy. Will these red spots go away?"

"They should fade soon," Ayla said, "though it may take a while before they are completely gone. I'll fix something to help the itch and bring the fever down a little."

Everyone had crowded into the tent by then. Jondalar and Kimeran were both standing by the taller pole, and the rest were crammed around them.

"I wonder why Beladora and the children got sick, but not the rest of us," Levela said. "At least not yet."

"If you haven't by now, you probably won't," Ayla said.

"I was worried that someone might have set evil spirits on us because they were jealous that we were making a Journey," Beladora said.

"I don't know," Ayla said. "Did you anger anyone?"

"If I did, I didn't mean to. I was excited about seeing my family and my Cave again. When I left with Kimeran, I didn't know if I ever would. It might have seemed like I was bragging," Beladora said.

"Did anyone at the First Cave of South Land Zelandonii talk about anyone who had stayed there before you? Or was anyone sick when you were there?" Ayla asked Kimeran.

"Now that you mention it, some people did make a crossing before us, more than one group, and I think their Zelandoni was taking care of someone who was sick," Kimeran said. "I didn't ask, though."

"If there were evil spirits present, they may not have been directed at you. It may be that they were left over from the people who were there before you, Beladora, but some sickness happens without anyone wishing it on you. It just seems to get passed around," Ayla said. "This fever with red spots might be one like that. If you get it when you are young, you don't usually get it after you are grown. That's what one Mamut told me. My guess is that all of you had it when you were children, or you'd be sick, too."

"I think I do remember a time when a lot of us were sick at a Summer Meeting," Jondecam said. "They put us all together in one tent, and once we got to feeling better, we felt special because we were getting so much attention. It was like a game; I think we had spots, too. Do any of you remember?"

"I was probably too young to remember," Levela said.

"And I was just enough older that I didn't pay any attention to younger children, sick or not," Jondalar said. "If I didn't get sick then, I must have had it when I was so young, I don't remember. What about you, Kimeran?"

"I think I do remember, sort of, but only because my sister was in the zelandonia," the other tall man said. "At a Summer Meeting, there's always so much going on, and youngsters from the same Cave tend to stay together. They don't always notice what others are doing. What about you, Ayla? Have you had the red-spot fever sickness?"

"I remember occasionally being sick and having a fever when I was growing up, but I don't remember if I ever had red spots with it," Ayla said. "But I didn't get sick when I went with a Mamut to the Mamutoi Camp that had the sickness, so that I could learn something about it, and how to treat it. And speaking of that, I want to go out and see what I can find to help you feel better, Beladora. I have some medicines with me, but the plants I want grow almost everywhere, and I'd rather have fresh ones if I can find some."

Everyone filed out of the tent except Kimeran, who stayed to look after Beladora and her children, as well as Levela's child.

"Can't I stay here, mother? With them?" Jonayla asked, indicating the other children.

"They can't play right now, Jonayla," her mother said. "They need to rest, and I'd like you to help me find some plants that I can use to make them feel better."

"What are you looking for?" Levela asked when they got outside. "Can I help you?"

"Do you know yarrow, or common coltsfoot? I also want willow bark, but I know where that is. I saw some just before we got here."

"Is yarrow the one with the fine leaves and tiny white flowers that grow together in a bunch? A little like carrots, with a stronger smell? That's one way you can tell the difference, from the smell," Levela asked.

"That is a very good description," Ayla said. "And coltsfoot?"

"Big roundish green leaves that are thick, white, and soft underneath."

"You know that one, too. Good. Let's go and find some," Ayla

said. Jondalar and Jondecam were standing by the fireplace outside the tent, talking, while Jonayla was nearby, listening. "Beladora and Gioneran still have some fever. We are going to look
for some plants to help bring down the heat. And something to
help the itchiness of all of them. I'll take Jonayla and Wolf."

"We were just saying we should collect more wood," Jondalar
said. "And I was thinking that I should look for some trees that
would make good poles for a pole-drag or two. Even when Beladora and the children get better, they might not be up to a long
walk, and we should start back to Camora's Cave before they
start worrying about us."

"Do you think Beladora will mind riding on a pole-drag?"
Ayla asked.

"We've all seen the First riding on one. She seems to like it. I
think it has made the idea less frightening," Levela said. "Why
don't we ask her?"

"I need to get my gathering basket anyway," Ayla said.

"I'll get mine, too, and we should let Kimeran and Beladora
know where we're going," Levela said. "And I'll tell Jonlevan
we're going to get something to make him feel better."

"He'll want to go, since he is better, especially when he finds
out that Jonayla is going with you," Jondecam said.

"I know he will," Levela said, "but I don't think he should yet.
What do you think, Ayla?"

"If I knew the area better and knew where we were going, it
might be all right, but I don't think so yet."

"That's what I'll tell him," Levela said.

"I'll take Beladora," Ayla said. "Whinney is more accustomed
to pulling a pole-drag," It had been several days since they found
the missing families, but Beladora still wasn't entirely recovered.
If she pushed herself too soon, Ayla was afraid she might end up
with a chronic problem that could make the rest of the Journey
more difficult.

She didn't add that Racer would not be a good horse to pull
her travois because he was harder to control. Even Jondalar,
who was very good with him, sometimes had difficulty when
the stallion got a bit fractious. Gray was still young, Jonayla

even younger in terms of ability, and with Whinney dragging
the travois behind her, it would be more difficult for Ayla to use
the lead rope to help her daughter control the horse. She wasn't
sure that they should make a pole-drag for Gray.

However, the large tent the other travelers had been camping
in while people were sick was assembled from their smaller traveling tents and some extra hides, and the third travois could hold
the tent poles and other things they had made while they had
stopped that they might otherwise have left behind. The children
were very much improved, but still tired easily. The pole-drags
would also provide a place for them to rest while they were traveling without having to stop. Ayla and Jondalar wanted to return
as quickly as possible. They were sure the ones who were waiting for them were wondering where they were.

The night before they planned to leave, they organized as
much as they could so they could leave quickly. Ayla, Jondalar,
Jonayla, and Wolf used their own traveling tent. In the morning,
they made a quick meal of the leftovers from the night before,
and packed everything on the pole-drags, including the backframes they usually wore to carry their essentials—shelter, additional clothing, and food—with them. Though the adults were
used to carrying them, they found it much easier to walk without the heavy loads. They got off to a good start and traveled
farther than they customarily did, but by evening, most people
were tired.

While they were drinking the last of their evening tea, Kimeran and Jondecam brought up the idea of stopping early to
go hunting so they would have something to bring with them
when they met Camora's relatives. Ayla was concerned. The
weather had cooperated so far. There had been a little shower
the night Ayla and Jondalar found the other travelers. It cleared
up after that, but Ayla didn't know how long it would stay that
way. Jondalar was aware that she had a good "nose" for weather,
and usually knew when rain was coming.

It wasn't exactly a smell that suggested rain; she thought of it
as a special tang in the air and often a damp feel. In later times,
some would refer to the ozone in the atmosphere before rain as
fresh air; others who had the ability to detect it thought it had a

metallic tinge. Ayla didn't have a name for it and found it hard to explain, but she knew it, and she had perceived that hint of coming rain recently. Slogging through mud and pouring rain was the last thing she wanted to do right now.

Ayla woke up when it was still dark. She got up to use the night basket, but stepped outside instead. There was still a glow from the coals in the fireplace in front of the tent that gave enough light for her to go to a nearby bush instead. The air was cool but fresh and as she headed back to the tent she noticed that the true black of night had shaded into the midnight blue of pre-dawn. She watched for a while as a rich deep red flooded the eastern sky, highlighting a mottled pattern of dark purple clouds, followed by a dazzling light that turned the red sky more fiery and spread the clouds out into bands of vibrant color.

"I'm sure it's going to rain soon," she said to Jondalar when she went back into the tent, "and it is going to be a big storm. I know they don't want to arrive empty-handed, but if we keep going we might get there before the rain starts. I would not want Beladora to get wet and cold just as she is getting better, and I dislike the idea of having everything get wet and muddy when if we hurry we might avoid it."

The rest woke up early, planning to start out not long after sunup. Everyone could see dark clouds gathering on the horizon, and Ayla was sure they would soon be in for a downpour.

"Ayla says a big storm is coming," Jondalar told the other two men when they brought up hunting. "She thinks it would be better to hunt later, after we get there."

"I know there are clouds in the distance," Kimeran said, "but that doesn't mean it will rain here. They look pretty far off."

"Ayla has a good sense of rain coming," Jondalar said. "I've seen it before. I don't necessarily want to have to dry out wet clothes and muddy footwear."

"But we only met them at the Matrimonial," Jondecam said. "I don't want to ask for their hospitality with nothing to give in return."

"We were only there a half a day before we left to look for you, but I noticed that they don't seem to be familiar with the spear-thrower. Why don't we ask them to come hunting with us and show them how to use it. That might be a better gift than just bringing them some meat," Jondalar said.

"I suppose . . . do you really think it's going to rain that soon?" Kimeran asked.

"I trust Ayla's 'nose' for rain. She is seldom wrong," Jondalar said. "She's been smelling rain for a few days and she thinks it will be a big storm. Not one that we'll want to get caught in without good shelter. She doesn't even want to stop to cook a midday meal; she says we should just drink water and eat traveling cakes along the way, so we can get there faster. Now that Beladora is getting well, I don't think you want her to get soaked." Suddenly he had another thought. "We could get there more quickly riding on the horses."

"How can we all ride on three horses?" Kimeran asked.

"Some people could ride on the pole-drags and others double up on the horses. Have you ever thought about sitting on a horse? You could sit behind Jonayla."

"Maybe someone else should sit on a horse. I've got long legs and I can run fast," Kimeran said.

"Not as fast as a horse," Jondalar said. "Her two children can ride on the pole-drag with Beladora. It would be a bumpy ride, but they have already done it a few times. We could move the gear on Racer's pole-drag to Gray's. Then Levela and Jonlevan can ride double on Racer with me. That leaves you and Jondecam. I thought he could ride on the pole-drag, or he can ride behind me, and Levela and her young one can be on the pole-drag. That leaves you riding double with Ayla or Jonayla. With your long legs, it would give you more room if you ride with Jonayla, since she rides so close to Gray's neck. Do you think you could hang on to a horse with your legs while you are sitting on her? You could also hold on to the pole-drag ropes. Whoever rides double with me can hang on to me. We won't ride too long like that—it would tire the horses—but we could cover a good bit of ground a lot faster if we let them run for a little while."

"I see you've been thinking about this," Jondecam said.

"Only since Ayla told me of her concerns," Jondalar said. "What do you think, Levela?"

"I don't want to get wet if I can avoid it," she said. "If Ayla says it's going to rain, I believe her. I'll ride a pole-drag with Jonvelan like Beladora if it means we'll get there faster, even if it is a little bumpy."

While the water was heating for tea, the loads on the pole-drags were rearranged, and Ayla and Jondalar got everyone settled. Wolf was watching from the side with his head tilted at an angle as though he was curious about what was going on, which was emphasized by his cocked ear. Ayla caught sight of him and smiled. They started out slowly at first, then with a look between them, Jondalar signaled Ayla, then gave a shout.

"Get ready, and hold on tight," he said.

Ayla leaned forward, instructing her horse to run. Whinney started into a fast trot; then her gait changed to a gallop. Though it wasn't as fast as it would have been if she hadn't been dragging the travois, she did gain considerable speed. The horses behind followed her lead and the urging of their usual riders, and picked up their pace. Wolf ran along beside them. It was exhilarating for Jondecam and Kimeran, and breathtaking, if a little frightening, for those holding on tight to the pole-drags as they bumped over the rough ground. Ayla paid close attention to her horse, and when Whinney started to labor under the strain, she slowed her down again.

"Well, that was exciting," Beladora said.

"That was fun!" both the twins said together. "Can we do it again?" Ginadela asked.

"Yes, can we do it again?" Gioneran asked.

"We'll do it again, but we have to let Whinney rest a little now," Ayla said. She was pleased with the distance they had traveled in their short burst of speed, but they still had some ways to go. They kept going, but at a walk. After she felt that her horse was rested, Ayla called out, "Let's do it again."

When the horses started running, the riders hung on, knowing now what to expect. The ones who had been frightened were not as frightened this time, but it was still exciting to move with greater speed than any of them could have run, even those with the longest of legs.

The native wild horses, which had been tamed but not do-mesticated, were very strong and tough. Their hooves needed no protection from rocky ground, they could carry or pull a surprisingly heavy load, and their endurance was well beyond what might be expected. Though they loved to run, the horses with the extra loads could sustain the pace for only a limited time, which Ayla watched very carefully. By the time she slowed them back to a walk, and after a while signaled them to take off in a run a third time, the horses even seemed to be enjoying it. Wolf did too. It seemed like some kind of game. He tried to anticipate when they would start to run again and get a head start, but he didn't want to get too far ahead because he was keeping pace and needed to predict when they would slow down.

By late afternoon Ayla and Jondalar were beginning to recognize the region though they weren't sure, and didn't want to miss the trail they needed to take to reach the Cave of Camora's people. It had been Willamar who knew the region. Going at a slower pace made everyone notice the changes in the weather. The air was damp and the wind had started to pick up. Then they heard a resounding rumble and the roaring crack of thunder and not long after saw a flash of lightning and it wasn't very far away. They all knew a big storm was almost upon them. Ayla began to shiver, but it wasn't just the sudden blast of cold damp air. The rumbling and roaring reminded her too much of an earthquake, and there was nothing she hated more than earthquakes.

They almost missed the trail, but Willamar and some of the others had been keeping a watch for them for several days. Jondalar was very relieved when he saw the familiar figure waving at them. The Trade Master had seen the horses approaching from some distance away, and had sent one of the people up to tell the Cave that the horses were returning. At a distance, when Willamar didn't see anyone walking alongside the horses, he was afraid they hadn't found anyone, but as they drew closer, he saw more than one head above the backs of the horses, and realized they were riding together. Then he saw the pole-drags and as they pulled up, people on them.

People from the Cave were rushing down the path. When Camora saw her brother and her uncle, she didn't know which to run to first. They solved her dilemma when both of them ran to her and hugged her together.

"Hurry, it's starting to rain," Willamar urged.

"We can leave the pole-drags here," Ayla said, then they all hurried up the trail.

The travelers stayed longer than planned, partly to give Camora a chance to visit with her kin, and for her mate and children to get to know them. The Cave was a more isolated band of people, and though they went to Summer Meetings, they didn't have any close neighbors. Jondecam and Levela considered staying with Jondecam's sister, perhaps until the travelers could stop and pick them up on their way back. She seemed hungry for company and news about people she knew. Kimoran and Beladora definitely planned to leave when the First did. Beladora's people lived at the end of their proposed Journey.

The First had been hoping to leave within a few days, but Jonayla came down with measles as they were getting ready to go, which delayed their departure. The three Zelandonia among the travelers gave remedies and instructions to the resident Cave on how to care for those who developed the contagious disease, explaining that they were likely to get sick, too, but that usually it wasn't too serious. The local Zelandoni had become acquainted with the First and Jonokol while Ayla and Jondalar were looking for the others, and had grown to respect their knowledge.

The people of the Ninth Cave told stories of their experiences with the sickness and made it seem so commonplace that the people didn't feel quite as nervous about getting sick with it. Even after Jonayla started to feel better, Zelandoni decided that they should postpone leaving until the people of the Cave started to show symptoms so the three of them could explain how to care for those who got sick and what herbs and poultices would be helpful. Many of the Cave did get sick, but not all of them, which made the First think that at least some of the people had been exposed to measles before.

Zelandoni and Willamar knew there were some Sacred Sites in the region and talked about them with Farnadal and their Donier. The First knew of them but had not seen them. Willamar had, but it had been many years before. The sites were related to the major painted cave near the Seventh Cave of South Land Zelandonii, just as the one near the Fourth South Land

Cave was, and they were Sacred Sites, but from the descriptions, there wasn't much to see, just a few rough paintings on stone walls.

They had already been delayed so long that the First decided they could omit those sites on this Donier Tour so they would have time to see some others. It was more important to see the very major Sacred Site that was not far from Amelana's Cave. And they still had to make a visit to the neighboring Giornadonii, and Beladora's Cave.

The wait gave the Ninth Cave an opportunity to get to know the people of Camora's Cave better, and Jondalar, in particular, the opportunity to demonstrate the spear-thrower and show how to make one to those who wanted to learn. The wait also gave Jondecam and Levela more time to visit with Camora and their relatives and when the travelers left, they were ready to go with them. During the extended visit, the two Caves had become quite friendly, and they talked about a reciprocal visit sometime.

For all the camaraderie, the visitors were anxious to be on their way, and the people of the Cave were thankful when they were gone. They were not accustomed to many visitors, unlike the Ninth Cave, which was located in the midst of a richly populated region. It was one reason that Camora still missed her family and friends. She was determined to make sure the Cave did make a return visit, and if she could, she was going to persuade her mate to stay.

After they started out again, it took the travelers a few days to settle back into a comfortable itinerant mode. The composition of the new group of travelers was quite different from the one they had started out with, primarily because there were more of them, and more children, which prolonged the time it took to move from place to place. As long as it had been just Jonayla, who often rode Gray, they moved at a fairly rapid pace, but with two more youngsters who were old enough to use their own legs, and a younger one who wanted to walk because the other children did, their rate of travel had inevitably slowed.

Ayla finally made the suggestion that Gray pull a pole-drag for the three children to use while Jonayla rode on her back. That helped the travelers to move a little faster. The trekkers settled into a very practical routine with all of them contributing to the well-being of the group in their own way.

As the season progressed and they continued in their southerly direction, the days grew warmer. It was generally pleasant, except for an occasional rainstorm or muggy heat spell. When they were traveling or working in warm weather, men often wore a breechclout and perhaps a vest, plus their decorative and identifying beads. Women usually wore a loose, comfortable sleeveless dress with slits up the sides for ease of walking, made of soft buckskin or woven fibers that went on over their head and tied at the waist. But as the weather warmed, even light clothing could be too much and they stripped down more. Both men and women sometimes wore only a thong or short fringed skirt and some beads, the children not even that, and their skins turned nut brown. A natural tan, slowly acquired, was the best protective sunscreen, and though they didn't know it, a healthy way to absorb certain essential vitamins.

Zelandoni was becoming more accustomed to walking and Ayla thought she was getting slimmer. She had little trouble keeping up, but she always insisted upon riding on her pole-drag when they arrived at a new location. People made a commotion when they saw her being pulled by a horse, which she felt added to the mystique of the zelandonia and to the position of the First Among Those Who Served The Great Earth Mother.

Their route, which was worked out by Zelandoni and Willamar, took them south through open woods and grasslands, along the west side of a massif, a highland that was the leftover stump of ancient mountains, ground down by the passage of time, with volcanoes forming new mountains on top of the old. Eventually they turned east, swinging around the bottom of the central highland, and then continued traveling east between the southern end of the highland and the north shore of the Southern Sea. As they traveled they often saw game, birds and animals of many kinds, but except when they stopped to visit settlements, no people crossed their path.

Ayla found herself truly enjoying the company of Levela, Beladora, and Amelana when they weren't visiting another Cave or Summer Meeting. They did things together with their children. Amelana's pregnancy was beginning to show, but she was no longer troubled by morning sickness and the walking was beneficial for her. She felt well and her vibrant good health along with her obvious show of maternity made her even more attractive to Tivonan and Palidar, Willamar's assistants. But as they continued the Donier Tour, stopping to visit various Caves, Summer Meetings, and Sacred Sites, there were many young men who found her equally attractive. And she enjoyed the attention.

Since Ayla was often with Zelandoni, the young women were learning some of the knowledge that Zelandoni was teaching her acolyte. They listened and sometimes joined in on their discussions about various things—medicinal practices, identifying plants, ways of counting, meanings of colors and numbers, stories and songs of the Histories and Elder Legends—and the Donier seemed to have no objection to passing her wisdom on to them. She knew that in times of emergency it wouldn't hurt to have some additional people around who knew something about what to do if they needed to act as assistants.

Traveling east, they found their way often blocked by rivers that came down from the massif and into the Southern Sea. Since none of the rivers were huge, they became adept at crossing them until they came to one that carved a large valley running from north to south. They turned and followed it north until they came to a tributary that joined it from the northeast and followed it.

A little beyond that, the traveling group came to a pleasant area of open woodland on the edge of an oxbow lake. Though it was early afternoon, they stopped and set up camp amid some brush and grass near a copse of trees. The children discovered a large patch of bilberries before the evening meal, and picked some to share with their elders, but they ate more as they picked. The women saw huge stands of cattails and phragmite reeds at the edge of the water, and the hunters found fresh signs of cloven hooves.

"We're getting close to the home of those that live the closest to the most important Sacred Cave of all the Zelandonii," Willamar said, after they built a fire and were relaxing with a drink of tea. "We're a large group to be visiting and asking for hospitality without bringing something to share equivalent to our size."

"It looks like a herd of aurochs or bison stopped here not too long ago, judging from those prints," Kimeran said.

"They may return to the water to drink here regularly. If we stay awhile, we could hunt them," Jonokol said.

"Or I could go look for them on Racer," Jondalar said.

"Most of us are running out of spears to hunt with," Jondecam said. "I broke another one the last time we went hunting, both the shaft and the point."

"This looks like a region that should have good flint," Jondalar said. "If I can find some, I'll make new points."

"I saw a stand of straight trees on our way here, younger than those in that copse, that would make good shafts," Palidar said. "It's not far away."

"Some of those bigger ones would make good shafts for a couple of new pole-drags to bring some fresh meat to the Cave we want to visit," Jondalar said.

"A few young bulls at this time of year would give us fresh meat and some for drying, and fat for traveling cakes and fuel for lamps, and a hide or two," Ayla said. "We can make new footwear from the skins. I don't mind walking barefoot most of the time, but sometimes I want protection for my feet and my footwear is wearing out."

"And look at all those cattails and reeds," Beladora said. "You can weave footwear from those, too, and we can make new sleeping rolls, and baskets and pads and many other things we need."

"Even gifts for the Cave we want to visit," Levela said.

"I hope we don't take too long. I'm awfully close to home, and I'm getting anxious," Amelana said. "I can't wait to see my mother."

"But you don't want to return empty-handed, do you?" the First said. "Wouldn't you like to bring a gift or two for your mother, and maybe some meat for your Cave?"

"You're right! I should do that, so it doesn't look like I'm just coming home begging," Amelana said.

"You know that you wouldn't be begging even if you didn't bring anything, but wouldn't it be nice to give them something?" Levela said.

24

They all decided it was time to take a few days to hunt and gather food to resupply their traveling larder, and restock equipment that was showing signs of hard use. They were excited about finding a place with such abundance.

"I want to get some of those berries. They look perfect for picking," Levela said.

"Yes, but first I want to make a picking basket, something to wear around my neck so I can use two hands to pick," Ayla said. "I want enough to dry some for traveling cakes, but then I need to weave a mat or two to dry them on."

"Will you make a basket for me?" Zelandoni said. "Picking is something I can do."

"I'd like to pick, too. Will you make a basket for me?" Amelana said.

"Show me how you make yours," Beladora said. "Picking with both hands is a good idea, but I always carried the basket on my arm."

"I'll show you all, including the children. They can help, too," Ayla said. "Let's go get some of those reeds and cattails."

"And collect the roots to eat with the evening meal," Beladora said.

Wolf was watching Ayla and Jonayla, and finally yipped to get the woman's attention. He was running toward the open field, then running back. "You want to do some exploring and hunting, too, Wolf? Well, go ahead," she said, giving him a hand signal that he knew meant he was free to go his own way.

The women spent the afternoon pulling and digging up plants from the muddy edge of the lake: the tall phragmite reeds, whose plume-like tops towered over both Jondalar and Kimeran, and slightly shorter cattails, whose spikes were fruiting with edible pollen. The fresh rootstalks and lower stems of both plants could also be eaten either raw or cooked, as well as the little bulblets that grew from the cattail rhizomes. Later the dried old stringy roots could be pounded into flour for making a kind of bread, especially good when mixed with the rich yellow pollen from the cattail spikes, but equally important were the nonedible parts.

The soft, hollow stems of the tall reeds could be woven into large baskets, or made into soft, springy bed mats, more comfortable to sleep on than fur bedrolls when it was warm, and into a ground mat for the furs when it was cold. The cattail leaves were also made into mats used for various purposes, including bedding and pads to kneel or sit upon. Besides being twined into baskets, they could be woven into dividing panels, waterproof coverings for dwellings, and rain cloaks and hats for people. The solid cattail stalk, when it became dry, made an excellent fire-drill. The brown "cat tail" tops would become fuzz that made good tinder, or stuffing for bedding, pads, and pillows, or absorbent material for babies' waste, or women's moontimes. They had found a veritable market of produce and products in the plants that grew so abundantly at the water's edge.

For the rest of the afternoon the women wove berry-picking baskets. The men spent the afternoon discussing hunting and collecting the straight new growths of young trees to make the dart-spears for the spear-throwers to replace those that had been lost or broken. Jondalar took off on Racer to follow the tracks and see if he could locate the herd that had made them. While he was at it, he looked for outcrops of flint, which he was sure could be found in this area. Ayla had seen him go and guessed he was looking for the herd, and for a brief moment considered going with him, but she was involved in making baskets and didn't want to interrupt her task.

Though Jondalar hadn't returned yet, they stopped for an evening meal and shared their plans. They were all laughing and talking when Jondalar rode into camp with a big grin.

"I found them, a sizable herd of bison," he said, "and I found some fresh flint that looks to be of good quality, for new spears."

He dismounted and took several large gray stones from the

carrying baskets that were tied onto Racer's back on each side for balance. Everybody clustered around him as he removed the carrying baskets, riding blanket, and halter from the stallion, then faced him toward the water, and slapped his rump. The brown horse waded into the lake and drank some water, then walked back out and on the sandy bank dropped down and rolled on his back, on one side, then the other. The people watching chuckled. It was amusing to watch the horse kicking his legs up in the air, obviously enjoying the good scratching he was giving himself.

Jondalar joined them around the fire and Ayla gave him a bowl of food that consisted of reconstituted dried meat, the lower stems and roots of cattail, and the budding tops of cattails, all cooked in the meat-flavored broth.

He smiled at Ayla. "And I also saw a covey of red grouse. That's the bird I told you about that looks like a ptarmigan except it doesn't turn white in winter. If we hunt them, we could use the feathers for the spears."

Ayla smiled back. "And I can make Creb's favorite dish."

"Do you want to hunt them tomorrow morning?" Jondalar said.

"Yes . . . ," Ayla said, then frowned. "Well, I was going to pick berries."

"Go ahead and hunt your grouse," Zelandoni said. "We have enough people picking."

"And I'll watch Jonayla, if you want," Levela said.

"You finish eating, Jondalar. I saw some nice round stones for my sling in that dry creek bed. I want to get them before it gets too dark," Ayla said, musing. "I should bring my spear-thrower, too. I have some spears left."

The next morning, instead of the usual dress, she put on a pair of soft buckskin leggings, which were similar to boy's winter underwear, then foot-coverings that consisted of a moccasin foot part that was attached to a soft upper that wrapped around the ankle. She finished with a sleeveless vestlike top made of the same material as the leggings and tied the lacings tightly closed in front; it offered some support for her breasts. Then she quickly braided her hair to get it out of her way, and wrapped her sling around her head. She put the holder for her spear-thrower and spears on her back, then tied on her waist thong, to which were attached a good knife in its sheath, a pouch that she filled with the stones she had collected, another pouch that held a few implements including her personal drinking cup, and finally a small medicine bag with a few emergency supplies.

She dressed quickly, feeling some excitement. She hadn't realized how much she wanted to go hunting. She picked up her riding blanket, stepped out of the tent, and whistled for Whinney, and with a different trill, whistled for Wolf, then walked to where the horses were grazing. Gray had a halter with a long lead that was attached to a peg pounded into the ground so she wouldn't stray too far; she had a tendency to wander off. She knew Whinney wouldn't go far from the younger mare. Jondalar had left Racer in the same area. She put the riding blanket on the dun-yellow horse and taking Gray's and Racer's lead ropes, she jumped on her mare and rode to the campfire. She lifted her leg over, slid down from the back of the horse, and went to her daughter, who was sitting beside Levela.

"Jonayla, hold on to Gray. She may want to follow us," Ayla said as she handed the lead to the girl. "We won't be gone too long." When she turned and looked up, she saw Wolf racing toward her. "There you are," she said.

While Ayla embraced her daughter, Jondalar pushed a last bite of cattail root in his mouth, and got a gleam in his eye when he looked at the woman so full of excitement dressed to go riding and hunting. She looks so fine, he thought. He went to the large waterbag, filled up smaller pouches with water to take with them, then poured some in his cup and drank it. He brought the rest to Ayla and gave her a small waterbag and put the cup back in his carrying pouch. They said a few parting words to the people around the fire, and both mounted their horses.

"I hope you find your ptarmigan," Beladora said, "or grouse."

"Yes, good hunting," Willamar said.

"In any case, have a good ride," the First added.

As the people watched the couple leave, each had their own thoughts and feelings about them. Willamar looked on Jondalar and his mate as Marthona's children, and therefore his, and felt the warmth of familial love. The First had a special feeling for Jondalar as a man she had once loved and still did in a way, though now it was as a friend and something more, almost as a son. She appreciated Ayla's many Gifts, loved her as a friend, and was glad to have a colleague whom she considered an equal. She was also glad that Jondalar had found a woman worthy of his love. Beladora and Levela had also grown to love Ayla as a good friend, though there were times when they felt a certain awe toward her. They understood the magnetism of Jondalar's appeal, but now that they both had mates and children whom they loved, they were not as overwhelmed and instead appreciated him as a caring friend who was willing to help whenever they asked.

Jonokol and the two young traders, and even Kimeran and Jondecam, appreciated Jondalar's skills especially with flint and the spear-thrower, and rather envied him. His mate was attractive and accomplished in so many ways, yet so devoted to him that even during Mother Festivals, she chose only him, but he had always been known to have his pick of women. Many women still found him almost irresistibly charismatic, though he did not encourage their advances.

Amelana was still in awe of Ayla and found it difficult to think of her as just a woman who could be a friend, but she admired her intensely, and wished she could be like her. The young woman was also one who found Jondalar tremendously attractive, and had tried on occasion to entice him, but he seemed not to notice. Every other man Amelana had met on this trip gave her at least an appreciative glance, but she never managed to get more than a friendly but detached smile from him and didn't know why. Actually, Jondalar was fully aware of her interest. In his younger days, more than one young woman with whom he had shared First Rites had tried to retain his interest afterward, though he was not allowed to have any further relations with them for a year. He had learned how to discourage such interest.

The two rode off on their horses, with Wolf following along. Jondalar led them west until he came to an area that looked familiar to him. He pulled up and showed her where he had found the flint, then looked around and started in a different direction. They came to an area of moorland, a tract of land covered with bracken, heather—the preferred food plant of red grouse—and coarse grasses with a few clumps of brush and brambles, not far from the western edge of the oxbow lake. Ayla smiled. It was similar to the tundra of ptarmigan habitat, and she could easily imagine that a southern variety of the birds could live in this region. They left the horses near a stand of hazelnut brush spreading out from a large center tree.

She could see that Wolf had taken notice of something ahead. He was alert, focused, and whining softly. "Go ahead, Wolf. Find them," Ayla said.

As he dashed off, Ayla slipped her sling off her head, reached in her pouch for two stones, set one in the soft cup of her sling, and gathered up both ends. She didn't have to wait long. With a sudden flurry of wings Wolf flushed out five red grouse. The birds lived close to the ground but could fly up in a burst of speed and then glide long. They resembled plump chickens with camouflage, brown and black flecked with white. Ayla hurled a stone the moment she saw the first bird, and delivered the second stone before the first one hit the ground. She heard a *swoosh* then saw Jondalar's spear pierce a third.

If it had been just the two of them traveling together, the way it was on their Journey, that would have been enough, but the travelers numbered sixteen in all, including four children. Because of the way Ayla cooked the birds, everyone always wanted a taste, and though they were of a decent size—a live weight of twelve or thirteen pounds full grown—three birds would hardly feed sixteen people. She wished it were the right season for eggs; she liked to stuff the birds with eggs and roast them together. The nests usually consisted of a depression on the ground lined with grass or leaves, but there were no eggs to find at this time of year.

Ayla whistled again for Wolf. He came bounding back. It seemed obvious that he was having fun chasing birds. "Maybe he can find some more," Ayla said, then looked at the four-legged hunter. "Wolf, find them. Find the birds."

The wolf dashed into the grassy field again and Ayla followed after him. Jondalar followed her. Before long another grouse flew up and although it was some distance away, Jondalar launched a spear with his thrower and managed to bring it down. Then, while Jondalar was looking for the one he killed, a lek of four males took to the sky, identified by black and brown with white markings on tail and wing plumage and the yellows and reds of the beaks and combs. Ayla got two more with stones from

her sling; she seldom missed. Jondalar had not seen the fly-up,
though he heard it, and was late getting his spear-thrower armed.
He wounded one, and heard it squawk.

"That should be enough," Ayla said, "even if we let Wolf have
that last one."

With Wolf's help, they found and gathered up seven birds. The
last had a broken wing but was still alive. Ayla wrung the bird's
neck and extracted the small spear, then signaled the wolf that he
could have it. Wolf picked it up in his mouth and carried it out of
sight into the field. Using tough grass as cordage, they tied the
rest of the grouse together by their feet in pairs and strolled back
to where the horses were grazing. She wrapped her sling around
her head again as they walked toward the horses.

When they returned to camp, the hunters were talking about
finding the bison while they were shaving the spear staffs
smooth. Jondalar joined them to finish making the many spears
they needed. After he knapped flint into points, they would attach them to the shafts and fletch them with the red grouse
feathers she would provide. In the meantime, Ayla got the
antler shovel that was used by everyone to clear the hearth of
ashes and various other tasks. But the broad, flat shovel was
not a spade for digging holes. For that she used a kind of awl, a
sturdy flint pointed blade attached to the end of a wooden handle that could be used to break up the ground. The shovel was
then used to remove the broken earth. She found a place off
to the side near the sandy beach and dug a fairly deep hole in
the sandy soil, built a fire nearby and placed several good-size
stones in it to heat them up, then started pulling the feathers
out of her grouse.

Most of the others came to help. The large, strong feathers
were given to the spear-makers, but Ayla wanted to keep the rest
of them, too. Beladora had a pouch that she emptied of some
implements and offered it to her for the feathers. They all helped
to eviscerate and clean the six grouse, saving the edible innards
like the hearts, gizzards, and livers. Ayla wrapped them in fresh
hay from the field and put them back inside each bird and then
wrapped the birds in more hay.

By then the stones were hot, and using bentwood tongs, Ayla
placed the stones in the bottom and along the sides of the pit.

She then covered them with dirt from the hole, and added green grass and leaves, which the children had helped to gather. The birds were placed on top of the greenery. Next, Ayla added vegetables—the lower stems of reeds and some ground nuts, good starchy roots that the other women had found—wrapped in edible green leaves, and put on top of the birds. These were covered by more green grass and leaves, another layer of dirt, then more hot stones. A last layer of dirt went on top to seal it off. It would all be left to cook undisturbed until time for the evening meal.

Ayla went to see how the spear-making was coming along. When she got there, some people were carving indentations in the butt ends of the shafts that would be placed against the hook at the back of the spear-thrower; others were gluing on the feathers with heated pitch from pine trees. The feathers were held in place with thin strings of sinew, which they had brought with them. Jonokol was grinding up charcoal that was added along with hot water to a chunk of warm pitch and stirred together. Then he dipped a stick in the thick black liquid and with it painted designs, abelans, on several spear shafts. An abelan signified both a person and his or her name, it meant the name of a life spirit, it was a personal symbol mark that was given to an infant shortly after birth by a Zelandoni. It wasn't writing, but it was a symbolic use of marks.

Jondalar had made spears for Ayla as well as himself, and gave them to her to mark with her own abelan. She counted them; there were twice ten, twenty. She made four lines close together on each of the shafts. That was her personal symbol mark. Since she wasn't born to the Zelandonii, she had chosen her own abelan and picked marks that matched the scars on her leg given to her by a cave lion when she was a little girl. It was how Creb had decided that the Cave Lion was her totem.

The marks would be used later to identify which hunter had slain a particular animal so the attribution of the kill could be made and the distribution of the meat would be equitable. It wasn't that the person who killed the animal got all the meat, but he or she would have first choice of the select parts and was credited with providing meat to the ones who were given a share, which could be even more important. It meant praise, recognition, and an obligation owed. The best hunters often gave most of their meat away just to acquire the credit, sometimes to the dismay of their mates, but it was expected of them.

Levela considered going on the hunt, and Beladora and Amelana said they would be happy to watch Jonlevan along with Jonayla, but in the end Levela decided not to go. She had only recently started weaning Jonlevan, and was still nursing him occasionally. She hadn't hunted since her son was born, and felt out of practice. She thought she might be more hindrance than help.

By the time the spears were completed, Jondalar had used up nearly all the flint he had found for the points, the best of the feathers were gone, applied to the spear shafts to help the weapons fly true, and it was nearly time to have the meal that Ayla had started. Several people had picked many more bilberries, most of which were drying on woven mats. The balance were being cooked into a sauce in a sturdy new bowl woven out of cattail leaves mixed with stems of rush plants that grew in a marsh near the lake, using stones heated in the fire. The only sweetening for the sauce came from the fruit itself, but flavorings from the flowers, leaves, and barks of various plants were often added. In this case Ayla had found meadowsweet, whose tiny flowers made a creamy, foaming display with a honey-sweet fragrance; the intensely aromatic blue flowers of hyssop, which was also a good cough remedy; and the leaves and scarlet flowers of bergamot. Rendered fat was added for a touch of richness.

The meal was pronounced a delicious success, almost a feast. The grouse provided a different meat, a new flavor, a change from the dried meat they so often had, and cooking in the ground oven had tenderized the birds, even the tough old males. The grass they were wrapped in had contributed its own flavor, and the fruit sauce added an agreeable piquant taste. There wasn't as much left over as usual for the morning meal, but enough, especially with the addition of the tender lower stems and rootstalks of cattails.

People were also excited about the hunt planned for the next day. Jondalar and Willamar started talking about it with the others, but until they saw exactly where the bison were, they couldn't decide what specific strategy to use. They would have to wait until they found the bovids. Since it was still daylight,

Jondalar decided on the spur of the moment to follow the trail again to see if he could still find the herd. He didn't know how much they might have moved. Ayla and Jonayla went with him on their horses, just to give the animals a run. They did find the bison, but not in quite the same place. Jondalar was glad he had decided to track them again, so he could lead the hunters directly to them.

There was always a little chill in the air in the early morning, even in the middle of summer. When Ayla stepped outside the tent the air felt fresh and damp. A cool mist hugged the ground and a layer of fog hung over the lake. Beladora and Levela were up already tending a new fire. Their children were up as well and Jonayla was with them. Ayla hadn't heard her get up, but the child could be very quiet when she wanted to be. When she spied her mother, she came running over.

"You're finally up, mother," she said, as Ayla reached down to pick her up and give her a hug. Ayla doubted that her daughter had been awake very long, but she knew that a child's sense of time was different from that of adults.

After she passed her water, Ayla decided to take a bathing swim in the lake before she went back into the tent. She emerged not long after dressed in her hunting outfit. Her activities woke Jondalar, who was content to lie in his bedroll and watch her; he had been well satisfied the night before. The sleeveless vest didn't offer much warmth, but the hunters didn't want to over-dress since they knew the temperature would rise later. On cool mornings they tended to stay close to the fire and drink hot tea. Their activity would warm them once they started out. The grouse tasted just as good cold as a morning meal as it did the night before. Once again Gray was left behind with Jonayla, but the child didn't want to stay.

"Mother, can't I go with you, please? You know I can ride Gray," the girl implored.

"No, Jonayla. It would be too dangerous for you. Things can happen that you don't expect, and sometimes you have to get your horse out of the way. And you don't know how to hunt yet," Ayla said.

"But when will I learn?" she said with great yearning.

Ayla remembered when she was eager to learn, even though women of the Clan weren't supposed to hunt. She'd had to teach herself, in secret. "I'll tell you what I'll do," she said. "I'll ask Jondy to make a spear-thrower for you, a small one that is your size, so you can begin practicing with it."

"Will you, mother? Promise?" the child said.

"Yes, I promise."

Jondalar and Ayla led their horses rather than riding them to make it easier for the rest to keep up. He found the huge ancient bison—six feet tall at the shoulder with gigantic horns, and with a coat that was a solid dark brown color—not far from where he had last seen them. It was a medium-size herd, but they didn't want the whole herd. They were a small group and only needed a few animals.

There was some discussion about the best way to hunt the bison and it was decided to walk around the herd, carefully so as not to disturb them, and see what the nearby lay of the land was like. There were no convenient blind canyons to drive them into, but there was a dry riverbed with fairly high banks on both sides in one place.

"This could work," Jondalar said, "if we build a fire at the lower end, but not until we drive them up close to it. So we'd have to get the fire ready to go and probably light it with a torch. Then we have to drive them this way."

"Do you really think that would work? How are we going to get them going?"

"With the horses and Wolf, we can drive them," Jondalar said. "Soon as they start into the narrow place, someone can start a fire at the end to slow them down. Others can wait on the high banks—probably best if you lie down on the ground—and when they're in front of you, jump up and use your spear-throwers. We should all gather some wood and pile it up at the end. Then get some tinder and other quick-burning fire-starting material."

"Sounds like you have it all worked out," Tivonan said.

"I've been thinking about it, and talking over some possibilities with Kimeran and Jondecam," Jondalar said. "On our Journey, with the horses and Wolf, we used to single out one or two animals from a herd. They're used to helping us hunt."

"That is how I learned to use the spear-thrower from horse-back," Ayla said. "We even got a mammoth once."

"It sounds like a good plan to me," Willamar said.

"And to me, but I'm not a good hunter," Jonokol said. "I haven't done much hunting, at least not until I came on this Donier Tour."

"Maybe you haven't done much before, but I think you are a more than adequate hunter now," Palidar said.

The rest of them agreed.

"Then I've gotten an extra benefit from this trip. Not only am I getting to see some fascinating Sacred Sites, I'm learning to be a better hunter," Jonokol said, grinning.

"Well, let's start collecting dry grass and wood to burn," Willamar said.

Ayla and Jondalar helped the group as they ranged out gathering wood and other burnable materials, and spread them across the end of the dry creek bed. At Willamar's suggestion they added a row of tinder and kindling at the front edge to help carry the fire along the extended pile. Then they mounted their horses, signaled Wolf, and started circling the herd. Willamar then assigned his apprentices, Palidar and Tivonan, to start a fire at both sides when he gave the word.

"As soon as the fire is well established, you can get into position to use your spear-throwers," Willamar said. The two young men nodded in agreement, and all of the group found places to wait.

And then they waited.

Each hunter was in his own silent space and listened in his own way. The two young men were excited, anticipating the hunt, and strained to hear Ayla and Jondalar rounding up the herd. Jonokol settled into a meditative state, which he had learned long ago kept him most alert and aware of what was going on around him. He heard Ayla and Jondalar shouting in the distance, but he also heard the loud ringing notes in slowing tempo and falling cadence of a kingfisher. He let his eyes search for the sound and caught a glimpse of the vibrant blue and chestnut-orange underparts of the fishing bird. Later, he heard the distinctive harsh call of a crow.

Kimeran let his mind wander back to the Second Cave of

the Zelandonii and hoped everyone was doing well in his absence . . . but perhaps not too well. He wouldn't want them to do better without his leadership. That could imply that he wasn't a very good leader. Jondecam was thinking about his sister, Camora, and wishing she lived closer. Levela, his mate, had said as much the night before.

The sounds of hooves pounding toward them caught everyone's attention. The two young men on either side of the long pile of wood looked at Willamar. He was holding up his hand but looking the other way, getting ready to signal. They both had a piece of flint in one hand and iron pyrite in the other, getting ready to strike them together, hoping they wouldn't fumble. They were all adept at making fire that way, but excitement could delay the procedure. The rest all had spear-throwers armed and ready.

As they started down the dry streambed, one wily old cow tried to turn aside but Wolf anticipated the move. He raced toward the bovine and, with a frightening show of teeth, snarled at the huge bison. It took the apparent path of least resistance and headed down the streambed.

Just then, Willamar gave the signal. Palidar struck first and his spark caught. He bent lower to blow it up into flame. It took Tivonan a second try, but he soon had a fire blazing toward the middle of the streambed. As the two fires joined, the larger dry wood flared up in back of the tinder. As soon as they were sure the fire was well established, they raced toward the higher ground, arming their throwing weapons on the way.

The other hunters were ready. The fire had already caused the bison to slow down in bawling confusion. They didn't want to run into the fire, but the ones at the rear of the stampeding herd were pushing them on.

The spears started to fly!

The air was full of wooden shafts with sharp flint points. Each hunter had selected a different animal to aim for and carefully watched it through the smoke and dust. When they cast a second spear, most were aimed at the same bison as the first. They had been hunting all summer along the way and all of their skills had improved.

Jondalar sighted a bull with a high humped back covered

with shaggy wool, and long sharp black horns. His first spear brought it down and a second kept it there. He quickly rearmed his spear-thrower and aimed for a cow but just wounded it.

Ayla's first spear found a young bull, not quite full grown. She watched it drop, then saw Jondalar's spear hit the cow. It staggered but didn't fall. She flung another spear at the wounded one, and saw it stumble. The first of the herd were breaking through the firewall. The rest were following, leaving behind their fallen brethren.

It was over.

It had happened so quickly, it was hard to believe. The hunters went to check the kills; nine bleeding bison littered the streambed. When they examined their spears, Willamar, Palidar, Tivonan, Jonokol, Kimeran, and Jondecam had each killed one animal. Jondalar and Ayla together had killed three.

"I didn't expect us to be quite so successful," Jonokol said, checking the marks on the spear to make sure the animal was his. "Maybe we should have coordinated our hunt beforehand. This is too much of a good thing."

"It's true, we didn't need so many," Willamar said, "but it means we have more to share. It won't go to waste." He always liked to bring something when he arrived at a new Cave.

"But how are we going to haul them all? Three horses can't pull nine huge bison on pole-drags," Palidar said. The young man's spear had hit a huge bull and he wasn't even sure how to begin to move the beast, much less the rest of them.

"I think someone is going to have to go ahead to the next Cave and bring some people back to help. I don't think they'll mind. They won't even have to hunt them," Jondalar said. He had been thinking along the same lines as Palidar, but he had more experience with such enormous beasts and knew that many hands made it easier.

"You're right," Jondecam said, "but I think we are going to have to move our camp here to butcher them." He wasn't really looking forward to moving.

"That might upset Beladora. She is working on several weaving projects that she won't want to relocate," Kimeran said. "Although she could come here to help with the skinning and butchering, I suppose."

"I think we can skin them here," Ayla said, "then cut them into large pieces, and make several trips to get them back to our camp, and start drying some of the meat. Then we can take some of the fresh meat to the next Cave and ask for help to move the rest of it."

"That would work," Willamar said. "I am going to use the horns to make a couple of drinking cups."

"I wouldn't mind keeping some of the hooves to boil into glue to attach spear points to shafts," Jondalar said. "Pitch is all right, but hooves and bones make a better glue."

"And we can make new waterbags out of the stomachs, and use the intestines to save the fat," Ayla added.

"Levela sometimes keeps chopped-up meat in cleaned-out intestines, too," Jondecam said, "and waterproof coverings for hats and footwear can be made from them."

Suddenly, Ayla realized how near they were to their destination. They would soon deliver Amelana to her Cave. Then they would go to see the very ancient Sacred Site that the First especially wanted Ayla to see; it wasn't far away. After that, it was only a couple of days farther to Beladora's people, according to Willamar. Then they would retrace their steps and return home.

It would be just as long a trek back as it was to get here, but as Ayla looked around, it seemed as though the Mother had provided them with the means to resupply all their needs for the return Journey. They had the materials they needed to replace their worn equipment, weapons, and clothing. There was more than enough meat to dry, and to make traveling cakes, which were essential for covering long distances in a hurry, by grinding up the dehydrated meat and adding fat and the dried berries. They had also dried roots and stems of certain vegetation, and common varieties of mushrooms that everyone knew.

"I've been here! I know this place!" Amelana said. She was so excited to see one familiar place, and then another, she couldn't erase her excited smile. There was no stopping to rest now; pregnant or not, she could hardly wait to get home.

The small group of travelers approached a well-marked trail that wound around a sharp U-shaped bend in the river. An old floodplain had left a broad, level grassy field somewhat above the swiftly flowing water that ended abruptly at the base of a steep cliff. A nice place for horses to graze, Ayla thought.

The wide trail gradually traversed up the side of the cliff around brush and small trees, some of whose roots were used as steps. It was not easy going for the horses, especially pulling the pole-drags, but Ayla remembered how sure-footed Whinney was when she had climbed up to her cave in the valley where Ayla had found her.

The trail leveled out, perhaps assisted by people, Ayla thought, as the travelers came to a sheltering overhanging shelf in an area that was obviously well inhabited. Many people, who had been engaged in various activities, all stopped and stared at the strange procession that was advancing toward them, which included people and surprisingly docile horses. Whinney was wearing the halter that Jondalar had made for her. Ayla liked to use it when they were heading into unknown and possibly unsettling situations, but she was leading both Whinney and Gray, who were both hauling pole-drags. Whinney was pulling the First; Gray's travois had a large load of bison meat. Willamar, his two assistants, and Amelana also accompanied them.

When the young woman among them who was obviously pregnant broke away from the visitors, it aroused attention. "Mother! Mother! It's me!" she called out as she ran toward a woman of substantial proportions.

"Amelana? Amelana, is that you? What are you doing here?" the woman said.

"I came home, mother, and I'm so glad to see you," Amelana cried.

She threw her arms around the woman, but her pregnant stomach made it difficult to stand close. The woman returned the embrace, then, holding her shoulders, pushed her back to look at the daughter she thought she would never see again.

"You're pregnant! Where's your mate? Why are you back? Did you do something wrong?" her mother said. She couldn't imagine why a woman would travel what she knew was a long distance—though she didn't know how long—when she was pregnant. She knew how impetuous her daughter could be and hoped she hadn't broken any social custom or taboo seriously enough that they would send her home.

"No, of course I didn't do anything wrong. If I had, the First Among Those Who Serve The Great Mother would not have brought me home. My mate walks the next world now, and I was pregnant and wanted to come home and have my baby near you," Amelana said.

"The First is here? The First brought you home?" the woman said.

She turned to look at the visitors. A woman was stepping down from some kind of contrivance that was pulled by a horse. She was a large woman, of a size greater than herself, and from the tattoo on the left side of her forehead, she knew the woman was a Zelandoni. The woman walked toward her with great dignity and a certain presence that conveyed authority. A closer look at her tattoo, plus the designs on her outfit and the chest plaque and other necklaces that she wore, made Amelana's mother understand that the woman was indeed the First.

"Why don't you introduce me to your mother, Amelana?" the First said.

"Mother, please greet the One Who Is First Among Those Who Serve The Great Earth Mother," Amelana began. "Zelandoni, this is Syralana of the Third Cave of the Zelandonii That Watches Over the Most Ancient Sacred Site, mated to Demoryn, leader of the Third Cave of the Zelandonii That Watches Over the Most Ancient Sacred Site, mother of Amelana and Alyshana." It gave her a certain sense of satisfaction to show her mother and those who were watching how well she knew the acknowledged leader of the zelandonia.

"I welcome you, First Among Those Who Serve The Great Mother," Syralana said, holding out both hands and walking toward her. "We are greatly honored that you have come."

The First grasped both hands and replied, "In the name of the Great Earth Mother, I greet you, Syralana of the Third Cave of the Zelandonii That Watches Over the Most Ancient Sacred Site."

"Did you travel this far just to bring my daughter home?" Syralana couldn't resist asking.

"I am taking my acolyte on her Donier Tour. She is the one with the horses. We have come to see your Most Ancient Sacred Site. It is known even to us, though we live far to the north."

25

Syralana looked at the tall woman, who was holding ropes that were attached to the two horses, with a bit of apprehension, which the First noticed.

"We can introduce you later, if you don't mind," she said. "You did say your mate is the leader of this Cave?"

"Yes, that is true," Syralana said. "Demoryn is the leader here."

"We have also come to ask your assistance, though it may also be a boon for you," the One Who Was First said.

A man stepped to the woman's side. "Here is my mate," Syralana said. "Demoryn, leader of the Third Cave of the Zelandonii That Watches Over the Most Ancient Sacred Site, please welcome the First Among Those Who Serve The Great Mother."

"Zelandoni the First, our Cave is pleased to welcome you and your friends," he said.

"Allow me to introduce our Trade Master. Willamar, please greet Demoryn, leader of the Third Cave of the Zelandonii That Watches Over the Most Ancient Sacred Site."

"I greet you, Demoryn," Willamar began, holding out both his hands, and continued with the formal greetings. Then he explained, "We stopped for a while just before we came here to hunt and replenish supplies, and to bring you a gift of some meat." He watched the leader and some others nod knowingly. It was the kind of thing they would have done. "We seem to have acquired an embarrassment of riches. We found a herd of bison and our hunters were exceptionally lucky. We counted nine bison killed when we were done, and our entire group only numbers sixteen, which includes four children. That is too much for us and in any case, even with the help of the horses, we cannot transport so much, but we don't want to waste the Gifts of the Mother. If you can send some people to help transport the meat here, we would like to share it with you. We brought some with us, but left some people behind to guard the rest."

"Yes, of course we'll help you, and will be pleased to share your good fortune," Demoryn said, then looked closely at Willamar and saw the tattoo in the middle of his forehead. "Master Trader, you have been here before, I think."

Willamar smiled. "Not to your particular Cave, but I have been in this region before. The First is taking her acolyte, the woman who controls the horses, on a Donier Tour. She is mated to the son of my mate. He is back at our campsite guarding the meat, along with my assistants, two young traders who will be following in my footsteps, and some others. I think Amelana was fortunate that we had planned this trek before she asked to come with us. She was eager to return to her home and have her baby here, near her mother."

"We are pleased to have her back with us. Her mother was very sad when she left, but she was so determined to go with the young man who came to visit, we couldn't refuse her. I am sorry that her mate now walks the next world. It must have been hard for his mother and family, but I'm not sorry to see Amelana. I didn't think I would ever see her again after she left," Demoryn said, "and she may not be so eager to leave home next time."

"I think you are right," Willamar said, with a knowing smile.

"I presume you will be going on to the First Cave to the meeting with all the other Zelandonia," the leader said.

"I haven't heard about any meeting," Willamar said.

"I thought that's why the First was here," Demoryn said.

"I don't know anything about it, but I don't know everything that the First knows." They both turned to look at the large woman. "Did you know there was a meeting of the zelandonia?" Willamar said.

"I certainly look forward to attending it," she said with an enigmatic smile.

Willamar just shook his head. Who could really know a Zelandoni? "Well, Demoryn, if you can get some people to help us unload the meat we brought, and go back with us to get what's left, then the rest of our travelers can come and visit, too."

As she helped Zelandoni unload her personal travel things, Ayla asked, "Did you know there was going to be a gathering of the zelandonia near here?"

"I wasn't certain, but meetings do tend to take place in a sequence of a certain number of years, and I thought this might be the right year for one in this region. I didn't mention it because I didn't want to create any expectations in case I was mistaken, or missed the timing."

"It looks like you were right," Ayla said.

"Amelana's mother seemed nervous about the horses, so I didn't rush to introduce you yet," the First said.

"If she's nervous about the horses, what is she going to think about Wolf?" Ayla said. "We can deal with formal introductions later. I'll take your pole-drag off Whinney and go back with her and Gray. We can make a new pole-drag for her to help bring the meat here. There's still so much left. I'd forgotten how big a bison was. Maybe we can bring some of it to the zelandonia gathering."

"That would be a good idea. I can ride in behind Whinney on my pole-drag, and Jondalar and Jonayla can bring in some meat on theirs," Zelandoni said.

Ayla thought a smile to herself. Arriving on the special travois with a horse pulling her always seemed to cause a commotion, and the First did like making an entrance. Everyone seemed to think it was some kind of magic. Why was it so amazing? Why couldn't people realize that they could make friends with a horse? Especially after seeing not only Jondalar and herself, but Jonayla riding? There was nothing magic about it. It took determination and effort and patience, but not magic.

When Ayla jumped up on Whinney's back, it brought even more expressions of surprise. She had been leading the horses, not riding, when they arrived. Since the rest of the visitors were walking, Ayla decided she would too. Tivonan and Palidar would walk back and lead the helpers from the Cave, but Ayla could get there faster and start making a new travois.

"Where is everyone else?" Jondalar said when she got to the campsite.

"They're coming. I came ahead to make another pole-drag for Whinney to help get the meat moved. We're going to bring some to another Cave. They call themselves the Zelandonii That Watches Over the Most Ancient Sacred Site. Amelana is from the Third Cave, but we're going to the First Cave. There is a gathering of the zelandonia, and the First knew it! Or at least she guessed there might be. It's hard to believe how much she knows. Where's Jonayla?"

"Beladora and Levela are watching her along with their children. That meat has drawn every meat-eater in the region, on legs and wings, and we thought it would be a good idea to keep the little ones in a tent, out of sight. It's been keeping all of us busy protecting that 'lucky' hunt," Jondalar said.

"Have you killed anything?" Ayla asked.

"Mostly we've just been trying to scare them off, shouting and throwing stones."

Just then a pack of hyenas appeared and, drawn by the scent of meat, went straight for the pile of bison. Without even giving it a second thought, Ayla pulled her sling off her head, reached for a couple of stones from her pouch, and in a smooth motion had a stone in the air aimed at the animal in the lead. A second stone quickly followed it. The leader was down when the second hyena gave a yelp that ended in the sound of a cackling laugh. The leaders of hyena packs were female, but all females had pseudo male organs and tended to be larger than the males. The hyena pack stopped advancing and were running back and forth thrashing about, grunting and howling their peculiar laughing sound, at a loss without their leader. The woman armed her spear-thrower and started for the indecisive pack.

Jondalar jumped in ahead of her. "What are you doing?" he said.

"Chasing off that dirty pack of hyenas," she said, her face screwed up in an expression of disgust and the sound of loathing in her voice.

"I know you hate hyenas, but you don't have to kill every one you see. They're just animals like any other, and have their place among the Mother's children. If we drag the leader off, the rest will likely follow," Jondalar said.

Ayla stopped and looked at him, then felt her tension leave. "You are right, Jondalar. They are just animals."

With spear-throwers armed, Jondalar picked up one hind foot and Ayla the other and started dragging. She noticed the hyena was still nursing, but she knew that hyenas often nursed for a year until the young were nearly full grown and the only way to tell the difference was in coat color. Young ones were darker. The snuffling, snorting, laughing pack followed; the other one she had hit was limping badly. They dumped the animal far away from the camp and as they walked back, they noticed that some of the other carnivores had followed them.

"Good!" Ayla said. "Maybe that will keep some of them away. I'm going to wash my hands. Those animals smell bad."

Most of the time Ayla's Zelandonii friends and relatives thought of her as an ordinary woman and mother, and didn't even notice her accent, but when she did something like walking into a pack of hungry hyenas and killing their leader with a stone from her sling without seeming to give it a second thought, then they suddenly became aware of her differences. She was not born to the Zelandonii, her upbringing had been totally unlike any of theirs, and her unusual way of speaking became noticeable.

"We need to cut down some small trees for a new pole-drag. It was Zelandoni's suggestion. I don't think she wants blood on hers. She does consider it hers, you know," Ayla said.

"It is hers. No one else would think of using it," Jondalar said.

It took two trips to haul all the meat from the auspicious hunt away, most of it dragged by the horns and pushed by the neighboring people. By the time the travelers had packed up their campsite, the sun was working its way down to meet the horizon, with shades of orange and red blazoned across the sky. They took the meat they were keeping for themselves and headed for the Cave. Ayla and Jondalar lingered for a while—with the horses they could catch up easily enough. They were making a final tour of the abandoned camp to see if anyone had left anything important behind.

It was obvious that people had been there. Trails between tents had worn paths that now led to flattened and yellow patches of

grass; fireplaces were black circles of charcoal; some trees had
raw scars of light-colored wood where branches had been torn
off and pointed stumps that looked as though they had been
chewed down by a beaver showed where trees had once grown.
There was some trash around, a shredded and torn basket near
one of the fireplaces, and a small and well-used sleeping roll
that Jonlevar had outgrown was open and discarded in the middle of a flattened patch where a tent had been. Scattered chips
of flint and broken points, and some piles of bone and vegetable
peelings were lying around, but they would soon degrade back
into the soil. Yet the vast stretches of cattails and reeds, though
well harvested, showed little change, the yellowed grass and the
black lenses of firepits would soon be covered with new green,
and the trees that were removed made room for new ones to
sprout. The people lived lightly on the land.

Ayla and Jondalar checked their waterbags and took a drink;
then Ayla felt the urge to pass her water before they started back,
and walked around the perimeter of the trees. If they were snow-
bound in the middle of winter, Ayla wouldn't hesitate to relieve
herself in a night basket no matter who was there watching, but
if it was possible, she preferred privacy, especially since she had
to take down her leggings and not just move aside a loose dress.

She untied the waist thong and squatted down, but when she
stood up to pull her leggings back on, she was surprised to see
four strange men staring at her. She was more offended than
anything. Even if they had come upon her accidentally, they
should not have stood there and stared at her. It was very rude.
Then she noticed details: a certain griminess in their clothing,
rather unkempt beards, stringy long hair, and mostly, lewd expressions. The last made her angry, though they expected her to
be frightened.

Perhaps she should have been.

"Don't you have the courtesy to look away when a woman
needs to pass her water?" Ayla said, giving them a look of disdain as she retied her waist thong.

Her disparaging remarks surprised the men. First because
they expected fear, then because they heard her accent. They
drew their own conclusions.

One looked at the others with a deriding grin. "She's a stranger. Probably visiting. Won't be many of her kind around."

"Even if there are, I don't see any around here," another man said, then turned to leer at her, as he started toward her.

Ayla suddenly remembered the time they stopped to visit the Losadunai on their Journey here; there had been a band of hoodlums who had been harassing women. She slipped her sling off her head and reached in her pouch for a stone, then whistled loud for Wolf, and followed it by the whistles for both horses.

The whistles startled the men, but the stones did more than startle. The man who was moving toward her yelped with pain as a stone landed soundly on his thigh; another stone hit the upper arm of a second man with a similar response. Both men grabbed their bodies at the points of impact.

"How in Mother's Underworld did she do that?" the first man said angrily. Then looking at the men he said, "Don't let her get away. I want to give her something back for that."

In the meantime Ayla had reached for her spear-thrower and armed it with a spear that was aimed at the first man. A voice came from the other side of the stand of trees.

"Just be glad she didn't aim for your head, or you'd be walking the next world now. She just killed a hyena with one of her stones."

The men turned to face a tall blond man who had a spear in another one of those strange devices aimed at them. He had spoken Zelandonii, but he too had an accent, not the same as the woman's but as though he came from some distance.

"Let's get away from here," another man said, and started running.

"Stop him, Wolf!" Ayla commanded.

Suddenly a large wolf they hadn't seen raced after the man. He grabbed an ankle with his teeth and brought him down, then stood over him snarling.

"Anyone else feel like running away?" Jondalar said. He looked the four men over and quickly summed up the situation. "I have a feeling you've been causing lots of trouble around here. I think we need to bring you to the nearest Cave and see what they think."

With Wolf nearby, he took away the few spears they had

among them, and their knives. They weren't used to being compelled to doing anything they didn't want to, but when they resisted, Ayla set Wolf on them again. None of them felt like going against the snarling beast. As they started walking, Wolf herded them, nipping at their heels and snarling. With Ayla on the back of her dun-yellow mare on one side of them and Jondalar on his dark brown stallion on the other, they had little chance to go anyplace but where they were led.

At one point along the way, two of the men decided to make a break for it running in different directions. Jondalar's spear whizzed just past the ear of the man who appeared to be the leader and stopped him short. Ayla's caught a flap of loose clothing of the other man and the momentum unbalanced him and brought him down to the ground.

"I think we should tie the hands of those two together, and maybe the other two as well," Jondalar said. "I don't think they want to face the people who live near here."

They were later coming back than expected. The sun was making a show of fading purples and deep reds in the western sky when they arrived at the stone shelter where the Cave lived.

"They're the ones who did it!" a woman cried when she saw the men. "They're the ones who forced me and killed my mate when he tried to stop them. Then they took our food and sleeping rolls, and left me there. I walked home, but I was pregnant and lost the baby."

"How did you meet up with them?" Demoryn asked Jondalar and Ayla.

"Just before we were ready to leave, Ayla went around the stand of trees near our camp to pass water; then I heard her whistle for Wolf and the horses. I went to see what was wrong and found her holding off these four. When I got there, two of them were nursing the bruises she gave them with stones from her sling and she had her spear-thrower armed and ready," Jondalar said.

"Bruises! Is that all? She killed a hyena with her stones," Tivonan said.

"I wasn't trying to kill them, just stop them," Ayla said.

"On our way home from our Journey, there were some young men causing trouble for the people on the other side of the glacier to the west. They had forced one young woman before her First Rites. I wondered if these men might be disturbing people around here," Jondalar said.

"They've been doing a lot more than disturbing, and they aren't young. It's been going on for years, stealing, forcing women, killing people, but no one has been able to find them," Syralana said.

"The question is, what do we do with them now?" Demoryn said.

"You take them to the meeting of the zelandonia," the First said.

"Good idea," Willamar said.

"But first you should tie them down better than they are. They already tried to run away on our way here. I took away the spears and knives I could find, but I might not have found them all. And someone should guard them overnight. Wolf can help," Ayla said.

"Yes, you are right. These are dangerous men," Demoryn said as he walked back toward the shelter. "The zelandonia can decide what to do, but they need to be stopped, whatever it takes."

"Remember Attaroa, Jondalar?" Ayla said, both of them falling in beside the leader of the Cave.

"I'll never forget her. She nearly killed you. If it hadn't been for Wolf, she would have. She was vicious, I'd even say evil. Most people are decent. They are willing to help people, especially if they are in trouble, but there always seems to be a few who take what they want and hurt people and don't seem to care," Jondalar said.

"I think Balderan enjoys hurting people," Demoryn said.

"So that's his name," Jondalar said.

"He always had a temper," Demoryn continued. "Even as a child he liked to pick on those who were weaker, and inevitably there were always a few boys who followed him, and did what he said."

"Why do some go along with people like that?" Ayla said.

"Who knows?" Jondalar said. "Maybe they're afraid of them and think if they go along, they won't be the ones who are picked on. Or maybe they don't have much status and making other people afraid makes them feel more important."

"I think we need to select some people to watch them closely," Demoryn said. "And guard them in shifts, so the watchers don't get sleepy."

"They should also be searched again. Some of them may keep hidden knives that they can use to cut the ropes and perhaps hurt people," Ayla said. "I'll take a shift, and as I said, Wolf can help. He's very good at guarding. It's like he sleeps with one eye open."

When they were searched, each of the men had hidden at least one knife, which they claimed were just eating knives. Demoryn had been considering whether to untie their hands at night so they could sleep more comfortably, but finding the knives made him change his mind. They were given a meal and watched closely while they ate. Ayla collected their eating knives when they were through. Balderan did not want to give his up, but a signal to Wolf, which brought him to his feet with a menacing snarl caused the man to let go of the sharp-edged tool. When she got close to him she could see his seething anger. He could barely keep it under control. He had been able to exercise his free will for most of his life. He had taken what he wanted with impunity, including the lives of other people. Now he was physically restrained and forced to do something he didn't want to do, and he didn't like it.

The visitors and most of the Third Cave of the Zelandonii That Watches Over the Most Ancient Sacred Site followed a trail upstream beside the meandering river that had cut deep into the limestone, creating a deep gorge that now constrained the river. Ayla noticed that the people of the local Cave began glancing at each other and smiling as though they shared a secret or were anticipating some amusing surprise. They rounded a sharp turn and behind the high gorge walls the visitors were astounded to see high above them a stone arch, a natural bridge spanning the river. The ones who had not seen it before stopped to gaze in wonder at the formation that had been created by the Great Earth Mother. They had never seen anything like it; no one had. It was unique.

"Does it have a name?" Ayla asked.

"It has many names," Demoryn said. "Some people name it

for the Mother, or for spirits of the next world. Some people think it looks something like a mammoth. We just call it the Arch or the Bridge."

Some four hundred thousand years before, the force of a subterranean stream carved through the limestone, eventually wearing the calcium carbonate rock away, creating caves and passageways. In the course of time, the level of the water lowered and the land uplifted, and the conduit that had broached the wall of stone had become a natural arch. The present river flowed through what had been a barrier and was now a bridge across the river, but so high it was seldom used. The high stone arch spanning the river was an awe-inspiring formation. Nothing like it existed anywhere else.

The top of the span was approximately on the same level as the top of the high cliffs closest to it, but the ancient channel had also carved out meanders nearer the river that had become level ground. During the wet season, when the river was running high, the sides of the limestone barrier sometimes restricted the flow of the water and caused flooding, but most of the time the river that had once created caves and worn its way through the limestone obstruction was placid and calm.

The field between the stone shelter of the First Cave of the Zelandonii Watchers and the river had a circular shape enclosed by the cliff walls of the deep gorge. Many eons before, it had been the loop of an oxbow that was the former riverbed, but it was now home to a meadow of mixed grasses, aromatic artemisia shrubs, and a plant whose edible green leaves resembled the feet of the ducks and geese that navigated the river waters in summer—goosefoot—and which bore multitudes of small black seeds that could also be ground between stones, then cooked and eaten.

An area toward the back of the field had a shallow talus slope, whose sharp-edged stones were mixed with enough soil to feed the roots of cold-loving pine, birch, and juniper trees, often dwarfed into brush. Above the field, the dark evergreen of trees and brush growing on the slopes and plateaus of the cliff made a strong contrast with the white limestone of the cliff. It also formed hillocks and terraces that provided a place for the people to gather when someone wanted to impart information to a group.

The First Cave of the Zelandonii That Watches Over the Most Ancient Sacred Site lived under a sheltering limestone ledge on a terrace above the floodplain. The zelandonia had gathered in the field below to hold their meeting.

The arrival of the visitors and the members of the Third Cave of Sacred Site Watchers created quite a stir. The zelandonia had set up a pavilion of sorts, a tentlike structure with a roof but only partial sides; the roof offered shade from the sun and the sidewalls blocked the wind blowing down the gorge. One of the acolytes had seen the approaching procession and rushed in, interrupting the meeting. A couple of the leading Zelandonia were annoyed for a moment, until they turned to look; then they felt a frisson of fear, which they tried not to show.

Ayla riding Whinney was in the lead. The First told her to ride up to the meeting tent, which she did. Then she moved her leg over and slid down and went to assist the First to step off the pole-drag. The First had a way of walking that was neither fast nor slow, but carried great authority. The two southern leaders immediately recognized the symbolism of her facial tattoos, clothing, and necklaces, and could hardly believe that the First Among Those Who Served The Great Earth Mother had come to their gathering. They had seen her so seldom that she was almost a mythical figure. They gave lip service to her existence, but thought themselves to be among the highest-ranking of the zelandonia, and they had selected a First of their own. To actually see her was a little overwhelming, but to see the manner of her arrival was even more so. The control of horses was unprecedented. She had to be extraordinarily powerful.

They approached with deference, greeted her with both hands extended, and welcomed her. She returned the greetings, and then proceeded to introduce several of her traveling companions: Ayla and Jonokol, Willamar and Jondalar, and then the rest of the travelers, with Willamar's assistants and the children last. Demoryn greeted the two most important of their zelandonia, the man who was the Zelandoni of his Cave, and the woman who was the Zelandoni of the First Cave of Sacred Site Watchers. Ayla had told Jonayla to keep Wolf out of sight, but after all the formal introductions were over, she and the child brought him out, and she saw another look of shock and fear. After persuading them to let her introduce them to the wolf, there was a little less fear, but some apprehension lingered. By this time the people from the First Cave had come down to the field from their living site on the side of the cliff, but Ayla was glad that formal introductions were held off until later.

The four men they were bringing for the zelandonia to deal with had been held back with the people from the Third Cave of Watchers until after all the formalities were over, but now Demoryn brought them forward. He approached his Zelandoni.

"You know the men who have been causing so much trouble, stealing and forcing women, and killing people?" he asked.

"Yes," the man replied. "We have just been talking about them."

"Well, we have them," Demoryn said, and signaled some men who had been designated to watch them. They were brought forward. The woman who had accused them of killing her mate and harming her came with them. "This one's name is Balderan. He's their leader."

All the zelandonia looked at the four men whose hands were tied together. They noted the unkempt look of the men, but the woman Zelandoni of the First Cave wanted something more than appearance upon which to judge them.

"How do you know they are the ones?" the woman Zelandoni asked.

"Because I was one who was forced, after they killed my mate," the woman said.

"And you are?"

"I am Aremina, of the Third Cave of the Zelandonii That Watches Over the Most Ancient Sacred Site," she said.

"What she says is true," the male Zelandoni of the Third Cave of Watchers said. "She was pregnant at the time and also lost her baby." He turned to Demoryn. "We have been talking about them, and were trying to think of a plan to find them. How did you catch them?"

"It was the First's acolyte," Demoryn said. "They tried to attack her, but didn't understand who she is."

"Who is she besides the First's acolyte?" the Zelandoni of the First Cave of Watchers said.

Demoryn turned to Willamar. "Why don't you explain?"

"Well," Willamar said, "I wasn't there, so I can only tell you what I was told, but I believe it. I know that Ayla is an extremely skilled hunter with both a stone-slinging weapon, and a spear-throwing weapon, which was devised by her mate, Jondalar. She's also the one who controls the wolf, and the horses, although her mate and child also do. Apparently, when these men tried to attack her, she bruised them with stones, although she can kill with stones if she chooses. Then Jondalar came with his spear-thrower. When one of them tried to run away, she sent the wolf to stop him. I've seen them work together hunting. Those men didn't have a chance."

"All the visitors use the spear-throwing weapon—Jondalar has promised to show us how—and when they went hunting, they were too lucky," Demoryn continued. "Each one brought down a bison. They killed nine of them. That's a lot of meat; bison are big animals. That's why we're bringing you a large load of meat, for your First Cave and for your zelandonia meeting.

"As for these men, once they were caught, we weren't sure what to do with them. Aremina thought they should be killed, since they killed her mate. Perhaps she's right. But we didn't know who should do the killing, or how. We all know how to kill animals that the Great Mother has given us so that we can live, but the Mother does not condone killing people. I didn't know if we should be the ones to kill them. It may bring bad luck to our Cave if we do, or if we didn't do it correctly. We thought the zelandonia should decide, so we brought them here."

"I think that was wise, don't you?" the First Among Those Who Served said. "It's fortunate that you are having a meeting so that all of you can discuss it and come to a decision."

She's letting them know that she doesn't plan to take over just because she's the First, Ayla thought, but she will be interested in what they do.

"I certainly hope you will be staying and will offer your counsel," said the Zelandoni of the First Cave of Sacred Site Watchers.

"Thank you. I would like that. This is not an easy problem to work out. We are here because I am taking my acolyte on her Donier Tour. I hope someone will be able to guide us through your Sacred Site. I have seen it only once before, but I have never forgotten it. Not only is it the Most Ancient, it is unbelievably beautiful, both the cave itself and the images that have been painted on the walls. They honor the Great Mother," the First said with feeling that conveyed her conviction.

"Of course. We have a Watcher at the Sacred Site who will be happy to guide you through it," the woman said, "but now let's see these men."

As the four men were brought forward, they were trying to resist, but Wolf was guarding them and herded Balderan back with snarls and nips to his ankles and legs when he tried to leave. It was obvious that Balderan was seething with rage. He particularly hated the foreign man and woman who could control horses and a wolf, and could therefore control him. For the first time in his life he was afraid, and what he feared most was Wolf. He wanted to kill the animal, but not any more than Wolf wanted to kill him. The four-legged hunter knew in the way that animals with senses more developed than those of humans know that this man was not like other men. He was born with too much or not enough of something that made him different, and Wolf innately knew that this man would not hesitate to harm the ones Wolf loved.

By now everyone from both Caves and all the neighboring zelandonia had gathered in the field in front of the cliffs, and when the men were brought forward, it caused quite a disturbance. Several people recognized Balderan and some shouted out accusations.

"He's the one!" a woman said. "He forced me! They all did."

"They stole meat from me that I had spread out to dry."

"He took my daughter and kept her for nearly a moon. I don't know what they did to her, but she was never right again and died the next winter. As far as I'm concerned, he killed her."

A middle-aged man came forward. "I can tell you about him. He was born to my Cave before I moved away," he said.

"I would like to hear what this man has to say," the First said.

"So would I," the Zelandoni from the Third Cave of Watchers said.

"Balderan was born to a woman who had no mate, and at first everyone was pleased that she had a son who seemed sound and healthy, a son who could one day make a contribution to the Cave, but from quite a young age, he was uncontrollable. He was a strong boy but he used his strength to take what he wanted whenever he wanted it. In the beginning his mother made excuses for him. Since she had no mate, she hoped her strong son, who quickly became a very good hunter because he liked killing things, would take care of her as she grew older, but eventually she came to recognize that he didn't care about her any more than anyone else," the man began.

"By the time he reached young manhood, all the people of the Cave were angry and afraid of him. It came to a head when he took some spears from a man who had made them for himself. When the man objected and tried to take them back, Balderan beat him so badly, he nearly died. I don't think he ever fully recovered. That was when everyone banded together and told him he had to leave. All the rest of the men and most of the women armed themselves and chased him away. Two friends left with him, young men who admired him for taking what he wanted and not having to work for anything. One of them returned before the summer was over and begged to be allowed to come back, but Balderan always managed to acquire a few followers.

"He would go to a Summer Meeting, settle into a fa'lodge, and challenge the other young men into reckless acts of danger to prove their manhood. He always bullied any who seemed weak or afraid, and when he left, he always had a few new followers charmed by his troublemaking ways. They would harass some new Caves until they finally got together to go looking for them. Then Balderan and friends would travel some distance away, and find other Caves from whom they could steal food, clothing, implements, weapons, and before long, women they could force."

Balderan sneered while the man related the story. He didn't care what anyone said about him. It was all true anyway, but he had never been caught before, and he didn't like it. Ayla observed him closely and saw that he was more than angry; she could see his fear and his hatred, and she was sure Wolf could smell it. She knew if Balderan made any attempt to hurt her, or Jonayla, or Jondalar, or any of the people traveling with them, Wolf would kill him. She knew that if she merely gave Wolf the signal to kill the man, he would, and the people would probably be grateful. But she didn't want Wolf to be the one to solve their problem and she didn't want Wolf to be known as a killer. Stories tended to grow out of proportion. Everyone knew wolves could kill. The fact that he helped to catch the man, and that he guarded the man and didn't kill him, that was the story she wanted people to tell about Wolf. The people needed to deal with Balderan themselves, and she was curious to see what they would do.

The other men with him weren't angry. They were just scared. They knew what they had done, and there were enough people here who knew it too. The man standing beside Balderan was thinking about the predicament he was in. It always seemed so easy following him, taking whatever they wanted, and frightening people. Of course, Balderan scared him too, sometimes, but it made him feel important to see people afraid of him. And when they saw that people who came after them were close and determined, and felt it was time to move on, they were nimble and quick and could always get away. They were sure they would never get caught, but the foreign woman with her weapons and her animals had changed that.

There was no doubt that she was a Zelandoni, and they should never have gone after One Who Serves The Mother. But how could they have known? She wasn't even tattooed. They said she was an acolyte, but an acolyte to the First? He didn't know the First really existed. He thought she was just a story like the Elder Legends. But now the most powerful Zelandoni on earth was here, with her acolyte, who had magic control of animals and had caught him. What were they going to do to him?

As though hearing his thoughts, one of the Zelandonia said, "Now that they're here, what are we going to do with them?"

"For now we have to feed them, find a place to keep them, and get some people to watch them until a decision can be made," the First said, then turned to the woman who was the Zelandoni of the First Cave of Ancient Sacred Site Watchers. "And perhaps you should divide out this bison meat."

She smiled at the First, acknowledging that she had turned over authority to her, as though she knew that she was the First in this region, although no one had told her. The woman called some names and delegated the responsibility to the leaders of the two Caves to decide how the meat should be parceled out, but assigned several other Zelandonia to supervise the actual work of skinning and butchering the beasts. Some had already been skinned, and they started cutting up that meat for their evening meal. Others were taking Balderan and his men toward the cliff.

Once he was in their hands, Ayla whistled Wolf to her and went to help Jondalar unhitch the pole-drags from the horses. She had seen a nice grassy area away from the people, but decided to ask if there was any reason she shouldn't use it for the horses. It was always a good idea not to make assumptions about the territory of other Caves. She first asked Demoryn, the leader of Amelana's Cave.

"We didn't have a Summer Meeting here this year so I think it just hasn't been trampled, but you might ask the Zelandoni First if you want to make sure," he said.

"Zelandoni First?" Ayla said. "Do you mean of the First Cave of the Watchers?"

"Yes, but that is not the reason she is called Zelandoni First. It's because she is our First," he said. "It is only coincidence that she happens to be the Zelandoni of that Cave. Which reminds me, I should also tell her that I sent a runner to tell one or two other Caves that Balderan has been caught. They were troubled more than most by him. A few more people may come."

Ayla frowned, and wondered how many other Caves would do the same. Maybe she should look for a more secluded spot, or perhaps make a fenced area for the horses the way she did at their Summer Meetings. She decided to talk to Jondalar about it after she talked to Zelandoni First.

Ayla and Jondalar talked to the rest of the travelers, and they decided to look for a choice spot to set up their camp, the way most Caves did when they arrived early at a Summer Meeting.

The First agreed with Ayla's intuition that there might be more people coming than anyone expected.

That evening, although meals were cooked by the families or groups that normally ate together, they all more or less sat together, rather like a feast. Balderan and his henchmen were given food, and their hands were untied so they could eat it. They spoke quietly to each other as they ate. There were several people watching them, but it was hard to maintain interest when there was nothing to watch except people eating their food. The night sky darkened as the meal progressed, and people who were friendly strangers were interested in getting to know each other.

Ayla and Jondalar left Wolf with Jonayla to give him a rest from his stressful vigilance and went for a walk together toward the zelandonia dwelling. The First had gone there to talk about making a special tour of the Sacred Cave with Ayla, Jonokol, and a few others, and another tour with the rest of the visitors, except for the children, which might not be as extensive.

The couple knew in general where the men they had captured were being held, but in the dark they didn't notice how carefully they were being watched by them. Balderan had been watching the tall man who was the mate of the woman acolyte, and as they approached, Balderan spoke to his men.

"We have to get away from here," he said. "If we don't, we won't live to see many more days."

"But how?" one of the men said.

"We need to get rid of that woman who controls the wolf," Balderan said.

"That wolf won't let us get close to her."

"Only when he's around. He isn't always with her. Sometimes he stays with the girl," Balderan said.

"But what about that man who's always around her? The visitor she came with. He's big."

"I've known men like him, tall and muscular, but too calm and mild. Have you ever seen him angry? I think he's one of those gentle giants who are so afraid they'll hurt someone they even avoid arguments. If we're quick, we can grab her before he knows it, and threaten to kill her if he makes a move. I don't think he'll take a chance that she might get hurt. By the time he thinks about it, it will be too late. We'll be gone and her with us."

"What are you going to threaten her with? They've taken our knives."

Balderan smiled, then loosened the leather thong that laced his shirt closed. "This," he said, pulling the thong out of its holes. "I'll wrap this around her neck."

"But what if your plan doesn't work?" another man asked.

"We won't be any worse off than we are now. We've got nothing to lose."

The next day one of the other Caves in the region arrived, and by evening, two more. The First came to see Ayla the morning of the following day. Jondalar stepped out to let them talk in private.

"We are going to have to think about how to deal with these men."

"Why do we have to?" Ayla said. "We don't live here."

"But you caught him. You're involved, whether you want to be or not. It could be the Mother wants you to be," the First added.

Ayla gave her a look of skepticism.

"Well, maybe not the Mother, but the people here want you to be. And I think you should. Besides, we need to talk to them about your tour of their Sacred Site. You will be amazed at this cave. I've seen it once and I know I'm going back in. There are some difficult places, but I'll never get another chance and I won't miss it," the First said.

That intrigued Ayla, and aroused her curiosity. All the walking on this Journey seemed to have improved the woman's health, but she still had problems and needed help when they got into rough terrain. She was a more than ample woman in spite of all her walking. She carried her weight with grace and assurance, and in many ways it added to her stature, but it could make moving around in tight places with uneven footing difficult.

"You're right, Zelandoni, but I don't want to make decisions about him. I don't think it's my place," Ayla said.

"You don't have to. We all know what has to be done. He

needs to be killed. If he isn't, he will kill more people. The question is, who will do it and how? Deliberately killing someone is not easy for most people. It's not supposed to be. It's not right for people to kill people. That's why we know he's not right inside. He doesn't know that, and that's why I'm glad all these Caves are coming together. It needs to be something they all participate in. I don't mean everyone has to kill him, but they all have to take responsibility for it. And they all have to know that it's the right thing to do in this particular case. A person shouldn't be killed out of anger, or for revenge. There are other ways to deal with those things. There is no other way where he's concerned," the First said, "but what is the best way to do it?"

They were both silent, then Ayla said, "There are plants . . ."

"I was going to say mushrooms," the First said. "They could be fed a meal with certain mushrooms."

"But what if they guess and decide not to eat them? Everyone knows there are poisonous mushrooms. They are easy to pick out and avoid," Ayla said.

"That's true, and while Balderan is not right, he's not stupid. What plants were you thinking of?"

"There are two plants that I know grow around here because I've seen them. One is called water parsnip. It grows in water," Ayla said.

"They are edible, especially the roots, when they are young and tender," the First said.

"Yes, but there is another plant that looks very similar and it's deadly poisonous," Ayla said. "I know the word in Mamutoi. I don't know what you call it, but I know it."

"I know the plant. It's poison hemlock," the First said. "That's our name for it. It also grows in water. So the same meal can be cooked for the whole Camp, everyone else will get water parsnip, but Balderan and his men will get hemlock." She paused, then said, "I was thinking, they could be served mushrooms, too, edible mushrooms. They may think they are poison and avoid them, and perhaps won't pay attention to the root vegetables, because it will look as though everybody is eating them."

"That's what I was thinking, unless someone can think of a better way," Ayla said.

The woman stopped to think again, then nodded. "Good, we

have a plan. It's always good to have a plan, to anticipate, if you can," said the Zelandoni Who Was First.

When the two women left the tent, no one was outside. The rest of their group of travelers had gone to see what was happening with the impromptu Summer Meeting, and to offer to help with the cooking or whatever needed doing. Except this wasn't a happy coming together of relatives, friends, and neighbors; this was a gathering to pass judgment for serious crimes.

More people were arriving and the field below the cliff was filling up. But the biggest surprise was late in the afternoon. Ayla and the First were in the zelandonia dwelling when Jonayla came running in interrupting the meeting.

"Mother, mother," she said. "Kimeran told me to come and tell you."

"Tell me what, Jonayla?" Ayla said with a stern tone to her voice.

"Beladora's family is here. And there is a strange person with them."

"Beladora's family? They aren't even Zelandonii; they're Giornadonii. They live far away, how could they have gotten here in just a day or so?" Ayla said. She turned to the others. "I think I have to go."

"I should go with you," the First said. "Please excuse us."

"They don't live that far," Zelandoni First said, walking them out, "and they often come to visit. At least every couple of years. I think they are as much Zelandonii as they are Giornadonii, but I doubt if they came because of the runners that were sent out. They were probably planning to visit anyway. They were likely as surprised to see their relative as she was to see them."

Kimeran was just outside and had heard Zelandoni First. "That's not entirely true," he said. "They went to the Giornadonii Summer Meeting, then decided to go to your Summer Meeting, and were planning on coming here later. They were at the Meeting Camp when the runner arrived and they found out from him that we were here. Of course, they also found out about Balderan. Did you know that he has caused trouble for some of the Giornadonii Caves? Is there anybody he hasn't harmed and alienated?"

"There will be a meeting about that soon," Zelandoni First

said. "We have to come to some kind of decision, shortly." As an afterthought, she said, "Did you say there was a strange person with them?"

"Yes, but you will see for yourself."

Ayla and the First were presented to Beladora's relatives with full formal introductions; then the First asked if they had set up their camp yet.

"No, we just arrived," said the woman they had just learned was Beladora's mother, Ginedora. Even without the introduction, it would have been obvious; she was an older, slightly plumper version of the woman they knew.

"I think there may be room near our camp," the First said. "Why don't we go claim it before someone else does."

When they reached the camp, there were more introductions and some initial hesitation about the animals, but then Ginedora saw a boy who looked as though he could have been born to her. She gave her daughter a questioning look. Beladora took her son's hand, and then her blond, blue-eyed daughter's hand.

"Come and meet your grandma," she said.

"You had two-born-together? They are both yours? And both healthy?" she said. Beladora nodded. "That's wonderful!" she said.

"This is Gioneran," the young mother said, holding up the hand of a five-year boy with the dark brown hair and brownish-green eyes like his mother.

"He is going to be tall, like Kimeran," Ginedora said.

"And this is Ginadela," Beladora said, holding up the hand of her fair daughter.

"She has Kimeran's coloring, and she's a beauty," the woman said. "Are they shy? Will they come and give me a hug?"

"Go and greet your grandma. We've come a long way to meet her," Beladora said, urging them forward. The woman got down on her knees and opened out her arms. Her eyes were feeling full and looked shiny. Somewhat reluctantly, the children gave her a cursory hug. She took one in each arm as a tear rolled down her cheek.

"I didn't know I had grandchildren. That's the trouble with your living so far away," Ginedora said. "How long are you staying here?"

"We don't know yet," Beladora said.

"Are you coming to our Cave?" Ginedela asked.

"We had planned to," she said.

"You've got to do more than visit for a few days. You've traveled this far—come back with us and stay for a year," the woman said.

"That's something we would have to think about," Beladora said. "Kimeran is the leader of our Cave. It would be hard for him to stay away for a year." When she saw tears starting in her mother's eyes, she added, "But we'll think about it."

Ayla glanced around at the other people who were beginning to set up camp. She noticed a man who was carrying someone on his shoulders. He bent down and helped the person off. At first she thought it was a child; then she looked again. It was a small person, but oddly shaped, with legs and arms too short. She tapped the First and moved her chin in the direction of the person.

The large woman looked, then looked more closely. She understood why Ayla had called her attention to the individual. She had never seen one, but she had heard about similar little people. "No wonder Beladora's mother seemed so relieved that her daughter's children, born at the same time, were normal. That person is an accident of birth. Like some dwarf trees whose growth becomes stunted, I think that is a dwarf person," she said.

"I would like to meet that person to learn more, but I don't want to make an issue of it. It would be like staring, and I think that person gets stared at enough," Ayla said.

26

Ayla had gotten up very early and gathered her collecting baskets and the panniers for Whinney. She told Jondalar that she was going to look for some greens and roots and whatever else she could find for tonight's feast, but she seemed distracted and uncomfortable.

"Would you like me to come along?" he asked.

"No!" Her answer was sharp and abrupt, and then she tried to soften it. "I was hoping you would watch Jonayla. Beladora is taking her children to spend some time with her mother this morning. Jondecam and Levela are also going and taking Jonlevan with them, because they are all related. I don't know what Kimeran is doing, but I think he may join them later. Jonayla is like family, but she is really just a friend and may feel left out because she won't have her usual friends to play with. I thought maybe you and Racer could go for a ride with her and Gray this morning."

"That's a good idea. We haven't been riding for a while. The exercise would do the horses good," Jondalar said. Ayla smiled at him and rubbed cheeks, but a frown still creased her forehead. She looked unhappy.

It was barely daylight when Ayla left, riding Whinney and whistling for Wolf. She rode along the riverbank looking over the vegetation. She knew the plants she was looking for grew near the place where they had camped, but she hoped she wouldn't have to ride that far. She rode past the Third Cave's location; it was deserted. Everyone was at the meeting that had spontaneously come about at the First Cave. She wondered how Amelana was doing, and if she would have her baby before they left. It could be any time now, she thought, and fervently hoped it would be a normal, healthy, happy baby.

She didn't find what she was looking for until she was close to their former campsite. It was the backwater of the river that had almost formed an oxbow lake that created the right kind of habitat for both water parsnip and water hemlock. She halted the horse and quickly slid off. Wolf seemed happy to have her to himself for a change and was a little frisky, but Ayla was in no mood for playfulness, so he began exploring the interesting smells coming from the small holes and hummocks.

She had her good sharp knife and a digging stick with her and first collected heaps of water parsnips. Then in another basket and with a new tool she had fashioned explicitly for the purpose, she dug up several roots and plants of the water hemlock. She wrapped them with long stems of grass and put them in a separate basket, again made expressly for the plants. She left it on the ground while she packed the parsnips in the panniers fastened to Whinney, then attached the separate basket on top. Then whistling for Wolf, she started back upstream; she was in a hurry to return. When she came to a place where the river flowed fresh and clean, she stopped to fill her waterbag. Then she saw the dry bed of a seasonal tributary stream that would be full of rushing water when rains came. The smooth, rounded stones on the bottom were perfect, and she carefully selected several of them to refill the pouch of stones for her sling.

She was near a stand of pines and noticed small mounds pushing up under a layer of needles and twigs beneath the trees and brushed them aside. She found a clump of pinkish-buff mushrooms hidden underneath. She searched and found more until she had collected quite a nice little pile of pine mushrooms. These were good mushrooms, white and firm of flesh with a rather nice, slightly spicy smell and taste, but not everyone knew them. She filled a third gathering basket with them. Then she mounted Whinney, whistled for Wolf, and rode back, pushing her mare to a gallop for part of the distance. People were in the midst of preparing or eating their morning meal when she arrived. She went straight to the zelandonia pavilion and brought in two of the baskets. Only the two "Firsts" were there.

"Did you find what you were looking for?" the One Who Was First asked.

"Yes," Ayla said. "Here are some good pine mushrooms, with a somewhat unusual flavor that I like very well," she said, then showing them the basket of water hemlock, she said, "I have never tasted these."

"That's good. I hope you never do," the large woman said.

"Outside, on Whinney's pannier is a big load of water parsnips. I was careful not to mix them," Ayla said.

"I'll give them to one of the people who is cooking," the taller, thinner Zelandoni First said. "If they are not cooked well, they can be unpalatable." She studied Ayla awhile. "This is uncomfortable for you, isn't it?"

"Yes. I have never deliberately collected something that I knew was harmful, especially knowing that it is intended to be given to someone, to kill him," Ayla said.

"But you know if he is allowed to live, he will only cause more harm."

"Yes, I know, but it still doesn't make me feel good about it."

"And it shouldn't," her First said. "You are helping your people and taking the onus on yourself. It's a sacrifice, but sometimes it's what a Zelandoni must do."

"I will make sure they go to the ones who should eat them," Zelandoni First said. "It is the sacrifice I must make. These are my people and he has hurt them long enough."

"What about his other men?" the First asked.

"One of them, Gahaynar, is asking what he can do to make reparations. He is saying how sorry he is," Zelandoni First said. "I don't know if he is just trying to talk his way out of the punishment he knows is coming, or if he means it. I think I will let the Mother decide. If he ends up not eating the root and lives, I will let him go. If Balderan doesn't eat it and lives, I have already spoken with several people who have been personally harmed by him and are eager to see him pay. Most have lost family members or have been attacked themselves. If necessary, I will turn him over to them, but I would prefer it if this more subtle approach works."

When Zelandonia First went to pick up the basket of hemlock she saw a slithering movement under the container. She quickly snatched the basket and moved it aside. Underneath was a snake, an extraordinary snake.

"Look at that!" the woman said.

Ayla and the First looked, then both took a small indrawn breath of surprise. It was a small snake, probably quite young, and the red stripes running the length of its body indicated it was a nonpoisonous type, but near the front of the body the stripes split into the shape of a Y. The snake had two heads! Both tongues slipped in and out of its mouths, sampling the air; then it started to move, but the movement was a bit erratic, as though it couldn't quite decide which way to go.

"Quick, get something to catch it before it gets away," the First said.

Ayla found a small watertight woven bowl. "Is this all right to use?" she asked Zelandonii First.

"Yes, that's fine," she said.

The snake started moving as Ayla approached, but she turned the basket upside down and clamped it over the snake. It pulled its own tail in as she held it down firmly so it couldn't get out under the edge.

"Now what do we do?" Zelandoni First said.

"Do you have something flat that I can slip under that?" Ayla asked.

"I don't know. Maybe the edge of a shovel that's been ground flat. Would that work? Like this one?" She picked up the shovel that was used to clean ashes out of the hearth.

"Yes, that's perfect," Ayla said. She took the shovel and slid the flat part under the basket, then picked them both up and held them together while she flipped them over. "Is there a lid for this bowl? And some twine to tie it on?"

Zelandoni First found a small shallow bowl and gave it to Ayla, who set the bowl with the snake down, removed the shovel and pressed the shallow bowl on top, then tied them together.

The three women left together to have a morning meal. They planned that the meeting should start when the sun was highest in the sky, but people started gathering on the slope earlier to find seating and standing places with enough elevation so they could see and hear better. Everyone knew this was a serious meeting, but there was still a feeling of celebration and festivity in the air, mostly because of the sociability of being together, especially since it was unplanned. And because people were glad that the vicious troublemaker had been caught.

By the time the sun was high, the meeting area was filled to overflowing. Zelandoni First started the meeting and began by welcoming the First Among Those Who Serve The Great Earth Mother, and the rest of the visitors. She explained that the First was accompanying her acolyte, and her former acolyte, who was now a Zelandoni, on their Donier Tour, and had come to see the Most Ancient Sacred Site. She also mentioned that the First's acolyte and her mate had captured Balderan and three of his men, when they tried to attack her. That information brought an undercurrent of voices from the audience.

"That is the main reason we called this gathering. Balderan has caused pain and suffering to many of you for many years. But now that we have him, we have to decide what to do with him. Whatever punishment we mete out to him should be something we all feel is appropriate," Zelandoni First said.

Someone in the audience said, "Kill him," in a loud whisper that everyone heard, including the zelandonia.

The One Who Was First responded, "That may well be the appropriate punishment, but who will do it, and how, is the question. It could be very unlucky if it is not handled properly," the large woman said, "for all of us. The Mother has declared strong prohibitions against people killing other people, except in extraordinary circumstances. In an effort to find a solution for coping with Balderan, we don't want to become what he is."

"How did she catch him?" someone asked.

"You should ask her," the First said, turning to Ayla.

This kind of situation always made her nervous, but she took a deep breath and tried to answer the question. "I have been a hunter since I was very young, and the weapon I first learned to use was a stone hurled with a sling," she began. For those who had not heard her speak before, her accent was a surprise. It was rare for a foreigner to become part of the zelandonia and she had to wait until people quieted down before she could continue. "Now you know, I was not born a Zelandonii," she said with a smile. Her comment brought a small chuckle from the audience.

"I was raised far to the east of here, and I met Jondalar when he was on his Journey." People were settling down, getting ready to listen to what could be a very good story.

"When Balderan and his men first saw me, I had gone behind the trees for some privacy, and when I stood up to pull my leggings back on, they were staring at me. It made me angry that they were so impolite, and I told them so. Not that it did any good." That brought a few chuckles from the group. "I usually keep my sling wrapped around my head; it is an easy way to carry it. When he came after me, I don't think Balderan understood that it was a weapon as I began to unwind it."

She unwound her sling as she was talking, then reached into her pouch and took out two of the stones she had collected from the dry streambed near their former camp earlier. She put the two ends of the sling together and placed a stone in the middle of a leather strap in a pocket that had formed from use. She had already selected a target: a varying hare in its brown summer coat sitting off to the side on a rock next to its hole. At the last minute, she also spied a pair of mallards, which had taken off from their nests near the river. With swift sure movements, she flung the first stone, and then the second.

People spoke out their surprise. "Did you see that!" "She killed that duck right out of the sky!" "She killed a rabbit, too!" The demonstration gave them a sense of her skill.

"I didn't want to kill Balderan," Ayla said.

"But she could have," Jonokol interjected, which brought another murmur of voices.

"I only wanted to stop him, so I aimed for his thigh. I think he may have a good bruise to show for it. I hit the other man on the arm." She whistled for Wolf, who came immediately at her call. That also brought a flurry of comments from the assembled group. "Balderan and the others didn't notice Wolf at first. This wolf is my friend and he will do what I ask him to. When a third man tried to run away, I told Wolf to stop him. He didn't attack him or try to kill him; he bit at the man's ankle and tripped him. Then Jondalar came around the trees with his spear-thrower.

"As we were bringing those men here, Balderan tried to run away. Jondalar used his spear-thrower to cast a spear. It just missed Balderan's ear. So he stopped," Ayla said. "Jondalar is very accurate with a spear-thrower." Again there were chuckles.

"I told you they didn't stand a chance," Willamar said to Demoryn, who was standing next to him. They were taking a turn at guarding Balderan and the others, who also heard everything that was said.

"When I saw how these men behaved toward me, I thought they were probably troublemakers. That's why we brought them with us, though they did not want to come. It was only after we arrived at the Third Cave of Watchers that we understood how much trouble they had caused over the years," Ayla said. She paused, looking down. It seemed obvious that she had more to say.

"I am a healer, a medicine woman. I have helped many women give birth. Fortunately, most babies are perfectly healthy when they are born, but some children of the Mother are not born right. I have seen some that are not. Usually, if the problem is serious, they don't survive. The Mother takes them back because only She can fix them, but some have a strong will to live. Even with serious problems, they live and often give much to their people," Ayla said.

"I was raised by a man who was a great Mog-ur, that is the word the people of the Clan use for Zelandoni. He had only one usable arm and walked with a limp, a problem from birth, and he had only one eye and his weak arm was further damaged when a cave bear chose him and became his totem. He was a very wise man who served his people, and was very well respected. There is also a boy who lives not far from our Cave, who was born with a deformed arm. His mother was afraid that he would never be able to hunt, and perhaps never become a real man, but he learned to use the spear-thrower with his good arm, became a good hunter and gained respect, and now has a fine young woman as his mate.

"When a child is born dead, or leaves this world and walks

the next soon after birth, it is because the only way a person
who is not born right can be fixed is to return to the Mother,
so She takes them back. Although it is much easier to say than
to do, one should not grieve for such children; the Mother has
taken them back so they can be made right."

Ayla reached into a haversack she wore over one shoulder
and took out a small bowl with a lid. She opened it and held
up the two-headed snake. There were startled *ooohs*. "Some
things are not right when they are born, and it is obvious." The
tongues flicked out of the mouths of both heads as she showed
the little creature. "The only way this snake can be fixed is
to return it to the Mother. Sometimes that is what should
be done.

"But sometimes someone is born wrong, and it is not obvious. When you look at them they seem normal, but they are
not right inside. Just like this little snake, the only way they
can be fixed is to return them to the Mother. Only She can fix
them."

Balderan and his men were also listening to Ayla's story.
"We're going to have to watch for our chance soon, if we're
going to get away from here," Balderan said, under his breath.
He had no desire to be returned to the Mother. For the first
time in his life he began to feel the fear he had so often caused
others to feel.

"I think that was a very appropriate way to talk about what
needs to be done," Zelandoni First said as she was walking
back to the zelandonia pavilion, along with the First, Ayla,
and Jonokol. Wolf was sedately following Ayla, as she had
signaled. She wanted people to know that while he was an
efficient four-legged hunter, unlike Balderan, he was not an
indiscriminate killer. "It will help people accept it if they can
think about sending Balderan back to the Mother to be made
right. What made you think of it?"

"I don't know," Ayla said, "but when I saw the dwarfed young
man who came with Beladora's people, I knew that there was
no medicine that could help him to grow into a normal size,
at least none that I knew of. Then that little snake made me

understand that there are some things only the Mother could fix, if not in this world, then perhaps in the next."

"Have you met the young man?" Zelandoni First asked.

"No, not yet."

"Nor have I," the First said.

"Then let's do it now."

The three women and the man walked toward the Giornadonii campsite. They stopped off at the Ninth Cave's camp and picked up Jondalar and Jonayla, and Willamar, the only ones who happened to be there. Beladora and Kimeran were at the camp with their children. Ayla wondered if Beladora's mother would succeed in persuading them to return with her and stay for a year. She couldn't blame her for trying, as she wanted to get to know her grandchildren, but Kimeran was the leader of the Second Cave.

The friends greeted each other with cheek rubs and then they went through a series of formal introductions to Beladora's mother, the leader of the Cave, and a few others. Then the young man came forward.

"I wanted to meet you," he said to Ayla. "I liked what you said about the snake and some of the people you know."

"I'm pleased that you did," Ayla said, then bent down and took both of his small, oddly shaped hands in hers. His arms were also too short. His head seemed almost too big for him. "I am Ayla of the Ninth Cave of the Zelandonii, mated to Jondalar, Master Flint-Knapper of the Ninth Cave of the Zelandonii, and Mother of Jonayla, Blessed of Doni, and I am Acolyte to the First Among Those Who Serve The Great Earth Mother. I was formerly of the Lion Camp of the Mamutoi, who live far to the east. I was adopted by the Mamut to be Daughter of the Mammoth Hearth, chosen by the spirit of the Cave Lion, protected by the Cave Bear, Friend of the Horses, Whinney, Racer, and Gray, and the four-legged hunter, Wolf."

"I am Romitolo of the Sixth Cave of the Giornadonii," he said in slightly accented Zelandonii. He was fluent in both languages. "I greet you, Ayla of the Ninth Cave of the Zelandonii. You have a lot of unusual ties. Perhaps you could explain them to me sometime," he said. "But first, I would like to ask you a question."

"By all means," Ayla said, noticing that he seemed to feel no need to recite all his names and ties. Well, he was unique enough, she thought. He seems young, yet ageless.

"What are you going to do with the little snake?" Romitolo asked. "Are you going to send him back to the Mother?"

"I don't think so. I think the Mother will take him when she's ready for him."

"You have horses and a wolf—would you let me have the little snake? I will take care of him."

Ayla paused for a while, then said, "I wasn't sure what to do with him, but I think that's a good idea, if it's all right with your leader. Some people fear snakes, even those that are not poisonous. You will have to learn what to feed him. I may be able to help you." She reached into her carrying sack and pulled out the woven bowl with the lid tied on and gave it to Romitolo. Wolf was leaning against her leg and whining slightly. "Would you like to meet the wolf? He won't hurt you. When he was growing up, he grew to love a boy who had some problems. I think you remind Wolf of him."

"Where is the boy now?" Romitolo asked.

"Rydag was very weak. He walks the next world now," Ayla said.

"I am getting weaker. I think I will walk the next world soon," Romitolo said. "Now I will think of it as returning to the Mother."

She didn't deny his assertion. He probably knew himself and his body better than anyone. "I am a medicine woman and was able to help Rydag be more comfortable. Can you tell me where you feel bad? I may be able to help you," Ayla said.

"We have a good healer and he has probably done everything that can be done. He gives me medicine to help the pain when I need it. I think I'll be ready to go back to the Great Mother when the time comes," Romitolo said, then changed the subject. "How can I meet your wolf? What do I have to do?"

"Just let him sniff you, and maybe lick your hand. You can pat him, if you like, and feel his fur. He's very gentle when I ask him to be. He adores babies," Ayla said. Then she added, "Have you seen the pole-drag that the One Who Is First rides on? If you would like to ride on it and be pulled around by a horse, I'd be happy to take you wherever you would like to go."

"Or, if you need anyone to help carry you," Jondalar added, "my shoulders are strong and I have carried people that way before."

"I thank you for your offers, but I have to tell you that it makes me tired to go visiting much. I used to love it. Now, even with someone carrying me, it's hard. I almost didn't come on this Journey, but if I hadn't, there would have been no one left to help me, and I can't manage without help. I do like it when people visit me, though."

"Do you know how many years you can count?" the One Who Was First asked.

"About fourteen years," he said. "I reached manhood two summers ago, but things have been getting worse since then."

The First nodded. "When a boy reaches manhood, his body wants to grow," she said.

"And mine doesn't know how to grow right," Romitolo said.

"But you know how to think, and that is more than many can say," the First said. "I hope you live many more years. I think you have much to offer."

The three women of the zelandonia rejoined each other later in the afternoon at the travelers' campsite. The large gathering area was too busy. What had started out to be a meeting of the neighboring zelandonia had turned into an unscheduled Summer Meeting, and those who were cooking meals had taken over the covered space of the pavilion. No one else was in camp at the moment, and Ayla's sleeping tent was being used as a quiet place to talk. Even then they spoke softly.

"Should the hemlock be served tonight, or should we wait until tomorrow night?" the First said.

"I don't think there is any need to wait. I think we should get it over with as quickly as possible," Zelandoni First said. "And the water parsnips should be cooked while they are fresh, although they will keep for a while. I have an assistant, not quite an acolyte, but a woman who helps me a lot. I will ask her to cook the hemlock roots."

"Will you tell her what they are and who they are for?" the First asked.

"Of course. It would be dangerous for her if she didn't know exactly what she was cooking and why."

"Is there anything you want me to do?" Ayla asked.

"You've done your share," the First said. "You gathered the plants to begin with."

"Then I think I will go and find Jondalar. I haven't seen him all day," Ayla said. "When are we going to visit the Sacred Site?"

"I think it's best to wait a few days, after this whole Balderan matter is finished," Zelandoni First said.

Balderan and his men had been watching both Ayla and Jondalar, and Wolf, very closely, though not overtly. It was getting dark and close to the time when the evening meal would be served. It wasn't officially being called a feast, but it would be a communal meal to which everyone was contributing, so it felt like a major celebration.

Ayla and Jondalar weren't entirely sure where the men were being held; it changed somewhat depending upon who was watching them. They were deeply involved in conversation with each other, and nearly walked into Balderan and his men.

Balderan looked around quickly, and noticed that the wolf was not with them. The men who were supposed to be watching them also seemed distracted and not paying attention. "Let's do it now!" he said.

Suddenly Balderan jumped out, grabbed Ayla, and the next instant had a leather thong around her neck. "Stay back or she dies!" Balderan shouted as he pulled tight on the cord. Ayla gasped, trying to breathe.

The other men had armed themselves with stones that they were threatening to throw or perhaps use to hit her or whoever came after them. Balderan had been waiting for this moment. He had planned how it would go in his mind, and now that he had her, he was enjoying it. He was going to kill her, maybe not right away, but he was going to enjoy it. He was sure he knew how the big "gentle giant" of a man would react.

But Balderan didn't know that Jondalar had cultivated that

calm and restrained demeanor as part of his need to keep himself under control at all times. He had allowed his temper to get control of him before and knew what he was capable of doing.

Jondalar's first thought was, how dare anybody try to harm Ayla! This time it wasn't temper, it was reaction.

In an instant, before any of the men even thought of moving, Jondalar took two long steps and was behind Balderan. He bent over and grabbed both his wrists and broke his hold, almost broke his arms. Then letting go of one arm, he spun him around and smashed him in the face with his fist. He was close to hitting him again, but the man slumped over in a daze, blood running down his face from his broken nose.

Balderan had misjudged Jondalar entirely. He was not only a big man, he was a powerful man with quick reflexes, a man who sometimes had to exert himself to control a spirited stallion. Racer was not a domesticated horse; he was a trained horse. Jondalar had lived with him from the day he was born and taught him, but Racer still had all the natural instincts of an extremely strong and sometimes willful wild stallion. It took a lot of strength to handle the horse, and it kept the man in shape.

Balderan had doubled the leather cord that had originally been used to tie his shirt together. It was still hanging loosely around Ayla's neck, but the marks it had made were bright red, even in the dim light of fireplaces that were some distance away. People were belatedly running in their direction. Everything had happened so fast. Several Zelandonia, including the First, went to help Ayla, and Jondalar wouldn't leave her side.

The people Zelandoni First had spoken to about how to deal with Balderan had gathered around him as he was lying on the ground. Suddenly Aremina, the woman who had been raped and whose mate he had killed, kicked him. Then the woman who had lost her daughter after she was held by them and badly mistreated suddenly kicked him too. Then a man who had been beaten by the men after watching his mate and young daughter being raped punched his face, breaking his nose again. Balderan's other men were trying to back away, but they were all surrounded now, and one of them was punched in the face.

There was no stopping the angry crowd now. Everyone who had been subject to the depredations of Balderan and his men was giving it back and then some. The crowd had turned into a mob. It had happened so fast, no one knew what to do at first; then the Zelandonia moved in to stop it. Ayla was among them shouting, "Stop it! Stop it now! You are acting like Balderan." But the people couldn't stop. All their frustrations, their feelings of impotence, humiliation, and powerlessness came out.

When the people settled down and looked around, all four men were sprawled on the ground, covered with blood. Ayla bent over Balderan to check him; he was dead and so were two others. One was barely hanging on to life, the one who had asked how he could make reparations. Wolf suddenly appeared and stayed with Ayla, watching the scene closely, a low growl in his throat, and she could tell he wasn't sure what to do. Ayla sat on the ground with her arms around his neck.

The First moved beside her. "That's not at all the way I expected it to happen," she said. "I didn't realize there was so much pent-up anger, but I should have."

"Balderan brought it on himself," Zelandoni First said. "If he hadn't attacked Ayla, Jondalar would not have hit him. Once he was down, the people who had been hurt by him couldn't hold back. They knew he wasn't invincible. I guess there is no need for the hemlock now. I will have to make sure it is disposed of properly."

Everyone was still tense and overexcited. It took a while for most people to understand what had happened. Those who had participated were beginning to feel a range of emotions. Some felt shame for what they had done; others felt relief, sorrow, excitement, even elation that Balderan had finally gotten back what he had given out.

Levela had kept Jonayla with her when Wolf ran out of the tent, though she wanted to follow him. Ayla had some of Balderan's blood on her when she returned, which upset her daughter. She assured Jonayla that it was not her own blood, but that of a man who was hurt.

The next morning Jondalar went to see the Zelandonia

who were both called First to tell them that Ayla wanted to stay in her tent and rest that day. Her throat still hurt from the attempted strangulation. All the local zelandonia had been discussing how to help the people, whether they should call another meeting, or wait until people came to them.

As Jondalar walked back, he was aware that people were watching him, but he didn't care. And he didn't hear the comments. Men admired his strength and his speed, his reaction had been so swift; the women just admired him. To have a man like that, so handsome, so quick to jump to his woman's defense, who wouldn't want such a man? If he had heard them talking, he wouldn't have cared. He just wanted to get to his Ayla and make sure she was well, and that everything was all right.

But after a while it was the story of Balderan's attack on Ayla and Jondalar's quick defense that was told several times, not the resulting melee that ended in the beating death of three men, and quite possibly a fourth, although Gahaynar was holding on to life. The zelandonia had to decide how they were going to dispose of the bodies. It posed a dilemma. They didn't want to honor them in any way; there would be no ceremony, but they did want to make sure their spirits were given back to the Mother. They ended up taking the bodies into the mountains and leaving them on the crest of a hill, exposed to every kind of scavenger.

The visitors from the nearby Caves spent a few more days camped in the field, then began to trickle away to get back into their normal routine now that the excitement was over. They would have many stories to tell about the visitors, the One Who Was First, and her acolyte who controlled a wolf and horses, and called up a two-headed snake, and who helped rid them of Balderan, but the versions of what happened to Balderan and his gang would likely be different depending upon what part each person had played in the events.

Ayla was getting restless and anxious to leave. She decided it was a good time to finish drying the bison meat—it would give her something to do—and laid out lines of cordage supported by sticks of wood, and built smoky fires in and around them.

Insects like gnats were drawn to the raw meat, where they liked to lay eggs that could cause it to spoil. The smoke kept them away, and incidentally flavored the meat. Then she set about slicing the sections of bison into thin, uniform pieces. Before long, Levela joined her, then Jondecam and Jondalar. Jonayla wanted to help, so Ayla showed her how to cut the meat and gave her a section of the corded lines to hang her pieces up to dry. Willamar and his two assistants strolled into camp around midday, quite excited.

"After we leave here, we were thinking it might be a good idea to go south along this river until we reach the Southern Sea," Willamar said. "After coming all this way, it would be a shame not to see it, and we've been told this is the time to trade for shells. They have many of the small round bead shells, and the pretty long dentalia, and some particularly nice scallop shells, even periwinkles, I'm told. We could keep some and trade some to the Fifth Cave."

"What do we have to trade with them for the shells?" Jondalar asked.

"I was going to talk to you about that. Do you think you could find some good flint and make some blades and points to exchange for shells? And maybe some of that meat you are drying, Ayla?" Willamar said.

"How do you know this is the time to trade, and about all these shell beads?" Levela asked.

"A man from the north just arrived. You'll have to meet him. He's a trader, too, and he has some fascinating ivory carvings," Willamar said.

"I knew a man who made ivory carvings," Ayla said, a little wistfully.

Jondalar's ears perked up. He knew that same ivory carver. He was a remarkable and talented artist, and the man to whom he almost lost Ayla. He still felt a lump in his throat at the thought.

"I would like to meet the man and see his carvings, and I wouldn't mind seeing the Southern Sea. I'm sure we can work something out in terms of trading. What else would make good trade goods?" he asked.

"Almost anything that is well made or useful, especially something unusual," Willamar said.

"Like Ayla's baskets," Levela said.

"Why my baskets?" Ayla said, a little surprised. "They're just plain baskets, not even any decoration on them."

"That's just it. They seem to be just plain baskets, until you look closely," Levela said. "They are made so well, absolutely tight and even, and the weave is so unusual. The ones that are watertight stay that way for a long time, the looser ones also hold up well. Anyone who knows anything about baskets would pick yours before a showier one that is not made as well. Even your throwaway baskets are too good to throw away."

Ayla blushed a little at all the praise. "I just make them the way I was taught," she said. "I didn't think there was anything special about them."

Jondalar smiled. "I remember when we first went to stay with the Mamutoi, and there was a festival where people were exchanging gifts. Tulie and Nezzie offered to give you some things that you could give as gifts, but you said you had many gifts you had made to keep yourself busy and wanted to go back to your valley and get them. So we went and got them. I think Tulie, in particular, was surprised at how beautiful and well made your gifts were. And Talut loved his bison robe. The things you make are beautiful, Ayla."

Now she was blushing bright red and at a loss as to what to say.

"If you don't think so, just look at Jonayla," Jondalar said with a grin.

"That's not just me. Jonayla has a lot of you in her, too," Ayla said.

"I certainly hope so," Jondalar said.

"There's no doubt the Mother used your spirit to blend with Ayla's," Levela said. "You can see it in Jonayla's eyes. They are exactly your color and that shade of blue is not very common."

"So everyone's agreed. We will go to the Southern Sea on our way home," Willamar interjected. "And I think you should make some baskets, Ayla. You can trade for salt, too, not just shells."

"When are we going to meet the man with the carvings?" Jondecam asked.

"If this is a good time to stop for a midday meal, you can meet him now," Willamar said.

"I just have a few more pieces to finish," Levela said.

"We can bring some of the bison with us to cook for our meal or contribute to a community meal," Jondalar said.

Jondalar picked up Jonayla and they all left with Willamar and walked to the zelandonia's covered shelter. Demoryn was talking to a stranger, and Amelana, obviously pregnant and fully aware of how attractive that made her, was smiling at him. He was smiling back. He was fairly tall and well built, with brown hair and blue eyes, an appealing friendly face, and to Ayla, there was something about him that seemed familiar.

"I brought the rest of our traveling group," Willamar said, and began the introductions. When he started with "Jondalar of the Ninth Cave of the Zelandonii," the man looked puzzled as Jondalar put Jonayla down in preparation for joining hands.

"And this is his mate, Ayla of the Ninth Cave of the Zelandonii, formerly of the Lion Camp of the Mamutoi, Daughter of the Mammoth Hearth . . ."

"You I know," the man said. "Or know of you. I am Conardi of the Losadunai and you both stayed with the Losadunai a few years ago?"

"Yes, we stayed with Laduni's Cave on our way back from our Journey," Jondalar said, with genuine excitement. Although anyone who made a Journey usually met many people, one seldom met them again, or even someone who knew someone a person had met.

"We all heard about both you at next Summer Meeting. You made big impression with horses and wolf I recall," Conardi said.

"Yes, the horses are at our camp, and Wolf is hunting," Ayla said.

"And this little beauty must be addition to family. You she resembles," Conardi said to the tall blond man with the vivid blue eyes. It sounded as though he was speaking Zelandonii with a slight shift in construction and a slightly different accent, but,

Ayla remembered, their languages were very close. He was actually speaking Zelandonii with some Losadunai, his own language, mixed in.

"Willamar said you brought carvings," Jondalar said.

"Yes. Here examples," Conardi said.

He untied a pouch from his waist ties, opened the top, and poured out several mammoth ivory figures onto an unused platter. Ayla picked one up. It was a mammoth with some extra lines incised on it, whose reason was not clear, so she asked him.

"I do not know," he said. "They always made that way. These not made by ancients, but made like ancients make, especially by young people who are learning."

Next, Ayla picked up a long, slender figure, and when she looked closely, she knew it was a bird, but a bird like a goose flying through the air. It was so simple, yet so full of life. The next figure was like a lion standing on its hind legs—at least the head was and the top of its body, and the upper arms seemed to be feline—but the legs were human. And in front of what would be the long underbelly of a cat, if it wasn't standing upright, was a clearly marked enlongated downward-pointing triangle, the pubic triangle, the unmistakable sign of a female. Though there were no humanlike breasts, the figure was a lion woman.

The last figure was definitely a woman, though she had no head, just a carved hole through which a cord was strung. The breasts were huge and quite high. The arms ended with the indication of a hand with fingers. The hips were broad and the buttocks large, with the line dividing them sharply incised all the way around to the front, ending with such an exaggerated depiction of a vulva, the female organ was almost everted.

"I think this was made by a woman who has been through childbirth," Ayla said. "That's sometimes how it feels, like you are being split in two."

"You may be right, Ayla. The breasts certainly appear to be full of milk," said the First.

"Are you offering these for trade?" Willamar asked.

"No, these my own. I carry for luck, but if you want one or more, could get some made," Conardi said.

"If it were me, I would get some extras made to take on trading missions. I'm sure they would trade well," Willamar said. "Are you a Trade Master, Conardi?" He had noticed the man did not have a trader's tattoo.

"I like travel, and trade some, but not Trade Master," Conardi said. "Everybody trades, but we have not such occupation as specialty."

"If you like to travel, you can make it be," Willamar said. "It is what I'm training my apprentices to be. This may be my last long trading mission. I'm at an age where traveling is losing its appeal. I'm ready to settle down at home with my mate and her children and grandchildren, like that pretty little one." He indicated Jonayla. "Some traders take their mates and families with them, but my mate was the leader of the Ninth Cave, and not as free to travel. So I always make sure I bring her something special. That's why I was asking if your carvings were available for trading. But I'm sure I'll find something when we go to the Southern Sea to trade for shells. Would you like to travel together with us?"

"When do you leave?" Conardi asked.

"Soon, but not before we see the Most Ancient Sacred Site," Willamar said.

"Is good you do. Beautiful cave, most extraordinary paintings, but I see several times. I go ahead, tell them you coming," Conardi said.

27

T he entrance to the cave was quite large but not symmetrical, and more wide than high. The right side was taller; the left lower section had a projecting ledge over part of it, creating a sheltered area that offered some protection from rain, and from the occasional rain of pebbles that cascaded down the cliff. A cone-shaped mound of gravel had accumulated at the far left end of the cave's mouth, falling from the rock face above, amassing on the ledge, and spilling over, creating a scree slope from the base of the cone that continued down the side of the cliff.

As a result of the capacious opening, light penetrated to some depth into the cave. Ayla thought it would make a good place to live, but it obviously was not used as such. Except for the corner under the ledge where a small fire was burning outside a sleeping shelter, there was little evidence of the things that people used to make their life comfortable. As they approached, a Zelandoni came out of the shelter and greeted them.

"In the name of the Great Earth Mother, you are welcome to Her Most Ancient Sacred Place, First Among Those Who Serve Her," she said, holding out both hands.

"I greet you, Watcher of Her Most Ancient Sacred Site," the First replied.

Jonokol was next. "I am Zelandoni of the Nineteenth Cave of the Zelandonii, and I greet you, Watcher of Her Most Ancient Sacred Site. I am told the images inside this Sacred Place are quite striking. I have also made some images, and I am honored to be invited to see this Sacred Site," he said.

The Watcher smiled. "So you are a Zelandoni Image Maker,"

she said. "I think you will be a little surprised at what you see in this cave, and perhaps you will appreciate the artistry more than most. The Ancients who worked here were quite skilled."

"Are all the images here made by the Ancients?" the Nineteenth asked.

The Watcher heard the unspoken plea in Jonokol's voice. She had heard it before from artists who came to visit. They wanted to know if they would be allowed to add to the work, and she knew what to say.

"Very nearly, though I do know of a few made more recently. If you feel equal to the task, and compelled to do so, you are free to make your mark here. We put no restrictions on anyone. The Mother chooses. You will know if you are chosen," the Watcher said. Though many asked, very few actually did feel equal to the task of contributing to the remarkable work inside.

Ayla was the next one. "In the name of the Great Mother of All, I greet you, Watcher of the Most Ancient Sacred Site," she said, holding out her hands. "I am called Ayla, acolyte to the First Among Those Who Serve The Great Earth Mother."

She's not ready to give up her name yet, was the Zelandoni's first thought. Then she grew conscious that the young woman had spoken with an unusual accent and knew she was the person she had been told about. Most of her Cave thought that all the visitors spoke Zelandonii with what they considered a northern accent, but the way this woman spoke was entirely different. She spoke well, and she obviously knew the language, but the way she made certain sounds was unlike anything she had heard before. There was no doubt that she came from a very distant place.

She looked at the young woman more carefully. Yes, she thought, she's attractive, but she has a foreign aspect, a different set to her features, a shorter face, wider space between her eyes. Even her hair, it's not fine, like so many Zelandonii women. It has a thicker texture, and though she is blond, the shade is distinctive, darker, rather like honey or amber. A foreigner and yet she is acolyte to the First. It's rare enough for a foreigner to become one of the zelandonia, much less acolyte to the First. But perhaps understandable since she's the one who can control horses and a wolf. And she's the one who stopped the men who have been causing so much trouble for so many years."

"You are welcome to this Most Ancient Sacred Site, Ayla, acolyte to the First," the Zelandoni said, grasping Ayla's hands. "I suspect you have traveled farther to see this site than anyone ever has."

"I came with the rest of . . ." Ayla started, then seeing the smile on the woman's face, she understood. It was her accent. The Watcher was talking about how far she had traveled on her Journey with Jondalar, and before that, from her home with the Clan, and perhaps even before that. "You could be right," she said, "but Jondalar may have traveled even farther. He Journeyed all the way from his home to the end of the Great Mother River far to the east, and beyond, where he found me, and then back again before we started on this Donier Tour."

Jondalar stepped closer at the sound of his name and grinned when he heard Ayla describe his travels. The woman was not young and immature and not old, but old enough so that she had the wisdom that came from experience and maturity, about the age he used to like women before he met Ayla.

"Greetings, respected Watcher of the Most Ancient Sacred Site," he said, holding out his hands. "I am Jondalar of the Ninth Cave of the Zelandonii, Flint-Knapper of the Ninth Cave. Mated to Ayla of the Ninth Cave of the Zelandonii, who is acolyte of the First. Son of Marthona, former leader of the Ninth Cave; brother of Joharran, leader of the Ninth Cave. Born to the Hearth of Dalanar, leader and founder of the Lanzadonii."

He recounted his important names and ties. It was one thing for members of the zelandonia to simply state their primary affiliations, but it would seem too casual and not very courteous for him to be so brief in a formal introduction, especially to a Zelandoni.

"You are welcome here, Jondalar of the Ninth Cave of the Zelandonii," she said, taking his hands and looking into eyes of an incredibly vivid shade of blue, eyes that seemed to see inside her very spirit, and cause her womanhood to quiver. She closed her eyes for a moment to regain her internal balance. No wonder she's not ready to give up her name yet, the Watcher thought. She's mated, and to one of the most fascinating men I have ever met. I wonder if anyone is planning a Mother Festival for these visitors from the north . . . too bad my time for serving as Watcher is not up yet. If someone needs me here, I can't go to Mother Festivals.

Willamar, who was waiting to introduce himself to the Watcher, ducked his head to smile to himself. It was a good thing that Jondalar hardly seemed to notice the impact he still had on women, he thought, and as perceptive as she was, Ayla seemed oblivious to it. Even though it was discouraged, he knew that jealousy still lived in the hearts of many.

"I am called Willamar, Master Trader of the Ninth Cave of the Zelandonii," he said, when his turn came, "mated to Marthona, the former leader of the Ninth Cave, who is the mother of this young man. Though he was not born to my hearth, he was raised there so I think of him as the son of my heart. I feel the same about Ayla and her little one, Jonayla."

She's not only mated, she has a child, a young child, the Watcher thought. How can she even think of becoming a Zelandoni? Much less as an acolyte to the the most powerful Zelandoni on earth? The First must see a lot of potential in her, but inside she must be pulled so many ways.

Only these five visitors would be going into the cave at this time. The rest of the visitors would go another time and might not see as much. The Caves that watched over the Sacred Site didn't like too many to go in at one time. There were torches and lamps near the fireplace. That was part of the Watcher's job, to gather and prepare them so they would be on hand when needed. Everyone took a torch. The Watcher handed out extras, put more of them in a pack, and added some stone lamps and small bladders of oil. When everyone had a fire holder to light the way, the Watcher started in.

There was enough daylight coming into the entrance chamber to get a sense of the huge size of the cave, and a first impression of its disorganized character. A chaotic landscape of stone formations filled the space. Columns of stalactites once attached to the ceiling and their stalagmitic mates had dropped down as though the floor had fallen out from under them, some tipped over, some collapsed, some shattered. There was a sense of immediacy in the way they were strewn about, yet everything was so frozen in time they were iced with a thick caramel layer of glistening stalagmitic frosting.

The Watcher started humming as she led them toward the left, staying close to the wall. The rest followed in single file, with the First next in line, then Ayla, followed by Jonokol and Willamar, with Jondalar at the end. He was tall enough to see over the heads of the rest and thought of himself as a sort of protective rear guard, though he had no idea from what they needed to be protected.

Even well into the cave there was still enough light coming in from the entrance that it was not entirely dark. Instead the cave was suffused with a kind of deep twilight, especially once eyes became accustomed to the shadowed ambience. As they moved inside and passed by with their lamps or torches, the coloration of the stone the light illuminated varied from thin new icicles of pure white to lumpy gray stumps hoary with age. Flowing draperies hung from above, striped along the folds in shades of yellow, orange, red, and white. Shining lights of crystal caught the eye, reflecting and amplifying the meager light, some glittering off the floor covered by a white film of calcite. They saw fantastical sculptures that kindled the imagination and colossal white columns that glowed with translucent mystery. It was an utterly beautiful cave.

In the vague light they reached a place where the space seemed to open out. The sides of the chamber disappeared and in front of them, except for a gleaming white disk, the emptiness seemed to go on and on. Ayla felt that they had entered another area that was even larger than the entrance chamber. Though the ceiling was hung with strange and magnificent stalactites that resembled long white hair, the floor was unusually level, like the calm, still lake it once was. But now the floor of the huge chamber was cluttered with skulls and bones and teeth, and the shallow depressions that had been the beds of hibernating cave bears.

The Watcher, who had been humming continuously, started increasing the volume of her sound until the intensity and force of the droning was louder than Ayla, who was standing

beside her, would have thought possible for anyone to make,
but there was no reverberation. The noise was swallowed by
the immensity of the empty space inside the stone cliff. Next
the One Who Was First started singing the Mother's Song in
her deep, rich operatic contralto.

> *Out of the darkness, the chaos of time,*
> *The whirlwind gave birth to the Mother sublime.*
> *She woke to Herself knowing life had great worth,*
> *The dark empty void grieved the Great Mother Earth.*
> *The Mother was lonely. She was the only.*

> *From the dust of Her birth She created the other,*
> *A pale shining friend, a companion, a brother.*
> *They grew up together, learned to love and to care,*
> *And when She was ready, they decided to pair.*
> *Around Her he'd hover. Her pale shining lover.*

> *She was happy at first with Her one counterpart . . .*

The First hesitated, then stopped. There was no resonance,
no echo coming back. The cave was telling them that this was
not the place for people. This space belonged to the cave bears.
She wondered if there were any images in the empty room. The
Watcher would know.

"Zelandoni who watches over this cave," she said formally,
"did the ancients make any images in the room ahead?"

"No," the woman said. "This room isn't ours to paint. We can
go into the room in spring, just as they often go into our place
in this cave, but the Mother has given this room to the cave
bears for their winter sleep."

"That must be why people decided not to live here," Ayla
said. "When I first saw this cave I thought it ought to be a
good place to live and wondered why a Cave had not chosen
it. Now I know."

The Watcher led them to the right. They passed by a small
opening that led to another chamber and a little farther on came
to a larger opening. Like the entrance chamber, this one was a
chaotic mass of fallen blocks of stalagmites and concretions.

The pathway went around these obstructions and led to a vast space with a high ceiling and a dark red floor. A promontory created by a huge cascade of stone dominated the chamber marked by several large red dots on a rock pendant suspended from the ceiling. They came to a large panel, a nearly vertical wall that continued up to the ceiling, covered by large red dots and various signs.

"How do you think these dots were made?" the Watcher asked.

"I suppose a big wad of leather or moss, or something similar could have been used," Jonokol said.

"I think the Zelandoni of the Nineteenth should look a little more closely," the First said. Ayla remembered that she had been here before and no doubt knew the answer. Willamar probably knew, too. Ayla did not volunteer a guess, nor did Jondalar. The Watcher held up her hand and stretched back her fingers, then held it up to a dot. It was just about the same size as her palm.

Jonokol peered at the large dots. They were a bit blurry but he could see faint impressions of the beginnings of fingers extending up from some of the dots. "You're right!" he said. "They must have made a very thick paste of red ocher, and dipped their palms in it. I don't think I have ever seen dots made that way!"

The Watcher smiled at his amazement, and looked rather pleased with herself. Seeing the smile made Ayla notice that the area they were in seemed to be more well lit. She looked around and realized they were close to the entrance again. They could have come this way in the beginning instead of going around by way of the extensive bear sleeping room, but she was sure the Watcher had her reasons for going the way she did. Next to the large dots was another painting that Ayla could not decipher except for the straight line of red paint above it with a crosspiece near the top.

The path led them around the blocks and concretions in the center of the room until they came to the head of a lion painted in black on the wall opposite. It was the only black painting she saw. Near it was a sign and some little dots, perhaps made with a finger. Somewhat farther on was a series of palm-size red dots. She counted them in her mind using the counting words. There were thirteen. Above them was another group of ten dots on the ceiling, but in order to make them someone had had to climb up on a concretion, with the help of some friends or apprentices, she supposed, so they must have been important to the maker, although she could not imagine why.

A little farther on was an alcove. A lobe of rock at the entrance was completely covered with the large red dots. Inside the alcove were more red dots on one wall and on the opposite wall, a group of dots, some lines and other markings, and three horse heads, two of them yellow. Within the central mass of blocks and stalagmites, opposite the alcove, the Watcher pointed out another sizable panel of large red dots behind some low concretions.

"Is there an animal head made of red dots in the middle of those dots?" Jonokol asked.

"Some people think so," the Watcher said, smiling at the image-making Zelandoni for seeing it.

Ayla tried to see an animal, but she only saw dots. She did, however, see a difference. "Do you think these dots were made by a different person than the other dots? They seem bigger."

"I think you are right," the Watcher said. "We think the others were made by a woman, these by a man. There are more images, but in order to see them, we need to go back the way we came."

She began humming again as she led them into a small chamber within the central concretions. A large drawing of the front part of a deer was painted there, probably a young megaceros. It had small, palmate antlers and a slight hump on the withers. While they were there, the Watcher raised the volume of her humming. The chamber resonated, crooned back to them. Jonokol joined in, singing scales that softly harmonized with the Watcher's tones. Ayla began whistling birdsongs that complemented the music. Then the First started singing the next verses of the Mother's Song, toning down her strong contralto so that it just lent a rich, deep intense note to the singing.

She was happy at first with Her one counterpart.
Then the Mother grew restless, unsure in Her heart.

She loved Her fair friend, Her dear complement,
But something was missing, Her love was unspent.
  She was the Mother. She needed another.

She dared the great void, the chaos, the dark,
To find the cold home of the life-giving spark.
The whirlwind was fearsome, the darkness complete.
Chaos was freezing, and reached for Her heat.
  The Mother was brave. The danger was grave.

She drew from cold chaos the creative source,
Then conceiving within, She fled with life force.
She grew with the life that She carried inside.
And gave of Herself with love and with pride.
  The Mother was bearing. Her life She was sharing.

The dark empty void and the vast barren Earth,
With anticipation, awaited the birth.
Life drank from Her blood, it breathed from Her bones.
It split Her skin open and sundered Her stones.
  The Mother was giving. Another was living.

Her gushing birth waters filled rivers and seas,
And flooded the land, giving rise to the trees.
From each precious drop more grass and leaves grew,
And lush verdant plants made all the Earth new.
  Her waters were flowing. New green was growing.

The First stopped at a place that felt like an ending to the impromptu chorus. Ayla stopped too, at the end of an extended melodious trill of a skylark, leaving Jonokol and the Watcher, who finished on a harmonizing tone. Jondalar and Willamar slapped their hands on their thighs in appreciation.

"That was marvelous," Jondalar said. "Just beautiful."

"Yes. That sounded quite good," Willamar said. "I'm sure the Mother appreciated it as much as we did."

The Watcher led them through the small chamber, then down to another recess. From the entrance the head of a bear painted in red could be seen. As they crouched down to get through a low corridor, more of the bear came into sight, and then the head of a second one appeared out of the darkness. Once they were through and could stand, they could see the head of a third bear lightly sketched under the head of the first one. The shape of the wall was skillfully used to add depth to the first bear, and although the second bear seemed to be complete, it was a hollow in the place of the hindquarters that gave that impression. It was almost as though the bear were emerging from the spirit world through the wall.

"Those are definitely cave bears," Ayla said. "The shape of their forehead is so distinctive. It's like that from the time they are little."

"Have you seen little cave bears?"

"Yes, occasionally. The people I grew up with had a special relationship with Cave Bears," Ayla said.

When they stood at the back of the niche, they could see two ibex partially painted in red on the right wall. The horns and the backs of the animals were formed by the natural fissures in the rock wall.

They went back through the corridor and climbed back up to the level of the deer, then followed the left-hand wall until they reached a large open area. As they walked around the chamber, Jonokol looked into a niche that held an ancient concretion with a top in the shape of a small basin. He took his waterbag and poured a little water in it. They went back out the way they went in and finally reached the large opening that led to the bears' sleeping room. Not far from the entrance of the cave, on a big rock pillar that separated the two chambers, opposite the other paintings in the room full of chaotic rock formations, was a panel some twenty feet long by ten feet high that was covered in large red dots. There were other markings and signs, including the straight line with a crossbar near the top.

The Watcher led them through the opening into the bears' sleeping room again, following the left wall. She stopped just before an opening. "There is much in here, but I wanted you to see certain things," the Zelandoni said, looking directly at Ayla. "First," she said, holding up the torch she was carrrying. There were some red marks on the wall that appeared to be random lines. Suddenly Ayla's mind filled in the gaps and she could see the head of a rhinoceros. She saw the forehead, the start of the two horns, a short line for its eye, the end of its muzzle with a line drawn for the mouth, and then the suggestion of its chest. It startled her in its simplicity, yet once she saw the animal, it was clear.

"It's a rhinoceros!" Ayla said.

"Yes, and you will not see any others inside this room," the Watcher said.

The floor was hard stone, calcite, and the left wall was blocked by white-and-orange-colored columns. Once past the columns, there were almost no concretions except for the ceiling, which held strange rounded stone shapes and reddish deposits. The floor was full of pieces of stone of every size that had fallen from the ceiling. A somewhat circular area was broken by the fall of a heavy fragment from above, which caused a tilt in the floor. Near the entrance, on a rock pendant was a small, rudimentary sketch in red of a mammoth.

Beyond that, high up on the wall was a small red bear. It was apparent that the artist had to climb up the wall to paint it. Below it, on a rock sticking out of the wall, were two mammoths that utilized the relief of rock wall, and beyond it on another protrusion was a strange sign. On the opposite wall was an extraordinary panel of red paintings, which included the forequarters of a well-made bear. The shape of the forehead and the way the head was carried identified it as a cave bear.

"Jonokol, doesn't this bear look very much like the red bear we just saw?" Ayla asked.

"Yes, it does. I suspect it was made by the same person," he said.

"But I don't understand the rest of the painting. It's like two different animals joined together so that it seems to have two heads, one of them coming out of the chest of the bear, but then there's a lion in the middle, and another lion head in front of the bear. I don't understand this painting at all," Ayla said.

"Perhaps it's not meant to be understood by anyone but the one who made it. The artist used a lot of imagination, and may have been trying to tell a story that is not known anymore.

There are no Elder Legends or Histories that I know of to explain it," the First said.

"I think we just have to appreciate the quality of the work," the Watcher said, "and let the Ancients keep their secrets."

Ayla nodded agreement. She had seen enough caves now to know that it wasn't so much how the images looked when they were done as what the artists accomplished while they were making the art. Farther into the gallery, beyond the second lion head and a fault in the wall was a panel painted with black: the head of a lion, a big mammoth, and finally a figure painted high above the floor on a pendant hanging from the ceiling; it was a large red bear, its back outlined with black. The mystery was how the artist painted it. It was easily visible from the floor, but whoever made it had to climb over many high concretions to reach it.

"Did you notice that all the animals are going out of the room, except for the mammoth?" Jonokol said. "It's as if they are coming into this world from the place of the spirit world."

The Watcher stood just outside the room they had been in and started humming again, but this time it was similar to the melody of the music of the Mother's Song the way the First sang it. Every Cave of the Zelandonii sang or recited the Mother's Song. It told the story of their beginnings, of the origin of the people, and while they were all similar and told the same story, each Cave's version was not exactly the same. That was especially true if they sang it. The melodies of the songs were often quite different, sometimes depending on who did the singing. Because she had been endowed with such an extraordinary voice, the First had composed her own unique way of singing it.

As if on signal, the First picked up the next verse of the Mother's Song from where she left off. Both Jonokol and Ayla refrained from joining in, and just enjoyed listening.

In violent labor spewing fire and strife,
She struggled in pain to give birth to new life.
Her dried clotted blood turned to red-ochered soil,
But the radiant child made it all worth the toil.
    The Mother's great joy. A bright shining boy.

Mountains rose up spouting flames from their crests,
She nurtured Her son from Her mountainous breasts.
He suckled so hard, the sparks flew so high,
The Mother's hot milk laid a path through the sky.
    His life had begun. She nourished Her son.

He laughed and he played, and he grew big and bright.
He lit up the darkness, the Mother's delight.
She lavished Her love, he grew bright and strong,
But soon he matured, not a child for long.
    Her son was near grown. His mind was his own.

She took from the source for the life She'd begun.
Now the cold empty void was enticing Her son.
The Mother gave love, but the youth longed for more,
For knowledge, excitement, to travel, explore.
    Chaos was Her foe. But Her son yearned to go.

He stole from Her side as the Great Mother slept,
While out of the dark swirling void chaos crept.
With tempting inducements the darkness beguiled.
Deceived by the whirlwind, chaos captured Her child.
    The dark took Her son. The young brilliant one.

The Mother's bright child, at first overjoyed,
Was soon overwhelmed by the bleak frigid void.
Her unwary offspring, consumed with remorse,
Could not escape the mysterious force.
    Chaos would not free. Her rash progeny.

But just as the dark pulled him into the cold,
The Mother woke up, reached out and caught hold.
To help Her recover Her radiant son,
The Mother appealed to the pale shining one.
    The Mother held tight. And kept him in sight.

The sound resonated. The song echoed back to them, not as
strongly as some, the First thought, but with interesting nuances, almost as though it were doubling back on itself. When

the First reached a place in the verse she felt was appropriate, she stopped. Silently, the group continued on.

On the right side of the cave they came to a large accumulation of stalagmitic stone along with collapsed blocks. This time the Watcher took them to the left side of the cave at the deepest part of the bears' sleeping room. Across from the stalagmites and stone blocks was a large rock pendant in the shape of a blade hanging from the ceiling. The stones defined the beginning of a new chamber with a high ceiling in the beginning, but decreasing toward the back. Many concretions hung from the roof and the walls, unlike the bears' sleeping place, which had no such concretions.

When they reached the hanging pendant, the Watcher knocked her torch against an edge of rock to make it burn cleaner, then held it up so the visitors could see the the surface of the panel. Closest to the bottom, facing left, painted in red, was a spotted leopard! Ayla, Jondalar, and Jonokol had never seen a leopard painted on the walls of a Sacred Site before. Its long tail made Ayla think it was probably a snow leopard. At the end of the leopard's tail was a thick flow of calcite and on the other side of it was one large red dot. No one understood the reason for the large red dots in this place, or even what the leopard meant, but there was no doubting that it was a leopard.

The same could not be said about the animal above it that faced right. The massive shoulders and shape of the head could almost be mistaken for a bear, but the thin body, long legs, and spots on the upper body made Ayla sure it was a cave hyena! She knew hyenas and they had massive shoulders. The shape of the head in the painted animal somewhat resembled that of a cave bear. The powerful teeth and jaw muscles of a hyena, which could crack the bones of a mammoth, had developed a more powerful bone structure, too, but its muzzle was longer. The coat of a hyena was stiff and coarse, especially around the head and shoulders.

"Do you see the other bear above it?" the Watcher said.

Suddenly Ayla caught sight of another figure above the hyena. In faint red lines Ayla could make out the distinctive shape of a cave bear facing left, in the opposite direction from the hyena, and she began making comparisons.

"I don't think the spotted animal is a bear. I think it is a cave hyena," Ayla said.

"Some people think so, but its head is so bearlike," the Watcher said.

"The heads of the two animals are similar," Ayla said, "but the hyena in the image has a longer muzzle, and no discernible ears. The tuft of bristly hair on the top of its head is typical of a hyena."

The Watcher didn't argue. People had a right to think what they wished, but the acolyte had made some interesting observations. The woman then pointed out another cat that was hidden on a narrow panel on the underside of the hanging stone and asked her what kind of cat she thought it was. Ayla wasn't sure; there were no distinctive marks on its coat and it was enlongated to fit the space, but it was very catlike—on second thought, maybe weasel-like. There were some other animals that she was told were ibex, but they weren't as clear to her. They were then led back to the left side of the chamber. At first there were many concretions, but no drawings.

As they continued down the passage they came to a long panel. A calcareous formation had decorated the wall with draperies and strings of red, orange, and yellow that didn't quite reach the thick conical mounds beneath them. Concretions like rivulets frozen in time seemed to run down the hanging drapes, leaving spaces between them on which strange signs had been painted.

One was a sort of long rectangular shape with lines coming out the sides. It reminded Ayla of a very large depiction of one of those creeping creatures with many legs, perhaps a caterpillar. In a space next to it was a shape that had something like wings on either side of the center. It could have been a butterfly, which was the next stage in the life of a caterpillar, but it wasn't as carefully done as many of the other paintings, so she wasn't sure. She thought of asking the Watcher, but doubted if she knew. Whatever she said would only be her guess.

As they continued, the wall became less extravagantly decorated. The Watcher started softly humming again. There was some resonance, but not much until they came to an area with overhanging rock. There clusters of red dots had been made. It was followed by a frieze of five rhinoceroses. There were other signs and animals in the area. Seven heads and one complete catlike animal, perhaps lions, plus a horse, a mammoth, a rhinoceros. Several positive images of handprints, plus dots forming lines and circular figures. Farther on were more signs and a sketch of a rhino in black.

Next they came to another blade of rock, a kind of partition on which were more signs, a partial outline of a mammoth in black with a red negative hand stencil inside the line of the body, and another on the flank of a horse. To the right of them, two clusters of large dots. On the other side of the panel of hand stencils was a drawing in red of a little bear. There was also a red deer and some other marks, but the bear was the predominant figure. It was drawn very much like the other red bears they had seen, but it was a miniature version. The panel marked the beginning of a small chamber straight ahead. As they looked in they could see that it had little headroom.

"I don't think we need to go in here," the Watcher said. "It's just a very small space without much in it, and we'd have to stoop or crouch once we were inside of it."

The First agreed. She had little desire to squeeze herself into a tiny space, and as she recalled, there wasn't much in it. Besides she knew what was coming and was more anxious to see that.

Instead of going straight ahead to visit the small chamber, the Watcher turned left, then followed the right wall. The next chamber was about five feet lower than the one they were in. The floor was slanted down, the ceiling was high in places and low in others, and the walls and ceiling had many concretions. There was some evidence that cave bears had been there—paw prints, claw marks, and bones. Ayla thought she saw the hint of a drawing some distance away, but the Watcher just walked through, not bothering to point it out. The space felt like an entryway to something else.

The entrance to the next chamber was low. In the center of the next room was a sinkhole, a depression that was about thirty feet around and over twelve feet deep. They passed around the right of it on a floor of brown earth.

"When did the floor collapse?" Jondalar asked. The floor

underfoot seemed solid enough, but he wondered if it could happen again.

"I don't know," the Watcher said, "but I do know it was after the Ancients were here."

"How do you know that?" Jondalar asked.

"Look above the hole," she said, pointing to a smooth, blade-like pendant of rock descending from the ceiling over the hole.

Everyone looked. Because the surfaces of most of the walls and descended ceiling rocks in this chamber were coated with a soft layer of light brown claylike material, vermiculite—a chemical alteration of the mineral constituents of the stone that softened the surface—the images were white. Drawings, engravings of a sort, could be made with a stick, or even a finger, displacing the brown-colored surface clay and leaving a pure white line underneath.

Ayla noticed that there were many white drawings in this room, but on the overhanging rock she could clearly see a horse, and an owl with its head turned around so that its face could be seen over its back. It was something owls were known to do, but she had never seen a drawing of it; she had never seen any owl drawings in any cave.

"You are right. That had to be made by the Ancients before the floor collapsed," Jondalar said, "because no one could reach it now."

The Watcher smiled at him, and enjoyed the incredulity in his voice. She pointed out several more of the finger-etched drawings in the large room. She took them around to the other side of the circular depression, the left wall. Although it was filled with hanging pendants of stalactites and stalagmitic pillars and circular pyramids built up on the floor, it was not difficult to move around in the room, and most of the decorations were at eye level. Even at a distance, the light from their torches showed many white engravings, some scraped to produce a white surface. Standing in the middle of the room they could see mammoths, rhinoceroses, bears, aurochs, bison, horses, and a series of curved lines and sinuous fingermarks drawn over bear claw marks.

"How many animals are in this room?" Ayla asked.

"I have counted almost twice twenty-five," the Watcher said,

holding up her left hand with all her fingers and her thumb
bent at the knuckles, then opening her hand and closing the
knuckles again.

Ayla remembered the other way to count with fingers. Counting with hands could be more complex than the simple counting
words, if one understood how to do it. The right hand counted
the words, and as each word was spoken, a finger was bent; the
left hand indicated the number of fives counted. The left hand,
held palm facing out, with all the fingers and thumbs bent at the
knuckles, counted not five, the way she had taught herself when
she first learned to count and the way Jondalar had once taught
her the counting words, but twenty-five. She had learned this
way of counting in her training, and the concept had astounded
her. It made the counting words so much more powerful when
used like that.

It occurred to her that the large dots could be a way of using
the counting words, too. One handprint could be counted as
five; one large dot made with only the palm of the hand could
mean twenty-five; two would be twice twenty-five, fifty; and
so many on the wall in one place would be a very large number, if one understood how to read it. But as with most things
associated with the zelandonia, it was probably more complex
than that. All signs had more than one meaning.

As they were walking around the room, Ayla saw a beautifully
made horse, and behind it two mammoths, one superimposed
on the other, with the line of their bellies drawn as a high arch,
which made Ayla think of the massive arch outside. Was the arch
supposed to represent a mammoth? Most of the animals in this
chamber seemed to be mammoths, but there were many rhinoceroses, too; one in particular captured Ayla's attention. Just
the front half was engraved and it seemed to be emerging from
a crack in the wall, emerging from the world behind the wall.
There were also a few horses, aurochs, and bison, but no felines
or deer. And while almost all of the images in the first part of the
cave were made with red paint—the red ocher from the floor and
walls—the images in this part were white, engraved with fingers
or another hard object, except for some made with black on the
right wall at the end, including a beautiful black bear nearby.

They looked interesting and she wanted to go see them, but

the Watcher led them around the left side of the large crater in the middle of the room toward another section of the cave. The left wall was hidden by a rocky mass of big blocks that she could barely make out in the light of the torches, which reminded her to knock off the excess burned ash from her torch. The light flared up and she realized that she would need to light another torch soon.

The Watcher began humming again as they approached another space defined by a much lower height. So low that someone had climbed up on the blocks and drawn a mammoth with a finger on the ceiling. On the right was the head of a bison, quickly done, followed by three mammoths, then several more drawings on rock pendants hanging from the ceiling. Ayla could see two big reindeer drawn in black and shaded to give them contours and, less detailed, a third one. On another part of the pendant, two black mammoths faced each other, but only the forequarters of the one on the left were made. The one on the right was filled in with black, and it had tusks—the only tusks she had seen on the mammoths in this cave. There were other drawings on pendants farther back, quite a distance above the floor: another mammoth engraved in left profile, a big lion, and then, surprisingly, a musk-ox identifiable by its down-curving horns.

Ayla had been so involved in trying to see the animals on the pendants in the back that it wasn't until she heard the First join in that she realized the Watcher, the First, and the Zelandoni of the Nineteenth Cave were singing to the cave again. She didn't join in this time. She could make bird and animal sounds, but she couldn't sing. But she did enjoy listening.

She welcomed him back, Her lover of old,
With heartache and sorrow, Her story She told.
Her dear friend agreed to join in the fight,
To rescue her child from his perilous plight.
    She told of Her grief. And the dark swirling thief.

The Mother was tired, She had to recover,
She loosened Her hold to Her luminous lover.

While She was sleeping, he fought the cold force,
And for a time drove it back to the source.
> *His spirit was strong. The encounter too long.*

Her fair shining friend struggled hard, gave his best,
The conflict was bitter, the struggle hard pressed.
His vigilance waned as he closed his great eye,
Then darkness crept close, stole his light from the sky.
> *Her pale friend was tiring. His light was expiring.*

When darkness was total, She woke with a cry.
The tenebrious void hid the light from the sky.
She joined in the conflict, was quick to defend,
And drove the dark shadow away from Her friend.
> *But the pale face of night. Let Her son out of sight.*

Trapped by the whirlwind, Her bright fiery son,
Gave no warmth to the Earth, cold chaos had won.
The fertile green life was now ice and snow,
And a sharp piercing wind continued to blow.
> *The Earth was bereft. No green plants were left.*

The Mother was weary, grieving and worn,
But She reached out again for the life She had borne.
She couldn't give up, She needed to strive,
For the glorious light of Her son to survive.
> *She continued the fight. To bring back the light.*

Suddenly something caught Ayla's eye, something that made her shiver, and gave her a frisson of not exactly fear, but recognition. She saw a cave bear skull, by itself, on top of the horizontal surface of a rock. She wasn't sure how the rock had found its way to the middle of the floor. There were a few other smaller rocks nearby and she assumed they had fallen from the ceiling, though none of the other rocks had a squared-off flat top surface, but she knew by what means the skull had found its place on the rock. Some human hand had put it there!

As she walked toward the rock, Ayla had sudden memories of the cave bear skull Creb had found with a bone forced through the opening formed by the eye socket and the cheek-bone. That skull had great significance to The Mog-ur of the Clan of the Cave Bear, and she wondered if any member of the Clan had ever been in this cave. This cave would certainly have held great meaning for them if they had. The Ancients who made the images in this cave were certainly people like her. The Clan didn't make images, but they could have moved a skull. And the Clan was here at the same time as the Ancient Painters. Could they have come into this cave?

As she drew closer and looked at the cave bear skull perched on the flat stone, with its two huge canine teeth extended over the edge, in her heart she believed that the Ancient who had put it there belonged to the Clan. Jondalar had seen her shake, and walked toward the center of the space. When he reached the stone, and saw the cave bear skull on the rock, he understood her reaction.

"Are you all right, Ayla?" he asked.

"This cave would have meant so much to the Clan," she said. "I can't help but think they knew about it. With their memories, maybe they still do."

The rest of them were now crowded around the stone with the skull.

"I see you have found the skull. I was going to show it to you," the Watcher said.

"Do any of the people of the Clan come here?" Ayla asked.

"The people of the Clan?" the Watcher said, shaking her head.

"The ones you call Flatheads. The other people," Ayla said.

"It's strange that you should ask," the Watcher said. "We do see Flatheads around here, but only at certain times of year, usually. They frighten the children, but we have come to a kind of understanding, if you can reach an understanding with animals. They stay away from us, and we don't bother them if all they want is to go into the cave."

"First I should tell you, they aren't animals; they are people. The cave bear is their primary totem—they call themselves the Clan of the Cave Bear," Ayla said.

"How can they call themselves anything? They don't talk," the Watcher said.

"They talk. They just don't talk the way we do. They use some words, but mostly they talk with their hands," Ayla said.

"How does one talk with hands?"

"They make gestures, motions with their hands and with their bodies," Ayla said.

"I don't understand," the Watcher said.

"I'll show you," Ayla said, handing her torch to Jondalar. "The next time you see a person of the Clan who wants to go into this cave, you could say this." Then she said the words as she made the gestures. "I would greet you, and I would tell you that you are welcome to visit this cave that is home to cave bears."

"Those motions, those hand wavings, they mean what you just said?" the Watcher asked.

"I've been teaching the Ninth Cave and our zelandonia, and anyone else who wants to learn," Ayla said, "how to make a few basic signs, so if they meet some people of the Clan when they are traveling, they can communicate, at least a little. I'll be happy to show you some signs, too, but it would probably be better if we wait until we get out of the cave where there is more light."

"I would like to see more, but how do you know so much?" the Watcher asked.

"I lived with them. They raised me. My mother, and whoever she was with—my people, I suppose—died in an earthquake. I was left alone. I wandered by myself until a clan found me and took me in. They took care of me, loved me, and I loved them back," Ayla said.

"You don't know who your people are?" the Watcher said.

"My people are the Zelandonii, now. Before that, my people were the Mamutoi, the mammoth hunters, and before that, my people were the Clan, but I don't remember the people I was born to," Ayla explained.

"I see," the Watcher said. "I would like to know more, but now we still have more of this cave to see."

"You are right," the First said. Once it came up, she had been interested in how this Zelandoni would react to the information that Ayla brought. "Let's continue."

While Ayla had been thinking about the bear skull on the

stone, the Watcher had shown the others more of the section they were in. Ayla noticed several areas as they walked on, a large scraped panel of mammoths, some horses, aurochs, and ibex.

"I should tell you, Zelandoni Who Is First," the Watcher said, "the last chamber along this axis that is going the length of the cave is rather difficult. It requires climbing up some high steps and stooping over to go through a place with a low ceiling, and there isn't much to see except some signs, a yellow horse, and some mammoths at the end. You might want to think about it before proceeding."

"Yes, I recall," the First said. "I don't need to see this last place this time. I'll let the more energetic ones go ahead."

"I'll wait with you," Willamar said. "I have seen it, too."

When the group got back together, they all started to walk along the wall that had been on the right and was now on their left. They passed the panel of scraped mammoths and finally came to the black paintings that they had only glimpsed from a distance. As they approached the first of the images, the Watcher started humming again, and the visitors could feel the cave responding.

28

The first images Ayla was drawn to were the horses, though they were by no means the first paintings on the wall. She had seen some beautiful art since she had come to know that visual representations existed, but she had never seen anything like the horse panel on this wall.

In this humid cave, the surface of the wall was soft. In this place, through chemical and bacterial agents that neither she nor the artists could begin to understand, the surface layer of the limestone had decomposed into mondmilch, a material with a soft, almost luxurious texture, and a pure white color. It could be scraped off a wall with almost anything, even a hand, and underneath was a hard white limestone, a perfect canvas for drawing. The ancients who painted these walls knew it, and knew how to use it.

There were four horse heads, painted in perspective, one on top of another, but the wall behind them had been scraped clean, which gave the artist the opportunity to show the detail, and the individual differences of each animal. The distinctive stand-up mane, the line of the jaw, the shape of the muzzle, an open or closed mouth, a flaring nostril, all were depicted with such accuracy, they seemed real.

Ayla turned to find the tall man to whom she was mated to share this moment with. "Jondalar, look at those horses! Have you ever seen anything like it? It's like they're alive."

He stood behind her and put his arms around her. "I have seen some beautiful horses painted on walls, but nothing like this. What do you think, Jonokol?"

Jonokol turned to the First. "Thank you for taking me with you on this trip. For this alone, the entire Journey would be worth it." He turned back to the painted wall. "And it's not just the horses. Look at those aurochs, and those rhinoceroses fighting."

"I don't think they are fighting," Ayla said.

"No, they do that before they share Pleasures, too," Willamar said. He looked at the First and felt they shared the same experience. Although both of them had been here before, seeing the images through Ayla's eyes was like seeing them for the first time.

The Watcher couldn't erase her smile of smug satisfaction. She didn't have to say, "I told you." This was the best part of being a Watcher. Not seeing the work herself—she had seen it many times—but seeing the way people responded to it. Most people. "Would you like to see more?"

Ayla just looked at her and smiled, but it was the loveliest smile she had ever seen. She really is a beautiful woman, the Watcher thought. I can understand Jondalar's attraction to her. If I were a man, I would be too.

Now that they had taken in the horses, Ayla could take the time to see the rest, and there was much more to see. The three aurochs to the left of the horses, mingled with the small rhinos, a deer, and below the confronting rhinos, a bison. On the right side of the horses there was an alcove, big enough for one at a time. Inside it were more horses, a bear or perhaps a big cat, an aurochs, and a bison with many legs.

"Look at that stampeding bison," Ayla said. "He's really running and breathing hard, and the lions," she added, first smiling, then laughing out loud.

"What's so funny?" Jondalar asked.

"See those two lions? That female sitting down is in heat, and the male is very interested, but she's not. He is not the one she wants to share Pleasures with, so she's sitting down and won't let him get close to her. The artist who made them was so good, you can see the disdain in her expression, and though the male is trying to look big and strong—see how he's baring his teeth?—he knows that she thinks he's not good enough for her, and is a little afraid of her," Ayla explained. "How can an artist do that? Get that look just right."

"How do you know all that?" asked the Watcher. No one had ever given that explanation before, but as Ayla spoke it seemed entirely right; they did seem to have those expressions.

"When I was teaching myself to hunt, I used to watch them," Ayla said. "I was living with the Clan then, and Clan women are not supposed to hunt, so I decided rather than hunt animals to eat, since I couldn't bring them back and they would go to waste, I'd hunt the meat-eaters that stole our food. I still got in bad trouble when they found out, though."

The Watcher had started humming again, and Jonokol was singing many notes of harmony around her tones. The First was getting ready to join in when Ayla stepped out of the alcove.

"I liked the lions best. I think that frustrated lion would sound like this," she said, then started the grunting buildup and let out a tremendous roar. It echoed off the rock of the cave all the way to the end of the passage ahead, then out toward the chamber with the bear skull.

The Watcher jumped back in shocked surprise and a little fear. "How does she do that?" She glanced at the First and Willamar with an incredulous look.

Both of them just nodded. "She still surprises us," Willamar said when Ayla and Jondalar moved on. "If you really listen, it's not as loud as it seems, but it is loud."

On the other side of the alcove was a panel of mostly reindeer, male reindeer. Even female reindeer had antlers, the only deer that did, but they were small. The six reindeer on the panel had well-developed antlers, with brow tines and a full curving backsweep. There were also a horse, a bison, and an aurochs. But she didn't think all the paintings were done by the same person. The bison was rather stiff, and the horse looked unrefined, especially after seeing the beautiful examples earlier. The person who made it was not as good an artist.

The Watcher walked to an opening at the right side that led to a narrow passageway that had to be taken single file because of the shape of the side walls and the rock pendants hanging from the ceiling. On the right side was a complete drawing in black of a megaceros, the giant deer whose defining characteristic was a hump on the withers, along with a small head and a sinuous neck. Ayla wondered why these artists showed them without antlers, since that was the defining characteristic to her, and the reason for the hump.

On the same panel, in a vertical position facing up, was the line of the back and two frontal horns of a rhinoceros, with its double arcs that represented ears. On the left side of the entrance was the shape of the head and back of two mammoths. Farther down the left wall were two more rhinos, facing in opposite directions. The one facing right was complete. It also had a broad dark stripe around its midsection as many rhinos in this cave did. Above it, the one facing left was only suggested by the line of the back and the little double-arc ears.

Even more interesting to Ayla was the line of hearths along the corridor, likely used to make the charcoal to make the drawings. The fires had blackened the walls near them. Were they the hearths of the Ancients, of the artists who created all the incredible paintings and drawings in this magnificent cave? It made them seem more real, like people, not like spirits from another world. The floor sloped down steeply and there were three abrupt drops of over three feet each along its length. The middle of the corridor had engravings made with fingers rather than black drawings. Just before the second drop in the level of the floor, there were three pubic triangles, with a vulvar cleft at the downward pointed end, on opposite sides, two on the left and one on the right.

The First was getting tired, but she knew she would never again make this trip, and even if she did, she wouldn't be able to walk the length of this cave. Jonokol and Jondalar, one on each side, had helped the First down the drops in the level of the floor, and when the floor of the corridor got especially steep. Although it was difficult going for her, Ayla noticed that she made no mention of not going on. At one point she heard the woman comment, almost to herself, that she would never see this cave again.

The amount of walking she had been doing on the Journey had made her healthier, but she was enough of a healer to know that she wasn't as well or as strong as she had been in her youth. She was determined to see this very special cave one last time in its entirety.

The last painted panel in the corridor was just before the last big drop in the floor level. On the right were four rhinoceroses that were partly painted and partly engraved. One was hard to see; two were quite small and had black bands circling their bellies, and had the typical ears. The last was much bigger but incomplete. A large male ibex, identified by the horns that swept back almost the full length of its body, was painted in black on a rock pendant that overlooked the group from its elevated position. On the left side, the wall had been scraped to prepare it for several animals: six full or partial horses, two bison and two megaceros, one of each complete, two little rhinos, and several lines and marks.

The biggest step down followed: a thirteen-foot progression of uneven terraces caused by flowing water and depressions in the fill dirt of the cave floor, with big bear nests dug into it. Jondalar, Jonokol, Willamar, and Ayla all helped the First get down. It would be just as difficult getting her up again, but they were all determined. Rock pendants hung from the ceiling, their fine, light surfaces reflecting the light from the torches, but they were not decorated. The right wall had very little art, but it did have some.

The Watcher started humming again, and the First joined her, and then Jonokol. Ayla waited. They faced the right wall first, but for no reason that Ayla could understand, it didn't resonate well. One panel had three black rhinoceroses—one complete with a black band around its middle, another that was just an outline, and a third that was just a head—three lions, a bear, the head of a bison, and a vulva. She had the feeling they were telling a story, perhaps about women, and she wished she knew what it was. They turned around and faced the left wall. Now the cave sang back.

At a quick look, the first part of the left wall seemed to be divided into three major sections. Very near the beginning of the space were three lions side by side facing right, shown in perspective by the line of the back. The biggest one farthest away was about eight feet long, painted in black and showing his scrotum so there was no doubt about his gender. The middle one was made with a red line, and also showed he was male. The one closest was smaller and female. As she looked at the drawing, Ayla wasn't sure about the middle one. There wasn't a third head, and it may have been there for perspective, and therefore it was just a lion couple. Though simple, the lines were very expressive. Above their backs, she could faintly make out three engraved mammoths made with a finger. Lions predominated in this part of the cave. To the right of the lions was a rhinoceros, and to the right of that were three more lions facing left that seemed to be staring at the other lions and two rhinos, which gave a certain balance to the panel.

All the paintings in this section were located at a level that could be reached by a person standing on the ground, except for one mammoth engraved high up on the wall. Many of the paintings were on top of bear claw markings, but there were also a few claw marks on top of them. So bears had visited after the people left.

There was a niche in the center of the next section. To the left of it were faded red lions and dots superimposed by black lions. Then a section with a rhino with multiple horns, eight in perspective, so that it appeared to be eight rhinos side by side and many more rhinos. To the right of the rhino panel was the niche, and painted inside it was a horse. Two black rhinos and a mammoth were painted above it, and impressions of animals emerging from deep in the rocks, the horse coming out of the niche, a massive bison coming from a crack, from the Other World, then mammoths, and a rhinoceros.

The section to the right of the niche had primarily two animals, lions and bison—lions hunting bison. The bison were crowded together in a herd on the left side, and the lions were straining toward them from the right, as though waiting for a signal to pounce. The lions were beautifully fierce, as she knew they should be; the Cave Lion was her totem. To Ayla, this was the most spectacular chamber in the whole cave. There was so much, she could not absorb it all, but she wanted to. The big panel ended at a ridge that formed a kind of second niche, a shallow one, with a complete black rhinoceros emerging from the world of the spirits. On the other side of the niche a bison was drawn with its head on one wall, seen full face, and its body in profile on another wall perpendicular to it, very effective.

Below the bison was a triangular cavity with two lion heads and the forequarters of another lion facing right. Above the lions was a black rhinoceros with streaks of red showing wounds and blood coming out of its mouth. Beyond that a wide rock pendant showed the place where the ceiling descended until it was perpendicular to the right wall. Three lions and another animal were painted on its internal surface, but visible from the chamber. Just before the ceiling descended, a protrusion of rock stood out and descended vertically, ending in a rounded point. It had four faces all richly decorated.

"To understand it fully, you need to see all the way around it," the Watcher said, showing Ayla the full composite figure: the forequarters of a bison on top of human legs with a large vulva between them, shaded black, with vertical engraving at the lower point. It was the bottom of a woman's body with a bison head above, and a lion around the back of the pendant. "The shape of that pendant has always looked to me like a man's organ."

"It does, doesn't it," Ayla agreed.

"There are a couple of small rooms that have some interesting paintings," the Watcher said. "If you like, I'll show you."

"Yes. I'd like to see as much as I can before we have to leave," Ayla said.

"You can see here, behind the male pendant, there are three lions. And after the bleeding rhino, there is a little corridor that leads to a beautiful horse," the Watcher said, leading her to show the way. "And here is the big bison at the end of the panel. Inside this area is a big lion, and some little horses. The area across the way is very hard to get into."

Ayla walked back toward the beginning of the chamber to

where the First was resting on a stone. The rest of the visitors were nearby.

"Well, what do you think, Ayla?" the woman asked.

"I am so glad you brought me here. I think this is the most beautiful cave I have ever seen. It's more than a cave, but I don't know a word for it. When I lived with the Clan I didn't know you could see something in real life and make something that looked like it out of something else." Ayla looked around for Jondalar, and smiled when she saw him. He came closer and stood with his arm around her, which was what she wanted. She needed to share this with him. "Then when I went to live with the Mamutoi and saw the things Ranec could make out of ivory, and others could make using leather and beads, and sometimes just a stick making marks on a smooth floor of dirt, I was amazed."

She stopped and looked down at the damp clay floor of the cave. All the people with their flickering torches were gathered together in one place. The pool of light didn't spread very far and the animals painted on the walls were just hints in the darkness, more like the fleeting glimpses that most people saw in the world outside.

"On this trip, and before, we have seen other paintings and drawings that were beautiful, and some that were not so beautiful, but remarkable just the same. I don't know how people do this, and I can't begin to know why. I think it's done to please the Mother and I'm sure it must, and maybe to tell Her story, or some other stories. Maybe people do it just because they can. Like Jonokol, he thinks of something to paint, and he can do it, so he does it. It's the same when you sing, Zelandoni. Most people can sing, more or less, but no one can sing like you. When you sing, I don't want to do anything but listen. It makes me feel good inside. That's how I feel when I look at these painted caves. It's how I feel when Jondalar looks at me with his eyes full of love. It feels like the ones who made these images are looking at me with eyes full of love."

She looked down at the floor because she was fighting back tears. She could usually control her tears, but she was having trouble this time.

"I think that's how the Mother must feel, too," Ayla finished, her eyes glistening in the flickering light.

Now I know why she's mated, the Watcher thought. She's going to be a remarkable Zelandoni; she already is, but she couldn't do it without him. Maybe that's what the Mother meant him to do. Then she started to hum. Jonokol joined her. His singing always seemed to make others' songs sound better. Then Willamar joined in just singing syllables. His voice was adequate, but it added to the music they sang together. Then Jondalar joined them. He had a good voice, but he didn't sing except when others did. Then with the voices making a background chorus that resonated inside the stone cave that was so beautifully decorated, the One Who Was First Among Those Who Served The Great Earth Mother began where she had left off with the Mother's Song.

And Her luminous friend was prepared to contest,
The thief who held captive the child of Her breast.
Together they fought for the son She adored.
Their efforts succeeded, his light was restored.
*   His energy burned. His brilliance returned.*

But the bleak frigid dark craved his bright glowing heat.
The Mother defended and would not retreat.
The whirlwind pulled hard, She refused to let go.
She fought to a draw with Her dark swirling foe.
*   She held darkness at bay. But Her son was away.*

When She fought the whirlwind and made chaos flee,
The light from Her son glowed with vitality.
When the Mother grew tired, the bleak void held sway,
And darkness returned at the end of the day.
*   She felt warmth from Her son. But neither had won.*

The Great Mother lived with the pain in Her heart,
That She and Her son were forever apart.
She ached for the child that had been denied,
So She quickened once more from the life force inside.
*   She was not reconciled. To the loss of Her child.*

When She was ready, Her waters of birth,
Brought back the green life to the cold barren Earth.
And the tears of Her loss, abundantly spilled,
Made dew drops that sparkled and rainbows that thrilled.
    Birth waters brought green. But Her tears could be seen.

With a thunderous roar Her stones split asunder,
And from the great cave that opened deep under,
She birthed once again from Her cavernous room,
And brought forth the Children of Earth from Her womb.
    From the Mother forlorn, more children were born.

Each child was different, some were large and some small,
Some could walk and some fly, some could swim and some
    crawl.
But each form was perfect, each spirit complete,
Each one was a model whose shape could repeat.
    The Mother was willing. The green earth was filling.

All the birds and the fish and the animals born,
Would not leave the Mother, this time, to mourn.
Each kind would live near the place of its birth,
And share the expanse of the Great Mother Earth.
    Close to Her they would stay. They could not run away.

They all were her children, they filled Her with pride,
But they used up the life force She carried inside.
She had enough left for a last innovation,
A child who'd remember Who made the creation.
    A child who'd respect. And learn to protect.

First Woman was born full grown and alive,
And given the Gifts she would need to survive.
Life was the First Gift, and like Mother Earth,
She woke to herself knowing life had great worth.
    First Woman defined. The first of her kind.

Next was the Gift of Perception, of learning,
The desire to know, the Gift of Discerning.

First Woman was given the knowledge within,
That would help her to live, and pass on to her kin.
   First Woman would know, how to learn, how to grow.

Her life force near gone, the Mother was spent,
To pass on Life's Spirit had been Her intent.
She caused all of Her children to create life anew,
And Woman was blessed to bring forth life, too.
   But Woman was lonely. She was the only.

The Mother remembered Her own loneliness,
The love of Her friend and his hovering caress.
With the last spark remaining, Her labor began,
To share life with Woman, She created First Man.
   Again She was giving. One more was living.

To Woman and Man the Mother gave birth,
And then for their home, She gave them the Earth,
The water, the land, and all Her creation.
To use them with care was their obligation.
   It was their home to use, but not to abuse.

For the Children of Earth the Mother provided,
The Gifts to survive, and then She decided
To give them the Gift of Pleasure and sharing,
That honors the Mother with the joy of their pairing.
   The Gifts are well earned, when honor's returned.

The Mother was pleased with the pair She created,
She taught them to love and to care when they mated.
She made them desire to join with each other,
The Gift of their Pleasures came from the Mother.
   Before She was through, Her children loved too.
   Earth's Children were blessed. The Mother could rest.

The silence was profound when they finished. Each person standing there felt the power of the Mother and the Mother's Song, more than they ever had. They looked at the paintings again and were more conscious of the animals that seemed to be emerging from the cracks and shadows of the cave, as though the Mother was creating them, giving birth to them, bringing them from the Other World, the spirit world, the Mother's Great Underworld.

Then they heard a sound that sent a chill through them, the mewling of a lion cub. It changed to the sounds a young lion made when it called for its mother, then to the first attempts of a young male lion trying to roar, and finally the huffing and grunting that led up to a full-blown roar of a male lion claiming his own.

"How does she do that?" the Watcher asked. "It sounds like a lion going through stages of growth. How does she know that?"

"She raised a lion, took care of him when he was growing up, and taught him to hunt with her," Jondalar said, "and roared with him."

"Did she tell you that?" the Watcher asked, a hint of doubt in her tone.

"Well, yes, sort of. He came back to visit her when I was healing in her valley, but he didn't like seeing me there, and attacked. Ayla stepped in front of me and he twisted himself around and stopped cold. Then she rolled around on the ground and hugged him, and got on his back and rode him, like she does Whinney. Except I don't think he would go where she wanted, only where he wanted to take her. He did bring her back, though. Then, after I asked her, she told me," Jondalar said.

His story was straightforward enough to be convincing. The Watcher just shook her head. "I think we should all light new torches," she said. "There should be at least one left for each of us, and I have some lamps, too."

"I think we should wait with the torches until we all get back out of this corridor," Willamar said.

"Yes, you're right," Jonokol said. "Will you hold mine?" he said to the Watcher.

Jonokol, Jondalar, Ayla, and Willamar literally lifted the First up some of the bigger drops, while the Watcher held up the torches to light the way. She threw one that had burned to almost nothing into one of the hearths that were lined up against the walls. When they reached the painted horses, everyone took a new torch. The Watcher stubbed out the ones that were partially burned and put them in her backframe; then they started back the way they had come. No one said much, just looked again at the animals as they passed by. Before they reached the entrance they noticed how much light found its way deeper into the cave.

At the entrance, Jonokol stopped. "Will you take me back into the large area in that other room?"

"Of course," she said without asking why. She knew.

"I'd like to go with you, Zelandoni of the Nineteenth Cave," Ayla said.

"I'm glad. I'd like you to. You can hold my torch," he said with a grin.

She was the one who found the white cave, and he was the first one she showed it to. She knew he was going to paint on those beautiful walls, although he might want some helpers. The three of them went back into the second room of the Bear Cave while the rest went out. The Watcher took them in a shorter way, and she knew where to take him, to the place where he had looked when they first went into this part of the cave. He found the secluded recess, and the ancient concretion he had seen before.

Taking out a flint knife, he went to the basin-topped stalagmite and in its base, in one accomplished movement, he carved the forehead, nose, mouth, jaw, and cheek, then two stronger lines for the mane and back of a horse. He looked at it a moment, then engraved the head of a second horse facing the opposite way on top of the first one. The stone of this one was a little harder to cut through, and the forehead line was not as precise, but he went back and cut individual hairs of a stand-up mane spaced at consistent intervals. Then he stepped back and looked.

"I wanted to add to this cave, but I wasn't sure if I should until after the First sang the Mother's Song deep in this cave," the Zelandoni of the Nineteenth Cave of the Zelandonii said.

"I told you it was the Mother's choice, and you would know. Now I know. It was appropriate," the Watcher said.

"It was the right thing to do," Ayla said. "Perhaps it is time for me to stop calling you Jonokol and start referring to you as the Zelandoni of the Nineteenth."

"Perhaps in public, but between us I hope I will always be Jonokol and you will be Ayla," he said.

"I would like that," Ayla said; then she turned to the Watcher. "In my mind I think of your name as the Watcher, as the one who watches over, but if you don't mind, I would like to know the name you were born with."

"I was called Dominica," she said, "and I will always think of you as Ayla no matter what happens, even if you become the First."

Ayla shook her head. "That is not likely. I am a foreigner with a strange accent."

"It doesn't matter," Dominica said. "We acknowledge the First, even if we don't know her or him. And I like your accent. I think it makes you stand out, as the One Who Is First should." Then she led them back out of the cave.

All that evening Ayla thought about the remarkable cave. There had been so much to see, to take in, it made her wish she could see it again. People were talking that evening about what to do with Gahaynar, and she kept finding her mind straying back to the cave. He appeared to be recovering from the severe beating he had received. Though he would carry the scars for the rest of his life, he seemed to hold no ill feelings toward the people who had done it. If anything, he seemed grateful not only to be alive, but that the zelandonia were taking care of him.

He knew what he had done, even if no one else did; Balderan and the others had died for not much worse. He didn't know why he had been spared, except that silently, while Balderan was planning how to kill the foreign woman, he had begged the Mother to save him. He knew they would never get away and he didn't want to die.

"He seems sincere in his wish to make reparations," Zelandoni First said. "Perhaps because he knows now that he can be made to pay for his actions, but it appears that the Mother has decided to spare him."

"Does anyone know to which Cave he was born?" the First asked. "Does he have relatives?"

"Yes, he has a mother," said one of the other Zelandonia. "I don't know of any other kin, but I think she's quite old and is losing her memories."

"That's the answer then," said the First. "He should be sent back to his Cave to care for his mother."

"But how is that reparations? It's his own mother," said another Zelandoni.

"It won't necessarily be easy if she continues to deteriorate, but it will relieve the Cave of having to look after her, and it will give him something worthwhile to do. I don't think it was something he planned to do as long as he was with Balderan, taking whatever he wanted without having to work for it. He should be made to work, to hunt for himself, or at least assist in communal hunts with his Cave, and to personally help his mother with whatever she needs."

"I guess that's not something a man necessarily likes to do, to take care of an old woman," the other Zelandoni said, "even his own mother."

Ayla had only been half listening, but she understood the gist of it and thought it was a good plan, and then went back to thinking about the Most Ancient Sacred Site. She finally decided that sometime in the next day or two, she would go back into the cave, alone, or perhaps with Wolf.

In the late morning the next day Ayla asked Levela if she would watch Jonayla again, and check to see how her meat was drying. She had put out another load of bison meat on the cords and thought this might be a good time to satisfy her desire to see the Most Ancient Sacred Site once more.

"I'm going to take Wolf and go back to the cave. I just want to see it again before we leave. Who knows how soon, if ever, we'll be back here again."

She packed several torches and a couple of stone lamps, along with some lichen wicks and some tied-off sections of intestine filled with fat that she put in a double-layered leather pouch. She checked her fire-making kit to make sure she had adequate materials—a firestone and flint, tinder, kindling, and some larger pieces of wood. She filled her waterbag and packed a cup for herself and a bowl for Wolf to drink from. She took her medicine bag with some extra packets of tea, although she doubted that she would make tea inside the cave, her good knife, and some warm clothes for wearing inside the cave, but she didn't bother with foot coverings. She was used to going barefoot and the soles of her feet were nearly as hard as hooves.

She whistled for Wolf and started walking up the path to the cave. When she reached the large entrance, she glanced at the sheltered corner. There was no fire burning in the fireplace and when she peeked into the sleeping structure, she saw that it was empty. The Watcher wasn't there this day. Usually she was told when people would be coming to visit the Most Ancient Sacred Site, and Ayla just decided to go without making prior arrangements.

She started a small fire in the fireplace and lit a torch, then holding it high, she started in, signaling Wolf to follow. She was aware again of how large the cave was, and of the disordered nature of the first rooms. Columns detached from the ceiling and tipped over, and huge blocks and fallen rock and rubble were scattered around the floor. The light penetrated into the cave quite a distance and she went in the way they originally had, to the left and straight ahead into the huge room with the bear wallows. Wolf stayed close to her side.

She kept to the right side of the passage, knowing that except for the large right-hand room, which she planned to visit on her way out, there would not be much to see until she was halfway into the cave. She did not plan to stay in the cave too long or to try to see everything again, just certain things. She proceeded into the chamber with the bear hollows and followed the right wall around until she came to the next room at the end of it, then looked for the thick blade-shaped rock that descended from the ceiling.

There it was as she remembered, painted in red, the leopard with the long tail and the hyena-bear. Was it a hyena or was it a bear? Yes, the shape of the head gave it the look of a cave bear, but the muzzle was longer and the tuft on the top of the head along with a bit of a mane looked like the stiff hair of a hyena. None of the other bears in this cave had that slender, long-legged shape—look at the second bear painted above it! I don't know what the artist was trying to say with this painting, she thought, but it looks to me like it is a painting of a hyena, even though it is the only hyena I have ever seen painted in any cave. But I've never seen a leopard, either. There are a bear, a hyena, and a leopard painted in this place, all strong, danger-ous animals. I wonder what the Traveling Storytellers would say about this scene?

Ayla passed by the next series of images, looking but not lingering—possible insects, a line of rhinoceroses, lions, horses, mammoths, signs, dots, handprints; she smiled at the red draw-ing of the little bear, so like the other bears in this cave, but smaller. She recalled that at this point in the cave the Watcher had turned left, then continued to follow the right wall. The next space had evidence of cave bears, and the floor was about five feet lower, which led to the next room, the one with the deep hole in the middle.

This was the room where all the drawings, or engravings, were white because the white surfaces were covered with ver-miculite. Of all the white engravings, she particularly noticed the rhinoceros emerging from a crack in the wall and stayed to look at it. Why did the Ancients paint these animals on the walls inside caves? she wondered. Why did Jonokol want to carve a drawing of two horses in that room near the entrance to this cave? His mind wasn't in any other place when he did it, like all the zelandonia who drank the tea in that Sacred Site of the Seventh Cave of the South Land Zelandonii. The art-ists probably wouldn't be capable of creating such remarkable images if they were. They had to think about what they were doing.

Did they make them for themselves or to show others? And what others? The other people of their cave or for the other zelandonia? Some of the larger rooms in certain caves could accommodate many people, and sometimes ceremonies were held in them, but many of the images were made in small caves or very cramped spaces in larger caves. They must have been made for themselves, for their own reasons. Were they looking for something in the spirit world? Perhaps a spirit animal of their own, like her lion totem, or a spirit animal that would bring them closer to the Mother? Whenever she tried to ask Zelandoni, she never got a satisfactory answer. Was that something she was supposed to find out for herself?

Wolf had been staying close, hugging the wall that Ayla was following. She carried the only light in the entire pitch-black cave; although his other senses gave him more information about his surroundings than her single torch, he liked being able to see as well.

The way that she knew she had reached the next section of the cave was the noticeable reduction in the height of the ceiling. There were more mammoths and bison and deer on the walls and pendants, some in white engraving, some in one area drawn in black. This was the room with the cave bear skull on the flat-topped rock, and Ayla walked over to see it again. She stayed awhile, thinking again of Creb and the Clan, before she continued. Banks of gray clay seemed to surround this chamber, which she climbed up to reach the last room, the one the First did not visit. She noticed traces of bear prints on the clay, which she hadn't seen the first time she was there. Two high steps brought her into the next space.

She found herself in the middle of the room; the ceiling was too low to walk along the sides. She decided it was time to light another torch, then wiped the remains of the first torch on the low ceiling to knock the fire off its small stub. Once she was certain the fire was out, she tucked what was left of the first torch into her backframe. She had to stoop in order to continue along the natural path, and at the base of a pendant she noticed a horizontal row of seven little red dots next to a series of black dots. Finally after another forty feet it was possible to stand erect again.

There were several more black torch marks; other people had evidently used this area to clean their torches. At the back the ceiling slanted down toward the floor. It was covered with a fine yellow coating of softened stone that had broken into vermiculations—little wormlike wavy lines. On this slanted

surface the simple outline of a horse had been drawn primarily
using two fingers. Because of the way the wall slanted, it was
very difficult for the artist to draw, requiring that his or her
head be bent backward the whole time, and never being able to
get an overall view while the drawing was being worked on. It
was slightly out of proportion, but it was the very last drawing
in the cave. She noticed a couple of mammoths had also been
outlined on the slanting ceiling.

Ayla detected an odor and looked around, then understood
that Wolf had passed some solid waste. She smiled. It couldn't
be helped. As she turned around to go back, she wondered if
there was a way out of the cave from here, but it was just a random thought. She wasn't going to look for it. As she walked
out closer to the wall, she felt her feet sink into the cold, soft
clay floor; Wolf followed after her, walking in the same soft
clay. After she climbed down out of this last room, the wall
that had been on her right was now on her left. She passed the
panel of scraped mammoths, then came to one of the sections
she was looking forward to seeing again—the horses painted
in black.

She studied the wall more carefully this time. She saw that
the soft brown layer had been scraped off a large section of
the wall to bring out the white limestone underneath, which
included most of the previous engraving of a rhinoceros and a
mammoth. The black coloring was charcoal, but because of the
way the artist used it, some places were darker and and some
lighter to make the horses and other animals look more lifelike.
Although the horses were what drew her, they were not the first
animals on the panel—aurochs were. And the lions inside the
niche made her smile again. That female just wasn't interested
in that young male. She was sitting down and not budging.

Ayla slowly walked the length of the painted wall until she
came to the entrance of the long gallery that led to the last
room of paintings, and saw the giant deer painted high up on
the right. This was also where the hearths to make charcoal
were lined up along the wall. The walkway started dropping
down. When she made the last big drop and came to the last
room, she walked even more slowly. She loved the lions, perhaps because they were her totem, but they were so real. She

reached the end and examined the final pendant, the one that looked like a male organ. It had a female vulva painted on it, with human legs, and was part bison and part lion. She felt sure someone had been telling a story there, too. Finally, she turned around and started back and when she reached the beginning of the chamber, she stopped and looked around.

She wanted to leave with a memory, the way the First sang to the cave. She couldn't sing, but she smiled when she thought of something she could do. She could roar like she did the first time she was here. Like lions often did, she began the *hunka-hunka* buildup to her roar. When she finally let it out, it was the best roar she could make; it even made Wolf cringe a little.

They had planned to get off to an early start, but Amelana started into labor early in the morning, so of course, the visiting Zelandonia couldn't leave. Amelana had a healthy baby boy by evening, and her mother provided a celebratory meal afterward. They didn't start off on their return trip until the following morning, and by then the leave-taking was rather anticlimactic.

The composition of the travelers had changed again. With Kimeran, Beladora, and the two children gone, and Amelana no longer traveling with them, there were only eleven left and they had to organize themselves differently. With only Jonlevan to play with, who was a year younger, Jonayla missed her friends. Jondecam felt the loss of Kimeran, his uncle who was more brother, and didn't realize how much they had understood each other when they worked together. It saddened him to think he might never see him again. The only women were Ayla, Levela, and the First and they felt the loss of Beladora, and the young antics of Amelana. It took a while to settle into a traveling routine again.

They followed the river downstream, and when it joined the larger river, continued to follow it as it made its way south. They could see the large expanse of the Southern Sea a full day before they reached it, but the panorama offered a glimpse of more than a vast stretch of water. They saw herds of reindeer and megaceroses, a matriarchal crowd of woolly mammoths along with their young of every age, and a collection of woolly rhinoceroses. There were also the beginnings of a coming together of various ungulates like aurochs and bisons in preparation for the fall, when throngs in the thousands would gather for the fighting and mating. Horses were moving toward their winter grazing grounds. There was a cool breeze blowing in from the sea; the Southern Sea was a cold sea, and looking out over the expanse of cold water made Ayla realize the season would be turning soon.

They found the traders Conardi had spoken of, and Conardi himself. He made the introductions, and it turned out that Ayla's baskets were a desirable item. For people who traveled with things, which traders did, well-made containers were a necessity. Ayla spent the first evening they were camped there making more baskets. Jondalar's flint points and tools were also well liked. Willamar's skill and experience as a trader came to the fore. He organized all of them into a trading bloc and included Conardi in it.

He would offer combinations of things, often to more than one person, like a supply of dry meat and a basket to carry it in. He acquired many shells for beads, and was grateful to have some of Ayla's baskets in which to hold them. He also got salt for Ayla and a necklace for Marthona made by one of the shell collectors, and some other things that he wasn't telling everyone about.

Once they were done with their trading, they began the return trip. They traveled faster than their initial journey. For one thing, they knew the way, and they weren't stopping to visit or to see painted caves. And the changing weather was pushing them. They were well stocked with provisions, so they didn't have to hunt as often. They did go to visit Camora again. She was very disappointed to learn that Kimeran had changed his plans and was staying with his mate's people. She and Jondecam were talking about him as though he were gone for good until the First reminded them that he did plan to return.

They had to wait again when they reached Big River because a storm had made the crossing too difficult until it settled down again. It was an anxious time because they didn't want to be stranded on the wrong side of the river for the season. Finally it cleared up and they made the crossing, although it was still rough. Once they reached The River they could hardly wait. They had to walk upstream because there were no rafts, and it would have been too strenuous to try to paddle upstream in any case.

When they finally spied the huge stone shelter that was the Ninth Cave, they were ready to break into a run, but they didn't have to. Lookouts had been posted to watch for them, and a signal fire was lit when they were spotted. Nearly the entire community of Caves turned out to meet them and welcome them back home.

Part Three

29

Ayla climbed the steep path to the top of the cliff. She carried a load of wood in a carrier that hung from a tumpline across her forehead and set it down near the battered column of basalt that seemed to grow at a precarious angle out of the edge of the limestone cliff. She stopped to gaze at the whole panorama. As often as she had seen it this past year that she had been marking the risings and settings of the moon and sun, the expansive view never failed to move her. She watched The River below flow in sinuous curves from north to south. Darkening clouds hugged the crests of the hills across The River to the east, obscuring their sharp outline. They would likely become more clear near dawn tomorrow, when she needed to see where the sun rose to compare it with the day before.

She turned the other way. The sun, blindingly brilliant, was on its downward path; it would soon be sunset and the bottoms of the few white fluffy clouds were tinged with pink, promising a grand show. Her eyes continued their movement to the horizon. She was almost sorry to see that the view toward the west was clear. She would have no excuse to avoid coming up tonight, she thought, as she headed back down to the Ninth Cave.

When she reached her dwelling under the sheltering limestone overhang, it was cold and empty. Jondalar and Jonayla must have gone to Proleva's for their meal tonight, Ayla thought, or maybe Marthona's. She was tempted to go look for them, but what was the use if she had to go out anyway?

She found tinder, flint, and a firestone near the cold hearth and started a fire. When it was well established, she added some cooking stones to it, then checked the waterbag and was glad to find it full. She poured some water into a wooden cooking bowl for tea. She searched around the hearth area and found some cold soup in a tightly woven basket that had been coated with river clay to make the cooking and storage pot even more watertight, something most of the women had started doing only within the last few years. With a ladle carved out of an ibex horn, she scooped up some of the contents from the bottom, and with her fingers picked out a few bites of cold meat and a rather soggy root of some kind, then moved the pot closer to the fire, and with bentwood tongs pushed some hot coals around it.

She added a few more sticks of wood to the fire, then sat down cross-legged on a low cushion while she waited for the stones to heat so she could bring the tea water to a boil, and closed her eyes. She was tired. The past year had been particularly difficult for her because she had to be awake during the night so much. She almost drifted off to sleep sitting up, but jerked awake when her head bobbed down.

With her fingers, she flicked a few drops of water on the cooking stones, watched them disappear with a hiss and a wisp of vapor, then using the bentwood tongs with the charred ends she picked up a cooking stone from the fire and dropped it into the bowl of water. The water roiled and sent up a cloud of steam. She added a second stone and when the water calmed down, she dipped her little finger in to test the heat. It was hot, but not as hot as she wanted. She added a third stone from the fire and waited for it to settle, then scooped out a large cupful of steaming water and dropped in a few pinches of dried leaves from a row of covered baskets on a shelf near the hearth and set down the tightly woven cup to wait for the tea to steep.

She checked a pouch that was dangling from a peg pounded into a support post. It held two small, flat sections of a megaceros antler and a flint burin that she had been using to gouge marks on the flat pieces cut out of the giant deer horn. She checked the tool to see if its chisel-like end was still sharp; with use, pieces spalled off. For a handle, the opposite end had been inserted into a section of antler from a roe deer that had been softened in boiling water. It hardened again when it dried. On one piece of flat antler she had been keeping a record of the sun's and moon's settings. On the second, she made tally marks to show the number of days from one full moon to the next—with the full moon, the absence of the moon, and the opposite-facing half disks indicated among the tally marks. She tied the pouch to her waist thong; then she ladled some warm soup into a wooden bowl and drank it down, stopping only to chew the pieces of meat.

From her sleeping room, she got her fur-lined cloak with the hood and wrapped it around her shoulders—it was cold at night even in summer—picked up the cup of hot tea, and left her dwelling. She again went toward the rising path at the back of the abri, just beyond the edge of the overhang, and started up, wondering where Wolf was. He was often her only companion on her long nightly vigils, lying on the ground at her feet as she sat on the top of the cliff bundled up in warm clothes.

When she came to the fork in the trail, she took a quick sip of tea, then put the cup down and hurried around to the trenches. Though they were moved to a slightly different place every year or so, they were always in the same general area. She quickly relieved herself, then hurried back to the path, picked up her cup, and followed the other fork, the steep narrow path that led up to the top of the cliff.

Not far from the strange leaning stone embedded deep into the top of the cliff face was the black circular lens of a charcoal-filled fireplace within a ring of stones, and a few smooth river rocks that made good cooking stones. Next to a natural outcrop of rock, a depression had been carved out of the frangible limestone beside the column. A large panel of dried grass woven so that rain ran off the overlapping rows was leaning against the stone. Under it were a couple of bowls, including a cooking bowl, and a leather pouch that held some odds and ends such as a flint knife, a couple of packets of tea, and some dried meat. Beside it was a rolled-up fur and inside that a rawhide packet containing fire-making materials, a crude stone lamp and a few wicks, and some torches.

Ayla put the packet aside; she would not light a fire until after the moon rose. She spread out the fur and settled herself down in her accustomed place, using the outcrop as a backrest, with her back to The River to watch the horizon to the west. She took the antler plaques and flint burin from the pouch, and looked closely at the record of the setting sun she had made so far, then back at the top edge of the western landscape.

Last night it set just to the left of that small rise, she said to herself, squinting her eyes to keep out the long, bright rays of the sun. The glowing hot light slipped behind a dusty haze near the ground, masking the searing incandescence to a glowing red disk. It was as perfectly round as its nighttime companion when it was full. Both celestial orbs were precisely circular, the only perfect circles in her environment. With the haze, the sun was easier to see, and it was easier to place its precise setting in relation to the silhouetted hilly line of the horizon in the distance. In the dimming light, Ayla gouged out a mark on her antler plaque.

Then she turned to face east, across The River. The first stars had made their appearance in the darkening sky. The moon would soon show his face, she knew, though sometimes it rose before the sun set, and sometimes it showed a paler face against a clear blue sky during the day. She had been watching the sun and moon rise and set for nearly a year, and while she hated the separation from Jondalar and Jonayla that her watch of the heavenly bodies had necessitated, she had been fascinated by the knowledge she had gained. Tonight, though, she felt unsettled. She wanted to go to her dwelling, crawl into her furs with Jondalar, and have him hold her, touch her, and make her feel as only he could. She stood up and sat back down, trying to find a more comfortable position, trying to prepare herself for her long, lonely night.

To pass the time and help keep herself awake, she concentrated on repeating in a low tone some of the many songs, and long histories and legends, often in rhyme, that she was committing to memory. Though she had an excellent memory, there was a lot of information she had to learn. She had no voice for melody and didn't try to sing them as many of the zelandonia did, but Zelandoni had told her singing wasn't necessary, so long as she knew the words and the meaning of them. The wolf seemed to enjoy the sound of her soft voice droning in metric monotony as he dozed beside her, but not even Wolf was with her tonight.

She decided to recite one of the Histories, a story that told about the before times, a story that was particularly difficult for her. It was an early reference to the ones the Zelandonii called Flatheads, the ones she thought of as her Clan, but her mind kept drifting away. The story was full of names that held no familiarity, events that had no meaning for her, and concepts that she didn't quite understand, or perhaps, with which she didn't agree. She kept thinking of her own memories, her own history, her early life with the Clan. Maybe she ought to switch to a legend. They were easier. They often told stories that were funny or sad, that explained or exemplified customs and behaviors.

She heard a faint sound, a panting breath, and turned to see Wolf coming up the path to join her. He bounded toward her, obviously happy to see her. She felt the same. "Hello, Wolf," she said, roughing up the thick fur around his neck and smiling as she held his head and looked into his eyes. "I'm so glad to see you. I'm in the mood for company tonight." He licked her face, then tenderly took her jaw in his teeth. When he let go, she gently held his furry muzzle in her teeth for a moment. "I think you are glad to see me, too. Jondalar and Jonayla must be back, and she is probably sleeping. It relieves my mind to know you are looking after her, Wolf, when I can't be there."

The wolf settled at her feet; she wrapped the cloak tightly around her, sat back down to wait for the moon to rise, and tried to concentrate on a legend about one of the Zelandonii ancestors, but instead she recalled the time that she nearly lost Wolf on their Journey. They were making a perilous crossing of a flooded river and had become separated from him. She remembered searching for him, cold and wet and nearly out of her mind with the fear that she had lost him. She felt again the sinking dread when she finally found him unconscious, afraid he was dead. Jondalar had found them both, and though he was cold and wet, too, he had done everything. She was so cold and exhausted, she was useless. He had put up the shelter, carried her and the half-drowned wolf inside, saw to the horses, took care of them all.

She wrenched her mind back to the present, feeling a need for Jondalar. Maybe the counting words, she thought. She started to say them, "One, two, three, four," and remembered how delighted she had been the first time Jondalar had explained them to her. She had understood the abstract concept immediately, counting things she could see in her cave: she had one sleeping place; one, two horses; one, two . . . Jondalar's eyes are so blue.

I must stop this, she thought. Ayla stood up and walked toward the columnar stone that seemed balanced so precariously close to the edge. Yet last summer when several men had tried to push it over, thinking it might pose a danger, they couldn't budge it. It was the stone that she had seen from below on the day she and Jondalar first arrived, she remembered, the one that made a distinctive outline against the sky. She vaguely recalled seeing it before in a dream.

She reached out and put her hand on the large stone near the base, and suddenly snatched it away. Her fingertips seemed to tingle where she had touched the stone. When she looked at it again, in the dim light of the moon, it felt as though the stone had moved slightly, leaned closer to the edge, and was it glowing? She backed away, staring at the peculiar stone. I must be imagining it, she thought. She shut her eyes and shook her head. When she opened them, the stone looked like any other stone. She reached out to touch it again. It felt like rock, but as she held her hand on the rough stone, she thought she felt a tingling again.

"Wolf, I think this is one night the sky can do without me," she said. "I'm starting to see things that aren't there. And look! The moon is already up, and I missed its rising. I'm not doing any good out here tonight anyway."

She thought about lighting a torch, but decided against taking the time to make a fire—the moon was bright enough. She picked her way carefully down the path by the light of the moon and stars with Wolf leading the way. She glanced back once more at the rock. It still seems to glow, she thought. Maybe I've been looking at the sun too much. Zelandoni did warn me to be careful.

It was much darker inside, but she could see by the reflection from the roof of the abri of a large communal fire that had been lit earlier in the evening and was still burning. Ayla entered her dwelling quietly. Everyone seemed to be sleeping, but a small lamp gave off a dim light. They often lit one for Jonayla. It took her longer to fall asleep when it was pitch dark. The lichen wick soaking in the melted fat burned for quite a while, and it had often served Ayla well when she came home late at night. She looked beyond the partition into the room where Jondalar was sleeping. Jonayla had crept in beside him again. She smiled at them, and started toward Jonayla's bed, not wanting to disturb them. Then she stopped and shaking her head, went to their bed.

"Is that you, Ayla?" Jondalar said sleepily. "Is it morning already?"

"No, Jondalar. I came in early tonight," she said as she picked up the towheaded child and put her in her own bed. She tucked her in and gave her a kiss on the cheek, then she went back to the bed she shared with Jondalar. When she got there, Jondalar was awake, propped up on one elbow.

"Why did you decide to come in early?"

"I couldn't seem to concentrate." She smiled at him sensuously, and removed her clothes, then crawled in beside him. The place was still warm from her sleeping daughter. "Do you remember that you once told me that anytime I wanted you, all I had to do was this?" she said as she gave him a long loving kiss.

He was quick to respond. "It's still true," he said, his voice gruff with his quickened desire. The nights had been long and lonely for him, too. Jonayla was cute and cuddly, and he loved her, but she was a little girl, and his mate's daughter, not his mate. Not the woman who aroused his passion and, until recently, had satisfied it so well.

He reached for her hungrily, kissing her mouth and her neck and then her body with starved ardor. She was equally hungry, equally ardent, and reached for his body in almost desperate need. He kissed her again, slowly, felt the inside of her mouth with his tongue, then her neck, and reached for her breast with his hand, then took the nipple into his mouth. She felt delicious jolts of pleasure race through her. It had been a long time since they had taken the time to explore the Mother's Gift of Pleasure.

He suckled one nipple, then the other, and caressed her breasts. She felt sensations that reached deep inside in the place that ached for him. He placed a hand on her stomach and massaged it gently. There was a softness to it that he liked, a slight roundness that made her seem even more womanly, if that was possible. She felt as though she were melting into a pool of delight, as his hand reached for the soft fur of her mound and then put a finger at the top of her slit, and began to draw circles inside. When he reached the spot that sent bolts of shudders through her, she moaned and arched into them.

He went lower, found the entrance to her warm, wet cave and reached inside. She spread her legs to give him more access. He got up and moved between them, then lowered himself and tasted her. That was the taste he knew, the taste of Ayla that he loved. With both hands he spread her petals wide and licked her with his warm tongue, explored her clefts and crevices until he found the nodule that had hardened a little. She felt each movement as a delicious flash of fire as the desire inside her grew. She was no longer conscious of anything except Jondalar and the mounting surge of exquisite Pleasure he made her feel.

His manhood had swelled to its fullness and strove for release. Her breathing quickened, each breath coming with a groan, until suddenly she reached a peak, and felt herself well up and overflow. He felt her warm wetness, then pulled back and entered her welcoming depths and plunged in deeply. She was ready for him, and arched to take him in. As he felt his member slide into her warm and welcoming well, he groaned with the Pleasure. It had been so long, or so it seemed.

She took him all, and as he felt her encompassing warmth, he felt a sudden gratefulness that the Mother had led him to her, that he had found this woman. He had almost forgotten how perfectly they fit together. He reveled in her as he plunged in again, and then again. She gave herself up to him, rejoiced in the sensations he made her feel. Suddenly, almost too soon, they felt the Pleasure mounting. It surged up, until with a volcanic release, it engulfed them. They held it and then let go.

Afterward, they rested, but their ravenous craving for each other was not quite satisfied. They loved again, languorously, drawing out each touch, each caress, until they could no longer resist and finished with a second burst of eager energy. Ayla could see a faint crack of morning light through a carelessly secured covering when she settled into the warm furs beside Jondalar to sleep. She was more than satisfied—she felt luxuriously satiated.

She looked at Jondalar. His eyes were closed, a relaxed and blissful smile on his face. She closed her eyes. Why had she waited so long? she thought. She tried to think how long it had been. Suddenly her eyes flew open. Her herbs! When was the last time she took her herbs? She hadn't had to worry about them when she was nursing—she knew it was unlikely that she would get pregnant then—but Jonayla had been weaned for several years. Making a tea of her contraceptive herbs was usually a habit, but she hadn't been as careful lately. She had forgotten them a few times before but she was convinced no new life could begin without a man, and since she had been spending her nights on the cliff, she hadn't shared Pleasures with Jondalar as often, so she wasn't concerned.

As an acolyte in training, her apprenticeship had been demanding, requiring periods of fasting, sleep deprivation, and other restrictions on her activities, including that she refrain from Pleasures for a period of time. For nearly a year, she had been staying awake at night to observe the movements of celestial objects. But her rigorous training was almost over. The year of studying the night sky would be finished soon, at the coming Summer Longday; then she would be considered for acceptance as a full acolyte. She was already skilled in healing or it would have taken much longer, although she would never stop learning.

Anytime after that, she could become Zelandoni, though she wasn't sure how. She had to be "called" to it, a mysterious process that no one could explain but that every Zelandoni had experienced. When an acolyte claimed a "calling," the potential Donier went through a probing interrogation by the other Zelandonia, who would then accept or reject the claim. If it was accepted, a place would be found for the new One To Serve The Mother, customarily as an assistant to an existing Zelandoni. If it was rejected, the acolyte would stay an acolyte, but an explanation was usually given so the next time a "calling" was felt it would be better understood. Some acolytes never reached the position of Zelandoni, and were happy with that, but most wanted to be called.

Before she fell asleep, she mused about the Pleasures. She was the only one who was convinced that they started new life growing inside a woman. If she was pregnant, it was likely she would be too busy with a new baby to think about any "calling." Well, time will tell, what's done is done; there's no point in worrying about whether or not I'm pregnant now. And would it really be so bad to have another child? A baby might be rather nice, Ayla thought. She closed her eyes and relaxed again, then drifted off to a contented sleep.

It was one of the children who first noticed the smoking signal fire from the Third Cave, and pointed it out to his mother. She showed it to her neighbor and both started toward Joharran's dwelling. Before they reached it, several others had seen it as well. Proleva and Ayla were just coming out as the crowd arrived. They looked up, rather surprised.

"Smoke from Two Rivers Rock," one said.

"Signal from the Third," said another at the same time.

Joharran was right behind his mate. He walked to the edge of the stone ledge. "They'll be sending a runner," he said.

The runner arrived not long after, somewhat out of breath. "Visitors!" he said. "From the Twenty-fourth Cave of the Southern Zelandonii, including their primary Zelandoni. They are going to our Summer Meeting, but wanted to visit some Caves along the way."

"They've come a long distance," Joharran said. "They will need a place to stay."

"I'll go tell the First," Ayla said. But I won't be going with everyone this year, she thought, as she started toward Zelandoni's dwelling. I have to wait for the Summer Longday. She felt a little sorry, and thought, I hope the visitors won't leave the Meeting too soon, but if they have come from very far, they might have to leave early to get back home before winter. That would be too bad.

"I'll check the large gathering area at the other end," Proleva said. "That will be a good place for them to stay, but they'll need water and firewood, at least. How many are there?"

"Perhaps as many as a small Cave," the runner said.

That could be as many as thirty, or more, Ayla thought, mentally using the special techniques she had learned in her training to count larger numbers. Counting with fingers and hands was more complicated than the simple counting words, if one understood how to do it, but as with most things associated with the zelandonia, it was even more complex than that. It could mean something entirely different. All signs had more than just one meaning.

After she told the First, Ayla followed Proleva to the other end of the large overhanging ledge, bringing some additional wood. Acquiring and supplying fuel for fire was a chore that required constant attention and effort. Everyone, including children, gathered anything that would burn: wood, brush, grasses, the dry dung of grazing animals, and the fat of any animal they hunted, including the random carnivore. In order to live in cold environments, fire was indispensable for both heat and light, not to mention using it to cook food to make it easier to chew and more digestible. Although some fat was used in cooking, most often it was used for the fire that provided light. Maintaining fire was demanding, but it was essential to maintain the life of the two-legged tropical omnivores who had evolved in warmer climes and walked their way around the world.

"There you are, Ayla! I thought we'd give the visitors the place next to the spring-fed creek that separates the Ninth Cave from Down River, but I've been wondering about the horses. Their place is so close to the area the visitors would be using, do you think they should be moved?" Proleva said. "The visitors might find it disconcerting to have horses so close."

"I was thinking the same thing, not only because of the visitors. The horses would not be happy to have so many strangers

close by. I think I'll move them to Wood Valley for now," Ayla
said.

"That would be a good place for them," Proleva said.

After the visitors arrived, were introduced, settled into their
temporary living space, and had eaten, the people broke into
several groups. An assemblage of the zelandonia, which included the First and Ayla, the Zelandoni of the visitors plus
her acolytes, the Zelandonia of the Third, the Fourteenth, and
the Eleventh Caves, plus a few others walked back to the gathering space at the other end of the huge abri. A fire had been
built and banked before the group of travelers left to eat, and
was stoked up again by one of them, who put water into a large
container and cooking stones into the fire. People brought out
their personal drinking cups in anticipation of a fresh cup of
hot tea, and conversations started or continued.

The visitors talked about their travels and they all exchanged
ideas about rituals and medicine. When the First mentioned the
contraceptive drink, there was great interest. Ayla told them
what herbs to use, in some cases describing them carefully so
there would be no confusion with similar plants. She talked a
little about her long Journey from the land of the mammoth
hunters, and they understood that she was a foreigner from a
long distance. Her accent wasn't quite as strange to the visitors
because they also spoke with an accent, although they thought
it was the northern Zelandonii who did. Ayla thought their way
of speaking was similar to, but not the same as, the way the
people they had met on her Donier Tour spoke, and the way
Kimeran's mate Beladora had said certain words.

When the evening was drawing to a close, the Zelandoni of
the visitors said, "I have been pleased to get better acquainted,
Ayla. Word of you has traveled even to our region, and I think
we are probably the most distant Cave who still call themselves
the Children of Doni. And who recognize the First Among
Those Who Serve The Mother," she added, addressing the large
woman.

"I suspect that you are counted as First among your group of
Southern Zelandonii. I am too far away."

"Perhaps I am, in our local territory, but we still acknowledge this region as our original homeland, and you as the First.

It is in our Histories, our Legends, our teachings. That's one reason we wanted to come, to reestablish our ties."

And to decide if you wanted to keep them, the First thought. She had noticed some facial expressions among some of the visitors that were, if not disdainful, then at least doubtful, and had overheard some quiet conversation in what was probably a local southern dialect questioning some of the northern zelandonia ways, especially from one young man. He very likely believed that no one there could understand the variation of Zelandonii they were speaking—few people they had met did—but the First had traveled quite a bit in her younger years, and more recently with Ayla, and she had welcomed many visitors from distant places. She was fairly adept at picking up languages, especially variations of Zelandonii. She glanced at Ayla, whom she knew had an almost uncanny knack for language, and could grasp even a strange one more quickly than anyone she knew.

Ayla caught the glance from her mentor, and the flick of her eyes toward the young man, and nodded slightly in an unobtrusive way, letting her know that she had also understood him. They would discuss it later.

"And I am pleased to know you," Ayla said. "Perhaps someday we can visit you."

"You would be welcome, both of you," the Zelandoni said, looking at the First.

The big woman smiled, but wondered how much longer she'd be able to make Journeys, especially long ones, and doubted that she would be the one to make a return visit. "You have brought some interesting new ideas that I am pleased to learn about, and I thank you for them," the large woman said.

"I have been very pleased to learn of your medicines," Ayla added.

"I have learned much, as well. I am especially grateful to know about the way to dissuade the Mother from Blessing a woman. There are those women who just should not bear another child, for her health and the sake of her family," the Zelandoni said.

"It was Ayla who brought that knowledge," the First admitted.

"Then I have something I would like to give to her in return, and to you, First Among Those Who Serve The Mother. I have a mixture that has some remarkable qualities. I think I will leave it with you to try out," the Southern Twenty-fourth said. "I hadn't planned to, I have only one pouch of it with me, but I can make up more when I get back."

She opened her traveling pack, took out her distinctive medicine box and removed a small pouch from it. She held it out. "I think you will find this quite interesting and perhaps useful." The First indicated that she should give it to Ayla. "It's very powerful. Be careful when you experiment with it," she said as she handed it to the younger woman.

"Do you prepare it as a decoction or infusion?" Ayla asked.

"It depends what you want," the woman said. "Each preparation gives it different properties. Later I'll show you what's in it, though I suspect you will have worked it out yourself by then."

Ayla couldn't wait to find out what was in it. She examined the pouch. It was made of soft leather and tied with a cord that she thought was made from the long hairs of the tail of a horse. She undid some interesting knots in the cord, which had been threaded through holes cut around the top of the soft leather pouch, and opened it. "One ingredient is certain," she said as she sniffed the contents. "Mint!" The scent also reminded her of the strong tea they had tried when they were visiting another one of the Southern Zelandonii. Ayla retied it with her own knots.

The woman smiled. Mint was the scent she used to distinguish this particular mixture, but it was far more powerful than that innocuous herb. She hoped she would still be here when someone began to experiment with it. That would be a test of the skill and knowledge of the northern zelandonia, she thought.

Ayla smiled at Zelandoni. "I may have another one on the way." They had been talking about children, though it was the First who had brought it up, she realized.

"I wondered about that. You didn't look like you were getting fat, like me—I doubt that you ever will—but you seem to be filling out in places. How many moontimes have you missed?"

"Just one. My moontime was due a few days ago. And though I'm not really getting sick, I feel a little nauseous in the morning sometimes," Ayla said.

"If I were to make a guess, I'd say you are going to have another baby. Are you happy about it?" Zelandoni asked.

"Oh, yes. I want another, although I hardly have time to take care of the one I have. I'm just glad Jondalar is so good with Jonayla."

"Have you told him yet?"

"No. It's too soon, I think. You never know—things can happen. I know he would like another child at his hearth. I wouldn't want him to get excited only to be disappointed. And it's a long enough wait even after you start showing—no reason to make him wait so long." Ayla thought about the night she came down from the cliff early, and how good it had been for both of them. Then she recalled the first time she had shared Pleasures with Jondalar. She laughed quietly, to herself.

"What's funny?" Zelandoni asked.

"I was just thinking about the first time Jondalar showed me the Gift of Pleasure, back in my valley. Until then, I didn't know it was supposed to be a Pleasure, or even that it could be. I could hardly communicate with him then. He had been teaching me to speak Zelandonii, but so much of his language, and most of his ways, were completely strange to me. As a mother was supposed to, Iza had explained how a woman of the Clan uses a certain signal to encourage a man, though I don't think she thought I'd ever really need it.

"I'd been making the signal to Jondalar, but it didn't mean anything to him. Later he showed me Pleasures again, because he wanted to, not because I did, and I kept thinking he would never understand my signals, when I wanted him again. I finally asked to speak to him the way the women of the Clan do. He didn't understand what I wanted when I sat down in front of him and bowed my head, waiting for him to tell me I could speak. Finally I just tried to tell him. When he understood the gist of it, he thought I wanted him to do it right away, and we had just finished. He said something like he didn't know if he could, but he would try. As it turned out, he didn't have any problem," Ayla said, smiling at her own innocence.

Zelandoni smiled, too. "He always was an obliging fellow," she said.

"I loved him the first time I saw him, before I even knew him, but he was so good to me, Zelandoni, especially when he showed me the Mother's Gift of Pleasures. I asked him once how he could know things about me that I didn't know about myself. He finally admitted that someone had taught him, an older woman, but I could tell he was greatly troubled. He really loved you, you know," Ayla said. "He still does, in his way."

"I loved him, too, and I still do, in my way. But I don't think he ever loved me the way he loves you."

"But I've been gone so much, especially at night. I'm surprised that I'm pregnant."

"Maybe you are wrong about his essence mixing with yours inside you, Ayla. Maybe new life is started by the Great Mother choosing a man's spirit and blending it with yours," Zelandoni said, with a wry smile.

"No. I think I know when this one was started." Ayla smiled. "I came home early one night, I just couldn't concentrate, and I forgot to make my special tea. Now I'm starting to love rain, especially at night, when I have to come in because I can't see anything anyway. I'll be glad when this watching year is over." The young woman studied her mentor, then asked the question she had wanted to ask. "You said you had thought about mating. Why didn't you?"

"Yes, I almost did mate once, but he was killed in a hunting accident. After he died, I buried myself in the training. No one else ever made me want to mate . . . except Jondalar. There was a time when I did consider him—he was so insistent, and he can be very persuasive—but you know it was forbidden. I was his donii-woman and, besides, he was so young. We would probably have had to move away from the Ninth Cave, and it might have been hard to find a place. I felt that it would be unfair to him; his family has always been important to him. It was hard enough for him to go to live with Dalanar," the Donier said. "And I didn't want to leave, either. Did you know I was selected for the zelandonia and started my training before I was a woman? I'm not sure when I finally realized that the

"If the things aren't all that much, why can't they carry them themselves?" Jonayla asked.

"That's just the point. They're not always so little. It's usually the bulky and the heavy things they want carried, things they probably wouldn't even take if they had to carry them by themselves," Jondalar said.

The next morning, Ayla accompanied the Ninth Cave part of the way, riding Whinney. "When do you think you'll be able to join us?" Jondalar asked.

"Sometime after the Summer Longday, but I'm not sure how long," Ayla said. "I am a little worried about Marthona. It may depend on how she feels, and who has come back to help her. When do you think Willamar will return?"

"It depends on where people have decided to hold their Summer Meetings. He hasn't made many long trips since your Donier Tour but he planned a longer than usual trip this year. He said he wanted to visit as many people as he could, both outlying Zelandonii and others. Several people went with him, and he was going to pick up a few more from other Caves along the way. This may be his last long trading circuit," Jondalar said.

"I thought that's what he said when he came along on my Donier Tour," Ayla said.

"He's been saying that every year for some time."

"I think he's finally going to name a new Trade Master, and he can't decide which one of his apprentices to choose. He's going to be observing them on this trip," Jondalar said.

"I think he should name both of them."

"I'll try to come back for a visit, but I'm going to be busy. I need to make arrangements to enlarge our place so Marthona and Willamar can move in with us in the fall."

Ayla turned to her daughter, and they embraced. "Be good, Jonayla. Mind Jondalar, and help Proleva," she said.

"I will, mother. I wish you were coming with us."

"I wish I were, too, Jonayla. I'm going to miss you," Ayla said.

She and Jondalar kissed, and she clung to him for a moment. "I'll miss you, too, Jondalar. I will even miss Racer and Gray." She gave each horse farewell strokes and a hug around the neck. "And I'm sure Whinney will, and Wolf, too."

Jonayla patted Whinney and scratched a favorite place, then bent down and gave Wolf a big hug. The animal wriggled with pleasure, and licked her face. "Can't we take Wolf with us, mother? I'm going to miss him so much," Jonayla asked, trying one last time.

"Then I would miss him, Jonayla. No, I think it's best if he stays here. You'll see him later in the summer," Ayla said.

Jondalar picked up Jonayla and put her on Gray. She could count six years now, and could mount the horse herself, if there was a stone or a stump nearby, but she still needed help out in the open. Jondalar mounted Racer, and taking Gray's lead rope, they quickly caught up with the rest. Ayla could not stop the tears as she stood with Whinney and Wolf watching Jondalar and Jonayla riding away from her.

Finally Ayla leaped up on the back of her dun-yellow mare. She rode partway, back toward home, then stopped and turned to look again at the departing Ninth Cave. They were moving along at a steady pace, strung out in a ragged line. At the rear she saw Jonayla and Jondalar on their horses, pulling the pole-drags.

The Summer Meeting was being held at the same place it had been held when Ayla first came. She had liked that location and hoped that Joharran would select the same site that the Ninth Cave had used for their camp when they were there before, if no one else had taken it. Joharran had always liked being in the thick of things, and the campsite was somewhat away from the major activities, but in the past few years, he had begun to select campsites that were closer to the edge so the horses wouldn't be surrounded by people. And he was learning to like having the space to spread out. If he chose the old campsite, there was plenty of room for their much larger than usual Cave to spread out, and a good place for the horses as well. And she could close her eyes and imagine them there. Ayla watched the people leaving for some time, then turned Whinney, signaled Wolf, and went back to the Ninth Cave.

Ayla hadn't known how lonely the huge abri could be with so many people gone, even though some people from the nearby

Caves had come to stay there. Most of the dwellings were closed up, and the abri had a deserted look. Tools and equipment from the large work area had been dismantled and taken along or put away, leaving empty spaces. Marthona's loom was one of the few remaining pieces of apparatus.

Ayla had asked Marthona to move in with them. She wanted to be nearby if Jondalar's mother needed help, especially at night, and the woman was quick to agree. Since she and Willamar were already planning to move in with them in the fall, it gave Marthona a chance to select which things she wanted to keep and which to give away; she couldn't move them all over to the smaller accommodations. They talked long together, and Marthona discovered a reason for happiness when she learned that Ayla was pregnant again.

Most of the people left behind were old or incapacitated in some way. Among them was a hunter with a broken leg, another recovering from a goring he suffered at the horns of an aurochs bull that had turned on him suddenly, and a pregnant woman who had already miscarried three times and been told that she had to stay off her feet if she ever expected to carry a baby full term. Her mother and her mate were staying with her.

"I am glad you are going to be here this summer, Ayla," Jeviva, the pregnant woman's mother, said. "Jeralda held her last one almost six moons, until Madroman came around. He told her to exercise. I think the reason she lost it was his fault. At least you know something about pregnancy—you've had a child of your own."

Ayla looked at Marthona, wondering if she knew anything about Madroman treating Jeralda. She hadn't heard anything. He had moved back to the Ninth Cave last year and brought many of his things with him as if he planned to stay for a while; then just a Moon or so ago, he left abruptly. A runner from another Cave had come to ask Ayla for help for someone who had broken his arm; her skill with fixing bones had spread wide. She stayed several days and when she returned, Madroman was gone.

"How far along is Jeralda now?" Ayla asked.

"Her moontimes were not regular and she was spotting blood so we weren't paying much attention and aren't sure when this life started. I think she's bigger than she was when she lost the last one, but maybe I'm just wishing," Jeviva said.

"I'll come by tomorrow and examine her, and see what I can find out, though I don't know if I'll be able to tell much. Did Zelandoni say anything about why she lost her first three?" Ayla asked.

"All she said is that Jeralda has a slippery womb and tends to drop them too easily. There didn't seem to be anything wrong with the last one, except that he was born too soon. He was alive when he was born and lived a day or so, then just stopped breathing." The woman turned her head aside and wiped away a tear.

Jeralda put her arm around her mother, and then her mate held her and her mother for a moment. Ayla watched the small family as they joined together in their remembered grief. She hoped this pregnancy would turn out to be more successful.

Joharran had designated two men to stay behind to hunt for the people left at the Ninth Cave and generally to help out where they could; they would be replaced in a Moon or so. There was also one hunter who had volunteered to stay, the mate of the pregnant woman who was having difficulties. The others had been unlucky enough to lose at the competitive games the leader had arranged to decide who had to remain behind. The older one was called Lorigan, and the younger, Forason. They had grumbled about it but since they would not have to take a turn in the competition the next year, they accepted their fate.

Ayla often joined the men on their hunts and enjoyed it, and just as often went out on her own with Whinney and Wolf. She hadn't hunted for some time, but she hadn't lost her skills. Forason, who was quite young, wasn't sure of the hunting ability of the Donier's acolyte in the beginning, and thought she'd get in the way, especially since she insisted on bringing the wolf. Lorigan only smiled. By the end of the first day, the young man was overwhelmed at her prowess with both spear-thrower and sling, and surprised at how well the animal worked with them. When they were returning, the older man explained to the youngster that it was she and Jondalar who had developed the spear-thrower and brought it with them when they returned from their Journey. Forason had the good sense to be embarrassed.

But, for the most part, Ayla stayed near the large abri. Those who were there usually shared their evening meal together. It tended to make the emptiness of the large area seem less when they were all together around one fire. The aged and infirm were overjoyed to have a real healer there to care for them. It gave them an unaccustomed sense of security. Most summers, instructions were left with those who were more fit or with the hunters. At most, there might be an acolyte who was staying behind for a similar reason that Ayla was, but generally not one so skilled.

Ayla fell into a routine. She slept late in the morning; then in the afternoon she visited with each person, listened to their complaints, gave them medicines or made poultices, or did whatever she could to make them feel better. It helped make the time pass for her. They all became closer, exchanged stories of their lives, or told stories they had heard. Ayla practiced telling the Elder Legends and the Histories she was learning, and told incidents from her early life, both of which people loved hearing. She still spoke with her unusual accent, but they were so accustomed to it, they didn't really hear it anymore, except that it tended to give her an appealing sense of the mysterious and exotic. They had fully accepted her as one of them, but they loved to tell stories about her to others because she was so unusual, and by association it made them feel special.

As they sat together in the warm sun of the late afternoon, Ayla's stories were in particular demand. She had led such an interesting life, and they never seemed to tire of asking her questions about the Clan or of asking her to show them how they would say certain words, or concepts. They also loved to hear the familiar songs and stories they had grown up with. Many of the older people knew some of the Legends as well as she, and were quick to point out any mistakes, but since several of the older ones came from other Caves, and each often had their own versions, there would be discussions or sometimes arguments about which interpretation was more correct. Ayla didn't mind. She was interested in the various renderings, and the discussions helped her to remember even better. It was a quiet, slow-paced time. The ones who were able often went out and gathered the fruits, vegetables, nuts, and seeds in season, to supplement their meals and to store for the winter.

Just before sunset each evening, Ayla climbed to the top of the cliff with the flat palmate sections of antler she had been marking. She had gotten in the habit of leaving Wolf with Marthona at night, showing her how to send Wolf to get her if she needed help. Ayla watched as the sun continued its almost imperceptible movement, setting just a little farther toward the right on the western horizon each night.

Until Zelandoni had set her to the task, she hadn't really paid that much attention to those kinds of celestial movements before. She had only noticed that the sun rose somewhere in the east and set in the west, and that the moon went through phases from full to dark and back to full again. Like most people, she was aware that the nighttime orb was in the sky during the day occasionally, and though people noticed it, they didn't often pay attention because it was so pale. There was a particular color, however, a shade of nearly transparent white, hardly more than a wash of water with a little white kaolin from a nearby deposit that was called "pale," after the pale moon of day.

Now she knew much more. That was why she was watching the place on the horizon where the sun rose and set, the placement of certain constellations and stars, and the different timings of the risings and settings of the moon. It was a full moon, and while it wasn't rare to have a full moon during the Winter Shortday or the Summer Longday, it was not especially common either. One of the events coincided with the full moon perhaps once every ten years, but since the full moon was always opposite the sun, it always rose at the same time that the sun set, and because the sun was high in the sky in summer, the full moon stayed low in the sky all night. She sat facing south and turning her head right and left to try to keep track of both of them.

The first night that the sun seemed to set in the same place
that it had the night before, she wasn't sure if she had seen it
right. Was it far enough to the right on the horizon? Had the
correct number of days passed? Was the time right? she wondered. She noted certain constellations, and the moon, and decided she'd wait until the next night. When the sun set at the
same place again, she was so excited, she wished Zelandoni
were with her so she could share it.

30

She could hardly wait until Marthona woke up the next morning to tell her that she thought it was the time of the Summer Longday. The woman's reaction was mixed. She was pleased for Ayla, but she also knew that it would not be long before Ayla would be going to the Summer Meeting and she'd be left alone. Not really alone, she knew; all the others would still be there, but Ayla had been wonderful company, enough so that she hardly noticed the absence of so many of her loved ones. She even noticed that the infirmities that kept her from the Summer Meeting seemed less. The young woman's medicinal skills, the special teas, poultices, massages, and other practices all seemed to help. She was feeling much better. Marthona was going to miss her greatly.

The sun seemed to stand still, to set in almost the same location for seven days, but only three that Ayla felt certain of. There did seem to be some movement on the two before and the two after, although less than normal, and then to her amazement, she could see that the place where the sun set had definitely reversed. It was exciting to watch the change in direction, and to realize that the sun would keep going back the way it had come until the Winter Shortday.

She had watched the previous Winter Shortday, along with Zelandoni and several other people, but she hadn't felt the same sense of excitement, although that one was always more important to most people. It was the Shortday that promised that the deep cold of winter would end and the warmth of summer would return, and was celebrated with great enthusiasm.

But this Summer Longday was very important to Ayla. She

had seen and verified it herself, and she felt a great sense of accomplishment, and relief. It also meant her year of watching was over. She would watch a few more days, and continue to mark, just to see if, and how, the setting places changed, but she was already thinking of leaving for the Summer Meeting.

The next night, after she had again verified that the sun had reversed its direction, Ayla was feeling restless up on the high cliff. She had been jumpy and nervous all day, and thought it might be her pregnancy, or perhaps the relief of knowing she would not have to spend many more lonely nights watching the skies. She tried to compose herself and began repeating the words to the Mother's Song to calm herself. It was still her favorite, but as she repeated the verses to herself, she only felt more tension.

"Why am I so jittery? I wonder if a storm is coming. That sometimes makes me tense," she said to herself. She realized she was talking to herself. Perhaps I should meditate, she thought. That should help me relax. Maybe I'll make a cup of tea.

She went back to the place where she had been sitting, stirred up the fire, filled a small cooking container with water from her waterbag, and sorted through the collection of herbs she kept in a medicine bag attached to her waist thong. She kept the dried leaves in packets, tied with various types and thicknesses of cord and twine, with various numbers of knots tied on the ends, so she could distinguish between them, the way Iza had taught her.

As she felt the various packets in the simple leather pouch, even with a fire and moonlight, it was too dark to see the differences, and she had to distinguish between the various herbs and medicines by feel and smell alone. She recalled her first medicine bag, given to her by Iza. It had been made from the entire waterproof hide of an otter with its innards removed through the large opening in the neck. She had made several reproductions of it and still had the last version of it that she had made. Though worn and shabby, she couldn't bear to throw it out. She had thought about making a new one again. It was a Clan medicine bag, and displayed a unique power. Even Zelandoni had been impressed when she first saw it, realizing it was special just from the look of it.

Ayla selected a couple of packets. Most of her herbs were medicinal, but some only mildly so and posed no harm if drunk for pleasure, such as mint or chamomile, which were good for soothing upset stomachs and aiding digestion, but were tasty in their own right. She decided on a mint mixture that included an herb to help her relax, and felt for the packet and sniffed it. It definitely was mint. Pouring some into the palm of her hand, she added it to the steaming water, and after it had steeped for a while, she poured herself a cup. She drank it down, partly for thirst, and then poured a second cup to sip on. The taste seemed a little off; she would have to get some fresher mint, she thought, but it wasn't that bad, and she was still thirsty.

When she finished it, she composed herself, then began to breathe deeply, the way she had been taught. Slowly, deeply, she said to herself. Think of Clear, think of the color called Clear, of a clear creek running over round stones, think of a clear cloudless sky with only the light of the sun, think of emptiness.

She found herself staring at the moon, less than a quarter last time she looked, but now big and round in the night sky. It seemed to grow larger, filling her vision, and she felt herself being pulled into it faster and faster. She tore her eyes away from the moon and got up.

She walked slowly toward the large, tilted boulder. "That stone is glowing! No, I'm imagining things again. It's just the moonlight. It's a different kind of stone from the rest; maybe it just shines more in the light of a full moon," she said out loud.

She closed her eyes, it seemed for a long time. When she opened them, the moon attracted her again; the large full moon was drawing her in. Then she looked around. She was flying! Flying without wind or sound. She looked down. The cliff and river were gone and the land below was unfamiliar. For an instant she thought she would fall. She felt dizzy. Everything was spinning. Bright colors formed a vortex of shimmering light around her, spinning faster and faster.

Ayla came to a sudden halt and was back on the top of the cliff again. She found herself concentrating on the moon, big and huge, and growing larger, filling her vision. She was pulled into it, and then she was flying again, flying the way she had done when she used to assist Mamut. She looked down and saw the stone. It was alive, glowing with spirals of pulsating light. She was drawn toward it, felt captured by the movement. She stared as lines of energy, emerging from the ground, wound around the huge, perilously balanced column, then disappeared into a corona of light at the top. She was floating just above the glowing rock, staring down into it.

It was brighter than the moon and lighted the landscape around it. No wind blew, not the slightest breeze, no leaf or branch stirred, but the ground and the air around her were alive with movement, filled with shapes and shadows flitting about, fleeting, insubstantial forms darting in random motion, glowing with faint energy akin to the light from the stone. As she watched, their motion took shape, developed purpose. The shapes were coming toward her, coming after her! She felt a tingling sensation; her hair rose straight up. Suddenly she was scrambling down the steep path, stumbling and slipping with fear. When she reached the abri, she ran toward the porch, lit by the moonlight.

Lying beside Marthona's bed where he had been told to stay, Wolf raised his head and whimpered.

Ayla raced across the porch toward Down River, then down to The River, and followed the path along it. She felt charged with energy, and ran now for the joy of it, no longer chased, but pulled by some incomprehensible attraction. She splashed across the river at the Crossing, and kept going, it seemed forever. She was approaching a tall cliff that jutted out by itself, a familiar cliff, yet totally unfamiliar.

She came to an inclined path and started climbing, her breath tearing from her throat in ragged gasps, but she was unable to stop. At the top of the path was the dark hole of a cave. She ran into it, into a black so thick she could almost grasp it in her hands, then stumbled on the uneven floor and fell heavily. Her head hit the stone wall.

When she woke, there was no light; she was in a long black tunnel, but somehow she could see. The walls glowed with faint iridescence. Moisture glistened. When she sat up, her head hurt, and for a moment she could only see red. She felt as though the walls were racing past her, but she hadn't moved. Then the iridescence shimmered again, and it was no longer dark. The rock walls glowed with eerie color, fluorescent greens, glowing reds, lustrous blues, pale luminous whites.

She got up and stood next to the wall, and felt the slick cold wetness as she followed the wall, which became an icy blue-green. She was no longer in a cave, but in a sheer crevasse deep in a glacier. Large plane surfaces reflected fleeting, darting, ephemeral shapes. Above her the sky was a deep purple blue. A glaring sun blinded her, and her head hurt. The sun came closer and filled the crevasse with light, but it was a crevasse no longer.

She was in a swirling river, being carried along in its current. Objects floated past, caught in eddies and whirling back-currents that turned faster and faster. She was caught in a whirlpool, turning, turning, round and round. It sucked her down. In a vertigo of spinning motion, the river closed over her head, and everything was black.

She was in a deep, empty, wrenching void, flying; flying faster than she could comprehend. Then her motion slowed and she found herself in a deep fog that glowed with light closing in on her. The fog opened to reveal a strange landscape. Geometric shapes in fluorescent greens, glowing reds, lustrous blues repeated themselves over and over again. Unfamiliar structures rose high in the air. Broad ribbons of white rolled out along the ground, luminous white, full of shapes speeding along it, speeding after her.

She was petrified with fear and felt a tickle probing the edge of her mind that seemed to recognize her. She shrank back, pulled away, feeling her way along the wall as fast as she could. She came to an end as panic filled her. She dropped down to the ground and felt a hole ahead. It was a small hole she could enter only by crawling. She skinned her knees on the rough ground, but didn't notice. The hole grew smaller; she could go no farther. Then she was speeding through a void again, so fast she lost all sense of motion.

She wasn't moving; the black around her was. It closed in, smothering her, drowning her, and she was in the river again and the current was pulling her. She was tired, exhausted; the river drew her into the current as it raced toward the sea, the warm sea. She felt a sharp pain deep inside, and felt the warm, salty waters flooding around her. She breathed in the smell of it, the taste of the waters, and felt she was floating peacefully in the tepid liquid.

But it wasn't water, it was mud. She gasped for breath as she tried to crawl out of the slime; then the beast that was chasing her grabbed her. She doubled up and cried out with pain as it crushed her. She was burrowing though the mud, trying to crawl out of the deep hole the crushing beast had pulled her into, trying to escape.

Then she was free, climbing a tree, swinging from its branches, driven by drought and thirst to the edge of the sea. She plunged in, embraced the water, and grew larger, more buoyant. Finally standing upright, she gazed out at a vast grassland and waded toward it.

But the water dragged against her. She fought to haul herself from the resistant tide; then exhausted, she collapsed. Waves lapping on the shore washed over her legs, pulling her back. She felt the pull, the pain, the grievous, wrenching, tearing pain that threatened to pull her insides out. With a gush of warm liquid, she gave in to the demand.

She crawled a little farther, leaned back against a wall, closed her eyes, and saw a rich steppeland, bright with spring flowers. A cave lion loped toward her in slow, graceful motion. She was in a tiny cave, crunched into a small declivity. She grew to fill the cave as the cave expanded. The walls breathed, expanding, contracting, and she was in a womb, a huge black womb deep in the earth. But she was not alone.

Their forms were vague, transparent; then the shapes coalesced into recognizable forms. Animals, every kind of animal she had ever seen, and birds, and fish, and insects, and some she was sure she had never seen before. They formed a procession, without order or pattern, one seeming to flow into the other. An animal became a bird or a fish, or another bird or animal or insect. A caterpillar became a lizard, then a bird, which grew into a cave lion.

The lion stood and waited for her to follow. Together they went through passages, tunnels, corridors, the walls becoming shapes that thickened and took form as they approached, and grew translucent, fading into the wall as they passed. A procession of woolly mammoths lumbered along through a vast, grassy steppe; then a herd of bison overtook them, and formed their own rank in their place.

She watched two reindeer approach each other. They touched noses; then the female dropped down to her knees, and the male reached down and licked her. Ayla was moved by the tender scene; then her attention was drawn by two horses, male and female. The female was in heat and moved in front of the male, making herself available as he prepared to mount.

She turned in another direction and followed the lion down another long corridor. At the end of the tunnel, she came to a rather large, rounded womb-like niche. She heard a distant pounding that drew closer as a bison herd appeared and filled the niche. They stopped to rest and graze.

But the pounding continued; the walls were throbbing in a slow, steady beat. The hard rock floor seemed to give under her feet and the throbbing became a deep, earthy voice, at first so faint she could hardly detect it. Then it grew louder and she recognized the sound. It was the talking drum of the Mamutoi! Only among the mammoth hunters had she ever heard a drum like that.

The instrument, made of a mammoth bone, had such tonal resonance and variation when hit with a modified antler beater that it could be rapidly tapped at variously discrete areas in such a way that it approximated the sound of a voice speaking words. The words, spoken with a staccato throbbing, did not quite match a human voice, but they were words. They had a slightly ambiguous vibrato quality, which added a touch of mystery and expressive depth, but played by someone with sufficient skill, they were distinctly words. The drum could literally be made to talk.

The rhythm and pattern of the words made by the drum began to sound familiar. Then she heard the high-pitched resonance of a flute, and singing along with it was a sweet, high voice, a voice that sounded like the Mamutoi woman Fralie, whom Ayla had known. Fralie had been pregnant, a precarious pregnancy that she nearly lost. Ayla had helped her, but even with her help, the baby had been born early. But her daughter had lived, and became healthy and strong.

Sitting inside the round niche, Ayla discovered her face was wet with tears. She was crying great, heaving sobs, as though she felt she had suffered a devastating loss. The sound of the drum grew stronger, overcoming her anguished lament. She was recognizing sounds, discerning words.

Out of the darkness, the chaos of time,
The whirlwind gave birth to the Mother sublime.
She woke to Herself knowing life had great worth,
The dark empty void grieved the Great Mother Earth.
    The Mother was lonely. She was the only.

It was the Mother's Song! Sung as she had never heard it sung before. If only she had the voice to sing, that's how she would sing it. It was both deep and earthy like a drum, and high and resonant like a flute, and the deep, rounded niche reverberated with the rich, vibrant sound.

The voice filled her head with the words; she felt them more than heard them, and the feeling was so much more than the words. She anticipated each line before it came, and when it came it was fuller, more eloquent, more profound. It seemed to go on forever, but she didn't want it to stop, and as it neared the end, she felt a deep sadness.

The Mother was pleased with the pair She created,
She taught them to love and to care when they mated.
She made them desire to join with each other,
The Gift of their Pleasures came from the Mother.
    Before She was through, Her children loved too.

But when Ayla anticipated no more, the voice did not stop.

Her last Gift, the Knowledge that man has his part.
His need must be spent before new life can start.
It honors the Mother when the couple is paired,
Because woman conceives when Pleasures are shared.
    Earth's Children were blessed. The Mother could rest.

The words came as a Gift, a benediction soothing her pain. The Mother was telling her she was right; she had been right all along. She'd always known; now it was confirmed. She was sobbing again, still feeling pain, but now it was mixed with joy. She was crying with grief and happiness both as the words repeated in her mind, over and over.

She heard the growl of a lion, and watched her Totem Spirit Lion turn to go. She tried to get up, but felt too weak, and called out to the animal.

"Baby! Baby, don't go! Who will lead me out of here?"

The animal loped down the tunnel, then stopped and was coming toward her, but it wasn't the lion that was approaching. Suddenly, the animal leaped at her, and began licking her face. Ayla shook her head, feeling shaky and confused.

"Wolf? Is it you, Wolf? How did you get here?" she said, hugging the great beast.

As she sat holding on to the wolf, her visions of the bison in the niche faded and grew dark. The scenes on the walls of the tunnels were getting dim, too. She reached for a wall to steady herself, then felt along the stone to move out of the niche. She sat on the ground and closed her eyes, trying to overcome her spinning head. When she tried to open her eyes, she wasn't sure that she had. It was absolutely dark, whether her eyes were open or closed, and she felt a tingling lick of fear crawl up her spine. How was she going to find her way out?

Then she heard Wolf whine, and felt his tongue on her face. She reached out for him and her nervousness eased. She groped for the stone wall beside her, and at first felt nothing, but as she kept reaching, her shoulder bumped the stone. There was a space under one wall, unnoticed because it was so close to the ground, but as she was feeling her way, her hand touched something that was not stone.

She pulled it back quickly, then realizing that it was familiar, she reached in again. The cave was blacker than night, and she tried to discover what it was by feel. It had a soft suede feel, like well-scraped buckskin leather. She pulled out a leather-wrapped bundle. Examining it in her hands, she located a thong or strap, unwrapped it, and found an opening. It seemed to be a carrier pack of some sort, a soft leather pouch suspended from a strap. Inside, she found an empty waterbag—it made her realize that she was thirsty—a fur something, perhaps a cloak, and she could feel and smell the remnants of some uneaten food.

She closed it and put it over her shoulder, then pulled herself up and stood next to the wall, fighting a wave of dizziness and nausea. She felt something warm run down the inside of her leg. The wolf was drawn to sniff her, but she had trained him away from that habit long before, and pushed his inquisitive nose aside.

"We need to find our way out of here, Wolf. Let's go home," she said, but as she started walking, feeling her way along the damp wall, she realized how weak and exhausted she was.

The floor was uneven and slippery, littered with broken pieces of stone intermixed with slick, clayey mud. Pillars of stalagmites, some as thin as twigs and some as massive as ancient trees, seemed to grow from the floor. The tops, when she happened to feel them, were wet from the inexorable drips of calcareous water falling from stalactites, their stone icicle counterparts reaching down from the ceiling. After hitting her head on one, she tried to be more careful. How had she ever gotten so far into the cave?

The wolf ranged ahead a short ways, then came back to her, and at one place urged her away from a wrong turn. When she felt the ground rise under her, she knew she was getting closer to the entrance. She had been in the cave often enough to recognize the place, but trying to climb up the tumbled stone, she felt a wave of dizziness that brought her to her knees. It seemed much farther than she remembered, and she had to stop and rest several times before reaching a smallish narrow opening. Although the entire cave was sacred, there was a natural barrier of rock that partitioned the cave, separating the more mundane beginning section from the inner profoundly sacred region. The hole was the only way through, an entrance into the Great Mother's Underworld.

She noticed the temperature starting to grow slightly warmer once she was beyond the obstruction, but it made her shiver as she became aware of how cold she was. After a turn, she thought she saw a hint of light ahead and tried to hurry. She was sure when she reached the next turn. She could see the wet texture of the cave walls glistening, and ahead the wolf jogging toward a faint glow. When she rounded a corner, she welcomed the dim light coming in from outside, though her eyes had become so accustomed to the dark, it was almost too brilliant. She almost ran when she saw the opening ahead.

Ayla staggered out of the cave, blinking her watering eyes, which washed streaks down her muddy cheeks. Wolf crowded in close to her. When she could finally see, she was surprised to discover the sun high overhead, and several people staring at her. The two hunters, Lorigan and Forason, and Jeviva, the pregnant woman's mother, held back at first, looking at her with a suggestion of awe, and their greeting was somewhat subdued, but when she stumbled and fell they rushed to help. They eased her to sit up, and when she saw their concern on their faces, she felt a great relief.

"Water," she said. "Thirsty."

"Let's get her some water," Jeviva said. She had noticed blood on Ayla's legs and clothing but didn't say anything.

Lorigan opened his waterbag and gave it to her. She drank greedily, letting it run out of her mouth in her hurry. Water had never tasted so good. She smiled when she finally stopped, but did not give up the waterbag.

"Thank you. I was ready to lick the water off the walls."

"There have been times when I felt that way," Lorigan said with a smile.

"How did you know where I was? And that I would be coming out?" Ayla asked.

"I saw the wolf run in this direction," Forason said, nodding in the animal's direction, "and when I told Marthona, she said you were probably in here. She told us to come and wait for you. She said you might need help. One or another of us has been here ever since. Jeviva and Lorigan just came to relieve me."

"I've seen some of the zelandonia come back from their 'calling' before. Some were so exhausted, they couldn't walk. Some don't come back," Jeviva said. "How do you feel?"

"Very tired," Ayla said. "And still thirsty." She took another drink, then handed the waterbag back to Lorigan. The carrier pack she had found inside slid off when Ayla put her arm down. She had forgotten she had it. Now that she was in the light, she could see that distinctive designs had been painted on it. She held it out. "I found this in there. Does anyone know who it belongs to? Someone may have tucked it out of the way and forgotten about it."

Lorigan and Jeviva looked at each other; then Lorigan said, "I've seen Madroman carrying that around."

"Have you looked inside it?" Jeviva said.

Ayla smiled. "I couldn't see to look. I didn't have a light, but I did try to feel," she said.

"You were in there in the dark?" Forason said, full of incredulous wonder.

"Never mind," Jeviva said, shushing him. "It's not your concern."

"I'd like to see what's in that," Lorigan said, giving Jeviva a significant glance. Ayla handed it to him. He pulled out the fur cloak and shook it out to expose it. The fur was made of squares and triangles of various types and shades from different animals sewn together into the characteristic pattern of a zelandonia acolyte.

"That does belong to Madroman. I saw him wearing it last year when he came around telling Jeralda what to do if she wanted to keep the baby," Jeviva said with a tone of disdain. "She held that one nearly six moons. He said she needed to appease the Mother, and told her to perform all kinds of rituals, but when Zelandoni found her walking in circles outside, she made her go in and lie down right away. Zelandoni said she needed to rest, or she would shake the baby loose too soon. The Donier said the only thing wrong with her was that she has a slippery womb and tends to drop them too easy. She lost that one. It would have been a boy." The woman looked at Lorigan. "What else is in there?"

He reached inside the pouch and pulled out the empty waterbag without comment, holding it up for all to see; then he looked inside and dumped the remaining contents out on top of the cloak. Partially chewed pieces of dried meat and a hunk of a traveling cake fell out, along with a small flint blade and a firestone. Among the crumbs there also appeared to be a few wood splinters and pieces of charcoal.

"Wasn't Madroman bragging before they left for the Summer Meeting that he had been 'called' and was finally going to be Zelandoni this year?" Lorigan said. He lifted the waterbag.

"I don't think he was very thirsty when he came out of that cave."

"Did you say you were planning to go to the Summer Meeting later, Ayla?" Jeviva said.

"I was thinking of going in a few days. Maybe now I'll wait awhile," Ayla said. "But yes, I do plan to go."

"I think you should take this with you," Jeviva said, carefully wrapping the food remains, splinters, fire-making equipment, and waterbag in the cloak, and stuffing the cloak back in the carrier pouch, "and tell Zelandoni where you found it."

"Can you walk?" the older hunter said.

Ayla tried to stand, and felt overcome with vertigo. For a moment everything went dark and she fell back. Wolf whimpered and licked her face.

"Stay there," the older hunter said. "Come on, Lorigan. We need to make a litter to carry her."

"If I rest, I think I can walk," Ayla said.

"No, I don't think you should," Jeviva said, then to the hunters, "I'll wait with her until you come back with the litter."

Ayla sat back against a stone, feeling grateful. Maybe she could have walked all the way to the Ninth Cave, but she was glad she wouldn't have to. "Perhaps you're right, Jeviva. I seem to get a little dizzy now and then."

"No wonder," Jeviva said under her breath. She had noticed a fresh bloodstain on the stone when Ayla tried to stand up. I think she lost a baby in there, the woman thought. What a terrible sacrifice to make to become Zelandoni, but she's not a cheat, not like that Madroman.

"Ayla? Ayla? Are you awake?"

Ayla opened her eyes and saw a blurry image of Marthona looking down at her with concern.

"How do you feel?"

Ayla thought about it. "I hurt. All over," she said in a hoarse whisper.

"I hope I didn't wake you. I heard you talking—maybe you were dreaming. Zelandoni warned me this might come. She didn't think it would be so soon, but she said it was possible. She told me not to stop you, and she told me not to let Wolf follow you, but she gave me some tea to fix for you when you came back." She had a steaming cup of liquid, but put it down to help prop Ayla up.

The tea was hot, but not too hot, and Ayla was grateful when she felt it slide down her throat. She was still thirsty, but she lay back down, too tired to sit up. Her head started to clear. She was in her dwelling, in her own bed. She looked around and saw Wolf beside Marthona. He whined with concern and drew closer to her. She reached out to touch him and he licked her hand.

"How did I get here?" she asked. "I don't remember much after I got out of the cave."

"The hunters carried you here on a litter. They said you tried to walk, and then fainted. You ran down from your watching place and apparently all the way to the Deep Hollow of Fountain Rocks. You weren't yourself and went in without a fire or anything. When Forason came and told me you had come out, I couldn't get there. I've never felt so useless in my life," Marthona said.

"I'm just glad you're here, Marthona," Ayla said, then closed her eyes again.

The next time she opened her eyes, only Wolf was there, keeping a vigil beside her bed. She smiled at him, reached over to pat his head, and scratched under his chin. He put his paws on the bed and tried to edge closer, close enough to lick her face. She smiled again, then pushed him away and tried to sit up. The groan of pain was involuntary, but it brought Marthona in a hurry.

"Ayla! What's wrong?" she said.

"I didn't know so many parts of me could hurt at the same time," Ayla said. The look of concern on Marthona's face was so strong, it was almost a caricature, and brought a smile to the young woman's face. "But I think I'll live."

"You have bruises and scrapes all over, but I don't think anything is broken," Marthona said.

"How long have I been here?"

"More than a day. You got here yesterday, late in the afternoon. The sun went down not long ago."

"How long was I gone?" Ayla asked.

"I don't know when you went into the cave, but from the time you left here until you got back, it was more than three days, almost four."

Ayla nodded. "I have no sense of the time that passed at all. I remember parts, some very clearly. It feels like something I dreamed, but different."

"Are you hungry? Thirsty?" Marthona asked.

"I'm thirsty," Ayla said, then felt an overwhelming dryness, as though the saying of it made her realize how dehydrated she was. "Very thirsty."

Marthona left and came back with a waterbag and a cup to drink from. "Do you want to sit up, or should I just prop up your head?"

"I'd rather try to sit up."

She rolled on her side, trying to muffle her groans, then got up on one elbow, breaking through a scab that had been forming over a bad scrape, and pushed herself up to sit on the edge of the bed platform. She felt a moment of dizziness, but it passed. She was more surprised at how much she hurt inside. Marthona poured water in the cup and Ayla took it in both hands. She drank it down without stopping, then held it out for more. She seemed to remember gulping down water from a waterbag when she first came into the light. She finished the second cup only a little more slowly.

"Are you hungry yet? You haven't had anything to eat," Marthona said.

"My stomach hurts," Ayla said.

"I imagine it does," Marthona said, looking away.

Ayla frowned. "Why should my stomach hurt?"

"You're bleeding, Ayla. You probably have cramps, and more."

"Bleeding? How can I be bleeding? I've missed three moontimes, I'm pregnant . . . Oh, no!" Ayla cried. "I've lost the baby, haven't I?"

"I think so, Ayla. I'm not expert in those things, but every woman knows you can't be pregnant and bleed at the same time, at least not as much as you have. You were bleeding when you came out, and a lot since then. I think it may take a while for you to regain your strength. I'm sorry, Ayla. I know you wanted this baby," Marthona said.

"The Mother wanted her more," Ayla said in a dry monotone of grief-stricken shock. She lay back down and stared up
at the underside of the limestone overhang. She didn't even
realize when she fell asleep again.

The next time she woke, Ayla had a strong urge to pass water.
It was obviously nighttime, dark, but several lamps were burning. She looked around and saw Marthona asleep on some cushions beside the bed platform. Wolf was beside the old woman
with his head up, looking at her. He's got two of us to worry and
watch over now, she thought. She rolled to her side and pulled
herself up again, sitting on the bed platform for a while before
she tried to get up. She was stiff, and still sore and achy, but she
felt stronger. Carefully, she eased herself to her feet. Wolf stood
up, too. She signaled him down again, then took a step toward
the night basket near the entrance.

She wished she had thought to take some changes of absorbent padding with her. She had been bleeding quite heavily. As
she started back to her sleeping place, Marthona approached,
bringing her a change.

"I didn't mean to wake you," Ayla said.

"You didn't. Wolf did, but you should have. Would you like
some water? I also have some stew, if you're ready to eat," Marthona said.

"Water would be nice, and maybe a little stew," Ayla said,
returning to the night basket to change to clean padding. Movement had eased her soreness.

"Where do you want to eat? In bed?" the woman asked as
she limped to the cooking area. She, too, was stiff and sore.
Her sleeping place and position had not been good for her
arthritis.

"No, I'd rather sit at the table." Ayla went into the cooking
area and poured a little water into a small basin bowl, then
rinsed her hands and using a small absorbent leather scrap
wiped off her face. She was sure Marthona had cleaned her
up a little, but she wanted to take a nice, refreshing swim with
some soaproot. Maybe in the morning, she thought.

The stew was cold, but tasty. Ayla thought she'd be able to
eat several bowls of it when she took the first few bites, but she
filled up sooner than she thought. Marthona made them both

some hot tea and joined Ayla at the table. Wolf slipped outside
while the two women were up, but was back before very long.

"Did you say Zelandoni expected that I would do something?"
Ayla asked.

"She didn't really expect it. She just thought it was possible."

"What did she expect? I don't really understand what happened," Ayla said.

"I think Zelandoni could tell you better. I wish she was here,
but I think you are Zelandoni now. I think you were 'called,' as
they say. Do you remember anything?" Marthona asked.

"I remember things, and then all of a sudden, I remember
something else, but I can't seem to sort it out," Ayla said,
frowning.

"I wouldn't worry about it yet. Wait until you have a chance
to talk to Zelandoni. I'm sure she'll be able to explain things
and help you. Right now, you just need to get your strength
back," Marthona said.

"You're probably right," Ayla said, relieved to have an excuse
to put off dealing with the whole thing. She didn't even want to
think about it, though she couldn't help remembering the baby
she had lost. Why did the Mother want to take her baby?

Ayla did little except sleep for several days, then one day
she woke up feeling starved, and couldn't seem to get enough
to eat for the next couple of days. When she finally emerged
from her dwelling and joined the small group, they all looked
at her with new respect, even awe, and a touch of apprehension. They knew she had been through an ordeal, which they
were convinced had changed her. And they all felt a certain
pride because they were there when it happened, and by association, they felt that they were somehow a part of it.

"How are you feeling?" Jeviva asked.

"Much better," Ayla said, "but hungry!"

"Come and join us. There is plenty of food and it's still warm,"
Jeviva said.

"I think I will." She sat down beside Jeralda, while Jeviva
prepared a dish for her. "And how are you feeling?"

"Bored!" Jeralda said. "I'm so tired of sitting and lying around.
I wish it was time for this baby to come."

"I think it is probably time for the baby to come. It wouldn't hurt if you took a walk now and then to encourage it. It's just a matter of waiting until the baby feels ready. I thought so the last time I examined you," Ayla said, "but I thought I'd wait before I said anything, and then I got distracted. I'm sorry."

That evening Marthona mentioned, with some hesitation, "I hope I didn't do anything wrong, Ayla."

"I don't understand."

"Zelandoni told me that if you did leave, not to try to stop you. When you didn't come back that morning, I was terribly worried, but Wolf was worse. You had told him to stay with me, but he was whining and wanting to go. Just the way he was looking at me, I could tell he wanted to go and look for you. I didn't want him to disturb anything, so I tied a rope around his neck, the way you would do sometimes when you wanted him to stay and not interrupt. But after a few days, he was so miserable, and I was so worried, I untied him. He raced out of here. Was I wrong to let him go?" the woman asked.

"No, I don't think so, Marthona," Ayla said. "I don't know if I was in a spirit world, but if I was and he found me there, I think I was already returning. Wolf helped me find my way out of the cave—at least he gave me the sense that I was going in the right direction. It was dark in there, but the passages are narrow, and I kept close to the wall. I think I might have been able to find my way out anyway, but it would have taken longer."

"I'm not sure if I should have tied him up in the first place. I don't know if it was my place to make that decision—I know I'm getting old, Ayla, when I can't even make a decision anymore." The former leader shook her head, looking disgusted with herself. "Things of the spirit world were never my strength. You were so weak when you got here, maybe She thought you needed a helper. Perhaps the Mother wanted me to let that animal go so he could find you and help you."

"I don't think anything you did was wrong. Things tend to happen the way She wants," Ayla said. "Right now, what I want is to go down to The River and take a long swim, and then have a good washing. Do you know if Zelandoni left behind

any of that Losadunai cleansing foam? The one I showed her
how to make from fat and ashes? She likes to use it for purify-
ing, especially to clean the hands of grave-diggers."

"I don't know about Zelandoni, but I have some," Marthona
said. "I like to use it on weavings, sometimes. I have even used
it on some of my platters, the ones I use for meat and to collect
clean fat. Can you use it for bathing, too?"

"The Losadunai did sometimes. It can be harsh and make
your skin red. Usually I prefer to use soaproot, or some other
plant, but right now, I just want to be clean," Ayla said.

"If only there was a well of Doni's healing hot waters nearby,"
Ayla said to herself as she headed toward The River with Wolf
at her side. "It would be perfect, but The River will do for now."
The wolf looked up at her at the sound of her voice. He had
stayed close to her, not wanting to let her out of his sight since
her return.

The hot sun felt good as she walked down the path toward
the swimming place. She lathered all over, and washed her
hair, then ducked under to rinse well and went for a long swim.
She climbed up and rested on a flat rock to let the sun dry her
while she combed her hair. The sun feels so good, she thought,
spreading out her drying buckskin and lying on top of it. When
was the first time I lay down on this rock? It was my first day
here, when Jondalar and I went swimming.

She thought of Jondalar, in her mind's eye seeing him lying
naked beside her. His yellow hair and darker beard . . . no,
it's summer. He'd be clean shaven. His broad, high forehead
beginning to show the lines caused by his habit of knotting it
in concentration or concern. His vivid blue eyes looking at her
with love and desire—Jonayla has his eyes. His straight fine
nose and strong jaw with a full, sensuous mouth.

Her thoughts lingered on his mouth, almost feeling it. His
broad shoulders, muscular arms, large, sensitive hands. Hands
that could feel a piece of flint and know how it would fracture,
or could caress her body with such perception that he would
know how she would react. His long, strong legs, the scar on
his groin from his encounter with her lion, Baby, and nearby,
his manhood.

She was feeling her desire for him build just thinking about him. She wanted to see him, to be near him. She hadn't even told him she had been expecting a baby; now she didn't have a baby to tell him about anymore. She felt a wave of grief. I wanted the baby, but the Mother wanted it more, she thought, frowning. She knew I wanted another baby, but I don't think the Mother would have wanted a baby that I didn't want.

For the first time since her ordeal, she began to think about the Mother's Song, and with a chill of recognition, remembered the verse, the new verse, the one that brought the new Gift, the Gift of Knowledge, the knowledge that men were necessary for new life to start.

Her last Gift, the Knowledge that man has his part.
His need must be spent before new life can start.
It honors the Mother when the couple is paired,
Because woman conceives when Pleasures are shared.
  Earth's Children were blessed. The Mother could rest.

I've known it for a long time. Now She has told me it is true. Why did She give me this Gift? So I could share it, so I could tell the others? That's why She wanted my baby! She told me first, told me Her last great Gift, but I had to be worthy. The cost was high, but maybe it had to be. Perhaps the Mother had to take something of great value so I would know that I had to appreciate the Gift. Gifts are not given without something of great value given back.

Have I been called? Am I Zelandoni now? Because I made the sacrifice of my baby, the Great Mother spoke to me, and gave me the rest of the Mother's Song, so I could share it, and bring this wonderful Gift to Her Children. Now Jondalar will know for certain that Jonayla is his as much as she is mine. And we'll know how to start a new baby when we want one. Now all men will know that it is more than spirits—it is him, his essence; his children are a part of him.

But what if a woman doesn't want another child? Or shouldn't have another one because she's too weak, or exhausted from having too many? Then she will know how to stop it! Now a woman will know how not to have a child if she is not ready, or doesn't want one. She doesn't have to ask the Mother, she won't have to take any special medicine, she will just have to stop sharing Pleasures and she won't have any more children. For the first time, a woman can be in control of her own body, her own life. This is very powerful knowledge . . . but there is another side. What about the man?

What if he doesn't want to stop sharing Pleasures? Or what if he wants a child that he knows comes from him? Or what if he doesn't want a child?

I want another baby, and I know Jondalar would want another baby, too. He's so good with Jonayla, and he's so good with the youngsters who are learning to knap flint, his apprentices. I'm sorry I lost this baby. Tears came to her eyes as she thought about the baby she miscarried. But I can have another one. If only Jondalar were here, we could begin to start another one now, but he's at the Summer Meeting. I can't even tell him about losing the baby if I'm here and he's at the Summer Meeting. He would feel bad, I know he would. He would want to start another one.

Why don't I go? I don't have to watch the sky anymore. I don't have to stay up late; my training is over. I have been "called." I am Zelandoni! And I need to tell the rest of the zelandonia. The Mother not only called me, She gave me a great Gift. A Gift for everyone. I need to go so I can tell all the Zelandonii about the Mother's wonderful new Gift. And so I can tell Jondalar, and maybe start another baby.

31

Ayla quickly got up from the rock, put on her clean clothes, gathered up her soiled ones and the drying skin, and whistled to Wolf as she hurried back along the path. As she walked up to the stone front porch of the shelter, she remembered her first swim with Jondalar, and then Marona and her friends offering to give her some new clothes.

Though Ayla had developed varying levels of tolerance toward the other women who were involved in the trick, she never got over her aversion to Marona, and avoided contact with her. The feeling was more than mutual. Marona had never made any effort to reconcile with the woman Jondalar brought home with him from his Journey. She had mated for a second time the same summer that Ayla and Jondalar did, but at the Second Matrimonial, and once again more recently. That mating had apparently not worked out, either; she had moved back to the Ninth Cave to stay with her cousin a year or so before. But for all her matings, she had no children.

Ayla couldn't abide the woman, and didn't know why she should be thinking of her. She shook off thoughts of Marona and concentrated on Jondalar. I'm so glad to finally be going to the Summer Meeting, she thought. I can ride Whinney, and it won't take long at all to get there, no more than a day, if I don't stop along the way.

The Summer Meeting was being held this year about twenty miles to the north along The River, at her favorite place for a Meeting. It was the same location as the first Zelandonii Summer Meeting she had ever gone to, and the one where she and Jondalar were mated. Such Meetings usually used up nearly all the resources around the area, but if enough time was allowed to pass, Mother Earth healed the place from the misuse caused by the large concentration of people and it was refreshed enough to host them again.

The young woman burst into her dwelling, full of vigor and enthusiasm, and began sorting through her clothes and possessions. She was humming her usual monotone under her breath when Marthona came in.

"You're suddenly full of excitement," the older woman said.

"I'm going to the Summer Meeting. I don't have to watch the sky anymore. I'm through with my training. There is no reason I can't go," Ayla said.

"Are you sure you're strong enough?" There was a note of regret in Marthona's voice.

"You've taken good care of me. I'm feeling fine, and I really want to see Jondalar, and Jonayla."

"I miss them too, but it's a long way to go alone. I thought you might wait until the next hunter comes to take a turn helping us. Then you could go back with Forason," Marthona suggested.

"I'm going to ride Whinney. It won't take long. I can probably get there in a day. Two at the most," Ayla said.

"Yes, you're probably right. I'd forgotten that you would be taking your horse, and Wolf, too," Marthona said.

Ayla noticed Marthona's disappointment, and suddenly realized how much the woman would like to go, and she was still concerned about her health. "How are you feeling? I don't want to leave if you are not well."

"No, don't stay on my behalf," Marthona said. "I'm much better. If I had felt this good at the beginning of the season, I might have considered going."

"Why don't you come with me? You could sit on Whinney's back. It might take a little longer, but only another day or so," Ayla said.

"No. I like the horse well enough, but I don't want to sit on her back. To be honest, it frightens me a little. You are right, though, you need to go. You need to tell Zelandoni that you were 'called.' Imagine what a surprise it will be."

"There's not much summer left anyway. Everyone will be coming back before long," Ayla said, trying to ease the separation.

"I feel two ways about that," Marthona said. "I'm anxious for the Summer Meeting to be over and for the Ninth Cave to come back, but I'm not looking forward to the return of winter. I suppose it's always that way when a person gets old."

Ayla's next step in preparing to leave was to look for Lorigan and Forason. She knew exactly where to find Jonclotan, with Jeralda. Almost everyone was sitting around the community fireplace, finishing up a meal.

"Ayla, come join us," Jeralda called. "Have something to eat. There is plenty left and it's still warm."

"I think I will. I've been so hungry the last few days," Ayla said.

"I can understand why," Jeviva said. "How do you feel?"

"Much more rested," Ayla said, then smiled. "I've decided that I'm going to go to the Summer Meeting soon. I've finished my sky watching, so there is no reason for me to stay, but I thought we ought to go hunting once more before I leave, both for those who are here, and for something to take with me to the Meeting. The animals around the Meeting Camp are likely to be almost gone, and those that haven't been killed are probably avoiding the area."

"You aren't going to leave before my baby comes, are you?" Jeralda said.

"If you don't have it in the next few days," Ayla said. "Though I would like to stay and see that nice healthy baby born. Have you been walking?"

"Yes, I have, but I was so looking forward to you being here to help me."

"Your mother is here, and several other women who know about babies, not to mention Jonclotan. I don't think you'll have any problems, Jeralda," Ayla said. Then she looked at the three hunters. "Would you like to go hunting with me tomorrow morning?"

"I hadn't planned on going for a few more days, but it doesn't matter to me," Lorigan said. "I can go tomorrow, especially if you're leaving soon. I have to admit, I've gotten used to our little hunting pack, including the wolf. I think we work together well."

"Which way do you want to go?" Jonclotan said.

"We haven't been north for a while," Forason said.

"I've been avoiding that direction because I don't know how far the hunters from the Summer Meeting are having to range now. I'm sure animals are gettting scarce around the Camp by now. That's why I want to bring something with me. I have Zelandoni's pole-drag, I can use it to haul a good-size carcass with me," Ayla said.

"Is that safe?" Jeviva said. "Won't you attract a hunting animal? Maybe you shouldn't go alone."

Marthona had joined them, but didn't say anything. She didn't think it was anything that would concern Ayla, if she had made up her mind to go.

"Wolf will warn me, and I think between us, we can drive off a four-legged hunter," Ayla said.

"Even a cave lion?" Jeralda asked. "Maybe you should wait until the hunters can go with you."

Ayla knew she was looking for a reason for her to stay so she'd be there to help her deliver her baby. "Don't you remember when we hunted a pride of cave lions who tried to settle too close to the Third Cave? It was too dangerous to allow that. Every child or elder would have been considered prey; we had to make them go. When we killed the lion and a couple of the lionesses, the rest of them left."

"Yes, but that was a whole hunting party. You are just one person," Jeralda said.

"No, Wolf will be with me, and Whinney. Lions like to go after something they know is weak. I think the scent of all of us together would confuse them, and I'll keep my spear-thrower close by. Besides, if I leave early in the morning, I should be able to get there before nightfall," Ayla said, then added to the hunters, "Tomorrow, let's plan to go southwest."

Marthona stayed back a ways listening to the conversation. She would make a good leader, the former leader of the Ninth Cave said to herself. She takes charge without even thinking about it, it just comes naturally. I think she's going to be a strong Zelandoni.

The hunters returned the next day hauling two large red deer with sizable racks. Ayla thought about going to get Whinney to help drag them back, but the other hunters didn't even think about it. They field-dressed the animals, emptied the stomachs, cleaned the intestines, and threw away the bowels, but saved the rest of the internal organs, then grabbed the antlers and started pulling them. They were used to getting their kills back home by themselves.

Two days later, Ayla was ready to leave. She packed everything on Zelandoni's large pole-drag, including the deer wrapped in a woven grass mat that Marthona had helped her make, and intended to leave the following morning, planning to reach the Summer Meeting Campsite by nightfall, without having to push Whinney too hard. But there was a delay, not exactly unexpected. Jeralda started labor in the middle of the night. Ayla was rather glad. She had been overseeing her pregnancy all summer, and didn't really want to leave her now that she was getting close. But she hadn't been entirely sure when the woman would deliver, a few days, or a whole Moon.

This time, luck was with Jeralda. She gave birth to a girl before midday. Her mate and her mother were as happy and excited as she was. After a meal, when the woman was resting comfortably, Ayla began to get restless. Everything was ready to go; besides, while letting the meat age a bit often added to its flavor, if too much time passed, it could get a little too high, at least to her taste. It wouldn't take much to pack up and leave; she could go now. But if she did, she would probably have to spend one night out along the way. She decided to leave anyway.

After farewells and last-minute instructions to Jeviva, Jeralda, and Marthona, Ayla started out. She enjoyed riding alone on Whinney, with Wolf loping beside them, and both the animals seemed to enjoy it as well. The weather was quite warm, but the riding blanket on Whinney's back added some comfort, and absorbed some of the sweat of woman and horse. She wore a short tunic and her loincloth skirt, similar to the one she had worn when she and Jondalar had traveled through the summer heat, and she was reminded of their Journey, but it made her miss him all the more.

Her body, which had thickened slightly from the lack of excercise during the past few years, had been thinned down by her ordeal in the cave. Her breasts, which had filled out when

she was heavy with milk while nursing Jonayla, and again with
early pregnancy, had gone back to normal size, and her muscle
tone was still good. She had always been firm and well shaped,
and though she could count twenty-six years now, she thought,
she looked very much the same as she had when she could
count only seventeen years.

She rode until sunset, then stopped and made camp beside
The River. Sleeping alone in her small tent made her think
about Jondalar again. She crawled into her furs and closed her
eyes, and kept seeing visions of the tall man with the thrilling
blue eyes, wishing he were there to wrap his arms around her,
wishing she could feel his mouth on hers. She rolled over,
closed her eyes, and tried again to go to sleep. She kept tossing
and turning but could not get to sleep. Wolf was beside her and
started whining.

"Am I keeping you awake, too, Wolf?" Ayla said.

He sat up and poked his nose out of the opening under the
closure, a growl deep in his throat. He squirmed his way under
the flap that was loosely tied across the triangular-shaped front
of the small tent, his growl becoming more menacing.

"Wolf! Where are you going? Wolf?"

She quickly untied the closure and started out, then turned
back and reached for her spear-thrower and a couple of spears.
The moon was waning, but there was still enough light to see
reflected shapes. She saw the pole-drag, then noticed that Whinney was moving away from it. Even in the limited moonglow,
she could tell from the way the mare moved that she was nervous. Wolf was crouching low, moving in the general direction
of the pole-drag, but slightly behind it. Then, for an instant, she
glimpsed a shape, a round head with two ears sticking up ending in tufts.

It's a lynx!

She'd had memories of the large cat with mottled whitish-
yellow fur, short stubby tail, and tufted ears. And long legs
that could run fast. It was her first encounter with a lynx that
had encouraged her to teach herself to cast two stones in rapid
succession with her sling, so she wouldn't be left weaponless
after one hurl. She checked to make sure that she had more

than one spear as she mounted one on her spear-thrower, ready to throw.

Then she saw his silhouette slinking toward the pole-drag.

"Aaaiiiii!" she screamed, running toward the cat. "Get out of there! That's not yours! Go away! Get out of here!"

The startled lynx leaped straight up in the air, then sped away. Wolf took off after it, but after a few moments, Ayla whistled. He slowed down, then stopped, and when she whistled again, finally turned around and headed back.

Ayla had brought along a little kindling. She used it to stir up the coals of the fire she had made earlier to heat some water for tea to drink with the traveling cake that she ate before going to bed. The coals had died, so she got her fire-making kit and started a new one. Once she had the kindling lit, she used a piece as a torch to search around for more fuel. She was on an open plain with The River running through it. There were a few trees near The River, but only green wood was available; dried grass was, though, and a few desiccated animal droppings, probably from a bison or an aurochs, she thought. It was enough to keep the small fire going for a while. She laid out her sleeping roll next to the fire and crawled into it with Wolf beside her. Whinney stayed close to Ayla and the fire as well.

She dozed a little during the night, but the least sound roused her. Without bothering to build up the fire, she was on her way again shortly after first light, stopping only long enough for the horse, the wolf, and herself to get a drink from The River. She ate another traveling cake along the way, and sighted the smoke of cooking fires from the Camp before noon. Ayla waved to a few friends as she rode along The River, pulling the pole-drag behind, heading first toward the place upstream where the Ninth Cave had camped before.

She went straight to the glen surrounded by trees. The simple corral made her smile. The horses nickered greetings at first scent. Wolf raced ahead to rub noses with Racer, who had been his friend since his puppy days, and Gray, whom he had watched over from the time she was born. He felt nearly as protective toward her as he did toward Jonayla.

Except for the horses, the camp of the Ninth Cave seemed to be deserted. Wolf began sniffing around a familiar tent, and when she brought in her sleeping roll, she saw Wolf near Jonayla's sleeping furs. He looked at her, whining with anxious need.

"Do you want to go find her, Wolf? Go ahead, Wolf, find Jonayla," she said, giving him the signal that he was free to go. He raced out of the tent, sniffed the ground to pick up her particular scent among all the others, then ran off, smelling the ground now and then. People had seen Ayla arriving, and before she could unpack the meat, relatives and friends came to greet her. Joharran was the first, Proleva close behind.

"Ayla! You finally made it," Joharran said, rushing toward her and giving her a big hug. "How's Mother? You have no idea how much she is missed. Both of you, in fact."

Proleva was next to embrace her. "Yes, how is Marthona?" she asked, giving Ayla time to answer.

"Better, I think. When I was leaving, she said if she had felt as good when everyone left, she might have come," Ayla said.

"How's Jeralda?" Proleva asked next.

Ayla smiled. "She had a girl, yesterday. The baby seems perfectly healthy—I don't think she was early. They both seem fine. Jeviva and Jonclotan are very happy."

"It looks like you brought something," Joharran said, motioning toward the travois.

"Lorigan, Forason, Jonclotan, and I did a little hunting," Ayla said. "We came upon a herd of red deer in Grass Valley, and got two stags. I left one there. It will hold them for a while. I brought the other one with me. I thought some fresh meat might be welcome about now. I know animals get a little scarce around here about this time. We had some before I left. They're good, already building up fat for winter."

Several more of the Ninth Cave arrived, and some others as well. Joharran and a couple of them started to unload the pole-drag.

Matagan, Jondalar's first apprentice, ran with a limp, but ran nonetheless, and greeted her enthusiastically. "People have been asking when you were coming. Zelandoni kept saying it could be anytime. But no one was expecting you in the middle of the day," Garthadal said. "Jondalar was sure that you wouldn't get here until evening or later. He said when you decided to come, you'd probably ride your horse and make the trip in one day."

"He was right. At least that's what I planned to do, but Jeralda went into labor in the middle of the night, and had her baby in the morning. I was too restless to wait, so I left in the afternoon and camped out last night," Ayla explained. Then, looking around, she asked, "Where is Jondalar? And Jonayla?"

Joharran and Proleva glanced at each other, then quickly looked away. "Jonayla is with the other girls her age," Proleva said. "The zelandonia had some things for them to do. They're going to take part in a special celebration Those Who Serve have planned."

"I'm not sure where Jondalar is," Joharran said, his brow knotted with the frown that was so like his brother's. He glanced up behind Ayla, and smiled. "But there is someone here who has been wanting to see you."

Ayla turned around and looked in the direction that Joharran had glanced. She saw a giant of a man with wild red hair and a bushy red beard. Her eyes opened wide.

"Talut? Talut, is it you?" she cried, rushing toward the burly man.

"No, Ayla. Not Talut. I am Danug, but Talut told me to give you a big hug for him, too," the young man said as he swept her up in a big, friendly embrace. She felt, not crushed—Danug had learned long ago to be careful of his overpowering strength—but enveloped, overwhelmed, almost smothered by the sheer size of the man. He was taller, by some measure, than Jondalar's six feet, six inches. His shoulders were nearly as broad as those of two ordinary men and his arms were the size of most men's thighs. She couldn't fully wrap her arms around his massive chest, and though his waist was slender enough in proportion, his muscular thighs and calves were huge.

Ayla had known only one other to match Danug's size: Talut, the man to whom Danug's mother was mated, the headman of the Lion Camp of the Mamutoi. And, if anything, the young man was bigger.

"I told you I was going to come and visit you someday," he said, when he put her down. "How are you, Ayla?"

"Oh, Danug," she said, tears filling her eyes. "I'm so glad to see you. How long have you been here? How did you get here? How did you get so big? I think you're bigger than Talut!" She easily slipped into speaking Mamutoi, but though her words were understood, it didn't make her questions follow any logical order.

"I think he is, too, but I'd never dare say that to Talut."

Ayla turned at the sound of the voice, and saw another young man. He seemed to be a stranger, but as she looked closer, she began to see similarities to others she had known. He resembled Barzec, though he was larger than the short, sturdy man who was mated to Tulie, the big headwoman of the Lion Camp. She was Talut's sister, and almost matched him in size. The young man bore a certain resemblance to both of them.

"Druwez?" Ayla said. "Are you Druwez?"

"It's hard to mistake the big galoot," the young man said, smiling at Danug, "but I didn't know if you would recognize me."

"You have changed," Ayla said, hugging him, "but I can see your mother, and Barzec, in you. How are they? And how's Nezzie, and Deegie, and everyone?" she asked, including both in her glance. "I can't tell you how much I've missed everyone."

"They miss you, too," Danug said. "But we have someone else with us who's been looking forward to meeting you."

A tall young man with a shy smile and curly brown hair was standing back a bit. He came forward at the prompting of the two young Mamutoi. Ayla knew she had never met him before, yet there was something strangely familiar about him—she just couldn't put her finger on it.

"Ayla of the Mamutoi . . . Zelandonii now, I guess, meet Aldanor of the S'Armunai," Danug said.

"S'Armunai!" Ayla said. Suddenly she realized what was so familiar about him. His clothing, especially his shirt. It was cut and decorated in the unique style of those people she and Jondalar had involuntarily visited on their Journey. Memories came rushing back. They were the people who had captured Jondalar, or rather, Attaroa's Camp of S'Armunai had. Ayla with Wolf and the horses had tracked them and found him. But that had not been the first time she had seen a shirt made in that style. Ranec, the Mamutoi man she almost mated, had one that he had traded carvings for.

Ayla suddenly realized they were staring at each other. She collected herself, stepped toward the young man with both hands held out in greeting. "In the name of Doni, the Great Earth Mother, also known as Muna, you are welcome here, Aldanor of the S'Armunai," she said.

"In the name of Muna, I thank you, Ayla." He smiled a shy grin. "You may be Mamutoi or Zelandonii, but did you know that among the S'Armunai you are known as 'S'Ayla, Mother of the Wolf Star, sent to destroy Attaroa, the Evil One'? There are so many stories about you, I didn't believe you were a real person. I thought you were a Legend. When Danug and Druwez stopped at our camp and said they were making a Journey to visit you, I asked if I could go along. Now I can't believe I'm actually meeting you!"

Ayla smiled and shook her head. "I don't know about stories or Legends," she said. "People often believe what they want to believe." He seems like a nice young man, she thought.

"I have something for you, Ayla," Danug said. "If you'll come inside, I'll give it to you." She followed Danug into a smallish hide-covered structure, apparently their traveling-tent, and watched as he rummaged through a pack. Finally he pulled out a small object carefully wrapped and tied with a cord. "Ranec told me to give this to you personally."

Ayla unwrapped the small package. Her eyes opened wide and she gasped with surprise as she held the object in her hand. It was a horse carved out of mammoth ivory, small enough to fit in her hand, but so exquisitely carved, it almost looked alive. Its head was thrust forward as though straining into the wind. The stand-up mane and shaggy coat were carved with a pattern of lines that suggested the rough texture of the horse's hide without hiding the stocky conformation of the small steppe horse. A shade of yellow ocher, the color of dry standing hay, had been rubbed onto the animal, matching the familiar color of one horse she knew, and a blackish color shaded the lower legs and the length of the spine.

"Oh, Danug. She's just beautiful. It's Whinney, isn't it?" Ayla smiled, but her eyes glistened with tears.

"Yes, of course. He started carving this horse right after you left."

"I think the hardest thing I ever did in my life was to tell Ranec that I was leaving to go with Jondalar. How is he, Danug?"

"He's fine, Ayla. He mated Tricie later that summer. You know, the woman who had the baby that probably came from his spirit? She has three children now. She's feisty, but she's good for him. She'll start raving about something, and he just smiles. He says he loves her spirit. She can't really resist his smile, and she really does love him. I don't think he will ever get over you completely, though. It caused a bit of trouble between them at first."

Ayla frowned. "What kind of trouble?"

"Well, he lets her have her way in almost everything, and I think in the beginning, she thought he was weak because he gave in so easily. She started pushing him, seeing how far she could go. Then she began demanding things, wanted him to get her this or that. He seemed to make a game out of it. No matter how outrageous, he would somehow manage to get whatever she asked for, and present it with one of those smiles of his. You know."

"Yes, I know," Ayla said, smiling through wet eyes as she remembered. "So pleased with himself, as though he had just won a competition, and was all full of his own cleverness."

"Then she started changing everything around," Danug continued. "His work space, his tools, all the special things he collected and arranged. He just let her. I think he was just seeing what she would do. But I happened to be in the lodge the day she decided to move this horse. I've never seen him so angry. He didn't raise his voice or anything—he just told her to put it back. She was surprised. I don't think she really believed him. He'd always given in to her. He told her again to put it back, and when she didn't, he grabbed her wrist, pretty hard, and took it from her. He told her never to touch that horse again. He said if she did, he would break the mating bond and pay the price. He said he loved her, but there was one piece of him she could never have. If she couldn't accept that she could leave.

"Tricie ran out of the lodge crying, but Ranec just put the horse back, then sat down and started carving. When she finally came back in, it was night. I couldn't help but overhear—their hearth is right next to ours—and well, I suppose I wanted to hear. She told him she wanted to stay with him. She said she loved him, had always loved him, and wanted to stay with him even if he did still love you. She promised never to touch the horse again. She didn't either. I think it gave her respect for him, and made her realize how she really felt about him. He's happy, Ayla. I don't think he'll ever forget you, but he's happy."

"I'll never forget him, either. I still think about him sometimes. If it hadn't been for Jondalar, I could have been happy with him. I did love him, I just loved Jondalar more. Tell me about Tricie's children," she said.

"That blending of spirits has produced an interesting mixture," Danug said. "The oldest is a boy—you saw him, didn't you? Tricie brought him to that Summer Meeting."

"Yes, I saw him. He was very fair. Is he still so fair?"

"His skin is the whitest I've ever seen, except where it's covered with freckles. Tricie has red hair and she's fair, but not as much as him. His eyes are pale blue, and he has fuzzy orangey-red hair. He can't stand the sun, he just burns, and if it's really bright, it hurts his eyes, but except for his color, he looks just like Ranec. It's strange to see them together, Ranec's brown skin next to Ra's white, but the same face. He's got Ranec's sense of humor, only more. Already, he can make anyone laugh, and he loves to travel. If he doesn't turn out to be a traveling storyteller, I'll be surprised. He can't wait until he's old enough to go off on his own. He wanted to come with us on our Journey. If he'd been a little older, I would have taken him. He'd have been good company.

"Tricie's little girl is a beauty. Her skin is dark, but not brown like Ranec's. Her hair is black as night, but her curls are softer. She has black eyes. Serious eyes. She's a quiet, delicate little thing, but I swear that there's not a man who sees her that isn't entranced by her. She'll have no trouble finding a mate.

"The baby is as dark as Ranec, and though it's hard to tell yet, I think his features are going to be more like Tricie's."

"It seems as though Tricie is a good addition to the Lion Camp, Danug. I wish I could see her children. I have a little girl, too," Ayla said, and suddenly remembered that she could have been having another one soon, were it not for her "call" to the deep cave. I would like to tell him that it is more than a blending of spirits that makes children, she thought.

"I know. I've met Jonayla. She looks just like you, except she has Jondalar's eyes. I wish I could take her back with me and let her meet everyone. Nezzie would love her. I've already fallen in love with her, just like I fell in love with you when I was a boy," Danug said with a delighted laugh.

Ayla looked so surprised, he laughed harder, and she could hear Talut's big, booming laughter coming from Danug. "In love with me?"

"I'm not surprised you didn't notice. Between Ranec and Jondalar, you had enough to think about, but I couldn't stop thinking about you. I dreamed about you. In fact, I still love you, Ayla. How would you like to come back to the Lion Camp with me?" There was a broad smile on his face and a twinkle in his eye, but something more, too. A hint of wistful longing, a wish that he knew would never be fulfilled.

She looked away for a moment, then changed the subject. "Tell me about the rest. How are Nezzie and Talut, Latie and Rugie?"

"Mother's fine. Getting older, that's all. Talut is losing his hair, and he hates it. Latie is mated, has a girl, and still talks about horses. Rugie is looking for a mate, or rather, the young men are looking at her. She's had her First Rites; Tusie did too, at the same time. Oh, and Deegie has two sons. She told me to give you her love. You never got to know her brother, Tarneg, did you? His mate has three little ones. You know they built another earthlodge nearby; Deegie and Tarneg are headwoman and headman. Tulie is pleased that she can see her grandchildren nearly every day. And she has taken another mate. Barzec says she's too much woman for only one man."

"Do I know him?" Ayla asked.

Danug smiled. "In fact, you do. It's Wymez."

"Wymez! You mean the man of Ranec's hearth, the flint-knapper Jondalar admires so much?" Ayla asked.

"Yes, that Wymez. He surprised us all, even Tulie, I think. And old Mamut has gone to the next world. We have a new one, but it's hard to get used to having someone else at the Third Hearth."

"I'm sorry to hear that. I loved that old man. I've been training to be One Who Serves The Mother, but he's the one who started it. My training is almost over," Ayla said. She didn't want to say too much until she talked to Zelandoni.

"That's what Jondalar said. I always thought you would serve the Mother. Mamut would never have adopted you if he didn't think so. There was a time when the Lion Camp thought you might be their Mamut, after the old man left this world. Ayla, you may be Zelandonii here, but you are still Mamutoi, still numbered among the Lion Camp."

"It makes me happy to hear that. No matter what names or ties I may acquire, in my heart I will always be Ayla of the Mamutoi," she said.

"You certainly did acquire some names and leave a trail of stories behind you on your Journey," Danug said. "Not just from the S'Armunai. I even heard about you from people who never met you. You were everything from a skilled healer and controller of surprising spiritual forces to the incarnation of the Great Earth Mother herself, a living muta—I guess here it's donii—come to help Her people. And Jondalar was her fair-haired and handsome mate—as they say here, 'Her pale shining lover.' Even Wolf was an incarnation, of the Wolf Star. The stories about him range from avenging beast to lovable creature who tended babies. The horses, too. They were animals of wonder that the Great Horse Spirit allowed to be controlled by you. There was one story—from Aldanor's people—that claimed the horses could fly, and carried you and Jondalar back to your homes in the next world. I was beginning to wonder if all the stories could be about the same people, but after talking to Jondalar, I think you both had some interesting adventures."

"I think people like to enlarge stories to make them seem more interesting," Ayla said. "And who's to prove them wrong once the people the stories are about are gone? We just traveled back here to Jondalar's home. You no doubt have had your share of adventures."

"But we didn't travel with a pair of magical horses and a wolf."

"Danug, you know there is nothing magical about those animals. You watched Jondalar train Racer, and you were there when I brought Wolf to the lodge as a tiny puppy. He's just a wolf that got used to people because he grew up with them."

"Which reminds me, where is that animal? I wonder if he'll still remember me," Danug said.

"As soon as we got here, he ran off to look for Jonayla," Ayla said. "Apparently, she is with her age-mates doing something for the zelandonia. But I still haven't seen Jondalar. Did he say anything about going hunting?"

"Not to me," Danug said, "but the three of us haven't been around here that much. We're strangers, from far away, but introduced by Jondalar as your kin, so we have been welcomed as kin. Everyone wants to hear our stories and ask questions about our people. We've all been asked to participate in First Rites. Even me, as big as I am, though I was questioned about my experience with such young women, and I think I was tested by one or two 'donii-women.'" The huge young man grinned with delight. "Jondalar translated for us in the beginning, but we've been learning Zelandonii, and can get by fairly well now on our own. People have been wonderful to us, but they keep wanting to give us things, and you know how hard it is to carry much when you're on a Journey. In fact, I did bring something that you left behind. I gave it to Jondalar. Do you remember the piece of ivory Talut gave you when you left? The one that showed landmarks to help to get started out right on your Journey?"

"Yes. We had to leave it behind to make room."

"Laduni gave it to me to give back to you."

"That must have made Jondalar happy. It was one thing he wanted to keep as a reminder of his stay with the Lion Camp."

"I understand that. The S'Armunai gave me something that I will definitely keep. I'll show you." Danug took out a figure of a mammoth made out of a very hard but strange kind of material. "I don't know what kind of stone it is. Aldanor says they make it, but I don't know whether to believe him."

"They do make that stone. They start with muddy clay, then shape it, and burn it in a very hot fire in a special enclosed space, like an oven built in the earth, until it turns to stone. I watched the S'Armuna of Three Sisters Camp do it. She is the one who discovered how to make that stone." Ayla paused, and her eyes took on a faraway look, as though she were looking inside at a memory. "She was not an evil person, but Attaroa did turn her the wrong way for a while. The S'Armunai are an interesting people."

"Jondalar told me what happened to both of you there. But Aldanor is from a different Camp. We stopped overnight at Three Sisters. I thought it was strange that there were so many women, but they were very hospitable. After I talked to Jondalar, I realized that I might not have made it this far if you hadn't passed that way first. I shudder to think about it," Danug said.

The leather entrance cover was moved aside. Danug and Ayla looked up and saw Dalanar looking in. "If I'd known you wanted to keep her to yourself, I might have thought again before taking you along with us to this Summer Meeting, young man," Dalanar said sternly, then smiled. "Can't say that I blame you. I know you haven't seen her in a long time, but there are many other people who want to talk to this young woman."

"Dalanar!" Ayla said, getting up and going outside the small tent to hug him. He'd aged, but he still looked so much like Jondalar, she felt a warm glow at the sight of him. "Did Danug and the other two come with you? How did they find you?"

"By accident—or it was meant to be—depending on who you ask. Some of us were out hunting. There's a river valley nearby that attracts a lot of passing herds. They saw us and indicated that they wanted to join in the hunt. We were more than happy to have three healthy young men help out. I had already been thinking that if we made some really successful hunts, enough to put some meat down for next winter and take some with us, we might go to the Zelandonii Meeting this year.

"Their help made a difference. We counted six bison kills. It wasn't until later that evening that this young man started asking about you and Jondalar, and how to find the Zelandonii," Dalanar said, indicating the huge red-haired man just emerging from the tent.

"Language was a bit of a problem. The only thing Danug could say was 'Jondalar of the Ninth Cave of the Zelandonii.' I tried to tell him Jondalar was the son of my hearth, but didn't have much luck," the older man continued. "Then Echozar returned from the flint mine, and Danug started talking to him in signs. He was surprised to find out Echozar could talk, but not nearly as surprised as Echozar was to see Danug and Druwez talk to him in signs. When Echozar asked where they learned it, he told us about his brother, a boy he said his mother adopted, who died. He said you were the one who taught everyone the hand signs so he could talk and be understood, Ayla.

"That's how we managed to communicate at first. Danug and Druwez talked to Echozar in signs, and he translated. I made up my mind then and told Danug we were going to the Zelandonii Summer Meeting and would take them with us. The next day Willamar and his party happened to arrive. It's amazing how good he is at communicating with people even if he doesn't know the language."

"Is Willamar here, too?" Ayla asked.

"Yes, I'm here."

Ayla spun around and smiled with delight to see the old Trade Master. They hugged with warmth and affection. "Did you come with the Lanzadonii, too?"

"No, we didn't arrive with them," Willamar said. "We still had a few other stops to make to finish out the round. We got here a few days ago. I was just getting ready to leave for the Ninth Cave."

"We actually came a little early this year," Dalanar said. "I knew where the Ninth would probably set up camp, so we're close by."

"I happened to be one of the people who saw the Ninth Cave coming," Danug said. "When I saw the horses from a distance, I knew it had to be your people, Ayla. I was really disappointed when you were not with them, though I was glad to see Jondalar. At least he could speak Mamutoi. I recognized Jonayla as your daughter right away, especially when I saw her sitting on the back of that gray horse. If you hadn't come, I was going to go back with the Ninth Cave and surprise you, but you surprised us instead," Danug said.

"You are a surprise, Danug, a welcome one. And you can still come and visit the Ninth Cave, you know," Ayla said, then turned to Dalanar. "I am glad you decided to come with the Lanzadonii. Is Jerika with you? Marthona will be so disappointed not to see all of you."

"I was sorry to hear she wasn't coming. Jerika was looking forward to seeing her, too. It's amazing what good friends they've turned out to be. How is Marthona?"

"Not entirely well," Ayla said, shaking her head. "She complains about her aching joints, but it's more than that. She has pain in her chest and trouble breathing when she exerts herself too much. I always did plan to come to the Meeting as soon as I could, but I hated to leave her. She did seem much better when I left, though."

"Do you really think she's better?" Willamar asked. His eyes had become serious.

"She said if she had felt as good earlier, when the Ninth Cave left, she might have come, but I don't think she could walk the whole way."

"Someone could have carried her," Dalanar said. "I carried Hochaman on my shoulders all the way to the Great Waters of the West, twice, before he died." Dalanar turned to Danug. "Hochaman was the mate of Jerika's mother. They traveled all the way from the Endless Seas of the East. His tears mingled with the salt of the Great Waters of the West, but they were tears of joy. It was his greatest wish to go as far as the land went, farther than anyone ever did. I've never heard of anyone who traveled farther."

"We remembered that story, Dalanar, and wanted to carry her," Ayla said, "but she didn't want to ride on Jondalar's shoulders. I think she felt it would be too undignified. She didn't want to ride on Whinney, either. I asked her, but she didn't want to do that either. She likes the horses, but the idea of riding one always did scare her." Ayla noticed the travois, the simple construction of poles and cross-mats, now unloaded on the ground. "I wonder . . . do you think she would mind riding on the pole-drag, Willamar?"

"For that matter, a few people could take turns carrying her on a litter," Dalanar volunteered. "With four people, one on each corner, it would be easy. She's not heavy."

"And she could sit up; she wouldn't have to look backward. I'm tempted to tell Jondalar to go back and get her, but I haven't seen him yet. Has he been with you, Dalanar?" Ayla asked.

"No, I haven't seen him all day. He could be anywhere. You know how it is at a Meeting like this," Dalanar said. "I haven't even seen Bokovan all day."

"Bokovan? Are Joplaya and Echozar here? I thought Echozar said he'd never come back after the big fuss that was made over his joining with Joplaya," Ayla said.

"It took a lot of persuading. Jerika and I thought he should come for Bokovan's sake. He's going to need to find a mate someday, too, and there aren't enough Lanzadonii yet. All the youngsters are raised like siblings, and you know how it is when children grow up together. They don't usually think of each other as potential mates. I told Echozar that it was only a few people who objected, but he wasn't convinced. It wasn't until this big Mamutoi and his cousin and friend came that he decided to go. They helped most of all."

"What did they do?"

"That's just it. They didn't do anything. You know how people always seem to feel uncomfortable around Echozar when they first meet him—you never did, but you were an exception," Dalanar said. "I think that's why he's always had a special fondness for you. Danug didn't either, just started talking to him in signs. The young S'Armunai didn't seem terribly bothered by Echozar either. Apparently they don't think of the ones of mixed spirits with as much antagonism as some of the Zelandonii."

"I think that's true," Ayla said. "Mixtures seem more common among them, and more accepted, though not entirely, especially when the look of the Clan is as strong as it is in Echozar. He might have some problem even there."

"Not with Aldanor. All three of those young men accepted him as easily as anyone else. They didn't make him an exception, or make special efforts to be nice to him. They just treated him like any other young man. It made Echozar realize, I think, that not everyone would hate him, or object to him. He could make friends, and so could Bokovan. In fact, that young couple that mated the same time you did, Jondecam and Levela? They have all but adopted Bokovan. He's over there all the time, playing with their youngsters, and all the rest of the children that always seem to be running around their camp. I wonder sometimes how they put up with having so many children there all the time," Dalanar said.

"Levela has no end of patience," Ayla said. "I think she loves it." She turned to Danug. "You will go with us back to the Ninth Cave, won't you? We haven't even started catching up on what everyone in the Lion Camp is doing."

"We were rather hoping to winter with you. I'd like to go all the way to the Great Waters of the West before I return. Besides, I don't think there is any way we're going to get Aldanor away from here before spring, and maybe not then," Danug said, smiling at his friend.

Ayla looked at him questioningly. "Why not?"

"When you see him around Jondalar's sister, you'll know."

"Folara?"

"Yes, Folara. He is absolutely smitten with her. Completely, totally, out of his mind over her, and I think the feeling may be mutual. At least she certainly doesn't seem to mind spending time with him. A lot of time with him." Though Danug had spoken Mamutoi, he was grinning. His language was similar, and he had learned quite a bit of Mamutoi on their Journey, and her name was the same word in any language. Ayla saw Aldanor's face flush. She raised her eyebrows and then smiled.

The tall, graceful young woman who Folara had become easily commanded attention everywhere she went. She had her mother's natural elegance and Willamar's easy charm, and as Jondalar had always predicted she would be, Folara was beautiful. Her beauty was not quite the consummate manifestation of perfection that Jondalar had been in his youth—and for the most part still was. Her mouth was a little too generous, her eyes were spaced a bit too wide, her light brown hair was a touch too fine, but the minor imperfections only made her more approachable and appealing.

Folara had had no lack of suitors, but none had quite excited her fancy, or fulfilled her unexpressed expectations. Her lack of interest in choosing a mate was driving her mother to distraction; she wanted to see a grandchild from her own daughter. After spending so much time with the woman, she had grown to understand her better, and knew that Folara's regard for the young S'Armunai would be of great consequence to

Marthona. The biggest question was would Aldanor decide to stay with the Zelandonii, or would Folara go with him back to the S'Armunai? Marthona needs to be here, Ayla thought.

"Willamar, have you noticed Folara's interest in this young S'Armunai?" Ayla asked, smiling at the self-consciously blushing visitor.

"Now that you mention it, I guess they have spent a lot of time together since I've been here,"

"You know Marthona, Willamar. You know she would want to be here if Folara is getting serious about a young man, especially one who may want her to go with him back to his home. I'm sure she would come here if she could."

"You're right, Ayla, but is she strong enough?"

"You said something about carrying her on a litter, Dalanar. How long do you think it would take for a few strong young men to run back to the Ninth Cave and bring her here?"

"No more than a few days for good runners, maybe twice that to bring her back, and however long it would take her to prepare. Do you really think she's well enough?" Dalanar said.

"Would Jerika be well enough if it was Joplaya?" Ayla asked.

Dalanar nodded with understanding.

"Marthona seemed much better when I left, and if she doesn't have to exert herself, I think she would be as well here, where there are so many people to help her, as she is at the Ninth Cave. She likes the horses, to watch them or pat them, and I think under the circumstances, she'd even ride the pole-drag to get here, but I believe she'd be more comfortable sitting up on a litter and able to talk to people along the way. I'd ask Jondalar, but he doesn't seem to be around anywhere. Could you and Dalanar, and maybe Joharran, arrange it, Willamar?"

"I think we could do that, Ayla. You're probably right. Folara's mother needs to be here if she is getting serious about mating, especially to a foreigner."

"Mother! Mother! You came! You finally came," a young voice called out. It was an interruption Ayla was delighted to hear. She turned and smiled, and her eyes lit up as she held out her arms to the young girl running toward her, with the wolf happily loping beside her. Her daughter fairly flew into her arms.

"I missed you so much," Ayla said, hugging her close; then she pulled back to look at her and hugged her again. "I can't believe how much you have grown, Jonayla!" she said when she put her down.

Zelandoni had followed the child back, at a slower pace, but smiled warmly at Ayla as she approached. After they had embraced in greeting she asked, "You finished your watching?"

"Yes, and glad of it, but it was exciting to see the sun stop and turn back, and mark it myself. The only problem was not having anyone there to share it with who really understood. I kept thinking of you," Ayla said.

Zelandoni observed the young woman closely. There was a different air about her; Ayla had changed. The woman tried to find it. Ayla has lost weight—has she been sick? She should be starting to show, but her waistline is thinner and her breasts are smaller. O, Doni, she thought. She isn't pregnant anymore! She must have miscarried.

But there was something else, a new assurance in her manner, an acceptance of the tragedy, a self-confident poise. She knew who she was—and who she was, was Zelandoni! She has been "called"! She must have lost the baby, then.

"We're going to have to talk, aren't we, Ayla?" Zelandoni Who Was First said, stressing her name. She could be called Ayla, but she wasn't Ayla anymore.

"Yes," the young woman said. She didn't have to say more. She knew that the One Who Was First Among Those Who Served The Mother understood.

"We should do it soon."

"Yes, we should."

"And, Ayla, I am sorry. I know you wanted the baby," she said quietly. Before Ayla could respond, more people crowded around.

Nearly all her close friends and kin came to the camp to greet her. Everyone seemed to be there except Jondalar, and no one seemed to know where he was. Usually when a person was leaving the Meeting Camp to go off by themselves or with just one or two others, someone was told where they were going. Ayla might have begun to worry, but no one else seemed to.

Most people stayed to have a meal or a snack. They recounted events that had taken place, talked about people, who was getting mated, who'd had another child or was expecting one, who had decided to sever the knot, or take a second mate—friendly gossip.

In the afternoon, people started wandering off to other activities. Ayla arranged her sleeping roll and the rest of the belongings that she had brought with her. She was glad she had taken the horses to the meadow in the woods earlier, and the corral that had been fenced for the horses, not so much to keep them in as to keep people out. Horses in a meadow were fair game under normal circumstances. Though everyone knew about the horses the Ninth Cave brought with them, just to leave no doubt that these were in fact those special horses, the area was conspicuously fenced. Jondalar and Jonayla often took them to the grassy steppes, to ride, or just to let them graze, but whenever they were not in the enclosure, she knew someone was with them.

Jonayla left with Zelandoni and Wolf to go back to the area of the zelandonia to finish working out the details of the special evening that was planned. Ayla decided to give Whinney a good grooming after the hot, dusty ride, and went to the horse meadow with soft pieces of leather and teasel brushes. She brushed Racer and Gray a bit, too, just to give them a scratching and some attention.

She looked at the small stream that flowed along the edge of the grassy glen before emptying into The River, and remembered the last time the Meeting was in this location. There was a swimming hole some distance upstream, she recalled. Not many people knew about it because it was far enough away from the Meeting Camp to make it inconvenient for general use. She hadn't known her adopted people as well then, and she and Jondalar used to go there when they wanted to get away from the crowds and spend some time alone together.

A swim would feel good right now, she thought, and the river is muddy from so much use. She started walking upstream toward the bend in the small stream that cut a deeper hole near the outside edge and left a grassy strand with a beach of small pebbles on the inside curve. She smiled thinking about

Jondalar and what they used to do beside that stream. She'd been thinking about him so much, thinking about how he could make her feel. She felt herself warming to his imagined touch, and even noticed a wetness between her legs. Wouldn't it be fun to try to make another baby? she thought.

As she approached the swimming hole, she heard splashing, and then voices, and almost turned back. Sounds like someone else has found this place, she thought. I'd hate to disturb another couple looking for a place to be alone. But it might not be a couple. It might just be some people going for a swim. As she approached, she heard a woman's voice, and then a man's. She couldn't make out the words, but something about that voice bothered her.

She moved as silently as she ever had when stalking an animal with her sling. She heard more talking, then a deep laugh of sheer abandon. She knew that laugh, though she hadn't heard it much recently, and it was rare enough in any case. Then she heard the woman's voice, and recognized it. She had a peculiar sinking feeling in the pit of her stomach as she looked through the bushes that skirted the small beach.

32

Jondalar and Marona were just coming out of the water as Ayla looked through the bushes. With a stab of anguish, she watched Marona turn to face Jondalar, put her arms around him and press her naked body close to his, then reach up to kiss him. Jondalar bent down to meet her lips. With fascinated horror, she watched his hands begin to caress her body. How many times had she felt his knowing hands?

Ayla wanted to run, but she couldn't move. They moved a few steps closer, toward a soft leather hide spread out on the grass just in front of her. She could see that he wasn't really aroused. But no one had seen him since she arrived, he'd been gone all day, and it was obvious to her that they had already used the leather blanket, at least once. Marona pressed against him again, kissed him deeply, as though with great hunger, then slowly dropped down in front of him. With a languid, knowing laugh, Marona enclosed her mouth around his flaccid manhood while Jondalar stood looking down at her.

Ayla could see his mounting excitement in his expression of intense pleasure. She had never seen his face when she did that to him—was that how he looked? As Marona moved rhythmically back and forth, his tumescent organ pushed her farther away from him as it began to extend.

It was an agony for Ayla to see him with her. She could hardly breathe, her stomach knotted in pain, her head pounded. She had never experienced this kind of feeling before. Was this anguish jealousy? Was this how Jondalar felt when I went to Ranec's bed? she thought. Why didn't he tell me? I didn't know then, I never felt jealousy before, and he never told me. He only said it was my right to choose who I wanted.

That means it's his right to be there with Marona!

Her eyes filled with tears, she couldn't stand it, she had to get away. She turned and started to run blindly through the small woods, but she tripped on an exposed root and crashed to the ground.

"Who's there? What's going on?" Ayla heard Jondalar's voice call out. She scrambled to her feet and started off again as Jondalar pushed the brush aside. "Ayla? Ayla!" he said in shocked surprise. "What are you doing here?"

She turned to face the man who was coming after her. "I didn't mean to interfere," she said, trying to compose herself. "You have the right to couple with whoever you want, Jondalar. Even Marona."

Marona pushed through the screen of bushes and stood close to Jondalar, pressing her body against him. "That's right, Ayla," she said with an exultant laugh. "He can couple with whoever he wants. What do you expect a man to do when his mate is too busy for him? We have coupled often, and not only this summer. Why do you think I moved back to the Ninth Cave? He didn't want me to tell you, but now that you've found out, you might as well know the whole story." She laughed again; then with a vicious sneer she said, "You may have stolen him from me, Ayla, but you haven't been able to keep him to yourself."

"I didn't steal him from you, Marona. I didn't even know you until I arrived here. Jondalar chose me of his own free will. Now he can choose you, if he wants, but tell me, do you really love him? Or are you just trying to cause trouble?" Ayla said. Then she turned and with as much dignity as she could gather, she hurried away.

Jondalar shrugged off the woman hanging on him and caught up with Ayla in a few strides. "Ayla, please wait! Let me explain!" he said.

"What is there to explain? Marona is right. How could I expect anything else? You were in the middle of something, Jondalar. Why don't you go back and finish it," she said, starting away again. "I'm sure Marona will be able to arouse you once more. She had you well on your way."

"I don't want Marona, not if I can have you, Ayla," Jondalar said, suddenly afraid he might lose her.

Marona looked at him with surprise. She meant nothing to him, she realized. She had meant nothing to him all along. She had made herself available, and he had found her an expedient way to take care of his urges. Marona glared at them both with anger, but Jondalar didn't notice.

He was concentrated on Ayla. Now he wished he hadn't given in to Marona's invitations, hadn't used her so casually. He was so intent on Ayla, on trying to think of something to say that could somehow explain how he felt, that he didn't even notice when the woman he had so recently been with stormed past him with her clothes bunched up in her arms. But Ayla did.

As a man, after he returned from his stay with Dalanar, Jondalar had always had his choice of women, but he had never really loved one. Nothing ever matched the powerful intensity of his first love, and his memory of those overwhelming emotions had been made stronger by the appalling scandal and disgrace it had brought on both Zolena and himself. She had been his donii-woman, his instructor and guide in the ways that a man should behave with a woman, but he was not supposed to fall in love with her. She was not supposed to allow it.

He had come to believe that he would never love a woman again. He had finally concluded that as a penalty imposed by the Mother for his youthful indiscretion, he would forever be unable to fall in love—until Ayla. And he'd had to travel for more than a year, to an entirely different and unfamiliar place, to find her. He loved Ayla more than his life. It overwhelmed him. He would do anything for her, go anyplace for her, he would give his life for her. The only person for whom he felt a love as strong, if of a different nature, was Jonayla.

"You should be grateful she is there to satisfy your needs, Jondalar," Ayla said, still hurting, and trying to cover the pain. "I am going to be even busier than ever now. I have been called. I will do as She wishes now. I will be as a child of the Great Earth Mother. I am Zelandoni."

"You were called? Ayla, when?" His voice was full of frantic worry. He'd seen some of the zelandonia returning from their first call, and he'd seen some, found later, who had not. "I should have been there, I could have helped you."

"No, Jondalar. You couldn't have helped me. No one can help. It must be done alone. I survived, and the Mother gave me a great Gift, but I had to make a sacrifice for it. She wanted our baby, Jondalar. I lost it in the cave," Ayla said with as much dignity as she could muster.

"Our baby? What baby? Jonayla was with me."

"The baby that was started when I came down from the cliff early one night. I suppose I should consider myself lucky that you hadn't already been with Marona that night, or I wouldn't have had a baby to sacrifice," she said with hollow bitterness.

"You were pregnant when you were called? Oh, Great Mother!" He was feeling panicky—he didn't want her to leave like that. What could he say to keep her there, to keep her talking? "Ayla, I know you think that's how new life starts, but you can't be sure."

"Yes, Jondalar, I can. The Great Mother told me. That was the Gift I received in exchange for my baby's life." She said it with such haunting, painful certainty, it left no room for doubt. "I thought we might try to start another, but I can see you are too busy for me." He stood there, stunned, as she walked away.

"O Doni, Great Mother, what have I done?" Jondalar cried out in anguish. "I've made her stop loving me. Oh, why did she have to see us?"

He stumbled after her, forgetting his clothes. Then, as she hurried away, he dropped to his knees, and followed her with only his eyes. Look at her, he thought, she's so thin! It must have been so hard for her. Some acolytes die. What if Ayla had died? I wasn't even there to help her. Why didn't I stay behind with her? I should have known she was almost ready, her training was nearly over, but I wanted to come to the Summer Meeting. I didn't think what might happen to her. All I could think of was myself.

As Ayla was lost to sight, he hunched forward, closed his eyes, and buried his face in his hands, as though trying not to see what he had done.

"Why did I couple with Marona?" he moaned aloud. Ayla has never coupled with anyone but me, he thought, not since

Ranec, not since we left the Mamutoi. Even at ceremonies and festivals to honor the Mother, when almost everyone chooses someone else, she has never chosen anyone but me. People talk about it. How many men have looked at me with envy, thinking what great Pleasure I must give her, for her never to choose anyone else.

"Why did Ayla have to see us?"

I never thought she would get here in the daytime. I thought she'd ride all day and get here late. I thought it was safe to come here during the day. I never wanted to cause Ayla pain. She's had enough pain. And now she's lost a baby. I didn't even know she was going to have another baby, and she lost it.

Did it really start that night? It was such an incredible night. I could hardly believe it when she came to bed and woke me up. Will it ever be like that again? She said the Mother wanted our baby. Was it our baby? In exchange Doni gave her a Gift. Ayla was given a Gift from the Mother? The Mother told her it was our baby, my baby and hers.

"Did Ayla lose my baby?" Jondalar said, his forehead knotted with the familiar frown.

Why did she come here? She said she wanted to start another baby. Was she looking for me? We always came to this swimming hole the last time the Meeting was here. I should have thought about that. I shouldn't have brought Marona here. Especially Marona. I knew how Ayla would feel if she found out about her, that's why I made Marona promise never to tell.

"Why did she have to see us?" he beseeched the vacant woods. "Have I become so used to her never choosing anyone else that I've forgotten what it was like for me?" He recalled the bitter pain and desolation he had felt the time she chose Ranec. I know how she must have felt when she saw me with Marona, he thought. Just the way I did when Ranec told her to come to his bed and she went, but she didn't know then. She thought she was supposed to go with him. How would I feel if she chose someone else now?

I tried to drive her away then because I was so hurt, but she still loved me. She made a Matrimonial tunic for me even when she was promised to Ranec. Jondalar felt the same wretched torment at the thought of losing her now as he had when he thought he was going to lose her to Ranec. Only this time it was worse. This time he was the one who had hurt her.

Ayla ran blindly ahead, tears clouding her vision, but they could not wash away her misery. She had thought about Jondalar at the Ninth Cave, dreamed about him at night, hungered for him on her way, and pushed herself to get here so she could be with him. She couldn't return to the camp and face all the people. She needed to be alone. She stopped at the horse enclosure and led Whinney out, put the horse blanket on her back, and climbed on, then raced her toward the open grassland.

Whinney was still tired from the trip, but responded to the woman's urging and galloped across the plains. Ayla could not get the picture of Marona and Jondalar out of her mind; she could think of nothing else, and soon forgot about directing the horse, but simply rode her. The mare slowed when she felt the woman cease to actively direct her and turned back toward the Camp at a slow walk, stopping to graze now and then. It was growing dark by the time they reached the Meeting site, and cooling down fast, but Ayla felt nothing except the deep numbing cold inside her. The horse did not feel her passenger take control again until they reached the horse grove and saw several people.

"Ayla, people have been wondering where you've been," Proleva said. "Jonayla was here looking for you, but after she ate, she went to Levela's to play with Bokovan when you didn't return."

"I've been riding," Ayla said.

"Jondalar finally turned up," Joharran said. "He came stumbling into the camp a while ago. I told him you were looking for him, but he just mumbled something incoherent."

Her eyes were glazed as she walked into the camp. She passed by Zelandoni without greeting her, without even seeing her.

The woman eyed her sharply. She knew something was wrong. "Ayla, we haven't seen much of you since you arrived," the Donier said, surprised that she'd had to speak first.

"I guess not," Ayla said.

It was plain to Zelandoni that Ayla's thoughts were somewhere else. Jondalar's "incoherent mumbling" hadn't been unclear to her, even if she hadn't understood the words. His actions were clear enough. She had also seen Marona emerge from the small wooded area looking disheveled, but not on the normal path used by most members of the Ninth Cave. She came to their camp from a different direction, went directly into the tent she had been sharing, and began to pack up her things. She told Proleva some friends from the Fifth Cave wanted her to stay with them.

Zelandoni had been aware of Jondalar's dalliance with Marona from the beginning. At first she thought there was little harm in it. She knew his true feelings for Ayla, and thought Marona would be just a passing fancy, something to relieve him at a time when Ayla had other demands on her and no choice but to be away at times. But she hadn't counted on Marona's obsession to get him back and to get back at Ayla, or her ability to insinuate herself upon him. Their physical attraction had always been strong. Even in the past, it had been the primary focus of their relationship. Sometimes, Zelandoni had suspected, it was the only thing they had had in common.

The Donier guessed that Ayla hadn't fully recovered from her ordeal in the cave. Her loss of weight and the gaunt hollows in her face would have given her away even if she hadn't seen it in Ayla's eyes. Zelandoni had seen too many acolytes return from a calling, emerging from a cave or returning from wandering the steppe, not to know the danger of the ordeal. She, herself, almost didn't survive. Since Ayla lost a baby at the same time, she would very likely also be suffering the melancholy most women felt after giving birth, which was often worse after miscarrying.

But the One Who Was First had seen more than the suffering Ayla had endured in the cave in her eyes now. She saw pain, the sharp chilling pain of jealousy with all the related feelings of betrayal, anger, doubt, and fear. She loves him too much; it's not hard to do, the woman once known as Zolena recalled. The First had often wondered during the past few years how a woman who loved a man so much could be Zelandoni, too, but Ayla's talent was formidable. In spite of her love for the man, it could not be ignored. And if anything, his feeling for her was even stronger.

But as much as he loved her, Jondalar was a man with strong drives. It was difficult for him to ignore them. It was especially true when there were no societal constraints against it, and someone as intimately familiar with him as Marona was using every faculty she possessed to encourage him. It was too easy to fall into the habit of going to her rather than bothering Ayla when she was busy.

Zelandoni knew Jondalar hadn't mentioned anything about his ongoing liaison to Ayla, and instinctively, others who cared about them had tried to shield her. They hoped Ayla would not find out, but the Donier knew if he continued, it was a vain hope. He should have known it, too.

In spite of how well she had learned the ways of the Zelandonii and seemed to fit in, Ayla had not been born to them. Their ways were not natural to her. Zelandoni almost wished the Summer Meeting were over. She would like to be able to watch the young woman, make sure she was all right, but the last part of the Summer Meeting was a very busy time for the One Who Was First. She observed the young woman, trying to discern the extent of her feelings over her discovery of Jondalar's encounters with Marona, and what effects it would have.

At Proleva's urging, Ayla accepted a plate of food, but she did little more than push it around. She dumped the food and cleaned the plate, then returned it. "I wish Jonayla would come back; do you know how long she'll be gone?" Ayla said. "I'm sorry I wasn't here when she came."

"You could go to Levela's and get her," Proleva said. "Levela would love it if you came to visit. I didn't see where Jondalar went. He may be there, too."

"I'm really tired," Ayla said. "I don't think I'd be very good company. I'm going to bed early, but will you send Jonayla in when she comes?"

"Are you feeling all right, Ayla?" Proleva asked, finding it hard to believe that she would just go to bed. She had been trying to find Jondalar all day, and now she wouldn't even walk a little ways to look for him.

"I'm fine. I'm just tired," Ayla said, heading for one of the large circular dwellings that ringed the central fireplace.

A wall of sturdy vertical panels made of overlapped cattail leaves, which shed rain, was attached to the outside of a circle of poles sunk into the ground. A second interior wall of panels woven out of flattened bulrush stems was attached to the inside of the poles, leaving an air space between for extra insulation to make it cooler on hot days and, with a fire inside, warmer on cool nights. The roof was a thick thatch of phragmite reeds, sloping down from a center pole, supported by a circular frame of slender alder poles lashed together. The smoke escaped through a hole near the center.

The construction provided a fairly large enclosed space that could be left open or divided into smaller areas with movable interior panels. Sleeping rolls were spread out on mats made of bulrushes, tall phragmite reeds, cattail leaves, and grasses around a central fireplace. Ayla partially undressed and crawled into her sleeping roll, but was far from ready to sleep. When she closed her eyes, all she could see was the scene of Jondalar with Marona, and her mind whirled with the implications.

Ayla knew that among the Zelandoni jealousy was not condoned, though she was not as aware that behavior designed to provoke it was even less acceptable. People recognized that jealousy existed and fully understood its cause, and more important, its often damaging effects. But in a harsh land often overwhelmed by long and bitter glacial winters, survival depended on mutual cooperation and assistance. The unwritten strictures against any behavior that could undermine the necessary goodwill required to maintain that unanimity and understanding were strongly enforced by social customs.

In such adverse conditions, children were especially at risk. Many died young, and while the community in general was important to their well-being, a close, caring family was considered essential. Though most commonly families began with a woman and man, they could be extended in any number of ways. Not only with grandparents, aunts, uncles, and cousins but, so long as it was agreeable to everyone involved, a woman might select more than one man, a man might choose two, or more, women, or even multiple couples might join. The only exception was the prohibition of close family members joining.

Siblings could not mate with each other, or those recognized as "close" cousins, for example. Other relationships were highly disapproved, though not expressly forbidden, such as a young man and his donii-woman.

Once the family was formed, customs and practices had developed to encourage its continuity. Jealousy did not favor long-term bonds, and various measures to alleviate its detrimental effects were understood. Passing attractions could often be appeased by the socially approved festivals to honor the Mother. Incidental relationships outside the family were usually overlooked, if they were conducted with restraint and discretion.

If the appeal of a mate was waning, or a stronger attraction developed, incorporation into the family was preferable to breaking it apart. And when nothing would serve except to sever the knot, there were always penalties of some sort levied against one or another or several of the people involved to discourage breaking apart, particularly when there were children.

Penalties might consist of continued assistance and support of the family for a period of time, sometimes coupled with restrictions against forming a new bond for a similar period of time. Or the penalty might be paid all at once, particularly if one or more of the people wanted to move away. There were no hard-and-fast rules. Each situation was judged individually within generally known customs by a number of people, usually those with no direct interest, who were known to have qualities of wisdom, fairness, and leadership.

If, for example, a man wanted to sever the knot with his mate and leave a family to mate with another woman, there would have to be a waiting period, the duration determined by several factors, one of which might be if the other woman was pregnant. During the wait, they would be urged to join the family rather than break the bond. If there was too much antipathy for the new woman to want to join or for her to be accepted into the family, the man could break the existing bond, but he could be required to assist in the support of the original family for some stated length of time. Or some total amount of stored foods, tools, implements, or whatever that could be traded could be paid at once.

A woman could also leave and, especially if she had children and was living at her mate's Cave, might return to the Cave she was born to, or move to the Cave of another man. If some or all of the children stayed with the mate, or if a woman left a mate who was sick, or disabled, a woman might have to pay a penalty. If they were living at her home Cave, she could ask for the Cave to make an unwanted mate leave—his mother's Cave would then be required to accept him. Usually there would be a reason given—a mate was cruel to her or her children, or he was lazy and didn't provide adequately—although it might not be the real reason. It could be that he wasn't paying enough attention to her, or that she was interested in pursuing someone else, or simply that she was no longer interested in living with him, or any other man.

Occasionally one or the other or both simply said they no longer wished to live together. The Cave's concern was, primarily, for the children and if they were provided for; if they were grown, almost any arrangement that people chose to make was acceptable. If there were no children involved, and no other extenuating circumstances, such as an illness of a family member, the knot could be severed—the relationship broken—with relative ease by either the woman or the man, usually involving little more than cutting a symbolic knot in a rope and moving out.

In any of those situations, jealousy could be most disruptive, but in any case, was not tolerated. The Cave would step in, if necessary. So long as it was agreeable and did not cause problems between Caves or disrupt the relationships of others, people could make almost any arrangements they wanted.

Of course, nothing kept anyone from avoiding a penalty by simply packing up and moving away, but other Caves usually learned about most separations sooner or later, and did not hesitate to exert social pressures as well. He or she would not be driven out, but would not be made very welcome either. A person would have to live alone, or move far away to avoid the penalties, and most people didn't want to be alone or live with strangers.

In the case of Dalanar, he had been more than willing to pay his penalty and then some. He didn't have another woman, and in fact still loved Marthona; he just couldn't bear to stay with her anymore when so much of her time and attention was directed toward the needs of the Ninth Cave. He traded belongings in order to pay the full penalty as soon as possible so he could leave, but he hadn't planned to stay away. He wanted to go only because the situation was too distressing for him to remain, and once he did leave, he just kept going until he found himself in the mountain foothills some distance to the east, where he stumbled across the flint mine, and stayed.

Ayla was still wide awake when Jonayla and Wolf came into the tent. She got up to help her daughter get ready for bed. After some attention from her, Wolf went to the place she had set out for him, using his blankets. She greeted some others who had just come into the large, sturdy, not-quite-permanent structure designed to sleep several, or to keep them dry when it rained.

"Where were you, mother?" Jonayla asked. "You weren't here when I came back with Zelandoni."

"I was out riding Whinney," Ayla explained. To the young girl who loved nothing more than riding her horse, the explanation was sufficient.

"Can I go out with you tomorrow? I haven't ridden Gray for a long time."

"How long?" Ayla asked with a smile.

"This many days." Jonayla held out two fingers on one hand and three fingers on the other. She didn't quite have the concept of counting yet, especially relating numbers of fingers to numbers of days.

Ayla smiled. "Can you say the counting words for how many that is?" She touched each finger to help her.

"One, two, four . . . ," Jonayla began.

"No, three, and then four."

"Three, four, five!" Jonayla finished.

"That's very good!" Ayla said. "Yes, I think we can go riding together tomorrow."

Children were not separated from adults and regularly taught in an organized way. They learned by observation and trial of adult activities, for the most part. Young children were with a caring adult most of the time, until they showed a desire to explore on their own, and whenever they expressed a desire to try something, they were usually given a tool and shown how. Sometimes they'd find their own tool and try to copy someone. If they really showed an aptitude or desire, child-size versions might be made for them, but they weren't toys so much as smaller-size fully functional tools.

The exception was dolls; it was not easy to create a small-size fully functional baby. Both girls and boys were given replicas of humans of various sizes and shapes when they were young, if they wanted them. In addition, real babies were often cared for by only slightly older siblings, usually under the watchful eye of an adult.

Community activities always included children. They were all encouraged to join in on the dancing and singing that were a part of various festivals, and some became quite good and were encouraged. Mental concepts like counting words were usually picked up incidentally, through storytelling, games, and conversation, although one or more of the zelandonia would occasionally take a group of children off to explain or show some particular concept or activity.

"Usually I go riding with Jondy," Jonayla said. "Can he come, too?"

Ayla hesitated a moment. "I suppose, if he wants to."

"Where is Jondy?" Jonayla said, looking around, suddenly realizing he wasn't there.

"I don't know," Ayla said.

"He was always here when I went to bed before. I'm glad you're here, mother, but I like it better when you're both here," Jonayla said.

The thought echoed through Ayla's mind. Yes, so do I, but he wanted to be with Marona.

When Ayla woke the next morning, it took her a few moments to recognize where she was. The inside of the structure was familiar; she had slept in similar ones often. Then it came to her. She was at the Summer Meeting. She glanced toward the place where her daughter usually slept. Jonayla was already gone. The child usually awoke suddenly, and was up and out of bed the next instant. Ayla smiled and looked beside her at Jondalar's place. He wasn't there, and it was obvious he had stayed away all night. Suddenly it all came crashing down on her again. Thinking where he might have been made the hot sting of tears rise and threaten to overflow.

Ayla had learned most of the customs of her adopted people, and had heard stories and Legends that helped to explain them, but she wasn't born into the culture, and appropriate behavior wasn't bred into her bones. She knew the general attitude about jealousy, but primarily in reference to Jondalar's lack of control as a youth. She felt that she had to demonstrate her ability to manage her emotions.

Her experience in the cave had been such a physically and emotionally wrenching ordeal, she was not thinking clearly. She was afraid to turn to anyone for help, afraid it would show that, like Jondalar, she could not control herself. But she was so devasted that, unconsciously, she wanted to strike out, make him feel her pain. She hurt, and she wanted to hurt back, make him sorry. She even considered going back into the cave and begging the Mother to take her, just to make Jondalar sorry.

She forced back her tears. I will not cry, she thought. She had learned to control her tears long ago, when she lived with the Clan. No one will know how I feel, she thought. I will act as though nothing happened. I will visit friends, I will join in the activities, I will meet with the other acolytes, I will do everything I'm supposed to.

Ayla lay awake, gathering courage to get up and face the day. I will have to talk to Zelandoni and tell her what happened in the cave. It will not be easy to keep anything from her. She always knows. But I can't let her know. I can't tell her that I know how jealousy feels.

Everyone who shared the tent with them knew something had happened between Ayla and Jondalar, and most had a fair idea what it was. For all that he thought he was being discreet, everyone knew about Marona and him—Marona enjoyed flaunting it too much. They had been glad to see Ayla come so things could get back to normal. But when Ayla stayed away all afternoon, a disheveled Marona tried to sneak back a different way, then packed up all her things and left, and Jondalar returned conspicuously disturbed and didn't come back that night to sleep, it wasn't hard to draw conclusions.

When Ayla finally got up, several people were sitting around a fire outside having a morning meal. It was still early, earlier than she thought. Ayla joined them.

"Proleva, do you know where Jonayla is? I promised her I'd go riding with her today, but I have to talk to Zelandoni first," Ayla said.

Proleva studied her closely. She was handling it much better today; someone who didn't know her might not realize anything was wrong, but Proleva knew her better than most.

"Jonayla went to Levela's again. She's been spending a lot of time there, and Levela loves it. That little sister of mine has loved having a camp full of children around since she was born, I think," Proleva said. "Zelandoni did ask me to tell you that she wants to see you as soon as you can. She said she'll be available all morning."

"I'll go after I eat, but I think I'll stop off and greet Marsheval and Levela on my way," Ayla said.

"They'd like that," Proleva said.

As Ayla approached the campsite, she heard childish voices raised in a squabble. "So you won. I don't care," Jonayla shouted at a boy somewhat bigger than her. "You can win all you want, you can take it all, but you can't have a baby, Bokovan. When I grow up I'm going to have lots of babies, but you can't have any at all. So there!"

Jonayla stood facing the boy, overpowering him in spite of his greater size. The wolf hovered close to the ground, his ears back, looking confused. He didn't know who to protect. Although the boy was bigger, he was younger. He looked hardly more than a baby, but an oversize baby. His chubby short legs were bowed, his body was long in proportion, and his big barrel chest was accentuated by a baby's pot belly. Wolf ran to Ayla when he saw her, and she put her arms around him to calm him down.

Bokovan's shoulders were already much broader than her daughter's, Ayla noticed. He had a big nose on a face that jutted out in the middle, accentuating that nose, and a receding chin. Though his forehead was straight and not sloped, he had a definite bony ridge over his eyes, not huge, but there.

To Ayla there was no question that he had the cast of the Clan, including his dark liquid eyes, but their shape was not quite Clan. Like his mother, he had a slight epicanthic fold, making his eyes seem slanted, and at that moment they were filled with tears. Ayla thought he was an exotically handsome child, though not many others agreed.

The boy ran to Dalanar. "Dalanah," he cried, "Jonayah say I can't ha'wa baby. Tell haw not twue."

Dalanar picked the boy up and put him on his lap. "I'm afraid it is true, Bokovan," Dalanar said. "Boys can't have babies. Only girls can grow up to have babies. But someday you can mate with a woman and help take care of her babies."

"But, I wan'na baby, too," Bokovan said, crying a new sob.

"Jonayla! That was a cruel thing to say," Ayla reprimanded. "Come here and say you're sorry to Bokovan. It's not nice to make him cry like that."

She did feel contrite; she really hadn't meant to make him cry. "I'm sorry, Bokovan," Jonayla said.

Ayla almost said that he would help to make babies when he grew up, but thought better of it. She hadn't even spoken to Zelandoni yet, and Bokovan wouldn't understand anyway, but her heart went out to the boy. She knelt down in front of him.

"Hello, Bokovan. My name is Ayla and I've been wanting to meet you. Your mother and Echozar are my friends."

"Can you say hello to Ayla, Bokovan?"

"He'wo, Ayla," the boy said, then buried his head in Dalanar's shoulder.

"Can I hold him, Dalanar?"

"I'm not sure if he'll let you. He's very shy and not used to people," Dalanar said.

Ayla held her arms out to the boy. He looked at her in serious contemplation. There was a liquid depth to his dark, slanted eyes, and something more, she felt. He reached out to her and she took the child from the man's arms. He was heavy! Ayla was surprised at his weight. "You are going to grow up to be a very big man, Bokovan. Do you know that?" Ayla hugged the boy to her.

"I'm really surprised he went to you," Dalanar said. "He never takes to strangers like that."

"How old is he now?" she asked.

"We can count just past three years for him, but he's big for his age. That can be a problem, especially for a boy. People think he's older than he is. I was always tall for my age when I was a youngster. Jondalar was, too," Dalanar said.

Why did it hurt so much just to hear Jondalar's name? Ayla thought. She must learn to overcome that. After all, if she was going to be Zelandoni now, she needed to show composure. She had been training to control her mind in many ways—why couldn't she control herself now?

Ayla held the boy as she greeted Levela and Marsheval. "I understand Jonayla has been here quite often. It seems she'd rather be here than any other place. Thank you for looking after her."

"We're happy to have her," Levela said. "She and my girls are good friends, but I'm glad you finally made it here this year. It was getting so late in the season, we didn't know if you were coming."

"I had planned to come before this, but things came up and I couldn't leave sooner," Ayla said.

"How's Marthona? Everyone has missed her," Levela said.

"She seems better . . . which reminds me . . ." She looked at Dalanar.

He spoke before she could ask. "Joharran sent some people for her yesterday, in the afternoon. If she's up to it, she should be here in a few days." He saw the questioning look on Levela's face. "They're going to carry her here on a litter, if she'll allow it. It was Ayla's idea. Folara and young Aldanor seem to be seeing a lot of each other, and she thought Marthona would want to be here if they are getting serious. I know how Jerika would feel if it were Joplaya." The young couple smiled and nodded. "Have you seen Jerika or Joplaya yet, Ayla?" Dalanar asked.

"No, I haven't, but I'm on my way to see Zelandoni; then I promised Jonayla we'd go riding together."

"Why don't you come back to the Lanzadonii camp this evening and stay for a meal?" Dalanar said.

Ayla smiled. "I'd like that," she said.

"Perhaps Jondalar can come, too. Do you know where he is?"

Ayla lost her smile, Dalanar noted with some concern.

"No, I'm afraid I don't," Ayla said.

"Well, there's always so much going on at Summer Meetings," Dalanar said, relieving her of Bokovan.

Yes, there certainly is, Ayla thought as she continued on her way to meet with the zelandonia.

33

"I really didn't think anyone would be so foolish as to think he could deceive the zelandonia like that," the huge woman said. She and Ayla were sitting together in the large structure that was used by the zelandonia for a variety of purposes. "Thank you for bringing these things to me." She paused. "You did know Madroman was the one who brought down all the difficulties on Jondalar and me? When he was young and I was his donii-woman?"

"Jondalar told me about it. Isn't that why he's missing his front teeth? Because Jondalar hit him?" Ayla asked.

"He did more than hit him. It was terrible. He became so violent, it took several men to stop him, and he was hardly more than a child then. That was the main reason Jondalar was sent away. He's learned to control himself now, but then his feelings, his anger and fury, were overpowering. I don't think he even knew what he was doing to Madroman. It was like something else had gotten inside of him and pushed his elan out; he was beside himself." The woman once known as Zolena closed her eyes, took a deep breath, and shook her head at the memory.

Ayla didn't know what to say, but the story disturbed her. She had seen Jondalar jealous and upset, but never that angry.

"It was probably for the best that someone brought it to the attention of the zelandonia. I had let it go too far," the First said, "but Madroman didn't do it because it was the right thing to do. He had watched us secretly and did it because he was jealous of Jondalar. But you can understand why I was beginning to wonder if I was letting personal feelings interfere with my judgment."

"I don't believe you would do that," Ayla said.

"I hope not. I've had my doubts about Madroman for some time. I think he lacks . . . something . . . a certain quality that is necessary to Serve The Mother, but he was admitted for training before I was First. When I originally questioned him about his call, I felt his story was too contrived. Several others thought the same, but some zelandonia wanted to give him every benefit. He's been an acolyte for so long, and he has yearned to be zelandoni from the beginning. That's why I felt it best to begin with an informal questioning; he has not had his final testing yet. These things you brought may help bring out the truth. That is all I want. He may have a good explanation for them. If so, then he will certainly be acknowledged, but if he is feigning his 'call,' we need to know."

"What will you do to him if the words he says are not true?"

"There isn't much we can do, except to forbid him from using any of the knowledge he gained as an acolyte, and tell his Cave about it. He will be disgraced, and that is hard punishment to bear, but there are no penalties. He really didn't harm anyone or commit any offense, except to lie. Maybe lying should be punishable, but I'm afraid everyone would have to be punished, then," Zelandoni said.

"Clan people don't lie. They can't. With their way of speaking, it's always known, so they never learned how," Ayla said.

"That's what you have said before. I sometimes wish that were so with us," the Donier said. "That's one reason the zelandonia never allow an acolyte to be present when we initiate a new zelandoni. It doesn't happen often, but every once in a while one tries to take a shortcut. It never works. We have ways of finding out."

Several of the zelandonia had come into the shelter while they were talking, including the visiting Zelandonia from the south who were still there. They were both curious and fascinated with the similarities and differences that the distance between them had created. They all chatted casually until everyone was there; then the large woman stood up, went to the entrance, and talked with a couple of newly initiated Zelandonia who were guarding the summer lodge to make sure no one tried to get close enough to listen. Ayla looked around the large summer dwelling.

The double-walled circular construction of vertical panels that enclosed the space was similar to the sleeping lodges, but larger. The movable interior panels had been stacked near the outer walls, in between the raised sleeping places that circled the large space, forming a single large room. Many of the mats that covered the ground were woven with intricate beautiful patterns, and various pads, pillows, and stools used for seating were scattered around near several low tables of various sizes. Most of them were graced with simple oil lamps, usually made of sandstone or limestone, that were lit day and night inside the windowless shelter.

Zelandoni closed the entrance flap and tied it shut, then walked back and sat down on a raised stool in the middle of the group. "Since it's so late in the season, and your call was rather unexpected, I think the choice should be yours, Ayla. Do you want to submit to informal questioning first? That can be easier to begin with, to get you used to the process. Or do you want a full formal testing?" the One Who Was First To Serve The Mother asked.

Ayla closed her eyes and bowed her head. "If we just talk about it informally, I'll have to go through it again, won't I?" she asked.

"Yes, of course."

She thought about the baby she had lost, and felt a stab of grief. She really didn't want to talk about it at all. "It was . . . hard," she said. "I don't want to go over it again and again. I think I was called. If not, I want to know as much as anyone. Can we just go ahead with it?"

A fire was burning in a fireplace that was slightly off-center toward the back of the fairly large round space, but the smoke found its way out of the central hole. Water was steaming in a waterbag that had been stretched across a frame and placed directly over the fire. The not-quite-waterproof, partially cured leather from a large animal seeped just enough so that it would not catch fire. The cooking skin had been used before. The outside was blackened and the bottom somewhat shrunk and misshapen from, in effect, being cooked by the boiling water inside and the fire outside, but it was an effective pot for keeping liquid simmering over the hot coals in the hearth.

The One Who Was First took a large pinch of some dried green plant material from a woven bowl and dropped it on the simmering water, then added three more pinches. The rather rank odor it gave off as it steamed was familiar to Ayla. The herb was datura and had not only been used by Iza, the Clan medicine woman who had cared for her, and trained her, it had also been used by The Mog-ur in special ceremonies with the men of the Clan. Ayla was very aware of its effects. She also knew it was not very prevalent in their immediate region. That meant it must have come from some distance away, making it rare and valuable.

"What is the name of that in Zelandonii?" Ayla asked, pointing at the dried material.

"It doesn't have a name in Zelandonii, and the foreign name is hard to pronounce," the First said. "We just call it the Southeast Tea."

"Where do you get it?"

"From our visiting Doniers of the Southern Cave, the Twenty-fourth, from the same person who gave you the herbs we were going to experiment with together. They live near the border of the territory of another people, and have more contact with their neighbors than they do with us. They even exchange mates. I'm surprised they haven't decided to affiliate, but they are fiercely independent, and take pride in their Zelandonii heritage. I don't even know what the plant looks like, or if it's more than one," the First explained.

Ayla smiled. "I do. It's one of the first plants I ever learned about from Iza. I've heard several names for it, datura, stink leaf; the Mamutoi have a name that would translate as 'thorn apple.' It's tall, rather coarse, with large strong-smelling leaves. It has big white—sometimes purple—flowers, shaped like funnels that flare out, and bears round prickly, thorny fruits. All parts of it are useful, including the roots. If used wrong, it can make people behave strangely, and of course, it can be fatally poisonous."

All the assembled zelandonia were suddenly very interested,
especially the visitors. They were surprised that the young woman
they had met earlier in the summer knew so much about it.

"Have you seen it around here?" Zelandoni of the Eleventh
asked.

"No, I haven't," Ayla said, "and I have been looking for it.
I had some with me when I came. But it's gone and I'd like to
replace it. It's very useful."

"How do you use it?" the visiting Donier pressed.

"It's a soporific; prepared one way, it can be used as an anes-
thetic, or when made another way, to help people relax, but it
can be very dangerous. It was used by the mog-urs of the Clan
for sacred ceremonies," Ayla said. It was just these kinds of
discussions that she loved best about being in the zelandonia.

"Do different parts of the plant have different uses, or different effects?" Zelandoni of the Third asked.

"I think we should put aside these questions for now," the
First interjected. "We are here for a different purpose."

Everyone settled back down, and those who had so eagerly
asked questions looked a bit embarrassed. The First dipped
out a cupful of the simmering liquid and set it aside to cool.
The remainder was passed around to the others, who each got
some but a smaller amount. When it was cool enough to drink,
the Donier gave the cup to Ayla.

"This testing could be done without this drink, using meditation, but it would take longer. The tea seems to help us relax
and get in the right state of mind," Zelandoni explained.

Ayla drank down the cup of tepid, rather foul-tasting tea and
then, along with everyone else, assumed whatever pose was
most conducive to meditation, and waited. Ayla was at first most
interested in consciously observing how the drink was affecting
her, thinking about how her stomach felt, how her breathing
was affected, whether she could notice a relaxation of her arms
and legs. But the effects were subtle. She didn't notice when
her mind wandered off and she found herself thinking about
something entirely unrelated. She was almost surprised—if she
could have felt surprise—when she became aware that the First
was talking to her, in a low, soft voice.

"Are you getting sleepy, Ayla? That's good. Just relax, let

yourself feel sleepy. Very sleepy. Empty your mind and rest. Don't think of anything, except my voice. Listen only to my voice. Let yourself be comfortable, relax, and hear only my voice," Zelandoni droned on. "Now, tell me, Ayla, where were you when you decided to go into the cave?"

"I was on top of the cliff," Ayla began, then stopped.

"Go on, Ayla, you were on top of the cliff. What were you doing? Take your time. Just tell the whole story in your own way. There's no hurry."

"The Shortday was already marked; the sun had turned around and was going back, heading for winter, but I thought I'd mark a few more days. It was quite late and I was tired. I decided to stir up the fire, make a little tea. I searched in my medicine bag for the mint. It was dark, but I was feeling the knots to find the right bag. I finally found the one by the strong smell of mint. While the tea was steeping, I decided to practice saying The Mother's Song." Ayla began to recite the song:

> Out of the darkness, the chaos of time,
> The whirlwind gave birth to the Mother sublime.
> She woke to Herself knowing life had great worth,
> The dark empty void grieved the Great Mother Earth.
> The Mother was lonely. She was the only.

"It's my favorite of all the Legends and Histories, so I repeated it while I was drinking the tea," Ayla said, continuing on with the next few verses.

> From the dust of Her birth She created the other,
> A pale shining friend, a companion, a brother.
> They grew up together, learned to love and to care,
> And when She was ready, they decided to pair.
> Around Her he'd hover. Her pale shining lover.

> She was happy at first with Her one counterpart.
> Then the Mother grew restless, unsure in Her heart.
> She loved Her fair friend, Her dear complement,
> But something was missing, Her love was unspent.
> She was the Mother. She needed another.

She dared the great void, the chaos, the dark,
To find the cold home of the life-giving spark.
The whirlwind was fearsome, the darkness complete.
Chaos was freezing, and reached for Her heat.
  The Mother was brave. The danger was grave.

She drew from cold chaos the creative source,
Then conceiving within, She fled with life force.
She grew with the life that She carried inside.
And gave of Herself with love and with pride.
  The Mother was bearing. Her life She was sharing.

It all seemed so clear in her mind, almost as though she were there again. "I was bearing, too, sharing my life with the growing life force inside. I felt so close to the Mother." She smiled dreamily.

Several of the zelandonia looked at each other with some surprise, then at the First. The big woman nodded, indicating that she knew Ayla was pregnant. "And then what happened, Ayla? What happened on that cliff?"

"The moon was so big, so bright. It filled the whole sky. I felt myself drawn to it, drawn up into it," Ayla continued, telling how she rose above the land, and how the column of rock glowed, then how she had become frightened and ran down to the Ninth Cave, then headed toward Down River and on to The River. She told how she had walked along a river, like The River but not quite the same, for a long, long time. It seemed like days and days, but the sun never shone. It was always night, lit only by the huge bright moon.

"I think Her shining lover, Her friend, was helping me to find my way," Ayla said. "Finally I came to the Place of the Sacred Fountain. I could see the path up to the cave glowing in the light of Lumi, Her shining friend. I knew he was telling me to go that way. I started up, but the path was so long, I wondered if I was going the right way, and then suddenly, I was there. I saw the dark opening of the cave, but I was afraid to go in. Then I heard, 'She dared the great void, the chaos, the dark' and I knew I had to be brave, like the Mother, and brave the dark, too."

* * *

Ayla continued her story, and the gathered zelandonia were completely enthralled. Whenever she stopped, or hesitated too long, Zelandoni encouraged her to go on in her low, soothing, unhurried voice.

"Ayla! Here, drink this!" It was Zelandoni's voice, but it sounded so far away. "Ayla! Sit up and drink this!" The voice was commanding now. "Ayla!"

She felt herself being raised up and opened her eyes. The big familiar woman held a cup to her lips. Ayla sipped it. It made her realize she was thirsty and she drank some more. The mist was beginning to clear. She was helped to sit up, and became aware of voices around her speaking softly, but with an undertone of excitement.

"How are you feeling, Ayla?" the First asked.

"I have a little headache, and I'm still thirsty," she said.

"This tea will make you feel better," the Donier of the Ninth Cave said. "Have some more."

Ayla drank it. "Now I think I have to pass water," she said, smiling.

"There's a night basket behind that screen," a zelandoni said, indicating the way.

Ayla stood up, felt slightly dizzy, but it cleared.

"I think we should let her get settled," Ayla heard the One Who Was First say. "She has been through a great deal, but I think there is little doubt she will be the next First."

"I believe you are right," she heard another voice say. She heard more of the zelandonia talking among themselves, but wasn't listening anymore. What did they mean? She wasn't sure she liked hearing them talk about "the next First."

When she returned, the Zelandoni of the Ninth Cave asked, "Do you remember everything you told us?"

Ayla closed her eyes, frowning with concentration. "I think so," she finally said.

"We would like to ask you some questions. Do you feel strong enough to answer, or would you like to rest longer?"

"I think I'm awake, and don't feel tired. I would like some more tea, though. My mouth still feels dry," Ayla said. Her cup was refilled.

"Our questions should help you to interpret your own experience," the Donier said. "No one else really can." Ayla nodded. "Do you know how long you were in the cave?" the First asked.

"Marthona said almost four days," Ayla said, "but I don't recall too much after I first came out. Some people were there waiting for me. They carried me back on a litter, and the next few days are not clear."

"Do you think you would be able to explain some things to us?"

"I'll try."

"The ice walls you spoke of—if I remember correctly, you told us once of falling down into a crevasse on your way across the glacier. By some miracle, you landed on a ledge and Jondalar pulled you out. Is that right?" the First asked.

"Yes. He threw me a rope and told me to wrap it around my waist. He attached the other end to his horse. Racer pulled me out," Ayla clarified.

"Few people who fall into crevasses are fortunate enough to get out. You came very close to death then. It is not uncommon for acolytes, when they are being called, to experience again those times when they were near the spirit world. Would you say that was a possible interpretation of the ice walls?" the First asked.

"Yes," Ayla said, then looked at the large woman. "I didn't think about it before, but that could explain some of the other things, too. I almost died crossing a flooded river on our way here, and I'm sure it was Attaroa's face I saw. She would have killed me for sure if Wolf hadn't saved me."

"I'm sure that accounts for some of the visions. Though I haven't heard the full story of your Journey here, obviously most people have," said the visiting Zelandoni. "But what was that black void? Was it a reference to the Mother's Song or did it have some other significance? You almost had me terrified." There was some quiet laughter and a few smiles at her comment, but some nods of agreement as well.

"And what about the warm sea, and the creatures burrowing in the mud and in the trees? That was all very strange," said another, "not to mention all the mammoths and reindeer, and the bison and horses."

"One question at a time, please," the First said. "There are many things we'd all like to know, but we are in no rush. Do you have any interpretations for those things, Ayla?"

"I don't have to interpret, I know what they are," Ayla said. "But I don't understand them."

"Well, what were they?" Zelandoni of the Third Cave asked.

"I think most people know that when I lived with the Clan, the woman who was like a mother to me was a medicine woman who taught me most of what I know about healing. She also had a daughter and we all lived at the hearth of her sibling, her brother, who was called Creb. Most people of the Clan knew Creb as The Mog-ur. A mog-ur was a man who knew the spirit world, and The Mog-ur was like the One Who Was First, the most powerful of all the mog-urs."

"He was like a zelandoni, then," the visiting Zelandoni said.

"In a sense. He wasn't a healer. The medicine women are the healers, they are the ones who know healing plants and practices, but it is the mog-ur who calls upon the spirit world to aid in the healing," Ayla explained.

"The two parts are separate? I always thought of them as inseparable," the woman unknown to Ayla said.

"You might also be surprised to know that only men were allowed to contact the spirit world, to be mog-urs, and only women were healers, medicine women," Ayla said.

"That is surprising."

"I don't know about the other mog-urs, but The Mog-ur had a special ability in the way he called upon the spirit world. He could go back to their beginnings and show others the way. He even took me back once, although he wasn't supposed to, and I think he was very sorry that he did. He changed after that; he lost something. I wish it had never happened."

"How did it happen?" the First asked.

"There was a root they used only for the special ceremony with all the mog-urs at the Clan Gathering. It had to be pre-pared a particular way, and only the medicine women of Iza's line knew how."

"You mean they have Summer Meetings, too?" the Zelandoni of the Eleventh asked.

"Not every summer, only once in seven years. When it was time for the Clan Gathering, Iza was sick. She couldn't make the trip, and her daughter was not yet a woman, and the root had to be prepared by a woman, not a girl. Although I didn't have the Clan memories, Iza had been training me to be a medicine woman. It was decided that I would have to be the one to prepare the root for the mog-urs. Iza explained how I would have to chew the root and then spit it out into a special bowl. She cautioned me not to swallow any of the juice while I was chewing. When we got to the Clan Gathering, the mog-urs were not going to allow me to make it. I was born to the Others, not to the Clan, but finally at the last moment Creb came for me and told me to prepare myself.

"I went through the ritual, but it was difficult for me and I ended up swallowing some, and I had made a little too much. Iza had told me it was too precious to be wasted, and by then I wasn't thinking clearly. I drank what was left in the bowl so it wouldn't go to waste, and without meaning to, I went into the cave nearby and deep inside I found the mog-urs. No woman was ever supposed to participate in the men's ceremonies, but I was there, and had also swallowed the drink.

"I can't really explain what happened after that, but somehow Creb knew I was there. I was falling into a deep black void; I thought I would be lost in it forever, but Creb came for me, pulled me back. I'm sure he saved my life. The people of the Clan have a special quality to their minds that we don't, just as we have a quality that they don't. They have memories; they can remember what their ancestors knew. They don't really have to learn what they need to know, like we do. They only have to need to know it, or to be 'reminded' to remember. They can learn something new, but it's more difficult for them.

"Their memories go back a long way. In certain circumstances they can go back to their beginnings, to a time so long ago, there were no people and the earth was different. Perhaps back to the time when the Great Earth Mother gave birth to her son and first made the land green with her birth waters. Creb had the ability to direct the other mog-urs and lead them back to those times. After he saved me, he took me with him and the other mog-urs back into the memories. If you go back far enough, we all have the same memories, and he helped me to find mine. I shared the experience with them.

"In the memories, when the earth was different, so long ago it is hard to imagine, those who came before people once lived in the depths of the ocean. When the water dried and they were stranded in the mud, they changed and learned to live on land. They changed many times after that, and with Creb, I was able to go there with them. It was not quite the same for me as it was for them, but still, I was able to go there. I saw the Ninth Cave before the Zelandonii lived there; I recognized the Falling Stone when I first arrived. And then I went someplace Creb was not able to go. He blocked out the other mog-urs so they wouldn't know I was there, and then he told me to leave, to get out of the cave before they discovered me. He never told them I was there. I would have been killed outright if they knew, but he was never the same after that."

There was a silence when Ayla finished. Zelandoni who was First broke the silence. "In our Histories and Legends, the Great Earth Mother gave birth to all life, and then to those like us who would remember Her. Who is to say how Doni formed us? What child remembers its life in the womb? Before it is born, a baby breathes water and struggles to breathe when first born. You have all seen and examined human life before it was fully formed, when it was expelled early. In the first stages, it does resemble a fish, and then animals. It may be she is remembering her own life in the womb, before she was born. Ayla's interpretation of her early experience with the ones she calls the Clan does not deny the Legends or the Mother's Song. It adds to them, explains them. But I am overwhelmed that those we have called animals for so long would have such great knowledge of the Mother, and having such knowledge in their 'memories,' how they could not recognize Her."

The zelandonia were relieved. The First had managed to take what at first seemed like a basic conflict of beliefs, told by Ayla with such credible conviction that it could almost create a schism, and instead blend them together. Her interpretation added strength to their beliefs rather than tearing them apart. They could, perhaps, accept that the ones they called Flatheads were intelligent in their own way, but the zelandonia had to maintain that the beliefs of those people were still inferior to their own. The Flatheads had not recognized the Great Earth Mother.

"So it was that root that brought on the black void and the strange creatures," Zelandoni of the Fifth said.

"It is a powerful root. When I left the Clan, I had taken some with me. I didn't plan to; it was just in my medicine bag. After I became a Mamutoi, I told Mamut about the root and my experience with Creb in the cave. As a young man, he had once been injured while traveling and a Clan medicine woman healed him. He stayed with them for a while, learned some of their ways, and participated at least once in a ceremony with the men of the Clan. He wanted us to try the root together. I think he felt that if Creb could control it, so could he, but there are some differences between the Clan and the Others. With Mamut we did not go back into past memories; we went somewhere else. I don't know where—it was very strange and frightening. We went through that void and almost didn't return, but . . . someone . . . wanted us back so much, his need overpowered everything else."

Ayla looked down at her hands. "His love was so strong . . . then," she said under her breath. Only Zelandoni noticed the pain in Ayla's eyes when she looked up. "Mamut said he would never use that root again. He said he was afraid he'd get lost in that void and never return, never find the next world. Mamut said that if I ever used that root again, I should make sure that I had strong protection or I might never return."

"You still have some of that root?" the First was quick to ask.

"Yes. I found more in the mountains near the Sharamudoi, but I haven't seen any since. I don't think it grows in this region," Ayla said.

"The root you have, is it still good? It's been a long time since your Journey," the large woman pressed.

"If it's dried properly and kept out of the light, Iza told me that the root concentrates, gets stronger with age," Ayla said. The One Who Was First nodded, more to herself than anyone.

"I got a strong impression that you felt the pain of childbirth," the visiting Zelandoni said. "Did you ever come near death giving birth?"

Ayla had told the First about her harrowing experience giving birth to her first child, her son of mixed spirits, and the large woman thought that might account for part of Ayla's ordeal of childbirth in the cave, but she didn't think it was necessary to tell everyone.

"I think the most important question is the one we have all been avoiding," the First interjected. "The Mother's Song is perhaps the oldest of the Elder Legends. Different Caves, different traditions often have minor variations, but the meaning is always the same. Would you recite it for us, Ayla? Not the whole song, just the last part of it."

Ayla nodded, closed her eyes, thought about where to begin.

With a thunderous roar Her stones split asunder,
And from the great cave that opened deep under,
She birthed once again from Her cavernous heart,
Bringing forth all the creatures of Earth from the start.
    From the Mother forelorn, more children were born.

Each child was different, some were large and some small,
Some could walk and some fly, some could swim and some
    crawl.
But each form was perfect, each spirit complete,
Each one was a model whose shape could repeat.
    The Mother was willing. The green earth was filling.

All the birds and the fish and the animals born,
Would not leave the Mother, this time, to mourn.
Each kind would live near the place of its birth,
And share the expanse of the Great Mother Earth.
    Close to Her they would stay. They could not run away.

Ayla had started out rather tentatively, but as she got into it, her voice gained more power; her delivery became more sure.

They all were her children, they filled her with pride
But they used up the life force she carried inside.

She had enough left for a last innovation,
A child who'd remember Who made the creation.
  A child who'd respect. And learn to protect.

First Woman was born full grown and alive,
And given the Gifts she would need to survive.
Life was the First Gift, and like Mother Earth,
She woke to herself knowing life had great worth.
  First Woman defined. The first of her kind.

Next was the Gift of Perception, of learning,
The desire to know, the Gift of Discerning,
First Woman was given the knowledge within,
That would help her to live, then impart to her kin.
  First Woman would know. How to learn, how to grow.

Her life force near gone, The Mother was spent,
To pass on Life's Spirit had been Her intent.
She caused all of Her children to create life anew,
And Woman was blessed to bring forth life, too.
  But Woman was lonely. She was the only.

The Mother remembered Her own loneliness,
The love of Her friend and his hovering caress.
With the last spark remaining, Her labor began,
To share life with Woman, She created First Man.
  Again She was giving. One more was living.

Ayla spoke the language so fluently, most people hardly noticed her accent anymore. They were used to the way she said certain words and sounds. It seemed normal. But as she repeated the familiar verses, her speech peculiarity seemed to add an exotic quality, a touch of mystery, that somehow made it seem that the verses came from some other place, perhaps some otherworldly place.

To Woman and Man the Mother gave birth,
And then for their home, She gave them the Earth,

The water, the land, and all Her creation.
To use them with care was their obligation.
  It was their home to use, but never abuse.

For the Children of Earth the Mother provided,
The Gifts to survive, and then She decided,
To give them the Gift of Pleasure and caring,
That honors the Mother with the joy of their sharing.
  The Gifts are well earned, when honor's returned.

The Mother was pleased with the pair She created,
She taught them to love and to care when they mated.
She made them desire to join with each other,
The Gift of their Pleasures came from the Mother.
  Before She was through, Her children loved too.

This was the place where the song usually ended, and Ayla
hesitated a moment before she continued. Then taking a breath,
she recited the verse that had filled her head with its booming
metered resonance deep in the cave.

Her last Gift, the Knowledge that man has his part.
His need must be spent before new life can start.
It honors the Mother when the couple is paired,
Because woman conceives when Pleasures are shared.
  Earth's Children were blessed. The Mother could rest.

There was an uneasy silence when she finished. Not one of
the powerful women and men there knew quite what to say.
Finally the Zelandoni from the Fourteenth Cave spoke up. "I
have never heard that verse or anything like it."

"Nor have I," said the First. "The question is, what does it
mean?"

"What do you think it means?" said the Fourteenth.

"I think it means that woman alone does not create new life,"
the First said.

"No, of course not. It has always been known that the spirit
of a man is blended with the spirit of a woman to make a new
life," the Eleventh protested.

Ayla spoke up. "The verse does not speak of 'spirit.' It says woman conceives when Pleasures are shared," she said. "It is not just a man's spirit; a new life will not start if a man's need is not spent. A child is as much a man's as it is a woman's, a child of his body as well as hers. It is the joining of man and woman that starts life."

"Are you saying that joining is not for Pleasures?" asked the Third with a tone of incredulous disbelief.

"No one doubts that joining is a Pleasure," the First said with a sardonic smile. "I think it means that Doni's Gift is more than the Gift of Pleasure. It is another Gift of Life. I think that is what the verse means. The Great Earth Mother did not create men just to share Pleasures with women, and to provide for her and her children. A woman is the Blessed of Doni because she brings forth new life, but a man is blessed too. Without him, no new life can start. Without men, and without the Pleasures, all life would stop."

There was an outburst of excited voices. "Surely there are other interpretations," said the visiting Zelandoni. "This seems too much, too hard to believe."

"Give me another interpretation," the First countered. "You heard the words. What is your explanation?"

The Zelandoni hesitated, paused. "I would have to think about it. It needs time for thought, for study."

"You can think about it for a day, or a year, or as many years as you can number; it will not change the interpretation. Ayla was given a Gift with her calling. She was chosen to bring this new Gift of the Knowledge of Life from the Mother," the One Who Was First said.

There was another buzz of commotion. "But gifts are always exchanged. No one receives a gift without the obligation of giving one in return, one of equal value," the Zelandoni of the Second Cave said. "It was the first time he had spoken. What Gift could Ayla give in return to the Mother that would be of equal value?" There was silence as everyone looked at Ayla.

"I gave Her my baby," she said, knowing in her heart that the child she had lost was one started by Jondalar, that it was her and Jondalar's child. Will I ever have another baby that will be Jondalar's, too? she wondered. "The Mother was honored deeply when that baby was started. It was a baby I wanted, wanted more than I can tell you. Even now, my arms ache with the emptiness of that loss. I may have another child someday, but I will never have that child."

Ayla fought back tears. "I don't know how much the Mother values the Gifts She gives Her children, but I know of nothing I value more than my children. I don't know why She wanted my child, but the Great Mother filled my head with the words of Her Gift after my baby was gone." Tears glistened in Ayla's eyes as much as she tried to control them. She bowed her head and said quietly, "I wish I could return Her Gift and have my baby back."

There was a gasp from several who were gathered. One did not take the Mother's Gifts lightly, nor did one openly wish to give them back. She might be greatly offended, and who could know what She might do then.

"Are you sure you were pregnant?" the Eleventh asked.

"I missed three moontimes, and I had all the other signs. Yes, I'm sure," Ayla explained.

"And I'm sure," the First said. "I knew she was carrying a child before I left for the Summer Meeting."

"Then she must have miscarried. That would account for the childbirth pain I thought I sensed in her telling," said the visiting Zelandoni.

"I think it's obvious that she miscarried. I believe the miscarriage brought her dangerously close to death while she was in the cave," the First said. "That must have been why the Mother wanted her baby. The sacrifice was necessary. It brought her close enough to the next world for the Mother to speak to her, to give her the verse for the Gift of Knowledge."

"I am sorry," said the Zelandoni of the Second Cave. "Losing a child can be a terrible burden to bear." He said it with such genuine feeling, it made Ayla wonder.

"If there are no objections, I think it is time for the ceremony," the One Who Was First said. There were nods of agreement. "Are you ready, Ayla?"

The young woman frowned with consternation as she looked around. Ready for what? It all seemed so sudden. The Donier could see her distress.

"You said you wanted to have the full formal testing. The understanding is that if you satisfied the zelandonia, you would progress to the next level. You would no longer be an acolyte. You would leave here zelandoni," the First explained.

"You mean, right now?" Ayla asked.

"The first mark of acceptance, yes," the First said, as she picked up a sharp flint knife.

34

"There will be a more public ceremony when you are presented to the people as a Zelandoni, but the marks are made with acceptance, in private with only the zelandonia. As you increase in rank, and marks are added, they are made in the presence of zelandonia and acolytes, but never in public," the Zelandoni Who Was First said. The large woman, who carried herself with the dignity and power her position conferred, asked, "Are you ready?"

Ayla swallowed, and frowned. "Yes," she said, and hoped she was.

The First looked around the gathering, making sure she had everyone's attention. Then she began. "This woman is fully trained to fulfill all the duties of the zelandonia, and it is the First Among Those Who Serve The Mother who attests to her knowledge."

There were nods and sounds of acknowledgment.

"She has been called and tested. Are there any among us who question her call?" Zelandoni asked.

There were no dissenters. There was never any doubt.

"Do all here agree to accept this woman as a Zelandoni into the ranks of the zelandonia?"

"We agree!" came the unanimous response.

Ayla watched as the man who was Zelandoni of the Second Cave came forward and held out a bowl of something dark. She knew what it was; a part of her mind was observing, not just participating. The bark of mountain ash, called a rowan tree, had been burned in a ceremonial fire and then sifted in the wind to a fine gray powder. The ashes of rowan bark were astringent, antiseptic. Then the woman who was the Zelandoni from a distant Cave, the one unknown to her, brought forth a steaming reddish liquid: last autumn's dried rowanberries, boiled down to a concentrated liquid and strained. Ayla knew the juice from the rowanberries was acidic and healing.

Zelandoni Who Was First picked up a bowl of soft, white, partially congealed pure tallow that had been rendered with boiling water from aurochs fat, and added a little to the powdered ashes, then some of the steaming red rowanberry juice. She mixed it with a small carved wooden spatula, adding more fat and liquid until it satisfied her. Then she faced the young woman and picked up the sharp flint knife.

"The mark you will receive can never be removed. It will declare to all that you acknowledge and accept the role of Zelandoni. Are you ready to accept that responsibility?"

Ayla took a deep breath and watched the woman with the knife approach, knowing what was coming. She felt a twinge of fear, swallowed hard, and closed her eyes. She knew it would hurt, but that wasn't what she was dreading. Once this was done, there was no going back. This was her last chance to change her mind.

Suddenly she recalled hiding in a shallow cave, trying to squeeze herself into the stone wall at her back. She saw the sharp, curved claws on the huge paw of a cave lion reaching in, and screamed with pain as four parallel gashes were raked across her left thigh. Squirming away, she found a small space to the side and pulled her legs in closer, away from the claws.

Her memory of being chosen and marked by her Cave Lion Totem had never been so clear and intense before. Reflexively, she reached for her left thigh to feel the different texture of the skin of the four parallel scars. They were recognized as Clan totem marks when she was accepted into Brun's clan, though traditionally a Cave Lion Totem chose male, not female.

How many marks had been carved into her body in her life? Besides the four marks of her protective totem spirit, Mog-ur had nicked the base of her throat to draw blood when she became the Woman Who Hunts. She was given her Clan hunting talisman, the red-stained oval of mammoth ivory, to show that in spite of the fact that she was a woman, she was accepted as a hunter of the Clan, though only allowed to use a sling.

She no longer carried the talisman with her, or her amulet with the rest of her signs either, though at that moment, she wished she had them. They were hidden behind the carved, woman-shaped donii figure in the niche that had been dug out of the limestone wall of her dwelling at the Ninth Cave. But she did have the scar.

Ayla touched the small mark, then reached for the scar on her arm. Talut had cut that mark, and with the bloody knife had notched an ivory plaque that he wore suspended from a fantastic necklace of amber and cave lion canine teeth and claws, to show that she was accepted into the Lion Camp, adopted by the Mamutoi.

She had never asked, she had always been chosen, and for each acceptance she bore a mark, a scar that she would carry always. It was the sacrifice she'd had to make. Now she was being chosen again. She could still decline, but if she didn't refuse now, she was committed for life. It crossed her mind that the scars would always remind her that there were consequences to being chosen, responsibilities that came with acceptance.

She looked into the eyes of the woman. "I accept, I will be Zelandoni," Ayla said, trying to sound firm and positive.

Then she closed her eyes and felt someone come up behind the stool on which she was seated. Hands, gentle but firm, pulled her back to rest on the soft body of a woman for support, then held her head and turned it so that her right forehead was presented. She felt a wash of liquid from something soft and wet wiped across her forehead, recognized the odor of iris root, a solution she had often used to clean wounds, and felt an anxious tension arise within her.

"Oh! Ow!" she cried out involuntarily as she felt the quick cut of a sharp blade, then fought to control such outbursts at a second cut, and then a third. The solution was applied again, then the cuts were dried, and another substance was rubbed in. This time the pain stung like a burn, but not for long; something in the stinging salve had numbed the pain.

"You can open your eyes, Ayla. It's over," the large woman said.

Ayla opened her eyes to see a rather dim, unfamiliar image. It took her a moment to realize what she was seeing. Someone was holding up a reflector and a lighted lamp so she could see herself in the oiled piece of sand-smoothed, black-stained wood. She seldom used a reflector, didn't even have one in her dwelling, and was always surprised to see her own face. Then her eyes were drawn to the marks on her forehead.

Just in front of her right temple was a short horizontal line with two vertical lines extending up from each end of about the same length, like a square with no top line or an open box. The three lines were black, with a little blood still oozing out around the edges. They looked so conspicuous, they seemed to diminish everything else. Ayla wasn't at all sure that she liked having her face marred like that. But there was nothing she could do about it now. It was done. She would carry those black marks on her face for the rest of her life.

She started to reach up to feel it, but the First stopped her. "It's best if you don't touch it just yet," she said. "It has almost stopped bleeding, but it's still fresh."

Ayla looked around at the rest of the zelandonia. They all had various marks on their foreheads, some more intricate than others, mostly square but with other shapes as well, many filled in with color. The markings of the First were the most elaborate of all. She knew they designated rank, position, affiliation of the zelandonia. She noticed, however, that the black lines faded to blue tattoos after they healed.

She was glad when they took the reflector away. She didn't like looking at herself. It made her uncomfortable to think that the strange, dim image of the face she saw belonged to her. She preferred to see herself reflected in the expressions of others: the happiness of her daughter when she saw her mother, the pleasure of seeing herself in the aspect and demeanor of people she cared about, like Marthona, and Proleva, Joharran, and Dalanar. And the look of love in Jondalar's eyes when he saw . . . not anymore . . . The last time he saw her, he was horrified. His look showed shock and dismay, not love.

Ayla closed her eyes to shut off impending tears, and tried to control her feelings of loss, disappointment, and pain. When she opened them and looked up, all the zelandonia were standing in front of her, including the two new ones, a woman and a man, who had been on guard outside, and all of them had warm smiles of anticipation and welcome. The One Who Was First spoke:

"You have traveled far, have belonged to many people, but your feet have always led you along the path the Great Earth Mother chose for you. It was your fate to lose your people at an early age, and then be taken in by a healer and a man who traveled the spirit world of those people you call the Clan. When you were adopted by the Mamut of the Mamutoi to the Mammoth Hearth that honors the Mother, your way was guided by She Who Gave Birth to All. Your destiny has always been to Serve Her.

"Ayla of the Ninth Cave of the Zelandonii, mated to Jondalar of the Ninth Cave, son of Marthona, former leader of the Ninth Cave of the Zelandonii; Mother of Jonayla, Blessed of Doni, of the Ninth Cave of the Zelandonii, who was born to the hearth of Jondalar; Ayla of the Mamutoi, member of the Lion Camp of the mammoth hunting people to the east, Daughter of the Mammoth Hearth, the zelandonia of the Mamutoi; Ayla, chosen by the Spirit of the Cave Lion and Protected by the Cave Bear of the Clan, your names and ties are many. Now they are no longer needed. Your new name means all of them, and more. Your name is one with all of Her creation. Your name is Zelandoni!"

"Your name is one with all of Her creation. Welcome Zelandoni!" the assembled group said in unison.

"Come, join with us in the Mother's Song, Zelandoni of the Ninth Cave," said the One Who Was First, and the group began entirely in unison.

Out of the darkness, the chaos of time,
The whirlwind gave birth to the Mother sublime . . .

When they reached the verse that had always been the last, only the One Who Was First continued in her beautiful rich voice:

The Mother was pleased with the pair She created,
She taught them to love and to care when they mated.
She made them desire to join with each other,
The Gift of their Pleasures came from the Mother.
    Before She was through, Her children loved too.

The whole group sang the last line; then they all looked expectantly at Ayla. It took her a moment to comprehend; then in a strong voice with an exotic accent, Ayla didn't sing, but spoke alone.

Her last Gift, the Knowledge that man has his part.
His need must be spent before new life can start.
It honors the Mother when the couple is paired,
Because woman conceives when Pleasures are shared.
    Earth's Children were blessed. The Mother could rest.

The group finished the final line, and stood silently for a while; then they broke up and relaxed. A large container of tea was brought out, and each one took out individual cups from pouches and pockets.

"The question now is, how do we tell the rest of the Zelandonii about the last Gift?" said the One Who Was First, as she casually sat on her stool.

The question brought an uproar. "Tell them!" "We can't tell them!" "It would be too much for them." "Think how much it would upset everything."

The First waited until the disturbance settled down; then she looked at the assembled zelandonia with a fierce glare. "Do you think Doni made this known so you could withhold it from Her Children? Do you think Ayla suffered those agonies, or that she was required to sacrifice her baby just so the zelandonia would have something to argue about? The zelandonia are Those Who Serve The Mother. It is not for us to say whether or not Her children may know. It is our task to decide how to tell them."

There was contrite silence; then the Zelandoni of the Fourteenth said, "It will take time to plan an appropriate ceremony.

Perhaps we should wait until next year. This season is almost over. Everyone will be going back soon."

"Yes," the Zelandoni of the Third quickly agreed. "Perhaps the best way would be to let each zelandoni tell his own Cave, in his own way, after he's had some time to think about it."

"The ceremony will be held three days from now and Ayla will tell them," the First announced unequivocally. "It was Ayla who was given the Gift. It is her place, her duty to tell the rest. She was called this season, and sent to this Summer Meeting for that reason." The First glared at her fellow Doniers; then her expression softened, and her tone became cajoling. "Wouldn't it be better to get it over with now? With the season so close to the end, there won't be time for too many difficulties to arise before we leave—and you can be sure there will be difficulties—but this way we will have all winter to get our own Caves used to the idea. By next season there shouldn't be any reason for problems."

The First wished she really believed that. Unlike the rest of the zelandonia, the First had thought about a man's contribution to creating new life for many years, even before her first conversation with Ayla. The fact that Ayla had come to her own similar conclusions was one of the reasons the woman had wanted her to become Zelandoni. Her observations were too perceptive, and she wasn't restricted by Zelandonii beliefs fed to her with mother's milk.

That was why Zelandoni had decided as soon as she heard Ayla tell about her experience in the cave, that the idea must be made known immediately, when everyone was still together. And while the zelandonia were still bewildered by it. She would have set the ceremony for the next day if she had thought it was possible to arrange it.

As she often did under the guise of resting or meditating, and seeming to ignore her surroundings, the woman waited and watched for a while as the zelandonia began to make plans. At first they were tentative.

She heard the Eleventh say, "Maybe a good approach might be to try to duplicate Ayla's own experience."

"We don't have to show her entire experience, just the essence of it," said the Twenty-third.

"If we had a cave large enough to hold everyone, it would help," the Zelandoni of the Second Cave said.

"We'll have to let the darkness of night act as the walls of a cave," the Fifth said. "If we have just one fire in the middle, it will help to concentrate everyone's attention."

Good, the First thought, listening to the Doniers speaking among themselves. They are starting to think of how to plan the ceremony rather than thinking of objections to it.

"We should have drums for the Mother's Song."

"And singing."

"The Ninth doesn't sing."

"Her voice is so distinctive, it doesn't matter."

"We can have singing in the background. Without words, just the sound."

"If we slow the cadence of the drums, the Mother's Song will have a greater impact, especially at the end when she speaks the last verse."

Ayla seemed at a loss with all the attention as more suggestions were made for her part, but after a while even she seemed to be getting involved with the arrangements. "The visitors from the Mamutoi, the two young men, Danug and Druwez, they know how to play drums so that they actually sound like a voice speaking. It's uncanny, but very mysterious. I think they could make the drums speak the final verse, if they brought their drums, or can find something similar."

"I would like to hear it first," said the Fourteenth.

"Of course," Ayla said.

More than she realized, Ayla was incredibly wise in the ways of people, and much more sophisticated and knowledgeable than she knew. The tactics of the Zelandoni Who Was First in pushing the zelandonia into creating the ceremony were not lost on Ayla. On a sometimes subliminal and sometimes fully aware level, she had watched the First mold the rest to her will. The woman was quick to press her advantage, knew when to bluster, when to threaten, when to cajole, wheedle, criticize, praise— and the zelandonia were not easily led. As a group they were clever, shrewd, often cynical, and on the whole more intelligent than most. Ayla remembered Jondalar asking Zelandoni once what made a Zelandoni First. Even then, she knew just how much to say, just how much to hold back.

Zelandoni relaxed. They were into it now. It would gain momentum of its own accord. Her problem most of the time was to keep them from getting too carried away. This time she was going to let them take on just as much as they wanted. The more spectacular, the better. *If I let them plan it big enough, and elaborate enough, they won't have time to think about anything else until after the ceremony.*

When the general outline for the ceremony had begun to take shape, and most of the zelandonia were developing a decided interest in the event, Zelandoni Who Was First hurled another surprise at them.

Getting up to get more tea, she made an ostensibly offhand comment. "I imagine we'll also have to make plans for a Camp Meeting a day or so after the ceremony to answer questions that are bound to come up. We might as well get them out of the way all at once. That's when we can announce the name for the relationship between a man and his children, and tell them that the men will name the boys from now on," she said.

The consternation of the zelandonia was immediate. Most hadn't had time to think about what changes the new knowledge was going to make.

"But a mother has always named her own children!" one of them said.

Zelandoni caught a few sharp looks. *That's what she had been afraid of; some of them were going to start thinking. As a group, it was not wise to underestimate the zelandonia.*

"How are the men going to realize that they are essential if we don't let them take some part?" the First asked. "It doesn't really change anything. Coupling will still be a Pleasure. Men are not going to start giving birth, and a man will still need to provide for the woman he has taken to his hearth and her children, especially while she is confined close to home and with small children. Naming a male child is a small thing; women will still name the females," the woman cajoled.

"In the Clan the mog-urs named all the children," Ayla mentioned. Everyone stopped and looked at her. "I was very pleased to be able to name my daughter. I was nervous about it, but it was very exciting, and it made me feel very important."

"I think the men would feel the same way," the First said, grateful for Ayla's unplanned support.

There were nods and grunts of approval. No one brought up any further objections, at least for the moment.

"What about the name of the relationship? Have you a name for it already?" the Zelandoni from the Twenty-ninth Cave asked, with a hint of suspicion.

"I thought I would meditate and see if I could think of something appropriate for children to call the men who shared in giving them life, to distinguish them from other men. Perhaps we should all think about it," the One Who Was First said.

The First had felt that she had to push them now, while the zelandonia were still overwhelmed, and at a disadvantage relative to herself, before they began to think about the possible consequences, and come up with some real objections that she couldn't confound with bluster. She had no doubt that this new Gift of the Knowledge of Life would have more profound repercussions than even she could imagine. It would change everything, and she wasn't entirely sure that she liked some of the very real possibilities that might develop.

The Zelandoni Who Was First was a keenly observant, intelligent woman. She had never had a child of her own, but in her case that was an advantage; she never had the distractions that children invariably entailed. But she had been midwife at more births than she cared to count, and had helped many women through miscarriages. As a result the First had more knowledge of the developmental stages of unborn fetuses than any mother.

The Doniers were also instrumental in helping some women end their pregnancies before full term. The most precarious time in the lives of infants was the first two years. Many children died then. Even with the help of mates, elder parents, or other extended family members, most mothers could not nurse and care for too many young children at one time if any were to survive.

Although nursing a baby, in itself, seemed to be a deterrent to starting another, it was sometimes necessary to terminate an unanticipated pregnancy if those who were already born were to live past infancy. Or if a woman was seriously ill, or had children who were nearly grown and was too old, or had had one or more harrowing deliveries in the past that had brought her close to death, and another pregnancy could deprive existing children of their mother. The mortality rate of children would have been appreciably higher if they did not practice such selective controls as were available to them. There might be other reasons, as well, for a woman to end her pregnancy.

And while the cause of pregnancy was not innately apparent, women did know that they were pregnant fairly soon. At some earlier time a woman, or women, had discovered how to know that a child was growing inside of her, before it was obvious. Perhaps she noticed that it had been some time since she had bled and she had learned that that could be a sign, or if she had been pregnant before, she might recognize certain symptoms. The knowledge had been passed down until all women learned it as part of their initiation into adulthood.

In the beginning, when a woman realized she was carrying a child, she might look back and try to think about what had caused it. Was it a certain food she ate? A special pool she had bathed in? A specific man she'd had relations with? A particular river she had crossed? A unique tree in whose shade she had slept?

If a woman wanted to have a baby, she might try repeating some or all of those activities, perhaps making it into a ritual. But she would learn that she could do any of those things any number of times and still not necessarily become pregnant. She then might wonder if it was a combination of actions, or the order in which they were done, or the time of day, or the cycle, or season, or year. Maybe just a strong desire to have a baby, or the concerted wishes of several people. Or perhaps it was unknown agents, emanations from rocks, or spirits from another world, or the Great Mother, the first Mother.

If she lived in a society that had developed a set of explanations that seemed reasonable, or even unreasonable, but that seemed to answer questions that were not accessible to her own observations, it would be easy to accept them if everyone else did.

But someone might be observant enough to begin to make connections and draw inferences that were close to the truth. Because of a unique set of circumstances, Ayla had come to such conclusions, though she'd had to overcome the strong urge to believe what others believed instead of her own observations and reasoning.

Even before talking to Ayla, the One Who Was First had also begun to suspect the true cause of conception. Ayla's belief, and explanation, was the final piece of information she needed to persuade herself, and she had felt for some time that people, women in particular, should know how new life was started.

Knowledge was power. If a woman knew what caused a baby to begin growing inside her, she could gain control over her own life. Instead of simply finding herself pregnant, whether she wanted a baby or not, whether the timing was right for her to have one, whether she was well enough, or had enough children already, she had a choice. If it was relations with a man that somehow caused the pregnancy, not something external and out of her hands, she could decide not to have a baby simply by choosing not to share Pleasures with a man. Of course, it wouldn't necessarily be easy for a woman to make that choice, and Zelandoni wasn't at all sure how the men would react.

Though there would likely be unknown repercussions, there was another reason that she wanted her people to know that children were the result of the union of women and men. The strongest reason of all: because it was true. And men needed to know it too. Men had been considered incidental to the process of procreation for too long. It was only right that men know that they were essential to the creation of life.

And Zelandoni believed the people were ready for it, more than ready. Ayla had already told Jondalar what she believed, and he was nearly convinced. More, he wanted to believe. This was the right time. If Zelandoni herself had guessed it and if Ayla could work it out, so could others. The First hoped that the consequences of telling everyone would not be too devastating, but if the zelandonia didn't tell them now, it was bound to come from someone else before long.

As soon as she heard Ayla recite the new final verse to the

Mother's Song, Zelandoni knew the truth had to be revealed now. But to be accepted, it could not be divulged casually or piecemeal. It needed dramatic impact. The One Who Was First was clever enough to understand that most of what happened to acolytes in the course of being "called" to serve the Mother was the products of their own minds. A few of the older zelandonia had become entirely cynical about the whole process, but there were always inexplicable events that were caused by unknown or unseen forces.

It was those events that revealed a true calling, and when Ayla talked about her experience in the cave, the First had never heard a truer calling. In particular, that final verse of the Mother's Song. Though Ayla's instinct for language and ability to memorize were phenomenal, and she had become a skillful and compelling teller of stories and speaker of Legends, she had never before displayed an ability to create verse, and she had said it filled her head, that she heard it complete. If she could explain it to the people with the same conviction, she would be very persuasive.

When it seemed to the First that everything was in motion and could not be stopped, she finally announced, "It's getting late. This has been a long meeting. I think we should go now and meet again tomorrow morning."

"I promised Jonayla I would go riding with her today," Ayla was explaining, "but the meeting took so long."

No wonder, Proleva thought to herself, eyeing the black marks on Ayla's forehead, but she refrained from saying anything. "Jondalar heard her talking to me about going out on the horses with you, wondering where you were and what was taking so long. Dalanar tried to explain to her that you were at a very important meeting, and no one knew how long you would be; then Jondalar offered to take her out."

"I'm glad he did," Ayla said. "I hated to disappoint her. Have they been gone long?"

"Most of the afternoon. I imagine they will be back soon," Proleva said. "Dalanar did ask me to remind you that the Lanzadonii are expecting you this evening."

"That's right! He did ask when I was on my way to the

meeting. I think I'll change clothes, and rest for a while. It's hard to believe that just sitting around at a meeting can make you so tired. Will you send Jonayla in to get me when she gets here?"

"Of course I will," Proleva said. It was a lot more than just a meeting, I'm sure, she thought. "Would you like something to eat? Maybe a little tea?"

"Yes, I think I would, Proleva, but I'd like to clean up a little first. I'd love to go for a swim . . . but I guess I should wait until later. I think I'll go check on Whinney first."

"They took her with them. Jondalar said she'd want to go with the other horses, and the run wouldn't hurt her."

"He's right. Whinney probably missed her children, too."

Proleva watched Ayla walk toward the sleeping lodge. She does look tired, the woman thought. Not surprising. Look what she's been through. Having a miscarriage, and now becoming our newest Zelandoni . . . and getting her call, whatever that really means.

The woman had seen the effects of getting too close to the spirit world. Everyone had. Anytime someone was seriously hurt, for example, or even more frightening, had an inexplicable critical illness, she knew they were near the next world. The idea that a person would purposely put themselves in contact with that world so that they could Serve The Mother was almost beyond her comprehension. Proleva felt a slight shudder. She was grateful that she would never have to go through such a harrowing experience. While she knew that someday everyone would have to move on to that fearful place, she had no desire whatever to join the ranks of the zelandonia.

She and Jondalar are having problems, too, Proleva thought. He's been avoiding her. I've watched him go the other way as soon as he sees her. I'm sure I know what his problem is. He's feeling ashamed. She caught him with Marona, and now he doesn't want to face her. This is not a good time for him to be avoiding Ayla. She needs everyone's help now, especially his.

If he didn't want Ayla to know about Marona, he shouldn't have started up with her again, even if she was encouraging him every way she could. He knew how Ayla would feel about her. He could have found some other woman, if he had to have one. It's not like he still couldn't have his pick of just about any woman in the whole camp. And it would have served that Marona woman right. She's so obvious, you'd think even he would see it.

As much as Proleva cared about him, there were times when her mate's younger brother exasperated her.

"Mother! Mother! Are you finally back? Proleva said you were here. You said we would go for a ride today, and I was waiting and waiting," Jonayla said. The wolf, who bounded in after her, was just as excited, trying to get Ayla's attention.

She gave the girl a big hug, then grabbed the head of the big carnivore and started to rub his face with hers, but her marks were feeling sore, so she just hugged him. He started to sniff her wound, but she pushed him away. He looked into his food dish instead, found a bone Proleva had left there earlier, and took it to his resting place.

"I'm sorry, Jonayla," Ayla said. "I didn't know the meeting with the zelandonia would take so long. I promise we'll do it another day, but it may not be tomorrow."

"It's all right, mother. The zelandonia do take a long time. They spent a whole day teaching us songs and dances and stuff, showing us where to stand and what steps to make. I did get to go riding anyway. Jondy took me."

"Proleva told me. I'm glad he did. I know how much you wanted to go," Ayla said.

"Does that hurt, mother?" Jonayla asked, pointing to Ayla's forehead.

Ayla was slightly taken aback that her daughter had noticed. "No, not now. It did a little at first, but not bad. That mark has a special meaning . . ."

"I know what it means," the girl said. "It means you're Zelandoni now."

"That's right, Jonayla."

"Jondy told me you won't have to be gone so much after you get a zelandoni mark. Is that true, mother?"

Ayla hadn't realized how much her daughter had missed her, and she felt a rush of gratitude that Jondalar had been there to take care of her, and explain things to her. She reached out to

hug the child. "Yes, it's true. I will still have to be gone sometimes, but not as much."

Maybe Jondalar missed her, too, but why did he have to turn
to Marona? He said he loved her, even after she found them
like that, but if he did, why was he staying away from her now?

"Why are you crying, mother?" the girl said. "Are you sure
that mark doesn't hurt? It looks sore."

"I'm just so glad to see you, Jonayla." She let go of the child,
but smiled at her through wet eyes. "I almost forgot to tell you.
We are going to visit the Lanzadonii camp and have a meal
with them tonight."

"With Dalanar and Bokovan?"

"That's right, and Echozar and Joplaya, and Jerika, and
everybody."

"Is Jondy coming?"

"I don't know, but I don't think so. He had to go someplace
else." Suddenly Ayla turned aside and seeing Jonayla's clothing
basket, started going through it. She didn't want her daughter
to see her in tears again. "It will get cold after it gets dark;
would you like to change into something warmer?"

"Can I wear the new tunic that Folara made for me?"

"That would be a good idea, Jonayla."

35

At first glance, in the distance, Ayla thought it was Jondalar carrying something, coming toward her along the well-worn main path between the camps of several friendly Caves. She felt her stomach tightening to a knot. The height, the shape of the body, the walk were so familiar, but as the man approached, she saw it was Dalanar, carrying Bokovan.

As soon as they neared, Dalanar saw the obvious black marks on her forehead. Ayla noted Dalanar's look of surprise when he first saw her, then his effort to avoid looking at her forehead, and remembered her marks. She didn't see them, and tended to forget them.

Is that why Jondalar is behaving so strangely? Dalanar wondered. When he had invited Jondalar to join the Lanzadonii for a meal, along with Ayla and Jonayla, Dalanar had been surprised by Jondalar's hesitation, and then refusal. He claimed he had already promised to be some other place, but he looked upset and embarrassed. It was as though he were looking for excuses not to join them this evening. He recalled his own reasons for leaving a woman he loved. But I didn't think Jondalar was bothered by her becoming zelandoni, the older man thought. He always seems to be proud of her skill as a healer, and content to be working the flint and training his apprentices.

"Would you let me carry you for a while, Bokovan? And give Dalanar a rest?" Ayla said, holding out her arms to him, and smiling. The youngster hesitated, then held out his arms to her. She remembered how much he weighed when she picked him up. Ayla, carrying Bokovan, walked alongside Dalanar, who was holding Jonayla's hand as they headed toward his camp. Wolf followed along behind.

The animal seemed to be perfectly comfortable wandering through the large Camp of people now, and none of the people appeared particularly concerned about him. Ayla had noticed, however, that the Zelandonii took a special delight in the reactions of visitors or strangers who were not accustomed to seeing a wolf mingle so freely with people.

When they arrived, Joplaya and Jerika came to greet her, and Ayla noticed their look of surprise, and not-quite-successful attempt to ignore her new forehead marks. Although there was still an air of sadness about the beautiful dark-haired young woman, whom Jondalar called cousin, Ayla noticed a smile of warm love light up her vivid green eyes as she took her son. Joplaya seemed more relaxed, more accepting of her life, and genuinely pleased to see Ayla.

Jerika also greeted her warmly. "Let me take Bokovan," she said, taking the child from his mother's arms. "I have some food ready for him. You and Ayla can visit."

Ayla spoke directly to the boy. "I am glad I met you, Bokovan. Will you come to visit me? I'm from the Ninth Cave. Do you know where it is?"

He stared at her for a while, then with great seriousness, he said, "Yeth."

Ayla could not help but notice both the similarities and the differences between Jerika, Joplaya, and Bokovan before his grandmother took him away. The older woman was short and sturdy, her movements quick and energetic. Her hair, once as dark as the night sky, was now showing sunset streaks of gray. Her face, round and flat with high cheekbones, was more wrinkled, but her black slanted eyes still sparkled with charm and wit.

Ayla remembered Hochaman, the man who had been mated to Jerika's mother. He had been the traveler, and his mate had chosen to go along with him. Jerika was born along the way. Ayla recalled Dalanar telling the S'Armunai visitor about Hochaman's long Journey, from the Endless Seas of the East all the way to the Great Waters of the West, with pride. It occurred to her that even though the truth was exceptional in itself, it was the kind of story that would be told and retold, probably growing with each telling until it became a legend or myth, with little resemblance to the original story.

Dalanar had met Jerika some time after he found his flint mine and had been at first intrigued and then captivated by the exotic woman. Several people had already gathered around Dalanar and his flint mine—beginning the nucleus of the Cave that would later be called the Lanzadonii—when Hochaman and Jerika arrived at his camp. They looked so unusual, it was obvious they had come from a great distance. Dalanar had never seen anyone like Jerika. She was tiny in comparison with most women, but intelligent and strong-minded, and he was captivated by the exotic young woman. It had taken someone that unusual to finally vanquish his great love for Marthona.

Joplaya was born to Dalanar's hearth. Ayla now knew that what she had long believed was true; Joplaya was as much Dalanar's child as she was Jerika's. But Jondalar had not gone to live with the Lanzadonii until he and Joplaya were both adolescents. They had not been raised together as sister and brother and Joplaya had fallen hopelessly in love with Jondalar, even though he was a "close cousin," an unmatable man.

Joplaya is as much his sister as Folara, Ayla thought, trying to sort out what the new relationships would mean. Jondalar and Folara are both children of Marthona, and Jondalar and Joplaya are both Dalanar's children. You can see him in both of them.

Jondalar was a younger replica of Dalanar, while Joplaya showed more of her mother's influence, but she was tall like Dalanar, and a more subtle contribution showed in other ways. Her hair was dark, but had light highlights. It was not the pure glossy sheen her mother's had been. Her face had the contours of Dalanar's people, with her mother's high cheekbones. But her most stunning feature was her eyes. Neither black like her mother's nor vivid blue like Dalanar's—and Jondalar's—Joplaya's eyes were a vivid green with accents of hazel, with a shape and epicanthic fold like her mother, but less pronounced. Jerika was obviously a foreigner, but in many ways Joplaya seemed more exotic than her mother because of her similarities.

Joplaya had decided to mate with Echozar because she knew she could never have the man she loved. She chose him, she once told Ayla, because she knew she'd never find a man who would love her more, and she was right. Echozar was one of "mixed spirits"—his mother had been Clan, and many people thought he was as ugly as Joplaya was beautiful. But not Ayla. She was sure Echozar looked the way her son would, when he grew up.

Bokovan exhibited all of the components of his unusual background. The physical strength of the Clan from Echozar along with the height of his mother, and Dalanar, were already obvious. His eyes were only slightly slanted and dark, nearly as dark as Jerika's, but not exactly black. Touches of a lighter shade or a reflective sparkle gave them a vivid quality she had never seen in such dark eyes. They were not only unusual, they were compelling. She sensed something special about Bokovan and wished the Lanzadonii lived closer; she would love to watch him grow up.

He was only a little younger than her son had been the last time she saw him, and he reminded her so much of Durc it almost hurt. Ayla wondered what kind of mind he would have. Would he have some aspect of the Clan memories along with the capacity to make art and speak with words? Like Dalanar's and Jerika's people? She had often thought about her son in the same way.

"Bokovan is a very special child, Joplaya," Ayla said. "When he's a little older, I wish you would consider sending him to the Ninth Cave for me to keep for a while."

"Why?" Joplaya asked.

"Partly because he may have some unique qualities that could lead to the zelandonia, and you might want to know about that, but mostly because I would love to get to know him better," Ayla said.

Joplaya smiled, then paused. "Would you be willing to send Jonayla to the Lanzadonii to stay with me for a while?"

"I never thought about it," Ayla said, "but that might be a

good idea . . . in a few years . . . if she'd be willing to go. Why do you want her?"

"I'll never have a girl. I'll never have another child. It was too hard on me giving birth to Bokovan," Joplaya said.

Ayla remembered the difficulty she had giving birth to her son Durc, the one born to the Clan, and she had heard about Joplaya's problems. "Are you sure, Joplaya? One difficult birth doesn't mean they all will be."

"Our Donier says she doesn't think I should try. She's afraid I would die. I came very close with Bokovan. I am taking the medicine that you gave the zelandonia—and mother tries to make sure I take it. I do it to please her, but even if I didn't, I don't think it would matter. I don't think I can get pregnant again. In spite of mother, I stopped taking the medicine for a while. I wanted another child, but Doni chose not to Bless me," Joplaya said.

Ayla didn't want to pry, but as a Zelandoni she felt she had to ask, especially now. "Do you honor the Mother frequently? It is important, if you want the Mother to Bless you, that you honor Her properly."

Joplaya smiled. "Echozar is a sweet and loving man. He may not be the one I wanted, Ayla . . ." She paused, and for a fleeting moment a look of desolation darkened her expression. Ayla matched it with one of her own, for an entirely different reason. "But I was right when I said no one could love me more than Echozar, and I have truly come to care for him. In the beginning, he could hardly bring himself to touch me, out of fear that he would somehow hurt me, and because, I think, he couldn't quite believe he had the right. We are beyond that now, although he still acts so grateful sometimes, I have to tease him out of it. He's even learning to laugh at himself. I think Doni is properly honored."

Ayla thought for a while. It was possible that the problem wasn't Joplaya's, but Echozar's. He was half Clan, and there could be a reason why a man who was Clan, or even just part, might experience some problem having a child with one of the Others. One child could have been just luck, though some would call him "abomination," not luck. She wasn't sure how often someone of the Clan actually coupled with one of the Others, or how many of the offspring lived, or were allowed to live.

Everyone knew about those with mixed spirits, but she hadn't seen very many. She stopped to consider them: There was her son, Durc, and Ura at the Clan Gathering. Rydag of the Mamutoi Lion Camp. Possibly Attaroa and others among the S'Armunai had Clan mixed in. Echozar was half, and of course, there was Bokovan. It was likely Brukeval's mother had been half, too, which accounted for his characteristic look.

She was going to ask how well the Mother was honored at ceremonies and festivals among the Lanzadonii. They were still a small group, although there had been some talk, she knew, about where they would locate a second Cave, sometime in the future. It occurred to her that perhaps she ought to talk to their Zelandoni first. After all, she was one of the ze-landonia and ought to discuss such things with another Zelan-doni. *Perhaps I should consult with the First. She may have some thoughts on the matter,* Ayla thought.

Echozar arrived at the camp then and the subject changed. She was glad for the chance to stop trying to be Zelandoni and just be a friend. He gave her a broad smile, which still startled her somewhat on a face so strongly Clan. An expression that bared the teeth had a different meaning in the clan she grew up with.

"Ayla! How good to see you!" Echozar said as they embraced. He too had noticed the fresh mark on her forehead, and though he understood what it meant, he had been adopted by Dalanar's people, and it didn't affect him quite the same way. He knew she was an acolyte, and expected her to become a Zelandoni someday. He might have commented on it, but he'd been exposed to more than his share of comment about the way he looked, and was reluctant to bring up any aspect of another person's appearance.

"And here's the wolf," he said, feeling just a touch of apprehension when Wolf sniffed him. The Lanzadonii were not as familiar with the animal, and though he did remember him, it took a while to get used to the idea of a wolf mingling freely with people. "I heard he was here; that's how I knew you had arrived. I was afraid we wouldn't see you after making the trip all the way here. Some of us were even considering going to the Ninth Cave to see you before we left. Your Mamutoi kin and their S'Armunai friend are definitely planning to go, and some of the Lanzadonii were thinking of going along," Echozar said.

Ayla thought he seemed much more confident and relaxed, and was sure Dalanar was right about how helpful it had been for Echozar to be accepted so easily by Danug and Druwez and—what was his name—Aldanor? She was sure Jondalar had welcomed him, too, along with their kin and several close friends. Jondalar would be very good about making Echozar feel welcome . . . but he hadn't said one single welcoming word to her. The only time she had seen him since she arrived was in the small woods, standing naked with Marona. Ayla had to look away to fight back the sudden tightness in her throat and sting of impending tears, feelings that seemed to come upon her at the most unexpected moments, lately. She said she had something in her eye.

"Just because I've come to the Summer Meeting doesn't mean you can't come to visit the Ninth Cave," Ayla said after a moment. "It's not very far from here, and since you are so close, you might as well. I think Dalanar and Joplaya would be interested in the way Jondalar has set up the training for his flint-knapping apprentices. He has six of them now," Ayla said, sounding almost normal. After all, she could hardly help talking about Jondalar to Dalanar and Joplaya. "And I'd love to see a little more of Bokovan, and of course, all the rest of you."

"I think that little one has charmed Ayla completely," Dalanar said. Everyone smiled benignly.

"He is going to be a big man," Echozar said. "And I want to teach him to be a good hunter."

Ayla grinned at him. For a moment, she could imagine that Echozar was a man of the Clan, proud of the son of his hearth. "He may turn out to be more than just a big man, Echozar. I think he's a very special child."

"Where is Jondalar?" Echozar asked. "Wasn't he supposed to come and share a meal with us tonight?"

"I saw him when he was taking Jonayla out with the horses after midday. He said he couldn't make it," Dalanar said, sounding disappointed.

"I was going to take Jonayla out, but the zelandonia meeting took longer than I expected," Ayla said. Everyone glanced up at her forehead.

"Did he say why he couldn't come?" Echozar asked.

"I don't know, something about other plans, and promises he made before Ayla came."

Ayla felt her stomach knot. I can imagine what promises he made, she thought.

It was nearly dark by the time Ayla insisted she had to go. Echozar walked back with her and Jonayla and Wolf, carrying a torch.

"You look happy, Echozar," Ayla said.

"I am happy, although I still find it hard to believe Joplaya is my mate. Sometimes I wake up at night and just look at her in the firelight. She is so beautiful, and she's wonderful. Kind and understanding. I feel so lucky, I sometimes wonder how I could deserve her."

"She's lucky, too, you know. I wish we lived closer."

"So you could see more of Bokovan?" he said. She saw his teeth gleaming with a smile.

"It's true, I would like to see more of Bokovan, and you and Joplaya, and everyone else," Ayla said.

"Have you considered coming back with us and staying over winter?" Echozar asked. "You know, Dalanar says you and Jondalar are always welcome."

Ayla frowned, staring into the dark. Yes, of course, Jondalar, she thought. "I don't think Jondalar would want to leave his apprentices. He has made promises, and winter is the best time to work on perfecting techniques," she said.

Echozar was silent for a few paces. "I don't suppose you'd want to leave Jondalar for a season and visit by yourself, with Jonayla and your animals, of course," he said. "As much as she loves Bokovan, I know Joplaya would love to have that little girl around. She and Bokovan spent a lot of time at Levela's camp and got to know her."

"I . . . don't know. I guess I never thought about it. I've been so busy training for the zelandonia . . . ," she said, then glanced around looking for her daughter, who was straggling behind. She has probably found something along the path to distract her, Ayla thought.

"We would never object to having another Donier," Echozar said.

Ayla smiled at him, then stopped. "Jonayla, why are you so far back?"

"I'm tired, mother," Jonayla whined. "Would you carry me?"

Ayla stopped to pick her daughter up, using a hip for support. The little girl's arms felt good around her neck. She had missed Jonayla, and hugged her little body close.

They continued in silence for a while, and began to hear raucous voices. Ahead they could see the light of a campfire behind a fairly dense stand of brush. It wasn't a regular Cave's site, Ayla gathered as they drew closer. Through the screen of brush, she noticed several men sitting around the fire. They were obviously gaming, and drinking something from miniature waterbags made from the nearly waterproof stomachs of small animals. She knew many of the men; several were from the Ninth Cave, but there was a sprinkling of others from several different Caves.

Laramar was there, the man who was known for making the potent alcoholic brew from almost anything that would ferment. While they didn't have the refinement of the wine that Marthona made, the drinks he produced weren't bad. He did very little of anything else and had perfected what had become his "craft," but he made it in quantity and many people regularly drank too much, creating problems. His only other claim to fame had been a hearthful of unkempt children, and a slovenly mate who indulged heavily in his product. Ayla and the rest of the Cave took more care of the children than either Laramar or Tremeda did.

Now the oldest girl, Lanoga, was mated to Lanidar and had a child of her own, but the young couple had adopted all her younger siblings. Her older brother, Bologan, also lived with them and helped to provide for the children. He had also helped to build their new dwelling, along with Jondalar and several others. Her mother, Tremeda, and Laramar also lived with them occasionally, when they chose to go to a place they called home, and both of them behaved as though it was theirs.

Besides Laramar, Ayla noticed the distinctive forehead markings of a Zelandoni on one man, but when he smiled, she saw the gap of his missing front teeth and frowned, realizing it was Madroman. Had he already been accepted into the zelandonia and tattooed? She didn't think so. She looked again and noticed that an edge of the "tattoo" was smeared. He must have painted it on, using the colors that some people used to temporarily decorate their faces for special occasions, but she had never seen anyone decorate with Zelandoni marks before.

Seeing him reminded her of the backpack she had found in the cave and had brought to the First. Though he invariably smiled and tried to engage her in conversation, she had always felt uneasy around Madroman. He disturbed her in a way that made her think of how a horse's fur looked when it was stroked opposite to the direction in which it grew; he rubbed her the wrong way.

She saw many young men, talking and laughing loudly, but there were other men of all ages. From what she knew of those she recognized, none of them contributed much. Some were not too bright, or were easily led. One of them spent most of his time drinking Laramar's brew, barely stumbling home each night, and often could be found in some out-of-the-way place completely unconscious, smelling of drink and vomit. Another was known to be unnecessarily brutal, especially to his mate and her children, and the zelandonia had talked of ways to intercede, waiting only for his mate to ask for help.

Then almost hidden in the shadows, she caught sight of Brukeval sitting somewhat off by himself with his back to a tall, roughly pointed stump, taking a drink from one of the bags. His temper still bothered her, but he was a cousin of Jondalar's and had always been kind to her. She hated to see him with such an unsavory lot.

She was about to turn away when she heard Wolf growl low in his throat. A voice spoke up loudly behind her back.

"Well, look what we have here. The animal lover, and a couple animals."

She spun around in surprise. A couple of animals, she thought, but I only have Wolf . . . it took her a moment before she realized that he had called Echozar an animal. She felt her anger rise.

"The only animal I see here is a wolf . . . or were you thinking of yourself?" Ayla countered.

There were a few guffaws from some who had heard the remarks and she saw the man frown. "I wasn't saying I was an animal," he said.

"That's good. I wouldn't put yourself in the same category as Wolf. You don't measure up," she said.

Some of the other men pulled the brush aside to see what was going on. They saw Ayla holding her daughter on one hip, her leg in front of the wolf to restrain him, and Echozar holding a torch.

"She sneaked up and was watching us," the man said defensively.

"I was walking along a main path and stopped to see who was making all the noise," Ayla said.

"Who is she? And why does she talk so funny?" asked a young man Ayla didn't know. Then he added with surprise, "That's a wolf!" Ayla had all but forgotten about her "accent" and so had most of the people who knew her, but occasionally a stranger brought it to her attention. From the pattern on the man's shirt, and the design of the necklace he wore, she guessed he was from a Cave that lived on another river to the north, a group that did not regularly attend their Summer Meeting. He must have arrived only recently.

"She's Ayla of the Ninth Cave, the one Jondalar brought back with him," Madroman said.

"And she's a Zelandoni who can control animals," another man said. Ayla thought he was from their neighbor, the Fourteenth Cave.

"She's not Zelandoni," Madroman said with an air of condescension. "She's an acolyte, still in training."

He had obviously not yet seen her new tattoo, Ayla thought.

"But when she came, she could already control that wolf and a couple of horses," the man from the Fourteenth Cave said.

"I told you she was an animal lover," the first man said with a sneer, looking pointedly at Echozar.

Echozar glared back, and moved toward Ayla protectively. This was a large group of men, and they had been drinking Laramar's brew. It had been known to bring out the worst in people.

"You mean like those horses from that Cave camped upstream?" the stranger said. "That's the first place I was taken when I got here. She's the one who controls them? I thought it was that man and the girl."

"Gray is my horse," Jonayla spoke up.

"They're all the same hearth," Brukeval said, strolling into the firelight.

Ayla glanced from Brukeval to Echozar, and saw their similarity immediately. Brukeval was clearly a modified version of Echozar, though neither of them was fully Clan.

"I think you should let Ayla get on her way," Brukeval continued. "And I think it might be smart to have our parties a little farther off the main path in the future."

"Yes, I think that is a good idea," said another voice that had suddenly appeared. Joharran, accompanied by some other men, stepped into the light of the torch held by Echozar. Several of them had unlit torches, which they immediately lit from Echozar's, showing how many there were. "We heard you, and came to see what was going on. There are plenty of places to have drinking parties, Laramar. I don't think you men need to be bothering people who are walking along main paths between camps. Perhaps you should move your party now. We don't need children stumbling over you in the morning."

"He can't tell us where to go," a slurred voice called out.

"That's right, he can't tell us where to go," said the first man who had seen Ayla.

"It's all right," Laramar said, picking up several of the small drinking bags that had not been unstoppered, and putting them in a backframe. "I'd rather find a place where we won't be bothered."

Brukeval began to help him. He glanced up at Ayla and caught her eye. She smiled at him with gratitude for taking her part and suggesting they move. He smiled back with a lingering expression that puzzled her, then frowned and looked away. She put Jonayla down and knelt to restrain Wolf while the men moved off.

"I was going to walk over to the Lanzadonii camp to talk to Dalanar, anyway, Echozar," Joharran said. "Why don't you walk back with me? Ayla can go on with Solaban and the others."

Ayla wondered what was so important that Joharran had to talk to Dalanar about that it couldn't wait until morning. Neither one was going anywhere in the dark. Then she noticed a few of the men who had been sitting around the fireplace move out from behind a bush and head in the direction the others had taken, their heads turning to watch Echozar, Joharran, and a couple of others go. She frowned with concern. Something did not feel right.

"I've never seen such goings-on with the zelandonia," Joharran commented. "Have you heard anything about the special ceremony everyone says they are planning? Ayla has her mark, but they haven't announced her yet. They usually do it right away. Has she said anything to you?"

"She's been so busy with the zelandonia, I haven't seen much of her," Jondalar said, which was not entirely true. He had not seen much of her, but not because she was so busy. He was the one who had been staying away and his brother knew it.

"Well, it looks like they must be planning something very big. Zelandoni spent a long time talking with Proleva, and she told me the zelandonia want a huge, elaborate feast. They are even talking to Laramar about supplying his brew for the festival. We're getting together a hunting party, probably be gone a day or two. Do you want to join us?" Joharran asked.

"Yes," Jondalar answered, almost too quickly, causing his brother to give him a questioning look. "I'd be glad to."

If he'd been thinking straight, Jondalar might have recalled that Ayla had said something to him when he first saw her, but he hadn't been able to think of anything but Ayla finding him with Marona since the incident. He just couldn't bring himself to simply crawl into the sleeping furs beside her under the circumstances. He didn't even know if she would let him. He was certain he had lost her, but was afraid to find out for sure.

He thought he had managed to find a plausible excuse for not returning to their camp another night, when Proleva asked him about it. He had actually slept near the horse enclosure, using horse blankets, and the ground covering he and Marona had used at the swimming place for bedding, to keep warm, but he didn't think he could continue staying away without arousing curiosity from the whole Camp. Being away on a hunting trip would solve the problem for the next day or two. He didn't even want to think beyond that.

Though Ayla was trying to behave as if nothing were wrong, and Jondalar thought his avoidance of her went unnoticed, in fact the whole camp was aware by now that something was wrong between the couple, and many guessed what it was. His clandestine trysts with Marona were not nearly so secret as he had thought. To most people, he was just being appropriately discreet and they ignored the affair. But the news that the formerly doting couple had not even shared the same bed since Ayla arrived, even though Marona had moved to a different camp, had spread quickly.

It was the kind of gossip people loved to speculate about. The fact that Ayla had been marked as a Zelandoni without being immediately announced, and that plans for a major ceremony were under way, only added to the delicious innuendos. People were guessing that the event had something to do with the newest Zelandoni, but no one seemed to know anything for sure. Usually one or another of the zelandonia would let something slip to an interested questioner, but this time none of them was talking. Some people were suggesting that even the acolytes didn't know the real reason for the big festival, though they all tried to act as if they did.

Jondalar was hardly aware that a celebration was being planned, and until Joharran had asked him to join the hunting party, he didn't care. Then it only became an excuse to get away for a while. He had seen Marona a few times. When she heard the rumors about the estrangement of Ayla and Jondalar, she had made a point of seeking him out, but he had lost all interest in her. He was little more than coldly polite when she spoke to him, but she was not the only one who tried to find out how serious their breach was. Brukeval also came to the camp of the Ninth Cave.

Though he had traveled to the Summer Meeting with the Ninth Cave, Brukeval had long since moved away to sleep in the men's summer lodges, the "far lodges" that were constructed around the periphery of the Summer Meeting Camp—commonly shortened to "fa'lodges." Some were used by young men recently elevated to manhood status, some by older men who were not yet mated or were between mates, or men who wished they were. Brukeval had never mated. He'd always had a secret fear of being refused, and had never asked anyone. Besides, none of the available women seemed all that interesting to him. Since he had no immediate family or children, he felt out of place at the Main Camp, and even around the more frequently used areas of the Ninth Cave. As the years went by and most of the men his age took mates, he avoided ordinary activities and familiar people more and more, and by default often ended up with the idlers who attached themselves to Laramar to partake of the brew he made, frequently imbibing of it himself for the forgetfulness it induced.

Brukeval had tried a few different men's tents at the Summer Meeting, but finally settled in the one that housed many of the men he knew from the Ninth Cave who enjoyed easy access to Laramar's brew. Laramar himself slept there most of the time rather than returning to the tent of his mate and her children. The children weren't very welcoming lately, especially since Lanoga mated that boy with the feeble arm. She'd grown up to be pretty enough, Laramar thought; she could have gotten a better man, though he'd heard the boy could hunt. Madroman often chose that men's tent as well, rather than the large dwelling of patronizing zelandonia, where he was still only an acolyte, even though he told everyone that he had been called.

Brukeval didn't much like the men he chose to live with, a shiftless bunch who had little to offer and even less respect. He knew he was brighter and more capable than most of them. He was related to the families of those who often became leaders and he had grown up with people who were responsible, intelligent, and often talented. The men with whom he shared a fa'lodge were essentially lazy, weak willed, or slow, with no generosity of spirit or heart and few other redeeming qualities.

As a result, in an effort to bolster their own self-worth and as an outlet for their frustrations, they fed each other's vanity and conceit with bragging contempt for something they could feel superior to: those dirty, stupid animals called Flatheads. They told each other that while they were not human, they could be tricky. Because Flatheads bore a vague resemblance to real people, they were sometimes clever enough to confuse the spirits that made a woman pregnant so that she gave birth to an abomination, and that was intolerable. For reasons of his own, the one thing Brukeval had in common with the men with whom he shared living space was a deep and abiding hatred for Flatheads.

Some of the men were brutal bullies, and in the beginning one or two had actually tried to bait and tease him about having a Flathead mother, but after he had demonstrated his irrational anger and powerful strength a few times, none dared to bother him again, and most came to treat him with more respect than anyone else who shared their fa'lodge. Besides, he did have some influence with the Cave leaders since he knew many of them, and had spoken up for one or another of the men who had gotten himself in deeper than usual trouble. Many of the men began to look to him as a leader of sorts. So did some of the Caves. They felt that he could be a restraining influence, and by the middle of the summer, if any of the men who lived there were being especially troublesome, Brukeval was the one people went to.

When he appeared at the Main Camp of the Ninth Cave, ostensibly to share a midday meal and visit with the people of his Cave, it caused some conjecture. Ayla had gone early. She was deeply involved with the activities of the zelandonia, and had taken Jonayla to stay with Levela along the way. In fact, most of the women were gone. With her usual organizing flair, Proleva had gathered up everyone she could find, assigning jobs here and delegating there, to begin the preparations for a great feast that would feed the entire Summer Meeting. The only women at the camp were the ones going on the hunt.

Proleva had left behind some food for the midday meal of the hunters who were gathering at the camp of the Ninth Cave. The hunting party would have to fend for themselves on the trail. Most of them had packed dried traveling food along with their equipment, tents, and sleeping rolls, though they did expect to eat fresh food they killed or collected most of the time.

Since he was there and was known to be a more than adequate hunter, Joharran invited him along on the hunt. Brukeval hesitated only a moment. He wondered about the situation between Ayla and Jondalar, and thought that perhaps during the camaraderie of a hunt, he might be able to find out.

Brukeval had never forgotten the way Ayla had faced them all down when Marona had tricked her into wearing entirely inappropriate clothing to her own welcoming party—now all the women were wearing similar outfits, he'd noticed. He remembered how warm she had been to him when they first met, the way she smiled, almost as though she knew him, with none of the hesitation or reservation most women showed. And he dreamed of her in her beautiful and unusual Matrimonial clothing, often seeing himself removing it, and after all these years, he still daydreamed about what it would be like if he were Jondalar lying beside her on soft furs.

Ayla had always been pleasant to him, but after that first night, he sensed a feeling of distance from her that was different from that first welcome. Brukeval had withdrawn more into himself as the years had gone by, but without their being aware of it, he knew a great deal about Jondalar and Ayla's life together, even intimate details. Among other things, he knew that Jondalar had been coupling with Marona—of all people—for some time. He also knew that Ayla never joined with anyone else, not even at Mother Festivals, and that she did not know about Jondalar and Marona.

Brukeval returned to the fa'lodge for his hunting gear, and by the time he got back to the Ninth Cave's camp, he was actually looking forward to the hunt. He hadn't really been included in one since he took up residence with the men he currently shared sleeping space with. As a rule, most hunting party leaders didn't bother asking the men from that tent to join them, and they seldom organized their own hunts, except for Brukeval, who had often gone off alone over the years and had learned to hunt or forage enough for himself when he wanted to.

The other men usually cadged something to eat from one Cave or another, often returning to the camps of their own Caves. Madroman had no concern about meals. He usually ate with the zelandonia, who were customarily supplied quite well by the Caves, usually in exchange for general services, but also for specific requests. Laramar also had his own resources. He traded his brew, and found no lack of willing consumers.

It was not uncommon for the youngest men staying in their own shelters to get food or a meal from one camp or another, although they usually tried to make some contribution in return, such as hunting or joining in other community work or food-gathering activities. And though it was not unusual for the men who had recently reached manhood to create a few problems now and then, it was generally ascribed to "high spirits" and tolerated, especially by older men recalling their own youth. If, however, they caused too much trouble, it could bring a visit from Cave leaders, who had the authority to impose penalties, including, at the worst, banishment from the Summer Meeting Camp.

Everyone knew that the men of Brukeval's fa'lodge—as people had started referring to the place—were not young, and they could seldom be found when there was work to do. But there was never a lack of food at Summer Meetings, and no one who showed up when it was time to eat was ever turned away, no matter how unwelcome. The men of that place were generally smart enough not to appear at the same camp too often. And they usually spread out so that all of them did not end up at one place at the same time, unless they learned of a rather lavish feast, as when one or more camps would have a large communal meal. But with their often loud parties, sometimes violent fights, slovenly ways, and unwillingness to contribute, that particular men's group skirted the very edge of tolerance.

But that tent was the only place where Brukeval could drown out his secret guilt and pain with Laramar's brew. In a drunken stupor, with his conscious mind no longer in control, then he was free to think of Ayla the way he wanted. He could think of the way she looked when she proudly faced down the laughter of the Ninth Cave, think of her smiling at him with her beautiful smile, laughing and a little tipsy, flirting with him, talking to him as if she thought he was an ordinary man, even a charming, handsome man, not ugly and short. People called him a Flathead, but it wasn't true, it wasn't. I am not a Flathead, he thought. It's only because I am short and . . . ugly.

Hidden in the dark, full of potent drink, he could dream of Ayla in her spectacular, exotic tunic with her beautiful golden hair falling around her face and the amber jewel nestled between her high, firm bare breasts. He could dream of holding those breasts, of touching those nipples, of taking them in his mouth. Just the thought would bring him to erection, and filled with his need, he barely had to touch himself to make his essence spurt.

Then he could crawl into his empty bed, and dream that he was the one who had stood in front of Zelandoni with Ayla at his side, not his cousin, the tall man with the yellow hair and vivid blue eyes, not that perfect man every woman wanted. But Brukeval knew he wasn't so perfect. Jondalar had been coupling with Marona, not telling Ayla, trying to hide it from everyone. He had guilty secrets, too, and now Ayla was sleeping alone. Jondalar had been sleeping outside in the horse place, using their riding blankets. Had Ayla stopped loving Jondalar? Had she found out about Marona and stopped loving that man who was everything Brukeval had ever wanted to be? The man who was mated to the woman he loved more than life itself? Did she need someone to love her now?

Even if she stopped loving Jondalar, he knew it wasn't likely that she would choose him, but she had smiled at him again, and didn't seem as distant. And with the arrival of Dalanar and the Lanzadonii, he was reminded that some beautiful women did choose men who were ugly. He was not a Flathead, and he hated to think of himself as having any similarity, but he was aware that Echozar, that ugly abomination of a man who was born of mixed spirits, whose mother was a Flathead, had mated the daughter of Dalanar's second woman, the one most people thought was so exotically beautiful. So it was possible. He tried not to get his hopes up, but if Ayla ever needed someone, someone who would never couple with anyone else, never, not as long as he lived, who would never love anyone else as long as he lived, he could be that man.

36

"Mother! Mother! 'Thona is here! Grandam finally came!" Jonayla cried, running into their lodge to announce the news, and then running out again. Wolf followed her in and out again.

Ayla stopped to think about how many days it had been since she had asked to have someone go for Marthona. She touched a finger to her leg as she thought about each day, and could count only four. Marthona must have been eager to come, as Ayla knew she would be, if a way could be found to get her here. She stepped out of the lodge just as four young men of approximately the same height lowered the litter on which Marthona was sitting from their shoulders to the ground. Two of them were Jondalar's apprentices; the other two were friends who happened to be nearby when the request for litter bearers was made.

Ayla looked at the contrivance upon which Marthona had been carried to the Summer Meeting. It consisted of two poles from straight young alder trees, placed parallel to each other with strong rope woven across them diagonally, creating a diamond pattern. Shorter shafts were woven through the ropes at intervals between the long poles to give some added stability. Ayla was sure that Marthona, who was an experienced weaver, had a hand in making it. The woman sat on a couple of cushions near the back and Ayla reached out a hand to help her stand up. Marthona thanked the young men as well as several others, who apparently had traded off the job of carrying the former leader.

They had spent the night before in the small valley of the Fifth Cave with the few people from that group who had stayed back from the meeting, along with one of their Zelandoni's acolytes. They were all quite interested in Marthona's mode of transportation. A couple of them wondered to themselves if they could find some young men who might be willing to carry them to a Summer Meeting. Most of them would have liked to attend; they all felt they were missing out when they had to stay back because they were not able to walk the distance on their own legs.

When Jondalar's apprentices brought the litter into the lodge, it occurred to Ayla that their services might still be needed. "Hartaman, would you and Zachadal, and maybe some of the others be willing to carry Marthona around the Camp, if she needs you? The walk from here to the zelandonia lodge and some of the other camps might be a little too far for her," Ayla said.

"Just let us know when you need us," Hartaman said. "It might be best if you could tell us in advance, but there is likely to be at least one of us around most of the time. I'll talk to some of the others and see if we can work out a way to make sure someone is here who can go and get more to help."

"That's very kind of you," Marthona said. She had heard Ayla's request as she walked in the entrance. "But I don't want to keep you from your own activities."

"There isn't that much to do anymore," Hartaman said. "Some people are planning to go hunting, or visiting relatives, or back home soon. Most of the ceremonies and feasts are over, except for the Late Matrimonial and whatever big event the zelandonia are preparing now, and no one seems able to find Jondalar lately, but he always does more training in the winter anyway. It's fun to carry you around, Marthona," Hartaman said, with a grin. "You can't believe how much attention we got just walking into Camp with you."

"Well, it seems I've become a new amusement," Marthona said, smiling back. "As long as you really don't mind, I may call upon you for your help now and then. I'll tell you the truth, I can walk much better for short distances, but I can't go very far even with a walking stick, and I hate slowing everyone else down."

Folara suddenly came bursting into the summer lodge. "Mother! You're here! Someone just told me you had come to the Summer Meeting. I didn't even know you were coming." They hugged in greeting, and touched cheeks.

"You can thank Ayla for that. When she heard that you might have found someone that you really care about, she suggested that someone go and get me. A young woman needs her mother if serious plans are being made," Marthona said.

"She's right," Folara said, and her smile was radiant, which made Marthona know that the possibility was true. "But how did you get here?"

"I think that was Ayla's idea, too. She told Dalanar and Joharran there was no reason that I couldn't be carried here on a stretcher by strong young men, so several of them came and got me. Ayla wanted me to come with her when she came, riding on Whinney's back, and I probably should have, but as much as I like the horses, the thought of riding one of them frightens me. I don't know how to control horses. Young men are easier. You just tell them what you want, and when you want to stop," Marthona said.

Folara hugged her brother's mate. "Thank you, Ayla. It takes another woman to understand. I did want my mother here, but I didn't know if she was well enough, and I knew she couldn't walk here." She turned to her mother. "How are you feeling?"

"Ayla took very good care of me when she was staying at the Ninth Cave, and I feel much better now than I did last spring," the woman said. "She really is a very good healer, and if you look closely, you will see that she is now a Zelandoni."

Marthona had noticed the mark on the side of her forehead, Ayla realized. It was healing and there was no pain, although it itched sometimes, and she had almost forgotten about it, unless someone mentioned it or made a point of staring.

"I know she is, mother," Folara said. "Everyone knows, even if they haven't announced it, but like all the rest of the zelandonia lately, she's been so busy, I haven't seen much of her. They're planning some kind of ceremony, but I don't know if it will be before or after the Second Matrimonial."

"Before," Ayla said. "You'll have time to talk to your mother and plan."

"So you are serious about someone," Marthona said. She paused and was quiet for a moment, thinking. Then she said. "Well, where is this young man? I'd like to meet him."

"He's waiting outside," Folara said. "I'll get him."

"Why don't I go out and meet him," Marthona said. It was dark in the summer lodge. There were no windows, only the entrance with its covering drape pulled back and tied, and the smoke hole in the middle of the roof, which was often left completely open during the day when the weather was nice. Her sight wasn't what it used to be and she wanted to get as good a look at this young man as she could.

When the three women went out of the entrance, Marthona saw three young men whom she didn't know, dressed in unfamiliar clothing, one of them a veritable giant with bright red hair. When Folara approached him first, Marthona took a deep breath. She had rather hoped he would not be the one her daughter had chosen. It wasn't that there was anything wrong with him. It was Marthona's aesthetic sense, which wasn't a deciding factor in any case, just that she always had hoped that the man Folara chose would fit well with her, that they would complement each other, and a man that big would make her tall and elegant daughter seem small. Folara began the introductions.

"Danug and Druwez of the Mamutoi are Ayla's kin. They came all this way to visit her. On their way they met another man and invited him to travel with them. Mother, please welcome Aldanor of the S'Armunai."

Ayla watched as a young man with the dark good looks of the S'Armunai came forward. "Aldanor, this is my mother, Marthona, former leader of the Ninth Cave of the Zelandonii, Mated to Willamar, Trade Master . . ."

Marthona breathed a sigh of relief when Folara started to formally introduce her to Aldanor, not the young red-haired giant, and began to recite the strange names and ties of the young man to the older woman.

"In the name of the Great Earth Mother, you are welcome here, Aldanor of the S'Armunai," Marthona said.

"In the name of Muna, Great Mother of the Earth, Her son Luma, bringer of warmth and light, and Her mate Bala, the watcher in the sky, I give you greetings," Aldanor said to Marthona, putting his hands up with arms bent at the elbow and palms facing her; then he remembered, and quickly changed the position so that his arms were stretched out and his palms were facing up, the way the Zelandonii made a greeting.

Both Marthona and Ayla knew that he must have been practicing the S'Armunai greeting so he could say it in Zelandonii, and they were both impressed. To Marthona, it spoke well of the handsome young man that he was willing to make the effort, and she had to admit he was a handsome young man. She could understand her daughter's attraction and, so far, was pleased with her choice.

Ayla had never heard the formal greeting of the S'Armunai; neither she nor Jondalar had ever been formally welcomed to a camp of the S'Armunai. Jondalar had been taken prisoner by Attaroa's Wolf Women and kept in a confined fenced area along with their men and boys. Ayla and the horses with the help of Wolf followed his trail to the camp.

After the formal greetings, Marthona and Aldanor began chatting, but Ayla recognized that while the former leader was being charming, she was also asking pointed questions to learn as much as she could about the stranger her daughter was planning to mate. Aldanor was explaining that he had met Danug and Druwez when they stopped to stay with his people for a while. He did not belong to Attaroa's Camp, but one farther north, for which he was grateful when it became known what had been going on there.

Ayla and Jondalar had become legendary figures to the S'Armunai. The tale was told of the beautiful S'Ayla, the Mother Incarnate, a living munai as fair as a summer day, and her mate, the tall, blond S'Elandon, who had come to earth to save the men of that southern camp. It was said that his eyes were the color of water in a glacier, more blue than the sky, and with his light hair, he was as handsome as only the shining moon would be if he came to earth and took human form. After the Mother's fierce Wolf, an incarnation of the Wolf Star, killed the evil Attaroa, S'Ayla and S'Elandon rode back up to the sky on their magic horses.

Aldanor had loved the stories when he first heard them, especially the idea that the visitors from the sky could control horses and wolves. He thought the legend came from a traveling storyteller, who must have had an inspiration of sheer genius to come up with such an innovative story. When the cousins claimed the two legendary figures were kin, and that they were on their way to visit them, he couldn't believe they were real. The young men got along well and when the two cousins extended the invitation, he decided to travel with them on their Journey to visit their Zelandonii kin, and see for himself. As the three young men traveled west, they heard more stories. The couple not only rode horses, but their wolf was so "fierce," he allowed babies to crawl all over him.

When they arrived at the Zelandonii Summer Meeting and he heard the true story of Attaroa and the people of her camp from Jondalar, Aldanor was amazed that the incidents in the legends were so accurate. He had planned to go back with Danug and Druwez just to tell everyone how true they were. A woman named Ayla did exist and was living with the Zelandonii, and her mate, Jondalar, was tall and blond with surprisingly blue eyes, and if a little older, still a most handsome man. Everyone said Ayla was beautiful, too.

But he decided not to go. No one would have believed him, any more than he had believed the stories that he heard were actually true. They were supernatural fables, which had a mystical kind of truth that helped to explain things that were unknown—myths. And besides, Jondalar's sister was a beauty in her own right, and she had captured his heart.

People had been gathering around as the stranger and Marthona talked, listening to the story Aldanor was telling.

"Why are the couple in the story called S'Ayla and S'Elandon, and not Ayla and Jondalar?" Folara asked.

"I think I can tell you that," Ayla said. "The S sound is an honorific; it is meant to express honor, show respect. The name S'Armunai means the 'honored people' or the 'special people.' When it is used in front of a person's name it means that person is held in great esteem."

"Why aren't we called 'special people'?" Jonayla asked.

"I think we are. I think their honorific is another way of saying 'Children of the Mother,' which is what we call ourselves," Marthona said. "Maybe we are related, or were long ago. It's interesting that they could take 'Zelandonii' and so easily change it to mean 'one who is honored,' or the 'special people.'"

"When they were confined to the fenced-in area," Ayla continued, "Jondalar started showing the men and boys how to do things, like make tools. He was the one who found a way to break everyone free. On our travels, when we would meet people, he often referred to himself as 'Jondalar of the Zelandonii.' One boy in particular took the Zelandonii part of Jondalar's name and started saying it 'S'Elandon,' giving him the honorific, because he honored and respected him so much. I think he believed that was what his name meant, 'Jondalar the honored one.' In the legend, they apparently gave me the honor, too."

Marthona was satisfied, for the present. She turned to Ayla. "I am being ill-mannered. I'm sorry. Please introduce me to your kin."

"This is Danug of the Mamutoi, son of Nezzie, who is mated to Talut, the leader of the Lion Camp, and this is his cousin Druwez, son of Talut's sister Tulie, co-leader of the Lion Camp of the Mamutoi," Ayla began. "Danug's mother, Nezzie, was the one who gave me my wedding outfit. You remember I told you she was going to adopt me, but then Mamut surprised everyone and adopted me instead."

Ayla knew Marthona had been very impressed by her wedding outfit, and she also knew that as the mother of the young woman who would soon be mated, she would want to know the standing of the young men, since it was likely they would be part of the Matrimonial Ceremony.

"I know others have welcomed you here," Marthona said, "but I want to add my greetings to theirs. I can understand how your people might miss Ayla. She would be a very worthwhile addition to any community, but if it's any compensation, you can tell them that we truly appreciate her. She has been a very welcome member of our Cave. Though a part of her heart will always belong to the Mamutoi, she is a very cherished Zelandonii."

"Thank you," Danug said. As the son of the leader's mate, he understood that this was part of the exchange of information that conveyed status and recognition of rank. "We have all missed her. My mother was very sorry when Ayla left, she was like a daughter to her, but she understood that her heart was with Jondalar. Nezzie will be very pleased to know that Ayla has found such a warm welcome among the Zelandonii, to know that her exceptional qualities are so well received." Even though his Zelandonii was not perfect, the young man was obviously well-spoken, and knew how to convey the position of his family among his people.

No one understood the value and importance of place and position better than Marthona. Ayla understood the concept of status. It had been important even to the Clan, and she was learning how the Zelandonii rated, ranked, and awarded significance to people, but she would never have the intuitive knowledge that someone like Marthona did, someone who was born into the highest position of her people.

In a society without currency, status was more than prestige, it was a form of wealth. People were eager to do favors for a person with standing because obligations always had to be repaid in kind. Debt was incurred when asking someone to make something, or to do something, or to go someplace, because of the implicit promise to return a favor of like value. No one really wanted to be in debt, but everyone was, and to have someone of high standing be in your debt gave you more status.

Many things had to be taken into account when appraising status, which was why people recited their "names and ties." Assigning value was one, as was effort. Even if the end product was not of the same quality, if the person gave it his or her best effort, the debt could be considered satisfied, though it didn't increase rank. Age was a factor; children up to a certain age did not accrue debts. In taking care of a child, even one's own, a debt to the community was paid, because children were the promise of continuity.

The reaching of a certain age, becoming an elder, also made a difference. Certain favors could be asked without accruing debt and without losing status, but as a person lost the ability to contribute, he or she didn't so much lose rank as shift position. An elder with knowledge and experience to offer could retain her status, but if she began to lose cognitive ability, she kept her position but only in name. He would still be respected for his past contributions, but his advice was no longer sought.

The system was complicated, but everyone learned its nuances the way they learned language, and by the time they reached the age of responsibility, most of them understood the fine distinctions. At any given time a person knew exactly what he owed and what was owed to him, the nature of the debts, and where she ranked within her own community.

Marthona also spoke with Druwez, whose position was equal to that of his cousin, since he was the son of Tulie, the sister of Talut and co-leader of the Lion Camp, but he tended to be more reticent. The sheer size of Danug made him more noticeable, and though shy in the beginning, he'd had to learn to be more forthcoming. A warm smile and willing conversation tended to alleviate any fears his size may have provoked.

Finally, Marthona turned to Ayla. "Where is that son of mine, who is so honored by Aldanor's people?"

Ayla turned aside. "I don't know," she said, trying to keep her sudden flush of emotion in check. Then she added, "I've been busy with the zelandonia."

Marthona knew immediately that something was very wrong. Ayla had been so excited about seeing Jondalar. Now she didn't even know where he was?

"I saw Jondy walking down by The River this morning," Jonayla said, "but I don't know where he's sleeping. I don't know why he won't sleep with us anymore. I like it better when he stays with us."

Although her face flushed, Ayla didn't say anything, and Marthona was certain something was seriously wrong. She'd have to find out just what was going on.

"Folara, would you and Marthona watch Jonayla, or drop her off at Levela's if you are going to the Main Camp? And take Wolf with you? I need to talk to Danug and Druwez, and maybe take them to the zelandonia lodge," Ayla said.

"Yes, of course," Folara said.

Ayla gave her daughter a hug. "I'll see you this evening," she said, then went up to the two young men and started speaking to them in Mamutoi.

"I was thinking about the talking drums and mentioned them to the First. Can either or both of you make the drums talk?" Ayla said.

"Yes," Danug said. "We both can, but we didn't bring any with us. Drums are not a necessary part of traveling gear when you go on a Journey."

"How long would it take to make a couple of them? I'm sure we can get people to help you if you need it. And would you be willing to play out a verse or two? As part of the ceremony we're planning?" Ayla said.

The two young men looked at each other, and shrugged. "If we can find the materials, they wouldn't take long to make, maybe a day or so. It's just rawhide stretched across a round frame, but it has to be a tight stretch so that the drum really resonates at different pitches. The frame has to be strong or it will break as the rawhide shrinks, especially if we use heat to shrink it faster," Druwez said. "They are small drums, and you play them with your fingers, very fast."

"I've seen some play them with a nicely balanced stick, but we learned to do it with the fingers," Danug said.

"Would you be willing to do it for the ceremony?" Ayla asked.

"Of course," they said in unison.

"Then come with me," she said as she headed toward the Main Camp.

On the way to the large zelandonia lodge, Ayla noticed how many people actually stopped and stared at them. Though often enough she had been, this time she wasn't the one who was the object of the gawks. It was Danug. It was rude, but in a way she couldn't blame them, he was a striking figure of a man. On the whole, the men of the Zelandonii tended to be tall, well-built men—Jondalar himself was six feet, six inches—but Danug stood head and shoulders above everyone else, and he was well proportioned to his size. If seen alone from some distance, he would have seemed to be an ordinary muscular man; it was when he stood in the midst of others that his great size was so noticeable. It made her recall the first time she saw Talut, the man of his hearth, the only man she ever saw who was of comparable dimensions. She had probably stared then, even though except for Jondalar, Talut was one of the first people of her own kind she had seen since she was a small child. Maybe that was why she stared.

When she reached the great lodge in the center of the Camp, two young female acolytes approached them. "I wanted to make sure we had all the ingredients for that special ceremonial drink you told us about," one of them said. "You said fermented birch sap, fruit juices scented with woodruff, and some herbs, right?"

"Yes, in particular, artemesia," Ayla said. "Sometimes called wormwood, or absinthe."

"I don't think I'm familiar with that drink," Druwez said.

"Did you stop and visit the Losadunai on your way here?" Ayla asked. "In particular, did you share a Mother Festival with them?"

"We stopped, but we didn't stay long," Druwez said, "and unfortunately, they did not have a Festival while we were there."

"Solandia, the mate of the Losaduna, told me how to make it. It tastes like a pleasant-tasting mild drink, but in fact, it is a potent mixture made especially to encourage the spontaneity and warm interaction that are wanted during a festival to honor the Mother," Ayla said. Then to the acolytes, she added, "I'll taste it when you are done and let you know if anything is missing."

As they turned to go, the two young women made some hand gestures to each other, and glanced back at Danug. Over the past few years, especially during Summer Meetings, Ayla had been teaching all the zelandonia some of the basic Clan signs. She thought it would help the Doniers to communicate, at least at a basic level, if they happened to meet some people of the Clan when they were traveling. Some picked it up better than others, but most of them seemed to enjoy having a silent secret method of talking that most people didn't understand. What the two young acolytes didn't know was that Ayla had taught Danug and Druwez the Clan signs long before when she lived with the Mamutoi.

Suddenly Danug looked at one of the young women and smiled. "Maybe you'd like to find out at the Mother Festival," he said, then turned to Druwez, and they laughed.

Both young women blushed; then the one who had first made the signs smiled at Danug with a suggestive look. "Maybe I would," she said. "I didn't know you understood the talking signs."

"Can you imagine anyone living around Ayla for very long without learning them?" Danug said, "Especially when my brother, the boy my mother adopted, was half Clan, and couldn't speak until Ayla came and taught us all to make the signs. I remember the first time Rydag made the sign for 'mother' to her. She cried."

People started milling around the ceremonial area early. The excitement in the air was tangible. The ceremony had been in stages of preparation for days and there was an incredible sense of expectation. This was going to be special, totally unique. Everyone knew it; they just didn't know what to expect. The suspense mounted as the sun began to sink. Never had the Zelandonii at the Summer Meeting wanted the sun to set quite so much. They wished it down from the sky.

Finally, as the sun settled down below the horizon and it grew dark enough to need fire, people began to settle down, waiting for the ceremonial fires to be lit. There was a natural amphitheater in the center of this area that was sufficiently large to hold the entire Camp of some two thousand people. Behind and toward the right of the Summer Meeting Camp, the limestone hills formed the general shape of a large scooped-out shallow bowl curving around on the sides but open in front. The base of the curved slopes converged to a small, relatively level field, which had been evened out with stones and packed earth over the many years the location had been used for meetings.

In a wooded copse near the rugged crest of the hill, a spring rose that filled a small pool, then spilled down the slope of the bowl shape, through the middle of the area at the bottom, and eventually into the larger stream of the camp. The spring-fed creek was so small, especially late in summer, that people stepped over it easily, but the clear, cold pool at the top supplied convenient drinking water. The grass-covered hillside within the partial bowl depression rose up in a gradual, irregular slope. Over the years, people had dug a little here, filled in a little there, until the slope of the hill had many small flattened sections that provided comfortable places for family groups or even whole Caves to sit together with a good view of the open space below.

People sat on the grass or spread out woven mats, stuffed pads, cushions, or furs on the ground. Fires were lit, mostly torches stuck into the ground, but also some small firepits encircling the entire gathering around the stagelike area, and one larger bonfire near the front and center of it; then several fires were lit throughout the area where people were sitting. Shortly afterward, quietly, the distinctive sound of young voices singing could be heard in the background of the conversation. People started shushing each other to hear the singing better. Then a parade of most of the youngsters of the entire Camp walked toward the central area singing a rhythmic song using the counting words. By the time they reached it, everyone else had stopped talking, although there were smiles and winks.

Beginning with the singing children had two purposes. The first was to let them show their elders what they were learning from the zelandonia. The second was a tacit understanding that a Mother Festival would take place along with the feasting and general revelry. When they were finished with their part, the children would be taken to one of the camps near the edge of the gathering where there would be games and their own feast separate from the adults, watched over by several Zelandonia and others, often older women and men, or new mothers who were not yet ready to participate, or women who had just begun their moontime, or those who just didn't feel like indulging in activities to honor the Mother at that time.

While most people looked forward to Mother Festivals, it was always voluntary, and it was easier for most people to participate if they knew they didn't have to worry about their children for an evening. The children were not prevented from going if they wanted to, and some of the older ones did, just to satisfy their curiosity, but watching adults talk, laugh, eat, drink, dance, and couple was not all that interesting if they weren't really ready for it and it wasn't forbidden. The close quarters in which they lived meant that children observed all adult activities all the time, from childbirth to death. No one made an issue of keeping them away; it was all a part of life.

When the children were done, most were led into the audience. Next, two men dressed as bison bulls with their heavy horned heads started at opposite sides and ran toward each other, slipping past but just barely missing each other, which captured people's attention. Then several people, including some children, dressed in the hides and horns of aurochs, started milling around like a herd. Some of the animal skins were hunting camouflages, some made just for this occasion. A lion came out, snarling and grunting, in a skin and tail, then attacked the cows with a roar so authentic, it made some people flinch.

"That was Ayla," Folara whispered to Aldanor. "No one can do a lion roar as well as she can."

The herd scattered, jumping over things and almost running into people. The lion chased after them. Then five people came out dressed in deer hides and holding antlers on their heads, and portrayed them jumping into a river as though running away from something, and swimming across. Horses were next, one of them whinnying so realistically, it got an answering whinny from a distance.

"That was Ayla, too," Folara informed the man beside her.

"She's very good," he said.

"She says she learned to mimic animals before she learned to speak Zelandonii."

There were other demonstrations portraying and depicting animals, all showing an event or story of some kind. The troupe of traveling storytellers were also a part of the presentation, pressed into service as various animals, and their skills added a vivid realism. Finally the animals started coming together. When they were all gathered, a strange animal appeared. It walked on four legs and had hooved feet, but it was covered with a strange spotted hide that hung down the sides almost to the ground and partially covered its head, to which two straight sticks had been attached that were meant to represent some kind of horns or antlers.

"What is that?" Aldanor asked.

"It's a magical animal, of course," Folara said. "But it's really Ayla's Whinney, who is being a Zelandoni. The First says all of her horses and Wolf are Zelandonia. That's why they choose to stay with her."

The strange Zelandoni animal led all the other animals away, then several of the zelandonia and storytellers hurried back as themselves and began playing drums and flutes. Some began singing some of the older Legends; then others narrated the Histories and lore that the people knew and loved so well.

The zelandonia had prepared well. They used every trick they knew to capture and hold the attention of the large crowd. When Ayla, with her face painted in Zelandoni designs—all except for the area around her new tattoo, which was left bare to show the permanent mark of acceptance—stepped in front of the group, all two thousand people held their breaths, ready to hang on to her every word, her every motion.

Drums resounded, high-pitched flutes interwove with the slow, steady, inexorable bass, with some tones below the range of hearing, but felt deep in the bone, *thrum, thrum, thrum.* The cadence changed in rhythm, then matched the meter of a verse so familiar, the people joined in singing or saying the beginning of the Mother's Song.

Out of the darkness, the chaos of time,
The whirlwind gave birth to the Mother sublime.
She woke to Herself knowing life had great worth,
The dark empty void grieved the Great Mother Earth.
The Mother was lonely. She was the only.

The First with her spectacular full, vibrant voice joined in. Drums and flutes played in between the singers and speakers as the Mother's Song continued. Near the middle, people began to take notice that the voice of the First was so markedly rich and rare, they stopped singing so they could listen. When she reached the last verse, she stopped and only the drums played by Ayla's visiting kin were left.

But the people almost thought they could hear the words. And then they were sure they could, but they were spoken with a strange, eerie vibrato. At first, the audience wasn't quite sure what they were hearing. The two young Mamutoi men stood in front of the crowd with their small drums and played the last verse of the Mother's Song in a strange staccato beat—drumbeats that sounded like words spoken in a throbbing voice as though someone were singing by rapidly varying the pressure of the breath, except it wasn't someone's breath, it was the drums! The drums were speaking words!

Th-e-e-e Mu-u-u-the-er wa-a-a-az pule-e-e-z-z-zed wi-i-i-ith ...

The silence of the listeners was perfect as everyone strained to hear the drums speak. Ayla, thinking about the way she had learned to throw her voice forward so that even those at the very back could hear her clearly, pitched her normally low voice slightly lower and spoke more loudly and more strongly into the dark stillness lit now by only one fire. The only sound the assembled crowd heard, seeming to come from the air around them on the beat of the drum, was Ayla speaking the last verse of the Mother's Song alone, repeating the words the drum had spoken.

The Mother was pleased with the pair She created,
She taught them to love and to care when they mated.
She made them desire to join with each other,
The Gift of their Pleasures came from the Mother.
Before She was through, Her children loved too.

The drumbeats slowed imperceptibly. Everyone knew this was the end; there was only one line left, yet somehow they were held waiting, not knowing why. It made them nervous, drove up the tension. When the drums got to the end of the verse, they didn't stop; instead the drums continued with unfamiliar words.

H-e-e-er la-a-ast G-i-i-ift, th-e-e-e ...

The people listened carefully, but still weren't sure what they had heard. Then Ayla stood alone, slowly repeating the verse, with emphasis.

> *Her last Gift, the Knowledge that man has his part.*
> *His need must be spent before new life can start.*
> *It honors the Mother when the couple is paired,*
> *Because woman conceives when Pleasures are shared.*
> *Earth's Children were Blessed. The Mother could rest.*

That didn't belong. That was new! They had never heard that part before. What did it mean? People felt uneasy. For as long as anyone knew or remembered, for long before anyone remembered, the Mother's Song had been the same, except for insignificant variations. Why was it different now? The meaning of the words hadn't yet penetrated. It was disquieting enough that new words were added, that the Mother's Song had changed.

Suddenly the last fire was put out. It was so black, no one dared move. "What does it mean?" a voice called out. "Yes, what does it mean?" came an echoing question.

But Jondalar was not asking. He knew. Then it's true, he thought. Everything Ayla has always said is true. Though he'd had time to think about it, even his mind struggled with the implications. Ayla had always told him Jonayla was his daughter, his true daughter, of his flesh, not just his spirit. She had been conceived because of his actions. Not some amorphous spirit that he couldn't see, mixed up in some vague way by the Mother inside Ayla with her spirit. He did it. He and Ayla both. He had given Ayla his essence with his manhood, his organ, and that was combined with something inside Ayla to make life begin.

Not every time. He had put a lot of his essence inside her. Maybe it took a lot of essence. Ayla had always said she wasn't sure exactly how it worked, only that it was a man and woman together that made life start. The Mother had given Her children the Gift of Pleasures to make life begin. Shouldn't starting a new life be a Pleasure? Is that why the urge to spend his essence inside a woman was so strong? Because the Mother wanted Her children to make their own children?

He felt as though his body had a new sense to it, as though it had come alive in some way. Men were necessary. He was necessary! Without him there would have been no Jonayla. If it had been some other man, she would not be Jonayla. She was who she was because of both of them, Ayla and him. Without men, there could be no new life.

Around the periphery, torches were being lit. People started getting up, milling around. Food was being uncovered and set out in several different areas. Each Cave, or group of related Caves, had a feasting place so no one would have to wait too long to eat. Except for children, most people hadn't eaten much all day. Some were too busy, some wanted to save room for the feast, and while it wasn't required, it was considered more proper to eat sparingly before the main meal on feast days.

People were talking as they headed toward the food, asking each other questions, still feeling uneasy.

"Come on, Jondalar," Joharran said. Jondalar didn't hear. He was so lost in his own thoughts, the crowd around him did not exist.

"Jondalar!" Joharran said again, and shook his shoulder.

"What?" Jondalar said.

"Come on, they are serving the food."

"Oh," the younger brother said, his mind still whirling as he stood up.

"What do you think it all means?" Joharran asked as they started walking.

"Did you see where Ayla went?" Jondalar said, still oblivious to everything except his own thoughts.

"I haven't seen her, but I imagine she'll join us before long. It was quite a ceremony. It took a lot of work and planning. Even the zelandonia need to relax and eat once in a while," Joharran said. They walked a few steps. "What do you think that meant, Jondalar? That last verse to the Mother's Song?"

Jondalar finally turned to look at his brother. "It meant what it said, 'man has his part.' It's not just women who are Blessed. No new life can begin without a man."

Joharran frowned, showing the furrows on his brow that matched his brother's. "Do you really think so?"

Jondalar smiled. "I know so."

As they approached the area where the Ninth Cave had gathered to feast, various strong drinks were being handed out. Someone put watertight woven cups in both Joharran's and Jondalar's hands. They took a taste, but it wasn't what either expected.

"What's this?" Joharran said. "I thought it would be Laramar's brew. It's nice, but it's rather light."

It was familiar to Jondalar, and he tasted again. Where had he tasted this before? "Ah! The Losadunai!"

"What?" Joharran said.

"This is the drink the Losadunai serve at their Mother Festivals. It tastes light, but don't underestimate it," Jondalar warned. "This is potent. It sneaks up on you. Ayla must have made it. Did you see where she went after the ceremony?"

"I thought I saw her a while ago coming out of the ceremonial tent. She had her regular clothes on," Joharran said.

"Did you see which direction she went?"

"There she is. Over there, where they are serving more of that new drink."

Jondalar headed toward a sizable group of people milling around a large kerfed box, dipping out cups of liquid. When he saw Ayla, she happened to be standing next to Laramar. She handed him a cup she had dipped. He said something, and she laughed, then smiled at him.

Laramar looked surprised, then leered in response. Maybe she wasn't so bad after all, he thought. She had always been so standoffish before, hardly ever said a word to him. But she is Zelandoni now; they are supposed to honor the Mother at festivals. This may turn out to be an interesting festival. Suddenly Jondalar appeared. Laramar frowned with disappointment.

"Ayla," Jondalar said. "I need to talk to you. Let's get away from here." He took her arm and tried to walk toward a less crowded place.

"Is there some reason you can't talk right here? I'm sure I'll be able to hear you. I haven't suddenly gone deaf," Ayla said, pulling her arm away.

"But I need to talk to you alone."

"You had plenty of opportunity to talk to me alone before, but you couldn't be bothered. Why is it suddenly so important now? This is the Mother Festival. I'm going to stay here and enjoy myself," she said, turning to smile rather suggestively at Laramar.

He forgot. In his excitement about his new depth of understanding, Jondalar forgot. Suddenly it all came back to him. She had seen him with Marona! And it was true, he hadn't spoken to her since then. Now she didn't want to talk to him. Ayla saw his face turn white. He reeled, as if someone had hit him, and stumbled away. He looked so beaten and confused, she almost called him back, but bit her tongue to keep from speaking.

Jondalar walked around in a daze, lost in his own thoughts. Someone put a cup of something in his hand. He drank it without thinking. Someone else filled it again. She was right, he thought. He'd had plenty of time to talk to her, to try to explain things to her. Why hadn't he done it? She had come looking for him, and found him with Marona. Why hadn't he gone looking for her? Because he was ashamed and afraid he'd lost her. What was he thinking? He'd tried to keep Marona a secret from Ayla. He should have just told her. In fact he shouldn't have been with Marona at all. Why had she been so appealing? Why did he want her so much then? Just because she was available? She didn't even interest him now.

Ayla said she'd lost a baby. His baby! "That baby was mine," he said aloud. "It was mine!" A few people passing by stared at him, staggering and talking to himself, and shook their heads.

That child she lost was his. She was called. He'd heard something about the terrible ordeal she went though. He'd wanted to go to her then, comfort her. Why hadn't he? Why had he tried so hard to stay away from her? Now she didn't want to talk to him. Could he blame her? He couldn't blame her if she never wanted to see him again.

What if she didn't? What if she really didn't ever want to see him again? What if she never wanted to share Pleasures with him again? Then the thought struck him. If she refused to share Pleasures with him, he'd never be able to start a baby with her. He would never have another child with Ayla.

Suddenly he didn't want to know that it was him. If it was a spirit that caused life to begin, it would just happen, no matter what anyone did. But if it was him, the essence of his manhood, and she didn't want him, there would be no more children for him. It didn't occur to him that he could have a child with another woman. It was Ayla he loved. She was his mate. It was her children he had promised to provide for. They would be the children of his hearth. He didn't want another woman.

As Jondalar stumbled around with a cup in his hand, he drew no more attention than any of the other celebrants who were staggering back and forth to the places where food and drink were supplied. Some laughing people bumped into him. They had just filled a waterbag with a potent drink of some kind.

"Uhhh, sorry. Lemme fill your cup. Can't have empty cups at a Mother Festival," one of them said.

Never had there been such a festival. There was more food than anyone could eat, more brew and wine and other beverages than anyone could drink. There were even leaves to smoke, certain mushrooms and other special things to eat. Nothing was forbidden. A few people had been chosen by lot or had volunteered to refrain from festival activities to make sure the Camp remained safe, to assist the few who inevitably got hurt, and to take care of those who got out of hand. And there were no young children around for the revelers to stumble over or worry about. They had all been gathered together to the camp at the edge of Summer Meeting Camp being looked after by Doniers and others.

Jondalar took a drink from his recently filled cup, unmindful that he was losing most of it as he walked around with the sloshing cupful. He hadn't eaten, and the liberally flowing beverages were having their effect. His head was swimming and his vision fuzzy, but his mind, still caught up in his private thoughts, was disassociated from everything. He heard dancing music and his feet took him toward the sound. Only vaguely did he see the dancers moving around in a circle in the flickering firelight.

Then a woman danced by and suddenly his vision cleared as he focused on her. It was Ayla. He watched her dance with several men. She laughed drunkenly. Staggering unsteadily, she broke away from the circle. Three men followed her, their hands all over her, tearing off her clothes. Unbalanced, she fell over in a heap with the three men. One of them climbed on top of her, roughly spread her legs apart, and jammed his engorged organ into her. Jondalar recognized him. It was Laramar!

Held by the sight, unable to move, Jondalar watched him moving up and down, in and out. Laramar! Filthy, drunken, lazy, shiftless Laramar! Ayla wouldn't even talk to him, but there she was with Laramar. She wouldn't let him love her, share Pleasures with her. She wouldn't let him start a baby with her.

What if Laramar is starting a baby with her!

Blood rushed to his head. All he could see in his red haze was Laramar, on top of Ayla, on top of *his* mate, bouncing up and down, up and down. Suddenly, in a blazing fury, Jondalar roared, "HE'S MAKING MY BABY!"

The tall man covered the distance between them in three strides. He pulled Laramar off Ayla, spun him around, and smashed his fist into the stunned man's face. Laramar crumpled to the ground, nearly unconscious. He didn't know who hit him, or even what had happened.

Jondalar jumped on top of him. In a savage, ravaging frenzy of jealousy and outrage, he was hitting Laramar, punching him, hammering him, unable to stop. His voice so tight with frustration, its pitch rose to a squeal, as Jondalar screamed, "He's making my baby! He's making my baby!" repeating it over and over again, "He's making my baby!"

Some men tried to drag him away, but he shook them off. In his maddened fury, his strength was almost superhuman. Several more tried to pull him away, but he was wild; they couldn't contain him.

Then, as Jondalar pulled back to pound his fist once more into the bloody mass of raw meat unrecognizable as a face, a massive hand grabbed his wrist. Jondalar struggled as he felt himself being pulled away from the unconscious man who was sprawled out on the ground, close to death. He fought to free himself from the two enormous, powerful arms that restrained him, but he couldn't break loose.

As Danug held him off, Zelandoni cried, "Jondalar! Jondalar! Stop! You'll kill him!"

He vaguely recognized the familiar voice of the woman he once knew as Zolena, and recalled hitting a young man over her; then his mind went blank. While several of the zelandonia rushed in to attend to Laramar, the burly red-haired giant picked Jondalar up in his arms like a baby and carried him away.

37

Zelandoni gave Ayla one of the tightly woven reed cups that had been specially made for the festival, nearly full of hot tea made of herbs that would be relaxing. She put another cup on a low table, then sat down on the large stool beside Ayla's stool. They were alone in the large zelandonia dwelling, except for the unconscious man, his face wrapped in soft skins that held healing poultices in place, lying on a nearby bed. Several lamps cast a warm glow of soft light around the injured man, and two more were on a low table that held the tea cups.

"I've never seen him like that," Ayla said. "Why did he do it, Zelandoni?"

"Because you were with Laramar."

"But it was a Mother Festival. I am Zelandoni now. I'm supposed to share the Mother's Gift at Festivals that Honor the Mother, aren't I?" Ayla said.

"Everyone is supposed to Honor the Mother at Her Festivals, and you always have, but never before with anyone except Jondalar," the large woman said.

"Just because I haven't done it before with anyone else shouldn't make any difference. After all, he's been coupling with Marona," Ayla said. Zelandoni noticed a touch of defensiveness in her voice.

"Yes, but you weren't available when he did. You know men often share the Mother's Gift of Pleasure with other women when their mates are not within easy reach, don't you?" the One Who Was First asked.

"Yes, of course," Ayla said, looking down quickly, then taking a sip of her tea.

"Does the thought of Jondalar choosing another woman bother you, Ayla?"

"Well, he never has chosen anyone else. Not as long as I've known him," Ayla said, looking at the woman with earnest concern. "How could I know him so little? I can't believe what he did. I wouldn't have believed it if I hadn't been there. First he sneaks around with Marona . . . and I found out he's been doing it for a long time. Then he . . . Why Marona?"

"How would you feel if it was someone else?"

Ayla looked down again. "I don't know." She looked up at Zelandoni again. "Why didn't he come to me if he wanted to satisfy his needs? I have never refused him. Never."

"Maybe that's why. Maybe he knew you were tired, or deeply involved in something you were learning, and he didn't want to impose himself on you, when he knew you would not refuse him," Zelandoni said. "And there were some times when you were required to forgo certain things for a period of time, Pleasures, food, even water."

"But why Marona? If it had been another woman, anyone else, I think I would have understood. I might not have liked it, but I would have understood. Why that woman?"

"Perhaps because she offered." Ayla looked so puzzled, Zelandoni went on to explain. "Everyone was aware that neither you nor Jondalar ever chose anyone else, Ayla, not even at Mother Festivals. Before he left, Jondalar was always available, especially then. He had such a strong drive, one woman was seldom enough for him. It was like he was never quite satisfied, until he came back with you. Not long after he returned, women stopped trying. If you don't make yourself available, no one offers. Most women don't like being refused. But Marona didn't care. It was so easy for her to have any man she wanted, a refusal just made it a challenge. Jondalar became a special challenge, I think."

"I can't believe how little I know him." Ayla shook her head, took another sip of tea. "Zelandoni, he almost killed Laramar. His face will never be the same. If Danug hadn't been here, I'm not sure Laramar would still be alive. No one else could stop him."

"It was one of the things I was afraid would happen after we told the people about a man's role in starting new life, though I didn't expect it to happen this way, or quite so soon. I knew problems would come up once we told the men, but I thought we'd have more time to work them out."

"I don't understand," Ayla said, frowning again. "I would have thought men would be happy to know that they were necessary for new life to begin, just as necessary as women, that it was the reason the Mother made them."

"They may be happy, but once they understand the implications, men may want to be sure that the children of their hearths are more than the children of their mates. They may want to know that the children they provide for came from them."

"Why should it matter? It never has before. Men have always provided for their mates' children. Most men have been pleased when their mates brought children to their hearths. Why would they suddenly want to provide for only their own?" Ayla said.

"It may turn out to be a thing of pride. They may get possessive of their mates and their children," the First said.

Ayla took a drink of tea and thought for a while, frowning. "How would they know for sure? It's the woman who gives birth. The only thing any man can know, without doubt, is that a baby is the child of his mate."

"The only way a man can be sure is if a woman shares Pleasures with only her mate," Zelandoni said. "Like you, Ayla."

Ayla's frown deepened. "But what about Mother Festivals? Most women look forward to them. They want to Honor the Mother, to share her Gift of Pleasures with more than one man."

"Yes, most women do, and men, too. It adds excitement and interest to their lives. Most women also want a mate to help take care of her children," Zelandoni said.

"Some women don't have mates. Their mothers, and aunts, and brothers help them, especially with a newborn. Even the Cave helps women take care of their children. Children have always been provided for," Ayla said.

"That's true, but things can change. There have been a few difficult years in the past, when animals were more scarce and plant food less abundant. When there is not as much, some people don't always want to share. If you only had enough food for one child, which child would you give it to?"

"I would give up my own food, for any child," Ayla said.

"For a while, yes. Most people would. But for how long? If you don't eat, you would become weak and sick. Then who would take care of your child?"

"Jonda . . ." Ayla started; then she stopped and put her hand to her mouth.

"Yes."

"But, Marthona would help, too, and Willamar, even Folara. The whole Ninth Cave would help," Ayla rushed ahead.

"That's true, Marthona and Willamar would, as long as they were able, but you know Marthona is not well, and Willamar is not getting younger. Folara is going to mate Aldanor in the Late Matrimonial this season. When she has a baby of her own, who will she feed first?"

"It's never that bad, Zelandoni. Sometimes things get a little scarce in the spring, but you can always find something to eat," Ayla said.

"And I hope that will always be true, but a woman usually feels more secure if she has a mate to help her."

"Sometimes two women share a hearth and help each other with their children," Ayla said. She was thinking about Aldanor's people, the S'Armunai, and Attaroa, who tried to get rid of all the men.

"And they may become mates to each other. It is always better to have someone around to help, someone who cares, but most women choose men. It's the way the Mother created most of us, and you have told us why, Ayla."

Ayla glanced over toward the man in the bed. "But if you knew everything was going to change, Zelandoni, why did you allow it to happen? You're the First. You could have stopped it," Ayla said.

"Perhaps, for a while. But the Mother would not have told you if She didn't want Her children to know. And once She decided, it was inevitable. It could not be kept a secret. When a truth is ready to be known, it may be delayed, but can't be stopped," Zelandoni said.

Ayla closed her eyes, thinking. Finally she opened them and said, "Jondalar was so . . . angry. So violent." Tears were welling up.

"The violence has always been there, Ayla. It is for most men. You know what Jondalar did to Madroman, and he was little more than a boy then. He has just learned to keep it under control, most of the time."

"But he couldn't stop hitting him. He nearly killed Laramar. Why?"

"Because you chose Laramar, Ayla. Everyone heard Jondalar yelling, 'He's making my baby.' You can be sure no man has forgotten those words. Why did you choose Laramar?"

Ayla bowed her head and tears tracked down her face as quiet sobs began. Finally she got it out. "Because Jondalar chose Marona." The tears she had held back for so long were suddenly flowing and there was no stopping them. "Oh, Zelandoni, I never knew what jealousy was until that moment when I saw them together. I'd just lost my baby, and I'd been thinking about Jondalar and looking forward to seeing him, and maybe starting another baby with him. It hurt so much to see him with Marona, and it made me so angry, I wanted to make him hurt, too." Zelandoni found a piece of soft bandaging material and gave it to her to wipe her eyes and her nose.

"And he wouldn't talk to me afterward. He didn't say he was sorry I lost the baby. Or hold me and comfort me. He didn't even touch me, not once. He never said one word to me. It hurt even more when he wouldn't talk to me. He didn't even give me a chance to be angry. To tell him how I felt. I wasn't even sure if he still loved me." She sniffled, and wiped away more tears, then continued.

"When Jondalar saw me at the feast, and finally came over to say he wanted to talk to me, Laramar happened to be nearby. I know Jondalar has no respect for Laramar. There is no man he dislikes more. He thinks Laramar not only treats his mate and her children badly, he causes other men to do the same. I knew it would make Jondalar angry if I chose Laramar instead of him, I knew it would hurt him. But I didn't know he would get so brutal. I didn't know he would try to kill him. I just didn't know."

Zelandoni reached for Ayla and held her while she cried. "I thought it was something like that," she said, patting her back and letting her get her tears out, but her mind was filling in details.

I should have paid closer attention, Zelandoni thought. I knew she had just miscarried, and that always brings on feelings of melancholy, and I knew Jondalar was not handling the problem well. He never does in this kind of situation, but Ayla seemed to be. I knew she was upset about Jondalar. I didn't realize how much. I should have, but she's hard to assess. It surprised me that she was called. I didn't think she was quite ready, but I knew it had happened the moment I saw her.

I thought it was difficult for her, especially with the miscarriage, but she has always been so strong. I didn't realize until I talked to Marthona just how bad it was. Then when she told her calling in front of the whole zelandonia—that caught me by surprise, too—I knew something had to be done about it right away. I should have talked to her first; then I would have known what to expect. It would have given me some time to think of the implications. But there is always so much going on at these Summer Meetings. It's not an excuse. I should have been there to help her, help them both, and I wasn't. I have to accept responsibility for a large part of this whole unfortunate affair.

While she was leaning on the soft shoulder of the large woman, sobbing and finally letting out the tears she had held back for so long, Ayla kept thinking about the question Zelandoni had asked. Why did I choose Laramar? Why did I choose the worst man in the whole Cave, probably the worst man at the whole Summer Meeting?

What a horrible Summer Meeting this has been. Instead of rushing to get here, it would have been better if I hadn't come at all, she said to herself. Then I wouldn't have seen them together. If I hadn't seen Marona and Jondalar, if someone had just told me, it would have been better. I still wouldn't have liked it, but at least every time I shut my eyes, I wouldn't see them.

Maybe that's what made me choose Laramar, what made

me want to hurt Jondalar so much. I wanted to make him feel
the way I was feeling. What does that make me? Wanting to
strike back, wanting to hurt. Is that worthy of a Zelandoni? If I
loved him so much, why should I want to hurt him? Because I
was jealous. Now I know why the Zelandonii try to prevent it.

Jealousy is a terrible thing, Ayla said to herself. I had no right
to feel so hurt. Jondalar didn't do anything wrong. It was his
right to choose Marona if he wanted to. He wasn't breaking
his bond; he was still contributing to the hearth, still helping to
provide for Jonayla and me. He has always done more than he
had to. He has probably taken care of Jonayla more than I have.
I know how bad he always felt about hitting Madroman when
he was younger. He hated himself for it; he must feel terrible
now. And what will happen to him? What will the Ninth Cave
do to him? Or the zelandonia, or all the Zelandonii, for almost
killing Laramar?

Ayla finally sat back, wiped her eyes and her nose, reached
for her tea. Zelandoni hoped the release had done her some
good, but Ayla's mind was still whirling. It's all my fault, she
thought. Tears started to fall again as she sat sipping cold tea,
almost without her noticing. Laramar is hurt so bad, he'll never
be the same, and it's my fault. He wouldn't be hurt if I hadn't
encouraged him, coaxed him, made him think I wanted him.

And she'd had to force herself to do it. She hated the thought
of his dirty, sweaty hands touching her. It made her skin crawl,
feel itchy, grimy, and she couldn't wash it away. She had
bathed, scrubbed herself nearly raw, flushed herself out. Even
though she knew it was dangerous, she drank a tea of mistle-
toe leaves and other herbs that made her vomit and gave her
painful cramps, to expel anything that may have started. But
nothing she did could rid her of the feel of Laramar.

Why had she done it? To hurt Jondalar? She was the one
who couldn't find time for him. She was the one who was
up all night and spent most of her waking hours memorizing
songs and Histories and symbols and counting words. If she
loved him so much, why didn't she find time for him, too?

Was it because she enjoyed her training? She did love it,
loved learning all the things she had to know to be zelandoni.

All the knowledge that could be revealed, and all that was hidden. The symbols that had secret meaning, symbols that she could scratch on a stone, or paint on a cloth, or weave into a mat. She knew what they meant. All the zelandonia knew what they meant. She could send a stone with symbols on it to another Zelandoni, and the person who carried it wouldn't have any idea that it meant anything at all, but the other zelandoni would know.

And she loved all the ceremony. Ayla remembered how moved and impressed she had been at her first ceremony with only the zelandonia that was held deep in that cave. Now she knew how to make them impressive. She had learned all the tricks, though it wasn't just tricks. Some of it was real, frighteningly real. She knew that some of the zelandonia, particularly the older ones, didn't really believe anymore. They had done it all so many times, they had grown accustomed to their own magic. Anyone could do it, they said. Maybe anyone could, but not without training. Not without help, or the magic medicines. What did it mean to fly with no wind, with your body still back with the zelandonia or the Cave, to someone who'd forgotten that not everyone could, or who did it only out of habit or duty?

Ayla remembered suddenly, at her initiation, hearing the One Who Was First say that she would be First someday. At the time Ayla had ignored it; she couldn't imagine herself as First, and besides she had a mate and a child. How could anyone be First and have a mate and family at the same time? Some of the zelandonia had families, but not many.

All she had ever really wanted, from the time she was little, was to have a mate and children, her own family. Iza had told her she would never have children—her Cave Lion totem was too strong—but she had surprised them. She'd had a son. Broud would have hated it if he'd known that by forcing her, he had given her the one thing she wanted. But it had been no Gift of Pleasures then. Broud didn't choose her because he cared about her. He loathed her. He forced her only to prove he could do whatever he wanted to her, and because he knew she detested it.

Now she had done it to herself. Forced herself to choose a man she detested to hurt a man she loved. Look what she had done to Jondalar because of her jealousy. It was her fault that he had almost killed a man. She didn't deserve a family. She couldn't even take care of her family as an acolyte. It would be much more difficult as a full-fledged Zelandoni. He'd be better off without her. Maybe she should let him go, let him find another mate.

But, how could she not be mated to Jondalar? How could she live without Jondalar? The thought brought on a freshet of new tears, which caused Zelandoni to wonder. It had seemed that Ayla had almost cried herself out. How could she live without Jondalar? Ayla thought. But how could Jondalar live with her now? She wasn't worthy of him. She had nearly driven him to kill, just because he needed to satisfy his needs. Needs she obviously wasn't satisfying. Even women of the Clan would do that, anytime their mates wanted. Jondalar deserves a better woman.

But what about Jonayla? She's his daughter, too, and he loves her so much. He's raised her more than I have. Jonayla deserves better than me for a mother. If I break the bond, he can mate again. He's still the most beautiful . . . no, the most handsome man of all the Caves. Everyone thinks so. He would have no trouble finding another woman, even a younger one. I am old already; a younger woman could have more children with him. He can even choose . . . Marona . . . if he wants to. It hurt her just to think it, but she felt a need to punish herself, and she could think of no worse pain to inflict on herself.

That's what I'll do. I'll break the bond and give Jonayla to Jondalar, and let him find another woman to have a family with. When I get back to the Ninth Cave, I won't move back into my home, I'll move in with Zelandoni, or I'll have another place built, or move away and be Zelandoni to another Cave . . . if any other Cave would have me. Maybe I should just go away, find another valley and live by myself.

Zelandoni watched the play of emotions across Ayla's face, but she couldn't quite decipher them. There always was something unfathomable about the woman, Zelandoni thought. But there is no doubt. Someday she will be First. Zelandoni had never forgotten that day in Marthona's dwelling when Ayla, young and untrained, had nevertheless overpowered the forceful mind of the First. It had shaken her more than she cared to admit.

"If you are feeling better, we should go, Ayla . . . Zelandoni of the Ninth Cave. We don't want to be late to the meeting. People will have a lot of questions, especially after what happened between Jondalar and Laramar," the One Who Was First Among Those Who Served The Great Earth Mother said.

"Come on, Jondalar. We need to get to the meeting. There are some questions I want to ask," Joharran said.

"You go on. I'll come later," Jondalar said, hardly looking up from the bedroll he was sitting on.

"No, I'm afraid not, Jondalar. I was specifically told to make sure you came with me," Joharran said.

"Told by whom?"

"Zelandoni and Marthona. Who do you think?"

"What if I don't want to go to this meeting?" Jondalar said, testing his prerogatives. He felt so miserable, he didn't want to move.

"Then I guess I'll have to ask this mighty Mamutoi friend of yours to carry you out there, the way he carried you here," Jondalar's brother said, grimly smiling at Danug. They were in the shelter that Danug, Druwez, Aldanor, and some other men used. Since only men used it, it was called a fa'lodge although it wasn't with the other fa'lodges on the outskirts of the Camp, or very far from the Ninth Cave's regular family dwellings. "You've hardly moved since. Whether you want to or not, Jondalar, you are going to have to face people. This is an open meeting. No one is going to discuss your situation. That will come later, after we see how well Laramar recovers."

"He should clean up a little," Solaban said. "He still has bloodstains on his clothes."

"I think you're right," Joharran said, then looked at Jondalar. "Are you going to do it yourself, or is somebody going to have to dunk you?"

"I don't care. If you want to dunk me, go ahead," Jondalar said.

"Jondalar, get a clean tunic and come to the river with me," Danug said, speaking Mamutoi. It was a way to let Jondalar know he had someone he could talk to in private, if he didn't want anyone else to know what he was saying; besides, he enjoyed the ease of speaking his own language rather than always struggling with Zelandonii.

"Fine," Jondalar said, sighing deeply, then hauling himself up. "It doesn't matter anyway." He really didn't care what happened to him. Jondalar was convinced that he had lost everything that mattered: his family, including Jonayla, the respect of his friends, and his people, but most of all, Ayla's love, and that he deserved to lose it.

Danug watched Jondalar plodding alongside him toward the river, oblivious to everything around him. The young Mamutoi had seen the same kind of problems between the two people he had come so far to see before, people he cared a great deal about and who, he knew, loved each other more than any two people he had ever met. He wished there was some way he could make them see what he and everyone around them knew, but just telling them wouldn't help. They would have to come to the realization on their own, and now it wasn't just them. Jondalar had seriously injured someone, and while Danug was not familiar with the details of Zelandonii customs, he knew there would be consequences.

Zelandoni moved the drape, pushed the screen aside, and peeked out of the concealed private access at the rear of the large zelandonia dwelling, directly opposite from the regular entrance. She scanned the assembly area that came down from the hillside behind and opened out onto the camp. People had been gathering all morning and it was nearly full.

She had been right about questions. The meaning of the ceremony and the new verse to the Mother's Song were beginning to be understood, but people were unsure. It was unsettling to think about what changes might happen, especially after Jondalar's behavior. Zelandoni looked again to make sure that certain people had arrived, and then waited a little longer to give the last stragglers a chance to get settled. Finally she gave a signal to a young zelandoni, who conveyed the "she's ready" sign to the others, and when everything was prepared, Zelandoni stepped outside.

Zelandoni Who Was First was a woman who exhibited great presence, and her magnificent size, both in height and mass, contributed to her bearing. She also commanded a large repertoire of techniques and tactics to keep gatherings focused on points she wanted to emphasize, and she would be using all her skills, both intuitive and learned, to project confidence and certainty to the large number of people who were watching her with such intensity.

Knowing how people had a tendency to speak out, she announced that since there were so many people, it would help keep things more orderly if questions were asked by the leaders of the Caves, or by only one member of each family. But if someone felt a strong need to say something, it should be brought up.

Joharran asked the first question, but it was a point everyone wanted clarified. "That new verse, I want to be sure I understand, does it mean that Jaradal and Sethona are my children, not just Proleva's?"

"Yes, that is right," Zelandoni who was First said. "Jaradal is your son, said Sethona is your daughter, Joharran, as much as they are Proleva's son and daughter."

"And it is the Gift of Pleasure from the Great Earth Mother that makes life begin inside a woman?" asked Brameval, the leader of the Fourteenth Cave.

"Doni's Gift to us is not only for Pleasure. It is also the Gift of Life."

"But Pleasures are shared often. Women don't get pregnant that often," said another voice, unable to wait.

"The Great Earth Mother still makes the final choice. Doni has not given up all Her knowledge, nor all Her prerogatives. She still decides when a woman will be Blessed with new life," the First said.

"Then what's the difference between using a man's spirit or the essense of his organ to start a baby?" Brameval asked.

"It's very clear. If a woman never shares Pleasure with a man, she will never have a child. She cannot just hope that someday the Mother will choose the spirit of some man and give her one. A woman must Honor the Mother by sharing Her Gift of Pleasures. The man must release his essense inside her, so that it can mix with the essense of a woman that is waiting for it," the Great Woman said.

"Some women never get pregnant," said Tormaden, the leader of the Nineteenth Cave.

"Yes, that's true. I have never had a child. Though I have Honored the Mother often, I have never become pregnant. I don't know why," the First said. "Perhaps because the Mother chose me for a different purpose. I know it would have been very difficult for me to Serve The Mother as I have, if I had a mate and children. That is not to say that zelandonia should not have children. Some zelandonia do and still Serve Her well, though it may be easier for a Zelandoni who is a man to be mated and have children at his hearth, than for a woman. A man does not have to bear a child, or give birth, or nurse. Some women are able to do both, especially if their calling is strong, but they must have mates and families who are very caring and willing to help."

Zelandoni noticed several people looking toward Jondalar, sitting with the Mamutoi visitors, somewhat uphill from the Ninth Cave, and not with the woman to whom he was mated. Ayla, who was holding Jonayla on her lap, sat beside Marthona, with the wolf between them near the front of the audience. She was close to the Ninth Cave, but also close to the ranks of the zelandonia. Most people believed that with her control of animals and her healing skills, even before she became an acolyte, Ayla's calling had to be strong, and until this summer when all their troubles began, everyone was aware of how caring Jondalar had been. Many people believed it was Marona who was at the root of their troubles—she was sitting with her cousin, Wylopa, and some friends from the Fifth Cave—but now it had escalated far beyond that. Although word had gone out that Laramar had regained consciousness, he was still recovering inside the zelandonia lodge and only they knew how badly he was hurt.

"My mate shares the Gift of Pleasures with other men, not just me, at Mother Festivals and ceremonies," a man in the audience said.

Now the questions are getting ticklish, Zelandoni thought. "Festivals and Ceremonies are held for sacred purposes. Sharing Pleasures is a sacred act. It honors the Great Earth Mother. If a child is conceived then, it is with her intention. It should be considered a favored child. Remember, Doni still chooses when a woman will become pregnant." There was a scattering of barely audible comments from the audience.

Kareja, the leader of the Eleventh Cave, stood up. "Willadan has asked me to ask a question for him, but I think he should ask it himself."

"If you think so, then certainly he should," Zelandoni said.

"My mate was a donii-woman one summer after we were mated," the man began. "She wasn't having any luck getting a baby started and wanted to make the offering to honor the Mother and encourage Her to start one. It seemed to work. She did have a child after that, and three more since then. But now I wonder, did any of those children come from me?"

This must be handled with great delicacy, Zelandoni thought. "All children born to your mate are your children," she said.

"But how do I know if they were started by me or some other man?"

"Tell me, Willadan, how old is your first child?"

"He can count twelve years. Almost a man." There was pride in his voice.

"Were you happy when your mate became pregnant with him, and when he was born?"

"Yes, we wanted children at our hearth."

"So you love him."

"Of course I love him."

"Would you love him more if you knew for sure that he was started by your essence?"

Willadan glanced at the boy. "No, of course not," he said, frowning.

"If you knew the rest of your children were started with your own essence, would you love them more?"

He paused, thinking about the point he knew she was making. "No. I could not love them more."

"Then does it make any difference if the essence that started them came from you or someone else?" Zelandoni noticed that his frown deepened. She decided to continue. "I have never been pregnant; I have never conceived a child, though there was a time when I wanted one, more than you will know. I am content now. I know the Mother chose what was best for me. But, it is possible, Willadan, that you were born as I was. Perhaps, for some reason known only to Doni, your essence could not start a child with your mate at that time. But the Great Earth Mother, in Her wisdom, gave you and your mate the children you wanted. If you were not the one who started them, would you be willing to give them back if you found the name of the man who may have started them?"

"No. I have provided for them all their lives," Willadan said.

"Exactly. You have cared for them, you love them, they are the children of your hearth. That means they are your children, Willadan."

"Yes, they are the children of my hearth, but you said *if* I am not the one who started them. Do you think they could have been started by my essence?" Willadan asked, a bit wistfully.

"It may well be that the honor your mate paid to the Mother was accepted as sufficient offering, and that she allowed your essence to start all of them. We don't know, but if you could not love them more, Willadan, does it make any difference?"

"No, I guess not."

"They may have been started by your essense, or they may not have," Zelandoni said, "but they will always be more than the children of your hearth. They are your children."

"Will we ever know for sure?"

"I don't know if we will ever know. With a woman, it is obvious. She is either pregnant or not. With a man, his children are always the children of his mate. That's the way it has always been. Nothing has changed. No man can be certain who started the children of his hearth."

"Jondalar can," came a voice from the audience. Everyone

stopped and stared at the one who had spoken. It was Jalodan, a young man from the Third Cave. He was sitting with Folara's friend, Galeya, whom he had mated two years before. He suddenly flushed from all the penetrating attention, including the hard look from Zelandoni. "Well, he can," he said defensively. "Everyone knows Ayla never chose anyone but him—until last night. If children are started from the essence of a man's organ, and Ayla never shared Pleasures with anyone but Jondalar, then the child of his hearth has to be his, had to come from his essence. That's what he was fighting about last night, wasn't he? He kept screaming, 'He's making my baby!' every time he hit Laramar."

Now all the attention was focused on Jondalar, and he squirmed under the intense scrutiny. Some people glanced at Ayla, but she was sitting rigidly still, looking down.

Suddenly Joharran stood up. "Jondalar was not in control of himself. He let himself drink too much, and it drowned his brains," he said with exasperated sarcasm.

There were smiles and snickers. "I'll wager his head was full of the 'morning-after' when the sun came up," another young man called out. There was a touch of admiration in his tone, as though he found Jondalar's violent behavior somehow laudable.

"Since both Jondalar and Laramar are from the Ninth Cave, this is an issue that will be settled by the Ninth Cave. This is not the place to discuss Jondalar's actions," Joharran said, trying to end the issue. He had heard the appreciation in the voices of some of the young men, and the last thing he wanted was for anyone to be emulating that kind of behavior.

"Except to say, Jemoral," Zelandoni added, "that Jondalar will be suffering from more than a morning-after headache, I'm afraid. There will be serious consequences to pay, you can be sure." It was difficult to know all the people at the meeting, though she tried. Their clothing was always a clue, as well as the beads and belts and other accoutrements they wore. This was a young man from the Fifth Cave, related to their Zelandoni. They all tended to be a little showier than most, and wore more beads, since they were known for making and trading them. And he was sitting closer to the front, which allowed her to see him clearly enough to recognize him.

"But I think I understand how he felt," Jemoral persisted. "What if I want the child of my mate to come from me?"

"Yes," another man spoke out, "what then?"

Another voice added, "What if I want the children of my hearth to be mine?"

Zelandoni waited until the commotion settled down, surveying the audience to see that most of the comments were coming from the Fifth Cave. Then she fixed the entire group with a stern look.

"You want the children of your hearth to be yours, Jemoral," she said, looking directly at the young man who had asked the question. "Do you mean like your clothes, or your tools, or your beads? You want to own them?"

"No-ah-no. I-ah-didn't mean that," the young man stuttered.

"I'm glad to hear that, because children cannot be owned. They can't be yours, or your mate's. No one can own them. Children are ours to love and care for, to provide for, to teach, as the Mother does for us, and you can do that whether they come from your essence, or from someone else's. We are all children of the Great Earth Mother. We learn from Her. Remember in the Mother's Song:

> To Woman and Man the Mother gave birth,
> And then for their home, She gave them the Earth,
> The water, the land, and all Her creation.
> To use them with care was their obligation.
>   It was their home to use, but not to abuse.

Several zelandonia joined in the response, then they continued.

> For the Children of Earth the Mother provided,
> The Gifts to survive, and then She decided,
> To give them the Gift of Pleasure and caring,
> That honors the Mother with the joy of their pairing.
>   The Gifts are well earned, when honor's returned.

"She provides for us, cares for us, teaches us, and in return for Her Gifts, we honor Her," the One Who Was First continued. "Doni's Gift of the Knowledge of Life was not given to you so that you might own the children born to your hearth, to claim them as yours." She looked at several of the young men who had spoken out. "It was given so that we would know that women are not the only ones who are the Blessed of Doni. Men have a purpose that is equal to that of women. They are not here just to provide and to help; men are necessary. Without men there would be no children. Isn't that enough? Do your children have to be yours? Do you have to own them?"

The young men exchanged sheepish looks, but Zelandoni wasn't sure if they truly understood. Then a young woman spoke up.

"What about before? We know our mothers and our grandmothers. I am my mother's daughter, but what about the men?"

The young woman wasn't immediately familiar to Zelandoni, but reflexively, the astute mind of the First tried to place her. She was sitting with the Twenty-third Cave, and the designs and patterns on her tunic and necklace indicated she was a member of that Cave, not from another Cave and sitting with friends. Though the outfit she wore indicated a woman and not a girl, she was obviously quite young. Probably just had her First Rites, the donier thought. For one so young to speak out in a large crowd indicated she was either brash and impetuous or brave and accustomed to being with people who spoke their minds, which would indicate leadership. The leader of the Twenty-third Cave was a woman, Dinara. Zelandoni recalled then that Dinara's eldest daughter was among those having First Rites this year, and Zelandoni noticed that Dinara was smiling at the young woman. Then she remembered the young woman's name.

"Nothing has changed, Diresa," the First said. "Children have always been the result of the joining of a man and a woman. Just because we didn't know before doesn't mean it hasn't always been that way. Doni just chose to tell us now. She must have felt we were ready for this knowledge. Do you know who your mother's mate was when you were born?"

"Yes, everyone knows who her mate is. It's Joncoran," Diresa said.

"Then Joncoran is your *Fa-ther.*" Zelandoni said. She had been waiting for the right opportunity to bring up the word that had been chosen. "Fa-ther is the name that has been given to a man who has children. A man is necessary for a life to begin, but he doesn't carry the baby inside him, nor does he give birth or nurse, but a man can love the child as much as a mother. He is a far-mother, a fa-ther. It was also chosen to indicate that while women are the Blessed of Doni, men may now think of themselves as the Favored of Doni. It is similar to 'mother,' but the *fa* sound was chosen to make it clear that it is a name for a man, just as 'fa'lodge' is the name for the men's place."

There was an immediate outburst of noisy talk from the gathering. In the audience, Ayla heard the new term being repeated several times, as though the people were tasting it, getting used to it. Zelandoni waited until the noise settled down.

"You, Diresa, are the daughter of your mother, Dinara, and you are the daughter of your father, Joncoran. Your mother has sons and daughters, and your father also has sons and daughters. Those children may call him 'father,' just as they call the woman who gave birth to them 'mother.'"

"What if the man who coupled with my mother and started me was not the man she mated?" asked Jemoral, the young man from the Fifth Cave.

"The man who is mated to your mother, the one who is the man of your hearth, is your father," Zelandoni said without hesitation.

"But if he didn't start me, how could he be my father?" Jemoral persisted.

That young man is going to be trouble, the One Who Was First thought. "You don't know who may have started you, but you know the man who lives with you and your mother. He is the one who is most likely to have 'fathered' you. If you don't know of anyone else for sure, he may as well not exist, and there is no point in naming a relationship that does not exist. Your mother's mate is the one who promised to provide for you. He's the one who cared for you, loved you, helped to raise you. It is not the coupling, it is the caring that makes a man your father. If the man to whom your mother was mated had died, and if she mated another man who loved you and cared for you, would you love him less?"

"But which one is the real 'father'?"

"You may always call the man who provides for you 'father.' When you name your ties, as in a formal introduction, your father is the man who was mated to your mother when you were born, the man you call 'the man of your hearth.' If the one who provides for you is not the one who was there when you were born, you will refer to him as your 'second father,' to distinguish between the two when it is necessary," Zelandoni explained. She was glad now that she spent a night, when she was unable to sleep, thinking about all the kinship ramifications this new knowledge would cause.

The One Who Was First had another announcement she wanted to make. "This may be a good time to bring up one more matter that needs to be mentioned. The zelandonia felt that the men need to be included in some of the rituals and customs associated with the welcoming of a new baby, to give them a deeper feeling and understanding of their part in the creation of new life. Therefore, from now on, the men will name the male children born to their hearths; the women will, of course, continue to name the female children."

Her statement was received with mixed feelings. The men looked surprised, but several of them were smiling. She could see by their expressions, however, that some of the women did not want to give up their prerogative of naming the children. No one wanted to make an issue of it just then, and no questions were asked, but she knew this idea was not settled. There would be problems, she was sure.

"What about children who are born to women who are not mated?" asked a very young-looking woman who was nevertheless cuddling a baby in her arms.

Second Cave, Zelandoni thought, looking at her clothing and jewelry. Could that be a child of last summer's First Rites? "The women who give birth before mating are Blessed, like the women who have new life started within them at the time they are mated. A woman who has been Blessed with a child has demonstrated that she can carry and deliver a healthy baby, and she is often the one who is chosen to be Blessed again. Until she mates, her children are provided for by her family or her Cave, and their 'father' is Lumi, the mate of Doni, the Great Earth Mother."

She smiled at the young woman. "Nothing has really changed, Shaleda." The name had suddenly come to her. "The Cave always provides for a woman with children who has no mate, whether her mate was lost to the next world or not yet chosen. But most men find a young woman with a baby very desirable. She usually mates quickly since she can bring a child to a man's hearth immediately, a child who is a favorite of Doni. The man she mates becomes the child's father, of course," the large woman explained, and watched the woman who was little more than a girl glancing shyly at a young man from the Third Cave who was staring at her with rapt adoration.

"But what about the man who is really the father?" said the familiar voice of the young man from the Fifth Cave who had been asking so many questions. "Isn't the man whose essence actually started the baby the father?"

Zelandoni noticed him glancing at the same young woman who was holding the baby. She was looking at the other man. Aah . . . Now I understand, the Donier thought. Maybe not a First Rites child, but a first infatuation. She was a little surprised at how easily she had fallen into the pattern of thinking about the birth of children being caused by the coupling of a man and a woman. It all seemed to fit into place so logically now.

Ayla had also been aware of the young man from the Fifth Cave, and had noticed the byplay between the young woman and the two men. Does he think he started her baby? Could he be jealous? she wondered. Ayla realized that she was now more aware not only of the concept, but of the intense feelings associated with jealousy. I didn't know this Gift of Knowledge from the Great Earth Mother would be so complicated. I'm not sure it's such a wonderful Gift at all, she said to herself.

"If a woman with a child has never been mated, then the man she mates, the one who promises to provide and care for the child, becomes the father of her baby. Of course, if a woman chooses to mate with more than one man, they would share the name 'father' equally," Zelandoni said, trying to show a possible alternative.

"But a woman doesn't have to mate with anyone she doesn't want, isn't that right?" the young woman said.

The First noticed that the Zelandoni of the Fifth Cave was climbing the hill toward the area where his Cave was gathered. "Yes, that has always been true and it hasn't changed." She saw that the Donier was sitting beside the young man who had so many questions, and turned to take a question from an entirely different segment of the audience.

"What is my father's father called?" asked a man from the Eleventh Cave.

Zelandoni breathed a quiet sigh of relief. An easy question. "A mother's mother is a grandmother, and is usually called grandma. A mother's father is a grandfather, or grandfa. A father's mother is a grandmother, too, but to distinguish between them, she will still be called grandam. A father's father is a grandfather, or grandaf. When you name your ties, your mother's mother is your close grandmother, or your grandma, and your mother's father is your close grandfather, or your grandfa, because you are always certain who your mother is."

"What if you don't know whose essence started your mother?" the leader of the Fifth Cave asked. "Or if they are walking in the next world, how can you name the tie?"

"If you know the man who was mated to your mother's mother, he would be your grandfather. The same is true for your father. Even if he is in the next world, your father was started by a man who coupled with his mother, just as your mother was started by a man who put the essence of his organ inside her mother," Zelandoni carefully explained.

"NO! Noooo!" came a cry from the audience. "It's not true! She has done it again. She has betrayed me, just when I was starting to trust her."

Everyone turned to look. On the far outside edge of the large group of people from the Ninth Cave, a man was standing. "It's a lie! It's all a lie! That woman is trying to trick you. The Mother would never have told her that," he screamed, pointing at Ayla. "She's a lying evil woman."

Shading her eyes, Ayla looked up and saw Brukeval. Brukeval? Why is he screaming at me like that? I don't understand, she thought. What did I do to him?

"I come from the spirit of a man who was chosen by the Great Mother to join with the spirit of my mother," Brukeval shrieked. "My mother came from the spirit of a *man* who was chosen by Doni to join with the spirit of her mother. She did not come from the organ of an animal! Not from the essence of any organ. I am a man! I am not a Flathead! I am *not* a Flathead!" His voice couldn't sustain the anguished scream; it cracked on the last words and ended on a sobbing wail.

38

Brukeval suddenly started running down the hill, then across the small field and kept on going, leaving the campsite behind without looking back. Several men, mostly from the Ninth Cave, started after him, Joharran and Jondalar among them, hoping that once he ran out of breath, they could talk to him, calm him down, bring him back. But Brukeval ran as though the spirit of the dead were chasing him. For all his resistance to it, he had inherited the strength and the stamina of the man of the Clan who was his grandfather. Though they ran faster in the beginning, and started to catch up, the men who were chasing after Brukeval did not have his endurance, and could not keep up the pace he set.

They finally stopped, gasping, bent over, some rolling on the ground, trying to catch their breaths in a collective agony of aching sides and raw throats. "I should have gotten Racer," Jondalar rasped, barely able to speak. "He couldn't have out-run a horse."

When they finally trudged back, the meeting was in disarray. People were standing up, walking around, talking. Zelandoni didn't want it to end like that, and had called for a pause until the men returned, hopefully with Brukeval. When they returned without him, she decided to finish up quickly.

"It is unfortunate that Brukeval of the Ninth Cave of the Zelandonii feels as he does. His sensitivity about his background is well known, but no one knows for sure what really happened to his grandmother. We only know that she was lost for some time, and finally found her way back, and later gave birth to Brukeval's mother. Anyone lost for so long is bound to have

adverse effects from the ordeal, and Brukeval's grandmother
was not in her right mind when she returned. She was so full
of fears, no one could believe, or even understand, much of
what she said.

"The daughter she bore was not physically strong, probably
because of her mother's ordeal, and her pregnancy and the
birth of her son was so hard for her, she died as a result. It's
likely that Brukeval bears the imprint of his mother's difficult
pregnancy in his stature and appearance, though it is fortunate
that he grew strong and healthy. I think Brukeval was entirely
right when he said he is a man. He is a Zelandonii man of the
Ninth Cave, a good man who has much to offer. I'm sure he
will decide to return to us after he's had time to reconsider, and
I know the Ninth Cave will welcome him back when he does,"
the One Who Was First said, then she continued.

"I think it is time to close this meeting. We all have much
to think about, and you can all continue the discussion we
started here with your own Zelandoni." As people were getting
up again to leave, the First signaled to the leader of the Fifth
Cave. "Will the Fifth Cave stay a little longer and join me here,
near the lodge?" she asked. "I have a matter of importance that
concerns you." Might as well get this unpleasant chore over
with while I'm at it, she thought. The meeting had not gone at
all the way she'd hoped. Jondalar's fight the night before had
set the wrong tone in the beginning, and Brukeval's abrupt
departure left people feeling unsettled at the end.

"I'm sorry I have to do this," the First said to the group of
people of all ages that constituted the Fifth Cave. Madroman
was among them as well as their Zelandoni. She picked up a
carry-sack that was on a table near the back of the lodge and
turned to face the acolyte. "Does this look familiar to you,
Madroman?" she asked.

He looked, and then he blanched, and glanced around looking worried and wary.

"It's yours, isn't it? It has your markings."

Several people were nodding their heads. Everyone knew
it was his. It was quite distinctive; they had seen him with it.

"Where did you get that?" he asked.

"Ayla found it hidden in the deep of Fountain Rock. After

you were 'called' to go in there," the First said, with heavy sarcasm.

"I might have guessed it was her," Madroman mumbled.

"She wasn't looking for anything. She was sitting on the floor near the large round niche at the back, and happened to feel it in a hidden space at the bottom of a wall. She thought someone had forgotten it, and wanted to return it to him," Zelandoni said.

"Why would she think someone had forgotten it if it was hidden?" Madroman said. There was no use pretending anymore.

"Because she wasn't thinking straight. She had just lost her baby, and very nearly her life, in that cave," the First said.

"What is this about?" the leader asked.

"Madroman has been an acolyte for a long time. He wanted to join the ranks of the zelandonia and was tired of waiting to be called." She emptied the carry-sack on the table. Out fell the remains of food, the waterbag, the lamp and fire-making equipment, and the cloak. "He hid this inside the cave, then pretended that he felt the call. He stayed inside a little more than two days, with plenty of food, water, light, and even a covering for warmth. He hid this, then came out acting groggy and disoriented, and claimed he was ready."

"You mean he lied about his call?" the leader asked.

"In a word, yes."

"If it hadn't been for her, you would never have known," Madroman spat out.

"You are wrong, Madroman. We knew. This only confirmed it. What makes you think you can fool the zelandonia? We have all been through it. Don't you think we'd know the difference?" Zelandoni said.

"Why didn't you say something before?"

"Some of us were trying to find a way to give you every opportunity. Some thought, or hoped, that it wasn't intentional. They wanted to make sure that you hadn't fooled yourself in your strong desire to become One Who Serves . . . until Ayla brought this to us. You would not have become zelandoni, in any case, but you might have remained an acolyte, Madroman. Now that is no longer possible. The Great Earth Mother doesn't want to be served by a liar and a cheat," the powerful woman said in tones that left no doubt about her feelings. "Kemordan, leader of the Fifth Cave of the Zelandonia," the First continued, "will you and your Cave bear witness?"

"We will," he replied.

"We will," said the Cave in unison.

"Madroman of the Fifth Cave of the Zelandonii, former acolyte," the First intoned, "you may never again put yourself out as a member of the zelandonia, not as an acolyte or in any other manner. You may never again attempt to treat someone's illness, or offer advice about the ways of the Mother, or in any way assume the duties of the zelandonia. Do you understand?"

"But what am I supposed to do now? That's all I've trained for. I don't know how to be anything but an acolyte," Madroman said.

"If you return everything you have received from the zelandonia, you can go back to your Cave and think about learning some other craft, Madroman. And be grateful I am not imposing a fine and announcing it to the whole Camp."

"They'll all find out anyway," Madroman said, then raising his voice, "You were never going to let me be a Zelandoni. You've always hated me. You and Jondalar, and your little favorite, Ayla, the Flathead lover. You've been out to get me from the beginning . . . Zolena."

There was a gasp from the Fifth Cave. Not one of them would have dared to be so disrespectful to the One Who Was First as to call her by her former name. Most would have been afraid to. Even Madroman paused in his tirade when he saw the expression on the face of the First. She was, after all, a woman of formidable powers.

He turned on his heel and stomped away, not sure what he was going to do as he headed for the fa'lodge he had sometimes shared with Laramar, Brukeval, and the rest. It was empty when he got there. Most camps were serving meals after the long meeting, and the rest of the men had gone to find something to eat. It suddenly came to him that neither Laramar or Brukeval would be back at all. Laramar would be a long time recovering, and who knew what Brukeval would do. Madroman walked over and took a small waterbag of barma from Laramar's travel-ing pack. He sat down on the sleeping roll and drank most of it down in a few gulps, then took a second one. Laramar will never know, he thought.

It's all the fault of that big dolt who knocked my teeth out. Madroman felt the hole in the front of his mouth with his tongue. He had learned to compensate for it, and didn't think about his missing teeth much anymore, though it had hurt when he was younger and women ignored him because of it. He'd since discovered that certain women were interested in him when they learned he was part of the zelandonia, even just an acolyte in training. None of those women would want him now. He flushed at the thought of his disgrace, and opened the second waterbag full of barma.

Why did Jondalar have to come back? he said to himself. If Jondalar hadn't returned from his Journey and brought that foreign woman here, she wouldn't have found that sack. Then the zelandonia never would have known, I don't care what that fat old woman says. I don't really want to go back to the Fifth Cave now, and I don't want to learn another trade. Why should I? I'm as good a Zelandoni as any of them, and I doubt that they've all been called, either. I'll bet a lot of them fake it. What is a call anyway? They probably all fake it. Even that Flathead lover. So what if she lost a baby. Women lose babies all the time. What's so special about that?

He took another drink, glanced over at Brukeval's place, then got up and walked over. Everything was there, neatly in order the way he always kept it. He didn't even come and get his gear, Madroman thought. He's going to sleep cold tonight without a sleeping roll. I wonder if I could find him. He might be grateful if I brought him his things. Madroman walked back to his place and looked at the paraphernalia he had acquired as an acolyte. That fat old woman wants me to give it all back.

I'm not going to do it! I'm going to pack up all my things and leave. He paused, looked over at Brukeval's sleeping place. If I can find him, maybe we could go on a Journey together, or something, find some other people. I could tell them I am Zelandoni; they'd never know.

That's what I'll do. I'll pack up Brukeval's gear, and go look for him. I know a few places he might be. He would be someone to stay with, and he's a better hunter than I am. I haven't done it in so long. Maybe I'll take some of Laramar's things, too. He'll never miss them. He won't even know who took them. It could be anyone in this lodge. They all know he won't be back.

And it's all Jondalar's fault. First he nearly kills me; then he nearly kills Laramar. He'll get away with it, too, just like he did before. I hate Jondalar, I've always hated Jondalar. Someone ought to hold him down and beat him up. Ruin his pretty face. See how he likes it. I'd like to give Ayla a few whacks, too. I know a few people who wouldn't mind holding her down. I'd give her something else, too, like a load of my "essence," he thought with an evil grin. Then she wouldn't walk so high. She never would share Pleasures with anyone else, not even at Mother Festivals. Thinks she's so perfect, finding my sack and bringing it to the zelandonia. If it weren't for her, I wouldn't be out. I'd be Zelandoni. I hate that woman!

Madroman finished up the second waterbag of barma, grabbed several more, then looked around to see what else he wanted to take. He found a spare outfit, used but still good. He tried it on; they were nearly the same size. He took it. His zelandonia clothing was decorative and distinctive, but not very practical for long hikes. The sleeping roll wasn't much good—it was an old throwaway to begin with; Laramar's good one was in his mate's tent—but there were several other very nice items, including a good fur cover. Then he found a real treasure, a new full winter outfit that Laramar had recently traded for. His barma was constantly in demand, and he had always been able to trade for whatever he wanted.

Next Madroman walked over to Brukeval's place and began hauling everything he saw back to his own place. He changed into the more practical outfit that he'd found at Laramar's place. It didn't matter that it had Ninth Cave decorations instead of Fifth Cave; he wasn't going to be staying at either place. He took food from both places, and then rummaged through the possessions of all the rest of the men, taking food and a few other items as well. He found a good, well-hafted knife, a small stone hatchet, and a new pair of warm mittens someone had just acquired. He didn't have any with him and winter was coming. Who knows where I'll be then? he thought. He had to repack a few times, eliminate a few things, but once he was ready, he was eager to leave.

He put his head out of the lodge and looked around. The Campsite was full of people, as usual, but none were nearby. He hoisted on the heavy backframe, and started out briskly. He planned on heading generally north, the direction he had seen Brukeval take. He was nearly beyond the boundary of the Summer Meeting Campsite, close to the camp of the Ninth Cave, when Ayla came out of a dwelling. She seemed to be distracted, preoccupied, but she glanced up and saw him. He flashed her a look of sheer hatred and kept on going.

The camp of the Ninth Cave looked deserted. Everyone had gone to the Lanzadoni camp for a joint midday meal, a feast they had been planning together for some time, but Ayla said she wasn't hungry, and promised she'd come later. She was sitting on her bedroll in the dwelling, feeling despondent, thinking about Brukeval and his outburst at the meeting, and wondering if there was anything she could have done. She didn't think Zelandoni had anticipated his reaction, and it didn't even occur to her to consider it, though now she was sure she should have. She knew how sensitive he was to inferences that he was in any way related to Flatheads.

He called them animals, she thought, but they aren't! Why do some people always say that? She wondered if Brukeval would still feel that way if he knew them better. It probably wouldn't make any difference. A lot of the Zelandonii feel that way.

The First reminded everyone that Brukeval's grandmother had not been in her right mind when she found her way home again, and that she was pregnant. Everyone says she was with the Clan, Ayla thought, and they're right. It's obvious that Brukeval has some Clan mixture in him, so she must have become pregnant while she was with them. That means some Clan man had to put his essence inside her.

A thought Ayla hadn't considered suddenly came to her. Did some man of the Clan force her over and over again, the way I was forced by Broud? I wasn't in my right mind when Broud was doing that to me and I didn't think they were animals. I was raised by them, I loved them. Not Broud. I hated him, even before he forced me, but I loved most of them.

Ayla hadn't thought of it quite that way when she first heard the story, but it was a possibility. The man might have forced her out of meanness, like Broud, or he might have thought he was doing her a favor, taking her as a second woman, perhaps, accepting her into the Clan, but it wouldn't have made any difference to her. That's not how she would have seen it, Ayla thought. She couldn't talk to them, or understand them. They were animals to her. Brukeval's grandmother must have hated it worse than I hated Broud doing it.

And as much as I wanted to have the baby when Iza told me I was pregnant, it was hard on me. I was sick all the time when I was expecting Durc, and I almost died delivering him. Clan women didn't have that much trouble, but Durc's head was so much bigger and harder than Jonayla's. Ayla had seen enough women into motherhood in the past few years to realize that her pregnancy and delivery of Jonayla was far more normal for women of the Others than her birthing of Durc had been. I don't know how I ever pushed him out, she thought, shaking her head. The heads of the Others are smaller, and the bone is thinner and more flexible. Our legs and arms are longer but those bones are thinner, too, Ayla said to herself, looking at her own limbs. All the bones of the Others are thinner.

Was Brukeval's grandmother sick during her pregnancy? Did she have a hard time delivering, like I did? Is that what happened to her? Is that why she died? Because it was so hard on her? Even Joplaya nearly died giving birth to Bokovan, and Echozar is only half Clan. Is a baby of "mixed spirits," a baby who's a mixture of the Clan and the Others, always hard on women of the Others? Ayla was brought up short with a new thought. Could that be why those babies were originally called abominations? Because they sometimes made their mothers die?

There are differences between the Clan and the Others. Maybe not enough to stop a baby from getting started, but enough to make it hard on the mother if she's one of the Others and used to birthing babies with smaller heads. It might not be so hard on Clan women. They're used to babies with big, long, hard heads and heavy brow ridges. It was probably easier for them to give birth to a mixed baby.

I don't think it's always good for the babies, though, whether the mother is Clan or Others. Durc was strong and healthy, even though I had a hard time, and so is Echozar, and his mother was Clan. Bokovan is healthy, but he's not quite the same. Echozar, his father, was the first mixture, so he's like Brukeval, but still Joplaya almost died. She realized she was using the word "father" with ease. It was so logical, and she had understood the relationship for a long time.

But Rydag was weak, and his mother was Clan. She died after giving birth, but Nezzie never said she had a hard time delivering. I don't think that's why she died. I think she'd been turned out of her clan and didn't want to live, especially since she must have thought her baby was deformed. Brukeval's mother was a first mixture, and her mother was one of the Others. She was weak, so weak she died giving birth to him. Whether he wants to admit it or not, Brukeval knows what happened to his grandmother; that's why he was so quick to understand the implications of the Gift of Life at the meeting. I wonder if he ever thought that his mother's weakness was somehow caused by the mixture.

I suppose I shouldn't blame Brukeval for hating the Clan. He didn't have a mother to love him, or to comfort him when people called him names because he looked a little different. It was hard for Durc, too. He looked enough different from the Clan that they thought he was deformed, and some of them didn't want to let him live, but at least he had people who loved him. I should have been more careful of Brukeval's feelings. I'm always so sure that I'm right. Always blaming people for calling the Clan Flatheads and animals. I know they aren't, but most people don't know them like I do. It was my fault Brukeval ran away. I don't blame him for hating me.

Ayla got up; she didn't want to sit inside anymore. It was dim and gloomy in the windowless dwelling, and the lamp was guttering out, adding to the darkness. She wanted to get out, do something besides think about her shortcomings. As she stepped out of the dwelling and looked around, she was surprised to see Madroman approaching in a big hurry. When he saw her, he gave her such a malicious glare, she felt the tingle of icy needles prickling up her spine, raising the hairs on the back of her neck, and a cold shudder of ominous apprehension.

Ayla watched him as he hurried on. Something's different about him, she said to herself. Then she noticed he was not wearing his acolyte clothing, but the clothes he had on were strangely familiar. She wrinkled her brow in concentration, then it came to her. Those are Ninth Cave patterns! But he's Fifth Cave; why is he wearing Ninth Cave clothes? And where is he going in such a hurry?

That look he gave me. Ayla shivered again at the thought. So full of hatred. Why should he hate me so much? And why wasn't he wearing his acoly . . . Oh . . . Suddenly it occurred to her. Zelandoni must have told him he can't be an acolyte anymore. Is he blaming me? But he's the one who lied; why should he blame me? It couldn't be because of Jondalar. He beat Madroman once—knocked his teeth out—but that was over Zelandoni, not me. Could he hate me because I found his leather sack in the cave? Maybe he hates me because he will never be a Zelandoni, and I just became one.

That's two of them who hate me, Madroman and Brukeval, Ayla thought. Three if I count Laramar; he must hate me, too. When he finally woke up, he said he didn't want to go back to the Ninth Cave when he felt good enough to leave the zelandonia lodge, and they decided that he could. I'm glad the Fifth Cave said they would be willing to take him. I couldn't blame him if he never wanted to see me again. I deserve his hatred. It is my fault that Jondalar beat him so badly. Jondalar probably hates me now, too. Ayla was feeling so despondent, she was beginning to think that everyone hated her.

Ayla started walking faster, unmindful of where she was going. She looked up when she heard a soft whicker, and found she was at the horse enclosure. She had been so busy the last few days, she had hardly seen the horses, and when she heard the welcoming whinny of her dun-yellow mare, tears brought a familiar ache behind her eyes. She climbed over the fencing, and hugged the sturdy neck of her old friend.

"Oh, Whinney! I'm so happy to see you," she said, talking in the strange language she always used with the mare, the one she had made up so long ago in the valley, before Jondalar came and taught her his language. "At least you still care about me," she said, as the tears overflowed. "You should probably hate me, too, I've been ignoring you so much. But I'm so glad you don't. You were always my friend, Whinney." She said the name the way she had learned from the mare, a remarkably close reproduction of the sound of a horse whinny. "When I didn't have anyone else, you were there. Maybe I should just go away with you. We could find a valley and live together, like we used to."

As she was sobbing into the thickening fur of the yellow horse, the young gray mare and the brown stallion joined them. Gray tried to get her nose under Ayla's hand while Racer bumped her back with his head to let her know he was there. Then he leaned against her, the way he had done so often before, keeping her between himself and his dam. Ayla hugged and stroked and scratched them all, then found a dried teasel to use as a currying brush and started to clean Whinney's coat.

It had always been a relaxing activity for her, to clean and care for the horses, and by the time she finished with Whinney and started on the impatient Racer, who had been nudging her for his share of her attention, her tears had dried and she was feeling better. She was working on Gray when Joharran and Echozar came looking for her.

"Everyone was wondering where you were, Ayla," Echozar said, smiling to see her standing in the middle of the three horses. It still amazed him to see her with the animals.

"I haven't spent much time with the horses lately, and their coats needed a good cleaning. They are already thickening up for winter," Ayla said.

"Proleva's been trying to keep the food warm for you, but she says it's drying out," Joharran said. "I think you should come and get something to eat."

"I'm almost through here. I've already brushed Whinney and Racer. I just have to finish up Gray. Then I probably should wash my hands," Ayla said, holding up her hand to show him her black palms, grimy with oily horse sweat and dirt.

"We'll wait," Joharran said. He had been given strict instructions not to return without her.

By the time Ayla arrived, people were finishing with the meal and starting to leave the Lanzadonii camp for various afternoon activities. Ayla had been disappointed that Jondalar was not at the big feast, but no one could get him out of the fa'lodge, short of picking him up and bodily carrying him. Once she was there Ayla was glad she went. After she picked up the plate piled high with food that had been saved for her, she had been pleased to have a little more time to talk to Danug and Druwez, and to get to know Aldanor a little better, although it appeared that she would have plenty of time for that.

Folara and Aldanor were going to be mated at the Late Matrimonial, just before the Summer Meeting ended, and he was going to become Zelandonii and a member of the Ninth Cave, much to Marthona's delight. Danug and Druwez promised to stop at his Camp on their way back home and tell his people, but that wouldn't be until next summer. They were wintering with the Zelandonii, and Willamar had promised to take them and a few others to see the Great Waters of the West, soon after they returned to the Ninth Cave.

"Ayla, will you walk with me back to the zelandonia lodge?" the First asked. "There are some things I'd like to talk over with you."

"Yes, of course, Zelandoni," Ayla said. "Let me talk to Jonayla first."

She found her daughter with Marthona, and inevitably with Wolf. "Do you know 'Thona is my grandmother? Not just my grandam?" Jonayla said when Ayla approached.

"Yes, I do," Ayla said. "Are you pleased to know that?" She reached to stroke the animal who was so excited to see her. Wolf had hardly left Jonayla for a moment since they arrived at the Campsite, as though trying to make up for their long separation earlier, but he seemed overjoyed to see Ayla whenever she was near, anxiously seeking her affection and

approval. He seemed most relaxed when they were both together with him, which usually was only at night.

"Although I've always felt that I was, it's nice to be acknowledged as the grandmother of the children of my sons," Marthona
said. "And though I've long thought of you as my daughter,
Ayla, it pleases me to know that Folara has finally found an acceptable man to mate, and may yet give me a grandchild before
I walk the next world."

She took Ayla's hand and looked at her. "I want to thank
you again for telling these men to come and get me." Smiling at Hartaman and some of the others who had carried her
on a litter to the Summer Meeting, and were often around
the Campsite since she arrived, she continued, "I'm sure they
were concerned about my health and meant well, but it takes a
woman to understand that a mother needs to be with her daughter when she's contemplating her Matrimonial."

"Everyone was pleased to think you might feel well enough
to come. You were greatly missed, Marthona," Ayla said.

Marthona avoided the subject of Jondalar's conspicuous
absence, and the probable reason for it, although it distressed
her greatly to think that her son had once again lost control of
himself, and caused great harm to another person. She was also
very concerned about Ayla. She had gotten to know the young
woman quite well, and knew how troubled she was, though she
handled herself remarkably well in spite of her anguish.

"Zelandoni asked me to walk with her to the zelandonia
lodge," Ayla said. "She said she wanted to talk about some
things. Will you take Jonayla back with you, Marthona?"

"I'll be happy to. I've missed this little one, although Wolf is
probably a better guardian than I am."

"Are you coming back to sleep with me tonight, mother?"
Jonayla said, with a worried look.

"Of course. I'm just going to talk to Zelandoni for a little
while," Ayla said.

"Is Jondy going to sleep with us tonight?"

"I don't know, Jonayla. He's probably busy."

"Why is he always so busy with those men in the fa'lodge
that he can't sleep with us?" the child asked.

"Sometimes men are just very busy," Marthona said, noticing that Ayla was struggling to keep her control. "You go ahead with Zelandoni; Ayla, we'll see you later. Come along, Jonayla. We should go and thank everyone for the wonderful feast; then, if you like, you can ride with me on the litter when they carry me back."

"Oh, could I?" Jonayla said. She thought it was particularly wonderful the way there were always a couple of young men nearby to carry Marthona wherever she wanted to go, especially if it was any distance.

As Ayla and Zelandoni walked toward the zelandonia lodge together, discussing the meeting and the things that might be done to create a more positive mood about the changes the Gift of Knowledge would bring about, Zelandoni thought that Ayla seemed quite despondent, though as usual she was covering it up well.

When they reached the lodge, Zelandoni started water heating for tea. They saw that Laramar had left the zelandonia lodge already, and must have been moved to the Fifth Cave's camp. When the tea was ready, she led Ayla to a quiet area where there were a few stools and a low table. She considered trying to get Ayla to talk about what was bothering her, but changed her mind. The First thought she had a good idea what was troubling Ayla, though she had not heard Jonayla question her mother about Jondalar's absence, and didn't know how much it added to her despair. The Donier decided it might be better to talk about something else to get Ayla's mind off her worries and concerns.

"I'm not sure if I heard you correctly at the time, Ayla . . . I should say Zelandoni of the Ninth Cave, but I thought you said you still had some of those roots that your Clan Zelandoni—what do you call him, Mogor?—used in his special ceremonies. Is that right?" The idea of them had intrigued the First ever since Ayla mentioned them. "Would they really still be good after all these years?"

"The Clan in this region call him Mogor, but we always said Mog-ur. And yes, I still have some of the roots, and I'm sure they're good. They get stronger with age, if stored properly. I know Iza often kept hers for the entire seven years between Clan Gatherings, and sometimes longer," Ayla said.

"What you said about them interests me. Though I do understand they can be hazardous, it might be a valuable experience to try a small experiment."

"I don't know," Ayla said. "They are dangerous, and I'm not sure if I'd know how to do a small experiment. I only know one way to prepare them." She felt nervous about the idea.

"If you don't think it's appropriate to experiment, that's fine." Zelandoni didn't want to distress her further. She took a sip of her tea to give herself a few moments to think. "Do you still have the pouch of mixed herbs that we were going to experiment on together? The ones you got from that visiting Zelandoni from the Cave that's so far away?"

"Yes, I'll get them," Ayla said, getting up to get the sack of medicinal herbs that she kept in her special place within the zelandonia lodge. She thought of it as her zelandonia medicine bag, though it did not resemble her Clan medicine bag.

Some years before, she had made a new one in the Clan style out of a whole otter skin, but it was in the lodge at the Ninth Cave's camp. Its distinctiveness gave it an unmistakable quality of something different. The one Ayla kept in the zelandonia lodge was similar to the ones used by all the doniers, a simple rawhide leather carrier, a smaller version of the one she used to carry meat. The decoration, however, was far from simple. Each of the medicine bags was unique, designed and made by each individual healer, bearing both required elements and others that were chosen by the user.

Ayla brought hers back to the area where Zelandoni was sipping tea while she waited. The young woman opened the leather packet and felt around inside. A frown creased her forehead. Finally she emptied it out onto the small table between them, and found the pouch she was looking for, but it was only half full.

"It looks like you have already experimented with that," Zelandoni said.

"I don't understand," Ayla said. "I don't recall opening this pouch. How did it get used?" She opened the container, poured a small amount in her palm, and sniffed. "It smells like mint."

"If I recall correctly, the Zelandoni who gave it to you said that the mint was put in as a way to identify this mixture. She doesn't keep mint in this kind of pouch, but in larger woven containers, so if it's in a pouch, and smells like mint, she knows it is this mixture," Zelandoni explained.

Ayla sat back and looked up at the ceiling with a deep frown, straining to remember. Suddenly she sat up. "I think I drank this the night I was watching the risings and settings. The night I was called. I thought it was mint tea." Suddenly she clasped her hand over her mouth. "Oh, Great Mother! Zelandoni, I might not have been called at all. It might have all been caused by this mixture!" Ayla said, appalled.

Zelandoni leaned forward, patted Ayla's hand, and smiled. "It's all right, Ayla. You don't need to be concerned about that. You were called; you are Zelandoni of the Ninth Cave. Many of the zelandonia have used similar herbs and mixtures to help them to find the Spirit World. A person may find herself in a different place as a result of using them, but only if you are ready for it are you called. There is no question that your experience was a true calling, though I must admit I didn't expect it to happen to you quite so soon. This mixture may have encouraged you to have it a little sooner than I anticipated, but that doesn't make it less meaningful."

"Do you know what was in it?" Ayla asked.

"She did tell me the ingredients, but I don't know the proportions. Even though we like to share our knowledge, most zelandonia like to keep a few secrets." The One Who Was First smiled. "Why do you ask?"

"I'm sure it must have been very strong," Ayla said, then looked down at the cup of tea in her hands. "I was wondering if there was anything in it that could have caused me to miscarry."

"Ayla, don't blame yourself," Zelandoni said, leaning forward and taking her hand. "I know it hurts to lose a baby, but you had no control over that. It was the sacrifice the Mother demanded of you, perhaps because She had to bring you close enough to the Next World to give you Her message. There may be something in this mixture that would cause a miscarriage, but perhaps there was no other way. It may have been She who caused you to take this when you did so that everything would happen as She wished."

"I've never made a mistake like that with the medicines in my bag. I was careless. So careless, I lost my baby," Ayla said, as though she hadn't even heard the First.

"Because you don't make those kind of mistakes is all the more reason to believe it was Her will. Whenever She calls someone to Serve Her, it is always unexpected, and the first time that one goes to the Spirit World alone is especially dangerous. Many never find their way back. Some leave something behind, as you did. It is always dangerous, Ayla. Even if you have gone there many times, you never know if this is the time that you will not find your way back."

Ayla was quietly sobbing, the tears glistening on her cheeks.

"It's good that you are letting go. You've held it in for too long, and you need to grieve for that baby," the Donier said. She got up, took both cups, and went to the back, where the bandaging skins were stored. When she returned, she poured more tea. "Here," she said, handing her the soft animal hide, and put the tea on the table.

Ayla wiped her eyes and her nose, took a deep breath to settle herself, then took a sip of the warmish tea, struggling to get herself under control again. It was more than losing the baby that had caused her tears, although that had been the catalyst. She couldn't seem to do anything right. Jondalar had stopped loving her, people hated her, and she had been so careless that she lost her baby. She had heard Zelandoni's words, but she didn't fully comprehend and it didn't change how she felt.

"Perhaps now you can understand why I'm so interested in those roots you talk about," the First said when it seemed that Ayla was feeling better. "If the experience can be carefully watched and controlled, we may have another helpful way to reach the Next World when we need to, like this mixture in the pouch, and some other herbs we sometimes use."

Ayla didn't hear her at first. When Zelandoni's words finally reached her, she recalled that she had never wanted to experiment with those roots again. Though The Mog-ur had been able to control the effects of the powerful substance, she was sure she would never be capable of it. She believed only a

Clan mind, with its unique differences, and the Clan memories, could control it. She didn't think anyone born to the Others could ever control the black void, no matter how well they were watched.

She knew that the First was fascinated. Mamut had been intrigued, too, about the special plants used only by the mog-urs of the Clan, but after their dangerous experience together, Mamut had said he would never use them again. He told her he was afraid he would lose his spirit in that paralyzing black void, and had warned her against them. Reliving the terrifying journey to that menacing unknown place when she was deep in the cave, and vividly recalling it during her initiation, made the memory too disturbingly fresh. And she knew that even her unnerving recollection was only a faint shadow of the real experience.

Yet, in the black despair of her present state of mind, she wasn't thinking clearly. She should have had time to regain her balance, but too much had happened too fast. Her ordeal in the cave when she was called, including the miscarriage, had weakened her both physically and emotionally. The pain and the jealousy, and the disappointment, of finding Jondalar with another woman were intensified by her experience in the cave, and by her loss. She had been looking forward to the knowing touch of his hands and the closeness of his body, to the thought of replacing the baby she had lost, to the healing comfort of his love.

Instead she found him with another woman, and not just any woman, the woman who had viciously and knowingly tried to hurt her before. Under normal circumstances, she might have been able to take his indiscretion in stride, especially if it had been with someone else. She might not have been happy about it. They had been too close. But she understood the customs. They were not so different from those of the men of the Clan, who could choose whatever woman they wanted.

She knew how jealous Jondalar had been about her and Ranec when they lived with the Mamutoi, even though she didn't know what was causing the barely controlled violence of his reaction. Ranec had told her to come with him, and she was raised by the

Clan. She hadn't learned yet that among the Others, she had the right to say no.

When they finally resolved the problem and she left with Jondalar back to his home, she had decided in her own mind that she would never give him cause to be jealous of her again. She never chose anyone else, even though she knew it would have been acceptable, and to her knowledge, he never did either. He certainly never did openly, as the other men did. When she was confronted with the fact that he not only had chosen someone else, but that he had been choosing that particular woman, in secret, for a long time, she felt utterly betrayed.

But Jondalar had not meant to betray her. He wanted to keep her from finding out so she wouldn't be hurt. He knew she never chose anyone else, and at a certain level, he even knew why. Though he would have struggled to control it, he knew how jealous he would have been if she had chosen someone else. He did not want her to experience the intensity of pain that he would have felt. When she found them together, he was beside himself. He simply didn't know what to do; he had never learned.

Jondalar was born to grow into a six-foot, six-inch tall, well-formed, incredibly handsome man, with an unconscious charisma enhanced by a vividly intense shade of blue eyes. His natural intelligence, innate manual dexterity, and intrinsic mechanical skill were discovered early, and he was encouraged to apply it in many areas until he discovered his love for knapping flint and making tools. But his powerful feelings were also stronger than most, far too intense, and his mother and those who cared about him struggled to teach him to keep them under control. Even as a child he wanted too much, cared too much, felt too much; he could be overcome with compassion, yearn with desire, rage with hate, or burn with love. He was given too much, too many Gifts, and few understood what a burden that could be.

When he was a young man, Jondalar had been taught how to please a woman, but that was a normal practice of his culture. It was something all young men were taught. The fact that he'd learned it so well was partly because he had been taught so well, and partly the result of his own natural inclination. He discovered young that he loved pleasing women, but he never had to learn how to interest a woman.

Unlike most men, he never had to find ways to make a woman notice him; he couldn't help but be noticed; he sought ways to get away, occasionally. He never had to think about how to meet a woman; women went out of their way to meet him; some threw themselves at him. He never had to entice a woman to spend her time with him; women couldn't get enough of him. And he never had to learn how to handle loss, or a woman's anger, or his own blundering mistakes. No one imagined that a man with his obvious Gifts wouldn't know how.

Jondalar's reaction when something didn't go right was to withdraw, try to keep his feelings under control, and hope that somehow it would sort itself out. He hoped that he would be forgiven, or his mistakes overlooked, and usually that was what happened. He didn't know what to do when Ayla saw him with Marona, and Ayla wasn't any more adept at handling those kinds of situations.

From the time she was first found by the Clan as a five-year, she had struggled to fit in, to make herself acceptable so they would not turn her out. The Clan didn't cry emotional tears and hers disturbed them, so she learned to hold them back. The Clan didn't display anger or pain or other strong emotions—it was not considered proper—so she learned not to show hers. To be a good Clan woman, she learned what was expected of her, and tried to behave the way she was expected to behave. She had tried to do the same with the Zelandonii.

But now she was at a loss. It seemed obvious to her that she had not learned how to be a good Zelandonii woman. People were upset with her, some people hated her, and Jondalar didn't love her. He had been ignoring her, and she had tried to provoke him to respond to her, but his brutal attack on Laramar was completely unexpected, and she felt, beyond all doubt, that it was entirely her fault. She had seen his compassion, and his love, and had seen him control his strong feelings when they were living with the Mamutoi. She thought she knew him. Now she was convinced she didn't know him at all. She had been trying to maintain a semblance of normality by sheer force of will, but she was tired from lying awake too many nights, too full of worry, pain, and anger to sleep, and what she needed desperately was calm surroundings and rest.

Perhaps Zelandoni had been a little too interested in learning about the Clan root, or she might have been more perceptive, but Ayla had always been a case apart. They didn't have enough common points of reference. Their backgrounds were far too different. Just when she thought she really understood the young woman, she'd find out that what she thought was true about Ayla was not.

"I don't want to make it a big issue if you really feel we shouldn't, Ayla, but if you could tell me something about how to prepare this root, perhaps we can work out a small experiment. Just to see if it might be useful. It would be just for the zelandonia, of course. What do you think?" Zelandoni said.

In Ayla's troubled state, even the terrifying black void struck her as a restful place, a place to get away from all the turmoil around her. And if she didn't come back, what difference would it make? Jondalar didn't love her anymore. She would miss her daughter—Ayla felt a tight knot grip her stomach—then thought Jonayla would probably be better off without her. The child was missing Jondalar. If she wasn't there, he would come back and take care of her again. And there were so many people who loved her, she would be well cared for.

"It's not that complicated, Zelandoni," Ayla said. "Essentially the roots are chewed to a mash and spit into a bowl of water. But they are hard to chew, and it takes a long time, and the one who is preparing it is not supposed to swallow any of the juice. It could be that it's a necessary ingredient, the juice that accumulates in the mouth," Ayla said.

"That's all? It seems to me if you just use a small amount, like one would test anything new, it shouldn't be that dangerous," Zelandoni said.

"There are some Clan rituals involved. The medicine woman who prepares the root for the mog-urs is supposed to purify herself first, bathe in a river using soaproot, and she is not supposed to wear clothing. Iza told me that was so the woman would be unsullied and open, with nothing hidden, so that she would not contaminate the holy men, the mog-urs. The Mog-ur,

Creb, painted my body with red and black colors, mostly circles around the female parts, to isolate them, I think," Ayla said. "It is a very sacred ceremony to the Clan."

"We could use the new cave you found. It is a very Sacred Place, and private. This would be a good use for it," the First said. "Anything else?"

"No, except when I tried the root with Mamut, he made sure that the people of the Lion Camp kept chanting so we would have something to hold on to, something that would keep us tethered to this world, and help us find our way back." She hesitated, looked down at the empty cup still in her hands, and added softly, "I'm not sure how, but Mamut said Jondalar may have helped bring us back."

"We will make sure all the zelandonia are there. They are very good at sustained chanting. Does it make any difference what is chanted?" the First asked.

"I don't think so. Just something familiar," Ayla said.

"When should we plan to do it?" Zelandoni asked, more excited than she thought she would be.

"I don't think it matters."

"Tomorrow morning? As soon as you can get everything ready?"

Ayla shrugged, as if she didn't care. At that moment, she didn't. "It's as good a time as any, I suppose," she said.

39

Jondalar was filled with as much anxiety and despair as Ayla. He had tried to avoid everyone as much as possible since the big ceremony where everyone was told about men and why they were created. He recalled parts of that night only vaguely. He did remember smashing Laramar in the face over and over again, and he couldn't erase from his mind the picture of that man moving up and down on top of Ayla. When he woke up the next day, his head was pounding, and he was still somewhat dizzy and very nauseous. He couldn't remember ever being so sick the next day, and wondered what was in the drinks he consumed.

Danug was there and he thought he ought to feel grateful to him, but he didn't know why. He asked Danug questions, trying to fill in the blanks. As Jondalar learned what he had done, he started to recall what had happened and was appalled, and full of remorse and shame. He had never much liked Laramar, but nothing he had ever done could be as bad as what Jondalar had done to him. He was so filled with self-hatred, he could not think of anything else. He was sure everyone felt the same way about him, and he was convinced that Ayla could not possibly love him anymore. How could anyone love someone so despicable?

Part of him wanted to leave everything behind and just go, as far away as he could get, but something held him back. He told himself he had to face his punishment, at least find out what it would be and somehow make amends, but it was more that things felt unfinished and he couldn't go leaving everything so unresolved. And deep inside, he wasn't sure he could simply walk away from Ayla and Jonayla. He couldn't bear the thought of never seeing them again, even if only from a distance.

His mind became a confusion of pain, guilt, and desperation. He could think of nothing he might do to make his life right again, and every time he saw anyone, he was sure they were looking at him with the same disgust and loathing that he felt about himself. Part of his self-recrimination stemmed from the fact that as dispicably as he'd behaved, and as ashamed as he was, every time he closed his eyes to try to sleep at night, he would see Laramar on top of Ayla, and feel the same rage and frustration he'd felt then. He knew in his heart that under the same circumstances, he would do it again.

Jondalar's mind dwelled on his problems constantly. He could hardly think of anything else. It was an incessant itch, like continually picking on the scab of a minor cut, never giving it a chance to heal, making it worse and worse until it became a running infection. He tried to get away from people as often as he could, and began taking long walks, usually beside the bank of The River, most often upstream. Each time he went he'd walk a little farther, stay a little longer, but he always reached a point where he could not go on and would have to turn around and walk back. Occasionally, he would get Racer and instead of walking along the river would ride out across the open grassland. He resisted taking his horse too often because it was then that he was most tempted to keep on going, but this day he wanted to ride out and put some distance between himself and the Camp.

As soon as she was fully awake, Ayla got up and went to The River. She hadn't slept well; at first she was too edgy and restless to fall asleep, and then she was awakened by dreams that she couldn't quite remember, but that left her uneasy. She thought about what she needed to do to make the Clan ceremony as close to correct as possible. While she looked for soaproot to purify herself, she also kept an eye out for a nodule of flint or even a leftover piece of reasonable size. She wanted to make a cutting tool in the Clan way that she could use to cut off a piece of leather to make a Clan amulet.

When she came to the mouth of the small stream as it emptied into The River, she turned to follow it instead. She had to walk upstream some distance before she found a few soaproot plants, in the woods behind the camp of the Ninth Cave. It was late in the season and most had been picked, and then the variety she found wasn't the same plant that the Clan used, and she had wanted the ritual to be right. Although, since she was a woman, it would never be a Clan ceremony anyway. Only men of the Clan consumed the roots. The woman's job was only to prepare them. As she stooped to pull the soaproots out, she thought she caught a glimpse of Jondalar in the woods, walking alongside the small stream, but when she stood up, she didn't see him and wondered if it was her imagination.

The stallion was glad to see Jondalar. The other horses were, too, but he didn't want to take them. He was in the mood for a long run alone. When they reached the open plains, Jondalar urged the horse into a thundering gallop across the land. Racer seemed just as eager to live up to his name. Jondalar wasn't paying much attention to where they were going, or where they were. Suddenly, he was literally jerked out of his moody meditation when he heard a loud belligerent neigh, the sound of hoofs, and felt his mount begin to rear. They were in the middle of a herd of horses. It was only his years of riding and quick reflexes that enabled him to keep his seat. He lunged forward and grabbed a handful of the stand-up mane of the steppe horse and held on, struggling to calm the stallion and get him back under control. Racer was a healthy stallion in his prime. Though he'd never had the experience of living in the auxiliary male herd that stayed near the fringes of a primary herd of females and young, keeping the herd stallion constantly on guard and ready to defend his own, or of the play-fighting with other young males as he was growing up, yet he was instinctively ready to challenge the herd male.

Jondalar's first thought was to get his horse as far away from the herd as possible, as fast as he could, but it was all he could do to turn the stallion around and head back toward the Campsite. When Racer settled down and they were finally heading steadily back, Jondalar began to wonder if it was fair to keep the virile stallion away from other horses, and for the first time, he seriously contemplated the idea of letting him go. He wasn't ready to give him up yet, but he began to rethink taking long rides alone on the brown stallion.

On the way back, he found himself moodily introspective again. He remembered the day of the big meeting, and watching Ayla sitting stiffly while Brukeval reviled her. He had ached to comfort her, to force Brukeval to stop, to tell him he was wrong. He had completely understood everything Zelandoni said; he'd heard most of it over the years from Ayla and he was more ready than most to accept it. The thing that was new to him was the name given to the relationship—"far mother," shortened to "fa'ther"—and he thought about Zelandoni's final words, that the men would name the boys; fathers would name their sons. He said the word over to himself. Father. He was a father. He was Jonayla's father.

He wasn't fit to be Jonayla's father! It would shame her to name him her father. He had nearly killed a man, with his fists. If it hadn't been for Danug, he would have. Ayla had lost a baby when she was alone, in the deep passages of Fountain Rocks Cave, and he wasn't there to help her. What if the child she had lost was a boy? If she hadn't lost it and it was a boy, would he have been the one to name him? What would it be like to decide on a name for a child?

What did it matter? He would never be able to name a child. He would never have any more children. He had lost his mate; he would have to leave his hearth. After Zelandoni had closed the meeting, he had avoided the conversations that everyone was having and had hurried back to the fa'lodge so he wouldn't have to see Ayla, or Jonayla.

He was still feeling the same when the rest of the fa'lodge started walking toward the Lanzadonii camp for the big feast the next day, but after everyone had been gone for some time, Jondalar couldn't seem to stop himself from dwelling on all his wrongs. Finally, he couldn't stand it inside the lodge, with his mind going over and over the same things, blaming himself, berating himself, scourging himself. He went out and headed for The River to take another long walk. Since his near encounter with the stallion when they ran into a herd of mares,

Racer seemed more excitable and Jondalar decided not to ride him. As he started walking upstream, he was surprised to see that Wolf had caught up with him. Jondalar was glad to see the carnivore and stopped to greet him, catching the great head by his ruff, which was growing thicker now and more luxurious.

"Wolf! What brings you here? Are you tired of all the noise and commotion, too? Well, you're welcome to join me," he said with enthusiasm. The animal responded with a low growl of pleasure.

Wolf had been so involved with Jonayla, after being away from her for so long, and with Ayla, who had been his primary focus since the day she pulled the frightened four-week pup from his cold and lonely den, that he hadn't spent much time with the third human he considered to be an essential member of his pack. On the way back to the camp of the Ninth Cave after the meal he'd been given, he saw Jondalar heading toward The River and ran after the man, ahead of Jonayla. He turned back to look at her, and whined.

"Go ahead, Wolf," the child said, signaling him on. "Go with Jondalar."

She had seen the man's great unhappiness, and she was more than aware that her mother was just as sad, for all that she tried not to show it. She didn't know exactly what, but the child knew something was terribly wrong and it gave her a fearful knot in the pit of her stomach. More than anything she wanted her family back together, and that included her 'Thona and Weemar, and Wolf and the horses, too. Maybe Jondy needs to see you, Wolf, and be with you, like I did, Jonayla thought.

Ayla had been thinking about Jondalar, or more precisely, about using the pool in the small river for her ceremonial bath, and that made her think of Jondalar. She wanted the quiet and privacy of the secluded place for the purification cleansing, but she hadn't been able to go back since she found Jondalar there with Marona. She knew there was flint in that area; Jondalar had found some, but she didn't see any, and didn't think she would have time to look farther afield. She knew Jondalar always had a few good hunks of flint around, but she didn't even consider asking him. He wasn't talking to her these days. She would just have to make do with a Zelandonii knife and awl to cut the hide and to pierce holes around the edge for the drawstring, even if it was another deviation from Clan custom.

She found a flattish rock, carried it closer to the pool in the small river and then with another rounder stone, she pounded the foamy saponifying ingredients from the soaproots on it, mixed with a little water. Then she stepped into the quiet backwater inside a curve at the edge of the pool and began to smooth the slippery foam on her body. The bottom dropped off quickly as she moved out from the bank to rinse. She ducked her head under, swam a few strokes, then returned to wash her hair. As Ayla bathed in the pool, she thought about the Clan.

She remembered her childhood with Brun's clan as peaceful and safe, with Iza and Creb there to love her and take care of her. Everyone knew from the time they were born what was expected of them, and there was no allowance for deviation. Roles were clearly defined. Everyone knew where they fit, knew their rank, knew their jobs, knew their place. Life was stable and secure. They didn't have to worry about new ideas changing things.

Why was she the one who had to bring changes that affected everyone? That some would hate her for? Looking back, her life with the Clan seemed so reassuring, she wondered why she had struggled so hard against the restrictions. The ordered life of the Clan appealed to her now. There was a comforting security to a strictly regulated life.

Yet, she was glad she had taught herself to hunt, though it was against Clan traditions. She was a woman and women of the Clan did not hunt, but if she hadn't known how, she wouldn't be alive now, even if she almost died for it after they found out. The first time she was cursed, when Brun expelled her from the clan, he limited the time to only one moon. It was the beginning of winter and they all expected her to die, but the hunting she was cursed for had saved her life from the curse. Maybe I should have died then, she thought.

She had defied the way of the Clan again when she ran away with Durc, but she couldn't let them expose her newborn son to the mercy of the elements and carnivores just because they thought he was deformed. Brun had spared them, though Broud objected. He had never made her life easy. When he became leader and cursed her, it was forever and for no good reason, and that time she was finally forced to leave the clan. Hunting saved her then, too. She would never have survived in the valley, if she wasn't a hunter, and if she hadn't known that she could live alone if she had to.

Ayla was still thinking about the Clan, and how to handle the rituals associated with the roots properly when she returned to the camp. She saw Jonayla sitting with Proleva and Marthona. They waved and beckoned to her.

"Come, have something to eat," Proleva said. Wolf had grown tired of walking with the melancholy man, who did nothing but shuffle along, and had come back to find Jonayla. He was on the other side of the fire gnawing a bone, and looked up. Ayla walked in their direction. She gave her daughter a hug, then held her off and looked at her with a strange sadness and hugged her again, almost too hard.

"Your hair is wet, mother," Jonayla said, squirming out of the way.

"I just washed it," Ayla said, petting the large wolf, who had come to greet her. She took the handsome head between her hands, looked deeply into his eyes, then hugged him with fervor. When she stood up, the wolf looked up at her with anticipation. She patted the front of her shoulders. He jumped up, steadied himself with his paws on her shoulders, licked her neck and face, then took her jaw gently in his teeth and held it. When he let go, she returned the wolf signal of pack membership, taking his muzzle in her teeth for a moment. She hadn't done that for a while and Ayla thought he seemed pleased.

Proleva let out the breath she'd been holding when Wolf dropped down. That particular bit of wolfish behavior from Ayla was disturbing no matter how many times she saw it. Watching the woman exposing her neck to the teeth of the huge wolf always unnerved her, and made her realize that the friendly, well-behaved animal was a powerful wolf who could easily kill any one of the humans he mingled with so freely.

After she caught her breath and settled her apprehensions, Proleva commented, "Help yourself, Ayla. There's plenty. This

morning's meal was easy to make. There was a lot left over
from yesterday's feast. I'm glad we decided to make a meal
together with the Lanzadonii. I liked working with Jerika and
Joplaya, and several of the other women. I feel as though I
know them better now."

Ayla felt a pang of regret. She wished she hadn't been so
busy with the zelandonia; she would have liked to help with
the feast. Working together was a good way to get to know
people better. Being wrapped up in her own problems didn't
help either; she could have gotten there earlier, she thought, as
she picked up one of the extra cups that were set out for those
who forgot their own, and dipped a cup of chamomile tea from
the large, kerfed wooden cooking box. Tea was always the first
thing made in the morning.

"The aurochs is particularly good and juicy, Ayla. They've
started to put on their winter fat, and Proleva just reheated
it. You should try some," Marthona urged, noticing that she
wasn't taking any food. "Food holders are over there." She
indicated a stack of odd-size but generally flat pieces of wood,
bone, and ivory that were used as plates.

Trees that had been felled and broken for firewood often
produced large splinters that could be quickly trimmed and
smoothed into plates and dishes; shoulder and pelvic bones
from various deer, bison, and aurochs were roughly shaped
to a reasonable size for the same purpose. The tusks of mammoths could be chipped off, much like flint, but making much
larger flakes that were used for plates as well.

Mammoth ivory could even be preshaped by cutting a circular groove first with a burin chisel. Then, using a solid end-
piece of antler or horn with the pointed tip held at just the right
angle in the groove of the circle, and with practice and a bit
of luck, a blow from a hammerstone on the back of it would
detach an ivory flake with the precut shape. But that much
work was usually done only for objects meant to be given as
gifts or for other special purposes. Such preshaped flakes of
ivory with smooth, slightly rounded outside surfaces could be
used for more than dishes. Decorative images could be etched
on them.

"Thank you, Marthona, but I have to get some things and go to see Zelandoni," Ayla said. Suddenly she stopped and hunkered down in front of the older woman, who was sitting on a small stool woven together out of reeds, cattail leaves, and flexible branches. "I really do want to thank you, for being so kind to me since the first day I arrived. I don't remember my own mother, only Iza, the Clan woman who raised me, but I like to think that my real mother would have been like you."

"I think of you as a daughter, Ayla," Marthona said, more moved than she would have expected. "My son was lucky to find you"; then she shook her head slightly. "Sometimes I wish he were more like you."

Ayla hugged her, then turned to Proleva. "Thank you, too, Proleva. You've been such a good friend to me, and I appreciate, more than I can say, the way you've taken care of Jonayla when I had to stay back at the Ninth Cave, and when I've been busy here." She hugged Proleva too. "I wish Folara were here, but I know she's busy with the preparations for her Matrimonial. I think Aldanor is a good man. I'm so happy for her. I have to go now," she said suddenly, hugged her daughter again, then hurried to the dwelling, misty-eyed with the tears she was holding back.

"I wonder what that was all about," Proleva said.

"If I didn't know better, I'd think she almost sounded like she was saying good-bye," Marthona said.

"Is mother going someplace, 'Thona?" Jonayla asked.

"I don't think so. At least no one has said anything to me."

Ayla stayed in the summer dwelling for a while making preparations. First she cut out a roughly circular shape from the belly of the skin of the red deer she had brought with her to the Summer Meeting. She had found the soft buckskin hide the day before folded up on her sleeping roll. When she asked Jonayla who had cured the deer skin, she was told, "Everybody did."

Cordage, fibrous rope, twine, thread, tough sinew, and strips of leather thong, in various sizes, were always useful and easy to make without having to think about it, once the techniques were learned. Most people busied themselves making things when they were sitting around talking or listening to stories, out of materials that were collected whenever they were found. So there was always some cordage around for anyone to use. Ayla got some strips of leather thong and a long piece of thin, flexible rope that were hanging on pegs pounded into posts near the entrance. After she had cut off the belly part into a circular shape, she folded the rest of the hide, then coiled up the rope and put it on top. She measured out a length of the leather thong around her neck, added additional length, then threaded it through the holes she cut around the edge of the leather circle.

She seldom wore her amulet anymore, not even her more modern one. Most Zelandonii wore necklaces, and it was hard to wear a lumpy leather pouch and a necklace at the same time. Instead, she usually kept her amulet in her medicine bag, which she customarily wore attached to a belt or waist thong. It wasn't a Clan medicine bag. She had thought about making another one several times, but never seemed to find the time. Releasing the drawstring that held her medicine bag closed, she searched inside and pulled out the small decorated pouch, her amulet, that was full of odd-shaped objects. She undid the knots and poured the strange collection of objects into her hand. They were the signs from her totem that signified important moments in her life. Most of them were given to her by the Spirit of the Great Cave Lion after she had made a critical decision as a sign that she had made the right choice, but not all.

The piece of red ocher that was the first object to go into the bag was worn smooth. It was given to her by Iza when she was accepted into the Clan. Ayla put it into the new amulet. The piece of black manganese dioxide that was given to her when she became a medicine woman was also worn down just from being inside the small pouch with the other objects for so long. The red and black material that was often used for coloration had left its residue on the other objects in the pouch. The mineral objects could be brushed off, such as the fossil cast of a seashell, the sign from her totem that her decision to hunt was proper for her, even though she was female.

He must have known even then that I would need to hunt if

I was going to survive, she thought. My Cave Lion even told Brun to let me hunt, although then, only with the sling. The disk of mammoth ivory, her hunting talisman that had been given to her when she was declared the Woman Who Hunts, had absorbed color that couldn't be brushed off, mostly red from the ocher.

She picked up the piece of iron pyrite and rubbed it against her tunic. It was her favorite sign; it was the one that told her she had been right to run away with Durc. If she hadn't, he would have been exposed without anyone thinking any more about it, since he had been judged deformed. When she took him and hid, knowing she could die as well, it made Brun and Creb stop and think.

The colored dust clung to the clear quartz crystal but didn't discolor it; that was the sign she found that told her she had made the right decision to stop looking for her people and stay in the valley of horses for a while. It always bothered her when she saw the black manganese stone. She picked it up again and held it in her closed fist. It held the spirits of all the people of the Clan. She had exchanged a piece of her spirit for it so that when she saved someone's life they incurred no obligation to her, since she already had a piece of everyone's spirit.

When Iza died, Creb, the Mog-ur, had taken her medicine woman stone from her before she was buried so she would not take the entire Clan to the spirit world with her, but no one took her stone when Broud cursed her with death. Goov had not been Mog-ur for very long, and it came as such a shock to everyone when Broud did it; no one remembered to get the stone from her, and she forgot to return it. What would happen to the Clan if she still had the stone when she passed to the next world?

She put all of her totem's signs into the new pouch, and knew she would keep them there from then on. It felt right for her Clan totem signs to be in a Clan amulet pouch. As she pulled the drawstring tight, she wondered, as she often had, why she had never been given a sign from her totem when she decided to leave the Mamutoi and go with Jondalar. Had she already become a child of the Mother? Had the Mother told her totem she didn't need a sign? Had she been given a more

subtle sign that she didn't recognize? Or—a new and more
frightening thought came to her—had she made the wrong decision? She felt a cold chill. For the first time in a long time,
Ayla clutched her amulet and sent a silent thought asking for
his protection to the spirit of the Great Cave Lion.

When she left the temporary dwelling, Ayla was carrying a
folded-up buckskin hide, a leather rucksack lumpy with the
objects it held, and her Clan medicine bag. There were several more people around the campfire, and she waved to them
as she left, but it wasn't the usual beckoning, "come-back"
motion with her palm facing inward, toward herself, which
commonly signified a temporary separation, acknowledging
that she would see them soon. She had raised her hand, palm
facing out, and moved it slightly from side to side. Marthona
frowned at the signal.

As she started walking upstream along the small river, a
quicker way toward the cave she had found a few years before,
Ayla was beginning to wonder whether she should go through
with this ceremony. Yes, Zelandoni would be disappointed,
and so would the rest of the zelandonia who were preparing
to assist, but it was more dangerous than they realized. When
she agreed to the ceremony the day before, she had been so
depressed, she didn't care if she got lost in the black void, but
she was feeling better this morning, especially after her bath
in The River, and seeing Jonayla, and Wolf, not to mention
Marthona and Proleva. She wasn't as ready to face that terrifying black void now. Maybe she should tell Zelandoni that she
had changed her mind.

She hadn't thought about the danger she was facing while
she was making her preliminary preparations, but she had felt
uncomfortable about her inability to perform all of the rituals
in the proper way. That was a very important aspect of Clan
ceremony, unlike the Zelandonii, who were more tolerant of
deviation. Even the words of the Mother's Song varied slightly
from Cave to Cave, which was a favored topic of discussion
among the zelandonia, and that was the most important Elder
Legend of all.

If such a Legend had been a sacred part of Clan ceremonies,
it would have been memorized and recited in precisely the

same way every time it was repeated, at least among the clans that had regular direct contact with each other. Even those clans from distant regions would have had a version that was very close. That was why she could communicate in the sacred sign language of the Clan with the clans in this region though it was a year's travel away from the clan she grew up with. There were minor differences, but it was amazingly similar.

Since it was a Clan ceremony she would be performing, using powerful roots prepared according to Clan procedures, she felt everything should be done as close as possible according to Clan tradition. She believed it was the only way she could hope to maintain any control, and she was beginning to have doubts if even that would help.

She was walking past the wooded area with her mind deep in thought, when she nearly bumped into someone coming out from behind a tree. She was startled to find herself practically in Jondalar's arms. He was even more surprised and at a complete loss about what to do. His first impulse was to finish what the accident had started and put his arms around her. He'd been longing to do it for so long, but catching a glimpse of her shocked expression, he jumped back, assuming somehow that her surprise meant revulsion, that she didn't want him to touch her. Her reaction to his instant avoidance was that he didn't want her, couldn't stand to be near her.

They stared at each other for a long moment. It was the closest they had been since she found him with Marona, and in their hearts, each yearned to prolong that moment, to broach the emotional distance that seemed to separate them. But a child running down the path they were on distracted them. They looked away for a moment and then couldn't quite look back.

"Uh, sorry," Jondalar said, aching to hold her but afraid she would rebuff him. He was so completely at a loss, he was looking around wildly, like an animal caught in a trap.

"Doesn't matter," Ayla said, looking down to hide the tears that were just too ready to flow these days. She didn't want him to see how terrible it made her feel to think that he couldn't stand to be close to her, that he couldn't wait to get away. Without looking up, she started walking again, hurrying before her overflowing eyes gave her away. Jondalar had to fight his own tears as he watched her almost running along the path in her hurry to get away from him.

Ayla continued along what had become a faint path toward the new cave. Although it was likely that every one of the entire family of Zelandonii people had been inside the new cave at least once, it wasn't used often. Because it was so beautiful and so unusual with its nearly white stone walls, it was considered a very spiritual, very sacred place, and still rather inviolable. The zelandonia and Cave leaders were still working out the appropriate times and ways to use it. Traditions hadn't been developed yet, it was too new.

As she approached the base of the small hill that held the cave, she noticed that the obstructing brush and the fallen tree, whose uplifted roots had originally exposed the opening to the underground chambers, were cleared away. Dirt and stones around the opening had also been removed, which enlarged the entrance.

Although she wasn't looking forward to the ceremony she had been preparing for, she had been excited about seeing the cave again, but the lighter mood that had almost made her decide to forgo this dangerous ceremony was gone. Her unhappiness matched the black void she was facing. What did it matter if she lost herself there? It couldn't be any worse than the way she felt at that moment. She was struggling to regain the self-control that seemed so elusive today. It almost seemed she had been on the verge of tears since she woke up.

She took a shallow stone bowl from her leather sack, and a fur package. Inside was a small, nearly watertight bag of fat with a stoppered end, which was wrapped and tied in the piece of fur to keep any seeping grease from damaging anything nearby. She found her package of lichen wicks, poured a little oil in the bowl, soaked a wick in it for a few moments, then pulled it out and leaned it against the edge of the bowl-shaped lamp. She was preparing to use her firestone to light it when she saw two more zelandonia walking up the path.

The sight of the zelandonia brought Ayla an added measure of composure. She was still new to their ranks, and wanted to keep their respect. They greeted each other and spoke of inconsequential matters; then one of them held the lamp while watching Ayla start a small fire on the ground with her fire-stone. Once the lamp was lit, she smothered the fire with dirt and all three entered the cave.

Once they passed through the warmth of the entrance area, and entered the total darkness of the inside, the temperature cooled to the ambient temperature of most caves, about fifty-five degrees. There was little conversation as they picked their way along exposed rocks and slippery clay with only a single lamp to show the way. By the time they reached a larger chamber, their eyes were so accustomed to the dark that the lights from many stone lamps seemed almost bright. Most of the zelandonia had already arrived and were waiting for Ayla.

"There you are, Zelandoni of the Ninth Cave," the First said. "Have you made all the preparations you think are necessary?"

"Not quite," Ayla said. "I still have to change. During the Clan ceremony, I would be naked except for my amulet and the colors painted on my body by the Mog-ur, when I make the drink. But it's too cold in the cave to be naked for very long, and besides, the mog-urs who drank the liquid wore clothes, so I will, too. I think it's important to stay as close to the Clan ceremony as possible, so I've decided to wear a wrap in the style of a Clan woman. I made a Clan amulet for my totem symbols, and to show that I am a medicine woman, I will wear my Clan medicine bag, although it is the objects in my amulet that are more important. It will enable the the Clan spirits to recognize me not only as a woman of the Clan, but as a medicine woman."

With all the zelandonia looking on with great curiosity, Ayla removed her clothing and began wrapping the soft, pliable deerhide around her, tying it on with a long cord in such a way as to leave pouches and folds to hold things. She thought about all the things she was doing that were not Clan, starting with her preparing the drink for herself instead of for the mog-urs. She was not a mog-ur—no woman of the Clan could be one—and she didn't know the rituals they performed to ready themselves for this ceremony, but she was a Zelandoni and she hoped that would make a difference once she reached the spirit world.

She took a small pouch out of her medicine bag. There was enough light from the many lamps to show its deep red ocher color, the color most sacred to the Clan, and then she took a wooden bowl out of the leather packframe. She had made the bowl some time ago in the style of the Clan to show Marthona, who, with her aesthetic sense, appreciated the simplicity and craftsmanship. Ayla had planned to give it to the woman and now she was glad she still had it. If it wasn't the special bowl that had been used only for this root for the many generations of Iza's ancestors, it was at least a wooden bowl made in the painstaking way the Clan made them.

"I will need some water," Ayla said as she undid the knots of the red pouch. She emptied the bag of roots into her hand.

"May I see them?" Zelandoni asked.

Ayla held them out to her, but there was nothing distinctive about them. They were just dried roots. "I'm not sure how much to use," she said, picking out two small pieces, hoping it would be correct. "I've only done this twice before, and I don't have Iza's memories."

A few of the zelandonia there had heard her speak about Clan memories, but most had no idea what she meant. She had tried to explain them to Zelandoni Who Was First, but since she didn't know exactly what they were herself, it was hard to explain to someone else.

Someone poured water into her wooden bowl, and Ayla drank a little to wet her mouth. She remembered how dry the roots were and how hard they were to chew. "I am ready," she said, and before she could change her mind, she put the roots in her mouth and began to chew.

It took a long time to soften them up enough to bite through, and though she did try to avoid swallowing her own saliva, it was difficult, and she thought to herself, since I'm the one who's going to drink it, maybe it doesn't matter too much. She chewed and chewed and chewed and chewed. It seemed to take forever, but finally her mouth held a soggy pulp, which she spit into the bowl. She stirred it with her finger, and watched the liquid turn a milky white.

Zelandoni was looking over her shoulder. "Is that what it's supposed to do?" She seemed to be trying to detect its odor.

"Yes," Ayla said. She could feel its primeval taste in her mouth. "Would you like to smell it?"

"It smells ancient," the woman said, "like a deep cool wet forest full of moss and mushrooms. May I taste it?"

She was going to refuse. It was so sacred to the Clan, Iza couldn't even make some just to show her how, and for a moment, Ayla was appalled that Zelandoni would ask. But then she realized this whole experiment was so far from anything the Clan would do that it could hardly matter if Zelandoni took a drink. Ayla held the bowl to the woman's lips and watched her take much more than a sip, and pulled it back before she took too much.

Then she held it to her own mouth and drank it down quickly, making sure there was none left for anyone else to sample. That was how she got in trouble the first time. Iza had told her there was not supposed to be any left, but she had made too much, and after his first taste, The Mog-ur knew it was too strong. He controlled how much each man drank, and left some in the bottom of the bowl. Ayla had found it later, after she had ingested too much from chewing the root and had too much of the women's drink besides. She was in such a confused state, she drank the rest down so none would be left. This time, she would make sure no one else would inadvertently be tempted to try it.

"When should we start to chant for you?" the First asked.

Ayla almost forgot about the chanting. "Probably should have started already," she said, a slight slur in her voice already.

The First was feeling the effects of her rather large taste as well, and struggled to keep her control as she signaled the zelandonia to begin chanting. That is a powerful root, she thought, and I only had one drink. What must Ayla be feeling now after all she drank? Zelandoni thought.

The ancient taste was familiar, and it brought on feelings Ayla would never forget, memories and associations of the other times she had tasted the drink, and of times long past. She felt the cool and damp of a deep forest, as though she were enveloped within it, with trees so huge it was difficult to find a way around and between them as she climbed up the steep side of a mountain followed by the horse. Lichen, damply soft and silvery grayish green, draped the trees, and moss covered the ground and rocks and logs of dead trees in a continuous carpet that ranged in shades from bright true green to deep pine green to rich earthy brownish green and all shades in between.

Ayla could smell fungus, mushrooms of every size and shape: fragile white wings sprouting from fallen trees, thick woody shelves attached to old stumps, large dense sponge-like brown capped, tiny delicate thin stemmed. There were honey-colored tight clusters, compact round spheres, shiny red tops with white spots, tall smooth caps that melted to black ooze, ghostly white perfect caps of death, and many more. She knew them all, tasted them all, felt them all.

She was in a great delta of a huge river, carried by a stream of muddy brown water, breaking through thick stands of tall phragmite reeds and cattails, and floating islands with trees and wolves that climbed them, spinning round and round in a small leather-covered bowl boat, rising up and floating on a cushion of air.

Ayla didn't know her knees had buckled as she went limp and dropped to the ground. She was picked up by several zelandonia and carried to a resting place that Zelandoni had thought to have brought into the cave for her. The First almost wished she had one as well as she reached for her strong padded wicker stool. She struggled to stay aware, to watch Ayla, and felt a dark tinge of worry start to develop in the back of her mind.

Ayla was feeling peaceful, quiet, sinking into a soft mist that was drawing her deeper in, until she was surrounded. It thickened around her into a fog that obscured all vision, then became a heavy damp cloud. She felt swallowed by it. She was suffocating, struggled to breathe, gasped for air, then felt herself begin to move.

She was moving faster and faster, caught in the middle of the suffocating cloud, rushing so fast it took her breath away, left her with no air. The cloud wrapped itself around her, squeezed her, pushing in from all sides, contracting, expanding, contracting, like something alive. It forced her to move with accelerating velocity until she fell into a deep, black empty space, a place as black as the inside of a cave, mindless, terrifying.

It would have been less terrifying if she had simply dropped into sleep, become unconscious, as it appeared she had to those watching, but she was not. She couldn't move, didn't really have a desire to move, but when she tried to focus her will to move something, even just a finger, she could not. She couldn't even feel her finger, or any other part of herself. She couldn't open her eyes, or turn her head; she had no volition, no will, but she could hear. At some level, she was aware. As though from a distance and yet with great clarity, she could hear the chant of the zelandonia; she could hear the faint murmur of voices from one corner, though she couldn't make out what they were saying; she could even hear her own heart beating.

Each donier chose a sound, a tone with a pitch and timbre each one was comfortable with on a sustained level. When they wanted to maintain a continuous chant, several of the doniers would begin to make their tone. The combination might or might not be harmonic; it didn't matter. Before the first one got out of breath, another voice would join in, and then another, and another at random intervals. The result was a droning interweaving fugue of tones that could go on indefinitely, if there were enough people to provide sufficient rest for those people who had to stop for a while.

For Ayla, it was a comforting sound that was there, but that tended to fade into the background as her mind observed scenes only she could see behind her closed eyelids, visions with the lucid incoherence of vivid dreams. It felt as though she were wide awake dreaming. At first, she kept gaining speed in the black space; she knew it though the void remained unchanged. She was terrified and alone. Achingly alone. There were no sensations, no taste, no smell, no sound, no sight, no touch, as though none ever existed or ever would, just her conscious, screaming mind.

An eternity passed. Then, at a great distance, barely discernible, a faint glimmer of light. She reached for it, strove for it. Anything, anything at all was better than nothing. Her striving pulled her faster, the light expanded into an amorphous, barely perceptible blur, and for a moment she wondered if her mind might have any other effects on the state she was in. The indistinct light thickened to a cloudiness and darkened with colors, alien colors with unknown names.

She was sinking into the cloud, falling through it, faster and faster, and then she fell out the bottom. A strangely familiar landscape opened up below her full of repetitive geometric shapes, squares and sharp angles, bright, shining, filled with light, repeating, climbing up. Nothing with such straight, sharp shapes existed in her familiar natural world. White ribbons seemed to flow along the ground in this strange place, reaching straight into the distance, with strange animals racing along it.

As she drew closer, she saw people, masses of squirming, wriggling people, all pointing their fingers at her. "Yoooou, yooou, yooou," they were saying; it was almost a chant. She saw a figure standing alone. It was a man, a man of mixed spirits. As she got closer, she thought he looked familiar, but not quite. At first she thought it was Echozar, but then it seemed to be Brukeval, and the people were saying, "Yoooou, yooou did it, yoooou brought the Knowledge, you did it."

"No!" her mind screamed. "It was the Mother. She gave me the Knowledge. Where's the Mother?"

"The Mother is gone. Only the Son remains," the people said. "You did it." She looked at the man and suddenly knew who he was, though his face was in shadow and she couldn't see him clearly.

"I couldn't help it. I was cursed. I had to leave my son. Broud made me go," her soundless voice cried out.

"The Mother is gone. Only the Son remains."

In her thoughts, Ayla frowned. What did it mean? Suddenly the world below took on different dimension, but still ominous and otherworldly. The people were gone, and the strange geometric shapes. It was an empty, desolate, windblown prairie. Two men appeared, brothers whom no one would guess were brothers. One was tall and blond like Jondalar, the other, older one, she knew was Durc though his face was still shadowed. The two brothers approached each other from opposite directions, and she felt great anxiety as though something terrible was about to happen, something she had to prevent. With a shock of terror, she was sure one of her sons would kill the other. With arms raised as though to strike, they drew closer. She strained to reach them.

Suddenly Mamut was there, holding her back. "It is not what you think. It is a symbol, a message," he said. "Watch and wait."

A third man appeared on the windblown steppes. It was Broud, looking at her with a glare of pure hatred. The first two men reached each other, then both turned to face Broud.

"Curse him, curse him, curse him with death," Durc motioned.

"But he is your father, Durc," Ayla thought with silent apprehension. "You should not be the one to curse him."

"He is cursed already," her other son said. "You did it, you kept the black stone. They are all cursed."

"No! No!" Ayla screamed. "I'll give it back. I can still give it back."

"There is nothing you can do, Ayla. It is your destiny," Mamut said.

When she turned to face him, Creb was standing beside him. "You gave us Durc," the old Mog-ur signed. "That was also your destiny. Durc is part of the Others, but he's Clan, too. The Clan is doomed, it will be no more, only your kind will go on, and the ones like Durc, the children of mixed spirits. Not many, perhaps, but enough. It won't be the same; he will become like the Others, but it is something. Durc is the son of the Clan, Ayla. He's the only son of the Clan."

Ayla heard a woman weeping, and when she looked, the scene had changed again. It was dark; they were deep in a cave. Then lamps were lit and she saw a woman holding a man in her arms. The man was her tall, blond son, and when the woman looked up, to her surprise Ayla saw herself, but she was not clear. It was as though she was seeing herself in a reflector. A man came and looked down at them. She looked up and saw Jondalar.

"Where is my son?" he asked her. "Where is my son?"

"I gave him to the Mother," the reflected Ayla cried. "The Great Earth Mother wanted him. She is powerful. She took him from me."

Suddenly, Ayla heard the crowd, and saw the strange geometric shapes. "The Earth Mother grows weak," the voices chanted. "Her children ignore Her. When they no longer Honor Her, She will be ravished."

"No," the reflected Ayla wailed. "Who will feed us? Who will care for us? Who will provide for us, if we don't Honor Her?"

"The Mother is gone. Only the Son remains. The Mother's children are no longer children. They have left the Mother behind. They have the Knowledge; they have come of age, as she knew someday they would." The woman still wept, but she wasn't Ayla anymore. She was the Mother, weeping because her children were gone.

Ayla felt herself being pulled out of the cave; she was weeping, too. The voices became faint, as though they were chanting from a great distance away. She was moving again, high above a vast grassy plain, full of great herds. Aurochs were stampeding, and horses were racing to keep up with them. Bison and deer were running, and ibex. She drew closer, began to see individual animals, the ones she had seen when she was called to the zelandonia, and the disguises that they had worn during the ceremony when they had given the Mother's new Gift to Her Children, when she recited the last verse of the Mother's Song.

Two bison bulls running past each other, great aurochs bulls marching toward each other, a huge cow almost flying in the air, and another one giving birth, a horse at the end of a passage falling down a cliff, many horses, most in colors, browns and reds and blacks, and Whinney with the spotted hide over her back and across her face, and the two sticklike antlers.

40

Zelandoni was not with Ayla on her arcane inward Journey, but she sensed it, and felt herself pulled toward it. Perhaps if she had consumed more of the drink, she might have been drawn in with Ayla and become lost in the enigmatic landscape induced by the root. As it was, she did lose control of her faculties for a period of time, and had her own difficulties.

The zelandonia weren't quite sure what was going on. Ayla appeared to be unconscious, and the First seemed close to it. She wasn't exactly dozing off, but she would slump down, and her eyes would glaze over as if she were gazing into some unseen distance. Then she would rouse herself and say things that didn't always make sense. She did not appear to be in control of the experiment, which was unusual in itself, and she definitely was not in control of herself, which made them all nervous. Those who knew her best were most alarmed, but they did not want to spread their concern among the rest.

The First shook herself awake, as if by an act of will. "Cold . . . cold . . . ," she said, then slumped over again and her eyes glazed. The next time she jerked herself awake, she shouted, "Cover . . . fur . . . cover Ayla . . . cold . . . so cold. Get hot . . ." Then she was gone again.

They had brought a few warm coverings with them, just because it was always cool in a cave. They had already put one on Ayla, but the Eleventh decided to add another one. When she happened to touch the young woman, she was surprised.

"She is cold, almost as cold as death," she said.

"Is she breathing?" the Third asked.

The Eleventh bent over and looked closely, noticed a slight

movement of her chest and felt a faint sigh of air from her barely open mouth. "Yes, she's breathing. But it's shallow."

"Do you think we should make some hot tea?" the Fifth asked.

"Yes, I think so, for both of them," the Third said.

"A stimulating tea or a soothing one?" said the Fifth.

"I don't know. Either one could react with that root in an unexpected way," the Third said.

"Let's try to ask the First. She's the one who should decide," the Eleventh said.

Her companions nodded. The three of them surrounded the large woman who was sitting on her stool, slumped over. The Third put her hand on the First's shoulder and gently nudged her, and then a little harder. Zelandoni jerked awake. "Do you want hot tea?" the Third asked.

"Yes! Yes!" the First said, loudly again, as though shouting helped her stay awake.

"Ayla, too?"

"Yes. Hot!"

"Tea to stimulate or soothe?" the Eleventh asked, also speaking loudly. The Zelandoni of the Fourteenth Cave walked over, frowning with concern.

"Stimul . . . No!" The First stopped, straining to concentrate. "Water! Just hot water!" she said. She shook herself again, trying to stay awake. "Help me up!"

"Are you sure you can stand?" the Third asked. "You don't want to fall."

"Help me up! Need to stay awake. Ayla needs . . . help." She started to fall off again, and shook herself violently. "Help me stand. Get hot . . . water. Not tea."

The Third, Eleventh, and Fourteenth all crowded around the hugely corpulent woman who was the First Among Those Who Served The Mother, and with some effort got her up on her feet. She wavered drunkenly, leaned heavily on two of the Zelandoni, and shook her head again. She closed her eyes and her expression took on a look of intense concentration. When she opened them, she was gritting her teeth with determination, but had stopped swaying.

"Ayla's in trouble," she said. "My fault. Should have known."

She was still having difficulty concentrating, thinking straight, but being up and moving around did help. The hot water did, too, if only to warm her. She felt cold, a deep, bone-chilling cold, and she knew it wasn't just being in the cave. "Too cold. Move her. Need fire. Warmth."

"You want us to move Ayla out of the cave?" the Fourteenth said.

"Yes. Too cold."

"Should we wake her?" the Eleventh asked.

"I don't think you can," the First said, "but try."

First they tried gently shaking her, then not so gently. Ayla didn't stir. They tried talking to her, then shouting, but they couldn't rouse her.

Zelandoni of the Third asked the First, "Should we continue chanting?"

"Yes! Chant! Don't stop! It's all she's got!" the Zelandoni who was First shouted.

The higher-ranked zelandonia gave a few instructions. Suddenly there was a flurry of activity as several people rushed outside and hurried to the zelandonia lodge, some to stir up a fire for hot water, others to get a litter to carry the young woman out of the cave. The rest renewed the chanting with fervor.

Several people were near the zelandonia lodge. A meeting of the couples planning to tie the knot at the Late Matrimonial had been planned later in the day, and a few of them had started to gather. Folara and Aldanor were among them. When several zelandonia came rushing toward the lodge, Folara and Aldanor looked at each other with concern.

"What's wrong? Why is everyone is such a hurry?" Folara asked.

"It's the new Zelandoni," a young man answered, one of the newer acolytes.

"You mean Ayla? Zelandoni of the Ninth?" Folara asked.

"Yes. She made a special drink using some kind of root, and the First said we have to get her out of the cave because it's too cold. She's not waking up," the acolyte answered.

They heard a commotion, and turned to look. A couple of strong young doniers were helping the First back from the cave.

She was having difficulty keeping her balance and finding her footing without stumbling. Folara had never seen Zelandoni so unstable. A wave of apprehension washed over her. The One Who Was First was always so completely self-assured, so positive. Even with her great size, she always moved with confidence and ease. It had been bad enough for the young woman to watch her mother weakening. It was utterly frightening to see someone she had always thought of as an unshakable force, a bulwark of security and strength, suddenly show such debility.

About the time that the First reached the lodge, another group of zelandonia appeared on the path leading down from the new cave carrying a litter, piled high with furs. As the procession approached, Folara and Aldanor could hear the distinctive interwoven sounds of zelandonia chanting. When the litter passed by, Folara looked at the young woman she had come to know and love, her brother's mate. Ayla's face was pasty white, and her breathing so shallow, she didn't seem to be moving at all.

Folara was horrified, and Aldanor could see her alarm. "We have to get mother, and Proleva, and Joharran," she said. "And Jondalar."

Although it was difficult, and even a little embarrassing, the walk down to the lodge from the cave had helped to clear Zelandoni's head. She dropped down on her large, comfortable stool gratefully and was glad for the cup of hot water. She hadn't dared to suggest an herb or medicinal to counteract the effects of the root, not when she wasn't thinking clearly, for fear its reaction in combination with the root might make the effects worse. Now that her head was more clear, though her body was still feeling the effects of the powerful root, she decided to experiment on herself. She added some stimulating herbs to a second cup of hot water, and sipped it slowly, trying to judge if she could feel anything. She wasn't sure if they helped, but at least they didn't seem to make things worse.

She stood up, and with a little assistance, went back to the bed, recently vacated by Laramar, where they had put Ayla. "Have you tried to give her hot water?" she asked.

"We haven't been able to get her mouth open," said a young acolyte who was standing nearby.

The First tried to pry Ayla's mouth open, but her jaws were clamped shut, as though she were straining against something with all her might. The Donier pulled back the covers and noticed her whole body was rigid. She was icy cold and clammy to the touch in spite of all the furs on her.

"Pour some hot water in that large bowl," she said to the young man. Several others who were standing around hurried to help him.

She hadn't been able to open the young woman's mouth. If she couldn't get any heat inside her, she would have to try to apply more heat from the outside. The First took several of the pieces of bandage material, both soft skins and fabric, that were still nearby and dumped them into the bowl of steaming water. Carefully, she squeezed the hot liquid out and applied a hot dressing to Ayla's arm. By the time she put another one on the other arm, the first one was cold.

"Keep more hot water coming," she said.

She untied the rope that was wrapped around Ayla's garment, and with the help of several zelandonia to lift her, unwound it from around her, noting the ingenious way it had secured the buckskin on her. Ayla was not quite naked, the First noted. She was wearing an arrangement of straps that held on the absorbent leather pad stuffed with cattail fuzz between her legs.

It is either her moontime, or she is still bleeding from the miscarriage, Zelandoni thought. If nothing else, it means Laramar did not start new life in her. Matter-of-factly, the Donier checked to see if she needed to be changed, but it appeared she was at the end of her flow. It was barely soiled, and she left the pad intact.

Then, with the help of several other doniers, she began placing hot, damp absorbent skins and cloths on Ayla in an attempt to drive away the deep cold that held the young woman. She herself had had only a taste of the internal chill, but it was enough to make her appreciate just how cold it felt. Finally, after many applications of heat, Ayla's rigid body seemed to relax; at least her jaw unclamped. Zelandoni hoped it was a

good sign, but she had no way of knowing for sure. She personally covered Ayla with warm furs. It was all she could do
for now.

Her large, sturdy stool was brought and the One Who Was
First sat beside the newest Zelandoni and began her anxious
vigil. For the first time, she became conscious of the chanting
that had been continuous from the beginning, with some joining in and others dropping out as they grew tired.

We may have to bring in more people to maintain it if this
wait goes on too long. Zelandoni didn't even want to think beyond the wait. When she did, she kept in her mind the thought
that Ayla would eventually wake up and she would be fine. Any
other outcome was too painful to comtemplate. If I hadn't been
so curious about those intriguing new roots, would I have been
more perceptive? the First wondered. Ayla did seem rather
upset and nervous when she arrived, but all the zelandonia
were there, and looking forward to this unique ceremony in the
new cave. She had watched Ayla chewing the roots for a long
time, and finally spitting them into the bowl of water, and then
she decided to try some herself.

That was her first warning. The effects that she felt from that
single drink were so much greater than she had anticipated.
Though she'd had some bad moments, she was glad now that
she did. It gave her a sense of what Ayla was going through.
Who would have thought that such innocuous-looking dried
roots could be so powerful? What were they? Did the plant
grow anywhere nearby? It obviously had some unique properties, some of which might be beneficial for specific uses, but
if there were to be any further experimentation, it would have
to be under much more careful and controlled circumstances.
It was a very dangerous root.

She had barely settled into the meditative state she usually assumed for long vigils when one of the zelandonia approached the First. Marthona and Proleva, along with Folara,
had arrived and were asking to come in.

"Of course they can come in," Zelandoni said. "They may
be of help, and we may need it before this is over."

When the three women were ushered in, they noticed several

zelandonia were chanting over a bed near the back. Zelandoni was sitting beside it.

"What happened to Ayla?" Marthona asked when she saw her lying pallid and unmoving on the bed.

"I wish I knew for sure," Zelandoni said. "And I'm afraid I may be largely to blame. Over the past few years, Ayla spoke occasionally about a root that was used by the . . . mog-urs, I think she calls them, the ones of her Clan who know of the spirits. They used it to help them enter the Spirit World, though only as part of special ceremonies, or so I understood. The way she talked about the root, I was sure she had used it, but she was always very cryptic about it. She did say that the effects were very powerful. I was intrigued, of course. Anything that can assist the zelandonia to communicate with the next world is always of interest."

Stools were brought for the three, and cups of chamomile tea. When they were settled, the First continued.

"I didn't know until recently that Ayla still had some of those roots, and that she believed they would still be effective. Frankly, I doubted it. Most herbs and medicinals lose strength over time. She claimed that if they were properly stored, they became concentrated, gained in strength over time. I thought perhaps a small experiment might get her to think about something besides her worries. I knew she was troubled over Jondalar, and that whole sad incident the night of the festival, especially after miscarrying when she was called . . ."

"You can't believe how difficult that was for her, Zelandoni," Marthona said. "I know it is never easy to be called—that's part of it, I suppose—but with the miscarriage and all, I will tell you, there were moments when I thought we'd lose her. She bled so heavily, I was afraid she was bleeding her life away. I was almost ready to send for you. If it had continued like that much longer, I would have, though I'm not sure you would have arrived in time."

Zelandoni nodded. "Perhaps you shouldn't have let her come so soon," she said.

"There was no way I could stop her. You know how she is when she decides she wants to do something," Marthona said. Zelandoni nodded in acknowledgment. "She couldn't wait to see

Jondalar, and Jonayla. Especially after losing one, she wanted to see her child, and I think she wanted to start another one. And she was sure she knew how. I think that's partly why she wanted to see Jondalar so bad."

"She saw him, all right," Proleva said, "with Marona."

"I don't understand Jondé sometimes," Folara said. "Of all people, why couldn't he leave her alone?"

"Probably because she wouldn't leave him alone," Proleva said. "His needs have always been strong. She made it too easy."

"And then what does he do when she decides to take her turn at the Festival?" Folara said. "It's not like she didn't have the right."

"Right or not, she didn't do it because she wanted to celebrate the Mother at the Festival," Zelandoni said. "She did it out of hurt and anger; that's why she chose the man she did. She didn't want Laramar, she wanted to get back at Jondalar. That doesn't Honor the Mother, and she knows it. Neither of them is without fault, but I think both of them are trying to take all the blame on themselves, and that doesn't help."

"No matter who takes the blame, Jondalar will still a have a harsh penalty to pay," Marthona said.

"I can't blame Laramar for not wanting to return to the Ninth Cave, and I'm glad the Fifth was willing to take him in, but his mate doesn't want to move," Proleva said. "She says the Ninth Cave is her home. She does have a good location, but if she stays without a mate, who's going to take care of that brood of hers?"

"Or supply the barma she drinks every day," Folara said.

"That may be what will encourage her to move to the Fifth," Zelandoni said.

"Unless her eldest son takes over," Proleva said. "He's been learning to make that barma for several years. Some say his is better than Laramar's, and there are enough people along our section of The River who would rather have a nearby source."

"Well, don't suggest it to him," Marthona said.

"It won't make any difference. If we can think of it, someone else is bound to as well," Proleva said.

Zelandoni noticed two more people joining the ones who

were chanting, and one leaving. She nodded her approval to them, then glanced at Ayla. Did her skin seem more gray? She hadn't moved but somehow she seemed to have sunk deeper into the bed. The Donier didn't like the way she looked. She went back to her explanation.

"I was saying that I wanted to try to help Ayla get her mind off her problems, to get her to talk about other things that are usually of great interest to her. That's why I asked her about this Clan root, but I'm not without fault, either. I was too anxious to learn about it. I should have been paying closer attention to her. I should have seen how upset she really was. And I should have believed her about the potency of the Clan root. I took only one drink, and had to struggle to maintain control. It is far more powerful than I ever imagined," Zelandoni said.

"I'm afraid Ayla is lost somewhere in the world of the spirits. The only thing I really remember her saying is that chanting was the tie that kept her bound to this world, and I could feel the pull of it when I was somewhat lost from just the one drink. I will be honest with you. I don't know what else to do for her, except to keep her warm and chant and hope it wears off soon."

"The Clan root—she told me about that," Marthona said. "The one she calls Mamut said he would never try that root again, that he was afraid he would be lost forever. He told her it was too powerful, and he warned Ayla never to use it again."

The First frowned. "Why didn't she tell me Mamut told her not to use that root? He was One Who Serves; he would know. Ayla was a little reluctant to try it at first, but she never told me why. And then she seemed perfectly willing, even performing Clan rituals for it. She didn't tell me Mamut had warned her against it," Zelandoni said, quite distraught.

The First got up and checked Ayla again. She was still cold and clammy, and her breath was hardly noticeable. If the Donier had just seen her, and touched her, she would have thought Ayla was dead. She lifted her eyelid. There was only a slight response. Zelandoni had thought, hoped, that all Ayla needed was time for the effects to wear off. Now she was beginning to wonder if anything would bring her out of it.

She looked around, beckoned to a particular acolyte. "Massage her, gently. Try to bring some color to her skin, and let's try to get some warm tea into her, something stimulating." And then louder, so everyone could hear, "Does anyone know where Jondalar is?"

"He's been taking long walks lately, usually by The River," Marthona said.

"I saw him practically running in that direction earlier," an acolyte said.

Zelandoni stood, and clapped her hands for everyone's attention. "Ayla's spirit is lost in the void, and she can't find her way back. She may not even be able to find her way to the Mother. We have to find Jondalar. If we don't get Jondalar here, she will never find her way back; she won't even have the will to try. Search the whole Campsite, every tent; get everyone looking for him. Search the woods, up and down The River; search in The River if we have to. Just get him here. Fast." Zelandoni was more agitated and upset than most people had ever seen her.

Everyone except for those who were needed to chant rushed out of the lodge and scattered in all directions. When they were gone, the One Who Was First To Serve The Mother examined Ayla again. She was still cold, and her skin was turning gray. *She's giving up,* the Donier thought. *I don't think she wants to live. Jondalar may already be too late.*

One of the acolytes burst into the fa'lodge used by Jondalar and the two Mamutoi visitors. Willamar and Dalanar were also in the lodge. They had come to look for Jondalar, too. The young acolyte had only seen the tall, red-haired man from a distance and didn't realize how big he was up close. He felt a bit overwhelmed.

"Do you know where Jondalar is?" the young man asked.

"No. I haven't seen him since early this morning," Danug replied. "Why?"

"It's the new Zelandoni. She drank some liquid that she made from a root and now her spirit is in some dark void and the First said we have to find Jondalar and bring him right away or she will die and her spirit will be lost forever," he said all in one breath without stopping. He finally caught his breath. "We're supposed to search everywhere, and ask everyone to help look for him," the acolyte said.

"Could it be that root she took with Mamut?" Danug asked, looking at Druwez with consternation.

"What root is that?" Dalanar asked, quick to notice their worry.

"Ayla had some root she brought with her from her Clan people," Danug explained. "Apparently it was used by the ones who talk to the spirit world. Mamut wanted to try it, so Ayla prepared it the way she had been taught. I don't know what happened, exactly, but no one could wake them up. Everyone was worried and we all had to chant. Finally Jondalar came and begged Ayla to come back, telling her how much he loved her. They'd been having some trouble—kind of like they are now. I don't understand how two people who love each other so much can be so blind to each other's feelings."

"He has always had trouble with women like that. I don't know if it's pride or lack of perception," Willamar said, shaking his head. "I thought when he brought Ayla home, he was past it. He's fine if he really doesn't care that much about a woman, but if he loves one, he seems to lose his sense and doesn't know what to do. You should hear the stories about him, but that's not important. What happened?"

"Jondalar just kept telling her he loved her and begging her to come back. Finally she woke up, and so did Mamut. Mamut told us later they would have been lost in some kind of a black void forever if Jondalar's love hadn't been so strong that it found its way to her; he brought her back, and him, too. Mamut said the roots were too strong; he could never control them, and would never try them again. He said he was afraid his spirit would be lost forever in that terrible place, and he warned Ayla against them, too." Danug felt the blood drain from his face. "She's done it again," he said as he ran out of the tent. Then he wasn't sure where to go. Finally he had an idea and he raced toward the camp of the Ninth Cave.

Several people were milling around the large cooking hearth, and he was relieved to see Jonayla. She had obviously been crying, and Wolf was whining and trying to lick the tears from her face. Marthona and Folara were trying to comfort her, too. They acknowledged the greeting of the big Mamutoi as he hunkered down in front of the little girl. He stroked Wolf's head when the animal nosed his way closer to the familiar man.

"How are you, Jonayla?" he said.

"I want my mother, Danug," she said, starting to cry. "My mother is sick. She won't wake up."

"I know she is. I think I know a way to help her," Danug said.

"How?" she said, looking at him with wide eyes.

"She got sick like this once before, when she lived with us at the Lion Camp. I think Jondalar could wake her up. He's the one who woke her up before. Do you know where Jondalar is, Jonayla?"

She shook her head. "I don't see Jondy very much anymore. He goes away, sometimes all day."

"Do you know where he goes?"

"Lots of times he walks up The River."

"Does he take Wolf with him sometimes?"

"Yes, but not today."

"Do you think Wolf could find him, if you told him to?"

Jonayla looked at Wolf, then back at Danug. "Maybe he could," she said, then, with a tremulous smile, "Yes, I think he could."

"If you tell Wolf to find Jondalar, I'll follow him, and tell Jondalar to come back and wake your mother up," Danug said.

"Mother and Jondy have not been talking very much. Maybe he won't want to," Jonayla said, with a worried frown. Danug thought that she looked exactly like Jondalar when she frowned like that.

"Don't worry about that, Jonayla. Jondalar loves your mother very much, and she loves him. If he knew she was in trouble, he would run here as fast as he could. I know it," Danug said.

"If he loves her, why doesn't he talk to her, Danug?"

"Because sometimes, even when you love someone, you don't always understand her. Sometimes you don't even understand yourself. Will you tell Wolf to find Jondalar?"

"Wolf, come here," the girl said. She stood up and took the great massive head between her little hands, just the way her mother would have. She looked so much like a little Ayla, Danug had to hide a smile. He wasn't alone. "Mother is sick and Jondalar has to come and help her, Wolf. You have to find him." She took her hands away and pointed toward The River. "Find Jondalar, Wolf. Go find Jondalar," she said.

It was not the first time the wolf had heard that command. Wolf and Ayla had had to follow Jondalar's trail before, on their Journey back, when he was captured by Attaroa's hunters. The anxious animal licked Jonayla's face, then started toward The River.

He turned around once and started back toward her, but she told him again, "Go, Wolf! Find Jondalar!" He looked back when Danug started after him, and then continued on in a fast trot, sniffing the ground.

Jondalar could hardly wait to get away from the Campsite after his brush with Ayla. Then, once he reached The River and started walking upstream, he couldn't stop thinking about it. He had almost done it, almost taken her in his arms. He had wanted to. Why didn't he? What would she have done if he had? Would she have gotten angry? Pushed him away? Or not? She had looked so surprised, so shocked, but wasn't he just as surprised to see her?

Why didn't he? What was the worst that could happen? If she had gotten angry and pushed him away, would things be any worse than they were now? At least he'd know that she didn't want him. You don't want to know, do you? But things can't go on the way they are now. Was she in tears when she ran away? Or did I imagine that? Why would she be in tears? Because she's upset, of course. But what would make her so upset? Just seeing you? Why should that upset her? She told me how she felt on the night of the Festival. She showed me, didn't she? She doesn't care about you anymore, but then why was she crying?

Usually when Jondalar walked along the river, he would think about starting back about the time that the sun reached its zenith, at midday. But on this day his mind was so lost in its ruminations, going over and over again each little nuance he could recall, or detail he thought he remembered, that he didn't even notice the passage of time or the height of the sun.

Danug, taking long strides to keep up with Wolf, began to wonder if the animal was on the right trail. Could Jondalar have traveled so far? It was well past noon when Danug stopped for a quick drink of water before continuing on. He stood up from the river's edge, and far in the distance, along a fairly straight stretch of the winding river, he thought he saw someone walking. He shaded his eyes, but could not see beyond what appeared to be a bend in the waterway. The wolf had rushed on ahead while he had stopped and was out of sight. Danug hoped he'd be able to catch up to him as he started out again, picking up the pace.

Jondalar was finally distracted from his intense preoccupation by movement in the brush near the water. He caught sight of the movement again. It's a wolf! I wonder if he's been stalking me, he said to himself, reaching for his spear-thrower. But he hadn't taken spears or spear-throwers. His eyes searched the ground, looking for a weapon, a heavy branch or large shed antler, or a good stone, something to defend himself, but when the huge animal finally broke cover, all he could do was throw up his arm in front of his face as he was knocked over by the charge.

But the animal wasn't biting him, he was licking him. Then he saw the ear cocked at a jaunty angle. It was not a wild wolf, he realized. "Wolf! Is it you? What are you doing here?" He sat up and had to fend off the exuberant advances of the excited animal. He sat for a while, petting the wolf and scratching him behind his ears, trying to calm him down. "Why aren't you with Jonayla, or Ayla? Why did you follow me all this way?" Jondalar said, beginning to have the inkling of alarm.

When he stood up and started on his way again, Wolf pranced nervously in front of him, then back in the direction he had come. "Do you want to go back, Wolf? Well, go ahead. You can go back." But when Jondalar started out again, the wolf jumped in front of him again. "What is it, Wolf?" Jondalar looked up at the sky, and for the first time noticed that the sun was well past its high point. "Do you want me to go back with you?"

"Yes, that's what he wants, Jondalar," Danug said.

"Danug! What are you doing here?" Jondalar said.

"Looking for you."

"Looking for me? Why?"

"It's Ayla, Jondalar. You have to come back right away."

"Ayla? What's wrong, Danug?"

"Remember that root? The one she made into juice for her and Mamut? She did it again, to show Zelandoni, but this time she drank it herself. No one can wake her up. Not even Jonayla. The Donier says you have to come right away, or Ayla will die and her spirit will be lost forever," Danug said.

Jondalar turned white. "No! Not that root! O, Great Mother, don't let her die. Please don't let her die," he said, and started running back the way he had come.

If he had been preoccupied on his way out, it was nothing compared to his single-minded intensity as he raced back. He tore along the edge of The River, scrambling through brush that tore at his bare legs and arms, and face. He didn't feel them. He ran until he was gasping for breath that rasped his throat raw, until he felt a pain in his side that was like a hot knife, until his legs knotted and ached. He hardly felt any of it; the pain in his mind was more. He even outdistanced Danug; only the wolf kept pace.

He couldn't believe how far he had come, and worse, how long it was taking him to get back. He slowed once or twice to catch his breath, but never stopped, and put on an extra burst of speed when the brush thinned out as he neared the Campsite.

"Where is she?" he asked the first person he saw.

"The zelandonia lodge," came the answer.

The whole Summer Meeting had been looking for him, waiting for him, and as he raced toward the lodge, several people actually cheered. He didn't hear it, and he didn't stop until he crashed through the entrance drape and saw her lying on the bed surrounded by lamps. And then, all he could do was gasp out her name.

"Ayla!"

41

Jondalar could hardly breathe, and every time he gasped for air, his throat felt raw. Sweat was pouring off him. He was bent over double from the pain in his side. His legs shook and could hardly support him as he approached the bed at the back of the lodge. Wolf had pressed in beside him, and with lolling tongue was panting heavily, too.

"Here, Jondalar, sit," Zelandoni said, standing up and giving him her own stool. She could see his extreme stress, and knew he must have run a great distance. "Get him some water," she said to the nearest acolyte. "Some for the wolf, too."

As he neared, he could see that Ayla's skin had a deathly gray pallor. "Ayla, oh, Ayla, why did you do it again?" he rasped, barely able to speak. "You know you almost died last time." He drank from the cup that was handed to him as a reflex, hardly realizing someone had given it to him. Then he literally climbed onto the bed. He pushed back the covers, picked Ayla up, and held her in his arms, shocked at how chilled she was. "She's so cold," he said, with a sobbing hiccup. He didn't know tears were streaming down his face. He wouldn't have cared if he did.

The wolf looked at the two people on the bed, lifted his muzzle into the air, and howled, a long eerie wolfsong that sent chills down the backs of the zelandonia who were in the lodge, and the people who were outside. It stunned the ones who were chanting, causing them to miss a pulse, and stop the continuous fugue for a heartbeat. It was only then that Jondalar became conscious of the zelandonia chanting. Then Wolf put his front paws on the bed, and whined for her attention.

"Ayla, Ayla, please come back to me," Jondalar pleaded. "You can't die. Who will give me a son? Oh, Ayla, what a thing to say. I don't care if you give me a son. It's you I want. I love you. I don't even care if you never talk to me again, just so I can look at you sometimes. Please come back to me. O Great Mother, send her back. Please send her back. I'll do anything you want, just don't take her away from me."

Zelandoni watched the tall, handsome man, face, chest, arms, and legs scratched and in places bleeding, sitting on the bed holding the nearly lifeless woman in his arms like a baby, rocking back and forth, tears streaming down his face, crying for her to come back. She hadn't seen him cry since he was a small boy. Jondalar didn't cry. He fought to control his emotions, keep them to himself. Very few people had ever gotten really close to him, except his family and her, and even then, once he reached manhood, there was always some distance, some reserve.

After he returned from his stay with Dalanar, she had often wondered if he would ever really love a woman again, and blamed herself. She knew he still loved her then, and she had been tempted, more than once, to give up the zelandonia and mate him, but as time went along and she never became pregnant, she knew she had made the right choice. She felt sure he would mate someday, and though she had often doubted that he would be capable of giving himself completely to any woman, Jondalar needed children. Children could be loved freely, completely, without reservation, and he needed to love like that.

She had been genuinely happy for him when he returned from his Journey with a woman whom he obviously loved, a woman who was worthy of his love. But she hadn't realized until then just how much he did love her. The First felt a small twinge of guilt. Maybe she shouldn't have pushed Ayla so hard to become Zelandoni. Maybe she should have just left the two of them alone. But it was the Mother's choice, after all.

"She's so cold. Why is she so cold?" Jondalar said. He stretched her out on the bed, lay down next to her, then half covered her naked body with his own, and pulled the furs over both of them. The wolf jumped up on the bed with them, crowding in close to her other side. Jondalar's heat filled the space quickly and the wolf's helped to hold it in. The man held her for a long time, looking at her, kissing her pale, still face, talking to her, pleading with her, begging the Mother for her, until finally his voice, his tears, and heat of his body and the wolf's began to penetrate her coldest depths.

Ayla wept silently. "You did it! You did it!" the people chanted, accusing her. Then only Jondalar stood there. She heard a wolf howl nearby.

"I'm sorry, Jondalar," she cried. "I'm sorry I hurt you."

He held out his arms to her. "Ayla," he gasped. "Give me a son. I love you."

She started toward the figure of Jondalar standing beside Wolf, and walked between them; then she felt something pulling. Suddenly she was moving, faster, much faster than before, though she felt rooted in place. The mysterious alien clouds appeared and were gone in an instant, yet seemed to take forever. The deep black void swooped by, engulfing her in an unearthly black emptiness that went on endlessly. She fell through the mist, and for a moment saw herself and Jondalar in a bed surrounded by lamps. Then she was inside a frigid, clammy shell. She struggled to move, but she was so stiff, so cold. Finally, her eyelids flickered. She opened her eyes and looked into the tearstained face of the man she loved, and a moment later felt the warm, licking tongue of the wolf.

"Ayla! Ayla! You're back! Zelandoni! She's awake! O Doni, Great Mother, thank you. Thank you for giving her back to me," Jondalar said with a heaving sob. He was holding her in his arms, crying his relief and his love, afraid to hold her too tight for fear he would hurt her, but not ever wanting to let her go. And she didn't want him to.

Finally he relaxed his embrace to let the Donier look at her. "Get down now, Wolf," Jondalar said, pushing the animal toward the edge. "You helped her; now let Zelandoni see her." The wolf jumped off the bed, but sat on the floor looking at them.

The First Among Those Who Served bent over Ayla, and saw open gray-blue eyes and a wan smile. She shook her head in amazement. "I didn't believe it was possible. I was sure she was gone, lost forever in some dark irretrievable place, where even I could not go to find her to lead her to the Mother. I was afraid the chanting was useless, that nothing could be done to save her. I doubted that anything would ever bring her back, not my most ardent hopes, nor the transcendent wish of every Zelandonii, not even your love, Jondalar. All the zelandonia combined could not have done what you did. I'm almost willing to believe you could have raised her from the Doni's deepest underworld. I've always said the Great Earth Mother would never refuse you anything you asked Her for. I think this proves it."

The news spread through the Campsite like a wildfire. Jondalar had brought her back. Jondalar had done what the zelandonia could not do. There wasn't a woman at the Summer Meeting who didn't wish in her heart that she was loved as much, or a man who didn't wish he knew a woman whom he could love so strongly. Stories were already beginning, stories that would be told around hearth fires and campfires for years, about Jondalar's love, so great it brought his Ayla back from the dead.

Jondalar thought about Zelandoni's comment. He had heard that before though he wasn't entirely sure what it meant, but it left him feeling uncomfortable to be told that he was so favored by the Mother that no woman could refuse him, not even Doni Herself; so favored that if he ever asked the Mother for anything, She would grant his request. He had also been warned to be careful of what he wished for, because he might get it, although he didn't really understand what that meant either.

For the first few days, Ayla was utterly exhausted, barely able to move and so weak, there were times when the Donier wondered if she would ever fully recover. She slept a great deal, sometimes lying so still, it was hard to tell if she was still breathing, but her sleep wasn't always restful. Occasionally, she would lapse into waves of delirium, tossing and turning and speaking out loud, but every time Ayla opened her eyes, Jondalar was there. He hadn't left her side since she awoke, except to take care of essential needs. He slept on his sleeping furs that he spread out on the floor beside her bed.

Zelandoni wondered, when Ayla seemed to falter, if he wasn't the only thing that kept her in the world of the living. In fact he was, along with her own inherent will to live, and her years of hunting and exercise, which had given her a strong, healthy body that could recover from devastating experiences, even those that brought her close to death.

Wolf stayed with her most of the time, as well, and seemed to sense when she was ready to wake up. After Jondalar stopped him from jumping up and putting his dirty paws on the bed, Wolf discovered that the height of the bed was just right for him to stand up and lay his head on it to watch her just before she opened her eyes. Jondalar and Zelandoni came to anticipate her waking by the actions of the animal.

Jonayla was so happy to have her mother awake, and Jondy and her mother back together, that she often came into the zelandonia lodge to be with them. Though she didn't sleep there, if they were both awake, she sometimes stayed awhile, sitting in Jondalar's lap, or lying beside her mother, even taking a nap with her. Other times she would run in for only a moment, as if to convince herself that all was still well. After she was recovered enough, Ayla usually sent Wolf out with Jonayla, although at first he was torn between staying with the woman and going with the child.

The Donier hovered nearby as well. The First blamed herself for not paying closer attention to the young woman's condition from the time she first arrived. But Summer Meetings required so much of her time and attention and Ayla had always been hard for her to read. She seldom talked about herself or her problems, and hid her feelings far too well. It was easy to overlook her symptoms of distress.

Ayla looked up from the bed and smiled at the bushy red-haired and bearded giant of a man who was looking down at her. Though not fully recovered, she had recently moved back to the camp of the Ninth Cave. She had been awake, earlier, when Jondalar told her Danug wanted to visit, but she dozed off momentarily before she heard her name softly spoken. Jondalar was sitting beside her, holding her hand, and Jonayla was sitting in his lap. Wolf pounded his tail on the floor beside her bed, in greeting to the young Mamutoi.

"I'm supposed to tell you, Jonayla, that Bokovan and some other children are going to Levela's hearth to play, and have something to eat. She has some bones for Wolf, too," Danug said.

"Why don't you go, Jonayla, and take Wolf," Ayla said, sitting up. "They would like to see you, and it won't be long before this Summer Meeting is over. After we go home, you probably won't see them again until next summer."

"All right, mother. I'm getting hungry, anyway, and maybe Wolf is too." The child gave her father and mother a hug, then walked toward the entrance with Wolf behind her. He whined back at Ayla before leaving the lodge, then followed after Jonayla.

"Sit down, Danug," Ayla said, motioning toward a stool. Then she looked around. "Where's Druwez?"

Danug sat down beside Ayla. "Aldanor needed a male friend who is not related for something having to do with his upcoming Matrimonial. Druwez agreed to be the one, since I have to fill in as an adopted relative," Danug said.

Jondalar nodded in understanding. "It's difficult learning a complete new set of customs. I remember how it was when Thonolan decided to mate Jetamio. Because I was his brother, it made me kin to the Sharamudoi, too, and since I was his only relative, I had to be a part of the ceremonies."

Though he could speak of the brother he'd lost more easily now, Ayla noticed his expression of regret. It would always be a great sadness to him, she knew.

Jondalar moved closer to Ayla and put his arm around her. Danug smiled at both of them. "First, there is something I need to say to you," he said with mock severity. "When are you two going to learn who you love? You both have to stop making problems for each other. Listen to me closely: Ayla loves Jondalar and no other man; Jondalar loves Ayla and no other woman. Do you think you can remember that? There never was and never will be anyone else for either one of you. I am going to make a rule that you have to follow for the rest of your lives. I don't care if everyone else couples with anyone they want; you may only couple with each other. If I ever hear differently, I am going to come back here and tie you both together. Is that understood?"

"Yes, Danug," Jondalar and Ayla said in unison. She turned to smile at Jondalar, who was smiling back at her; then both grinned at Danug.

"And I'll tell you a secret. As soon as we can, we're going to start a baby together," Ayla said.

"Not yet, though," Jondalar said. "Not until Zelandoni says you are well enough. But woman, just wait until you are."

"I'm not sure which Gift is better," Danug said with a big smile. "The Gift of Pleasure, or the Gift of Knowledge. I think the Mother must love us a lot to make starting a new life such a Pleasure!"

"I think you're right," Jondalar said.

"I have tried to translate the Zelandonii Mother's Song into Mamutoi so I can tell everyone, and when I get back, I'm going to start looking for a mate so I can start a son," Danug said.

"What's wrong with a daughter?" Ayla said.

"There's nothing wrong with a daughter, except I wouldn't be able to name her. I want a son so I can name him. I've never named a child before," Danug said.

"You've never had a child to name before," Ayla said, laughing.

"Well, that's true," Danug said a bit chagrined. "At least none I've known of, but you know what I mean. I've never had the chance before."

"I understand how he feels. It doesn't matter to me whether we have another girl or a boy, but I wonder what it would be like to name a son," Jondalar said. "But Danug, what if the Mamutoi do not accept the idea that men should name the boys?"

"I just have to make sure that the woman I decide to mate agrees," Danug said.

"That's true," Ayla said. "But why do you have to go back to find a mate, Danug? Why don't you stay here, like Aldanor? I'm sure you could find a Zelandonii woman who would be pleased to be your mate."

"And Zelandonii women are certainly beautiful, but in many ways, I'm like Jondalar. Traveling can be exciting, but I need to return to my own people to settle down. Besides, there's only one woman I would stay here to mate, Ayla," Danug said, with a wink at Jondalar, "and she's already claimed."

Jondalar chuckled, but there was a look in Danug's eye, a tone in his voice that made Ayla wonder if his jocular statement was said entirely in jest.

"I'm just glad she was willing to come home with me," Jondalar said. The way Jondalar looked at her with his vivid blue eyes made her tingle all the way to her innermost place. "Danug is right. Doni must really love us to have made making children such a Pleasure."

"It isn't all Pleasure for a woman, Jondalar. Giving birth can be very painful," Ayla said.

"But I thought you said giving birth to Jonayla was easy, Ayla," Jondalar said, his forehead creased with his familiar frown.

"Even an easy childbirth has some pain, Jondalar. It just wasn't as bad as I expected," Ayla said.

"I don't want to cause you pain," he said, turning to look at her. "Are you sure we should have another?" Jondalar suddenly remembered that Thonolan's mate had died giving birth.

"Don't be silly, Jondalar. Of course we're going to have another baby. I want one, too, you know. It's not just you. And it's not that bad. If you don't want to start one, though, maybe I can find another man who will," she said with a teasing smile.

"Oh no you can't," Jondalar said, giving her shoulder a hug. "Danug just told you that you may not couple with anyone except me, remember?"

"I never wanted to couple with anyone but you, Jondalar. You are the one who taught me the Mother's Gift of Pleasure. No one could possibly give me more, maybe because I love you so much," Ayla said.

Jondalar turned his face away to hide the tears that had come to his eyes, but Danug had looked in another direction and affected not to notice. When Jondalar turned back, he looked at Ayla with great seriousness. "I never told you how sorry I am about Marona. I didn't really want her that much. She just made it so easy. I didn't want to tell you because I was afraid it would hurt you. When you found us together, I kept thinking how much you must hate me. I want you to know, I love only you."

"I know you love me, Jondalar," Ayla said. "Everyone at this whole Summer Meeting knows you love me. I wouldn't be here if you didn't love me. In spite of what Danug said, if you ever need to, even if you just want to, you can couple with anyone you want, Jondalar. I don't even hate Marona anymore. I don't blame her for wanting you. Who wouldn't want you? Sharing the Gift of Pleasure isn't what makes love. It makes babies, but not love. Love can make Pleasures better, but if you love someone, what difference does coupling with someone else once in a while make? Coupling takes a few moments. How can that be more important than a lifetime of love? Even in the Clan, coupling was done just to relieve a man's needs. You wouldn't expect me to break our bond just because you coupled with someone else, would you?"

Danug laughed. "If that were a reason, everyone would have to break his bond. People look forward to Festivals to Honor the Mother, to share Pleasures with someone else once in a while. I've heard stories that Talut can still couple with as many as six women in a row at Festivals. Mother always said it just gave her a chance to see if any other man could match him. None ever could."

"Talut is a better man than I am," Jondalar said. "There was a time, maybe, but I don't have the stamina anymore. And to be honest, I don't have the desire."

"It may just be stories," Danug said. "I can't say that I've ever seen him with any woman except mother. He spends a lot of time with other leaders, and she spends most of her time at Meetings visiting with relatives and friends. I think most people just like to tell stories."

There was a pause in the conversation and each of the young people looked at each other. Then Danug spoke up. "I wouldn't break the mating bond over it, but to be honest, I really would like it better if the woman I mate would share Pleasures with no one except me."

"What about during Festivals to Honor the Great Earth Mother?" Jondalar asked.

"I know we should all Honor the Mother at festivals and such, but how would I know the children my mate brought to my hearth were mine if she shares Pleasures with someone else?" Danug said.

Ayla looked at them both, and remembered the words of the First. "If a man loves the children a woman brings to his hearth now, why should knowing who started them make any difference?"

"Maybe it shouldn't, but I would still want them to be mine," Danug said.

"If you start a child, does that make him yours? Would you own him, like a personal possession?" Ayla asked. "Would you not love a child you didn't own, Danug?"

"I don't mean mine in the sense of owning, but mine in the sense that the child would have come from me," Danug tried to explain. "I probably would grow to care for any child of my hearth, one that didn't come from me or even one that did not come from my mate. I loved Rydag as a brother, more than a brother, and he was not Talut's or Nezzie's, but I would like to know if a child of my hearth was started by me. A woman doesn't have to worry. She always knows."

"I understand how Danug feels, Ayla. It makes me happy to know Jonayla came from me. And everyone knows she did because everyone knows you never chose anyone but me. We always Honored the Mother at Festivals, but we always chose each other."

"I wonder if you'd be so eager to have children of your own if you had to go through the pain along with your mate," Ayla said. "Some women would be happy if they never had to have children. Not many, but some."

The men glanced at each other, but neither one looked at Ayla, feeling slightly embarrassed at voicing personal thoughts that seemed to contradict the customs and beliefs of their people.

"By the way, have you heard that Marona is going to mate again?" Danug said, changing the subject.

"She is?" Jondalar said. "No, I didn't know. When?"

"In a few days, at the Late Matrimonial, when Folara and Al- danor mate," Proleva said, just coming in. She was followed by Joharran.

"That's what Aldanor told me," Danug said.

Greetings were exchanged, the women hugged, and the leader of the Ninth Cave bent down and touched her cheek with his. Low stools were dragged close to Ayla's bed.

"Who is she mating?" Ayla asked, after everyone was settled, picking up the thread of the recent disclosure.

"Some friend of Laramar's who was staying with him and that bunch at the fa'lodge, the one they aren't using anymore," Proleva said. "He's a stranger, but Zelandonii, I understand."

"He comes from a group of Caves that lie along Big River to the west of here. I heard he came to our Summer Meeting with a message for someone, and decided to stay. I don't know if he knew them before, but he got along well with Laramar and the rest of that bunch," Joharran said.

"I think I know the one," Jondalar said.

"He's been staying at the camp of the Fifth Cave, since they left that fa'lodge, and Marona has been staying there, too. That's where he met her," Proleva said.

"I didn't think Marona wanted to mate again, and he seems rather young. I wonder why she would choose him," Jondalar said.

"Maybe she didn't have much choice," Proleva said.

"But everyone says she's so beautiful, she could have almost anyone she wanted," Ayla said.

"For a night, but not for a mate," Danug said. "I hear people talk. The men she's mated before don't speak very well of her."

"And she's never had any children," Proleva said. "Some people say she can't have any. That could make her less desirable to some men, but I guess it doesn't matter to her intended. She is going with him to his Cave."

"I think I met him," Ayla said, "when I was walking back from the Lanzadonii camp with Echozar one night. I can't say that I cared much for him. Why did he move out of that fa'lodge?"

"They all did after their personal things were taken," Joharran said.

"I heard something about that, but I wasn't paying much attention at the time," Jondalar said.

"Someone took things?" Ayla said.

"Someone took personal things from just about everyone who was staying at that fa'lodge," Joharran said.

"Why would anyone do something like that?" Ayla asked.

"I don't know, but Laramar was pretty upset when he found out that a new winter outfit he'd just traded for was missing, not to mention his pack carrier and most of his barma. Someone else was missing new mittens, another man lost a good knife, and almost all the food was gone," Joharran said.

"Does anyone know who did it?" Jondalar asked.

"Two people are missing, Brukeval and Madroman," Joharran said. "Brukeval left without anything, as far as anyone knows. The other men who were staying at the fa'lodge claim most of his things were still there after he left, but later most of them were missing, and so are Madroman's."

"I heard Zelandoni tell someone that Madroman did not return the sacred objects he received as an acolyte," Proleva said.

"I saw Madroman leaving!" Ayla said, suddenly remembering.

"When?" Joharran asked.

"It was the day the Ninth Cave shared a feast with the Lanzadonii. I was the only one at camp, and just coming out of the lodge. He gave me a look of such hatred, it actually frightened me, but he seemed to be in a big hurry. I remember thinking there was something odd about him. Then I realized I hardly ever saw him without his acolyte tunic, but this time he was wearing regular clothes, except I thought it was strange that his outfit was decorated with Ninth Cave symbols, not Fifth Cave."

"That's where Laramar's new outfit went," Joharran said. "I wondered if it was him."

"Do you think Madroman took it?" Ayla said.

"Yes, and everything else that was taken."

"I think you're right, Joharran," Jondalar said.

"I would guess he didn't want to face people after the disgrace of being rejected by the zelandonia, at least not the people who knew him," Danug said.

"I wonder where he went," Proleva said.

"He's probably going to try to find some other people to live with," Joharran said. "That's why he took the things. He knows winter is coming and he didn't know where he would be staying."

"What will he do to get some strange group to accept him? He doesn't have a skill, and he never was much of a hunter. I heard he never went out hunting again after he joined the zelandonia, not even on a drive," Jondalar said.

"Anyone can do that and almost everyone does. Children love going out and beating the bushes, and making a lot of noise to flush rabbits and other animals out and then chasing them toward hunters or into a net," Proleva said.

"Madroman does have a skill. That's why he didn't return the sacred objects he got from the zelandonia," Joharran said. "That's what he'll do. He'll be a Zelandoni."

"But he's not a Zelandoni!" Ayla said. "He lied about being called."

"But some strange group of people won't know that," Danug said.

"He's been around the zelandonia for so many years, he knows how to act like one. He'll lie again," Proleva said.

"Do you think he would really do that?" Ayla asked, appalled at the very idea.

"You should tell Zelandoni you saw him leave, Ayla," Proleva said.

"And the other leaders should know," Joharran said. "Maybe we can bring it up before your meeting tomorrow, Jondalar. At least it will give people something else to talk about besides you."

Ayla's eyes opened wide. "So soon?" she said. "Proleva, I am going to be there."

They were outside on the level ground in front of the sloping sides of the large natural amphitheater. Laramar was seated, and though his face was still somewhat swollen, he appeared to have essentially recovered from the beating he had received at the hands of the man facing him, except for the scars and battered nose from which he would never recover. Jondalar tried not to flinch as he stood in the bright afternoon sunlight looking at the man whose face was so badly damaged. He would not have been recognized by people who knew him well, if they hadn't known who he was. Originally there had been some talk that Laramar might lose an eye, and Jondalar was grateful that he had not.

It was ostensibly a meeting of the Ninth Cave and the Fifth Cave, with the zelandonia as mediators, but since any interested parties were free to attend, nearly everyone who had come to the Summer Meeting was curious and had indicated "interest." Though the Ninth Cave would have preferred to have waited until later for this confrontation, after the summer gathering of Zelandonii was over, the Fifth Cave had insisted. Since they were being asked to accept Laramar, they wanted to know what they and Laramar could expect as compensation from Jondalar and the Ninth Cave.

Jondalar and Laramar had met for the first time since the incident just before the public meeting inside the zelandonia lodge, along with Joharran, Kemordan, the leader of the Fifth Cave, each Cave's Zelandoni, and several other leaders and zelandonia. They knew Marthona was not strong, and she was told that she did not need to be at the meeting, especially since Laramar's mother was no longer alive, but she would have none of it. Jondalar was her son and she was going to be there. The mates of both of them were not a part of the first meeting either since they both presented complications. Ayla, because she had played such a large role in the incident, and Laramar's mate, because she did not want to move to the Fifth Cave with him, another aspect that would have to be dealt with.

Jondalar was quick to say how sorry he was, and how much he regretted his actions, but Laramar had nothing but disdain for the tall, handsome brother of the leader of the Ninth Cave. For one of the first times in his life, Laramar had the high ground; he was in the right, he had done nothing wrong, and he wasn't going to give up any of his advantage.

There was a slight buzz of conversation among the audience when the participants walked out of the lodge as news that Ayla had seen Madroman leaving the Campsite wearing clothing he had very likely stolen from Laramar was passed around. It was followed by an undercurrent of comment speculating about the various ramifications: Jondalar's and the First's past history with Madroman, his rejection from the zelandonia and Ayla's role in it, and why she was the only one who saw him leave. People settled in to watch the events full of anticipation. It wasn't often that they were presented with the opportunity to observe so much high drama. The whole summer was proving to be an exciting one that would fill many long slow winter days with meat for discussion, and stories for seasoning.

"We have some serious matters to resolve today," the First started. "These are not matters of the Spirit World but problems between Her children and we ask that Doni observe our deliberations and help us to speak the truth, to think clearly, and to reach fair decisions."

She took out a small carved sculpture and held it up. It was the figure of a full-bodied woman with the legs tapering to barely suggested feet. Though they could not distinctly see the object she held in her hand, they all knew that it was a donii, a place for the all-encompassing spirit of the Great Earth Mother or at least some essential part of Her nature, to reside. A tall cairn of stones, almost a pillar, with a large base of fairly big stones tapering up to a flattened top of sandy gravel, had been constructed in the center of the level area.

With a decided flourish, the First Among Those Who Served The Mother planted the feet of the donii into the gravel and propped Her up for all to see. The primary purpose of the donii in this context was to prevent deliberate lying, and She was a strong deterrent. When the Mother's spirit was expressly invoked to watch, everyone knew any lies would be seen by Her and brought to light; while someone might lie and get away with it for the moment, eventually the truth would come out, and usually with far worse repercussions. Not that there was not any great danger of anyone lying today, but it could still be a limiting influence on any tendency to exaggerate.

"Shall we begin," the First said. "There were many witnesses, so I don't think we need to go into any great detail about the circumstances. During the recent Festival to Honor the Mother, Jondalar found his mate Ayla sharing the Mother's Gift of Pleasures with Laramar. Both Ayla and Laramar joined together of their own desire. There was no force, no compulsion. Is that correct, Ayla?"

She hadn't expected to be questioned so quickly, to have all the attention of the people suddenly brought to bear on her. It caught her by surprise, but she wouldn't have known how to lie about it if she had wanted to.

"Yes, Zelandoni. That is true."

"Is that true, Laramar?"

"Yeah, she was more than willing. She came after me," he said.

The First fought a slight urge to caution him about exaggeration, but continued on. "And then what happened?" She was deciding whether to ask Ayla or Jondalar, but Laramar jumped in.

"You can see what happened. The next thing I know, Jondalar was punching me in the face," he said.

"Jondalar?"

The tall man bowed his head and swallowed. "That's what happened. I saw him with Ayla, and I dragged him off her and started hitting him. I know it was wrong. I have no excuse," Jondalar said, knowing in his heart even as he said it that he would do it again.

"Do you know why you hit him, Jondalar?" the First asked.

"I was jealous," he mumbled.

"You were jealous, is that what you said?"

"Yes, Zelandoni."

"If you had to express your jealousy, Jondalar, couldn't you have just pulled them apart? Did you have to hit him?"

"I couldn't stop myself. And once I started . . ." Jondalar shook his head.

"Once he started, no one could stop him, he even hit me!" the leader of the Fifth said. "He was beside himself, in some kind of a frenzy. I don't know what we would have done if that big Mamutoi hadn't got hold of him."

"That's why he's so ready to take in Laramar," Folara whispered to Proleva, but easily heard by those around her. "He's mad that he couldn't stop Jondé, and got hit when he tried."

"He also likes Laramar's barma, but he may discover that Laramar is no shiny piece of amber," Proleva said. "He is not exactly the first one I would ask to join my Cave." She turned her attention back to the center.

"This is the reason," Zelandoni was saying, "that we try to teach the senselessness of jealousy. It can get out of hand. Do you understand that, Jondalar?"

"Yes, I do. It was stupid of me, and I'm very sorry. I'll do whatever you say to make up for it. I want to make amends."

"He can't make up for it," Laramar said. "He can't fix my face, just like he couldn't put the teeth back in Madroman's mouth."

The First gave Laramar a look of annoyance. That was uncalled for, she thought. It wasn't necessary to bring that up. He doesn't have the least idea how much Jondalar was provoked in that situation. But she kept her thoughts to herself.

"But reparations were paid," Marthona said loudly.

"And I expect them to be paid again!" Laramar retorted.

"What *do* you expect?" the First asked. "What redress are you asking? What do you want, Laramar?"

"What I want is to punch *his* pretty face in," Laramar said.

There was a gasp from the audience.

"That is no doubt true, but it is not a remedy allowed by the Mother. Do you have any other thoughts about how you would like him to make amends?" the Donier asked.

Laramar's mate stood up. "He keeps making bigger dwellings for himself. Why don't you ask him to make a big new dwelling for your family, Laramar?" she called out.

"That might be a possibility, Tremeda," the First said, "but where would you want it made, at the Ninth Cave, or the Fifth Cave, Laramar?"

"That's no compensation for me," Laramar said. "What do I care what kind of dwelling she lives in? She'll just turn it into a filthy mess anyway."

"You don't care about where your children live, Laramar?" the First asked.

"My children? They're not mine, not if what you say is true. If coupling is the way they start, I didn't start any of them . . . except maybe the first. I haven't coupled, much less had any 'Pleasures' with her in years. Believe me, she's no Pleasure. I don't know where those children came from, maybe Mother Festivals—give a man enough to drink and even she mig t look good—but whoever started them, it wasn't me. The onl ng that woman is good for is drinking my barma," Laramar sneered.

"That is certainly true. Lanoga has taken care of her siblings more than her mother and now Lanidar is helping. But they are too young to take on so much responsibility," Proleva said from the audience.

"Laramar, they are still the children of your hearth. It is your responsibility to provide for them," the One Who Was First said. "You cannot just decide you don't want them."

"Why not? I don't want them. They never meant anything to me. She doesn't even care about them. Why should I?"

The leader of the Fifth Cave was looking just as horrified as everyone else at Laramar's callous denunciation of the children of his hearth, and in the audience, Proleva whispered, "I told you he was no shiny piece of amber."

"Then who do you expect to take care of the children of your hearth, Laramar?" Zelandoni said.

The man stopped and frowned. "For all I care, Jondalar can. There's nothing he can give me that I want. He can't give me back my face, and I can't have the satisfaction of giving him what he gave me. He's so eager to take care of things, to make amends, let him take care of that lazy, loud-mouthed, manipulating shrew and her brood," Laramar said.

"He may owe you a lot, Laramar, but that's too much to ask of a man who has a family of his own, to take on the responsibility of a family the size of yours," Joharran said.

"Never mind, Joharran. I'll do it," Jondalar said. "If that's what he wants, I'll do it. If he isn't going to take responsibility for his own hearth, someone has to. Those children need someone to care about them."

"Don't you think you should talk to Ayla about it first?" Proleva said from the audience. "That much responsibility will take away from her own family." Not that they don't already take more care of that family than either Laramar or Tremeda, the woman thought, but didn't say aloud.

"No, Proleva. He's right," Ayla said. "I'm responsible, too, for what Jondalar did to Laramar. I didn't realize what it would come to, but I'm just as much at fault. If taking on the responsibility for his family will satisfy Laramar, then we should do it."

"Well, Laramar, is that what you want?" the First said.

"Yeah, if it will keep the rest of you off me, why not?" Laramar said, then he laughed. "You're welcome to her, Jondalar."

"What about you, Tremeda? Is that satisfactory to you?" Zelandoni said.

"Will he build me a new dwelling, like the one he's making for her?" she asked, pointing at Ayla.

"Yes, I will make sure you have a new dwelling," Jondalar said. "Do you want it made at the Ninth Cave or the Fifth?"

"Well, if I'm going to be your second woman, Jondalar," she said, trying to be coy, "I might as well stay at the Ninth. That's my home, anyway."

"Hear me, Tremeda," Jondalar said, looking directly at her. "I am not taking you as a second woman. I said I would assume the responsibility to provide for you and your children. I said I would build you a dwelling. That is the full extent of my obligation to you. I am doing this as reparation for the injury I did to your mate. In no way are you anything close to a second woman to me, Tremeda! Is that understood?"

Laramar laughed. "Don't say I didn't warn you, Jondalar. I told you she was a manipulating shrew. She'll use you any way she can." He laughed again. "You know, maybe this isn't going to be so bad. It just might give me some satisfaction to see you have to put up with her."

"Are you sure you want to go swimming there, Ayla?" Jondalar asked.

"It was our place before you took Marona there, and it's still the best place to swim, especially now when the river is so stirred up and muddy downstream. I haven't had the chance for a good swim since I arrived, and we'll be leaving soon," Ayla said.

"But are you sure you're strong enough to swim?"

"Yes, I am sure, but don't worry. I plan to spend most of the time lying on the bank in the sun. All I want is to get out of this lodge and spend some time with you away from people for a while, now that I finally got Zelandoni to agree that I'm well enough," Ayla said. "I was getting ready to get on Whinney and go someplace anyway before too long. I know she's concerned, but I'm fine. I just need to get out and move around."

Zelandoni had blamed herself for not paying close enough attention to Ayla and was being—rather uncharacteristically—overprotective. She felt more than a little responsible for the fact that they had almost lost the young woman, and she wasn't going to let that happen again. Jondalar was in full agreement, and for a while Ayla enjoyed their unaccustomed close attention, but as she gained her strength back, she began to find such doting concern vexing. Ayla had been trying to convince the Donier that she was completely rested and strong enough to ride and swim again, but it wasn't until the First wanted Wolf out of the way for a while that she finally agreed.

Jonayla and the youngsters her age were again involved with the zelandonia in preparations for a small part they would play in the farewell ceremonies that were being planned to close the Summer Meeting. Wolf was not only a distraction when all the children were together, making it hard for them to concentrate, but it was difficult for Jonayla to both control him and learn what she was supposed to do. When Zelandoni had intimated to Ayla that, while the wolf was certainly welcome, perhaps she could keep the animal with her, it had been the edge Ayla needed to persuade the Donier that she ought to take Wolf, and the horses, away from the Campsite for some exercise.

Ayla was anxious to leave as early as possible the next morning before Zelandoni changed her mind. Jondalar had watered and brushed the horses before the morning meal, and when he tied riding blankets on Whinney and Racer, and fitted halters on Racer and Gray, they knew they were going out, and pranced with anticipation. Though they didn't plan to ride her, Ayla didn't want to leave the young mare alone. She was sure Gray would be lonely if she were left behind; horses liked companionship, especially of their own kind, and Gray needed the exercise, too.

The wolf looked up with expectation when Jondalar picked up a pair of pack baskets made to hang across the back of a horse. The carriers were full of various implements and mysterious packages wrapped in pieces of the pale brown material woven from flax fibers that Ayla had made as training samplers, to pass the time while she was recovering. Marthona had arranged to have a small loom made and was teaching her to weave. One of the baskets was covered by a leather hide to spread out on the ground, and the other by the soft yellowish toweling skins that had been gifts of the Sharamudoi.

Wolf bounded on ahead when the man signaled that he could go with them as they left the lodge. Near the horse enclosure, Ayla stopped to pick a few ripe berries hanging from red-stemmed bushes. She brushed the round, powdery blue fruit against her tunic, noticed the deeper blue skin, then popped it in her mouth and, smiling with satisfaction, savored the sweet, juicy taste. As she climbed up on a stump to mount Whinney, she felt good just being outside, knowing she didn't have to go back in the lodge right away. She was sure she knew every crack that cut through every painted or carved design on the sturdy wooden poles that supported the roof thatch, every smudge of soot that blackened the edges of the smoke hole. She wanted to look at sky and trees, and a landscape uncluttered with lodges.

As they started out, Racer was unusually boisterous and a bit fractious, and communicated some of his unruliness to the two mares, making them harder to handle. Once they got beyond the wooded area, Ayla slipped the halter off Gray so she could go at her own pace, and by tacit agreement, Ayla and Jondalar urged their mounts to a gallop and let them go at full speed. By the time the animals eased off of their own accord, they had worked off their excess energy and were more relaxed, but not Ayla. She was exhilarated. She had always loved riding fast, and after being kept close to camp, it was especially exciting.

They rode along at a more leisurely pace across a landscape contoured by the deep relief of high hills, limestone cliffs, and river-cut valleys. Though the noon sun was still hot most days, the season was turning. Mornings were often cool and crisp, and evenings overcast or rainy. Leaves were transforming their lush green of full summer into the yellows and occasional reds of autumn. The grasses of the open plains shaded from deep gold and rich brown to the pale yellow and grayish dun of the natural hay that would stand in the fields throughout most of the winter, but the leaves of certain forbs had turned to shades of red. Single plants or small clumps of the herbs suddenly appearing along their way stood out as bright spots of color that delighted Ayla, but it was the occasional south-facing wooded hillside that made her catch her breath with its dazzling display. From a distance, the colorful brush and trees gave an impression of large bouquets of bright flowers.

Gray was content to follow along riderless, stopping now and then to graze, and Wolf poked his nose into hillocks, pockets of brush, and patches of tall grass as he traced his own path of invisible scents and secret sounds. Their route traced a broad circle that eventually took them back toward the Meeting Campsite from the upstream direction of The River. But they didn't return to camp. They cut in alongside the smaller waterway that wound through the woods to the north of the Ninth Cave's camp and, near the time the sun reached its zenith, they found their way to the deep swimming hole at a sharp bend in the smaller stream. The trees provided dappled shade for the secluded beach of sandy gravel.

The sun felt pleasantly warm as Ayla lifted her leg over and slid down from Whinney. She unfastened the pack baskets and untied the riding blanket, and while Jondalar spread out the large hide, she pulled out a leather drawstring bag and hand-fed the dun-yellow mare some mixed grains, mostly oats, then gave her some affectionate strokes and scratches. After a few more handfuls she did the same for Gray, who had been nudging her for attention.

Jondalar fed and fondled Racer. The stallion was still more unmanageable than usual, though he calmed down with the food and handling, but Jondalar didn't want to go after him if he decided to wander off. With a long rope attached to his halter, he hitched the horse to a small tree. Jondalar suddenly recalled that he had been considering letting the stallion go to find a place for himself with other horses on the open plains, and wondered if he should, but the man wasn't ready yet to give up the company of the magnificent animal.

Wolf, who had been chasing his own whims, suddenly appeared from behind a screen of brush. Ayla had brought a meaty bone for him, but before she pulled it out of the pack basket, she decided to give him some attention, too. She tapped her shoulder and braced herself to receive the weight of the huge wolf as he jumped up on his hind legs and supported himself with his paws in front of her shoulders. He licked her neck, then gently held her jaw in his teeth. She returned the gesture in kind, then signaled him down, and hunkered in front of him, taking his head between her hands. She rubbed and scratched behind his ears and roughed up the thickening fur around his neck, then sat down on the ground and just hugged him. She knew the wolf had been there for her, too, as much as Jondalar, when she was recovering from her perilous Journey to the world of the spirits.

As often as he'd seen it, the tall man still marveled at her way with the wolf, and as comfortable as he was with the animal himself, he still reminded himself occasionally that Wolf was a hunting animal. A killing animal. Others of his kind stalked, killed, and ate animals larger than themselves. Wolf could as easily tear Ayla's throat out as caress it gently with his teeth, yet he trusted this animal completely with his woman and his child. He had seen the love Wolf felt for them both and though he couldn't fathom how it was possible, at a basic level, he understood it. He firmly believed that Wolf's feeling for him was very much like his feeling for the wolf. The animal trusted him with the woman and child he loved, but Jondalar had no doubt that if Wolf ever thought that the man would cause harm to either one of them, he wouldn't hesitate to stop him any way he could, even if it meant killing him. He would do the same.

Jondalar enjoyed watching Ayla with the wolf. But then he loved watching her no matter what she was doing, especially now that she was nearly her old self and they were back together. He'd hated leaving her behind when he left with the Ninth Cave for the Summer Meeting, and had missed her terribly, in spite of his diversion with Marona. After feeling sure he had lost her, first because of his own actions, and then, more desperately, because of the juice from the roots she had taken, he could hardly believe they were together again. He had so thoroughly persuaded himself that she was forever gone from him that he had to keep looking at her, smiling at her, watching her smile back to believe that she was still his mate, his woman; that they were riding the horses, going for a swim, being together just as though nothing had happened.

It made him think of their long Journey together, their adventures, and the people they had met along the way. There were the Mamutoi, the mammoth hunters who had adopted Ayla, and the Sharamudoi, among whom his brother Thonolan had found a mate, though her death had killed his spirit. Tholie and Markeno, as well as the others, had wanted Ayla and him to stay, especially after she had used her medicine skills to straighten Rosharío's broken arm, which had been healing badly. They had even met Jeran, a hunter from the Hadumai, the people he and Thonolan had visited. And of course the S'Armunai, whose hunters, the Wolf Women, had captured him, and Attaroa, their headwoman, who had tried to kill Ayla, until Wolf stopped her the only way he could, by killing her. And the Losadunai . . .

He suddenly remembered when they had stopped to visit the Losadunai on their long Journey from the land of the mammoth hunters. They lived on the other side of the glaciered highland to the east, where the Great Mother River began, and their language had enough similarities to Zelandonii that he could understand most of it, although Ayla with her Gift for languages had quickly learned it even better. The Losadunai were among the best known of the Zelandonii neighbors, and travelers from both often visited with each other, although crossing the glacier could be an obstacle.

There had been a Mother Festival while they were visiting, and just before it started, Jondalar and Losaduna had conducted a private ceremony. Jondalar had asked the Great Mother for a child, born to Ayla, to be born to his hearth, one born of his spirit, or his essence, as Ayla always said it. He had also made a special request. He had asked that if Ayla ever became pregnant with a child of his spirit, he wanted to know for sure that it was from him. Jondalar had often been told that he was favored by the Mother, so favored that no woman could refuse him, not even Doni Herself.

He fully believed that when Ayla was lost in the void after using the dangerous roots again, the Great Mother had granted his impassioned entreaty; she had given him what he wished for, longed for, what he had asked for, and in his mind he fervently thanked her again. But suddenly he understood that the Mother had also granted the request he had made in the special ceremony with the Losaduna. He knew that Jonayla was his child, the child of his essence, and he was happy for that.

He knew that all the children born to Ayla would be of his spirit, his essence, because of who she was, because she loved only him, and it pleased him to know that. And he knew he would love only her, no matter what. But this new Gift of Knowledge, he knew it would change things and couldn't help but wonder how much.

He wasn't the only one. Everyone was thinking about it, but one in particular. The woman who was the First Among Those Who Served The Great Earth Mother was sitting quietly in the zelandonia lodge thinking about the new Gift of Knowledge and knew it would change the world.